V

EVERYMAN'S LIBRARY

EVERYMAN,
I WILL GO WITH THEE,
AND BE THY GUIDE,
IN THY MOST NEED
TO GO BY THY SIDE

P. G. WODEHOUSE

THE BEST
OF
WODEHOUSE

AN ANTHOLOGY

WITH AN INTRODUCTION BY
JOHN MORTIMER

EVERYMAN'S LIBRARY
Alfred A. Knopf   New York   London   Toronto
306

THE BEST OF WODEHOUSE

—

CONTENTS

INTRODUCTION

It's a serious fault in our approach to literature, that we don't take comedy seriously. How impossible to imagine any really funny book winning the Booker Prize, yet much of life is essentially comic and our greatest writers, Shakespeare and Dickens, excelled in the creation of humorous characters and were always ready to laugh at the pomposity of our world's most self-important people. And yet P. G. Wodehouse, whom Evelyn Waugh rightly called one of the best writers of the first half of the twentieth century, is relegated to a brief entry in *The Oxford Companion to English Literature* as though making people laugh was not one of the greatest favours a writer can bestow on the world.

Pelham Grenville Wodehouse was born in 1881, the son of a good-natured colonial administrator serving as a magistrate in Hong Kong, and a more formidable mother who might have been a model for the strong-minded aunts in so many of his stories. Eleanor Deane, known as 'Shanghai Lil', met Ernest Wodehouse when she travelled to the Far East in search of a husband. She was a talented artist and one of a large family with artistic and literary pretensions. Young Pelham, even from his childhood known as 'Plum', was sent to Dulwich College, a remarkable institution which also nurtured the talents of Raymond Chandler and C. S. Forester. It was a time when hansom cabs, of the sort that brought troubled spirits to seek the advice of Sherlock Holmes in Baker Street, clattered through London, and Kipling's soldiers served an empire on which the sun never set.

I've had the privilege of looking through the Wodehouse archive in the home of Sir Edward Cazalet, a retired High Court judge whose grandmother married Wodehouse. So I've been able to see Plum's school reports, all excellent, which show that he not only studied Shakespeare but Greek drama and Latin poetry. In time, these great works would echo through his books. He also read Browning and Tennyson and the works of Jerome K. Jerome, and was captivated by the operas of

ix

P. G. WODEHOUSE

Gilbert and Sullivan. When he saw *Patience* he was, he wrote, 'absolutely drunk with ecstasy'. Gilbert's lyrics not only had a profound affect on Gershwin's songs, but also inspired Wodehouse when he came to write for the musical theatre.

In his excellent *Life of Wodehouse* Robert McCrum identifies the masters at Dulwich who most influenced the author. Among them was Philip Hope, who could rattle off sentences in Greek or Latin. Wodehouse apparently shared this ability, and was able to construct the most complicated sentences with grammatical accuracy.

*

After school came work in a bank, which Wodehouse seems to have enjoyed, and then the early stories concerning the witty and imperturbable Psmith ('the p is silent as in phthisis, psychic and ptarmigan'), the absent-minded Lord Emsworth and the ever resourceful Ukridge, who keeps a chicken farm and was based on a friend who followed this dangerous occupation. From then on his productivity was amazing. According to Robert McCrum, in the decade following World War I Wodehouse composed lyrics for some twelve musicals, wrote or adapted four plays, and published twenty books in London and New York.

Then came the stories about the unforgettable partnership of Bertie Wooster and Jeeves, which I see as his masterpieces. It may not have been a new idea to write a book about the master–servant relationship in which the servant is, inevitably, the master. It inspired Don Quixote and Sancho Panza, but, in my view, you can have a lot more fun with Jeeves and Bertie Wooster than with their Spanish forefathers. Wodehouse spoke of the achievement with his usual modesty, saying that he had managed to sell a number of short stories to the *Saturday Evening Post* about 'a bloke called Bertie Wooster and his valet'. What he had done was to discover two characters fit to join the immortals.

Bertie Wooster is a usually well-meaning character, but not, we would have to admit, the Brain of Britain. As Jeeves describes him he is 'an exceedingly pleasant and amiable young gentleman, but not intelligent. By no means intelligent.' Bertie is in perpetual trouble – about his clothes, his ineffectual attempts to help his friends, his efforts to woo girls or to escape the tyranny of his ruthless aunts.

And Jeeves is, of course, inimitable. He is a mastermind, more intelligent, and far more entertaining, than any encountered by James Bond. Bertie Wooster puts his brain power down to the fact that Jeeves consumes a good deal of fish. Be that as it may, as a plotter he is an even brighter version of Psmith from the other side of the green baize door. He glides in and out of bedrooms, draws the curtains and provides the first enlivening cup of tea; is able to advise his master in the choice of socks, gentlemen's suitings or even an over-expressive tie. He will put up with most things except, on one famous occasion, his master's desire to play upon some type of banjo.

Jeeves is not only a richly comic character, he fulfils a desperate need in all of us. What would we not do for an enigmatic presence to glide in with a cup of early-morning tea, solve all our problems, correct our mistakes and even give us sound advice on the choice of shirts?

Jeeves is also a walking dictionary of quotations, and as such very useful to his employer who is partial to a literary allusion but whose grasp of the classics is rather tenuous. In an early story, 'Jeeves and the Unbidden Guest', Bertie has an amusing slant on the role of unexpected doom in Greek drama: 'I'm not absolutely certain of my facts, but I rather fancy it's Shakespeare – or, if not, it's some equally brainy lad – who says that it's always just when a chappie is feeling particularly tophole and more than usually braced with things in general that Fate sneaks up behind him with the bit of lead piping.' In *Thank You, Jeeves*, his recollection of poetry learnt at school is even more vague. After he meets a striking girl he says, 'Jeeves, who was the fellow who on looking at something felt like somebody looking at something?' Of course Jeeves knows the quotation: 'I fancy the individual you have in mind, sir, is the poet Keats, who compared his emotions on first reading Chapman's Homer to those of stout Cortez when with eagle eyes he stared at the Pacific.'

When Wodehouse went to work in Hollywood he said he turned all the characters in the scripts he was given from doctors to earls and valets. His earl, Lord Emsworth, worried owner of the prize pig Empress of Blandings, may not be as fascinating and original a character as the immortal Jeeves, but *Blandings Castle* can still provide more hilarity and better entertainment than most Hollywood movies.

*

Wodehouse married Ethel Wayman in 1919. Born Ethel Newton, she had led an eventful life, having been twice married and widowed. She had a young daughter, Leonora Rowley, by her first husband, a civil engineer with whom she had gone to live in India. Her second marriage was to a Jermyn Street tailor who, after a painful bankruptcy, committed suicide. Ethel then went to New York to pursue a career as an actress, and it was there she met Wodehouse and they fell in love.

In the course of time Leonora married, to Wodehouse's great delight, an English landowner named Peter Cazalet. They set up home on a large estate and, again in the course of time, Leonora gave birth to Edward Cazalet. It was from Sir Edward's archive I learned that Wodehouse, before he started work every morning, would always write a love letter to his wife still, no doubt, asleep upstairs.

Ethel was funny, apparently not beautiful but with an excellent figure, mad about dancing and described by Malcolm Muggeridge as a 'mixture of Mistress Quickly and Florence Nightingale, with a touch of Lady Macbeth thrown in'. It's a tribute to their love that the marriage survived the difficulties that afflicted the couple during World War II.

When war broke out the Wodehouses were living in a villa they had bought in Le Touquet. As the German armies swept through France, many British residents fled to the coast and managed to return home. The Wodehouses were amongst those who preferred to wait. There was a novel to work on (*Joy in the Morning*) and a beloved dog that would be quarantined as soon as they returned to England. They did keep in daily contact with British army officers who promised to advise them when it would be sensible to leave, but they were taken aback by the speed of the German advance and their belated attempts to flee were unsuccessful. The Germans duly arrived, requisitioning

the Wodehouses' stores, cars and bicycle and even making use
of their bathroom. Perhaps because he saw life as a comedy
and thought in his innocence that his presence could harm
no one, the author showed considerable sangfroid, taking a
'business as usual' line which can be seen as a kind of courage.
Throughout the early summer of 1940 he continued with his
writing, walked the dogs, enjoyed crumpets for tea and hoped
for the best. He also had to report to the German authorities
every day. Then one morning he was escorted home and given
a short time to pack up his belongings. Characteristically he
said he had not experienced such a feeling of dread since he
had to appear to receive his D. Litt. at Oxford. He packed his
clothes, pens and scribbling pads together with the complete
works of Shakespeare and the poems of Tennyson. While Ethel
was allowed to remain free in occupied France, he now found
himself in a prison in Loos which he described in great detail
in his notebook.

His cell was '12 foot long by about 8 foot wide, whitewashed
walls, bed in corner under window ... toilet in corner near
door', and so on. Having given up the bed to another prisoner,
Wodehouse slept on a straw mattress on the floor. He had been
wise enough to pack certain items such as half a pound of tea,
to which Ethel had added a cold mutton chop and a slab of
chocolate. Later he was moved to a former Belgian army barracks in Liège where a German soldier shook his hand and
said, 'Thank you for Jeeves.' This recognition didn't, however,
prevent his further incarceration in various barracks, spending
cold nights without a blanket and sickened by the stench from
the drains. He behaved, it has to be said, with outstanding
stoicism and even found, in spite of everything, cheerfulness
breaking through. 'Suddenly,' he wrote, 'for no reason, I got a
sort of exalted feeling – definitely happy' .This burst of emotional elation was apparently brought about by a prisoner paying back the five francs he had lent him. His final internment
was in Tost, in Germany. From there he wrote letters to friends
in England, although he knew they might never get them,
asking for pipe tobacco and more chocolate. He also
announced that he was quite happy and had started work on
a new novel.

Wodehouse was interviewed by an American journalist (before his country had entered the war). His surprisingly contented attitude, and the fact that he refused the privilege of a private room, reinforced the feeling that he didn't take the war entirely seriously and contributed to his subsequent disgrace. Nor was his ability to concentrate on writing a comic novel in such alarming circumstances thought to be in his favour. He did, however, accept some privileges. He had the use of a typewriter and was able to make contributions to American magazines such as the *Saturday Evening Post*, and it was in the office of the prison governor that the fatal suggestion was made to him, 'Why don't you do some broadcasts ... for your American readers?' To which Wodehouse was unwise enough to reply that there was nothing he would like better. It was clear that these broadcasts would deal with his experiences as a prisoner and it should have been obvious to everyone that his approach to this subject would be humorous.

The Gestapo interrupted a game of cricket Wodehouse was playing with fellow inmates and removed him from prison. He was taken to Berlin, where he was confined, under constant supervision, in more luxurious quarters in the Hotel Adlon. There followed the series of broadcasts that had such dire consquences for the author. Their tone was, of course, far from serious. He spoke of his situation as a comic interlude in his busy life. He described his arrest at the Le Touquet villa, and said that he advised anyone who wanted to be arrested by the Germans to buy a villa in Le Touquet. He told his listeners that there was a good deal to be said for internment as it allowed you to get on with your reading; 'the chief drawback is that it means your being away from home a good deal'. He described the sergeant in charge of the internees in Le Touquet as 'a genial soul ... infusing the whole thing [with] a pleasant atmosphere of the school treat'. His general attitude was self-deprecating and he showed his determination to make the best of things. He joked that in prison all he had wanted was for the guards to look the other way 'and leave the rest to me', in return for which he offered to hand over 'India [and] an autographed set of my books'. The price he had to pay turned out to be much higher. He remained at the Hotel Adlon and elsewhere until 1943 (when he was allowed to transfer to another hotel in Paris), paying for it himself from his European royalties, and he made it clear that he could be happy anywhere given a large supply of pens and paper.

England had endured the Blitz and rationing, and faced a long war which had already cost many lives. It was understandable that people should disapprove of Wodehouse's broadcasts. What was not excusable was that he should be damned as a traitor. The attack was led by a journalist, William Connor, who wrote under the name of 'Cassandra' in the *Daily Mirror*. In a broadcast, Connor accused Wodehouse of selling his country to the Nazis for the price of a soft bed in a luxury hotel. He said that Wodehouse was a traitor and compared him, unfavourably, to many anti-Nazis confined in prisons who hadn't sold their souls for 'thirty pieces of silver'. Connor continued his attack in the *Daily Mirror* and by the end of the war Wodehouse's reputation was at its lowest ebb. Trying, as usual, to take the light-hearted view, he wrote that he had not experienced such unusual displeasure since, as a boy, he broke the curate's umbrella.

In 1947 Wodehouse left France and set up home in America. His routine remained the same, he wrote in the mornings and walked the dogs in the afternoons. Times had, however, changed. 'The world of which I had been writing since I was so high,' he wrote 'had gone with the wind and is one with Nineveh and Tyre. Young men no longer lazed in the Drones Club or even had valets.' But he wrote on, dealing with the change as best he could, ever conscious of the writer's first duty which is to entertain his audience.

I learnt a most astonishing thing from Edward Cazalet's archive. After the war Wodehouse met William Connor, his principal persecutor. They had lunch, 'Cassandra' was unable to resist the Wodehouse charm and they became friends. This fact also seems to prove that P. G. Wodehouse was a very nice man indeed.

In time, England forgave his broadcasts. He was made a knight and, to his great amusement, his effigy was exhibited in Madame Tussaud's. In February 1975 he was taken into hospital for tests. He was found there one evening, dead in his armchair, with a pipe and tobacco on his lap and a piece of manuscript within easy reach. He had never stopped writing.

*

Was he a great writer? Perhaps Evelyn Waugh was exaggerating when he rated him above his heavyweight contemporaries. He may not have been as profound as James Joyce or E. M. Forster but he gave more pleasure to a wider public. This collection will give you an opportunity to judge him. Jeeves and Bertie Wooster, Lord Emsworth, Ukridge and Uncle Fred can be called as witnesses in his trial. Or, of course, you may have had such a good time reading the evidence that the verdict seems irrelevant.

Like Dickens, Wodehouse created a world of his own, and he achieved a totally individual style. In Jeeves he created a character so alive he can be mentioned in the same breath as Sam Weller or Malvolio. He easily achieved the hardest of all literary tasks, which is to make readers laugh. He is enjoyed as much as ever over thirty years after his death. If that doesn't make him a great writer it will have to do, until the next one comes along.

John Mortimer

JOHN MORTIMER is a playwright, a best-selling novelist, screenwriter and former barrister and QC. His plays include *A Voyage Round My Father* and *The Dock Brief*. His novels *Summer's Lease, Paradise Postponed* and all the Rumpole stories have been adapted for television. He has also written three volumes of memoirs, *Clinging to the Wreckage, The Summer of a Dormouse* and *Where There's a Will*. He lives in a house built by his father in the Chilterns.

SELECT BIBLIOGRAPHY

The best introduction to Wodehouse is more of his own fiction, but for those who want to probe a little deeper, the following may be of use.

David Jasen, Frances Donaldson, Owen Dudley Edwards, Joseph Connolly and Benny Green have written interesting biographies but all are superseded by Robert McCrum's *Wodehouse, A Life*, Viking Penguin and W. W. Norton & Company, 2004.

Among Wodehouse's autobiographical writings, *Over Seventy* (quoted in this anthology) is the most revealing, though that is not saying much. It does, however, throw light on his methods.

An affectionate overview of the œuvre can be found in Richard Usborne's *Wodehouse at Work to the End*, Barrie and Jenkins, 1976. This is a light-hearted but level-headed commentary by an expert on English popular fiction, at his best on Wodehouse's literary sources.

Among reference books, *Wooster's World* by Geoffrey Jaggard, Macdonald and Co., 1967, explores every aspect of its subject. More comprehensive still is *The Millennium Wodehouse Concordance* in several volumes from 1994, Porpoise Books, Maidenhead, edited by Tony Ring and Geoffrey Jaggard. Besides complete lists of characters and places featured in the stories, these guides include essays on relevant topics of interest, and first publication details for all books discussed,

Finally, there is *In Search of Blandings* by N. T. P. Murphy, Secker and Warburg, 1986, an investigation into possible models for the famous castle which includes a commentary on Wodehouse's early life and times.

CHRONOLOGY

DATE	AUTHOR'S LIFE	LITERARY CONTEXT
1881	Pelham Grenville born 15 October in Guildford, Surrey, third son of Eleanor (*née* Deane) and Henry Ernest Wodehouse. Taken to live in Hong Kong where his father works as a magistrate.	Gilbert and Sullivan: *Patience* (opera). Collins: *The Black Robe*. James: *The Portrait of a Lady*. Twain: *The Prince and the Pauper*.
1882		F. Anstey: *Vice Versa*.
1883	Children placed in care of a nanny, Miss Roper, in England; PGW does not see his parents again for 3 years.	Stevenson: *Treasure Island*. Henty: *Under Drake's Flag*.
1884		First edition of Oxford English Dictionary published. F. Anstey: *The Black Poodle*. Henty: *With Clive in India*.
1885		F. Anstey: *The Tinted Venus*. Twain: *Huckleberry Finn*. Meredith: *Diana of the Crossways*. Haggard: *King Solomon's Mines*. Gilbert and Sullivan: *The Mikado* (opera).
1886	Sent with brothers Philip Peveril ('Pev') and Armine as boarder to a small school in Croydon, Surrey.	Stevenson: *Dr Jekyll and Mr Hyde*. James: *The Bostonians*. F. Anstey: *A Fallen Idol*. Jerome: *Idle Thoughts of an Idle Fellow*.
1887		Haggard: *She*. Hardy: *The Woodlanders*. Stevenson: *Kidnapped*. Conan Doyle: *A Study in Scarlet*.
1888		Barrie: *When a Man's Single*. Stevenson: *The Black Arrow*.
1889	Pev is diagnosed with a weak chest, for which sea air is prescribed; the brothers are moved to Elizabeth College in St Peter Port, Guernsey.	Twain: *A Connecticut Yankee at King Arthur's Court*. Jerome: *Three Men in a Boat*. Stevenson and Osbourne: *The Wrong Box*. Stevenson: *The Master of Ballantrae*.

HISTORICAL EVENTS

British force defeated at Battle of Majuba Hill, bringing first Boer War to an end. Convention of Pretoria. Tsar Alexander II assassinated in Russia. Second Irish Land Act passed by prime minister Gladstone.

Irish republicans murder Lord Frederick Cavendish, chief secretary for Ireland, and under-secretary Thomas Henry Burke. Triple Alliance defence pact signed by Germany, Austria and Italy. Britain occupies Egypt and the Sudan.

Siege of Khartoum, Sudan by al-Mahdi and supporters (to 1885). 'Scramble for Africa' begins; Berlin Conference held to regulate European colonization of the continent and trade.

Uprising in north-west Canada ends in failure for rebelling Métis people. Lord Salisbury forms Conservative ministry. Statue of Liberty arrives in New York harbour.

Britain annexes Upper Burma; long period of guerrilla warfare ensues. Nationwide strike in US in support of 8-hour working day; rally in Haymarket Square, Chicago ends in violence when a bomb is thrown at police. Newly elected prime minister Gladstone resigns when his first Home Rule Bill for Ireland is defeated; Salisbury returns to office (to 1892). Queen Victoria's Golden Jubilee. Secret Reinsurance Treaty between Germany and Russia. Britain annexes Zululand to impede Transvaal's access to the African coast. 'Bloody Sunday' clashes between police and pro-Irish independence demonstrators in Trafalgar Square, London. Match girls' strike in London. Wilhelm II succeeds to the throne, becoming last German monarch.
Eiffel Tower built in Paris. Great Dock Strike, London.

DATE	AUTHOR'S LIFE	LITERARY CONTEXT
1890		Conan Doyle: *The Sign of Four.* Kipling: *The Light that Failed*; *Soldiers Three.*
1891		George Newnes launches the *Strand Magazine* (to 1950). Barrie: *The Little Minister.* Wilde: *The Picture of Dorian Gray.* Zangwill: *The Big Bow Mystery.* Hardy: *Tess of the d'Urbervilles.*
1892	PGW attends Malvern House naval preparatory school in Kearnsey, Kent. Younger brother Richard Lancelot Deane is born.	Wilde: *Lady Windermere's Fan.* Conan Doyle: *The Adventures of Sherlock Holmes.* Grossmith brothers: *The Diary of a Nobody.* Stevenson and Osbourne: *The Wrecker.* Zangwill: *Children of the Ghetto.*
1893		Wilde: *A Woman of No Importance.* Benson: *Dodo.*
1894	Joins Armine at Dulwich College, London (to 1900).	G. du Maurier: *Trilby.* Hope: *The Prisoner of Zenda.* Kipling: *The Jungle Book.* Twain: *Pudd'nhead Wilson.*
1895	Parents return from Hong Kong and take a house in Dulwich; Armine and Plum become day boys.	Wilde: *The Importance of Being Earnest*; *An Ideal Husband.* Trial and conviction of Oscar Wilde. Hardy: *Jude the Obscure.* Wells: *The Time Machine.*
1896	Wodehouses buy a home in Shropshire; PGW becomes a boarder again at Dulwich.	Wells: *The Island of Doctor Moreau.* Stevenson: *Weir of Hermiston.* Beerbohm: *The Works of Max Beerbohm.* Belloc: *The Bad Child's Book of Beasts.*
1897		F. Anstey: *Baboo Jabberjee, B.A.* Wells: *The Wheels of Chance.*
1898	Shares a study with William Townend, lifelong friend and fellow writer.	Relaunch of the *Saturday Evening Post* as a journal. James: *The Turn of the Screw.* Wells: *The War of the Worlds.* Belloc: *The Modern Traveller.*

CHRONOLOGY

HISTORICAL EVENTS

Bismarck forced to resign as prime minister of Germany. Parnell loses his leadership of Irish Nationalist Party. Treaties with Belgium, France, Germany and Portugal define and extend British interests in African continent. New York's Carnegie Hall opens with a public performance conducted by Tchaikovsky. Education Act abolishes fees for elementary schooling in England and Wales.

Resignation of Salisbury; Gladstone becomes prime minister for fourth and last time.

Independent Labour Party founded, led by James Keir Hardie. Gladstone's second Irish Home Rule Bill rejected by Lords. Crash on New York Stock Exchange triggers economic crisis.
Gladstone resigns, having split Liberals over Home Rule. Outbreak of bubonic plague in Tain Ping Shan area of Hong Kong, killing over 2,500 people. First Sino-Japanese War (to 1895). Dreyfus Affair. Nicholas II becomes Russian tsar.
Conservatives win general elections in Britain; third Salisbury ministry begins. First Proms concert at Queen's Hall, London. Lumière brothers give first public screening of projected motion film in Paris.

First US screening of motion pictures at Koster and Bial's Music Hall in New York. Anglo-French conflict on the Upper Nile. Anglo-Egyptian troops under General Kitchener begin reconquest of the Sudan.

Queen Victoria's Diamond Jubilee. Wilhelm II and naval adviser Tirpitz launch policy of *Weltpolitik*; German naval laws (1898, 1900) instigate arms race with Britain.
Consolidation of Manhattan, Brooklyn, Bronx, Queens and Staten Island as Greater New York. Spanish-American War. 'New Territories' are leased to Britain by the Qing Dynasty for 99 years under Convention for the Extension of Hong Kong Territory. Annexation of Hawaii by US. Fashoda Incident in the Sudan.

DATE	AUTHOR'S LIFE	LITERARY CONTEXT
1899	Editor of school magazine the *Alleynian* (to 1900).	George Horace Lorimer appointed editor of the *Saturday Evening Post* (to 1937). Kipling: *Stalky & Co.* Hornung: *The Amateur Craftsman.*
1900	First paid article 'Some Aspects of Game-Captaincy' appears in the *Public School Magazine*. Enters employment at the Lombard Street, London branch of Hong Kong and Shanghai Bank.	Jerome: *Three Men on the Bummel.* Chesterton: *The Wild Knight and Other Poems.* Wells: *Love and Mr Lewisham.*
1901	Suffers an attack of mumps. Begins contributing articles to the *Globe and Traveller* newspaper.	Hornung: *The Black Mask.* Butler: *Erewhon Revisited.* Kipling: *Kim.*
1902	Resigns from the bank in order to write full-time. First article for *Punch*, 'An Unfinished Collection', is printed. A. & C. Black publish PGW's first novel *The Pothunters*.	James: *The Wings of the Dove.* Barr McCutcheon: *Brewster's Millions.* Conan Doyle: *The Hound of the Baskervilles.* Kipling: *Just So Stories.* Barrie: *The Admirable Crichton.*
1903	Takes lodgings above the stables at Emsworth House School, Hampshire where friend Herbert Westbrook teaches. Joins permanent staff of the *Globe*, working on the 'By the Way' column. *A Prefect's Uncle*; *Tales of St Austin's* (stories).	James: *The Ambassadors.* Butler: *The Way of All Flesh.*
1904	Boards the SS *St Louis* to New York for first US visit. Promoted editor of the *Globe*'s 'By the Way' column (to 1909); appoints Westbrook his deputy. *The Gold Bat*; *William Tell Told Again* (children's); 'Put Me in My Little Cell' (song lyric for *Sergeant Blue*).	James: *The Golden Bowl.* Saki: *Reginald.* Chesterton: *The Napoleon of Notting Hill.* Barr McCutcheon: *The Day of the Dog.* Barrie: *Peter Pan.* Shaw: *John Bull's Other Island.*
1905	Sells first story to the *Strand*, 'The Wirepullers'. *The Head of Kay's*.	Forster: *Where Angels Fear to Tread.* Wells: *Kipps.* Le Queux: *The Czar's Spy.* Chesterton: *The Club of Queer Trades.* Orczy: *The Scarlet Pimpernel.* Wallace: *The Four Just Men.*

HISTORICAL EVENTS

Anglo-Egyptian Sudan established under British governor-general Reginald
Wingate. First Peace Conference at the Hague. Second Boer War (to 1902);
Kimberley and Mafeking besieged by Boers.

Relief of Kimberley and Mafeking. Britain claims victory in Orange Free
State and the Transvaal. World exhibition in Paris attracts over 50 million
visitors in 6 months. Russia occupies Manchuria. Boxer Rebellion in China
(to 1901). Demonstrations for home rule in Phoenix Park, Dublin.

Death of Queen Victoria; accession of Edward VII. Assassination of
President McKinley in US; succeeded by Theodore Roosevelt. Marconi
transmits messages across the Atlantic.
Anglo-Japanese Treaty signed. Triple Alliance between Germany, Austria-
Hungary and Italy renewed. Salisbury retires; Balfour becomes prime
minister in UK.

Anti-immigration law passed by US Congress. Murder of Alexander I and
Queen Draga of Serbia. Emmeline Pankhurst founds Women's Social and
Political Union. Formation of Bolshevik party, led by Lenin. Wright brothers
make first powered aircraft flight.

Russo-Japanese War (to 1905). Signing of Entente Cordiale between Britain
and France. Dogger Bank incident creates Anglo-Russian tensions. Opening
of New York subway.

First Russian Revolution. Trades Union Congress demands 8-hour day and
free trade for UK. Sinn Fein independence party is founded in Dublin.

DATE	AUTHOR'S LIFE	LITERARY CONTEXT
1906	Signed up by Seymour Hicks as resident lyricist at the Aldwych Theatre, London. Makes acquaintance with American composer Jerome Kern while working on *The Beauty of Bath*, for which PGW writes lyric 'Mister Chamberlain'. Publishes first novel for adults, *Love Among the Chickens*.	Galsworthy: *The Forsyte Saga* (to 1921).
1907	'Now That My Ship's Come Home' and 'You, You, You' (lyrics for *The Gay Gordons*). *The White Feather*; *Not George Washington* (with H. Westbrook). Joins the Gaiety Theatre as lyricist.	Molnár: *The Paul Street Boys*; *The Devil*. Belloc: *Cautionary Tales for Children*.
1908	*The Globe By the Way Book* (with H. Westbrook); *The Luck Stone* serialized in *Chums* (published as a book 1997).	Forster: *A Room with a View*. Chesterton: *The Man Who Was Thursday*. Bennett: *The Old Wives' Tale*.
1909	Second visit to America; sells stories to *Colliers* and *Cosmopolitan*. First book published in US, *Love Among the Chickens*, by Circle Publishing Co. *The Swoop!*; *Mike* (later published in 2 parts, the second under the title *Enter Psmith*, 1935; the 2 vols were republished in 1953 as *Mike at Wrykyn* and *Psmith and Mike*). Serialization of *Psmith, Journalist* in *The Captain* from October (published as a book 1915).	Wells: *Tono-Bungay*. Le Queux: *Spies of the Kaiser*; *The House of Whispers*. Molnár: *Liliom*. Walpole: *The Wooden Horse*. Chesterton: *The Ball and the Cross*.
1910	*Psmith in the City*; *A Gentleman of Leisure* (US title *The Intrusion of Jimmy*).	Forster: *Howards End*. Bennett: *Clayhanger*. Saki: *Reginald in Russia*.
1911	First play, *A Gentleman of Leisure* (with John Stapleton), opens in New York.	Chesterton: *The Innocence of Father Brown*. Walpole: *Mr Perrin and Mr Traill*. Bennett: *The Card*. Saki: *The Chronicles of Clovis*. Beerbohm: *Zuleika Dobson*.
1912	Two very different versions of *The Prince and Betty* published in UK and USA.	Doyle: *The Lost World*. Cobb: *Back Home*. Benson: *Mrs Ames*.

CHRONOLOGY

Liberals come to power under Campbell-Bannerman in UK election. Launch of HMS *Dreadnought*, world's most powerful warship. Earthquake in San Francisco devastates the city and kills at least 1,000. German Naval Bill passed, accelerating armaments race between Britain and Germany.

Renewal of Triple Alliance (Germany, Austria-Hungary and Italy). Conclusion of Anglo-Russian Entente, aligning Russia with France and Britain as the Triple Entente. Second Hague Conference.

Campbell-Bannerman resigns because of bad health; Asquith takes over. Signature of the Baltic Convention and North Sea Convention. Austria annexes Bosnia and Herzegovina. Suffragette protests in London.

Settlement of crisis between Austria and Serbia over annexation of Bosnia-Herzegovina. Amalgamation of Customs with Excise department of Inland Revenue under one board. First crossing of English Channel by air by Louis Blériot. House of Lords rejects Lloyd George's 'People's Budget'; constitutional crisis arises, with Liberals demanding abolition of Lords' veto.

Death of Edward VII. Union of South Africa established, with dominion status.

Parliament Bill restricting power of House of Lords is passed. Agadir crisis. Coronation of George V. Nestor Film Company opens first motion picture studio in Hollywood. Chinese Revolution.

British explorer Scott reaches South Pole. Hong Kong's first tertiary institution, the University of Hong Kong, opens. Third Home Rule Bill for Ireland meets with opposition from Ulster Unionists. SS *Titanic* sinks. Dockers strike in London. First Balkan War (to 1913). Democrat Woodrow Wilson elected US president.

DATE	AUTHOR'S LIFE	LITERARY CONTEXT
1913	First play in London, *Brother Alfred*, lasts just 14 performances. *The Little Nugget*.	Walpole: *Fortitude*. Phillips Oppenheim: *The Double Life of Mr Alfred Burton*. Shaw: *Pygmalion*. Saki: *When William Came*.
1914	*The Man Upstairs and other Stories*. Marries Ethel Wayman (*née* Newton) in New York, gaining a stepdaughter, Leonora.	Saki: *Beasts and Super-Beasts*. Barr McCutcheon: *The Prince of Graustark*. Chesterton: *The Wisdom of Father Brown*.
1915	First serial, *Something New* (UK title *Something Fresh*), is published in US magazine the *Saturday Evening Post*. Appointed drama critic for *Vanity Fair*. *Psmith, Journalist* (book form).	Buchan: *The Thirty-Nine Steps*. Cobb: *Old Judge Priest*; *Speaking of Operations*. Maugham: *Of Human Bondage*. Firbank: *Vainglory*.
1916	*Uneasy Money* (first published in US; UK publication 1917). Collaborates with Jerome Kern and playwright Guy Bolton for first time on hit musical *Miss Springtime*.	Buchan: *Greenmantle*.
1917	*Piccadilly Jim* (first published in US; UK publication 1918). *The Man with Two Left Feet* (stories). Works with Bolton and Kern on musicals *Have a Heart, Oh, Boy!, Leave It To Jane, The Riviera Girl* and *Miss 1917*.	Kipling: *A Diversity of Creatures*. Barrie: *Dear Brutus*.
1918	*Oh, Lady! Lady!* (lyrics); *See You Later* (lyrics).	W. Lewis: *Tarr*.
1919	Returns to London. *My Man Jeeves* (stories); *Their Mutual Child* (first published in US; UK publication 1920 as *The Coming of Bill*); *A Damsel in Distress*; *The Rose of China* (lyrics).	Maugham: *The Moon and Sixpence*. Firbank: *Valmouth*. Beerbohm: *Seven Men*. Shaw: *Heartbreak House*.
1920	*The Little Warrior* (first published in US; UK publication 1921 as *Jill the Reckless*).	Benson: *Queen Lucia*. Fitzgerald: *This Side of Paradise*. Phillips Oppenheim: *The Great Impersonation*. S. Lewis: *Main Street*. Christie: *The Mysterious Affair at Styles*.

CHRONOLOGY

xxvii

DATE	AUTHOR'S LIFE	LITERARY CONTEXT
1921	*The Indiscretions of Archie* (stories); *The Golden Moth* (lyrics – music by Ivor Novello).	Le Queux: *Mademoiselle of Monte Carlo.* Benchley: *Of All Things!*. Buchan: *The Path of the King.* Huxley: *Crome Yellow.*
1922	*The Clicking of Cuthbert* (US title *Golf Without Tears* – stories); *The Girl on the Boat* (US title *Three Men and a Maid*); *The Cabaret Girl* (lyrics – music by J. Kern); *The Adventures of Sally* (US title *Mostly Sally*).	S. Lewis: *Babbitt.* Fitzgerald: *The Beautiful and the Damned.* Cobb: *J. Poindexter, Colored.* Walpole: *The Cathedral.* Benson: *Miss Mapp.*
1923	Knocked down by a car while staying on Long Island but escapes major injury. *The Inimitable Jeeves* (US title *Jeeves* – stories); *The Beauty Prize* (lyrics); *Leave it to Psmith.*	Firbank: *The Flower Beneath the Foot.* Huxley: *Antic Hay.*
1924	Final Bolton-Wodehouse-Kern collaboration, *Sitting Pretty*. *Ukridge* (US title *He Rather Enjoyed It* – stories); *Bill the Conqueror.*	Forster: *A Passage to India.*
1925	*Carry On, Jeeves* (stories); *Sam the Sudden* (US title *Sam in the Suburbs*).	Fitzgerald: *The Great Gatsby.* Woolf: *Mrs Dalloway.* Mackail: *Greenery Street.* S. Lewis: *Arrowsmith.* Wallace: *The Mind of Mr J. G. Reader.*
1926	*The Heart of a Goof* (US title *Divots* – stories); *Hearts and Diamonds* (libretto and one lyric); *The Play's the Thing* (play). Elected a Fellow of the Royal Society of Literature.	Chesterton: *The Incredulity of Father Brown.* Parker: *Enough Rope.* Green: *Blindness.* Firbank: *Concerning the Eccentricities of Cardinal Pirelli.* Kipling: *Debits and Credits.* Milne: *Winnie-the-Pooh.*
1927	Wodehouses lease 17 Norfolk Street as London home. *The Nightingale* (lyrics – libretto by G. Bolton); *Her Cardboard Lover* (play, with Valeric Wyngate); *The Small Bachelor*; *Meet Mr Mulliner* (stories). Best-known lyric 'Bill' interpolated into Broadway hit *Showboat*.	Benson: *Lucia in London.* Woolf: *To the Lighthouse.* Chesterton: *The Secret of Father Brown.* Kern: *Showboat* (musical).

CHRONOLOGY

Southern Ireland becomes free state with dominion status.

Civil war in Ireland (to 1923). Stalin becomes general secretary of Russian Bolshevik party's Central Committee. Fascist uprising in Italy; Mussolini granted dictatorial powers. First broadcast of British Broadcasting Company.

Baldwin elected prime minister. Failure of Hitler's coup in Munich.

Death of Lenin. First Labour government formed by Ramsay MacDonald; Baldwin returns to office after Conservative election victory. Hollywood motion picture studio Metro-Goldwyn-Mayer, Inc. (MGM) founded.

Treaty of Locarno.

General strike in Britain. Germany admitted to League of Nations. First television demonstrated.

British Broadcasting Company receives royal charter, becoming British Broadcasting Corporation. German economy collapses. Lindbergh flies the Atlantic solo. Warner Bros. release *The Jazz Singer*, first successful feature-length 'talkie'.

DATE	AUTHOR'S LIFE	LITERARY CONTEXT
1928	*Rosalie* (lyrics, with Ira Gershwin); *The Three Musketeers* (lyrics, with Clifford Grey); *Money for Nothing*; *A Damsel in Distress* (play, with Ian Hay).	Woolf: *Orlando.* Maugham: *Ashenden.* W. Lewis: *The Childermass.* Waugh: *Decline and Fall.*
1929	Death of Ernest Wodehouse. *Mr Mulliner Speaking* (stories); *Baa, Baa, Black Sheep* (play, with Ian Hay); *Summer Lightning* (US title *Fish Preferred*); *Candle-Light* (play).	Remarque: *All Quiet on the Western Front.* Green: *Living.* Priestley: *The Good Companions.*
1930	Signs first contract with MGM in Hollywood; PGW and Leonora take a house in Beverly Hills. *Very Good, Jeeves*; *Leave it to Psmith* (play, with Ian Hay). *Those Three French Girls*, first film with MGM, released to mixed reviews.	Waugh: *Vile Bodies.* Hammett: *The Maltese Falcon.* Wallace: *The Terror.* Walpole: *Rogue Herries.* Christie: *Murder at the Vicarage.*
1931	MGM contract is not renewed. *Big Money*; *If I Were You*.	Parker: *Death and Taxes.* Woolf: *The Waves.* Betjeman: *Mount Zion.* Benson: *Mapp and Lucia.*
1932	PGW and Ethel lease a house in Auribeau, France. Leonora marries Peter Cazalet. *Louder and Funnier* (articles); *Doctor Sally*; *Hot Water*.	Priestley: *Dangerous Corner.* Runyon: *Guys and Dolls.* Waugh: *Black Mischief.* Gibbons: *Cold Comfort Farm.*
1933	*Mulliner Nights* (stories); *Heavy Weather*.	Parker: *After Such Pleasures.* Thurber: *My Life and Hard Times.* Maugham: *Ah King.* Coward: *Private Lives.*
1934	Successfully challenges Inland Revenue's attempts to claim more tax on his earnings. Birth of first grandchild Sheran Cazalet. *Thank You, Jeeves*; *Right Ho, Jeeves* (US title *Brinkley Manor*); *Anything Goes* (libretto, with G. Bolton).	Christie: *Murder on the Orient Express.* Fitzgerald: *Tender is the Night.* Hilton: *Good-bye Mr Chips.* Graves: *I, Claudius.* Waugh: *A Handful of Dust.* Porter: *Anything Goes* (musical).
1935	Buys villa Low Wood in Le Touquet, France. *Blandings Castle and Elsewhere* (US title *Blandings Castle* – stories); *The Luck of the Bodkins*; *The Inside Stand* (play).	Compton-Burnett: *A House and its Head.* Benson: *Lucia's Progress.* Chesterton: *The Scandal of Father Brown.* Thurber: *The Middle-Aged Man on the Flying Trapeze.*

CHRONOLOGY

Women receive full suffrage in Britain. Stalin introduces first Five-Year Plan in USSR. Radio-Keith-Orpheum (RKO) Pictures formed in US. Hoover becomes US president. Fleming discovers penicillin.

Wall Street crash. Beginning of worldwide economic depression. Second Labour government under MacDonald.

Nazis win seats from the moderates in German election.

The viceroy and Gandhi agree Delhi Pact. Opening of world's tallest structure, the Empire State Building. Japanese invasion of Manchuria. Labour government resigns; replaced by a National Coalition under MacDonald.
Hunger marches in Britain. Landslide victory for Democrat F. D. Roosevelt in US presidential election.

Roosevelt's 'New Deal' strategies announced. Hitler becomes chancellor of Germany; National Socialist party declared only legal party. Japan withdraws from League of Nations.

Night of the Long Knives in Germany. Unrest in Spain.

20th Century Fox formed in Los Angeles. German government announces Nuremberg Laws, legitimizing persecution of Jews. Italy invades Abyssinia; League of Nations applies economic sanctions. Baldwin succeeds MacDonald as prime minister.

DATE	AUTHOR'S LIFE	LITERARY CONTEXT
1935 *cont.*		Isherwood: *Mr Norris Changes Trains.*
		Forester: *The African Queen.*
1936	Leonora's son Edward is born. PGW's elder brother Armine dies. Starts second contract with MGM. *Young Men in Spats* (stories); *Laughing Gas.* 20th Century Fox produces *Thank You, Jeeves!*, with Arthur Treacher as Jeeves. MGM adaptations of *Piccadilly Jim* and *Anything Goes* are released.	Benchley: *My Ten Years in a Quandary and How They Grew.* D. du Maurier: *Jamaica Inn.* Hay: *The Housemaster.*
1937	Parts with MGM; works on film version of *A Damsel in Distress* for RKO, starring Fred Astaire. Leaves Hollywood for Le Touquet. *Lord Emsworth and Others* (US title *The Crime Wave at Blandings* – stories); *Summer Moonshine* (first published in US; UK publication 1938).	Christie: *Death on the Nile.* American composer George Gershwin dies, aged 38. Priestley: *Time and the Conways.* Forester: *The Happy Return* (first Hornblower novel). Tolkien: *The Hobbit.* Rome: *Pins and Needles* (musical).
1938	*The Code of the Woosters.*	D. du Maurier: *Rebecca.* Greene: *Brighton Rock.* Waugh: *Scoop.* Runyon: *Take It Long.* Pritchett: *You Make Your Own Life.*
1939	Awarded a D. Litt. from the University of Oxford. *Uncle Fred in the Springtime.*	Chandler: *The Big Sleep.* Green: *Party Going.* Isherwood: *Goodbye to Berlin.* West: *The Day of the Locust.* Benson: *Trouble for Lucia.*
1940	Younger brother Dick dies of leukaemia. Unsuccessful attempts to escape the Nazi advance. Low Wood is requisitioned and PGW detained by Germans in a succession of internment camps. *Eggs, Beans and Crumpets* (stories); *Quick Service.*	Chandler: *Farewell, My Lovely.* Greene: *The Power and the Glory.* Thomas: *Portrait of the Artist as a Young Dog.* Green: *Pack My Bag: A Self-Portrait.*
1941	Released from internment and taken to Berlin; reunited with Ethel. Makes 5 broadcasts for US fans on German radio; provokes allegations of treachery in UK. Eleanor Wodehouse dies.	D. du Maurier: *Frenchman's Creek.* Coward: *Blithe Spirit* (play). Fitzgerald: *The Last Tycoon.* Kern: *Last Time I Saw Paris* (musical).

CHRONOLOGY

German troops enter Rhineland. Spanish Civil War (to 1939). Rome-Berlin Axis allies Hitler with Mussolini. Anti-Comintern Pact agreed by Germany and Japan. Abdication of Edward VIII. Pinewood Film Studios open in England.

Basque village of Guernica destroyed by German bomber planes. Chamberlain becomes prime minister. Japan invades China.

Germany annexes Austria. Munich crisis.

Nazi-Soviet Pact. Hitler invades Poland; World War II begins.

Churchill becomes prime minister. Dunkirk invasion. Fall of France. Temporary Purchase Tax imposed in UK. Battle of Britain. The Blitz. Italy joins the war as ally to Germany.

Germans invade USSR. Japanese attack Pearl Harbor; US enters war.

DATE	AUTHOR'S LIFE	LITERARY CONTEXT
1942	*Money in the Bank* (first published in US; UK publication 1946).	Waugh: *Put Out More Flags*. Chandler: *The High Window*.
1943	Leaves Germany for France with Ethel.	Rodgers and Hammerstein: *Oklahoma* (musical). Benchley: *Benchley Beside Himself*. Perelman and Weill: *One Touch of Venus* (musical). Chandler: *The Lady in the Lake*. Green: *Caught*.
1944	Leonora Cazalet dies. Major Cussen of MI5 flies to Paris to question PGW on his wartime relations with the Nazis; he is not prosecuted.	Hartley: *The Eustace and Hilda Trilogy* (to 1947). Runyon: *Runyon à la Carte*. Compton-Burnett: *Elders and Betters*.
1945		Thurber: *The Thurber Carnival*. Orwell: *Animal Farm*. Waugh: *Brideshead Revisited*. Green: *Loving*. Mitford: *The Pursuit of Love*. Priestley: *An Inspector Calls*.
1946	*Joy in the Morning* (first published in US; UK publication 1947).	Berlin: *Annie Get Your Gun* (musical). Hodgins: *Mr Blandings Builds His Dream House*. Dahl: *Over to You*. Larkin: *Jill*.
1947	Sells home in France and embarks for New York on SS *America*. *Full Moon*.	Mortimer: *Charade*.
1948	*Spring Fever*, *Don't Listen, Ladies* (play, with G. Bolton); *Uncle Dynamite*.	Greene: *The Heart of the Matter*. Perelman: *Westward Ha!* Waugh: *The Loved One*. Green: *Concluding*.
1949	Reaches settlement with US tax authorities in the Supreme Court. *The Mating Season*.	Rodgers and Hammerstein: *South Pacific* (musical). Orwell: *Nineteen Eighty-Four*. Greene: *The Third Man*. Mitford: *Love in a Cold Climate*. Smith: *I Capture the Castle*.
1950	*Nothing Serious* (stories).	Green: *Nothing*.
1951	*The Old Reliable*.	Salinger: *The Catcher in the Rye*. Greene: *The End of the Affair*. Pritchett: *Mr Beluncle*.

CHRONOLOGY

Germans reach Stalingrad. North Africa campaign; battle of El-Alamein.

Germans retreat in Russia, Africa and Italy.

Normandy landings. Liberation of Paris. Red Army reaches Belgrade and Budapest.

Unconditional surrender of Germany; Hitler commits suicide. US drops atomic bombs on Hiroshima and Nagasaki. End of World War II. United Nations founded. Death of Roosevelt; Truman becomes US president.

BBC resumes television broadcasting. Nuremberg trials. 'Iron Curtain' speech by Churchill.

The Marshall Plan to aid postwar Europe is rejected by USSR as threat to Communism. India and Pakistan gain independence.

Communist coup in Czechoslovakia. Jewish state of Israel established. Russian blockade of West Berlin. Assassination of Gandhi in India. Apartheid introduced in South Africa.

North Atlantic Treaty signed. Germany is divided into East and West. Communists win Chinese civil war.

UK formerly recognizes People's Republic of China. McCarthy 'Witch Trials' in USA. Korean War (to 1953); UN imposes trade embargo on China for its involvement on the side of Kim ll-sung.
Festival of Britain; inauguration of Royal Festival Hall in London. Wartime prime minister Winston Churchill re-elected.

P. G. WODEHOUSE

DATE	AUTHOR'S LIFE	LITERARY CONTEXT
1952	Ethel purchases new house in Basket Neck Lane, Remsenburg, Long Island. *Barmy in Wonderland* (US title *Angel Cake*); *Pigs Have Wings*.	Waugh: *Men at Arms*, first novel in the *Sword of Honour Trilogy* (to 1961). Christie: *The Mouse Trap*. Green: *Doting*.
1953	*Ring for Jeeves* (US title *Return of Jeeves*); *Performing Flea* (US title *Author! Author!* – autobiographical, with W. Townend).	Fleming: *Casino Royale*. Dahl: *Someone Like You*. Hartley: *The Go-Between*.
1954	*Bring on the Girls!* (autobiographical, with G. Bolton); *Jeeves and the Feudal Spirit* (US title *Bertie Wooster Sees It Through*).	K. Amis: *Lucky Jim*. Chandler: *The Long Goodbye*. Tolkien: *The Lord of the Rings*.
1955	Earns legal status as a US citizen.	Cecil: *Brothers in Law*. K. Amis: *That Uncertain Feeling*. Greene: *The Quiet American*.
1956	*French Leave* (with G. Bolton); *America I Like You* (first published in US; UK publication 1957 as *Over Seventy* – autobiographical).	Fleming: *Diamonds are Forever*. K. Amis: *That Uncertain Feeling*.
1957	*Something Fishy* (US title *The Butler Did It*).	Perelman: *The Road to Milltown*. Fleming: *From Russia with Love*. Spark: *The Comforters*. Christie: *4.50 From Paddington*. Hartley: *The Hireling*.
1958	*Cocktail Time*.	Chandler: *Playback*. Capote: *Breakfast at Tiffany's*.
1959	*A Few Quick Ones* (stories).	Fleming: *Goldfinger*. Böll: *Billiards at Half-Past Nine*. Southern: *The Magic Christian*. Spark: *Memento Mori*.
1960	*Jeeves in the Offing* (US title *How Right You Are, Jeeves*).	Betjeman: *Summoned by Bells*. Spark: *The Ballad of Peckham Rye*. Lee: *To Kill a Mockingbird*. Dahl: *Kiss Kiss*. Updike: *Rabbit, Run*.
1961	BBC broadcasts *An Act of Homage and Reparation* by Evelyn Waugh to celebrate PGW's 80th birthday. *Ice in the Bedroom* (US title *The Ice in the Bedroom*); *Service with a Smile* (first published in US; UK publication 1962).	Fleming: *Thunderball*. Heller: *Catch-22*. Spark: *The Prime of Miss Jean Brodie*.

CHRONOLOGY

DATE	AUTHOR'S LIFE	LITERARY CONTEXT
1962	Long-standing friend William Townend dies. Ethel undergoes successful operation for cancer. Film version of *The Girl on the Boat*, starring Norman Wisdom and Richard Briers.	Kesey: *One Flew Over the Cuckoo's Nest*. Burgess: *A Clockwork Orange*. Deighton: *The Ipcress File*.
1963	*Stiff Upper Lip, Jeeves*.	Le Carré: *The Spy Who Came in from the Cold*. Burgess: *Inside Mr Enderby*. Spark: *The Girls of Slender Means*.
1964	*Frozen Assets* (US title *Biffen's Millions*); *The Brinkmanship of Galahad Threepwood* (first published in US; UK publication 1965 as *Galahad at Blandings*).	Fleming: *Chitty Chitty Bang Bang*. Isherwood: *A Single Man*.
1965	Television series *The World of Wooster*, based on Jeeves and Wooster stories (to 1967).	Nichols: *The Sterile Cuckoo*.
1966	*Plum Pie* (stories and essays).	Deighton: *Billion-Dollar Brain*. Stoppard: *Rosencrantz and Guildenstern are Dead*.
1967	Founds the P. G. Wodehouse Animal Shelter in Remsenburg. *Company for Henry* (US title *The Purloined Paperweight*). Television mini-series *Blandings Castle* airs on BBC.	
1968	*Do Butlers Burgle Banks?*	Burgess: *Enderby Outside*.
1969	*A Pelican at Blandings* (US title *No Nudes is Good Nudes*).	The *Saturday Evening Post* ceases publication. Pritchett: *Blind Love and Other Stories*. K. Amis: *The Green Man*.
1970	*The Girl in Blue*.	Updike: *Bech: A Book*. Spark: *The Driver's Seat*.
1971	*Much Obliged, Jeeves* (US title *Jeeves and the Tie That Binds*).	Updike: *Rabbit Redux*.
1972	Invited to attend Sunday Service with President Nixon, but declines offer. *Pearls, Girls and Monty Bodkin* (US title *The Plot That Thickened*).	Stoppard: *Jumpers*.

CHRONOLOGY

HISTORICAL EVENTS

UK announces controls on illegal entry into Hong Kong from China.
Cuban missile crisis. Anglo-French agreement on construction of Concorde.

Profumo affair; prime minister Macmillan resigns. Assassination of Kennedy;
Johnson becomes president.

British and French governments agree to construct Channel Tunnel. US
Civil Rights Act prohibits discrimination in employment on basis of race or
gender. House of Commons votes to abolish death penalty for murder.
Nobel Peace Prize awarded to Martin Luther King.

Death of Winston Churchill. Civil war breaks out in Dominican Republic;
Johnson orders US intervention. Sustained bombing of targets in North
Vietnam by US aircraft. Largest recorded power failure blacks out all of
New York City.
Mao launches Cultural Revolution in China.

Labour disputes in Hong Kong erupt into violent riots against British
colonial rule. Six-Day War between Israel and Arab states. Argentinian-born
guerrilla hero Che Guevara shot dead in Bolivia.

Student unrest throughout Europe. Martin Luther King assassinated; violent
reaction throughout US. Czechoslovakia invaded by Soviet troops. Richard
Nixon elected US president.
US troops begin to withdraw from Vietnam. Astronaut Neil Armstrong
becomes first man on the moon. British troops assume responsibility for
security in Northern Ireland.

Black September conflict in Jordan (to 1971). Chilean Salvador Allende
becomes world's first democratically elected Marxist head of state.
India recognizes independence of East Pakistan as Bangladesh.

'Bloody Sunday' in Londonderry, Northern Ireland; direct rule imposed by
British government. Israeli building at Olympic Village near Munich
attacked by Arab guerrillas. Strategic Arms Limitation Treaty (SALT I)
signed by US and USSR.

DATE	AUTHOR'S LIFE	LITERARY CONTEXT
1973	*Bachelors Anonymous.*	Pynchon: *Gravity's Rainbow.* Ayckbourn: *The Norman Conquests.* M. Amis: *The Rachel Papers.*
1974	Sits for a Madame Tussaud's wax likeness. *Aunts Aren't Gentlemen* (US title *The Cat-Nappers*).	McDonald: *Fletch.* Sharpe: *Porterhouse Blue.* Le Carré: *Tinker, Tailor, Soldier, Spy.*
1975	Receives KBE. Dies aged 93 on 14 February. BBC's television series *Wodehouse Playhouse* airs, featuring recorded introductions by PGW (to 1978).	Dexter: *Last Bus to Woodstock.* McEwan: *First Love, Last Rites.*
1976		Sharpe: *Wilt.*
1977	Inauguration of P. G. Wodehouse Memorial Corner of the Dulwich College Library; the library itself is officially christened The Wodehouse Library in 1981. *Sunset at Blandings.*	Stoppard: *Every Good Boy Deserves Favour.* P. Fitzgerald: *The Golden Child.*

HISTORICAL EVENTS

Chilean president Allende and at least 2,700 others killed in coup led by General Pinochet. Energy crisis prompts state of emergency in Britain.

Coalminers hold full-scale strike in UK. Resignation of Nixon following Watergate scandal.

End of Vietnam War. USSR and Western powers sign Helsinki Accords. Civil war in Lebanon (to 1990).

Death of Chairman Mao in China. Jimmy Carter elected US president.

THE CODE OF THE
WOOSTERS

CHAPTER I

I REACHED out a hand from under the blankets, and rang the bell for Jeeves.

'Good evening, Jeeves.'

'Good morning, sir.'

This surprised me.

'Is it morning?'

'Yes, sir.'

'Are you sure? It seems very dark outside.'

'There is a fog, sir. If you will recollect, we are now in Autumn – season of mists and mellow fruitfulness.'

'Season of what?'

'Mists, sir, and mellow fruitfulness.'

'Oh? Yes. Yes, I see. Well, be that as it may, get me one of those bracers of yours, will you?'

'I have one in readiness, sir, in the ice-box.'

He shimmered out, and I sat up in bed with that rather unpleasant feeling you get sometimes that you're going to die in about five minutes. On the previous night, I had given a little dinner at the Drones to Gussie Fink-Nottle as a friendly send-off before his approaching nuptials with Madeline, only daughter of Sir Watkyn Bassett, CBE, and these things take their toll. Indeed, just before Jeeves came in, I had been dreaming that some bounder was driving spikes through my head – not just ordinary spikes, as used by Jael the wife of Heber, but red-hot ones.

He returned with the tissue-restorer. I loosed it down the hatch, and after undergoing the passing discomfort, unavoidable when you drink Jeeves's patent morning revivers, of having the top of the skull fly up to the ceiling and the eyes shoot out of their sockets and rebound from the opposite wall like racquet balls, felt better. It would have been overstating it to say that even now Bertram was back again in mid-season form, but I had at least slid into the convalescent class and was equal to a spot of conversation.

'Ha!' I said, retrieving the eyeballs and replacing them in position. 'Well, Jeeves, what goes on in the great world? Is that the paper you have there?'

'No, sir. It is some literature from the Travel Bureau. I thought that you might care to glance at it.'

'Oh?' I said. 'You did, did you?'

And there was a brief and – if that's the word I want – pregnant silence.

I suppose that when two men of iron will live in close association with one another, there are bound to be occasional clashes, and one of these had recently popped up in the Wooster home. Jeeves was trying to get me to go on a Round-The-World cruise, and I would have none of it. But in spite of my firm statements to this effect, scarcely a day passed without him bringing me a sheaf or nosegay of those illustrated folders which the Ho-for-the-open-spaces birds send out in the hope of drumming up custom. His whole attitude recalled irresistibly to the mind that of some assiduous hound who will persist in laying a dead rat on the drawing-room carpet, though repeatedly apprised by word and gesture that the market for same is sluggish or even non-existent.

'Jeeves,' I said, 'this nuisance must now cease.'

'Travel is highly educational, sir.'

'I can't do with any more education. I was full up years ago. No, Jeeves, I know what's the matter with you. That old Viking strain of yours has come out again. You yearn for the tang of the salt breezes. You see yourself walking the deck in a yachting cap. Possibly someone has been telling you about the Dancing Girls of Bali. I understand, and I sympathize. But not for me. I refuse to be decanted into any blasted ocean-going liner and lugged off round the world.'

'Very good, sir.'

He spoke with a certain what-is-it in his voice, and I could see that, if not actually disgruntled, he was far from being gruntled, so I tactfully changed the subject.

'Well, Jeeves, it was quite a satisfactory binge last night.'

'Indeed, sir?'

'Oh, most. An excellent time was had by all. Gussie sent his regards.'

'I appreciate the kind thought, sir. I trust Mr Fink-Nottle was in good spirits?'

'Extraordinarily good, considering that the sands are running out and that he will shortly have Sir Watkyn Bassett for a father-in-law. Sooner him than me, Jeeves, sooner him than me.'

I spoke with strong feeling, and I'll tell you why. A few months before, while celebrating Boat Race night, I had fallen into the clutches of the Law for trying to separate a policeman from his helmet, and after sleeping fitfully on a plank bed had been hauled up at Bosher Street next morning and fined five of the best. The magistrate who had inflicted this monstrous sentence – to the accompaniment, I may add, of some very offensive remarks from the bench – was none other than old Pop Bassett, father of Gussie's bride-to-be.

As it turned out, I was one of his last customers, for a couple of weeks later he inherited a pot of money from a distant relative and retired to the country. That, at least, was the story that had been put about. My own view was that he had got the stuff by sticking like glue to the fines. Five quid here, five quid there – you can see how it would mount up over a period of years.

'You have not forgotten that man of wrath, Jeeves? A hard case, eh?'

'Possibly Sir Watkyn is less formidable in private life, sir.'

'I doubt it. Slice him where you like, a hellhound is always a hellhound. But enough of this Bassett. Any letters today?'

'No, sir.'

'Telephone communications?'

'One, sir. From Mrs Travers.'

'Aunt Dahlia? She's back in town, then?'

'Yes, sir. She expressed a desire that you would ring her up at your earliest convenience.'

'I will do even better,' I said cordially. 'I will call in person.'

And half an hour later I was toddling up the steps of her residence and being admitted by old Seppings, her butler. Little knowing, as I crossed that threshold, that in about two shakes of a duck's tail I was to become involved in an imbroglio that would test the Wooster soul as it had seldom been tested before. I allude to the sinister affair of Gussie Fink-Nottle, Madeline Bassett, old Pop Bassett, Stiffy Byng, the Rev. H. P. ('Stinker') Pinker, the eighteenth-century cow-creamer and the small, brown, leather-covered notebook.

*

No premonition of an impending doom, however, cast a cloud on my serenity as I buzzed in. I was looking forward with bright anticipation to the coming reunion with this Dahlia – she, as I may have mentioned before, being my good and deserving aunt, not to be confused with Aunt Agatha, who eats broken bottles and wears barbed wire next to the skin. Apart from the mere intellectual pleasure of chewing the fat with her, there was the glittering prospect that I might be able to cadge an invitation to lunch. And owing to the outstanding virtuosity of Anatole, her French cook, the browsing at her trough is always of a nature to lure the gourmet.

The door of the morning room was open as I went through the hall, and I caught a glimpse of Uncle Tom messing about with his collection of old silver. For a moment I toyed with the idea of pausing to pip-pip and enquire after his indigestion, a malady to which he is extremely subject, but wiser counsels prevailed. This uncle is a bird who, sighting a nephew, is apt to buttonhole him and become a bit informative on the subject of sconces and foliation, not to mention scrolls, ribbon wreaths in high relief and gadroon borders, and it seemed to me that silence was best. I whizzed by, accordingly, with sealed lips, and headed for the library, where I had been informed that Aunt Dahlia was at the moment roosting.

I found the old flesh-and-blood up to her Marcel-wave in proof sheets. As all the world knows, she is the courteous and popular proprietress of a weekly sheet for the delicately nurtured entitled *Milady's Boudoir*. I once contributed an article to it on 'What The Well-Dressed Man Is Wearing'.

My entry caused her to come to the surface, and she greeted me with one of those cheery view-halloos which, in the days when she went in for hunting, used to make her so noticeable a figure of the Quorn, the Pytchley and other organizations for doing the British fox a bit of no good.

'Hullo, ugly,' she said. 'What brings you here?'

'I understood, aged relative, that you wished to confer with me.'

'I didn't want you to come barging in, interrupting my work. A few words on the telephone would have met the case. But I suppose some instinct told you that this was my busy day.'

'If you were wondering if I could come to lunch, have no anxiety. I shall be delighted, as always. What will Anatole be giving us?'

'He won't be giving you anything, my gay young tapeworm. I am entertaining Pomona Grindle, the novelist, to the midday meal.'

'I should be charmed to meet her.'

'Well, you're not going to. It is to be a strictly *tête-à-tête* affair. I'm trying to get a serial out of her for the *Boudoir*. No, all I wanted was to tell you to go to an antique shop in the Brompton Road — it's just past the Oratory — you can't miss it — and sneer at a cow-creamer.'

I did not get her drift. The impression I received was that of an aunt talking through the back of her neck.

'Do what to a what?'

'They've got an eighteenth-century cow-creamer there that Tom's going to buy this afternoon.'

The scales fell from my eyes.

'Oh, it's a silver whatnot, is it?'

'Yes. A sort of cream jug. Go there and ask them to show it to you, and when they do, register scorn.'

'The idea being what?'

'To sap their confidence, of course, chump. To sow doubts and misgivings in their mind and make them clip the price a bit. The cheaper he gets the thing, the better he will be pleased. And I want him to be in cheery mood, because if I succeed in signing the Grindle up for this serial, I shall be compelled to get into his ribs for a biggish sum of money. It's sinful what these best-selling women novelists want for their stuff. So pop off there without delay and shake your head at the thing.'

I am always anxious to oblige the right sort of aunt, but I was compelled to put in what Jeeves would have called a *nolle prosequi*. Those morning mixtures of his are practically magical in their effect, but even after partaking of them one does not oscillate the bean.

'I can't shake my head. Not today.'

She gazed at me with a censorious waggle of the right eyebrow.

'Oh, so that's how it is? Well, if your loathsome excesses have left you incapable of headshaking, you can at least curl your lip.'

'Oh, rather.'

'Then carry on. And draw your breath in sharply. Also try clicking the tongue. Oh, yes, and tell them you think it's Modern Dutch.'

'Why?'

'I don't know. Apparently it's something a cow-creamer ought not to be.'

She paused, and allowed her eye to roam thoughtfully over my perhaps somewhat corpse-like face.

'So you were out on the tiles last night, were you, my little chickadee? It's an extraordinary thing – every time I see you, you appear to be recovering from some debauch. Don't you ever stop drinking? How about when you are asleep?'

I rebutted the slur.

'You wrong me, relative. Except at times of special revelry, I am exceedingly moderate in my potations. A brace of cocktails, a glass of wine at dinner and possibly a liqueur with the coffee – that is Bertram Wooster. But last night I gave a small bachelor binge for Gussie Fink-Nottle.'

'You did, did you?' She laughed – a bit louder than I could have wished in my frail state of health, but then she is always a woman who tends to bring plaster falling from the ceiling when amused. 'Spink-Bottle, eh? Bless his heart! How was the old newt-fancier?'

'Pretty roguish.'

'Did he make a speech at this orgy of yours?'

'Yes. I was astounded. I was all prepared for a blushing refusal. But no. We drank his health, and he rose to his feet as cool as some cucumbers, as Anatole would say, and held us spellbound.'

'Tight as an owl, I suppose?'

'On the contrary. Offensively sober.'

'Well, that's a nice change.'

We fell into a thoughtful silence. We were musing on the summer afternoon down at her place in Worcestershire when Gussie, circumstances having so ordered themselves as to render him full to the back teeth with the right stuff, had addressed the young scholars of Market Snodsbury Grammar School on the occasion of their annual prize giving.

A thing I never know, when I'm starting out to tell a story about a chap I've told a story about before, is how much explanation to bung in at the outset. It's a problem you've got to look at from every angle. I mean to say, in the present case, if I take it for granted that my public knows all about Gussie Fink-Nottle and just breeze ahead, those publicans who weren't hanging on my lips the first time are apt to be fogged. Whereas if before kicking off I give about eight volumes of the man's life and history, other bimbos who were so hanging will stifle yawns and murmur 'Old stuff. Get on with it.'

I suppose the only thing to do is to put the salient facts as briefly as possible in the possession of the first gang, waving an apologetic hand at the second gang the while, to indicate that they had better let their attention wander for a minute or two and that I will be with them shortly.

This Gussie, then, was a fish-faced pal of mine who, on reaching man's estate, had buried himself in the country and devoted himself entirely to the study of newts, keeping the little chaps in a glass tank and observing their habits with a sedulous eye. A confirmed recluse you would have called him, if you had happened to know the word, and you would have been right. By all the rulings of the form book, a less promising prospect for the whispering of tender words into shell-like ears and the subsequent purchase of platinum ring and licence for wedding it would have seemed impossible to discover in a month of Sundays.

But Love will find a way. Meeting Madeline Bassett one day and falling for her like a ton of bricks, he had emerged from his retirement and started to woo, and after numerous vicissitudes had clicked and was slated at no distant date to don the spongebag trousers and gardenia for buttonhole and walk up the aisle with the ghastly girl.

I call her a ghastly girl because she was a ghastly girl. The Woosters are chivalrous, but they can speak their minds. A droopy, soupy, sentimental exhibit, with melting eyes and a cooing voice and the most extraordinary views on such things as stars and rabbits. I remember her telling me once that rabbits were gnomes in attendance on the Fairy Queen and that the stars were God's daisy chain. Perfect rot, of course. They're nothing of the sort.

Aunt Dahlia emitted a low, rumbling chuckle, for that speech of Gussie's down at Market Snodsbury has always been one of her happiest memories.

'Good old Spink-Bottle! Where is he now?'

'Staying at the Bassett's father's place – Totleigh Towers, Totleigh-in-the-Wold, Glos. He went back there this morning. They're having the wedding at the local church.'

'Are you going to it?'

'Definitely no.'

'No, I suppose it would be too painful for you. You being in love with the girl.'

I stared.

'In love? With a female who thinks that every time a fairy blows its wee nose a baby is born?'

'Well, you were certainly engaged to her once.'

'For about five minutes, yes, and through no fault of my own. My dear old relative,' I said, nettled, 'you are perfectly well aware of the inside facts of that frightful affair.'

I winced. It was an incident in my career on which I did not care to dwell. Briefly, what had occurred was this. His nerve sapped by long association with newts, Gussie had shrunk from pleading his cause with Madeline Bassett, and had asked me to plead it for him. And when I did so, the fat-headed girl thought I was pleading mine. With the result that when, after that exhibition of his at the prize giving, she handed Gussie the temporary mitten, she had attached herself to me, and I had had no option but to take the rap. I mean to say, if a girl has got it into her nut that a fellow loves her, and comes and tells him that she is returning her *fiancé* to store and is now prepared to sign up with him, what can a chap do?

Mercifully, things had been straightened out at the eleventh hour by a reconciliation between the two pills, but the thought of my peril was one at which I still shuddered. I wasn't going to feel really easy in my mind till the parson had said: 'Wilt thou, Augustus?' and Gussie had whispered a shy 'Yes.'

'Well, if it is of any interest to you,' said Aunt Dahlia, 'I am not proposing to attend that wedding myself. I disapprove of Sir Watkyn Bassett, and don't think he ought to be encouraged. There's one of the boys, if you want one!'

'You know the old crumb, then?' I said, rather surprised, though of course it bore out what I often say – viz. that it's a small world.

'Yes, I know him. He's a friend of Tom's. They both collect old silver and snarl at one another like wolves about it all the time.

We had him staying at Brinkley last month. And would you care to hear how he repaid me for all the loving care I lavished on him while he was my guest? Sneaked round behind my back and tried to steal Anatole!'

'No!'

'That's what he did. Fortunately, Anatole proved staunch – after I had doubled his wages.'

'Double them again,' I said earnestly. 'Keep on doubling them. Pour out money like water rather than lose that superb master of the roasts and hashes.'

I was visibly affected. The thought of Anatole, that peerless disher-up, coming within an ace of ceasing to operate at Brinkley Court, where I could always enjoy his output by inviting myself for a visit, and going off to serve under old Bassett, the last person in the world likely to set out a knife and fork for Bertram, had stirred me profoundly.

'Yes,' said Aunt Dahlia, her eye smouldering as she brooded on the frightful thing, 'that's the sort of hornswoggling high-binder Sir Watkyn Bassett is. You had better warn Spink-Bottle to watch out on the wedding day. The slightest relaxation of vigilance, and the old thug will probably get away with his tie-pin in the vestry. And now,' she said, reaching out for what had the appearance of being a thoughtful essay on the care of the baby in sickness and in health, 'push off. I've got about six tons of proofs to correct. Oh, and give this to Jeeves, when you see him. It's the "Husbands' Corner" article. It's full of deep stuff about braid on the side of men's dress trousers, and I'd like him to vet it. For all I know, it may be Red propaganda. And I can rely on you not to bungle that job? Tell me in your own words what it is you're supposed to do.'

'Go to antique shop –'

'– in the Brompton Road –'

'– in, as you say, the Brompton Road. Ask to see cow-creamer –'

'– and sneer. Right. Buzz along. The door is behind you.'

It was with a light heart that I went out into the street and hailed a passing barouche. Many men, no doubt, might have been a bit sick at having their morning cut into in this fashion, but I was conscious only of pleasure at the thought that I had it in my power to perform this little act of kindness. Scratch Bertram Wooster, I often say, and you find a Boy Scout.

The antique shop in the Brompton Road proved, as fore-shadowed, to be an antique shop in the Brompton Road and, like all antique shops except the swanky ones in the Bond Street neighbourhood, dingy outside and dark and smelly within. I don't know why it is, but the proprietors of these establishments always seem to be cooking some sort of stew in the back room.

'I say,' I began, entering; then paused as I perceived that the bloke in charge was attending to two other customers.

'Oh, sorry,' I was about to add, to convey the idea that I had horned in inadvertently, when the words froze on my lips.

Quite a slab of misty fruitfulness had drifted into the emporium, obscuring the view, but in spite of the poor light I was able to note that the smaller and elder of these two customers was no stranger to me.

It was old Pop Bassett in person. Himself. Not a picture.

There is a tough, bulldog strain in the Woosters which has often caused comment. It came out in me now. A weaker man, no doubt, would have tiptoed from the scene and headed for the horizon, but I stood firm. After all, I felt, the dead past was the dead past. By forking out that fiver, I had paid my debt to Society and had nothing to fear from this shrimp-faced son of a whatnot. So I remained where I was, giving him the surreptitious once-over.

My entry had caused him to turn and shoot a quick look at me, and at intervals since then he had been peering at me side-ways. It was only a question of time, I felt, before the hidden chord in his memory would be touched and he would realize that the slight, distinguished-looking figure leaning on its umbrella in the background was an old acquaintance. And now it was plain that he was hep. The bird in charge of the shop had pottered off into an inner room, and he came across to where I stood, giving me the up-and-down through his wind-shields.

'Hullo, hullo,' he said. 'I know you, young man. I never forget a face. You came up before me once.'

I bowed slightly.

'But not twice. Good! Learned your lesson, eh? Going straight now? Capital. Now, let me see, what was it? Don't tell me. It's coming back. Of course, yes. Bag-snatching.'

'No, no. It was –'

'Bag-snatching,' he repeated firmly. 'I remember it distinctly. Still, it's all past and done with now, eh? We have turned over a new leaf, have we not? Splendid. Roderick, come over here. This is most interesting.'

His buddy, who had been examining a salver, put it down and joined the party.

He was, as I had already been able to perceive, a breath-taking cove. About seven feet in height, and swathed in a plaid ulster which made him look about six feet across, he caught the eye and arrested it. It was as if Nature had intended to make a gorilla, and had changed its mind at the last moment.

But it wasn't merely the sheer expanse of the bird that impressed. Close to, what you noticed more was his face, which was square and powerful and slightly moustached towards the centre. His gaze was keen and piercing. I don't know if you have even seen those pictures in the papers of Dictators with tilted chins and blazing eyes, inflaming the populace with fiery words on the occasion of the opening of a new skittle alley, but that was what he reminded me of.

'Roderick,' said old Bassett, 'I want you to meet this fellow. Here is a case which illustrates exactly what I have so often maintained – that prison life does not degrade, that it does not warp the character and prevent a man rising on stepping-stones of his dead self to higher things.'

I recognized the gag – one of Jeeves's – and wondered where he could have heard it.

'Look at this chap. I gave him three months not long ago for snatching bags at railway stations, and it is quite evident that his term in jail has had the most excellent effect on him. He has reformed.'

'Oh, yes?' said the Dictator.

Granted that it wasn't quite 'Oh, yeah?' I still didn't like the way he spoke. He was looking at me with a nasty sort of supercilious expression. I remember thinking that he would have been the ideal man to sneer at a cow-creamer.

'What makes you think he has reformed?'

'Of course he has reformed. Look at him. Well groomed, well dressed, a decent member of Society. What his present walk in life is, I do not know, but it is perfectly obvious that he is no longer stealing bags. What are you doing now, young man?'

'Stealing umbrellas, apparently,' said the Dictator. 'I notice he's got yours.'

And I was on the point of denying the accusation hotly – I had, indeed, already opened my lips to do so – when there suddenly struck me like a blow on the upper maxillary from a sock stuffed with wet sand the realization that there was a lot in it.

I mean to say, I remembered now that I had come out without my umbrella, and yet here I was, beyond any question of doubt, umbrellaed to the gills. What had caused me to take up the one that had been leaning against a seventeenth-century chair, I cannot say, unless it was the primeval instinct which makes a man without an umbrella reach out for the nearest one in sight, like a flower groping toward the sun.

A manly apology seemed in order. I made it as the blunt instrument changed hands.

'I say, I'm most frightfully sorry.'

Old Bassett said he was, too – sorry and disappointed. He said it was this sort of thing that made a man sick at heart.

The Dictator had to shove his oar in. He asked if he should call a policeman, and old Bassett's eyes gleamed for a moment. Being a magistrate makes you love the idea of calling policemen. It's like a tiger tasting blood. But he shook his head.

'No, Roderick. I couldn't. Not today – the happiest day of my life.'

The Dictator pursed his lips, as if feeling that the better the day, the better the deed.

'But listen,' I bleated, 'it was a mistake.'

'Ha!' said the Dictator.

'I thought that umbrella was mine.'

'That,' said old Bassett, 'is the fundamental trouble with you, my man. You are totally unable to distinguish between *meum* and *tuum*. Well, I am not going to have you arrested this time, but I advise you to be very careful. Come, Roderick.'

They biffed out, the Dictator pausing at the door to give me another look and say 'Ha!' again.

A most unnerving experience all this had been for a man of sensibility, as you may imagine, and my immediate reaction was a disposition to give Aunt Dahlia's commission the miss-in-balk and return to the flat and get outside another of Jeeves's pick-me-ups. You know how harts pant for cooling streams when heated in the chase. Very much that sort of thing. I realized now what madness it had been to go into the streets of London with only one of them under my belt, and I was on the point of melting away and going back to the fountain head, when the proprietor of the shop emerged from the inner room, accompanied by a rich smell of stew and a sandy cat, and enquired what he could do for me. And so, the subject having come up, I said that I understood that he had an eighteenth-century cow-creamer for sale.

He shook his head. He was a rather mildewed bird of gloomy aspect, almost entirely concealed behind a cascade of white whiskers.

'You're too late. It's promised to a customer.'

'Name of Travers?'

'Ah.'

'Then that's all right. Learn, O thou of unshuffled features and agreeable disposition,' I said, for one likes to be civil, 'that the above Travers is my uncle. He sent me here to have a look at the thing. So dig it out, will you? I expect it's rotten.'

'It's a beautiful cow-creamer.'

'Ha!' I said, borrowing a bit of the Dictator's stuff. 'That's what you think. We shall see.'

I don't mind confessing that I'm not much of a lad for old silver, and though I have never pained him by actually telling him so, I have always felt that Uncle Tom's fondness for it is evidence of a goofiness which he would do well to watch and check before it spreads. So I wasn't expecting the heart to leap up to any great extent at the sight of this exhibit. But when the whiskered ancient pottered off into the shadows and came back with the thing, I scarcely knew whether to laugh or weep. The thought of an uncle paying hard cash for such an object got right in amongst me.

It was a silver cow. But when I say 'cow', don't go running away with the idea of some decent, self-respecting cudster such as you may observe loading grass into itself in the nearest meadow. This was a sinister, leering, Underworld sort of animal, the kind that would spit out of the side of its mouth for twopence. It was about four inches high and six long. Its back opened on a hinge. Its tail was arched, so that the tip touched the spine – thus, I suppose, affording a handle for the cream-lover to grasp. The sight of it seemed to take me into a different and dreadful world.

It was, consequently, an easy task for me to carry out the programme indicated by Aunt Dahlia. I curled the lip and clicked the tongue, all in one movement. I also drew in the breath sharply. The whole effect was that of a man absolutely out of sympathy with this cow-creamer, and I saw the mildewed cove start, as if he had been wounded in a tender spot.

'Oh, tut, tut, tut!' I said, 'Oh, dear, dear, dear! Oh, no, no, no, no, no! I don't think much of this,' I said, curling and clicking freely. 'All wrong.'

'All wrong?'

'All wrong. Modern Dutch.'

'Modern Dutch?' He may have frothed at the mouth, or he may not. I couldn't be sure. But the agony of spirit was obviously intense. 'What do you mean, Modern Dutch? It's eighteenth-century English. Look at the hallmark.'

'I can't see any hallmark.'

'Are you blind? Here, take it outside in the street. It's lighter there.'

'Right ho,' I said, and started for the door, sauntering at first in a languid sort of way, like a connoisseur a bit bored at having his time wasted.

I say 'at first', because I had only taken a couple of steps when I tripped over the cat, and you can't combine tripping over cats with languid sauntering. Shifting abruptly into high, I shot out of the door like someone wanted by the police making for the car after a smash-and-grab raid. The cow-creamer flew from my hands, and it was a lucky thing that I happened to barge into a fellow citizen outside, or I should have taken a toss in the gutter.

Well, not absolutely lucky, as a matter of fact, for it turned out to be Sir Watkyn Bassett. He stood there goggling at me with horror and indignation behind the pince-nez, and you could almost see him totting up the score on his fingers. First, bag-snatching, I mean to say; then umbrella-pinching; and now this. His whole demeanour was that of a man confronted with the last straw.

'Call a policeman, Roderick!' he cried, skipping like the high hills.

The Dictator sprang to the task.

'Police!' he bawled.

'Police!' yipped old Bassett, up in the tenor clef.

'Police!' roared the Dictator, taking the bass.

And a moment later something large loomed up in the fog and said: 'What's all this?'

Well, I dare say I could have explained everything, if I had stuck around and gone into it, but I didn't want to stick around and go into it. Side-stepping nimbly, I picked up the feet and was gone like the wind. A voice shouted 'Stop!' but of course I didn't. Stop, I mean to say! Of all the damn silly ideas. I legged it down byways and along side streets, and eventually fetched up somewhere in the neighbourhood of Sloane Square. There I got aboard a cab and started back to civilization.

My original intention was to drive to the Drones and get a bite of lunch there, but I hadn't gone far when I realized that I wasn't equal to it. I yield to no man in my appreciation of the Drones Club...its sparkling conversation, its camaraderie, its atmosphere redolent of all that is best and brightest in the metropolis...but there would, I knew, be a goodish bit of bread thrown hither and thither at its luncheon table, and I was in no vein to cope with flying bread. Changing my strategy in a flash, I told the man to take me to the nearest Turkish bath.

It is always my practice to linger over a Turkish b., and it was consequently getting late by the time I returned to the flat. I had managed to put in two or three hours' sleep in my cubicle, and that, taken in conjunction with the healing flow of persp. in the hot room and the plunge into the icy tank, had brought the roses back to my cheeks to no little extent. It was, indeed, practically with a merry tra-la-la on my lips that I latchkeyed my way in and made for the sitting room.

And the next moment my fizziness was turned off at the main by the sight of a pile of telegrams on the table.

CHAPTER 2

I DON'T know if you were among the gang that followed the narrative of my earlier adventures with Gussie Fink-Nottle – you may have been one of those who didn't happen to get around to it – but if you were you will recall that the dirty work on that occasion started with a tidal wave of telegrams, and you will not be surprised to learn that I found myself eyeing this mound of envelopes askance. Ever since then, telegrams in any quantity have always seemed to me to spell trouble.

I had had the idea at first glance that there were about twenty of the beastly things, but a closer scrutiny revealed only three. They had all been despatched from Totleigh-in-the-Wold, and they all bore the same signature.

They ran as follows:

The first:

> Wooster,
> Berkeley Mansions,
> Berkeley Square,
> London.
> Come immediately. Serious rift Madeline and self. Reply.
> *Gussie*

The second:

> Surprised receive no answer my telegram saying Come immediately serious rift Madeline and self. Reply.
> *Gussie*

And the third:

> I say, Bertie, why don't you answer my telegrams? Sent you two today saying Come immediately serious rift Madeline and self. Unless you come earliest possible moment prepared lend every effort effect reconciliation, wedding will be broken off. Reply.
> *Gussie*

I have said that that sojourn of mine in the T. bath had done much to re-establish the *mens sana in corpore* whatnot. Perusal of these frightful communications brought about an instant relapse. My misgivings, I saw, had been well founded. Something had whispered to me on seeing those bally envelopes that here we were again, and here we were.

The sound of the familiar footsteps had brought Jeeves floating out from the back premises. A glance was enough to tell him that all was not well with ye employer.

'Are you ill, sir?' he enquired solicitously.

I sank into a c. and passed an agitated h. over the b.

'Not ill, Jeeves, but all of a twitter. Read these.'

He ran his eye over the dossier, then transferred it to mine, and I could read in it the respectful anxiety he was feeling for the well-being of the young seigneur.

'Most disturbing, sir.'

His voice was grave. I could see that he hadn't missed the gist. The sinister import of those telegrams was as clear to him as it was to me.

We do not, of course, discuss the matter, for to do so would rather come under the head of speaking lightly of a woman's name, but Jeeves is in full possession of the facts relating to the Bassett–Wooster mix-up and thoroughly cognizant of the peril which threatens me from that quarter. There was no need to explain to him why I now lighted a feverish cigarette and hitched the lower jaw up with a visible effort.

'What do you suppose has happened, Jeeves?'

'It is difficult to hazard a conjecture, sir.'

'The wedding may be scratched, he says. Why? That is what I ask myself.'

'Yes, sir.'

'And I have no doubt that that is what you ask yourself?'

'Yes, sir.'

'Deep waters, Jeeves.'

'Extremely deep, sir.'

'The only thing we can say with any certainty is that in some way – how, we shall presumably learn later – Gussie has made an ass of himself again.'

I mused on Augustus Fink-Nottle for a moment, recalling how he had always stood by himself in the chump class. The best judges had been saying it for years. Why, at our private school, where I had first met him, he had been known as 'Fat-head', and that was in competition with fellows like Bingo Little, Freddie Widgeon and myself.

'What shall I do, Jeeves?'

'I think it would be best to proceed to Totleigh Towers, sir.'

'But how can I? Old Bassett would sling me out the moment I arrived.'

'Possibly if you were to telegraph to Mr Fink-Nottle, sir, explaining your difficulty, he might have some solution to suggest.'

This seemed sound. I hastened out to the post office, and wired as follows:

> Fink-Nottle,
>   Totleigh Towers,
>   Totleigh-in-the-Wold.
> Yes, that's all very well. You say come here immediately, but how dickens can I? You don't understand relations between Pop Bassett and self. These not such as to make him welcome visit Bertram. Would inevitably hurl out on ear and set dogs on. Useless suggest putting on false whiskers and pretending be fellow come inspect drains, as old blighter familiar with features and would instantly detect imposture. What is to be done? What has happened? Why serious rift? What serious rift? How do you mean wedding broken off? Why dickens? What have you been doing to the girl? Reply.
>
>   *Bertie*

The answer to this came during dinner:

> Wooster,
>   Berkeley Mansions,
>   Berkeley Square,
>   London.
> See difficulty, but think can work it. In spite strained relations, still speaking terms Madeline. Am telling her have received urgent letter from you pleading be allowed come here. Expect invitation shortly.
>
>   *Gussie*

And on the morrow, after a tossing-on-pillow night, I received a bag of three.

The first ran:

> Have worked it. Invitation dispatched. When you come, will you bring book entitled *My Friends The Newts* by Loretta Peabody published Popgood and Grooly get any bookshop.
>
> *Gussie*

The second:

> Bertie, you old ass, I hear you are coming here. Delighted, as something very important want you do for me.
>
> *Stiffy*

The third:

> Please come here if you wish, but, oh Bertie, is this wise? Will not it cause you needless pain seeing me? Surely merely twisting knife wound.
>
> *Madeline*

Jeeves was bringing me the morning cup of tea when I read these missives, and I handed them to him in silence. He read them in same. I was able to imbibe about a fluid ounce of the hot and strengthening before he spoke.

'I think that we should start at once, sir.'

'I suppose so.'

'I will pack immediately. Would you wish me to call Mrs Travers on the telephone?'

'Why?'

'She has rung up several times this morning.'

'Oh? Then perhaps you had better give her a buzz.'

'I think it will not be necessary, sir. I fancy that this would be the lady now.'

A long and sustained peal had sounded from the front door, as if an aunt had put her thumb on the button and kept it there. Jeeves left the presence, and a moment later it was plain that his intuition had not deceived him. A booming voice rolled through the flat, the voice which once, when announcing the advent of a fox in their vicinity, had been wont to cause members of the Quorn and Pytchley to clutch their hats and bound in their saddles.

'Isn't that young hound awake yet, Jeeves?...Oh, there you are.'

Aunt Dahlia charged across the threshold.

At all times and on all occasions, owing to years of fox-chivvying in every kind of weather, this relative has a fairly purple face, but one noted now an even deeper mauve than usual. The breath came jerkily, and the eyes gleamed with a goofy light. A man with far less penetration than Bertram Wooster would have been able to divine that there before him stood an aunt who had got the pip about something.

It was evident that information which she yearned to uncork was bubbling within her, but she postponed letting it go for a moment in order to reproach me for being in bed at such an hour. Sunk, as she termed it in her forthright way, in hoggish slumber.

'Not sunk in hoggish slumber,' I corrected. 'I've been awake some little time. As a matter of fact, I was just about to partake of the morning meal. You will join me, I hope? Bacon and eggs may be taken as read, but say the word and we can do you a couple of kippers.'

She snorted with a sudden violence which twenty-four hours earlier would have unmanned me completely. Even in my present tolerably robust condition, it affected me rather like one of those gas explosions which slay six.

'Eggs! Kippers! What I want is a brandy and soda. Tell Jeeves to mix me one. And if he forgets to put in the soda, it will be all right with me. Bertie, a frightful thing has happened.'

'Push along into the dining saloon, my fluttering old aspen,' I said. 'We shall not be interrupted there. Jeeves will want to come in here to pack.'

'Are you off somewhere?'

'Totleigh Towers. I have had a most disturbing –'

'Totleigh Towers? Well, I'm dashed! That's just where I came to tell you you had jolly well got to go immediately.'

'Eh?'

'Matter of life and death.'

'How do you mean?'

'You'll soon see, when I've explained.'

'Then come along to the dining room and explain at your earliest convenience.'

'Now then, my dear old mysterious hinter,' I said, when Jeeves had brought the foodstuffs and withdrawn, 'tell me all.'

For an instant, there was silence, broken only by the musical sound of an aunt drinking brandy and soda and self lowering a cup of coffee. Then she put down her beaker, and drew a deep breath.

'Bertie,' she said, 'I wish to begin by saying a few words about Sir Watkyn Bassett, CBE. May greenfly attack his roses. May his cook get tight on the night of the big dinner party. May all his hens get the staggers.'

'Does he keep hens?' I said, putting a point.

'May his cistern start leaking, and may white ants, if there are any in England, gnaw away the foundations of Totleigh Towers. And when he walks up the aisle with his daughter Madeline, to give her away to that ass Spink-Bottle, may he get a sneezing fit and find that he has come out without a pocket handkerchief.'

She paused, and it seemed to me that all this, while spirited stuff, was not germane to the issue.

'Quite,' I said. 'I agree with you *in toto*. But what has he done?'

'I will tell you. You remember that cow-creamer?'

I dug into a fried egg, quivering a little.

'Remember it? I shall never forget it. You will scarcely believe this, Aunt Dahlia, but when I got to the shop, who should be there by the most amazing coincidence but this same Bassett —'

'It wasn't a coincidence. He had gone there to have a look at the thing, to see if it was all Tom had said it was. For — can you imagine such lunacy, Bertie? — that chump of an uncle of yours had told the man about it. He might have known that the fiend would hatch some devilish plot for his undoing. And he did. Tom lunched with Sir Watkyn Bassett at the latter's club yesterday. On the bill of fare was a cold lobster, and this Machiavelli sicked him on to it.'

I looked at her incredulously.

'You aren't going to tell me,' I said, astounded, for I was familiar with the intensely delicate and finely poised mechanism of his tummy, 'that Uncle Tom ate lobster? After what happened last Christmas?'

'At this man's instigation, he appears to have eaten not only pounds of lobster, but forests of sliced cucumber as well. According to his story, which he was able to tell me this morning — he could only groan when he came home yesterday — he resisted at first. He was strong and resolute. But then circumstances were too much for him. Bassett's club, apparently, is one of those clubs where they have the cold dishes on a table in the middle of the room, so placed that wherever you sit you can't help seeing them.'

I nodded.

'They do at the Drones, too. Catsmeat Potter-Pirbright once hit the game pie from the far window six times with six consecutive rolls.'

'That was what caused poor old Tom's downfall. Bassett's lobster sales-talk he might have been strong enough to ignore, but the sight of the thing was too much for him. He yielded, tucked in like a starving Eskimo, and at six o'clock I got a call from the hall porter, asking me if I would send the car round to fetch away the remains, which had been discovered by the page boy writhing in a corner of the library. He arrived half an hour later, calling weakly for bicarbonate of soda. Bicarbonate of soda, my foot!' said Aunt Dahlia, with a bitter, mirthless laugh. 'He had to have two doctors and a stomach-pump.'

'And in the meantime –?' I said, for I could see whither the tale was tending.

'And in the meantime, of course, the fiend Bassett had nipped down and bought the cow-creamer. The man had promised to hold it for Tom till three o'clock, but naturally when three o'clock came and he didn't turn up and there was another customer clamouring for the thing, he let it go. So there you are. Bassett has the cow-creamer, and took it down to Totleigh last night.'

It was a sad story, of course, and one that bore out what I had so often felt about Pop Bassett – to wit, that a magistrate who could nick a fellow for five pounds, when a mere reprimand would more than have met the case, was capable of anything, but I couldn't see what she thought there was to be done about it. The whole situation seemed to me essentially one of those where you just clench the hands and roll the eyes mutely up to heaven and then start a new life and try to forget. I said as much, while marmalading a slice of toast.

She gazed at me in silence for a moment.

'Oh? So that's how you feel, is it?'

'I do, yes.'

'You admit, I hope, that by every moral law that cow-creamer belongs to Tom?'

'Oh, emphatically.'

'But you would take this foul outrage lying down? You would allow this stick-up man to get away with the swag? Confronted with the spectacle of as raw a bit of underhanded skulduggery as has ever been perpetrated in a civilized country, you would just sit tight and say "Well, well!" and do nothing?'

I weighed this.

'Possibly not "Well, well!" I concede that the situation is one that calls for the strongest comment. But I wouldn't do anything.'

'Well, I'm going to do something. I'm going to pinch the damn thing.'

I started at her, astounded. I uttered no verbal rebuke, but there was a distinct 'Tut, tut!' in my gaze. Even though the provocation was, I admitted, severe, I could not approve of these strong-arm methods. And I was about to awaken her dormant conscience by asking her gently what the Quorn would think of these goings-on – or, for the matter of that, the Pytchley – when she added:

'Or, rather, you are!'

I had just lighted a cigarette as she spoke these words, and so, according to what they say in the advertisement, ought to have been nonchalant. But it must have been the wrong sort of cigarette, for I shot out of my chair as if somebody had shoved a bradawl through the seat.

'Who, me?'

'That's right. See how it all fits in. You're going to stay at Totleigh. You will have a hundred excellent opportunities of getting your hooks on the thing –'

'But, dash it!'

'– and I must have it, because otherwise I shall never be able to dig a cheque out of Tom for that Pomona Grindle serial. He simply won't be in the mood. And I signed the old girl up yesterday at a fabulous price, half the sum agreed upon to be paid in advance a week from current date. So snap into it, my lad. I can't see what you're making all this heavy weather about. It doesn't seem to me much to do for a loved aunt.'

'It seems to me a dashed lot to do for a loved aunt, and I'm jolly well not going to dream –'

'Oh, yes you are, because you know what will happen, if you don't.' She paused significantly. 'You follow me, Watson?'

I was silent. She had no need to tell me what she meant. This was not the first time she had displayed the velvet hand beneath the iron glove – or, rather, the other way about – in this manner.

For this ruthless relative has one all-powerful weapon which she holds constantly over my head like the sword of – of who was the chap? – Jeeves would know – and by means of which she can always bend me to her will – viz. the threat that if I don't kick in she will bar me from her board and wipe Anatole's cooking from my lips. I shall not lightly forget the time when she placed sanctions on me for a whole month – right in the middle of the pheasant season, when this superman is at his incomparable best.

I made one last attempt to reason with her.

'But why does Uncle Tom want his frightful cow-creamer? It's a ghastly object. He would be far better without it.'

'He doesn't think so. Well, there it is. Perform this simple, easy task for me, or guests at my dinner table will soon be saying: "Why is it that we never seem to see Bertie Wooster here any more?" Bless my soul, what an amazing lunch that was that Anatole gave us yesterday! "Superb" is the only word. I don't wonder you're fond of his cooking. As you sometimes say, it melts in the mouth.'

I eyed her sternly.

'Aunt Dahlia, this is blackmail!'

'Yes, isn't it?' she said, and beetled off.

I resumed my seat, and ate a moody slice of cold bacon.

Jeeves entered.

'The bags are packed, sir.'

'Very good, Jeeves,' I said. 'Then let us be starting.'

'Man and boy, Jeeves,' I said, breaking a thoughtful silence which had lasted for about eighty-seven miles, 'I have been in some tough spots in my time, but this one wins the mottled oyster.'

We were bowling along in the two-seater on our way to Totleigh Towers, self at the wheel, Jeeves at my side, the personal effects in the dicky. We had got off round about eleven-thirty, and the genial afternoon was now at its juiciest. It was one of those crisp, sunny, bracing days with a pleasant tang in the air, and had circumstances been different from what they were, I should no doubt have been feeling at the peak of my form, chatting gaily, waving to passing rustics, possibly even singing some light snatch.

Unfortunately, however, if there was one thing circumstances weren't, it was different from what they were, and there was no suspicion of a song on the lips. The more I thought of what lay before me at these bally Towers, the bowed-downer did the heart become.

'The mottled oyster,' I repeated.

'Sir?'

I frowned. The man was being discreet, and this was no time for discretion.

'Don't pretend you don't know all about it, Jeeves,' I said coldly. 'You were in the next room throughout my interview with Aunt Dahlia, and her remarks must have been audible in Piccadilly.'

He dropped the mask.

'Well, yes, sir, I must confess that I did gather the substance of the conversation.'

'Very well, then. You agree with me that the situation is a lulu?'

'Certainly a somewhat sharp crisis in your affairs would appear to have been precipitated, sir.'

I drove on, brooding.

'If I had my life to live again, Jeeves, I would start it as an orphan without any aunts. Don't they put aunts in Turkey in sacks and drop them in the Bosphorus?'

'Odalisques, sir, I understand. Not aunts.'

'Well, why not aunts? Look at the trouble they cause in the world. I tell you, Jeeves, and you may quote me as saying this – behind every poor, innocent, harmless blighter who is going down for the first time in the soup, you will find, if you look carefully enough, the aunt who shoved him into it.'

'There is much in what you say, sir.'

'It is no use telling me that there are bad aunts and good aunts. At the core, they are all alike. Sooner or later, out pops the cloven hoof. Consider this Dahlia, Jeeves. As sound an egg as ever cursed a foxhound for chasing a rabbit, I have always considered her. And she goes and hands me an assignment like this. Wooster, the pincher of policemen's helmets, we know. We are familiar with Wooster, the supposed bag-snatcher. But it was left for this aunt to present to the world a Wooster who goes to the houses of retired magistrates and, while eating their bread and salt, swipes their cow-creamers. Faugh!' I said, for I was a good deal overwrought.

'Most disturbing, sir.'

'I wonder how old Bassett will receive me, Jeeves.'

'It will be interesting to observe his reactions, sir.'

'He can't very well throw me out, I suppose, Miss Bassett having invited me?'

'No sir.'

'On the other hand, he can – and I think he will – look at me over the top of his pince-nez and make rummy sniffing noises. The prospect is not an agreeable one.'

'No, sir.'

'I mean to say, even if this cow-creamer thing had not come up, conditions would be sticky.'

'Yes, sir. Might I venture to enquire if it is your intention to endeavour to carry out Mrs Travers's wishes?'

You can't fling the hands up in a passionate gesture when you are driving a car at fifty miles an hour. Otherwise, I should have done so.

'That is the problem which is torturing me, Jeeves. I can't make up my mind. You remember that fellow you've mentioned to me once or twice, who let something wait upon something? You know who I mean – the cat chap.'

'Macbeth, sir, a character in a play of that name by the late William Shakespeare. He was described as letting "I dare not" wait upon "I would", like the poor cat i' th' adage.'

'Well, that's how it is with me. I wobble, and I vacillate – if that's the word?'

'Perfectly correct, sir.'

'I think of being barred from those menus of Anatole's, and I say to myself that I will take a pop. Then I reflect that my name at Totleigh Towers is already mud and that old Bassett is firmly convinced that I am a combination of Raffles and a pea-and-thimble man and steal everything I come upon that isn't nailed down –'

'Sir?'

'Didn't I tell you about that? I had another encounter with him yesterday, the worst to date. He now looks upon me as the dregs of the criminal world – if not Public Enemy Number One, certainly Number Two or Three.'

I informed him briefly of what had occurred, and conceive my emotion when I saw that he appeared to be finding something

humorous in the recital. Jeeves does not often smile, but now a
distinct simper had begun to wreathe his lips.

'A laughable misunderstanding, sir.'

'Laughable, Jeeves?'

He saw that his mirth had been ill-timed. He reassembled the
features, ironing out the smile.

'I beg your pardon, sir. I should have said "disturbing".'

'Quite.'

'It must have been exceedingly trying, meeting Sir Watkyn in
such circumstances.'

'Yes, and it's going to be a dashed sight more trying if he
catches me pinching his cow-creamer. I keep seeing a vision of
him doing it.'

'I quite understand, sir. And thus the native hue of resolution is
sicklied o'er with the pale cast of thought, and enterprises of great
pitch and moment in this regard their currents turn awry and lose
the name of action.'

'Exactly. You take the words out of my mouth.'

I drove on, brooding more than ever.

'And here's another point that presents itself, Jeeves. Even if
I want to steal cow-creamers, how am I going to find the time? It
isn't a thing you can just take in your stride. You have to plan and
plot and lay schemes. And I shall need every ounce of concentration for this business of Gussie's.'

'Exactly, sir. One appreciates the difficulty.'

'And, as if that wasn't enough to have on my mind, there is that
telegram of Stiffy's. You remember the third telegram that came
this morning. It was from Miss Stephanie Byng, Miss Bassett's
cousin, who resides at Totleigh Towers. You've met her. She
came to lunch at the flat a week or two ago. Smallish girl of
about the tonnage of Jessie Matthews.'

'Oh, yes, sir. I remember Miss Byng. A charming young lady.'

'Quite. But what does she want me to do for her? That's the
question. Probably something completely unfit for human consumption. So I've got that to worry about, too. What a life!'

'Yes, sir.'

'Still, stiff upper lip, I suppose, Jeeves, what?'

'Precisely, sir.'

During these exchanges, we had been breezing along at a
fairish pace, and I had not failed to note that on a signpost

which we had passed some little while back there had been inscribed the words 'Totleigh-in-the-Wold, 8 miles'. There now appeared before us through the trees a stately home of E.

I braked the car.

'Journey's End, Jeeves?'

'So I should be disposed to imagine, sir.'

And so it proved. Having turned in at the gateway and fetched up at the front door, we were informed by the butler that this was indeed the lair of Sir Watkyn Bassett.

'Childe Roland to the dark tower came, sir,' said Jeeves, as we alighted, though what he meant I hadn't an earthly. Responding with a brief 'Oh, ah,' I gave my attention to the butler, who was endeavouring to communicate something to me.

What he was saying, I now gathered, was that if desirous of mixing immediately with the inmates I had chosen a bad moment for hitting the place. Sir Watkyn, he explained, had popped out for a breather.

'I fancy he is somewhere in the grounds with Mr Roderick Spode.'

I started. After that affair at the antique shop, the name Roderick was, as you may imagine, rather deeply graven on my heart.

'Roderick Spode? Big chap with a small moustache and the sort of eye that can open an oyster at sixty paces?'

'Yes, sir. He arrived yesterday with Sir Watkyn from London. They went out shortly after lunch. Miss Madeline, I believe, is at home, but it may take some little time to locate her.'

'How about Mr Fink-Nottle?'

'I think he has gone for a walk, sir.'

'Oh? Well, right ho. Then I'll just potter about a bit.'

I was glad of the chance of being alone for a while, for I wished to brood. I strolled off along the terrace, doing so.

The news that Roderick Spode was on the premises had shaken me a good deal. I had supposed him to be some mere club acquaintance of old Bassett's, who confined his activities exclusively to the metropolis, and his presence at the Towers rendered the prospect of trying to carry out Aunt Dahlia's com-mission, always one calculated to unnerve the stoutest, twice as intimidating as it had been before, when I had supposed that I should be under the personal eye of Sir Watkyn alone.

Well, you can see that for yourself, I mean to say. I mean, imagine how some unfortunate Master Criminal would feel, on coming down to do a murder at the old Grange, if he found that not only was Sherlock Holmes putting in the weekend there, but Hercule Poirot, as well.

The more I faced up to the idea of pinching that cow-creamer, the less I liked it. It seemed to me that there ought to be a middle course, and that what I had to do was explore avenues in the hope of finding some formula. To this end, I paced the terrace with bent bean, pondering.

Old Bassett, I noted, had laid out his money to excellent advantage. I am a bit of a connoisseur of country houses, and I found this one well up to sample. Nice façade, spreading grounds, smoothly shaven lawns, and a general atmosphere of what is known as old-world peace. Cows were mooing in the distance, sheep and birds respectively bleating and tootling, and from somewhere near at hand there came the report of a gun, indicating that someone was having a whirl at the local rabbits. Totleigh Towers might be a place where Man was vile, but undoubtedly every prospect pleased.

And I was strolling up and down, trying to calculate how long it would have taken the old bounder, fining, say, twenty people a day five quid apiece, to collect enough to pay for all this, when my attention was arrested by the interior of a room on the ground floor, visible through an open French window.

It was a sort of minor drawing room, if you know what I mean, and it gave the impression of being overfurnished. This was due to the fact that it was stuffed to bursting point with glass cases, these in their turn stuffed to bursting point with silver. It was evident that I was looking at the Bassett collection.

I paused. Something seemed to draw me through the French window. And the next moment, there I was, *vis-à-vis*, as the expression is, with my old pal the silver cow. It was standing in a smallish case over by the door, and I peered in at it, breathing heavily on the glass.

It was with considerable emotion that I perceived that the case was not locked.

I turned the handle. I dipped in, and fished it out.

Now, whether it was my intention merely to inspect and examine, or whether I was proposing to shoot the works, I do not know. The nearest I can remember is that I had no really settled plans. My frame of mind was more or less that of a cat in an adage.

However, I was not accorded leisure to review my emotions in what Jeeves would call the final analysis, for at this point a voice behind me said 'Hands up!' and, turning, I observed Roderick Spode in the window. He had a shotgun in his hand, and this he was pointing in a negligent sort of way at my third waistcoat button. I gathered from his manner that he was one of those fellows who like firing from the hip.

CHAPTER 3

I HAD described Roderick Spode to the butler as a man with an eye that could open an oyster at sixty paces, and it was an eye of this nature that he was directing at me now. He looked like a Dictator on the point of starting a purge, and I saw that I had been mistaken in supposing him to be seven feet in height. Eight, at least. Also the slowly working jaw muscles.

I hoped he was not going to say 'Ha!' but he did. And as I had not yet mastered the vocal cords sufficiently to be able to reply, that concluded the dialogue sequence for the moment. Then, still keeping his eyes glued on me, he shouted:

'Sir Watkyn!'

There was a distant sound of Eh-yes-here-I-am-what-is-it-ing.

'Come here, please. I have something to show you.'

Old Bassett appeared in the window, adjusting his pince-nez.

I had seen this man before only in the decent habiliments suitable to the metropolis, and I confess that even in the predicament in which I found myself I was able to shudder at the spectacle he presented in the country. It is, of course, an axiom, as I have heard Jeeves call it, that the smaller the man, the louder the check suit, and old Bassett's apparel was in keeping with his lack of inches. Prismatic is the only word for those frightful tweeds and, oddly enough, the spectacle of them had the effect of steadying my nerves. They gave me the feeling that nothing mattered.

'Look!' said Spode. 'Would you have thought such a thing possible?'

Old Bassett was goggling at me with a sort of stunned amazement.

'Good God! It's the bag-snatcher!'

'Yes. Isn't it incredible?'

'It's unbelievable. Why, damn it, it's persecution. Fellow follows me everywhere, like Mary's lamb. Never a free moment. How did you catch him?'

'I happened to be coming along the drive, and I saw a furtive figure slink in at the window. I hurried up, and covered him with my gun. Just in time. He had already begun to loot the place.'

'Well, I'm most obliged to you, Roderick. But what I can't get over is the chap's pertinacity. You would have thought that when we foiled that attempt of his in the Brompton Road, he would have given up the thing as a bad job. But no. Down he comes here next day. Well, he will be sorry he did.'

'I suppose this is too serious a case for you to deal with summarily?'

'I can issue a warrant for his arrest. Bring him along to the library, and I'll do it now. The case will have to go to the Assizes or the Sessions.'

'What will he get, do you think?'

'Not easy to say. But certainly not less than –'

'Hoy!' I said.

I had intended to speak in a quiet, reasonable voice – going on, after I had secured their attention, to explain that I was on these premises as an invited guest, but for some reason the word came out like something Aunt Dahlia might have said to a fellow member of the Pytchley half a mile away across a ploughed field, and old Bassett shot back as if he had been jabbed in the eye with a burned stick.

Spode commented on my methods of voice production.

'Don't shout like that!'

'Nearly broke my ear-drum,' grumbled old Bassett.

'But listen!' I yelled. 'Will you listen!'

A certain amount of confused argument then ensued, self trying to put the case for the defence and the opposition rather harping a bit on the row I was making. And in the middle of it all, just as I was showing myself in particularly good voice, the door opened and somebody said 'Goodness gracious!'

I looked round. Those parted lips...those saucer-like eyes... that slender figure, drooping slightly at the hinges...

Madeline Bassett was in our midst.

'Goodness gracious!' she repeated.

I can well imagine that a casual observer, if I had confided to him my qualms at the idea of being married to this girl, would have raised his eyebrows and been at a loss to understand. 'Bertie,' he would probably have said, 'you don't know what's good for you,' adding, possibly, that he wished he had half my complaint. For Madeline Bassett was undeniably of attractive exterior – slim, *svelte*, if that's the word, and bountifully equipped with golden hair and all the fixings.

But where the casual observer would have been making his bloomer was in overlooking that squashy soupiness of hers, that subtle air she had of being on the point of talking baby-talk. It was that that froze the blood. She was definitely the sort of girl who puts her hands over a husband's eyes, as he is crawling in to breakfast with a morning head, and says: 'Guess who!'

I once stayed at the residence of a newly married pal of mine, and his bride had had carved in large letters over the fireplace in the drawing room, where it was impossible to miss it, the legend: 'Two Lovers Built This Nest,' and I can still recall the look of dumb anguish in the other half of the sketch's eyes every time he came in and saw it. Whether Madeline Bassett, on entering the marital state, would go to such an awful extreme, I could not say, but it seemed most probable.

She was looking at us with a sort of pretty, wide-eyed wonder.

'Whatever is all the noise about?' she said. 'Why, Bertie! When did you get here?'

'Oh, hallo. I've just arrived.'

'Did you have a nice journey down?'

'Oh, rather, thanks. I came in the two-seater.'

'You must be quite exhausted.'

'Oh, no, thanks, rather not.'

'Well, tea will be ready soon. I see you've met Daddy.'

'And Mr Spode.'

'And Mr Spode.'

'I don't know where Augustus is, but he's sure to be in to tea.'

'I'll count the moments.'

Old Bassett had been listening to these courtesies with a dazed expression on the map – gulping a bit from time to time, like a fish that has been hauled out of a pond on a bent pin and isn't at all sure it is equal to the pressure of events. One followed the mental processes, of course. To him, Bertram was a creature of the underworld who stole bags and umbrellas and, what made it worse, didn't even steal them well. No father likes to see his ewe lamb on chummy terms with such a one.

'You don't mean you know this man?' he said.

Madeline Bassett laughed the tinkling, silvery laugh which was one of the things that had got her so disliked by the better element.

'Why, Daddy, you're too absurd. Of course I know him. Bertie Wooster is an old, old, a very dear old friend of mine. I told you he was coming here today.'

Old Bassett seemed not abreast. Spode didn't seem any too abreast, either.

'This isn't your friend Mr Wooster?'

'Of course.'

'But he snatches bags.'

'Umbrellas,' prompted Spode, as if he had been the King's Remembrancer or something.

'And umbrellas,' assented old Bassett. 'And makes daylight raids on antique shops.'

Madeline was not abreast – making three in all.

'Daddy!'

Old Bassett stuck to it stoutly.

'He does, I tell you. I've caught him at it.'

'*I've* caught him at it,' said Spode.

'We've both caught him at it,' said old Bassett. 'All over London. Wherever you go in London, there you will find this fellow stealing bags and umbrellas. And now in the heart of Gloucestershire.'

'Nonsense!' said Madeline.

I saw that it was time to put an end to all this rot. I was about fed up with that bag-snatching stuff. Naturally, one does not expect a magistrate to have all the details about the customers at his fingers' ends – pretty good, of course, remembering his *clientèle* at all – but one can't just keep passing a thing like that off tactfully.

'Of course it's nonsense,' I thundered. 'The whole thing is one of those laughable misunderstandings.'

I must say I was expecting that my explanation would have gone better than it did. What I had anticipated was that after a few words from myself, outlining the situation, there would have been roars of jolly mirth, followed by apologies and back-slappings. But old Bassett, like so many of these police court magistrates, was a difficult man to convince. Magistrates' natures soon get warped. He kept interrupting and asking questions, and cocking an eye at me as he asked them. You know what I mean – questions beginning with 'Just one moment –' and 'You say –' and 'Then you are asking us to believe –' Offensive, very.

However, after a good deal of tedious spadework, I managed to get him straight on the umbrella, and he conceded that he might have judged me unjustly about that.

'But how about the bags?'

'There weren't any bags.'

'I certainly sentenced you for something at Bosher Street. I remember it vividly.'

'I pinched a policeman's helmet.'

'That's just as bad as snatching bags.'

Roderick Spode intervened unexpectedly. Throughout this – well, dash it, this absolute Trial of Mary Dugan – he had been standing by, thoughtfully sucking the muzzle of his gun and listening to my statements as if he thought it all pretty thin; but now a flicker of human feeling came into his granite face.

'No,' he said, 'I don't think you can go so far as that. When I was at Oxford, I once stole a policeman's helmet myself.'

I was astounded. Nothing in my relations with this man had given me the idea that he, too, had, so to speak, once lived in Arcady. It just showed, as I often say, that there is good in the worst of us.

Old Bassett was plainly taken aback. Then he perked up.

'Well, how about that affair at the antique shop? Hey? Didn't we catch him in the act of running off with my cow-creamer? What has he got to say to that?'

Spode seemed to see the force of this. He removed the gun, which he had replaced between his lips, and nodded.

'The bloke at the shop had given it to me to look at,' I said shortly. 'He advised me to take it outside, where the light was better.'

'You were rushing out.'

'Staggering out. I trod on the cat.'

'What cat?'

'It appeared to be an animal attached to the personnel of the emporium.'

'H'm! I saw no cat. Did you see a cat, Roderick?'

'No, no cat.'

'Ha! Well, we will pass over the cat –'

'But I didn't,' I said, with one of my lightning flashes.

'We will pass over the cat,' repeated old Bassett, ignoring the gag and leaving it lying there, 'and come to another point. What were you doing with that cow-creamer? You say you were looking at it. You are asking us to believe that you were merely subjecting it to a perfectly innocent scrutiny. Why? What was your motive? What possible interest could it have for a man like you?'

'Exactly,' said Spode. 'The very question I was going to ask myself.'

This bit of backing-up from a pal had the worst effect on old Bassett. It encouraged him to so great an extent that he now yielded completely to the illusion that he was back in his bally police court.

'You say the proprietor of the shop handed it to you. I put it to you that you snatched it up and were making off with it. And now Mr Spode catches you here, with the thing in your hands. How do you explain that? What's your answer to that? Hey?'

'Why, Daddy!' said Madeline.

I dare say you have been wondering at this pancake's silence during all the cut-and-thrust stuff which had been going on. It is readily explained. What had occurred was that shortly after saying 'Nonsense!' in the earlier portion of the proceedings, she had happened to inhale some form of insect life, and since then had been choking quietly in the background. And as the situation was far too tense for us to pay any attention to choking girls, she had been left to carry on under her own steam while the men threshed out the subject on the agenda paper.

She now came forward, her eyes still watering a bit.

'Why, Daddy,' she said, 'naturally your silver would be the first thing Bertie would want to look at. Of course, he is interested in it. Bertie is Mr Travers's nephew.'

'What!'

'Didn't you know that? Your uncle has a wonderful collection hasn't he, Bertie? I suppose he has often spoken to you of Daddy's.'

There was a pause. Old Bassett was breathing heavily. I didn't like the look of him at all. He glanced from me to the cow-creamer, and from the cow-creamer to me, then back from me to the cow-creamer again, and it would have taken a far less astute observer than Bertram to fail to read what was passing in his mind. If ever I saw a bimbo engaged in putting two and two together, that bimbo was Sir Watkyn Bassett.

'Oh!' he said.

Just that. Nothing more. But it was enough.

'I say,' I said, 'could I send a telegram?'

'You can telephone it from the library,' said Madeline. 'I'll take you there.'

She conducted me to the instrument and left me, saying that she would be waiting in the hall when I had finished. I leaped at it, established connection with the post office, and after a brief conversation with what appeared to be the village idiot, telephoned as follows:

> Mrs Travers,
>   47, Charles Street,
>   Berkeley Square,
>   London.

I paused for a moment, assembling the ideas, then proceeded thus:

> Deeply regret quite impossible carry out assignment re you know what. Atmosphere one of keenest suspicion and any sort of action instantly fatal. You ought to have seen old Bassett's eye just now on learning of blood relationship of self and Uncle Tom. Like ambassador finding veiled woman snooping round safe containing secret treaty. Sorry and all that, but nothing doing. Love.
>
> *Bertie*

I then went down to the hall to join Madeline Bassett.

She was standing by the barometer, which, if it had had an ounce of sense in its head, would have been pointing to 'Stormy' instead of 'Set Fair': and as I hove alongside she turned and gazed at me with a tender goggle which sent a thrill of dread creeping down the Wooster spine. The thought that there stood one who was on distant terms with Gussie and might ere long return the ring and presents afflicted me with a nameless horror.

I resolved that if a few quiet words from a man of the world could heal the breach, they should be spoken.

'Oh, Bertie,' she said, in a low voice like beer trickling out of a jug, 'you ought not to be here!'

My recent interview with old Bassett and Roderick Spode had rather set me thinking along those lines myself. But I hadn't time to explain that this was no idle social visit, and that if Gussie hadn't been sending out SOSs I wouldn't have dreamed of coming within a hundred miles of the frightful place. She went on, looking at me as if I were a rabbit which she was expecting shortly to turn into a gnome.

'Why did you come? Oh, I know what you are going to say. You felt that, cost what it might, you had to see me again, just once. You could not resist the urge to take away with you one last memory, which you could cherish down the lonely years. Oh, Bertie, you remind me of Rudel.'

The name was new to me.

'Rudel?'

'The Seigneur Geoffrey Rudel, Prince of Blay-en-Saintonge.'

I shook my head.

'Never met him, I'm afraid. Pal of yours?'

'He lived in the Middle Ages. He was a great poet. And he fell in love with the wife of the Lord of Tripoli.'

I stirred uneasily. I hoped she was going to keep it clean.

'For years he loved her, and at last he could resist no longer. He took ship to Tripoli, and his servants carried him ashore.'

'Not feeling so good?' I said, groping. 'Rough crossing?'

'He was dying. Of love.'

'Oh, ah.'

'They bore him into the Lady Melisande's presence on a litter, and he had just strength enough to reach out and touch her hand. Then he died.'

She paused, and heaved a sigh that seemed to come straight up from the cami-knickers. A silence ensued.

'Terrific,' I said, feeling I had to say something, though personally I didn't think the story a patch on the one about the travelling salesman and the farmer's daughter. Different, of course, if one had known the chap.

She sighed again.

'You see now why I said you reminded me of Rudel. Like him, you came to take one last glimpse of the woman you loved. It was dear of you, Bertie, and I shall never forget it. It will always remain with me as a fragrant memory, like a flower pressed between the leaves of an old album. But was it wise? Should you not have been strong? Would it not have been better to have ended it all cleanly, that day when we said goodbye at Brinkley

Court, and not to have reopened the wound? We had met, and you have loved me, and I had had to tell you that my heart was another's. That should have been our farewell.'

'Absolutely,' I said. I mean to say, all that was perfectly sound, as far as it went. If her heart really was another's, fine. Nobody more pleased than Bertram. The whole nub of the thing was – was it? 'But I had a communication from Gussie, more or less indicating that you and he were *p'fft.*'

She looked at me like someone who has just solved the crossword puzzle with a shrewd 'Emu' in the top right-hand corner.

'So that was why you came! You thought that there might still be hope? Oh, Bertie, I'm sorry…sorry…so sorry.' Her eyes were misty with the unshed, and about the size of soup plates. 'No, Bertie, really there is no hope, none. You must not build dream castles. It can only cause you pain. I love Augustus. He is my man.'

'And you haven't parted brass rags?'

'Of course not.'

'Then what did he mean by saying "Serious rift Madeline and self"?'

'Oh, that?' She laughed – another tinkling, silvery one. 'That was nothing. It was all too perfectly silly and ridiculous. Just the teeniest, weeniest little misunderstanding. I thought I had found him flirting with my cousin Stephanie, and I was silly and jealous. But he explained everything this morning. He was only taking a fly out of her eye.'

I suppose I might legitimately have been a bit shirty on learning that I had been hauled all the way down here for nothing, but I wasn't. I was amazingly braced. As I have indicated, that telegram of Gussie's had shaken me to my foundations, causing me to fear the worst. And now the All Clear had been blown, and I had received absolute inside information straight from the horse's mouth that all was hotsy-totsy between this blister and himself.

'So everything's all right, is it?'

'Everything. I have never loved Augustus more than I do now.'

'Haven't you, by Jove?'

'Each moment I am with him, his wonderful nature seems to open before me like some lovely flower.'

'Does it, egad?'

'Every day I find myself discovering some new facet of his extraordinary character. For instance…you have seen him quite lately, have you not?'

'Oh, rather. I gave him a dinner at the Drones only the night before last.'

'I wonder if you noticed any difference in him?'

I threw my mind back to the binge in question. As far as I could recollect, Gussie had been the same fish-faced freak I had always known.

'Difference? No, I don't think so. Of course, at that dinner I hadn't the chance to observe him very closely – subject his character to the final analysis, if you know what I mean. He sat next to me, and we talked of this and that, but you know how it is when you're a host – you have all sorts of things to divert your attention…keeping an eye on the waiters, trying to make the conversation general, heading Catsmeat Potter-Pirbright off from giving his imitation of Beatrice Lillie…a hundred little duties. But he seemed to me much the same. What sort of difference?'

'An improvement, if such a thing were possible. Have you not sometimes felt in the past, Bertie, that, if Augustus had a fault, it was a tendency to be a little timid?'

I saw what she meant.

'Oh, ah, yes, of course, definitely.' I remembered something Jeeves had once called Gussie. 'A sensitive plant, what?'

'Exactly. You know your Shelley, Bertie.'

'Oh, am I?'

'That is what I have always thought him – a sensitive plant, hardly fit for the rough and tumble of life. But recently – in this last week, in fact – he has shown, together with that wonderful dreamy sweetness of his, a force of character which I had not suspected that he possessed. He seems completely to have lost his diffidence.'

'By Jove, yes,' I said, remembering. 'That's right. Do you know, he actually made a speech at that dinner of mine, and a most admirable one. And, what is more –'

I paused. I had been on the point of saying that, what was more, he had made it from start to finish on orange juice, and not – as had been the case at the Market Snodsbury prize giving – with about three quarts of mixed alcoholic stimulants lapping about inside him: and I saw that the statement might be injudicious.

That Market Snodsbury exhibition on the part of the adored object was, no doubt, something which she was trying to forget.

'Why, only this morning,' she said, 'he spoke to Roderick Spode quite sharply.'

'He did?'

'Yes. They were arguing about something, and Augustus told him to go and boil his head.'

'Well, well!' I said.

Naturally, I didn't believe it for a moment. Well, I mean to say! Roderick Spode, I mean – a chap who even in repose would have made an all-in wrestler pause and pick his words. The thing wasn't possible.

I saw what had happened, of course. She was trying to give the boyfriend a build-up and, like all girls, was overdoing it. I've noticed the same thing in young wives, when they're trying to kid you that Herbert or George or whatever the name may be has hidden depths which the vapid and irreflective observer might overlook. Women never know when to stop on these occasions.

I remember Mrs Bingo Little once telling me, shortly after their marriage, that Bingo said poetic things to her about sunsets – his best friends being perfectly well aware, of course, that the old egg never noticed a sunset in his life and that, if he did by a fluke ever happen to do so, the only thing he would say about it would be that it reminded him of a slice of roast beef, cooked just right.

However, you can't call a girl a liar; so, as I say, I said: 'Well, well!'

'It was the one thing that was needed to make him perfect. Sometimes, Bertie, I ask myself if I am worthy of so rare a soul.'

'Oh, I wouldn't ask yourself rot like that,' I said heartily. 'Of course you are.'

'It's sweet of you to say so.'

'Not a bit. You two fit like pork and beans. Anyone could see that it was a what-d'you-call-it…ideal union. I've known Gussie since we were kids together, and I wish I had a bob for every time I've thought to myself that the girl for him was somebody just like you.'

'Really?'

'Absolutely. And when I met you, I said: "That's the bird! There she spouts!" When is the wedding to be?'

'On the twenty-third.'

'I'd make it earlier.'

'You think so?'

'Definitely. Get it over and done with, and then you'll have it off your mind. You can't be married too soon to a chap like Gussie. Great chap. Splendid chap. Never met a chap I respected more. They don't often make them like Gussie. One of the fruitiest.'

She reached out and grabbed my hand and pressed it. Unpleasant, of course, but one had to take the rough with the smooth.

'Ah, Bertie! Always the soul of generosity!'

'No, no, rather not. Just saying what I think.'

'It makes me so happy to feel that…all this…has not interfered with your affection for Augustus.'

'I should say not.'

'So many men in your position might have become embittered.'

'Silly asses.'

'But you are too fine for that. You can still say these wonderful things about him.'

'Oh, rather.'

'Dear Bertie!'

And on this cheery note we parted, she to go messing about on some domestic errand, I to head for the drawing room and get a spot of tea. She, it appeared, did not take tea, being on a diet.

And I had reached the drawing room, and was about to shove open the door, which was ajar, when from the other side there came a voice. And what it was saying was:

'So kindly do not talk rot, Spode!'

There was no possibility of mistake as to whose voice it was. From his earliest years, there has always been something distinctive and individual about Gussie's *timbre*, reminding the hearer partly of an escape of gas from a gas pipe and partly of a sheep calling to its young in the lambing season.

Nor was there any possibility of mistake about what he had said. The words were precisely as I have stated, and to say that I was surprised would be to put it too weakly. I saw now that it was perfectly possible that there might be something, after all, in that wild story of Madeline Bassett's. I mean to say, an Augustus Fink-Nottle who told Roderick Spode not to talk rot was an Augustus Fink-Nottle who might quite well have told him to go and boil his head.

I entered the room, marvelling.

Except for some sort of dim female abaft the teapot, who looked as if she might be a cousin by marriage or something of that order, only Sir Watkyn Bassett, Roderick Spode and Gussie were present. Gussie was straddling the hearth rug with his legs apart, warming himself at the blaze which should, one would have said, have been reserved for the trouser seat of the master of the house, and I saw immediately what Madeline Bassett had meant when she said that he had lost his diffidence. Even across the room one could see that, when it came to self-confidence, Mussolini could have taken his correspondence course.

He sighted me as I entered, and waved what seemed to me a dashed patronizing hand. Quite the ruddy Squire graciously receiving the deputation of tenantry.

'Ah, Bertie. So here you are.'

'Yes.'

'Come in, come in and have a crumpet.'

'Thanks.'

'Did you bring that book I asked you to?'

'Awfully sorry. I forgot.'

'Well, of all the muddle-headed asses that ever stepped, you certainly are the worst. Others abide our question, thou art free.'

And dismissing me with a weary gesture, he called for another potted-meat sandwich.

I have never been able to look back on my first meal at Totleigh Towers as among my happiest memories. The cup of tea on arrival at a country house is a thing which, as a rule, I particularly enjoy. I like the crackling logs, the shaded lights, the scent of buttered toast, the general atmosphere of leisured cosiness. There is something that seems to speak to the deeps in me in the beaming smile of my hostess and the furtive whisper of my host, as he plucks at my elbow and says 'Let's get out of here and go and have a whisky and soda in the gun room.' It is on such occasions as this, it has often been said, that you catch Bertram Wooster at his best.

But now all sense of *bien-être* was destroyed by Gussie's peculiar manner – that odd suggestion he conveyed of having bought the place. It was a relief when the gang had finally drifted away, leaving us alone. There were mysteries here which I wanted to probe.

I thought it best, however, to begin by taking a second opinion on the position of affairs between himself and Madeline. She had told me that everything was now hunky-dory once more, but it was one of those points on which you cannot have too much assurance.

'I saw Madeline just now,' I said. 'She tells me that you are sweethearts still. Correct?'

'Quite correct. There was a little temporary coolness about my taking a fly out of Stephanie Byng's eye, and I got a bit panicked and wired you to come down. I thought you might possibly plead. However, no need for that now. I took a strong line, and everything is all right. Still, stay a day or two, of course, as you're here.'

'Thanks.'

'No doubt you will be glad to see your aunt. She arrives tonight, I understand.'

I could make nothing of this. My Aunt Agatha, I knew, was in a nursing home with jaundice. I had taken her flowers only a couple of days before. And naturally it couldn't be Aunt Dahlia, for she had mentioned nothing to me about any plans for infesting Totleigh Towers.

'Some mistake,' I said.

'No mistake at all. Madeline showed me the telegram that came from her this morning, asking if she could be put up for a day or two. It was dispatched from London, I noticed, so I suppose she has left Brinkley.'

I stared.

'You aren't talking about my Aunt Dahlia?'

'Of course I'm talking about your Aunt Dahlia.'

'You mean Aunt Dahlia is coming here tonight?'

'Exactly.'

This was nasty news, and I found myself chewing the lower lip a bit in undisguised concern. This sudden decision to follow me to Totleigh Towers could mean only one thing, that Aunt Dahlia, thinking things over, had become mistrustful of my will to win, and had felt it best to come and stand over me and see that I did not shirk the appointed task. And as I was fully resolved to shirk it, I could envisage some dirty weather ahead. Her attitude towards a recalcitrant nephew would, I feared, closely resemble that which in the old tally-ho days she had been wont to adopt towards a hound which refused to go to cover.

'Tell me,' continued Gussie, 'what sort of voice is she in these days? I ask, because if she is going to make those hunting noises of hers at me during her visit, I shall be compelled to tick her off pretty sharply. I had enough of that sort of thing when I was staying at Brinkley.'

I would have liked to go on musing on the unpleasant situation which had arisen, but it seemed to me that I had been given the cue to begin my probe.

'What's happened to you, Gussie?' I asked.

'Eh?'

'Since when have you been like this?'

'I don't understand you.'

'Well, to take an instance, saying you're going to tick Aunt Dahlia off. At Brinkley, you cowered before her like a wet sock. And, to take another instance, telling Spode not to talk rot. By the way, what was he talking rot about?'

'I forget. He talks so much rot.'

'I wouldn't have the nerve to tell Spode not to talk rot,' I said frankly. My candour met with an immediate response.

'Well, to tell you the truth, Bertie,' said Gussie, coming clean, 'neither would I, a week ago.'

'What happened a week ago?'

'I had a spiritual rebirth. Thanks to Jeeves. There's a chap, Bertie!'

'Ah!'

'We are as little children, frightened of the dark, and Jeeves is the wise nurse who takes us by the hand and –'

'Switches the light on?'

'Precisely. Would you care to hear about it?'

I assured him that I was all agog. I settled myself in my chair and, putting match to gasper, awaited the inside story.

Gussie stood silent for a moment. I could see that he was marshalling his facts. He took off his spectacles and polished them.

'A week ago, Bertie,' he began, 'my affairs had reached a crisis. I was faced by an ordeal, the mere prospect of which blackened the horizon. I discovered that I would have to make a speech at the wedding breakfast.'

'Well, naturally.'

'I know, but for some reason I had not foreseen it, and the news came as a stunning blow. And shall I tell you why I was so overcome by stark horror at the idea of making a speech at the wedding breakfast? It was because Roderick Spode and Sir Watkyn Bassett would be in the audience. Do you know Sir Watkyn intimately?'

'Not very. He once fined me five quid at his police court.'

'Well, you can take it from me that he is a hard nut, and he strongly objects to having me as a son-in-law. For one thing, he would have liked Madeline to marry Spode – who, I may mention, has loved her since she was so high.'

'Oh, yes?' I said, courteously concealing my astonishment that anyone except a certified boob like himself could deliberately love this girl.

'Yes. But apart from the fact that she wanted to marry me, he didn't want to marry her. He looks upon himself as a Man of Destiny, you see, and feels that marriage would interfere with his mission. He takes a line through Napoleon.'

I felt that before proceeding further I must get the low-down on this Spode. I didn't follow all this Man of Destiny stuff.

'How do you mean, his mission? Is he someone special?'

'Don't you ever read the papers? Roderick Spode is the founder and head of the Saviours of Britain, a Fascist organization better known as the Black Shorts. His general idea, if he doesn't get knocked on the head with a bottle in one of the frequent brawls in which he and his followers indulge, is to make himself a Dictator.'

'Well, I'm blowed!'

I was astounded at my keenness of perception. The moment I had set eyes on Spode, if you remember, I had said to myself 'What ho! A Dictator!' and a Dictator he had proved to be. I couldn't have made a better shot, if I had been one of those detectives who see a chap walking along the street and deduce that he is a retired manufacturer of poppet valves named Robinson with rheumatism in one arm, living at Clapham.

'Well, I'm dashed! I thought he was something of that sort. That chin…Those eyes…And, for the matter of that, that moustache. By the way, when you say "shorts", you mean "shirts", of course.'

'No. By the time Spode formed his association, there were no shirts left. He and his adherents wear black shorts.'

'Footer bags, you mean?'

'Yes.'

'How perfectly foul.'

'Yes.'

'Bare knees?'

'Bare knees.'

'Golly!'

'Yes.'

A thought struck me, so revolting that I nearly dropped my gasper.

'Does old Bassett wear black shorts?'

'No. He isn't a member of the Saviours of Britain.'

'Then how does he come to be mixed up with Spode? I met them going around London like a couple of sailors on shore leave.'

'Sir Watkyn is engaged to be married to his aunt – a Mrs Wintergreen, widow of the late Colonel H. H. Wintergreen, of Pont Street.'

I mused for a moment, reviewing in my mind the scene in the antique-bin.

When you are standing in the dock, with a magistrate looking at you over his pince-nez and talking about you as 'the prisoner Wooster', you have ample opportunity for drinking him in, and what had struck me principally about Sir Watkyn Bassett that day at Bosher Street had been his peevishness. In that shop, on the other hand, he had given the impression of a man who has found the blue bird. He had hopped about like a carefree cat on hot bricks, exhibiting the merchandise to Spode with little chirps of 'I think your aunt would like this?' and 'How about this?' and so forth. And now a clue to that fizziness had been provided.

'Do you know, Gussie,' I said, 'I've an idea he must have clicked yesterday.'

'Quite possibly. However, never mind about that. That is not the point.'

'No, I know. But it's interesting.'

'No, it isn't.'

'Perhaps you're right.'

'Don't let us go wandering off into side issues,' said Gussie, calling the meeting to order. 'Where was I?'

'I don't know.'

'I do. I was telling you that Sir Watkyn disliked the idea of having me for a son-in-law. Spode also was opposed to the match. Nor did he make any attempt to conceal the fact. He used to come popping out at me from round corners and muttering threats.'

'You couldn't have liked that.'

'I didn't.'

'Why did he mutter threats?'

'Because, though he would not marry Madeline, even if she would have him, he looks on himself as a sort of knight, watching over her. He keeps telling me that the happiness of that little girl is very dear to him, and that if ever I let her down, he will break my neck. That is the gist of the threats he mutters, and that was one of the reasons why I was a bit agitated when Madeline became distant in her manner, on catching me with Stephanie Byng.'

'Tell me, Gussie, what were you and Stiffy actually doing?'

'I was taking a fly out of her eye.'

I nodded. If that was his story, no doubt he was wise to stick to it.

'So much for Spode. We now come to Sir Watkyn Bassett. At our very first meeting I could see that I was not his dream man.'

'Me, too.'

'I became engaged to Madeline, as you know, at Brinkley Court. The news of the betrothal was, therefore, conveyed to him by letter, and I imagine that the dear girl must have hauled up her slacks about me in a way that led him to suppose that what he was getting was a sort of cross between Robert Taylor and Einstein. At any rate, when I was introduced to him as the man who was to marry his daughter, he just stared for a moment and said "What?" Incredulously, you know, as if he were hoping that this was some jolly practical joke and that the real chap would shortly jump out from behind a chair and say "Boo!" When he at last got on to it that there was no deception, he went off into a corner and sat there for some time, holding his head in his hands. After that I used to catch him looking at me over the top of his pince-nez. It unsettled me.'

I wasn't surprised. I have already alluded to the effect that over-the-top-of-the-pince-nez look of old Bassett's had had on me, and I could see that, if directed at Gussie, it might quite conceivably have stirred the old egg up a good deal.

'He also sniffed. And when he learned from Madeline that I was keeping newts in my bedroom, he said something very derogatory – under his breath, but I heard him.'

'You've got the troupe with you, then?'

'Of course. I am in the middle of a very delicate experiment. An American professor has discovered that the full moon influences the love life of several undersea creatures, including one species of fish, two starfish groups, eight kinds of worms and a ribbon-like seaweed called Dictyota. The moon will be full in two or three days, and I want to find out if it affects the love life of newts, too.'

'But what *is* the love life of newts, if you boil it right down? Didn't you tell me once that they just waggled their tails at one another in the mating season?'

'Quite correct.'

I shrugged my shoulders.

'Well, all right, if they like it. But it's not my idea of molten passion. So old Bassett didn't approve of the dumb chums?'

'No. He didn't approve of anything about me. It made things most difficult and disagreeable. Add Spode, and you will understand why I was beginning to get thoroughly rattled. And then, out of a blue sky, they sprang it on me that I would have to make a speech at the wedding breakfast – to an audience, as I said before, of which Roderick Spode and Sir Watkyn Bassett would form a part.'

He paused, and swallowed convulsively, like a Pekingese taking a pill.

'I am a shy man, Bertie. Diffidence is the price I pay for having a hyper-sensitive nature. And you know how I feel about making speeches under any conditions. The mere idea appals me. When you lugged me into that prize-giving affair at Market Snodsbury, the thought of standing on a platform, faced by a mob of pimply boys, filled me with a panic terror. It haunted my dreams. You can imagine, then, what it was like for me to have to contemplate that wedding breakfast. To the task of haranguing a flock of aunts and cousins I might have steeled myself. I don't say it would have been easy, but I might have managed it. But to get up with Spode on one side of me and Sir Watkyn Bassett on the other…I didn't see how I was going to face it. And then, out of the night that covered me, black as the pit from pole to pole, there shone a tiny gleam of hope. I thought of Jeeves.'

His hand moved upwards, and I think his idea was to bare his head reverently. The project was, however, rendered null and void by the fact that he hadn't a hat on.

'I thought of Jeeves,' he repeated, 'and I took the train to London and placed my problem before him. I was fortunate to catch him in time.'

'How do you mean, in time?'

'Before he left England.'

'He isn't leaving England.'

'He told me that you and he were starting off almost immediately on one of those Round-The-World cruises.'

'Oh, no, that's all off. I didn't like the scheme.'

'Does Jeeves say it's all off?'

'No, but I do.'

'Oh?'

He looked at me rather oddly, and I thought he was going to say something more on the subject. But he only gave a rummy sort of short laugh, and resumed his narrative.

'Well, as I say, I went to Jeeves, and put the facts before him. I begged him to try to find some way of getting me out of this frightful situation in which I was enmeshed – assuring him that I would not blame him if he failed to do so, because it seemed to me, after some days of reviewing the matter, that I was beyond human aid. And you will scarcely credit this, Bertie: I hadn't got more than halfway through the glass of orange juice with which he had supplied me, when he solved the whole thing. I wouldn't have believed it possible. I wonder what that brain of his weighs?'

'A good bit, I fancy. He eats a lot of fish. So it was a winner, was it, this idea?'

'It was terrific. He approached the matter from the psychological angle. In the final analysis, he said, disinclination to speak in public is due to fear of one's audience.'

'Well, I could have told you that.'

'Yes, but he indicated how this might be cured. We do not, he said, fear those whom we despise. The thing to do, therefore, is to cultivate a lofty contempt for those who will be listening to one.'

'How?'

'Quite simple. You fill your mind with scornful thoughts about them. You keep saying to yourself: "Think of that pimple on Smith's nose"…"Consider Jones's flapping ears"…"Remember the time Robinson got hauled up before the beak for travelling first-class with a third-class ticket"…"Don't forget you once saw the child Brown being sick at a children's party"…and so on. So that when you are called upon to address Smith, Jones, Robinson and Brown, they have lost their sting. You dominate them.'

I pondered on this.

'I see. Well, yes, it sounds good, Gussie. But would it work in practice?'

'My dear chap, it works like a charm. I've tested it. You recall my speech at that dinner of yours?'

I started.

'You weren't despising us?'

'Certainly I was. Thoroughly.'

'What, me?'

'You, and Freddie Widgeon, and Bingo Little, and Catsmeat Potter-Pirbright, and Barmy Fotheringay-Phipps, and all the rest of those present. "Worms!" I said to myself. "What a crew!" I said to myself. "There's old Bertie," I said to myself. "Golly!" I said to myself, "what I know about *him*!" With the result that I played on you as on a lot of stringed instruments, and achieved an outstanding triumph.'

I must say I was conscious of a certain chagrin. A bit thick, I mean, being scorned by a goof like Gussie – and that at a moment when he had been bursting with one's meat and orange juice.

But soon more generous emotions prevailed. After all, I told myself, the great thing – the fundamental thing to which all other considerations must yield – was to get this Fink-Nottle safely under the wire and off on his honeymoon. And but for this advice of Jeeves's, the muttered threats of Roderick Spode and the combined sniffing and looking over the top of the pince-nez of Sir Watkyn Bassett might well have been sufficient to destroy his morale entirely and cause him to cancel the wedding arrangements and go off hunting newts in Africa.

'Well, yes,' I said, 'I see what you mean. But dash it, Gussie, conceding the fact that you might scorn Barmy Fotheringay-Phipps and Catsmeat Potter-Pirbright and – stretching the possibilities a bit – me, you couldn't despise Spode.'

'Couldn't I?' He laughed a light laugh. 'I did it on my head. And Sir Watkyn Bassett, too. I tell you, Bertie, I approach this wedding breakfast without a tremor. I am gay, confident, debonair.

There will be none of that blushing and stammering and twiddling the fingers and plucking at the tablecloth which you see in most bridegrooms on these occasions. I shall look these men in the eye, and make them wilt. As for the aunts and cousins, I shall have them rolling in the aisles. The moment Jeeves spoke those words, I settled down to think of all the things about Roderick Spode and Sir Watkyn Bassett which expose them to the just contempt of their fellow men. I could tell you fifty things about Sir Watkyn alone which would make you wonder how such a moral and physical blot on the English scene could have been tolerated all these years. I wrote them down in a notebook.'

'You wrote them down in a notebook?'

'A small, leather-covered notebook. I bought it in the village.'

I confess that I was a bit agitated. Even though he presumably kept it under lock and key, the mere existence of such a book made one uneasy. One did not care to think what the upshot and outcome would be were it to fall into the wrong hands. A brochure like that would be dynamite.

'Where do you keep it?'

'In my breast pocket. Here it is. Oh, no, it isn't. That's funny,' said Gussie. 'I must have dropped it somewhere.'

CHAPTER 4

I DON'T know if you have had the same experience, but a thing I have found in life is that from time to time, as you jog along, there occur moments which you are able to recognize immediately with the naked eye as high spots. Something tells you that they are going to remain etched, if etched is the word I want, for ever on the memory and will come back to you at intervals down the years, as you are dropping off to sleep, banishing that drowsy feeling and causing you to leap on the pillow like a gaffed salmon.

One of these well-remembered moments in my own case was the time at my first private school when I sneaked down to the headmaster's study at dead of night, my spies having informed me that he kept a tin of biscuits in the cupboard under the bookshelf; to discover, after I was well inside and a modest and unobtrusive withdrawal impossible, that the old bounder was seated at his desk and – by what I have always thought a rather odd coincidence – actually engaged in the composition of my end-of-term report, which subsequently turned out a stinker.

It was a situation in which it would be paltering with the truth to say that Bertram retained unimpaired his customary *sang-froid*. But I'm dashed if I can remember staring at the Rev. Aubrey Upjohn on that occasion with half the pallid horror which had shot into the map at these words of Gussie's.

'Dropped it?' I quavered.

'Yes, but it's all right.'

'All right?'

'I mean, I can remember every word of it.'

'Oh, I see. That's fine.'

'Yes.'

'Was there much of it?'

'Oh, lots.'

'Good stuff?'

'Of the best.'

'Well, that's splendid.'

I looked at him with growing wonder. You would have thought that by this time even this pre-eminent sub-normal would have spotted the frightful peril that lurked. But no. His tortoiseshell-rimmed spectacles shone with a jovial light. He was full of *élan* and *espièglerie*, without a care in the world. All right up to the neck, but from there on pure concrete – that was Augustus Fink-Nottle.

'Oh, yes,' he said, 'I've got it all carefully memorized, and I'm extremely pleased with it. During this past week I have been subjecting the characters of Roderick Spode and Sir Watkyn Bassett to a pitiless examination. I have probed these two gumboils to the very core of their being. It's amazing the amount of material you can assemble, once you begin really analysing people. Have you ever heard Sir Watkyn Bassett dealing with a bowl of soup? It's not unlike the Scottish express going through a tunnel. Have you ever seen Spode eat asparagus?'

'No.'

'Revolting. It alters one's whole conception of Man as Nature's last word.'

'Those were two of the things you wrote in the book?'

'I gave them about half a page. They were just trivial, surface faults. The bulk of my researches went much deeper.'

'I see. You spread yourself?'

'Very much so.'

'And it was all bright, snappy stuff?'

'Every word of it.'

'That's great. I mean to say, no chance of old Bassett being bored when he reads it.'

'Reads it?'

'Well, he's just as likely to find the book as anyone, isn't he?'

I remember Jeeves saying to me once, apropos of how you can never tell what the weather's going to do, that full many a glorious morning had he seen flatter the mountain tops with sovereign eye and then turn into a rather nasty afternoon. It was the same with Gussie now. He had been beaming like a searchlight until I mentioned this aspect of the matter, and the radiance suddenly disappeared as if it had been switched off at the main.

He stood gaping at me very much as I had gaped at the Rev. A. Upjohn on the occasion to which I have alluded above. His expression was almost identical with that which I had once surprised on the face of a fish, whose name I cannot recall, in the royal aquarium at Monaco.

'I never thought of that!'

'Start now.'

'Oh, my gosh!'

'Yes.'

'Oh, my golly!'

'Quite.'

'Oh, my sainted aunt!'

'Absolutely.'

He moved to the tea table like a man in a dream, and started to eat a cold crumpet. His eyes, as they sought mine, were bulging.

'Suppose old Bassett does find that book, what do you think will ensue?'

I could answer that one.

'He would immediately put the bee on the wedding.'

'You don't really think that?'

'I do.'

He choked over his crumpet.

'Of course he would,' I said. 'You say he has never been any too sold on you as a son-in-law. Reading that book isn't going to cause a sudden change for the better. One glimpse of it, and he will be countermanding the cake and telling Madeline that she shall marry you over his dead body. And she isn't the sort of girl to defy a parent.'

'Oh, my gosh!'

'Still, I wouldn't worry about that, old man,' I said, pointing out the bright side, 'because long before it happened, Spode would have broken your neck.'

He plucked feebly at another crumpet.

'This is frightful, Bertie.'

'Not too good, no.'

'I'm in the soup.'

'Up to the thorax.'

'What's to be done?'

'I don't know.'

'Can't you think of anything?'

'Nothing. We must just put our trust in a higher power.'

'Consult Jeeves, you mean?'

I shook the lemon.

'Even Jeeves cannot help us here. It is a straight issue of finding and recovering that notebook before it can get to old Bassett. Why on earth didn't you keep it locked up somewhere?'

'I couldn't. I was always writing fresh stuff in it. I never knew when the inspiration would come, and I had to have it handy.'

'You're sure it was in your breast pocket?'

'Quite sure.'

'It couldn't be in your bedroom, by any chance?'

'No. I always kept it on me – so as to have it safe.'

'Safe. I see.'

'And also, as I said before, because I had constant need of it. I'm trying to think where I saw it last. Wait a minute. It's beginning to come back. Yes, I remember. By the pump.'

'What pump?'

'The one in the stable yard, where they fill the buckets for the horses. Yes, that is where I saw it last, before lunch yesterday. I took it out to jot down a note about the way Sir Watkyn slopped his porridge about at breakfast, and I had just completed my critique when I met Stephanie Byng and took the fly out of her eye. Bertie!' he cried, breaking off. A strange light had come into his spectacles. He brought his fist down with a bang on the table. Silly ass. Might have known he would upset the milk. 'Bertie, I've just remembered something. It is as if a curtain had been rolled up and all was revealed. The whole scene is rising before my eyes. I took the book out, and entered the porridge item. I then put it back in my breast pocket. Where I keep my handkerchief.'

'Well?'

'Where I keep my handkerchief,' he repeated. 'Don't you understand? Use your intelligence, man. What is the first thing you do, when you find a girl with a fly in her eye?'

I uttered an exclamash.

'Reach for your handkerchief!'

'Exactly. And draw it out and extract the fly with the corner of it. And if there is a small, brown leather-covered notebook alongside the handkerchief –'

'It shoots out –'

'And falls to earth –'

'– you know not where.'

'But I do know where. That's just the point. I could lead you to the exact spot.'

For an instant I felt braced. Then moodiness returned.

'Yesterday before lunch, you say? Then someone must have found it by this time.'

'That's just what I'm coming to. I've remembered something else. Immediately after I had coped with the fly, I recollect hearing Stephanie saying "Hullo, what's that?" and seeing her stoop and pick something up. I didn't pay much attention to the episode at the time, for it was just at that moment that I caught sight of Madeline. She was standing in the entrance of the stable yard, with a distant look on her face. I may mention that in order to extract the fly I had been compelled to place a hand under Stephanie's chin, in order to steady the head.'

'Quite.'

'Essential on these occasions.'

'Definitely.'

'Unless the head is kept rigid, you cannot operate. I tried to point this out to Madeline, but she wouldn't listen. She swept away, and I swept after her. It was only this morning that I was able to place the facts before her and make her accept my explanation. Meanwhile, I had completely forgotten the Stephanie-stooping-picking-up incident. I think it is obvious that the book is now in the possession of this Byng.'

'It must be.'

'Then everything's all right. We just seek her out and ask her to hand it back, and she does so. I expect she will have got a good laugh out of it.'

'Where is she?'

'I seem to remember her saying something about walking down to the village. I think she goes and hobnobs with the curate. If you're not doing anything, you might stroll and meet her.'

'I will.'

'Well, keep an eye open for that Scottie of hers. It probably accompanied her.'

'Oh, yes. Thanks.'

I remembered that he had spoken to me of this animal at my dinner. Indeed, at the moment when the *sole meunière* was being served, he had shown me the sore place on his leg, causing me to skip that course.

'It biteth like a serpent.'

'Right ho. I'll be looking out. And I might as well start at once.'

It did not take me long to get to the end of the drive. At the gates, I paused. It seemed to me that my best plan would be to linger here until Stiffy returned. I lighted a cigarette, and gave myself up to meditation.

Although slightly easier in the mind than I had been, I was still much shaken. Until that book was back in safe storage, there could be no real peace for the Wooster soul. Too much depended on its recovery. As I had said to Gussie, if old Bassett started doing the heavy father and forbidding banns, there wasn't a chance of Madeline sticking out her chin and riposting with a modern 'Is zat so?' A glance at her was enough to tell one that she belonged to that small group of girls who still think a parent should have something to say about things: and I was willing to give a hundred to eight that, in the circumstances which I had outlined, she would sigh and drop a silent tear, but that when all the smoke had cleared away Gussie would be at liberty.

I was still musing in sombre and apprehensive vein, when my meditations were interrupted. A human drama was developing in the road in front of me.

The shades of evening were beginning to fall pretty freely by now, but the visibility was still good enough to enable me to observe that up the road there was approaching a large, stout, moon-faced policeman on a bicycle. And he was, one could see, at peace with all the world. His daily round of tasks may or may not have been completed, but he was obviously off duty for the moment, and his whole attitude was that of a policeman with nothing on his mind but his helmet.

Well, when I tell you that he was riding without his hands, you will gather to what lengths the careless gaiety of this serene slop had spread.

And where the drama came in was that it was patent that his attention had not yet been drawn to the fact that he was being chivvied – in the strong, silent, earnest manner characteristic of this breed of animal – by a fine Aberdeen terrier. There he was, riding comfortably along, sniffing the fragrant evening breeze; and there was the Scottie, all whiskers and eyebrows, haring after him hell-for-leather. As Jeeves said later, when I described the scene to him, the whole situation resembled some great moment in a Greek tragedy, where somebody is stepping high, wide and handsome, quite unconscious that all the while Nemesis is at his heels, and he may be right.

The constable, I say, was riding without his hands: and but for this the disaster, when it occurred, might not have been so complete. I was a bit of a cyclist myself in my youth – I think I have mentioned that I once won a choir boys' handicap at some village sports – and I can testify that when you are riding without your hands, privacy and a complete freedom from interruption are of the essence. The merest suggestion of an unexpected Scottie connecting with the ankle bone at such a time, and you swoop into a sudden swerve. And, as everybody knows, if the hands are not firmly on the handlebars, a sudden swerve spells a smeller.

And so it happened now. A smeller – and among the finest I have ever been privileged to witness – was what this officer of the law came. One moment he was with us, all merry and bright; the next he was in the ditch, a sort of *macédoine* of arms and legs and wheels, with the terrier standing on the edge, looking down at him with that rather offensive expression of virtuous smugness which I have often noticed on the faces of Aberdeen terriers in their clashes with humanity.

And as he threshed about in the ditch, endeavouring to un-scramble himself, a girl came round the corner, an attractive young prune upholstered in heather-mixture tweeds, and I recognized the familiar features of S. Byng.

After what Gussie had said, I ought to have been expecting Stiffy, of course. Seeing an Aberdeen terrier, I should have gathered that it belonged to her. I might have said to myself: If Scotties come, can Stiffy be far behind?

Stiffy was plainly vexed with the policeman. You could see it in her manner. She hooked the crook of her stick over the Scottie's collar and drew him back; then addressed herself to the man, who had now begun to emerge from the ditch like Venus rising from the foam.

'What on earth,' she demanded, 'did you do that for?'

It was no business of mine, of course, but I couldn't help feeling that she might have made a more tactful approach to what threatened to be a difficult and delicate conference. And I could see that the policeman felt the same. There was a good deal of mud on his face, but not enough to hide the wounded expression.

'You might have scared him out of his wits, hurling yourself about like that. Poor old Bartholomew, did the ugly man nearly squash him flat?'

Again I missed the tactful note. In describing this public servant as ugly, she was undoubtedly technically correct. Only if the competition had consisted of Sir Watkyn Bassett, Oofy Prosser of the Drones, and a few more fellows like that, could he have hoped to win to success in a beauty contest. But one doesn't want to rub these things in. Suavity is what you need on these occasions. You can't beat suavity.

The policeman had now lifted himself and bicycle out of the abyss, and was putting the latter through a series of tests, to ascertain the extent of the damage. Satisfied that it was slight, he turned and eyed Stiffy rather as old Bassett had eyed me on the occasion when I had occupied the Bosher Street dock.

'I was proceeding along the public highway,' he began, in a slow, measured tone, as if he were giving evidence in court, 'and the dorg leaped at me in a verlent manner. I was zurled from my bersicle –'

Stiffy seized upon the point like a practised debater.

'Well, you shouldn't ride a bicycle. Bartholomew hates bicycles.'

'I ride a bersicle, miss, because if I didn't I should have to cover my beat on foot.'

'Do you good. Get some of the fat off you.'

'That,' said the policeman, no mean debater himself, producing a notebook from the recesses of his costume and blowing a water-beetle off it, 'is not the point at tissue. The point at tissue is that this makes twice that the animal has committed an aggravated assault on my person, and I shall have to summons you once more, miss, for being in possession of a savage dorg not under proper control.'

The thrust was a keen one, but Stiffy came back strongly.

'Don't be an ass, Oates. You can't expect a dog to pass up a policeman on a bicycle. It isn't human nature. And I'll bet you started it, anyway. You must have teased him, or something, and I may as well tell you that I intend to fight this case to the House of Lords. I shall call this gentleman as a material witness.' She turned to me, and for the first time became aware that I was no gentleman, but an old friend. 'Oh, hallo, Bertie.'

'Hallo, Stiffy.'

'When did you get here?'

'Oh, recently.'

'Did you see what happened?'

'Oh, rather. Ringside seat throughout.'

'Well, stand by to be subpoenaed.'

'Right ho.'

The policeman had been taking a sort of inventory and writing it down in the book. He was now in a position to call the score.

'Piecer skin scraped off right knee. Bruise or contusion on left elbow. Scratch on nose. Uniform covered with mud and'll have to go and be cleaned. Also shock – severe. You will receive the summons in due course, miss.'

He mounted his bicycle and rode off, causing the dog Bartholomew to make a passionate bound that nearly unshipped him from the restraining stick. Stiffy stood for a moment looking after him a bit yearningly, like a girl who wished that she had half a brick handy. Then she turned away, and I came straight down to brass tacks.

'Stiffy,' I said, 'passing lightly over all the guff about being charmed to see you again and how well you're looking and all that, have you got a small, brown, leather-covered notebook that Gussie Fink-Nottle dropped in the stable yard yesterday?'

She did not reply, seeming to be musing – no doubt on the recent Oates. I repeated the question, and she came out of the trance.

'Notebook?'

'Small, brown, leather-covered one.'

'Full of a lot of breezy personal remarks?'

'That's the one.'

'Yes, I've got it.'

I flung the hands heavenwards and uttered a joyful yowl. The dog Bartholomew gave me an unpleasant look and said something under his breath in Gaelic, but I ignored him. A kennel of Aberdeen terriers could have rolled their eyes and bared the wisdom tooth without impairing this ecstatic moment.

'Gosh, what a relief!'

'Does it belong to Gussie Fink-Nottle?'

'Yes.'

'You mean to say that it was Gussie who wrote those really excellent character studies of Roderick Spode and Uncle Watkyn? I wouldn't have thought he had it in him.'

'Nobody would. It's a most interesting story. It appears –'

'Though why anyone should waste time on Spode and Uncle Watkyn when there was Oates simply crying out to be written about, I can't imagine. I don't think I have ever met a man, Bertie, who gets in the hair so consistently as this Eustace Oates. He makes me tired. He goes swanking about on that bicycle of his, simply asking for it, and then complains when he gets it. And why should he discriminate against poor Bartholomew in this sickening way? Every red-blooded dog in the village has had a go at his trousers, and he knows it.'

'Where's that book, Stiffy?' I said, returning to the *res*.

'Never mind about books. Let's stick to Eustace Oates. Do you think he means to summons me?'

I said that, reading between the lines, that was rather the impression I had gathered, and she made what I believe is known as a *moue*...Is it *moue*?...Shoving out the lips, I mean, and drawing them quickly back again.

'I'm afraid so, too. There is only one word for Eustace Oates, and that is "malignant". He just goes about seeking whom he may devour. Oh, well, more work for Uncle Watkyn.'

'How do you mean?'

'I shall come up before him.'

'Then he does still operate, even though retired?' I said, remembering with some uneasiness the conversation between this ex-beak and Roderick Spode in the collection room.

'He only retired from Bosher Street. You can't choke a man off magistrating, once it's in his blood. He's a Justice of the Peace now. He holds a sort of Star Chamber court in the library. That's where I always come up. I'll be flitting about, doing the flowers, or sitting in my room with a good book, and the butler comes and says I'm wanted in the library. And there's Uncle Watkyn at the desk, looking like Judge Jeffreys, with Oates waiting to give evidence.'

I could picture the scene. Unpleasant, of course. The sort of thing that casts a gloom over a girl's home life.

'And it always ends the same way, with him putting on the black cap and soaking me. He never listens to a word I say. I don't believe the man understands the ABC of justice.'

'That's how he struck me, when I attended his tribunal.'

'And the worst of it is, he knows just what my allowance is, so can figure out exactly how much the purse will stand. Twice this year he's skinned me to the bone, each time at the instigation of this man Oates – once for exceeding the speed limit in a built-up area, and once because Bartholomew gave him the teeniest little nip on the ankle.'

I tut-tutted sympathetically, but I was wishing that I could edge the conversation back to that notebook. One so frequently finds in girls a disinclination to stick to the important subject.

'The way Oates went on about it, you would have thought Bartholomew had taken his pound of flesh. And I suppose it's all going to happen again now. I'm fed up with this police persecution. One might as well be in Russia. Don't you loathe policemen, Bertie?'

I was not prepared to go quite so far as this in my attitude towards an, on the whole, excellent body of men.

'Well, not *en masse*, if you understand the expression. I suppose they vary, like other sections of the community, some being full of quiet charm, others not so full. I've met some very decent policemen. With the one on duty outside the Drones I am distinctly chummy. *In re* this Oates of yours, I haven't seen enough of him, of course, to form an opinion.'

'Well, you can take it from me that he's one of the worst. And a bitter retribution awaits him. Do you remember the time you gave me lunch at your flat? You were telling me about how you tried to pinch that policeman's helmet in Leicester Square.'

'That was when I first met your uncle. It was that that brought us together.'

'Well, I didn't think much of it at the time, but the other day it suddenly came back to me, and I said to myself: "Out of the mouths of babes and sucklings!" For months I had been trying to think of a way of getting back at this man Oates, and you had showed it to me.'

I started. It seemed to me that her words could bear but one interpretation.

'You aren't going to pinch his helmet?'

'Of course not.'

'I think you're wise.'

'It's man's work. I can see that. So I've told Harold to do it. He has often said he would do anything in the world for me, bless him.'

Stiffy's map, as a rule, tends to be rather grave and dreamy, giving the impression that she is thinking deep, beautiful thoughts. Quite misleading, of course. I don't suppose she would recognize a deep, beautiful thought, if you handed it to her on a skewer with tartare sauce. Like Jeeves, she doesn't often smile, but now her lips had parted – ecstatically, I think – I should have to check up with Jeeves – and her eyes were sparkling.

'What a man!' she said. 'We're engaged, you know.'

'Oh, are you?'

'Yes, but don't tell a soul. It's frightfully secret. Uncle Watkyn mustn't know about it till he has been well sweetened.'

'And who is this Harold?'

'The curate down in the village.' She turned to the dog Bartholomew. 'Is lovely kind curate going to pinch bad, ugly policeman's helmet for his muzzer, zen, and make her very, very happy?' she said.

Or words to that general trend. I can't do the dialect of course.

I stared at the young pill, appalled at her moral code, if you could call it that. You know, the more I see of women, the more I think that there ought to be a law. Something has got to be done about this sex, or the whole fabric of Society will collapse, and then what silly asses we shall all look.

'Curate?' I said. 'But, Stiffy, you can't ask a curate to go about pinching policemen's helmets.'

'Why not?'

'Well, it's most unusual. You'll get the poor bird unfrocked.'

'Unfrocked?'

'It's something they do to parsons when they catch them bending. And this will inevitably be the outcome of the frightful task you have apportioned to the sainted Harold.'

'I don't see that it's a frightful task.'

'You aren't telling me that it's the sort of thing that comes naturally to curates?'

'Yes, I am. It ought to be right up Harold's street. When he was at Magdalen, before he saw the light, he was the dickens of a chap. Always doing things like that.'

Her mention of Magdalen interested me. It had been my own college.

'Magdalen man, is he? What year? Perhaps I know him.'

'Of course you do. He often speaks of you, and was delighted when I told him you were coming here. Harold Pinker.'

I was astounded.

'Harold Pinker? Old Stinker Pinker? Great Scott! One of my dearest pals. I've often wondered where he had got to. And all the while he had sneaked off and become a curate. It just shows you how true it is that one-half of the world doesn't know how the other three-quarters lives. Stinker Pinker, by Jove! You really mean that old Stinker cures souls?'

'Certainly. And jolly well, too. The nibs think very highly of him. Any moment now, he may get a vicarage, and then watch his smoke. He'll be a Bishop some day.'

The excitement of discovering a long-lost buddy waned. I found myself returning to the practical issues. I became grave.

And I'll tell you why I became grave. It was all very well for Stiffy to say that this thing would be right up old Stinker's street. She didn't know him as I did. I had watched Harold Pinker through the formative years of his life, and I knew him for what he was – a large, lumbering, Newfoundland puppy of a chap – full of zeal, yes: always doing his best, true; but never quite able to make the grade; a man, in short, who if there was a chance of bungling an enterprise and landing himself in the soup, would snatch at it. At the idea of him being turned on to perform the extraordinarily delicate task of swiping Constable Oates's helmet, the blood froze. He hadn't a chance of getting away with it.

I thought of Stinker, the youth. Built rather on the lines of Roderick Spode, he had played Rugby football not only for his University but also for England, and at the art of hurling an opponent into a mud puddle and jumping on his neck with cleated boots had had few, if any, superiors. If I had wanted someone to help me out with a mad bull, he would have been my first choice. If by some mischance I had found myself trapped in the underground den of the Secret Nine, there was nobody I would rather have seen coming down the chimney than the Rev. Harold Pinker.

But mere thews and sinews do not qualify a man to pinch policemen's helmets. You need finesse.

'He will, will he?' I said. 'A fat lot of bishing he's going to do, if he's caught sneaking helmets from members of his flock.'

'He won't be caught.'

'Of course he'll be caught. At the old Alma Mater he was always caught. He seemed to have no notion whatsoever of going about a thing in a subtle, tactful way. Chuck it, Stiffy. Abandon the whole project.'

'No.'

'Stiffy!'

'No. The show must go on.'

I gave it up. I could see plainly that it would be mere waste of time to try to argue her out of her girlish daydreams. She had the same type of mind, I perceived, as Roberta Wickham, who once persuaded me to go by night to the bedroom of a fellow guest at a country house and puncture his hot-water bottle with a darning needle on the end of a stick.

'Well, if it must be, it must be, I suppose,' I said resignedly. 'But at least impress upon him that it is essential, when pinching policemen's helmets, to give a forward shove before applying the upwards lift. Otherwise, the subject's chin catches in the strap. It was to overlooking this vital point that my own downfall in Leicester Square was due. The strap caught, the cop was enabled to turn and clutch, and before I knew what had happened I was in the dock, saying "Yes, your Honour" and "No, your Honour" to your Uncle Watkyn.'

I fell into a thoughtful silence, as I brooded on the dark future lying in wait for an old friend. I am not a weak man, but I was beginning to wonder if I had been right in squelching so curtly Jeeves's efforts to get me off on a Round-The-World cruise. Whatever you may say against these excursions – the cramped conditions of shipboard, the possibility of getting mixed up with a crowd of bores, the nuisance of having to go and look at the Taj Mahal – at least there is this to be said in their favour, that you escape the mental agony of watching innocent curates dishing their careers and forfeiting all chance of rising to great heights in the Church by getting caught bonneting their parishioners.

I heaved a sigh, and resumed the conversation.

'So you and Stinker are engaged, are you? Why didn't you tell me when you lunched at the flat?'

'It hadn't happened then. Oh, Bertie, I'm so happy I could bite a grape. At least, I shall be, if we can get Uncle Watkyn thinking along "Bless you, my children" lines.'

'Oh, yes, you were saying, weren't you? About him being sweetened. How do you mean, sweetened?'

'That's what I want to have a talk with you about. You remember what I said in my telegram, about there being something I wanted you to do for me?'

I started. A well-defined uneasiness crept over me. I had forgotten all about that telegram of hers.

'It's something quite simple.'

I doubted it. I mean to say, if her idea of a suitable job for curates was the pinching of policemen's helmets, what sort of an assignment, I could not but ask myself, was she likely to hand to me? It seemed that the moment had come for a bit of in-the-bud-nipping.

'Oh, yes?' I said. 'Well, let me tell you here and now that I'm jolly well not going to do it.'

'Yellow, eh?'

'Bright yellow. Like my Aunt Agatha.'

'What's the matter with her?'

'She's got jaundice.'

'Enough to give her jaundice, having a nephew like you. Why, you don't even know what it is.'

'I would prefer not to know.'

'Well, I'm going to tell you.'

'I do not wish to listen.'

'You would rather I unleashed Bartholomew? I notice he has been looking at you in that odd way of his. I don't believe he likes you. He does take sudden dislikes to people.'

The Woosters are brave, but not rash. I allowed her to lead me to the stone wall that bordered the terrace, and we sat down. The evening, I remember, was one of perfect tranquillity, featuring a sort of serene peace. Which just shows you.

'I won't keep you long,' she said. 'It's all quite simple and straightforward. I shall have to begin, though, by telling you why we have had to be so dark and secret about the engagement. That's Gussie's fault.'

'What has he done?'

'Just been Gussie, that's all. Just gone about with no chin, goggling through his spectacles and keeping newts in his bedroom. You can understand Uncle Watkyn's feelings. His daughter tells him she is going to get married. "Oh, yes?" he says. "Well, let's have a dekko at the chap." And along rolls Gussie. A nasty jar for a father.'

'Quite.'

'Well, you can't tell me that a time when he is reeling under the blow of having Gussie for a son-in-law is the moment for breaking it to him that I want to marry the curate.'

I saw her point. I recollected Freddie Threepwood telling me that there had been trouble at Blandings about a cousin of his wanting to marry a curate. In that case, I gathered, the strain had been eased by the discovery that the fellow was the heir of a Liverpool shipping millionaire; but, as a broad, general rule, parents do not like their daughters marrying curates, and I take it that the same thing applies to uncles with their nieces.

'You've got to face it. Curates are not so hot. So before anything can be done in the way of removing the veil of secrecy, we have got to sell Harold to Uncle Watkyn. If we play our cards properly, I am hoping that he will give him a vicarage which he has in his gift. Then we shall begin to get somewhere.'

I didn't like her use of the word 'we', but I saw what she was driving at, and I was sorry to have to insert a spanner in her hopes and dreams.

'You wish me to put in a word for Stinker? You would like me to draw your uncle aside and tell him what a splendid fellow Stinker is? There is nothing I would enjoy more, my dear Stiffy, but unfortunately we are not on those terms.'

'No, no, nothing like that.'

'Well, I don't see what more I can do.'

'You will,' she said, and again I was conscious of that subtle feeling of uneasiness. I told myself that I must be firm. But I could not but remember Robert Wickham and the hot-water bottle. A man thinks he is being chilled steel – or adamant, if you prefer the expression – and suddenly the mists clear away and he finds that he has allowed a girl to talk him into something frightful. Samson had the same experience with Delilah.

'Oh?' I said, guardedly.

She paused in order to tickle the dog Bartholomew under the left ear. Then she resumed.

'Just praising Harold to Uncle Watkyn isn't any use. You need something much cleverer than that. You want to engineer some terrifically brainy scheme that will put him over with a bang. I thought I had got it a few days ago. Do you ever read *Milady's Boudoir*?'

'I once contributed an article to it on "What The Well-Dressed Man Is Wearing", but I am not a regular reader. Why?'

'There was a story in it last week about a Duke who wouldn't let his daughter marry the young secretary, so the secretary got a friend of his to take the Duke out on the lake and upset the boat, and then he dived in and saved the Duke, and the Duke said "Right ho".'

I resolved that no time should be lost in quashing this idea.

'Any notion you may have entertained that I am going to take Sir W. Bassett out in a boat and upset him can be dismissed instanter. To start with, he wouldn't come out on a lake with me.'

'No. And we haven't a lake. And Harold said that if I was thinking of the pond in the village, I could forget it, as it was much too cold to dive into ponds at this time of year. Harold is funny in some ways.'

'I applaud his sturdy common sense.'

'Then I got an idea from another story. It was about a young lover who gets a friend of his to dress up as a tramp and attack the girl's father, and then he dashes in and rescues him.'

I patted her hand gently.

'The flaw in all these ideas of yours,' I pointed out, 'is that the hero always seems to have a half-witted friend who is eager to place himself in the foulest positions on his behalf. In Stinker's case, this is not so. I am fond of Stinker – you could even go so far as to say that I love him like a brother – but there are sharply defined limits to what I am prepared to do to further his interests.'

'Well, it doesn't matter, because he put the presidential veto on that one, too. Something about what the vicar would say if it all came out. But he loves my new one.'

'Oh, you've got a new one?'

'Yes, and it's terrific. The beauty of it is that Harold's part in it is above reproach. A thousand vicars couldn't get the goods on him. The only snag was that he has to have someone working with him, and until I heard you were coming down here I couldn't think who we were to get. But now you have arrived, all is well.'

'It is, is it? I informed you before, young Byng, and I now inform you again that nothing will induce me to mix myself up with your loathsome schemes.'

'Oh, but Bertie, you must! We're relying on you. And all you have to do is practically nothing. Just steal Uncle Watkyn's cow-creamer.'

I don't know what you would have done, if a girl in heather-mixture tweeds had sprung this on you, scarcely eight hours after a mauve-faced aunt had sprung the same. It is possible that you would have reeled. Most chaps would, I imagine. Personally, I was more amused than aghast. Indeed, if memory serves me aright, I laughed. If so, it was just as well, for it was about the last chance I had.

'Oh, yes?' I said. 'Tell me more,' I said, feeling that it would be entertaining to allow the little blighter to run on. 'Steal his cow-creamer, eh?'

'Yes. It's a thing he brought back from London yesterday for his collection. A sort of silver cow with a kind of blotto look on its face. He thinks the world of it. He had it on the table in front of him at dinner last night, and was gassing away about it. And it was then that I got the idea. I thought that if Harold could pinch it, and then bring it back, Uncle Watkyn would be so grateful that he would start spouting vicarages like a geyser. And then I spotted the catch.'

'Oh, there was a catch?'

'Of course. Don't you see? How would Harold be supposed to have got the thing? If a silver cow is in somebody's collection, and it disappears, and next day a curate rolls round with it, that curate has got to do some good, quick explaining. Obviously, it must be made to look like an outside job.'

'I see. You want me to put on a black mask and break in through the window and snitch this *objet d'art* and hand it over to Stinker? I see. I see.'

I spoke with satirical bitterness, and I should have thought that anyone could have seen that satirical bitterness was what I was speaking with, but she merely looked at me with admiration and approval.

'You are clever, Bertie. That's exactly it. Of course, you needn't wear a mask.'

'You don't think it would help me throw myself into the part?' I said with s. b., as before.

'Well, it might. That's up to you. But the great thing is to get through the window. Wear gloves, of course, because of the fingerprints.'

'Of course.'

'Then Harold will be waiting outside, and he will take the thing from you.'

'And after that I go off and do my stretch at Dartmoor?'

'Oh, no. You escape in the struggle, of course.'

'What struggle?'

'And Harold rushes into the house, all over blood –'

'Whose blood?'

'Well, I said yours, and Harold thought his. There have got to be signs of a struggle to make it more interesting, and my idea was that he should hit you on the nose. But he said the thing would carry greater weight if he was all covered with gore. So how we've left it is that you both hit each other on the nose. And then Harold rouses the house and comes in and shows Uncle Watkyn the cow-creamer and explains what happened, and everything's fine. Because, I mean, Uncle Watkyn couldn't just say "Oh, thanks" and leave it at that, could he? He would be compelled, if he had a spark of decency in him, to cough up that vicarage. Don't you think it's a wonderful scheme, Bertie?'

I rose. My face was cold and hard.

'Most. But I'm sorry –'

'You don't mean you won't do it, now that you see that it will cause you practically no inconvenience at all? It would only take about ten minutes of your time.'

'I do mean I won't do it.'

'Well, I think you're a pig.'

'A pig, maybe, but a shrewd, level-headed pig. I wouldn't touch the project with a bargepole. I tell you I know Stinker. Exactly how he would muck the thing up and get us all landed in the jug, I cannot say, but he would find a way. And now I'll take that book, if you don't mind.'

'What book? Oh, that one of Gussie's.'

'Yes.'

'What do you want it for?'

'I want it,' I said gravely, 'because Gussie is not fit to be in charge of it. He might lose it again, in which event it might fall into the hands of your uncle, in which event he would certainly kick the stuffing out of the Gussie–Madeline wedding arrangements, in which event I would be up against it as few men have ever been up against it before.'

'You?'

'None other.'

'How do you come into it?'

'I will tell you.'

And in a few terse words I outlined for her the events which had taken place at Brinkley Court, the situation which had arisen from those events and the hideous peril which threatened me if Gussie's entry were to be scratched.

'You will understand,' I said, 'that I am implying nothing derogatory to your cousin Madeline, when I say that the idea of being united to her in the bonds of holy wedlock is one that freezes the gizzard. The fact is in no way to her discredit. I should feel just the same about marrying many of the world's noblest women. There are certain females whom one respects, admires, reveres, but only from a distance. If they show any signs of attempting to come closer, one is prepared to fight them off with a blackjack. It is to this group that your cousin Madeline belongs. A charming girl, and the ideal mate for Augustus Fink-Nottle, but ants in the pants to Bertram.'

She drank this in.

'I see. Yes, I suppose Madeline is a bit of a Gawd-help-us.'

'The expression "Gawd-help-us" is one which I would not have gone so far as to use myself, for I think a chivalrous man ought to stop somewhere. But since you have brought it up, I admit that it covers the facts.'

'I never realized that that was how things were. No wonder you want that book.'

'Exactly.'

'Well, all this has opened up a new line of thought.'

That grave, dreamy look had come into her face. She massaged the dog Bartholomew's spine with a pensive foot.

'Come on,' I said, chafing at the delay. 'Slip it across.'

'Just a moment. I'm trying to straighten it all out in my mind. You know, Bertie, I really ought to take that book to Uncle Watkyn.'

'What!'

'That's what my conscience tells me to do. After all, I owe a lot to him. For years he has been a second father to me. And he ought to know how Gussie feels about him, oughtn't he? I mean to say, a bit tough on the old buster, cherishing what he thinks is a harmless newt-fancier in his bosom, when all the time it's a snake that goes about criticizing the way he drinks soup. However, as you're being so sweet and are going to help Harold and me by stealing that cow-creamer, I suppose I shall have to stretch a point.'

We Woosters are pretty quick. I don't suppose it was more than a couple of minutes before I figured out what she meant. I read her purpose, and shuddered.

She was naming the Price of the Papers. In other words, after being blackmailed by an aunt at breakfast, I was now being blackmailed by a female crony before dinner. Pretty good going, even for this lax post-war world.

'Stiffy!' I cried.

'It's no good saying "Stiffy!" Either you sit in and do your bit, or Uncle Watkyn gets some racy light reading over his morning egg and coffee. Think it over, Bertie.'

She hoisted the dog Bartholomew to his feet, and trickled off towards the house. The last I saw of her was a meaning look, directed at me over her shoulder, and it went through me like a knife.

I had slumped back on to the wall, and I sat there, stunned. Just how long, I don't know, but it was a goodish time. Winged creatures of the night barged into me, but I gave them little attention. It was not till a voice suddenly spoke a couple of feet or so above my bowed head that I came out of the coma.

'Good evening, Wooster,' said the voice.

I looked up. The cliff-like mass looming over me was Roderick Spode.

I suppose even Dictators have their chummy moments, when they put their feet up and relax with the boys, but it was plain from the outset that if Roderick Spode had a sunnier side, he had not come with any idea of exhibiting it now. His manner was curt. One sensed the absence of the bonhomous note.

'I should like a word with you, Wooster.'

'Oh, yes?'

'I have been talking to Sir Watkyn Bassett, and he has told me the whole story of the cow-creamer.'

'Oh, yes?'

'And we know why you are here.'

'Oh, yes?'

'Stop saying "Oh, yes?" you miserable worm, and listen to me.'

Many chaps might have resented his tone. I did myself, as a matter of fact. But you know how it is. There are some fellows you are right on your toes to tick off when they call you a miserable worm, others not quite so much.

'Oh, yes,' he said, saying it himself, dash it, 'it is perfectly plain to us why you are here. You have been sent by your uncle to steal this cow-creamer for him. You needn't trouble to deny it. I found you with the thing in your hands this afternoon. And now, we learn, your aunt is arriving. The muster of the vultures, ha!'

He paused a moment, then repeated 'The muster of the vultures,' as if he thought pretty highly of it as a gag. I couldn't see that it was so very hot myself.

'Well, what I came to tell you, Wooster, was that you are being watched – watched closely. And if you are caught stealing that cow-creamer, I can assure you that you will go to prison. You need entertain no hope that Sir Watkyn will shrink from creating a scandal. He will do his duty as a citizen and a Justice of the Peace.'

Here he laid a hand upon my shoulder, and I can't remember when I have experienced anything more unpleasant. Apart from what Jeeves would have called the symbolism of the action, he had a grip like the bite of a horse.

'Did you say "Oh, yes?"' he asked.

'Oh, no,' I assured him.

'Good. Now, what you are saying to yourself, no doubt, is that you will not be caught. You imagine that you and this precious aunt of yours will be clever enough between you to steal the cow-creamer without being detected. It will do you no good, Wooster. If the thing disappears, however cunningly you and your female accomplice may have covered your traces, I shall know where it has gone, and I shall immediately beat you to a jelly. To a jelly,' he repeated, rolling the words round his tongue as if they were vintage port. 'Have you got that clear?'

'Oh, quite.'

'You are sure you understand?'

'Oh, definitely.'

'Splendid.'

A dim figure was approaching across the terrace, and he changed his tone to one of a rather sickening geniality.

'What a lovely evening, is it not? Extraordinarily mild for the time of year. Well, I mustn't keep you any longer. You will be

wanting to go and dress for dinner. Just a black tie. We are quite
informal here. Yes?'

The word was addressed to the dim figure. A familiar cough
revealed its identity.

'I wished to speak to Mr Wooster, sir. I have a message for him
from Mrs Travers. Mrs Travers presents her compliments, sir, and
desires me to say that she is in the Blue Room and would be glad if
you could make it convenient to call upon her there as soon as
possible. She has a matter of importance which she wishes to
discuss.'

I heard Spode snort in the darkness.

'So Mrs Travers has arrived?'

'Yes, sir.'

'And has a matter of importance to discuss with Mr Wooster?'

'Yes, sir.'

'Ha!' said Spode, and biffed off with a short, sharp laugh.

I rose from my seat.

'Jeeves,' I said, 'stand by to counsel and advise. The plot has
thickened.'

CHAPTER 5

I SLID into the shirt, and donned the knee-length under-wear.

'Well, Jeeves,' I said, 'how about it?'

During the walk to the house I had placed him in possession of the latest developments, and had left him to turn them over in his mind with a view to finding a formula, while I went along the passage and took a hasty bath. I now gazed at him hopefully, like a seal awaiting a bit of fish.

'Thought of anything, Jeeves?'

'Not yet, sir, I regret to say.'

'What, no results whatever?'

'None, sir, I fear.'

I groaned a hollow one, and shoved on the trousers. I had become so accustomed to having this gifted man weigh in with the ripest ideas at the drop of the hat that the possibility of his failing to deliver on this occasion had not occurred to me. The blow was a severe one, and it was with a quivering hand that I now socked the feet. A strange frozen sensation had come over me, rendering the physical and mental processes below par. It was as though both limbs and bean had been placed in a refrigerator and overlooked for several days.

'It may be, Jeeves,' I said, a thought occurring, 'that you haven't got the whole scenario clear in your mind. I was able to give you only the merest outline before going off to scour the torso. I think it would help if we did what they do in the thrillers. Do you ever read thrillers?'

'Not very frequently, sir.'

'Well, there's always a bit where the detective, in order to clarify his thoughts, writes down a list of suspects, motives, times when, alibis, clues and what not. Let us try this plan. Take pencil and paper, Jeeves, and we will assemble the facts. Entitle the thing "Wooster, B. – position of." Ready?'

'Yes, sir.'

'Right. Now, then. Item One – Aunt Dahlia says that if I don't pinch that cow-creamer and hand it over to her, she will bar me from her table, and no more of Anatole's cooking.'

'Yes, sir.'

'We now come to Item Two – viz., if I do pinch the cow-creamer and hand it over to her, Spode will beat me to a jelly.'

'Yes, sir.'

'Furthermore – Item Three – if I pinch it and hand it over to her and don't pinch it and hand it over to Harold Pinker, not only shall I undergo the jellying process alluded to above, but Stiffy will take that notebook of Gussie's and hand it over to Sir Watkyn Bassett. And you know and I know what the result of that would be. Well, there you are. That's the set-up. You've got it?'

'Yes, sir. It is certainly a somewhat unfortunate state of affairs.'

I gave him one of my looks.

'Jeeves,' I said, 'don't try me too high. Not at a moment like this. Somewhat unfortunate, forsooth! Who was it you were telling me about the other day, on whose head all the sorrows of the world had come?'

'The Mona Lisa, sir.'

'Well, if I met the Mona Lisa at this moment, I would shake her by the hand and assure her that I knew just how she felt. You see before you, Jeeves, a toad beneath the harrow.'

'Yes, sir. The trousers perhaps a quarter of an inch higher, sir. One aims at the carelessly graceful break over the instep. It is a matter of the nicest adjustment.'

'Like that?'

'Admirable, sir.'

I sighed.

'There are moments, Jeeves, when one asks oneself "Do trousers matter?"'

'The mood will pass, sir.'

'I don't see why it should. If you can't think of a way out of this mess, it seems to me that it is the end. Of course,' I proceeded on a somewhat brighter note, 'you haven't really had time to get your teeth into the problem yet. While I am at dinner, examine it once more from every angle. It is just possible that an inspiration might pop up. Inspirations do, don't they? All in a flash, as it were?'

'Yes, sir. The mathematician Archimedes is related to have discovered the principle of displacement quite suddenly one morning, while in his bath.'

'Well, there you are. And I don't suppose he was such a devil of a chap. Compared with you, I mean.'

'A gifted man, I believe, sir. It has been a matter of general regret that he was subsequently killed by a common soldier.'

'Too bad. Still, all flesh is as grass, what?'

'Very true, sir.'

I lighted a thoughtful cigarette and, dismissing Archimedes for the nonce, allowed my mind to dwell once more on the ghastly jam into which I had been thrust by young Stiffy's ill-advised behaviour.

'You know, Jeeves,' I said, 'when you really start to look into it, it's perfectly amazing how the opposite sex seems to go out of its way to snooter me. You recall Miss Wickham and the hot-water bottle?'

'Yes, sir.'

'And Gwladys what-was-her-name, who put her boyfriend with the broken leg to bed in my flat?'

'Yes, sir.'

'And Pauline Stoker, who invaded my rural cottage at dead of night in a bathing suit?'

'Yes, sir.'

'What a sex! What a sex, Jeeves! But none of that sex, however deadlier than the male, can be ranked in the same class with this Stiffy. Who was the chap, lo! whose name led all the rest – the bird with the angel?'

'Abou ben Adhem, sir.'

'That's Stiffy. She's the top. Yes, Jeeves?'

'I was merely about to enquire, sir, if Miss Byng, when she uttered her threat of handing over Mr Fink-Nottle's notebook to Sir Watkyn, by any chance spoke with a twinkle in her eye?'

'A roguish one, you mean, indicating that she was merely pulling my leg? Not a suspicion of it. No, Jeeves, I have seen untwinkling eyes before, many of them, but never a pair so totally free from twinkle as hers. She wasn't kidding. She meant business. She was fully aware that she was doing something which even by female standards was raw, but she didn't care. The whole fact of the matter is that all this modern emancipation of women has resulted in them getting it up their noses and not giving a damn what they do. It was not like this in Queen Victoria's day. The Prince Consort would have had a word to say about a girl like Stiffy, what?'

'I can conceive that His Royal Highness might quite possibly not have approved of Miss Byng.'

'He would have had her over his knee, laying into her with a slipper, before she knew where she was. And I wouldn't put it past him to have treated Aunt Dahlia in a similar fashion. Talking of which, I suppose I ought to be going and seeing the aged relative.'

'She appeared very desirous of conferring with you, sir.'

'Far from mutual, Jeeves, that desire. I will confess frankly that I am not looking forward to the *séance*.'

'No, sir?'

'No. You see, I sent her a telegram just before tea, saying that I wasn't going to pinch that cow-creamer, and she must have left London long before it arrived. In other words, she has come expecting to find a nephew straining at the leash to do her bidding, and the news will have to be broken to her that the deal is off. She will not like this, Jeeves, and I don't mind telling you that the more I contemplate the coming chat, the colder the feet become.'

'If I might suggest, sir – it is, of course, merely a palliative – but it has often been found in times of despondency that the assumption of formal evening dress has a stimulating effect on the morale.'

'You think I ought to put on a white tie? Spode told me black.'

'I consider that the emergency justifies the departure, sir.'

'Perhaps you're right.'

And, of course, he was. In these delicate matters of psychology he never errs. I got into the full soup and fish, and was immediately conscious of a marked improvement. The feet became warmer, a sparkle returned to the lack-lustre eyes, and the soul seemed to expand as if someone had got to work on it with a bicycle pump. And I was surveying the effect in the mirror, kneading the tie with gentle fingers and running over in my mind a few things which I proposed to say to Aunt Dahlia if she started getting tough, when the door opened and Gussie came in.

At the sight of this bespectacled bird, a pang of compassion shot through me, for a glance was enough to tell me that he was not abreast of stop-press events. There was visible in his demeanour not one of the earmarks of a man to whom Stiffy had been confiding her plans. His bearing was buoyant, and I exchanged a swift, meaning glance with Jeeves. Mine said 'He little knows!' and so did his.

'What ho!' said Gussie. 'What ho! Hallo, Jeeves.'

'Good evening, sir.'

'Well, Bertie, what's the news? Have you seen her?'

The pang of compash became more acute. I heaved a silent sigh. It was to be my mournful task to administer to this old friend a very substantial sock on the jaw, and I shrank from it.

Still, these things have to be faced. The surgeon's knife, I mean to say.

'Yes,' I said. 'Yes, I've seen her. Jeeves, have we any brandy?'

'No, sir.'

'Could you get a spot?'

'Certainly, sir.'

'Better bring the bottle.'

'Very good, sir.'

He melted away, and Gussie stared at me in honest amazement.

'What's all this? You can't start swigging brandy just before dinner.'

'I do not propose to. It is for you, my suffering old martyr at the stake, that I require the stuff.'

'I don't drink brandy.'

'I'll bet you drink this brandy – yes, and call for more. Sit down, Gussie, and let us chat awhile.'

And depositing him in the armchair, I engaged him in desultory conversation about the weather and the crops. I didn't want to spring the thing on him till the restorative was handy. I prattled on, endeavouring to infuse into my deportment a sort of bedside manner which would prepare him for the worst, and it was not long before I noted that he was looking at me oddly.

'Bertie, I believe you're pie-eyed.'

'Not at all.'

'Then what are you babbling like this for?'

'Just filling in till Jeeves gets back with the fluid. Ah, thank you, Jeeves.'

I took the brimming beaker from his hand, and gently placed Gussie's fingers round the stem.

'You had better go and inform Aunt Dahlia that I shall not be able to keep our tryst, Jeeves. This is going to take some time.'

'Very good, sir.'

I turned to Gussie, who was now looking like a bewildered halibut.

'Gussie,' I said, 'drink that down, and listen. I'm afraid I have bad news for you. About that notebook.'

'About the notebook?'

'Yes.'

'You don't mean she hasn't got it?'

'That is precisely the nub or crux. She has, and she is going to give it to Pop Bassett.'

I had expected him to take it fairly substantially, and he did. His eyes, like stars, started from their spheres and he leaped from the chair, spilling the contents of the glass and causing the room to niff like the saloon bar of a pub on a Saturday night.

'What!'

'That is the posish, I fear.'

'But, my gosh!'

'Yes.'

'You don't really mean that?'

'I do.'

'But why?'

'She has her reasons.'

'But she can't realize what will happen.'

'Yes, she does.'

'It will mean ruin!'

'Definitely.'

'Oh, my gosh!'

It has often been said that disaster brings out the best in the Woosters. A strange calm descended on me. I patted his shoulder.

'Courage, Gussie! Think of Archimedes.'

'Why?'

'He was killed by a common soldier.'

'What of it?'

'Well, it can't have been pleasant for him, but I have no doubt he passed out smiling.'

My intrepid attitude had a good effect. He became more composed. I don't say that even now we were exactly like a couple of French aristocrats waiting for the tumbril, but there was a certain resemblance.

'When did she tell you this?'

'On the terrace not long ago.'

'And she really meant it?'

'Yes.'

'There wasn't –'

'A twinkle in her eyes? No. No twinkle.'

'Well, isn't there any way of stopping her?'

I had been expecting him to bring this up, but I was sorry he had done so. I foresaw a period of fruitless argument.

'Yes,' I said. 'There is. She says she will forgo her dreadful purpose if I steal old Bassett's cow-creamer.'

'You mean that silver cow thing he was showing us at dinner last night?'

'That's the one.'

'But why?'

I explained the position of affairs. He listened intelligently, his face brightening.

'Now I see! Now I understand! I couldn't imagine what her idea was. Her behaviour seemed so absolutely motiveless. Well, that's fine. That solves everything.'

I hated to put a crimp in his happy exuberance, but it had to be done.

'Not quite, because I'm jolly well not going to do it.'

'What! Why not?'

'Because, if I do, Roderick Spode says he will beat me to a jelly.'

'What's Roderick Spode got to do with it?'

'He appears to have espoused that cow-creamer's cause. No doubt from esteem for old Bassett.'

'H'm! Well, you aren't afraid of Roderick Spode.'

'Yes, I am.'

'Nonsense! I know you better than that.'

'No, you don't.'

He took a turn up and down the room.

'But, Bertie, there's nothing to be afraid of in a man like Spode, a mere mass of beef and brawn. He's bound to be slow on his feet. He would never catch you.'

'I don't intend to try him out as a sprinter.'

'Besides, it isn't as if you had to stay on here. You can be off the moment you've put the thing through. Send a note down to this curate after dinner, telling him to be on the spot at midnight, and then go to it. Here is the schedule, as I see it. Steal cow-creamer – say, twelve-fifteen to twelve-thirty, or call it twelve-forty, to allow for accidents. Twelve-forty-five, be at stables, starting up your car. Twelve-fifty, out on the open road, having accomplished a nice, smooth job. I can't think what you're worrying about. The whole thing seems childishly simple to me.'

'Nevertheless –'

'You won't do it?'

'No.'

He moved to the mantelpiece, and began fiddling with a statuette of a shepherdess of sorts.

'Is this Bertie Wooster speaking?' he asked.

'It is.'

'Bertie Wooster whom I admired so at school – the boy we used to call "Daredevil Bertie"?'

'That's right.'

'In that case, I suppose there is nothing more to be said.'

'No.'

'Our only course is to recover the book from the Byng.'

'How do you propose to do that?'

He pondered, frowning. Then the little grey cells seemed to stir.

'I know. Listen. That book means a lot to her, doesn't it?'

'It does.'

'This being so, she would carry it on her person, as I did.'

'I suppose so.'

'In her stocking, probably. Very well, then.'

'How do you mean, very well, then?'

'Don't you see what I'm driving at?'

'No.'

'Well, listen. You could easily engage her in a sort of friendly romp, if you know what I mean, in the course of which it would be simple to…well, something in the nature of a jocular embrace…'

I checked him sharply. There are limits, and we Woosters recognize them.

'Gussie, are you suggesting that I prod Stiffy's legs?'

'Yes.'

'Well, I'm not going to.'

'Why not?'

'We need not delve into my reasons,' I said, stiffly. 'Suffice it that the shot is not on the board.'

He gave me a look, a kind of wide-eyed, reproachful look, such as a dying newt might have given him, if he had forgotten to change its water regularly. He drew in his breath sharply.

'You certainly have altered completely from the boy I knew at school,' he said. 'You seem to have gone all to pieces. No pluck. No dash. No enterprise. Alcohol, I suppose.'

He sighed and broke the shepherdess, and we moved to the door. As I opened it, he gave me another look.

'You aren't coming down to dinner like that, are you? What are you wearing a white tie for?'

'Jeeves recommended it, to keep up the spirits.'

'Well, you're going to feel a perfect ass. Old Bassett dines in a velvet smoking-jacket with soup stains across the front. Better change.'

There was a good deal in what he said. One does not like to look conspicuous. At the risk of lowering the morale, I turned to doff the tails. And as I did so there came to us from the drawing room below the sound of a fresh young voice chanting, to the accompaniment of a piano, what exhibited all the symptoms of being an old English folk song. The ear detected a good deal of 'Hey nonny nonny', and all that sort of thing.

This uproar had the effect of causing Gussie's eyes to smoulder behind the spectacles. It was as if he were feeling that this was just that little bit extra which is more than man can endure.

'Stephanie Byng!' he said bitterly. 'Singing at a time like this!'

He snorted, and left the room. And I was just finishing tying the black tie, when Jeeves entered.

'Mrs Travers,' he announced formally.

An 'Oh, golly!' broke from my lips. I had known, of course, hearing that formal announcement, that she was coming, but so does a poor blighter taking a stroll and looking up and seeing a chap in an aeroplane dropping a bomb on his head know that that's coming, but it doesn't make it any better when it arrives.

I could see that she was a good deal stirred up – all of a doodah would perhaps express it better – and I hastened to bung her civilly into the armchair and make my apologies.

'Frightfully sorry I couldn't come and see you, old ancestor,' I said. 'I was closeted with Gussie Fink-Nottle upon a matter deeply affecting our mutual interests. Since we last met, there have been new developments, and my affairs have become somewhat entangled, I regret to say. You might put it that Hell's foundations are quivering. That is not overstating it, Jeeves?'

'No, sir.'

She dismissed my protestations with a wave of the hand.

'So you're having your troubles, too, are you? Well, I don't know what new developments there have been at your end, but there has been a new development at mine, and it's a stinker. That's why I've come down here in such a hurry. The most rapid action has got to be taken, or the home will be in the melting-pot.'

I began to wonder if even the Mona Lisa could have found the going so sticky as I was finding it. One thing after another, I mean to say.

'What is it?' I asked. 'What's happened?'

She choked for a moment, then contrived to utter a single word.

'Anatole!'

'Anatole?' I took her hand and pressed it soothingly. 'Tell me, old fever patient,' I said, 'what, if anything, are you talking about? How do you mean, Anatole?'

'If we don't look slippy, I shall lose him.'

A cold hand seemed to clutch at my heart.

'Lose him?'

'Yes.'

'Even after doubling his wages?'

'Even after doubling his wages. Listen, Bertie. Just before I left home this afternoon, a letter arrived for Tom from Sir Watkyn Bassett. When I say "just before I left home", that was what made me leave home. Because do you know what was in it?'

'What?'

'It contained an offer to swap the cow-creamer for Anatole, and Tom is seriously considering it!'

I stared at her.

'What? Incredulous!'

'Incredible, sir.'

'Thank you, Jeeves. Incredible! I don't believe it. Uncle Tom would never contemplate such a thing for an instant.'

'Wouldn't he? That's all you know. Do you remember Pomeroy, the butler we had before Seppings?'

'I should say so. A noble fellow.'

'A treasure.'

'A gem. I never could think why you let him go.'

'Tom traded him to the Bessington-Copes for an oviform chocolate pot on three scroll feet.'

I struggled with a growing despair.

'But surely the delirious old ass – or, rather Uncle Tom – wouldn't fritter Anatole away like that?'

'He certainly would.'

She rose, and moved restlessly to the mantelpiece. I could see that she was looking for something to break as a relief to her surging emotions – what Jeeves would have called a palliative – and courteously drew her attention to a terra cotta figure of the Infant Samuel at Prayer. She thanked me briefly, and hurled it against the opposite wall.

'I tell you, Bertie, there are no lengths to which a really loony collector will not go to secure a coveted specimen. Tom's actual words, as he handed me the letter to read, were that it would give him genuine pleasure to skin old Bassett alive and personally drop him into a vat of boiling oil, but that he saw no alternative but to meet his demands. The only thing that stopped him wiring him there and then that it was a deal was my telling him that you had gone to Totleigh Towers expressly to pinch the cow-creamer, and that he would have it in his hands almost immediately. How are you coming along in that direction, Bertie? Formed your schemes? All your plans cut and dried? We can't afford to waste time. Every moment is precious.'

I felt a trifle boneless. The news, I saw, would now have to be broken, and I hoped that that was all there would be. This aunt is a formidable old creature, when stirred, and I could not but recall what had happened to the Infant Samuel.

'I was going to talk to you about that,' I said. 'Jeeves, have you that document we prepared?'

'Here it is, sir.'

'Thank you, Jeeves. And I think it might be a good thing if you were to go and bring a spot more brandy.'

'Very good, sir.'

He withdrew, and I slipped her the paper, bidding her read it attentively. She gave it the eye.

'What's all this?'

'You will soon see. Note how it is headed. "Wooster, B. – position of." Those words tell the story. They explain,' I said, backing a step and getting ready to duck, 'why it is that I must resolutely decline to pinch that cow-creamer.'

'What!'

'I sent you a telegram to that effect this afternoon, but, of course, it missed you.'

She was looking at me pleadingly, like a fond mother at an idiot child who has just pulled something exceptionally goofy.

'But, Bertie, dear, haven't you been listening? About Anatole? Don't you realize the position?'

'Oh, quite.'

'Then have you gone cuckoo? When I say "gone", of course –'

I held up a checking hand.

'Let me explain, aged r. You will recall that I mentioned to you that there had been some recent developments. One of these is that Sir Watkyn Bassett knows all about this cow-creamer-pinching scheme and is watching my every movement. Another is that he has confided his suspicions to a pal of his named Spode. Perhaps on your arrival here you met Spode?'

'That big fellow?'

'Big is right, though perhaps "supercolossal" would be more the *mot juste*. Well, Sir Watkyn, as I say, has confided his suspicions to Spode, and I have it from the latter personally that if that cow-creamer disappears, he will beat me to a jelly. That is why nothing constructive can be accomplished.'

A silence of some duration followed these remarks. I could see that she was chewing on the thing and reluctantly coming to the conclusion that it was no idle whim of Bertram's that was causing him to fail her in her hour of need. She appreciated the cleft stick in which he found himself and, unless I am vastly mistaken, shuddered at it.

This relative is a woman who, in the days of my boyhood and adolescence, was accustomed frequently to clump me over the side of the head when she considered that my behaviour warranted this gesture, and I have often felt in these days that she was on the point of doing it again. But beneath this earhole-sloshing exterior there beats a tender heart, and her love for Bertram is, I know, deep-rooted. She would be the last person to wish to see him get his eyes bunged up and have that well-shaped nose punched out of position.

'I see,' she said, at length. 'Yes. That makes things difficult, of course.'

'Extraordinarily difficult. If you care to describe the situation as an *impasse*, it will be all right with me.'

'Said he would beat you to a jelly, did he?'

'That was the expression he used. He repeated it, so that there should be no mistake.'

'Well, I wouldn't for the world have you manhandled by that big stiff. You wouldn't have a chance against a gorilla like that. He would tear the stuffing out of you before you could say "Pip-pip". He would rend you limb from limb and scatter the fragments to the four winds.'

I winced a little.

'No need to make a song about it, old flesh and blood.'

'You're sure he meant what he said?'

'Quite.'

'His bark may be worse than his bite.'

I smiled sadly.

'I see where you're heading, Aunt Dahlia,' I said. 'In another minute you will be asking if there wasn't a twinkle in his eye as he spoke. There wasn't. The policy which Roderick Spode outlined to me at our recent interview is the policy which he will pursue and fulfil.'

'Then we seem to be stymied. Unless Jeeves can think of something.' She addressed the man, who had just entered with the brandy – not before it was time. I couldn't think why he had taken so long over it. 'We are talking of Mr Spode, Jeeves.'

'Yes, madam?'

'Jeeves and I have already discussed the Spode menace,' I said moodily, 'and he confesses himself baffled. For once, that substantial brain has failed to click. He has brooded, but no formula.'

Aunt Dahlia had been swigging the brandy gratefully, and there now came into her face a thoughtful look.

'You know what has just occurred to me?' she said.

'Say on, old thicker than water,' I replied, still with that dark moodiness. 'I'll bet it's rotten.'

'It's not rotten at all. It may solve everything. I've been wondering if this man Spode hasn't some shady secret. Do you know anything about him, Jeeves?'

'No, madam.'

'How do you mean, a secret?'

'What I was turning over in my mind was the thought that, if he had some chink in his armour, one might hold him up by means of it, thus drawing his fangs. I remember, when I was a girl, seeing your Uncle George kiss my governess, and it was amazing how it eased the strain later on, when there was any question of her keeping me in after school to write out the principal imports and exports of the United Kingdom. You see what I mean? Suppose we knew that Spode had shot a fox, or something? You don't think much of it?' she said, seeing that I was pursing my lips dubiously.

'I can see it as an idea. But there seems to me to be one fatal snag – viz. that we don't know.'

'Yes, that's true.' She rose. 'Oh, well, it was just a random thought, I merely threw it out. And now I think I will be returning to my room and spraying my temples with *eau-de-Cologne*. My head feels as if it were about to burst like shrapnel.'

The door closed. I sank into the chair which she had vacated, and mopped the b.

'Well, that's over,' I said thankfully. 'She took the blow better than I had hoped, Jeeves. The Quorn trains its daughters well. But, stiff though her upper lip was, you could see that she felt it deeply, and that brandy came in handy. By the way, you were the dickens of a while bringing it. A St Bernard dog would have been there and back in half the time.'

'Yes, sir. I am sorry. I was detained in conversation by Mr Fink-Nottle.'

I sat pondering.

'You know, Jeeves,' I said, 'that wasn't at all a bad idea of Aunt Dahlia's about getting the goods on Spode. Fundamentally, it was sound. If Spode had buried the body and we knew where, it would unquestionably render him a negligible force. But you say you know nothing about him.'

'No, sir.'

'And I doubt if there is anything to know, anyway. There are some chaps, one look at whom is enough to tell you that they are pukka sahibs who play the game and do not do the things that aren't done, and prominent among these, I fear, is Roderick Spode. I shouldn't imagine that the most rigorous investigation would uncover anything about him worse than that moustache of his, and to the world's scrutiny of that he obviously has no objection, or he wouldn't wear the damned thing.'

'Very true, sir. Still, it might be worth while to institute enquiries.'

'Yes, but where?'

'I was thinking of the Junior Ganymede, sir. It is a club for gentlemen's personal gentlemen in Curzon Street, to which I have belonged for some years. The personal attendant of a gentleman of Mr Spode's prominence would be sure to be a member, and he would, of course, have confided to the secretary a good deal of material concerning him, for insertion in the club book.'

'Eh?'

'Under Rule Eleven, every new member is required to supply the club with full information regarding his employer. This not only provides entertaining reading, but serves as a warning to members who may be contemplating taking service with gentlemen who fall short of the ideal.'

A thought struck me, and I started. Indeed, I started rather violently.

'What happened when you joined?'

'Sir?'

'Did you tell them all about me?'

'Oh, yes, sir.'

'What, everything? The time when old Stoker was after me and I had to black up with boot polish in order to assume a rudimentary disguise?'

'Yes, sir.'

'And the occasion on which I came home after Pongo Twistleton's birthday party and mistook the standard lamp for a burglar?'

'Yes, sir. The members like to have these things to read on wet afternoons.'

'They do, do they? And suppose some wet afternoon Aunt Agatha reads them? Did that occur to you?'

'The contingency of Mrs Spenser Gregson obtaining access to the club book is a remote one.'

'I dare say. But recent events under this very roof will have shown you how women do obtain access to books.'

I relapsed into silence, pondering on this startling glimpse he had accorded of what went on in institutions like the Junior Ganymede, of the existence of which I had previously been unaware. I had known, of course, that at nights, after serving the frugal meal, Jeeves would put on the old bowler hat and slip round the corner, but I had always supposed his destination to have been the saloon bar of some neighbouring pub. Of clubs in Curzon Street I had had no inkling.

Still less had I had an inkling that some of the fruitiest of Bertram Wooster's possibly ill-judged actions were being inscribed in a book. The whole thing to my mind smacked rather unpleasantly of Abou ben Adhem and Recording Angels, and I found myself frowning somewhat.

Still, there didn't seem much to be done about it, so I returned to what Constable Oates would have called the point at tissue.

'Then what's your idea? To apply to the Secretary for information about Spode?'

'Yes, sir.'

'You think he'll give it to you?'

'Oh, yes, sir.'

'You mean he scatters these data – these extraordinarily dangerous data – these data that might spell ruin if they fell into the wrong hands – broadcast to whoever asks for them?'

'Only to members, sir.'

'How soon could you get in touch with him?'

'I could ring him up on the telephone immediately, sir.'

'Then do so, Jeeves, and if possible chalk the call up to Sir Watkyn Bassett. And don't lose your nerve when you hear the girl say "Three minutes". Carry on regardless. Cost what it may, ye Sec. must be made to understand – and understand thoroughly – that now is the time for all good men to come to the aid of the party.'

'I think I can convince him that an emergency exists, sir.'

'If you can't, refer him to me.'

'Very good, sir.'

He started off on his errand of mercy.

'Oh, by the way, Jeeves,' I said, as he was passing through the door, 'did you say you had been talking to Gussie?'

'Yes, sir.'

'Had he anything new to report?'

'Yes, sir. It appears that his relations with Miss Bassett have been severed. The engagement is broken off.'

He floated out, and I leaped three feet. A dashed difficult thing to do, when you're sitting in an armchair, but I managed it.

'Jeeves!' I yelled.

But he had gone, leaving not a wrack behind.

From downstairs there came the sudden booming of the dinner gong.

IT HAS always given me a bit of a pang to look back at that dinner and think that agony of mind prevented me sailing into it in the right carefree mood, for it was one which in happier circumstances I would have got my nose down to with a will. Whatever Sir Watkyn Bassett's moral shortcomings, he did his guests extraordinarily well at the festive board, and even in my preoccupied condition it was plain to me in the first five minutes that his cook was a woman who had the divine fire in her. From a Grade A soup we proceeded to a toothsome fish, and from the toothsome fish to a salmi of game which even Anatole might have been proud to sponsor. Add asparagus, a jam omelette and some spirited sardines on toast, and you will see what I mean.

All wasted on me, of course. As the fellow said, better a dinner of herbs when you're all buddies together than a regular blow-out when you're not, and the sight of Gussie and Madeline Bassett sitting side by side at the other end of the table turned the food to ashes in my m. I viewed them with concern.

You know what engaged couples are like in mixed company, as a rule. They put their heads together and converse in whispers. They slap and giggle. They pat and prod. I have even known the female member of the duo to feed her companion with a fork. There was none of this sort of thing about Madeline Bassett and Gussie. He looked pale and corpse-like, she cold and proud and aloof. They put in the time for the most part making bread pills and, as far as I was able to ascertain, didn't exchange a word from start to finish. Oh, yes, once – when he asked her to pass the salt, and she passed the pepper, and he said 'I meant the salt,' and she said, 'Oh, really?' and passed the mustard.

There could be no question whatever that Jeeves was right. Brass rags had been parted by the young couple, and what was weighing upon me, apart from the tragic aspect, was the mystery of it all. I could think of no solution, and I looked forward to the conclusion of the meal, when the women should have legged it and I would be able to get together with Gussie over the port and learn the inside dope.

To my surprise, however, the last female had no sooner passed through the door than Gussie, who had been holding it open, shot through after her like a diving duck and did not return, leaving me alone with my host and Roderick Spode. And as they sat snuggled up together at the far end of the table, talking to one another in low voices, and staring at me from time to time as if I had been a ticket-of-leave man who had got in by crashing the gate and might be expected, unless carefully watched, to pocket a spoon or two, it was not long before I, too, left. Murmuring something about fetching my cigarette case, I sidled out and went up to my room. It seemed to me that either Gussie or Jeeves would be bound to look in there sooner or later.

A cheerful fire was burning in the grate, and to while away the time I pulled the armchair up and got out the mystery story I had brought with me from London. As my researches in it had already shown me, it was a particularly good one, full of crisp clues and meaty murders, and I was soon absorbed. Scarcely, however, had I really had time to get going on it, when there was a rattle at the door handle, and who should amble in but Roderick Spode.

I looked at him with not a little astonishment. I mean to say, the last chap I was expecting to invade my bedchamber. And it wasn't as if he had come to apologize for his offensive attitude on the terrace, when in addition to muttering menaces he had called me a miserable worm, or for those stares at the dinner table. One glance at his face told me that. The first thing a chap who has come to apologize does is to weigh in with an ingratiating simper, and of this there was no sign.

As a matter of fact, he seemed to me to be looking slightly more sinister than ever, and I found his aspect so forbidding that I dug up an ingratiating simper myself. I didn't suppose it would do much towards conciliating the blighter, but every little helps.

'Oh, hallo, Spode,' I said affably. 'Come on in. Is there something I can do for you?'

Without replying, he walked to the cupboard, threw it open with a brusque twiddle and glared into it. This done, he turned and eyed me, still in that unchummy manner.

'I thought Fink-Nottle might be here.'

'He isn't.'

'So I see.'

'Did you expect to find him in the cupboard?'

'Yes.'

'Oh?'

There was a pause.

'Any message I can give him if he turns up?'

'Yes. You can tell him that I am going to break his neck.'

'Break his neck?'

'Yes. Are you deaf? Break his neck.'

I nodded pacifically.

'I see. Break his neck. Right. And if he asks why?'

'He knows why. Because he is a butterfly who toys with women's hearts and throws them away like soiled gloves.'

'Right ho.' I hadn't had a notion that that was what butterflies did. Most interesting. 'Well, I'll let him know if I run across him.'

'Thank you.'

He withdrew, slamming the door, and I sat musing on the odd way in which history repeats itself. I mean to say, the situation was almost identical with the one which had arisen some few months earlier at Brinkley, when young Tuppy Glossop had come in to my room with a similar end in view. True, Tuppy, if I remembered rightly, had wanted to pull Gussie inside out and make him swallow himself, while Spode had spoken of breaking his neck, but the principle was the same.

I saw what had happened, of course. It was a development which I had rather been anticipating. I had not forgotten what Gussie had told me earlier in the day about Spode informing him of his intention of leaving no stone unturned to dislocate his cervical vertebrae should he ever do Madeline Bassett wrong. He had doubtless learned the facts from her over the coffee, and was now setting out to put his policy into operation.

As to what these facts were, I still had not the remotest. But it was evident from Spode's manner that they reflected little credit on Gussie. He must, I realized, have been making an ass of himself in a big way.

A fearful situation, beyond a doubt, and if there had been anything I could have done about it, I would have done same without hesitation. But it seemed to me that I was helpless, and that Nature must take its course. With a slight sigh, I resumed my goose-flesher, and was making fair progress with it, when a hollow voice said: 'I say, Bertie!' and I sat up quivering in every limb. It was as if a family spectre had edged up and breathed down the back of my neck.

Turning, I observed Augustus Fink-Nottle appearing from under the bed.

Owing to the fact that the shock had caused my tongue to get tangled up with my tonsils, inducing an unpleasant choking sensation, I found myself momentarily incapable of speech. All I was able to do was goggle at Gussie, and it was immediately evident to me, as I did so, that he had been following the recent conversation closely. His whole demeanour was that of a man vividly conscious of being just about half a jump ahead of Roderick Spode. The hair was ruffled, the eyes wild, the nose twitching. A rabbit pursued by a weasel would have looked just the same – allowing, of course, for the fact that it would not have been wearing tortoiseshell–rimmed spectacles.

'That was a close call, Bertie,' he said, in a low, quivering voice. He crossed the room, giving a little at the knees. His face was a rather pretty greenish colour. 'I think I'll lock the door, if you don't mind. He might come back. Why he didn't look under the bed, I can't imagine. I always thought these Dictators were so thorough.'

I managed to get the tongue unhitched.

'Never mind about beds and Dictators. What's all this about you and Madeline Bassett?'

He winced.

'Do you mind not talking about that?'

'Yes, I do mind not talking about it. It's the only thing I want to talk about. What on earth has she broken off the engagement for? What did you do to her?'

He winced again. I could see that I was probing an exposed nerve.

'It wasn't so much what I did to her – it was what I did to Stephanie Byng.'

'To Stiffy?'

'Yes.'

'What did you do to Stiffy?'

He betrayed some embarrassment.

'I – er…Well, as a matter of fact, I…Mind you, I can see now that it was a mistake, but it seemed a good idea at the time…You see, the fact is…'

'Get on with it.'

He pulled himself together with a visible effort.

'Well, I wonder if you remember, Bertie, what we were saying up here before dinner…about the possibility of her carrying that notebook on her person…I put forward the theory, if you recall, that it might be in her stocking…and I suggested, if you recollect, that one might ascertain…'

I reeled. I had got the gist. 'You didn't –'

'Yes.'

'When?'

Again that look of pain passed over his face.

'Just before dinner. You remember we heard her singing folk songs in the drawing room. I went down there, and there she was at the piano, all alone…At least, I thought she was all alone… And it suddenly struck me that this would be an excellent opportunity to…What I didn't know, you see, was that Madeline, though invisible for the moment, was also present. She had gone behind the screen in the corner to get a further supply of folk songs from the chest in which they are kept … and … well, the long and short of it is that, just as I was… well, to cut a long story short, just as I was…How shall I put it?…Just as I was, so to speak, getting on with it, out she came…and…Well, you see what I mean… I mean, coming so soon after that taking-the-fly-out-of-the-girl's-eye-in-the-stable-yard business, it was not easy to pass it off. As a matter of fact, I didn't pass it off. That's the whole story. How are you on knotting sheets, Bertie?'

I could not follow what is known as the transition of thought.

'Knotting sheets?'

'I was thinking it over under the bed, while you and Spode were chatting, and I came to the conclusion that the only thing to be done is for us to take the sheets off your bed and tie knots in them, and then you can lower me down from the window. They do it in books, and I have an idea I've seen it in the movies. Once outside, I can take your car and drive up to London. After that, my plans are uncertain. I may go to California.'

'California?'

'It's seven thousand miles away. Spode would hardly come to California.'

I stared at him aghast.

'You aren't going to do a bolt?'

'Of course I'm going to do a bolt. Immediately. You heard what Spode said?'

'You aren't afraid of Spode?'

'Yes, I am.'

'But you were saying yourself that he's a mere mass of beef and brawn, obviously slow on his feet.'

'I know. I remember. But that was when I thought he was after you. One's views change.'

'But, Gussie, pull yourself together. You can't just run away.'

'What else can I do?'

'Why, stick around and try to effect a reconciliation. You haven't had a shot at pleading with the girl yet.'

'Yes, I have. I did it at dinner. During the fish course. No good. She just gave me a cold look, and made bread pills.'

I racked the bean. I was sure there must be an avenue some-where, waiting to be explored, and in about half a minute I spotted it.

'What you've got to do,' I said, 'is to get the notebook. If you secured that book and showed it to Madeline, its contents would convince her that your motives in acting as you did towards Stiffy were not what she supposed, but pure to the last drop. She would realize that your behaviour was the outcome of…it's on the tip of my tongue…of a counsel of desperation. She would understand and forgive.'

For a moment, a faint flicker of hope seemed to illumine his twisted features.

'It's a thought,' he agreed. 'I believe you've got something there, Bertie. That's not a bad idea.'

'It can't fail. *Tout comprendre, c'est tout pardonner* about sums it up.'

The flicker faded.

'But how can I get the book? Where is it?'

'It wasn't on her person?'

'I don't think so. Though my investigations were, in the circumstances, necessarily cursory.'

'Then it's probably in her room.'

'Well, there you are. I can't go searching a girl's room.'

'Why not? You see that book I was reading when you popped up. By an odd coincidence – I call it a coincidence, but probably these things are sent to us for a purpose – I had just come to a bit where a gang had been doing that very thing. Do it now, Gussie. She's probably fixed in the drawing room for the next hour or so.'

'As a matter of fact, she's gone to the village. The curate is giving an address on the Holy Land with coloured slides to the Village Mothers at the Working Men's Institute, and she is playing the piano accompaniment. But even so…No, Bertie, I can't do it. It may be the right thing to do…in fact, I can see that it is the right thing to do…but I haven't the nerve. Suppose Spode came in and caught me.'

'Spode would hardly wander into a young girl's room.'

'I don't know so much. You can't form plans on any light-hearted assumption like that. I see him as a chap who wanders everywhere. No. My heart is broken, my future a blank, and there is nothing to be done but accept the fact and start knotting sheets. Let's get at it.'

'You don't knot any of my sheets.'

'But, dash it, my life is at stake.'

'I don't care. I decline to be a party to this craven scooting.'

'Is this Bertie Wooster speaking?'

'You said that before.'

'And I say it again. For the last time, Bertie, will you lend me a couple of sheets and help knot them?'

'No.'

'Then I shall just have to go off and hide somewhere till dawn, when the milk train leaves. Goodbye, Bertie. You have disappointed me.'

'You have disappointed *me*. I thought you had guts.'

'I have, and I don't want Roderick Spode fooling about with them.'

He gave me another of those dying-newt looks, and opened the door cautiously. A glance up and down the passage having apparently satisfied him that it was, for the moment, Spodeless, he slipped out and was gone. And I returned to my book. It was the only thing I could think of that would keep me from sitting torturing myself with agonizing broodings.

Presently I was aware that Jeeves was with me. I hadn't heard him come in, but you often don't with Jeeves. He just streams silently from spot A to spot B, like some gas.

CHAPTER 7

I WOULDN'T say that Jeeves was actually smirking, but there was a definite look of quiet satisfaction on his face, and I suddenly remembered what this sickening scene with Gussie had caused me to forget – viz. that the last time I had seen him he had been on his way to the telephone to ring up the Secretary of the Junior Ganymede Club. I sprang to my feet eagerly. Unless I had misread that look, he had something to report.

'Did you connect with the Sec., Jeeves?'

'Yes, sir. I have just finished speaking to him.'

'And did he dish the dirt?'

'He was most informative, sir.'

'Has Spode a secret?'

'Yes, sir.'

I smote the trouser leg emotionally.

'I should have known better than to doubt Aunt Dahlia. Aunts always know. It's a sort of intuition. Tell me all.'

'I fear I cannot do that, sir. The rules of the club regarding the dissemination of material recorded in the book are very rigid.'

'You mean your lips are sealed?'

'Yes, sir.'

'Then what was the use of telephoning?'

'It is only the details of the matter which I am precluded from mentioning, sir. I am at perfect liberty to tell you that it would greatly lessen Mr Spode's potentiality for evil, if you were to inform him that you know all about Eulalie, sir.'

'Eulalie?'

'Eulalie, sir.'

'That would really put the stopper on him?'

'Yes, sir.'

I pondered. It didn't sound much to go on.

'You're sure you can't go a bit deeper into the subject?'

'Quite sure, sir. Were I to do so, it is probable that my resignation would be called for.'

'Well, I wouldn't want that to happen, of course.' I hated to think of a squad of butlers forming a hollow square while the Committee snipped his buttons off. 'Still, you really are sure that if I look Spode in the eye and spring this gag, he will be baffled? Let's get this quite clear. Suppose you're Spode, and I walk up to you and say "Spode, I know all about Eulalie," that would make you wilt?'

'Yes, sir. The subject of Eulalie, sir, is one which the gentleman, occupying the position he does in the public eye, would, I am convinced, be most reluctant to have ventilated.'

I practised it for a bit. I walked up to the chest of drawers with my hands in my pockets, and said, 'Spode, I know all about Eulalie.' I tried again, waggling my finger this time. I then had a go with folded arms, and I must say it still didn't sound too convincing.

However, I told myself that Jeeves always knew.

'Well, if you say so, Jeeves. Then the first thing I had better do is find Gussie and give him this life-saving information.'

'Sir?'

'Oh, of course, you don't know anything about that, do you? I must tell you, Jeeves, that, since we last met, the plot has thickened again. Were you aware that Spode has long loved Miss Bassett?'

'No, sir.'

'Well, such is the case. The happiness of Miss Bassett is very dear to Spode, and now that her engagement has gone phut for reasons highly discreditable to the male contracting party, he wants to break Gussie's neck.'

'Indeed, sir?'

'I assure you. He was in here just now, speaking of it, and Gussie, who happened to be under the bed at the time, heard him. With the result that he now talks of getting out of the window and going to California. Which, of course, would be fatal. It is imperative that he stays on and tries to effect a reconciliation.'

'Yes, sir.'

'He can't effect a reconciliation, if he is in California.'

'No, sir.'

'So I must go and try to find him. Though, mark you, I doubt if he will be easily found at this point in his career. He is probably on the roof, wondering how he can pull it up after him.'

My misgivings were proved abundantly justified. I searched the house assiduously, but there were no signs of him. Somewhere, no doubt, Totleigh Towers hid Augustus Fink-Nottle, but it kept its secret well. Eventually, I gave it up, and returned to my room, and stap my vitals if the first thing I beheld on entering wasn't the man in person. He was standing by the bed, knotting sheets.

The fact that he had his back to the door and that the carpet was soft kept him from being aware of my entry till I spoke. My 'Hey!' – a pretty sharp one, for I was aghast at seeing my bed thus messed about – brought him spinning round, ashen to the lips.

'Woof!' he exclaimed. 'I thought you were Spode!'

Indignation succeeded panic. He gave me a hard stare. The eyes behind the spectacles were cold. He looked like an annoyed turbot.

'What do you mean, you blasted Wooster,' he demanded, 'by sneaking up on a fellow and saying "Hey!" like that? You might have given me heart failure.'

'And what do you mean, you blighted Fink-Nottle,' I demanded in my turn, 'by mucking up my bed linen after I specifically forbade it? You have sheets of your own. Go and knot those.'

'How can I? Spode is sitting on my bed.'

'He is?'

'Certainly he is. Waiting for me. I went there after I left you, and there he was. If he hadn't happened to clear his throat, I'd have walked right in.'

I saw that it was high time to set this disturbed spirit at rest.

'You needn't be afraid of Spode, Gussie.'

'What do you mean, I needn't be afraid of Spode? Talk sense.'

'I mean just that. Spode, *qua* menace, if *qua* is the word I want, is a thing of the past. Owing to the extraordinary perfection of Jeeves's secret system, I have learned something about him which he wouldn't care to have generally known.'

'What?'

'Ah, there you have me. When I said I had learned it, I should have said that Jeeves had learned it, and unfortunately Jeeves's lips are sealed. However, I am in a position to slip it across the man in no uncertain fashion. If he attempts any rough stuff, I will give him the works.' I broke off, listening. Footsteps were coming along the passage. 'Ah!' I said. 'Someone approaches. This may quite possibly be the blighter himself.'

An animal cry escaped Gussie.

'Lock that door!'

I waved a fairly airy hand.

'It will not be necessary,' I said. 'Let him come. I positively welcome this visit. Watch me deal with him, Gussie. It will amuse you.'

I had guessed correctly. It was Spode, all right. No doubt he had grown weary of sitting on Gussie's bed, and had felt that another chat with Bertram might serve to vary the monotony. He came in, as before, without knocking, and as he perceived Gussie, uttered a wordless exclamation of triumph and satisfaction. He then stood for a moment, breathing heavily through the nostrils.

He seemed to have grown a bit since our last meeting, being now about eight foot six, and had my advice *in re* getting the bulge on him proceeded from a less authoritative source, his aspect might have intimidated me quite a good deal. But so sedulously had I been trained through the years to rely on Jeeves's lightest word that I regarded him without a tremor.

Gussie, I was sorry to observe, did not share my sunny confidence. Possibly I had not given him a full enough explanation of the facts in the case, or it may have been that, confronted with Spode in the flesh, his nerve had failed him. At any rate, he now retreated to the wall and seemed, as far as I could gather, to be trying to get through it. Foiled in this endeavour, he stood looking as if he had been stuffed by some good taxidermist, while I turned to the intruder and gave him a long, level stare, in which surprise and hauteur were nicely blended.

'Well, Spode,' I said, 'what is it now?'

I had put a considerable amount of top spin on the final word, to indicate displeasure, but it was wasted on the man. Giving the question a miss like the deaf adder of Scripture, he began to advance slowly, his gaze concentrated on Gussie. The jaw muscles, I noted, were working as they had done on the occasion when he had come upon me toying with Sir Watkyn Bassett's collection of old silver: and something in his manner suggested that he might at any moment start beating his chest with a hollow drumming sound, as gorillas do in moments of emotion.

'Ha!' he said.

Well, of course, I was not going to stand any rot like that. This habit of his of going about the place saying 'Ha!' was one that had got to be checked, and checked promptly.

'Spode!' I said sharply, and I have an idea that I rapped the table.

He seemed for the first time to become aware of my presence. He paused for an instant, and gave me an unpleasant look.

'Well, what do *you* want?'

I raised an eyebrow or two.

'What do I want? I like that. That's good. Since you ask, Spode, I want to know what the devil you mean by keeping coming into my private apartment, taking up space which I require for other purposes and interrupting me when I am chatting with my personal friends. Really, one gets about as much privacy in this house as a strip-tease dancer. I assume that you have a room of your own. Get back to it, you fat slob, and stay there.'

I could not resist shooting a swift glance at Gussie, to see how he was taking all this, and was pleased to note on his face the burgeoning of a look of worshipping admiration, such as a distressed damsel of the Middle Ages might have directed at a knight on observing him getting down to brass tacks with the dragon. I could see that I had once more become to him the old Daredevil Wooster of our boyhood days, and I had no doubt that he was burning with shame and remorse as he recalled those sneers and jeers of his.

Spode, also, seemed a good deal impressed, though not so favourably. He was staring incredulously, like one bitten by a rabbit. He seemed to be asking himself if this could really be the shrinking violet with whom he had conferred on the terrace.

He asked me if I had called him a slob, and I said I had.

'A fat slob?'

'A fat slob. It is about time,' I proceeded, 'that some public-spirited person came along and told you where you got off. The trouble with you, Spode, is that just because you have succeeded in inducing a handful of half-wits to disfigure the London scene by going about in black shorts, you think you're someone. You hear them shouting, "Heil, Spode!" and you imagine it is the Voice of the People. That is where you make your bloomer. What the Voice of the People is saying is: "Look at that frightful ass Spode swanking about in footer bags! Did you ever in your puff see such a perfect perisher?"'

He did what is known as struggling for utterance.

'Oh?' he said. 'Ha! Well, I will attend to you later.'

'And I,' I retorted, quick as a flash, 'will attend to you now.' I lit a cigarette. 'Spode,' I said, unmasking my batteries, 'I know your secret!'

'Eh?'

'I know all about —'

'All about what?'

It was to ask myself precisely that question that I had paused. For, believe me or believe me not, in this tense moment, when I so sorely needed it, the name which Jeeves had mentioned to me as the magic formula for coping with this blister had completely passed from my mind. I couldn't even remember what letter it began with.

It's an extraordinary thing about names. You've probably noticed it yourself. You think you've got them, I mean to say, and they simply slither away. I've often wished I had a quid for every time some bird with a perfectly familiar map has come up to me and Hallo-Woostered, and had me gasping for air because I couldn't put a label to him. This always makes one feel at a loss, but on no previous occasion had I felt so much at a loss as I did now.

'All about what?' said Spode.

'Well, as a matter of fact,' I had to confess, 'I've forgotten.'

A sort of gasping gulp from up-stage directed my attention to Gussie again, and I could see that the significance of my words had not been lost on him. Once more he tried to back: and as he realized that he had already gone as far as he could go, a glare of despair came into his eyes. And then, abruptly, as Spode began to advance upon him, it changed to one of determination and stern resolve.

I like to think of Augustus Fink-Nottle at that moment. He showed up well. Hitherto, I am bound to say, I had never regarded him highly as a man of action. Essentially the dreamer type, I should have said. But now he couldn't have smacked into it with a prompter gusto if he had been a rough-and-tumble fighter on the San Francisco waterfront from early childhood.

Above him, as he stood glued to the wall, there hung a fairish-sized oil painting of a chap in knee-breeches and a three-cornered hat gazing at a female who appeared to be chirruping to a bird of sorts — a dove, unless I am mistaken, or a pigeon. I had noticed it once or twice since I had been in the room, and had, indeed, thought of giving it to Aunt Dahlia to break instead of the Infant Samuel at Prayer. Fortunately, I had not done so, or Gussie would not now have been in a position to tear it from its moorings and bring it down with a nice wristy action on Spode's head.

I say 'fortunately', because if ever there was a fellow who needed hitting with oil paintings, that fellow was Roderick Spode. From the moment of our first meeting, his every word and action had proved abundantly that this was the stuff to give him. But there is always a catch in these good things, and it took me only an instant to see that this effort of Gussie's, though well meant, had achieved little of constructive importance. What he should have done, of course, was to hold the picture sideways, so as to get the best out of the stout frame. Instead of which, he had used the flat of the weapon, and Spode came through the canvas like a circus rider going through a paper hoop. In other words, what had promised to be a decisive blow had turned out to be merely what Jeeves would call a gesture.

It did, however, divert Spode from his purpose for a few seconds. He stood there blinking, with the thing round his neck like a ruff, and the pause was sufficient to enable me to get into action.

Give us a lead, make it quite clear to us that the party has warmed up and that from now on anything goes, and we Woosters do not hang back. There was a sheet lying on the bed where Gussie had dropped it when disturbed at his knotting, and to snatch this up and envelop Spode in it was with me the work of a moment. It is a long time since I studied the subject, and before committing myself definitely I should have to consult Jeeves, but I have an idea that ancient Roman gladiators used to do much the same sort of thing in the arena, and were rather well thought of in consequence.

I suppose a man who has been hit over the head with a picture of a girl chirruping to a pigeon and almost immediately afterwards enmeshed in a sheet can never really retain the cool, intelligent outlook. Any friend of Spode's, with his interests at heart, would have advised him at this juncture to keep quite still and not stir till he had come out of the cocoon. Only thus, in a terrain so liberally studded with chairs and things, could a purler have been avoided.

He did not do this. Hearing the rushing sound caused by Gussie exiting, he made a leap in its general direction and took the inevitable toss. At the moment when Gussie, moving well, passed through the door, he was on the ground, more inextricably entangled than ever.

My own friends, advising me, would undoubtedly have recommended an immediate departure at this point, and looking back, I can see that where I went wrong was in pausing to hit the bulge which, from the remarks that were coming through at that spot, I took to be Spode's head, with a china vase that stood on the mantelpiece not far from where the Infant Samuel had been. It was a strategical error. I got home all right and the vase broke into a dozen pieces, which was all to the good – for the more of the property of a man like Sir Watkyn Bassett that was destroyed, the better – but the action of dealing this buffet caused me to over-balance. The next moment, a hand coming out from under the sheet had grabbed my coat.

It was a serious disaster, of course, and one which might well have caused a lesser man to feel that it was no use going on struggling. But the whole point about the Woosters, as I have had occasion to remark before, is that they are not lesser men. They keep their heads. They think quickly, and they act quickly. Napoleon was the same. I have mentioned that, at the moment when I was preparing to inform Spode that I knew his secret, I had lighted a cigarette. This cigarette, in its holder, was still between my lips. Hastily removing it, I pressed the glowing end on the ham-like hand which was impeding my getaway.

The results were thoroughly gratifying. You would have thought that the trend of recent events would have put Roderick Spode in a frame of mind to expect anything and be ready for it, but this simple manœuvre found him unprepared. With a sharp cry of anguish, he released the coat, and I delayed no longer. Bertram Wooster is a man who knows when and when not to be among those present. When Bertram Wooster sees a lion in his path, he ducks down a side street. I was off at an impressive speed, and would no doubt have crossed the threshold with a burst which would have clipped a second or two off Gussie's time, had I not experienced a head-on collision with a solid body which hap-pened to be entering at the moment. I remember thinking, as we twined our arms about each other, that at Totleigh Towers, if it wasn't one thing, it was bound to be something else.

I fancy that it was the scent of *eau-de-Cologne* that still clung to her temples that enabled me to identify this solid body as that of

Aunt Dahlia, though even without it the rich, hunting-field expletive which burst from her lips would have put me on the right track. We came down in a tangled heap, and must have rolled inwards to some extent, for the next thing I knew, we were colliding with the sheeted figure of Roderick Spode, who when last seen had been at the other end of the room. No doubt the explanation is that we had rolled nor'-nor'-east and he had been rolling sou'-sou'-west, with the result that we had come together somewhere in the middle.

Spode, I noticed, as Reason began to return to her throne, was holding Aunt Dahlia by the left leg, and she didn't seem to be liking it much. A good deal of breath had been knocked out of her by the impact of a nephew on her midriff, but enough remained to enable her to expostulate, and this she was doing with all the old fire.

'What is this joint?' she was demanding heatedly. 'A loony bin? Has everybody gone crazy? First I meet Spink-Bottle racing along the corridor like a mustang. Then you try to walk through me as if I were thistledown. And now the gentleman in the burnous has started tickling my ankle – a thing that hasn't happened to me since the York and Ainsty Hunt Ball of the year nineteen-twenty-one.'

These protests must have filtered through to Spode, and presumably stirred his better nature, for he let go, and she got up, dusting her dress.

'Now, then,' she said, somewhat calmer. 'An explanation, if you please, and a categorical one. What's the idea? What's it all about? Who the devil's that inside the winding-sheet?'

I made the introductions.

'You've met Spode, haven't you? Mr Roderick Spode, Mrs Travers.'

Spode had now removed the sheet, but the picture was still in position, and Aunt Dahlia eyed it wonderingly.

'What on earth have you got that thing round your neck for?' she asked. Then, in more tolerant vein: 'Wear it if you like, of course, but it doesn't suit you.'

Spode did not reply. He was breathing heavily. I didn't blame him, mind you – in his place, I'd have done the same – but the sound was not agreeable, and I wished he wouldn't. He was also gazing at me intently, and I wished he wouldn't do that, either. His face was flushed, his eyes were bulging, and one had the odd illusion that his hair was standing on end – like quills upon the fretful porpentine, as Jeeves once put it when describing to me the reactions of Barmy Fotheringay-Phipps on seeing a dead snip, on which he had invested largely, come in sixth in the procession at the Newmarket Spring Meeting.

I remember once, during a temporary rift with Jeeves, engaging a man from the registry office to serve me in his stead, and he hadn't been with me a week when he got blotto one night and set fire to the house and tried to slice me up with a carving knife. Said he wanted to see the colour of my insides, of all bizarre ideas. And until this moment I had always looked on that episode as the most trying in my experience. I now saw that it must be ranked second.

This bird of whom I speak was a simple, untutored soul and Spode a man of good education and upbringing, but it was plain that there was one point at which their souls touched. I don't suppose they would have seen eye to eye on any other subject you could have brought up, but in the matter of wanting to see the colour of my insides their minds ran on parallel lines. The only difference seemed to be that whereas my employee had planned to use a carving knife for his excavations, Spode appeared to be satisfied that the job could be done all right with the bare hands.

'I must ask you to leave us, madam,' he said.

'But I've only just come,' said Aunt Dahlia.

'I am going to thrash this man within an inch of his life.'

It was quite the wrong tone to take with the aged relative. She has a very clannish spirit and, as I have said, is fond of Bertram. Her brow darkened.

'You don't touch a nephew of mine.'

'I am going to break every bone in his body.'

'You aren't going to do anything of the sort. The idea!... Here, you!'

She raised her voice sharply as she spoke the concluding words, and what had caused her to do so was the fact that Spode at this moment made a sudden move in my direction.

Considering the manner in which his eyes were gleaming and his moustache bristling, not to mention the gritting teeth and the sinister twiddling of the fingers, it was a move which might have been expected to send me flitting away like an adagio dancer. And had it occurred somewhat earlier, it would undoubtedly have done so. But I did not flit. I stood where I was, calm and collected. Whether I folded my arms or not, I cannot recall, but I remember that there was a faint, amused smile upon my lips.

For that brief monosyllable 'you' had accomplished what a quarter of an hour's research had been unable to do – viz. the unsealing of the fount of memory. Jeeves's words came back to me with a rush. One moment, the mind a blank: the next, the fount of memory spouting like nobody's business. It often happens this way.

'One minute, Spode,' I said quietly. 'Just one minute. Before you start getting above yourself, it may interest you to learn that I know all about Eulalie.'

It was stupendous. I felt like one of those chaps who press buttons and explode mines. If it hadn't been that my implicit faith in Jeeves had led me to expect solid results, I should have been astounded at the effect of this pronouncement on the man. You could see that it had got right in amongst him and churned him up like an egg whisk. He recoiled as if he had run into something hot, and a look of horror and alarm spread slowly over his face.

The whole situation recalled irresistibly to my mind something that had happened to me once up at Oxford, when the heart was young. It was during Eights Week, and I was sauntering on the river-bank with a girl named something that has slipped my mind, when there was a sound of barking and a large, hefty dog came galloping up, full of beans and buck and obviously intent on mayhem. And I was just commending my soul to God, and feeling that this was where the old flannel trousers got about thirty bob's worth of value bitten out of them, when the girl, waiting till she saw the whites of its eyes, with extraordinary presence of mind suddenly opened a coloured Japanese umbrella in the animal's face. Upon which, it did three back somersaults and retired into private life.

Except that he didn't do any back somersaults, Roderick Spode's reactions were almost identical with those of this non-plussed hound. For a moment, he just stood gaping. Then he said 'Oh?' Then his lips twisted into what I took to be his idea of a conciliatory smile. After that, he swallowed six – or it may have been seven – times, as if he had taken aboard a fish bone. Finally, he spoke. And when he did so, it was the nearest thing to a cooing dove that I have ever heard – and an exceptionally mild-mannered dove, at that.

'Oh, do you?' he said.

'I do,' I replied.

If he had asked me what I knew about her, he would have had me stymied, but he didn't.

'Er – how did you find out?'

'I have my methods.'

'Oh?' he said.

'Ah,' I replied, and there was silence again for a moment.

I wouldn't have believed it possible for so tough an egg to sidle obsequiously, but that was how he now sidled up to me. There was a pleading look in his eyes.

'I hope you will keep this to yourself, Wooster? You will keep it to yourself, won't you, Wooster?'

'I will –'

'Thank you, Wooster.'

'– provided,' I continued, 'that we have no more of these extraordinary exhibitions on your part of – what's the word?'

He sidled a bit closer.

'Of course, of course. I'm afraid I have been acting rather hastily.' He reached out a hand and smoothed my sleeve. 'Did I rumple your coat, Wooster? I'm sorry. I forgot myself. It shall not happen again.'

'It had better not. Good Lord! Grabbing fellows' coats and saying you're going to break chaps' bones. I never heard of such a thing.'

'I know, I know. I was wrong.'

'You bet you were wrong. I shall be very sharp on that sort of thing in the future, Spode.'

'Yes, yes, I understand.'

'I have not been at all satisfied with your behaviour since I came to this house. The way you were looking at me at dinner. You may think people don't notice these things, but they do.'

'Of course, of course.'

'And calling me a miserable worm.'

'I'm sorry I called you a miserable worm, Wooster. I spoke without thinking.'

'Always think, Spode. Well, that is all. You may withdraw.'

'Good night, Wooster.'

'Good night, Spode.'

He hurried out with bowed head, and I turned to Aunt Dahlia, who was making noises like a motor-bicycle in the background.

She gazed at me with the air of one who has been seeing visions. And I suppose the whole affair must have been extraordinarily impressive to the casual bystander.

'Well, I'll be –'

Here she paused – fortunately, perhaps, for she is a woman who, when strongly moved, sometimes has a tendency to forget that she is no longer in the hunting-field, and the verb, had she given it utterance, might have proved a bit too fruity for mixed company.

'Bertie! What was all that about?'

I waved a nonchalant hand.

'Oh, I just put it across the fellow. Merely asserting myself. One has to take a firm line with chaps like Spode.'

'Who is this Eulalie?'

'Ah, there you've got me. For information on that point you will have to apply to Jeeves. And it won't be any good, because the club rules are rigid and members are permitted to go only just so far. Jeeves,' I went on, giving credit where credit was due, as is my custom, 'came to me some little while back and told me that I had only to inform Spode that I knew all about Eulalie to cause him to curl up like a burnt feather. And a burnt feather, as you have seen, was precisely what he did curl up like. As to who the above may be, I haven't the foggiest. All that I can say is that she is a chunk of Spode's past – and, one fears, a highly discreditable one.'

I sighed, for I was not unmoved.

'One can fill in the picture for oneself, I think, Aunt Dahlia? The trusting girl who learned too late that men betray…the little bundle…the last mournful walk to the river-bank… the splash… the bubbling cry…I fancy so, don't you? No wonder the man pales beneath the tan a bit at the idea of the world knowing of that.'

Aunt Dahlia drew a deep breath. A sort of Soul's Awakening look had come into her face.

'Good old blackmail! You can't beat it. I've always said so and I always shall. It works like magic in an emergency. Bertie,' she cried, 'do you realize what this means?'

'Means, old relative?'

'Now that you have got the goods on Spode, the only obstacle to your sneaking that cow-creamer has been removed. You can stroll down and collect it tonight.'

I shook my head regretfully. I had been afraid she was going to take that view of the matter. It compelled me to dash the cup of joy from her lips, always an unpleasant thing to have to do to an aunt who dandled one on her knee as a child.

'No,' I said. 'There you're wrong. There, if you will excuse me saying so, you are talking like a fathead. Spode may have ceased to be a danger to traffic, but that doesn't alter the fact that Stiffy still has the notebook. Before taking any steps in the direction of the cow-creamer, I have got to get it.'

'But why? Oh, but I suppose you haven't heard. Madeline Bassett has broken off her engagement with Spink-Bottle. She told me so in the strictest confidence just now. Well, then. The snag before was that young Stephanie might cause the engagement to be broken by showing old Bassett the book. But if it's broken already –'

I shook the bean again.

'My dear old faulty reasoner,' I said, 'you miss the gist by a mile. As long as Stiffy retains that book, it cannot be shown to Madeline Bassett. And only by showing it to Madeline Bassett can Gussie prove to her that his motive in pinching Stiffy's legs was not what she supposed. And only by proving to her that his motive was not what she supposed can he square himself and effect a reconciliation. And only if he squares himself and effects a reconciliation can I avoid the distasteful necessity of having to marry this bally Bassett myself. No, I repeat. Before doing anything else, I have got to have that book.'

My pitiless analysis of the situation had its effect. It was plain from her manner that she had got the strength. For a space, she sat chewing the lower lip in silence, frowning like an aunt who has drained the bitter cup.

'Well, how are you going to get it?'

'I propose to search her room.'

'What's the good of that?'

'My dear old relative, Gussie's investigations have already revealed that the thing is not on her person. Reasoning closely, we reach the conclusion that it must be in her room.'

'Yes, but, you poor ass, whereabouts in her room? It may be anywhere. And wherever it is, you can be jolly sure it's carefully hidden. I suppose you hadn't thought of that.'

As a matter of fact, I hadn't, and I imagine that my sharp 'Oh ah!' must have revealed this, for she snorted like a bison at the water trough.

'No doubt you thought it would be lying out on the dressing table. All right, search her room, if you like. There's no actual harm in it, I suppose. It will give you something to do and keep you out of the public houses. I, meanwhile, will be going off and starting to think of something sensible. It's time one of us did.'

Pausing at the mantelpiece to remove a china horse which stood there and hurl it to the floor and jump on it, she passed along. And I, somewhat discomposed, for I had thought I had got everything neatly planned out and it was a bit of a jar to find that I hadn't, sat down and began to bend the brain.

The longer I bent it the more I was forced to admit that the flesh and blood had been right. Looking round this room of my own, I could see at a glance a dozen places where, if I had had a small object to hide like a leather-covered notebook full of criticisms of old Bassett's method of drinking soup, I could have done so with ease. Presumably, the same conditions prevailed in Stiffy's lair. In going thither, therefore, I should be embarking on a quest well calculated to baffle the brightest bloodhound, let alone a chap who from childhood up had always been rotten at hunt-the-slipper.

To give the brain a rest before having another go at the problem, I took up my goose-flesher again. And, by Jove, I hadn't read more than half a page when I uttered a cry. I had come upon a significant passage.

'Jeeves,' I said, addressing him as he entered a moment later, 'I have come upon a significant passage.'

'Sir?'

I saw that I had been too abrupt, and that footnotes would be required.

'In this thriller I'm reading,' I explained. 'But wait. Before showing it to you, I would like to pay you a stately tribute on the accuracy of your information *re* Spode. A hearty vote of thanks, Jeeves. You said the name Eulalie would make him wilt, and it did. Spode, *qua* menace…is it *qua*?'

'Yes, sir. Quite correct.'

'I thought so. Well, Spode, *qua* menace, is a spent egg. He has dropped out and ceased to function.'

'That is very gratifying, sir.'

'Most. But we are still faced by this Becher's Brook, that young Stiffy continues in possession of the notebook. That notebook, Jeeves, must be located and re-snitched before we are free to move in any other direction. Aunt Dahlia has just left in despondent mood, because, while she concedes that the damned thing is almost certainly concealed in the little pimple's sleeping quarters, she sees no hope of fingers being able to be laid upon it. She says it may be anywhere and is undoubtedly carefully hidden.'

'That is the difficulty, sir.'

'Quite. But that is where this significant passage comes in. It points the way and sets the feet upon the right path. I'll read it to you. The detective is speaking to his pal, and the "they" refers to some bounders at present unidentified, who have been ransacking a girl's room, hoping to find the missing jewels. Listen attentively, Jeeves. "They seem to have looked everywhere, my dear Postlethwaite, except in the one place where they might have expected to find something. Amateurs, Postlethwaite, rank amateurs. They never thought of the top of the cupboard, the thing any experienced crook thinks of at once, because" – note carefully what follows – "because he knows it is every woman's favourite hiding-place."'

I eyed him keenly.

'You see the profound significance of that, Jeeves?'

'If I interpret your meaning aright, sir, you are suggesting that Mr Fink-Nottle's notebook may be concealed at the top of the cupboard in Miss Byng's apartment?'

'Not "may", Jeeves, "must". I don't see how it can be concealed anywhere else but. That detective is no fool. If he says a thing is so, it is so. I have the utmost confidence in the fellow, and am prepared to follow his lead without question.'

'But surely, sir, you are not proposing –'

'Yes, I am. I'm going to do it immediately. Stiffy has gone to the Working Men's Institute, and won't be back for ages. It's absurd to suppose that a gaggle of Village Mothers are going to be sated with coloured slides of the Holy Land, plus piano accompaniment, in anything under two hours. So now is the time to operate while the coast is clear. Gird up your loins, Jeeves, and accompany me.'

'Well, really, sir –'

'And don't say "Well, really, sir". I have had occasion to rebuke you before for this habit of yours of saying "Well, really, sir" in a soupy sort of voice, when I indicate some strategic line of action. What I want from you is less of the "Well, really, sir" and more of the buckling-to spirit. Think feudally, Jeeves. Do you know Stiffy's room?'

'Yes, sir.'

'Then Ho for it!'

I cannot say, despite the courageous dash which I had exhibited in the above slab of dialogue, that it was in any too bobbish a frame of mind that I made my way to our destination. In fact, the nearer I got, the less bobbish I felt. It had been just the same the time I allowed myself to be argued by Roberta Wickham into going and puncturing that hot-water bottle. I hate these surreptitious prowlings. Bertram Wooster is a man who likes to go through the world with his chin up and both feet on the ground, not to sneak about on tiptoe with his spine tying itself into reef knots.

It was precisely because I had anticipated some such reactions that I had been so anxious that Jeeves should accompany me and lend moral support, and I found myself wishing that he would buck up and lend a bit more than he was doing. Willing service and selfless co-operation were what I had hoped for, and he was not giving me them. His manner from the very start betrayed an aloof disapproval. He seemed to be dissociating himself entirely from the proceedings, and I resented it.

Owing to this aloofness on his part and this resentment on mine, we made the journey in silence, and it was in silence that we entered the room and switched on the light.

The first impression I received on giving the apartment the once-over was that for a young shrimp of her shaky moral outlook Stiffy had been done pretty well in the matter of sleeping accommodation. Totleigh Towers was one of those country houses which had been built at a time when people planning a little nest had the idea that a bedroom was not a bedroom unless you could give an informal dance for about fifty couples in it, and this sanctum could have accommodated a dozen Stiffys. In the rays of the small electric light up in the ceiling, the bally thing seemed to stretch for miles in every direction, and the thought that if that detective had not called his shots correctly, Gussie's notebook might be concealed anywhere in these great spaces, was a chilling one.

I was standing there, hoping for the best, when my meditations were broken in upon by an odd, gargling sort of noise, something like static and something like distant thunder, and to cut a long story short this proved to proceed from the larynx of the dog Bartholomew.

He was standing on the bed, stropping his front paws on the coverlet, and so easy was it to read the message in his eyes that we acted like two minds with but a single thought. At the exact moment when I soared like an eagle on to the chest of drawers, Jeeves was skimming like a swallow on to the top of the cupboard. The animal hopped from the bed and, advancing into the middle of the room, took a seat, breathing through the nose with a curious whistling sound, and looking at us from under his eyebrows like a Scottish elder rebuking sin from the pulpit.

And there for a while the matter rested.

CHAPTER 8

JEEVES WAS the first to break a rather strained silence.

'The book does not appear to be here, sir.'

'Eh?'

'I have searched the top of the cupboard, sir, but I have not found the book.'

It may be that my reply erred a trifle on the side of acerbity. My narrow escape from those slavering jaws had left me a bit edgy.

'Blast the book, Jeeves! What about this dog?'

'Yes, sir.'

'What do you mean – "Yes, sir"?'

'I was endeavouring to convey that I appreciate the point which you have raised, sir. The animal's unexpected appearance unquestionably presents a problem. While he continues to main-tain his existing attitude, it will not be easy for us to prosecute the search for Mr Fink-Nottle's notebook. Our freedom of action will necessarily be circumscribed.'

'Then what's to be done?'

'It is difficult to say, sir.'

'You have no ideas?'

'No, sir.'

I could have said something pretty bitter and stinging at this – I don't know what, but something – but I refrained. I realized that it was rather tough on the man, outstanding though his gifts were, to expect him to ring the bell every time, without fail. No doubt that brilliant inspiration of his which had led to my signal victory over the forces of darkness as represented by R. Spode had taken it out of him a good deal, rendering the brain for the nonce a bit flaccid. One could but wait and hope that the machinery would soon get going again, enabling him to seek new high levels of achievement.

And, I felt as I continued to turn the position of affairs over in my mind, the sooner, the better, for it was plain that nothing was going to budge this canine excrescence except an offensive on a major scale, dashingly conceived and skilfully carried out. I don't think I have ever seen a dog who conveyed more vividly the impression of being rooted to the spot and prepared to stay there till the cows – or, in this case, his proprietress – came home. And what I was going to say to Stiffy if she returned and found me roosting on her chest of drawers was something I had not yet thought out in any exactness of detail.

Watching the animal sitting there like a bump on a log, I soon found myself chafing a good deal. I remember Freddie Widgeon, who was once chased on to the top of a wardrobe by an Alsatian during a country house visit, telling me that what he had disliked most about the thing was the indignity of it all – the blow to the proud spirit, if you know what I mean – the feeling, in fine, that he, the Heir of the Ages, as you might say, was camping out on a wardrobe at the whim of a bally dog.

It was the same with me. One doesn't want to make a song and dance about one's ancient lineage, of course, but after all the Woosters did come over with the Conqueror and were extremely pally with him: and a fat lot of good it is coming over with Conquerors, if you're simply going to wind up by being given the elbow by Aberdeen terriers.

These reflections had the effect of making me rather peevish, and I looked down somewhat sourly at the animal.

'I call it monstrous, Jeeves,' I said, voicing my train of thought, 'that this dog should be lounging about in a bedroom. Most unhygienic.'

'Yes, sir.'

'Scotties are smelly, even the best of them. You will recall how my Aunt Agatha's McIntosh niffed to heaven while enjoying my hospitality. I frequently mentioned it to you.'

'Yes, sir.'

'And this one is even riper. He should obviously have been bedded out in the stables. Upon my Sam, what with Scotties in Stiffy's room and newts in Gussie's, Totleigh Towers is not far short of being a lazar house.'

'No, sir.'

'And consider the matter from another angle,' I said, warming to my theme. 'I refer to the danger of keeping a dog of this nature and disposition in a bedroom, where it can spring out ravening on anyone who enters. You and I happen to be able to take care of ourselves in an emergency such as has arisen, but suppose we had been some highly strung house-maid.'

'Yes, sir.'

'I can see her coming into the room to turn down the bed. I picture her as a rather fragile girl with big eyes and a timid expression. She crosses the threshold. She approaches the bed. And out leaps this man-eating dog. One does not like to dwell upon the sequel.'

'No, sir.'

I frowned.

'I wish,' I said, 'that instead of sitting there saying "Yes, sir" and "No, sir", Jeeves, you would do something.'

'But what can I do, sir?'

'You can get action, Jeeves. That is what is required here – sharp, decisive action. I wonder if you recall a visit we once paid to the residence of my Aunt Agatha at Woollam Chersey in the county of Herts. To refresh your memory, it was the occasion on which, in company with the Right Honourable A. B. Filmer, the Cabinet Minister, I was chivvied on to the roof of a shack on the island in the lake by an angry swan.'

'I recall the incident vividly, sir.'

'So do I. And the picture most deeply imprinted on my mental retina – is that the correct expression?'

'Yes, sir.'

'– is of you facing that swan in the most intrepid "You-can't-do-that-there-here" manner and bunging a raincoat over its head, thereby completely dishing its aims and plans and compelling it to revise its whole strategy from the bottom up. It was a beautiful bit of work. I don't know when I have seen a finer.'

'Thank you, sir. I am glad if I gave satisfaction.'

'You certainly, did, Jeeves, in heaping measure. And what crossed my mind was that a similar operation would make this dog feel pretty silly.'

'No doubt, sir. But I have no raincoat.'

.'Then I would advise seeing what you can do with a sheet. And in case you are wondering if a sheet would work as well, I may tell you that just before you came to my room I had had admirable results with one in the case of Mr Spode. He just couldn't seem to get out of the thing.'

'Indeed, sir?'

'I assure you, Jeeves. You could wish no better weapon than a sheet. There are some on the bed.'

'Yes, sir. On the bed.'

There was a pause. I was loath to wrong the man, but if this wasn't a *nolle prosequi*, I didn't know one when I saw one. The distant and unenthusiastic look on his face told me that I was right, and I endeavoured to sting his pride, rather as Gussie in our *pourparlers* in the matter of Spode had endeavoured to sting mine.

'Are you afraid of a tiny little dog, Jeeves?'

He corrected me respectfully, giving it as his opinion that the undersigned was not a tiny little dog, but well above the average in muscular development. In particular, he drew my attention to the animal's teeth.

I reassured him.

'I think you would find that if you were to make a sudden spring, his teeth would not enter into the matter. You could leap on to the bed, snatch up a sheet, roll him up in it before he knew what was happening, and there we would be.'

'Yes, sir.'

'Well, are you going to make a sudden spring?'

'No, sir.'

A rather stiff silence ensued, during which the dog Bartholomew continued to gaze at me unwinkingly, and once more I found myself noticing — and resenting — the superior, sanctimonious expression on his face. Nothing can ever render the experience of being treed on top of a chest of drawers by an Aberdeen terrier pleasant, but it seemed to me that the least you can expect on such an occasion is that the animal will meet you halfway and not drop salt into the wound by looking at you as if he were asking if you were saved.

It was in the hope of wiping this look off his face that I now made a gesture. There was a stump of candle standing in the parent candlestick beside me, and I threw this at the little blighter. He ate it with every appearance of relish, took time out briefly in order to be sick, and resumed his silent stare. And at this moment the door opened and in came Stiffy — hours before I had expected her.

The first thing that impressed itself upon one on seeing her was that she was not in her customary buoyant spirits. Stiffy, as a rule, is a girl who moves jauntily from spot to spot — youthful elasticity is,

I believe, the expression – but she entered now with a slow and dragging step like a Volga boatman. She cast a dull eye at us, and after a brief 'Hullo, Bertie. Hullo, Jeeves,' seemed to dismiss us from her thoughts. She made for the dressing-table and, having removed her hat, sat looking at herself in the mirror with sombre eyes. It was plain that for some reason the soul had got a flat tyre, and seeing that unless I opened the conversation there was going to be one of those awkward pauses, I did so.

'What ho, Stiffy.'

'Hullo.'

'Nice evening. Your dog's just been sick on the carpet.'

All this, of course, was merely by way of leading into the main theme, which I now proceeded to broach.

'Well, Stiffy, I suppose you're surprised to see us here?'

'No, I'm not. Have you been looking for that book?'

'Why, yes. That's right. We have. Though, as a matter of fact, we hadn't got really started. We were somewhat impeded by the bow-wow.' (Keeping it light, you notice. Always the best way on these occasions.) 'He took our entrance in the wrong spirit.'

'Oh?'

'Yes. Would it be asking too much of you to attach a stout lead to his collar, thus making the world safe for democracy?'

'Yes, it would.'

'Surely you wish to save the lives of two fellow creatures?'

'No, I don't. Not if they're men. I loathe all men. I hope Bartholomew bites you to the bone.'

I saw that little was to be gained by approaching the matter from this angle. I switched to another *point d'appui*.

'I wasn't expecting you,' I said. 'I thought you had gone to the Working Men's Institute, to tickle the ivories in accompaniment to old Stinker's coloured lecture on the Holy Land.'

'I did.'

'Back early, aren't you?'

'Yes. The lecture was off. Harold broke the slides.'

'Oh?' I said, feeling that he was just the sort of chap who would break slides. 'How did that happen?'

She passed a listless hand over the brow of the dog Bartholomew, who had stepped up to fraternize.

'He dropped them.'

'What made him do that?'

'He had a shock, when I broke off our engagement.'

'What!'

'Yes.' A gleam came into her eyes, as if she were reliving unpleasant scenes, and her voice took on the sort of metallic sharpness which I have so often noticed in that of my Aunt Agatha during our get-togethers. Her listlessness disappeared, and for the first time she spoke with a girlish vehemence. 'I got to Harold's cottage, and I went in, and after we'd talked of this and that for a while, I said "When are you going to pinch Eustace Oates's helmet, darling?" And would you believe it, he looked at me in a horrible, sheepish, hang-dog way and said that he had been wrestling with his conscience in the hope of getting its OK, but that it simply wouldn't hear of him pinching Eustace Oates's helmet, so it was all off. "Oh?" I said, drawing myself up. "All off, is it? Well, so is our engagement," and he dropped a double handful of coloured slides of the Holy Land, and I came away.'

'You don't mean that?'

'Yes, I do. And I consider that I have had a very lucky escape. If he is the sort of man who is going to refuse me every little thing I ask, I'm glad I found it out in time. I'm delighted about the whole thing.'

Here, with a sniff like the tearing of a piece of calico, she buried the bean in her hands, and broke into what are called uncontrollable sobs.

Well, dashed painful, of course, and you wouldn't be far wrong in saying that I ached in sympathy with her distress. I don't suppose there is a man in the W1 postal district of London more readily moved by a woman's grief than myself. For two pins, if I'd been a bit nearer, I would have patted her head. But though there is this kindly streak in the Woosters, there is also a practical one, and it didn't take me long to spot the bright side to all this.

'Well, that's too bad,' I said. 'The heart bleeds. Eh, Jeeves?'

'Distinctly, sir.'

'Yes, by Jove, it bleeds profusely, and I suppose all that one can say is that one hopes that Time, the great healer, will eventually stitch up the wound. However, as in these circs you will, of course, no longer have any use for that notebook of Gussie's, how about handing it over?'

'What?'

'I said that if your projected union with Stinker is off, you will, of course, no longer wish to keep that notebook of Gussie's among your effects –'

'Oh, don't bother me about notebooks now.'

'No, no, quite. Not for the world. All I'm saying is that if – at your leisure – choose the time to suit yourself – you wouldn't mind slipping it across –'

'Oh, all right. I can't give it you now, though. It isn't here.'

'Not here?'

'No. I put it…Hallo, what's that?'

What had caused her to suspend her remarks just at the point when they were becoming fraught with interest was a sudden tapping sound. A sort of tap-tap-tap. It came from the direction of the window.

This room of Stiffy's, I should have mentioned, in addition to being equipped with four-poster beds, valuable pictures, richly upholstered chairs and all sorts of things far too good for a young squirt who went about biting the hand that had fed her at luncheon at its flat by causing it the utmost alarm and despondency, had a balcony outside its window. It was from this balcony that the tapping sound proceeded, leading one to infer that someone stood without.

That the dog Bartholomew had reached this conclusion was shown immediately by the lissom agility with which he leaped at the window and started trying to bite his way through. Up till this moment he had shown himself a dog of strong reserves, content merely to sit and stare, but now he was full of strange oaths. And I confess that, as I watched his champing and listened to his observations, I congratulated myself on the promptitude with which I had breezed on to that chest of drawers. A bone-crusher, if ever one drew breath, this Bartholomew Byng. Reluctant as one always is to criticize the acts of an all-wise Providence, I was dashed if I could see why a dog of his size should have been fitted out with the jaws and teeth of a crocodile. Still, too late of course to do anything about it now.

Stiffy, after that moment of surprised inaction which was to be expected in a girl who hears tapping sounds at her window, had risen and gone to investigate. I couldn't see a thing from where I was sitting, but she was evidently more fortunately placed. As she drew back the curtain, I saw her clap a hand to her throat, like someone in a play, and a sharp cry escaped her, audible even above the ghastly row which was proceeding from the lips of the frothing terrier.

'Harold!' she yipped, and putting two and two together I gathered that the bird on the balcony must be old Stinker Pinker, my favourite curate.

It was with a sort of joyful yelp, like that of a woman getting together with her demon lover, that the little geezer had spoken his name, but it was evident that reflection now told her that after what had occurred between this man of God and herself this was not quite the tone. Her next words were uttered with a cold, hostile intonation. I was able to hear them, because she had stooped and picked up the bounder Bartholomew, clamping a hand over his mouth to still his cries – a thing I wouldn't have done for a goodish bit of money.

'What do you want?'

Owing to the lull in Bartholomew, the stuff was coming through well now. Stinker's voice was a bit muffled by the intervening sheet of glass, but I got it nicely.

'Stiffy!'

'Well?'

'Can I come in?'

'No, you can't.'

'But I've brought you something.'

A sudden yowl of ecstasy broke from the young pimple.

'Harold! You angel lamb! You haven't got it, after all?'

'Yes.'

'Oh, Harold, my dream of joy!'

She opened the window with eager fingers, and a cold draught came in and played about my ankles. It was not followed, as I had supposed it would be, by old Stinker. He continued to hang about on the outskirts, and a moment later his motive in doing so was made clear.

'I say, Stiffy, old girl, is that hound of yours under control?'

'Yes, rather. Wait a minute.'

She carried the animal to the cupboard and bunged him in, closing the door behind him. And from the fact that no further bulletins were received from him, I imagine he curled up and went to sleep. These Scotties are philosophers, well able to adapt themselves to changing conditions. They can take it as well as dish it out.

'All clear, angel,' she said, and returned to the window, arriving there just in time to be folded in the embrace of the Incoming Stinker.

It was not easy for some moments to sort out the male from the female ingredients in the ensuing tangle, but eventually he disengaged himself and I was able to see him steadily and see him whole. And when I did so, I noticed that there was rather more of him than there had been when I had seen him last. Country butter and the easy life these curates lead had added a pound or two to an always impressive figure. To find the lean, finely trained Stinker of my nonage, I felt that one would have to catch him in Lent.

But the change in him, I soon perceived, was purely superficial. The manner in which he now tripped over a rug and cannoned into an occasional table, upsetting it with all the old thoroughness, showed me that at heart he still remained the same galumphing man with two left feet, who had always been constitutionally incapable of walking through the great Gobi desert without knocking something over.

Stinker's was a face which in the old College days had glowed with health and heartiness. The health was still there − he looked like a clerical beetroot − but of heartiness at this moment one noted rather a shortage. His features were drawn, as if Conscience were gnawing at his vitals. And no doubt it was, for in one hand he was carrying the helmet which I had last observed perched on the dome of Constable Eustace Oates. With a quick, impulsive movement, like that of a man trying to rid himself of a dead fish, he thrust it at Stiffy, who received it with a soft, tender squeal of ecstasy.

'I brought it,' he said dully.

'Oh, Harold!'

'I brought your gloves, too. You left them behind. At least, I've brought one of them. I couldn't find the other.'

'Thank you, darling. But never mind about gloves, my wonder man. Tell me everything that happened.'

He was about to do so, when he paused, and I saw that he was staring at me with a rather feverish look in his eyes. Then he turned and stared at Jeeves. One could read what was passing in his mind. He was debating within himself whether we were real, or whether the nervous strain to which he had been subjected was causing him to see things.

'Stiffy,' he said, lowering his voice, 'don't look now, but is there something on top of that chest of drawers?'

'Eh? Oh, yes, that's Bertie Wooster.'

'Oh, it is?' said Stinker, brightening visibly. 'I wasn't quite sure. Is that somebody on the cupboard, too?'

'That's Bertie's man, Jeeves.'

'How do you do?' said Stinker.

'How do you do, sir?' said Jeeves.

We climbed down, and I came forward with outstretched hand, anxious to get the reunion going.

'What ho, Stinker.'

'Hullo, Bertie.'

'Long time since we met.'

'It is a bit, isn't it?'

'I hear you're a curate now.'

'Yes, that's right.'

'How are the souls?'

'Oh, fine, thanks.'

There was a pause, and I suppose I would have gone on to ask him if he had seen anything of old So-and-so lately or knew what had become of old What's-his-name, as one does when the conversation shows a tendency to drag on these occasions of ancient College chums meeting again after long separation, but before I could do so, Stiffy, who had been crooning over the helmet like a mother over the cot of her sleeping child, stuck it on her head with a merry chuckle, and the spectacle appeared to bring back to Stinker like a slosh in the waistcoat the realization of what he had done. You've probably heard the expression 'The wretched man seemed fully conscious of his position.' That was Harold Pinker at this juncture. He shied like a startled horse, knocked over another table, tottered to a chair, knocked that over, picked it up and sat down, burying his face in his hands.

'If the Infants' Bible Class should hear of this!' he said, shuddering strongly.

I saw what he meant. A man in his position has to watch his step. What people expect from a curate is a zealous performance of his parochial duties. They like to think of him as a chap who preaches about Hivites, Jebusites and what not, speaks the word in season to the backslider, conveys soup and blankets to the deserving bed-ridden and all that sort of thing. When they find him de-helmeting policemen, they look at one another with the raised eyebrow of censure, and ask themselves if he is quite the right man for the job. That was what was bothering Stinker and preventing him being the old effervescent curate whose jolly laugh had made the last School Treat go with such a bang.

Stiffy endeavoured to hearten him.

'I'm sorry, darling. If it upsets you, I'll put it away.' She crossed to the chest of drawers, and did so. 'But why it should,' she said, returning, 'I can't imagine. I should have thought it would have made you so proud and happy. And now tell me everything that happened.'

'Yes,' I said. 'One would like the first-hand story.'

'Did you creep up behind him like a leopard?' asked Stiffy.

'Of course he did,' I said, admonishing the silly young shrimp. 'You don't suppose he pranced up in full view of the fellow? No doubt you trailed him with unremitting snakiness, eh, Stinker, and did the deed when he was relaxing on a stile or somewhere over a quiet pipe?'

Stinker sat staring straight before him, that drawn look still on his face.

'He wasn't on the stile. He was leaning against it. After you left me, Stiffy, I went for a walk to think things over, and I had just crossed Plunkett's meadow and was going to climb the stile into the next one, when I saw something dark in front of me, and there he was.'

I nodded. I could visualize the scene.

'I hope,' I said, 'that you remembered to give the forward shove before the upwards lift?'

'It wasn't necessary. The helmet was not on his head. He had taken it off and put it on the ground. And, I just crept up and grabbed it.'

I started, pursing the lips a bit.

'Not quite playing the game, Stinker.'

'Yes, it was,' said Stiffy, with a good deal of warmth. 'I call it very clever of him.'

I could not recede from my position. At the Drones, we hold strong views on these things.

'There is a right way and a wrong way of pinching policemen's helmets,' I said firmly.

'You're talking absolute nonsense,' said Stiffy. 'I think you were wonderful, darling.'

I shrugged my shoulders.

'How do you feel about it, Jeeves?'

'I scarcely think that it would be fitting for me to offer an opinion, sir.'

'No,' said Stiffy. 'And it jolly well isn't fitting for you to offer an opinion, young pie-faced Bertie Wooster. Who do you think you are,' she demanded, with renewed warmth, 'coming strolling into a girl's bedroom, sticking on dog about the right way and wrong way of pinching helmets? It isn't as if you were such a wonder at it yourself, considering that you got collared and hauled up next morning at Bosher Street, where you had to grovel to Uncle Watkyn in the hope of getting off with a fine.'

I took this up promptly.

'I did not grovel to the old disease. My manner throughout was calm and dignified, like that of a Red Indian at the stake. And when you speak of me hoping to get off with a fine –'

Here Stiffy interrupted, to beg me to put a sock in it.

'Well, all I was about to say was that the sentence stunned me. I felt so strongly that it was a case for a mere reprimand. However, this is beside the point – which is that Stinker in the recent encounter did not play to the rules of the game. I consider his behaviour morally tantamount to shooting a sitting bird. I cannot alter my opinion.'

'And I can't alter my opinion that you have no business in my bedroom. What are you doing here?'

'Yes, I was wondering that,' said Stinker, touching on the point for the first time. And I could see, of course, how he might quite well be surprised at finding this mob scene in what he had supposed the exclusive sleeping apartment of the loved one.

I eyed her sternly.

'You know what I am doing here. I told you. I came –'

'Oh, yes. Bertie came to borrow a book, darling. But' – here her eyes lingered on mine in a cold and sinister manner – 'I'm afraid I can't let him have it just yet. I have not finished with it myself. By the way,' she continued, still holding me with that compelling stare, 'Bertie says he will be delighted to help us with that cow-creamer scheme.'

'Will you, old man?' said Stinker eagerly.

'Of course he will,' said Stiffy. 'He was saying only just now what a pleasure it would be.'

'You won't mind me hitting you on the nose?'

'Of course he won't.'

'You see, we must have blood. Blood is of the essence.'

'Of course, of course, of course,' said Stiffy. Her manner was impatient. She seemed in a hurry to terminate the scene. 'He quite understands that.'

'When would you feel like doing it, Bertie?'

'He feels like doing it tonight,' said Stiffy. 'No sense in putting things off. Be waiting outside at midnight, darling. Everybody will have gone to bed by then. Midnight will suit you, Bertie? Yes, Bertie says it will suit him splendidly. So that's all settled. And now you really must be going, precious. If somebody came in and found you here, they might think it odd. Good night, darling.'

'Good night, darling.'

'Good night, darling.'

'Good night, darling.'

'Wait!' I said, cutting in on these revolting exchanges, for I wished to make a last appeal to Stinker's finer feelings.

'He can't wait. He's got to go. Remember, angel. On the spot, ready to the last button, at twelve pip emma. Good night, darling.'

'Good night, darling.'

'Good night, darling.'

'Good night, darling.'

They passed on to the balcony, the nauseous endearments receding in the distance, and I turned to Jeeves, my face stern and hard.

'Faugh, Jeeves!'

'Sir?'

'I said "Faugh!" I am a pretty broadminded man, but this has shocked me — I may say to the core. It is not so much the behaviour of Stiffy that I find so revolting. She is a female, and the tendency of females to be unable to distinguish between right and wrong is notorious. But that Harold Pinker, a clerk in Holy Orders, a chap who buttons his collar at the back, should countenance this thing appals me. He knows she has got that book. He knows that she is holding me up with it. But does he insist on her returning it? No! He lends himself to the raw work with open enthusiasm. A nice look-out for the Totleigh-in-the-Wold flock, trying to keep on the straight and narrow path with a shepherd like that! A pretty example he sets to this Infants' Bible Class of which he speaks! A few years of sitting at the feet of Harold Pinker and imbibing his extraordinary views on morality and ethics, and every bally child on the list will be serving a long stretch at Wormwood Scrubs for blackmail.'

I paused, much moved. A bit out of breath, too.

'I think you do the gentleman an injustice, sir.'

'Eh?'

'I am sure that he is under the impression that your acquies-cence in the scheme is due entirely to goodness of heart and a desire to assist an old friend.'

'You think she hasn't told him about the notebook?'

'I am convinced of it, sir. I could gather that from the lady's manner.'

'I didn't notice anything about her manner.'

'When you were about to mention the notebook, it betrayed embarrassment, sir. She feared lest Mr Pinker might enquire into the matter and, learning the facts, compel her to make restitution.'

'By Jove, Jeeves, I believe you're right.'

I reviewed the recent scene. Yes, he was perfectly correct. Stiffy, though one of those girls who enjoy in equal quantities the gall of an army mule and the calm *insouciance* of a fish on a slab of ice, had unquestionably gone up in the air a bit when I had seemed about to explain to Stinker my motives for being in the room. I recalled the feverish way in which she had hustled him out, like a small bouncer at a pub ejecting a large customer.

'Egad, Jeeves!' I said, impressed.

There was a muffled crashing sound from the direction of the balcony. A few moments later, Stiffy returned.

'Harold fell off the ladder,' she explained, laughing heartily. 'Well, Bertie, you've got the programme all clear? Tonight's the night!'

I drew out a gasper and lit it.

'Wait!' I said. 'Not so fast. Just one moment, young Stiffy.'

The ring of quiet authority in my tone seemed to take her aback. She blinked twice, and looked at me questioningly, while I, drawing in a cargo of smoke, expelled it nonchalantly through the nostrils.

'Just one moment,' I repeated.

In the narrative of my earlier adventures with Augustus Fink-Nottle at Brinkley Court, with which you may or may not be familiar, I mentioned that I had once read a historical novel about a Buck or Beau or some such cove who, when it became necessary for him to put people where they belonged, was in the habit of laughing down from lazy eyelids and flicking a speck of dust from the irreproachable Mechlin lace at his wrists. And I think I stated that I had had excellent results from modelling myself on this bird.

I did so now.

'Stiffy,' I said, laughing down from lazy eyelids and flicking a speck of cigarette ash from my irreproachable cuff, 'I will trouble you to disgorge that book.'

The questioning look became intensified. I could see that all this was perplexing her. She had supposed that she had Bertram nicely ground beneath the iron heel, and here he was, popping up like a two-year-old, full of the fighting spirit.

'What do you mean?'

I laughed down a bit more.

'I should have supposed,' I said, flicking, 'that my meaning was quite clear. I want that notebook of Gussie's, and I want it immediately, without any more back chat.'

Her lips tightened.

'You will get it tomorrow – if Harold turns in a satisfactory report.'

'I shall get it now.'

'Ha jolly ha!'

'"Ha jolly ha!" to you, young Stiffy, with knobs on,' I retorted with quiet dignity. 'I repeat, I shall get it now. If I don't, I shall go to old Stinker and tell him all about it.'

'All about what?'

'All about everything. At present, he is under the impression that my acquiescence in your scheme is due entirely to goodness of heart and a desire to assist an old friend. You haven't told him about the notebook. I am convinced of it. I could gather that from your manner. When I was about to mention the notebook, it betrayed embarrassment. You feared lest Stinker might enquire into the matter and, learning the facts, compel you to make restitution.'

Her eyes flickered. I saw that Jeeves had been correct in his diagnosis.

'You're talking absolute rot,' she said, but it was with a quaver on the v.

'All right. Well, toodle-oo. I'm off to find Stinker.'

I turned on my heel and, as I expected, she stopped me with a pleading yowl.

'No, Bertie, don't! You mustn't!'

I came back.

'So! You admit it? Stinker knows nothing of your...' The powerful phrase which Aunt Dahlia had employed when speaking of Sir Watkyn Bassett occurred to me – 'of your underhanded skulduggery.'

'I don't see why you call it underhanded skulduggery.'

'I call it underhanded skulduggery because that is what I consider it. And that is what Stinker, dripping as he is with high principles, will consider it when the facts are placed before him.' I turned on the h. again. 'Well, toodle-oo once more.'

'Bertie, wait!'

'Well?'

'Bertie, darling –'

I checked her with a cold wave of the cigarette-holder.

'Less of the "Bertie, darling". "Bertie, darling", forsooth! Nice time to start the "Bertie, darling"-ing.'

'But, Bertie darling, I want to explain. Of course I didn't dare tell Harold about the book. He would have had a fit. He would have said it was a rotten trick, and of course I knew it was. But there was nothing else to do. There didn't seem any other way of getting you to help us.'

'There wasn't.'

'But you are going to help us, aren't you?'

'I am not.'

'Well, I do think you might.'

'I dare say you do, but I won't.'

Somewhere about the first or second line of this chunk of dialogue, I had observed her eyes begin to moisten and her lips to tremble, and a pearly one had started to steal down the cheek. The bursting of the dam, of which that pearly one had been the first preliminary trickle, now set in with great severity. With a brief word to the effect that she wished she were dead and that

I would look pretty silly when I gazed down at her coffin, knowing that my inhumanity had put her there, she flung herself on the bed and started going *oomp*.

It was the old uncontrollable sob-stuff which she had pulled earlier in the proceedings, and once more I found myself a bit unmanned. I stood there irresolute, plucking nervously at the cravat. I have already alluded to the effect of a woman's grief on the Woosters.

'Oomp,' she went.

'Oomp...Oomp...'

'But, Stiffy, old girl, be reasonable. Use the bean. You can't seriously expect me to pinch that cow-creamer.'

'It oomps everything to us.'

'Very possibly. But listen. You haven't envisaged the latent snags. Your blasted uncle is watching my every move, just waiting for me to start something. And even if he wasn't, the fact that I would be co-operating with Stinker renders the thing impossible. I have already given you my views on Stinker as a partner in crime. Somehow, in some manner, he would muck everything up. Why, look at what happened just now. He couldn't even climb down a ladder without falling off.'

'Oomp.'

'And, anyway, just examine this scheme of yours in pitiless analysis. You tell me the wheeze is for Stinker to stroll in, all over blood, and say he hit the marauder on the nose. Let us suppose he does so. What ensues? "Ha!" says your uncle, who doubtless knows a clue as well as the next man. "Hit him on the nose, did you? Keep your eyes skinned, everybody, for a bird with a swollen nose." And the first thing he sees is me with a beezer twice the proper size. Don't tell me he wouldn't draw conclusions.'

I rested my case. It seemed to me that I had made out a pretty good one, and I anticipated the resigned 'Right ho. Yes, I see what you mean. I suppose you're right.' But she merely oomped the more, and I turned to Jeeves, who hitherto had not spoken.

'You follow my reasoning, Jeeves?'

'Entirely, sir.'

'You agree with me, that the scheme, as planned, would merely end in disaster?'

'Yes, sir. It undoubtedly presents certain grave difficulties. I wonder if I might be permitted to suggest an alternative one.'

I stared at the man.

'You mean you have found a formula.'

'I think so, sir.'

His words had de-oomped Stiffy. I don't think anything else in the world would have done it. She sat up, looking at him with a wild surmise.

'Jeeves! Have you really?'

'Yes, miss.'

'Well, you certainly are the most wonderfully woolly baa-lamb that ever stepped.'

'Thank you, miss.'

'Well, let us have it, Jeeves,' I said, lighting another cigarette and lowering self into a chair. 'One hopes, of course, that you are right, but I should have thought personally that there were no avenues.'

'I think we can find one, sir, if we approach the matter from the psychological angle.'

'Oh, psychological?'

'Yes, sir.'

'The psychology of the individual?'

'Precisely, sir.'

'I see. Jeeves,' I explained to Stiffy, who, of course, knew the man only slightly, scarcely more, indeed, than as a silent figure that had done some smooth potato-handing when she had lunched at my flat, 'is and always has been a whale on the psychology of the individual. He eats it alive. What individual, Jeeves?'

'Sir Watkyn Bassett, sir.'

I frowned doubtfully.

'You propose to try to soften that old public enemy? I don't think it can be done, except with a knuckleduster.'

'No, sir. It would not be easy to soften Sir Watkyn, who, as you imply, is a man of strong character, not easily moulded. The idea I have in mind is to endeavour to take advantage of his attitude towards yourself. Sir Watkyn does not like you, sir.'

'I don't like him.'

'No, sir. But the important thing is that he has conceived a strong distaste for you, and would consequently sustain a severe shock, were you to inform him that you and Miss Byng were betrothed and were anxious to be united in matrimony.'

'What! You want me to tell him that Stiffy and I are that way?'

'Precisely, sir.'

I shook the head.

'I see no percentage in it, Jeeves. All right for a laugh, no doubt – watching the old bounder's reactions I mean – but of little practical value.'

Stiffy, too, seemed disappointed. It was plain that she had been hoping for better things.

'It sounds goofy to me,' she said. 'Where would that get us, Jeeves?'

'If I might explain, miss. Sir Watkyn's reactions would, as Mr Wooster suggests, be of a strongly defined character.'

'He would hit the ceiling.'

'Exactly, miss. A very colourful piece of imagery. And if you were then to assure him that there was no truth in Mr Wooster's statement, adding that you were, in actual fact, betrothed to Mr Pinker, I think the overwhelming relief which he would feel at the news would lead him to look with a kindly eye on your union with that gentleman.'

Personally, I had never heard anything so potty in my life, and my manner indicated as much. Stiffy, on the other hand, was all over it. She did the first few steps of a Spring dance.

'Why, Jeeves, that's marvellous!'

'I think it would prove effective, miss.'

'Of course, it would. It couldn't fail. Just imagine, Bertie, darling, how he would feel if you told him I wanted to marry you. Why, if after that I said "Oh, no, it's all right, Uncle Watkyn. The chap I really want to marry is the boy who cleans the boots," he would fold me in his arms and promise to come and dance at the wedding. And when he finds that the real fellow is a splendid, wonderful, terrific man like Harold, the thing will be a walk-over. Jeeves, you really are a specific dream-rabbit.'

'Thank you, miss. I am glad to have given satisfaction.'

I rose. It was my intention to say goodbye to all this. I don't mind people talking rot in my presence, but it must not be utter rot. I turned to Stiffy, who was now in the later stages of her Spring dance, and addressed her with curt severity.

'I will now take the book, Stiffy.'

She was over by the cupboard, strewing roses. She paused for a moment.

'Oh, the book. You want it?'

'I do. Immediately.'

'I'll give it you after you've seen Uncle Watkyn.'

'Oh?'

'Yes. It isn't that I don't trust you, Bertie, darling, but I should feel much happier if I knew that you knew I had still got it, and I'm sure you want me to feel happy. You toddle off and beard him, and then we'll talk.'

I frowned.

'I will toddle off,' I said coldly, 'but beard him, no. I don't seem to see myself bearding him!'

She stared.

'But Bertie, this sounds as if you weren't going to sit in.'

'It was how I meant it to sound.'

'You wouldn't fail me, would you?'

'I would. I would fail you like billy-o.'

'Don't you like the scheme?'

'I do not. Jeeves spoke a moment ago of his gladness at having given satisfaction. He has given me no satisfaction whatsoever. I consider that the idea he has advanced marks the absolute zero in human goofiness, and I am surprised that he should have entertained it. The book, Stiffy, if you please – and slippily.'

She was silent for a space.

'I was rather asking myself,' she said, 'if you might not take this attitude.'

'And now you know the answer,' I riposted. 'I have. The book, if you please.'

'I'm not going to give you the book.'

'Very well. Then I go to Stinker and tell him all.'

'All right. Do. And before you can get within a mile of him, I shall be up in the library, telling Uncle Watkyn all.'

She waggled her chin, like a girl who considers that she has put over a swift one: and, examining what she had said, I was compelled to realize that this was precisely what she had put over. I had overlooked this contingency completely. Her words gave me pause. The best I could do in the way of a comeback was to utter a somewhat baffled 'H'm!' There is no use attempting to disguise the fact – Bertram was nonplussed.

'So there you are. Now, how about it?'

It is never pleasant for a chap who has been doing the dominant male to have to change his stance and sink to ignoble pleadings, but I could see no other course. My voice, which had been firm and resonant, took on a melting tremolo.

'But, Stiffy, dash it! You wouldn't do that?'

'Yes, I would, if you don't go and sweeten Uncle Watkyn.'

'But how can I go and sweeten him? Stiffy, you can't subject me to this fearful ordeal.'

'Yes, I can. And what's so fearful about it? He can't eat you.'

I conceded this.

'True. But that's about the best you can say.'

'It won't be any worse than a visit to the dentist.'

'It'll be worse than six visits to six dentists.'

'Well, think how glad you will be when it's over.'

I drew little consolation from this. I looked at her closely, hoping to detect some signs of softening. Not one. She had been as tough as a restaurant steak, and she continued as tough as a restaurant steak. Kipling was right. D. than the m. No getting round it.

I made one last appeal.

'You won't recede from your position?'

'Not a step.'

'In spite of the fact – excuse me mentioning it – that I gave you a dashed good lunch at my flat, no expense spared?'

'No.'

I shrugged my shoulders, as some Roman gladiator – one of those chaps who threw knotted sheets over people, for instance – might have done on hearing the call-boy shouting his number in the wings.

'Very well, then,' I said.

She beamed at me maternally.

'That's the spirit. That's my brave little man.'

At a less preoccupied moment, I might have resented her calling me her brave little man, but in this grim hour it scarcely seemed to matter.

'Where is this frightful uncle of yours?'

'He's bound to be in the library now.'

'Very good. Then I will go to him.'

I don't know if you were ever told as a kid that story about the fellow whose dog chewed up the priceless manuscript of the book he was writing. The blow-out, if you remember, was that he gave the animal a pained look and said: 'Oh, Diamond,

Diamond, you – or it may have been thou – little know – or possibly knowest – what you – or thou – has – or hast – done.' I heard it in the nursery, and it has always lingered in my mind. And why I bring it up now is that this was how I looked at Jeeves as I passed from the room. I didn't actually speak the gag, but I fancy he knew what I was thinking.

I could have wished that Stiffy had not said 'Yoicks! Tally-ho!' as I crossed the threshold. It seemed to me in the circumstances flippant and in dubious taste.

IT HAS been well said of Bertram Wooster by those who know him best that there is a certain resilience in his nature that enables him as a general rule to rise on stepping-stones of his dead self in the most unfavourable circumstances. It isn't often that I fail to keep the chin up and the eye sparkling. But as I made my way to the library in pursuance of my dreadful task, I freely admit that Life had pretty well got me down. It was with leaden feet, as the expression is, that I tooled along.

Stiffy had compared the binge under advisement to a visit to the dentist, but as I reached journey's end I was feeling more as I had felt in the old days of school when going to keep a tryst with the headmaster in his study. You will recall me telling you of the time I sneaked down by night to the Rev. Aubrey Upjohn's lair in quest of biscuits and found myself unexpectedly cheek by jowl with the old bird, I in striped non-shrinkable pyjamas, he in tweeds and a dirty look. On that occasion, before parting, we had made a date for half-past four next day at the same spot, and my emotions were almost exactly similar to those which I had experienced on that far-off afternoon, as I tapped on the door and heard a scarcely human voice invite me to enter.

The only difference was that while the Rev. Aubrey had been alone, Sir Watkyn Bassett appeared to be entertaining company. As my knuckles hovered over the panel, I seemed to hear the rumble of voices, and when I went in I found that my ears had not deceived me. Pop Bassett was seated at the desk, and by his side stood Constable Eustace Oates. It was a spectacle that rather put the lid on the shrinking feeling from which I was suffering. I don't know if you have ever been jerked before a tribunal of justice, but if you have you will bear me out when I say that the memory of such an experience lingers, with the result that when later you are suddenly confronted by a sitting magistrate and a standing policeman, the association of ideas gives you a bit of a shock and tends to unman.

A swift keen glance from old B. did nothing to still the fluttering pulse.

'Yes, Mr Wooster?'

'Oh – ah – could I speak to you for a moment?'

'Speak to me?' I could see that a strong distaste for having his sanctum cluttered up with Woosters was contending in Sir Watkyn Bassett's bosom with a sense of the obligations of a host. After what seemed a nip-and-tuck struggle, the latter got its nose ahead. 'Why, yes…That is…If you really…Oh, certainly…Pray take a seat.'

I did so, and felt a good deal better. In the dock, you have to stand. Old Bassett, after a quick look in my direction to see that I wasn't stealing the carpet, turned to the constable again.

'Well, I think that is all, Oates.'

'Very good, Sir Watkyn.'

'You understand what I wish you to do?'

'Yes, sir.'

'And with regard to that other matter, I will look into it very closely, bearing in mind what you have told me of your suspicions. A most rigorous investigation shall be made.'

The zealous officer clumped out. Old Bassett fiddled for a moment with the papers on his desk. Then he cocked an eye at me.

'That was Constable Oates, Mr Wooster.'

'Yes.'

'You know him?'

'I've seen him.'

'When?'

'This afternoon.'

'Not since then?'

'No.'

'Are you quite sure?'

'Oh, quite.'

He fiddled with the papers again, then touched on another topic.

'We were all disappointed that you were not with us in the drawing room after dinner, Mr Wooster.'

This, of course, was a bit embarrassing. The man of sensibility does not like to reveal to his host that he has been dodging him like a leper.

'You were much missed.'

'Oh, was I? I'm sorry. I had a bit of a headache, and went and ensconced myself in my room.'

'I see. And you remained there?'

'Yes.'

'You did not by any chance go for a walk in the fresh air, to relieve your headache?'

'Oh, no. Ensconced all the time.'

'I see. Odd. My daughter Madeline tells me that she went twice to your room after the conclusion of dinner, but found it unoccupied.'

'Oh, really? Wasn't I there?'

'You were not.'

'I suppose I must have been somewhere else.'

'The same thought had occurred to me.'

'I remember now. I did saunter out on two occasions.'

'I see.'

He took up a pen and leaned forward, tapping it against his left forefinger.

'Somebody stole Constable Oates's helmet tonight,' he said, changing the subject.

'Oh, yes.'

'Yes. Unfortunately he was not able to see the miscreant.'

'No?'

'No. At the moment when the outrage took place, his back was turned.'

'Dashed difficult, of course, to see miscreants, if your back's turned.'

'Yes.'

'Yes.'

There was a pause. And as, in spite of the fact that we seemed to be agreeing on every point, I continued to sense a strain in the atmosphere, I tried to lighten things with a gag which I remembered from the old *in statu pupillari* days.

'Sort of makes you say to yourself *Quis custodiet ipsos custodes*, what?'

'I beg your pardon?'

'Latin joke,' I exclaimed. '*Quis* – who – *custodiet* – shall guard – *ipsos custodes* – the guardians themselves? Rather funny, I mean to say,' I proceeded, making it clear to the meanest intelligence, 'a chap who's supposed to stop chaps pinching things from chaps having a chap come along and pinch something from him.'

'Ah, I see your point. Yes, I can conceive that a certain type of mind might detect a humorous side to the affair. But I can assure you, Mr Wooster, that that is not the side which presents itself to me as a Justice of the Peace. I take the very gravest view of the matter, and this, when once he is apprehended and placed in custody, I shall do my utmost to persuade the culprit to share.'

I didn't like the sound of this at all. A sudden alarm for old Stinker's well-being swept over me.

'I say, what do you think he would get?'

'I appreciate your zeal for knowledge, Mr Wooster, but at the moment I am not prepared to confide in you. In the words of the late Lord Asquith, I can only say "Wait and see". I think it is possible that your curiosity may be gratified before long.'

I didn't want to rake up old sores, always being a bit of a lad for letting the dead past bury its dead, but I thought it might be as well to give him a pointer.

'You fined me five quid,' I reminded him.

'So you informed me this afternoon,' he said, pince-nezing me coldly. 'But if I understood correctly what you were saying, the outrage for which you were brought before me at Bosher Street was perpetrated on the night of the annual boat race between the Universities of Oxford and Cambridge, when a certain licence is traditionally granted by the authorities. In the present case, there are no such extenuating circumstances. I should certainly not punish the wanton stealing of Government property from the person of Constable Oates with a mere fine.'

'You don't mean it would be chokey?'

'I said that I was not prepared to confide in you, but having gone so far I will. The answer to your question, Mr Wooster, is in the affirmative.'

There was a silence. He sat tapping his finger with the pen, I, if memory serves me correctly, straightening my tie. I was deeply concerned. The thought of poor old Stinker being bunged into the Bastille was enough to disturb anyone with a kindly interest in his career and prospects. Nothing retards a curate's advancement in his chosen profession more surely than a spell in the jug.

He lowered the pen.

'Well, Mr Wooster, I think that you were about to tell me what brings you here?'

I started a bit. I hadn't actually forgotten my mission, of course, but all this sinister stuff had caused me to shove it away at the back of my mind, and the suddenness with which it now came popping out gave me a bit of a jar.

I saw that there would have to be a few preliminary *pourparlers* before I got down to the nub. When relations between a bloke and another bloke are of a strained nature, the second bloke can't charge straight into the topic of wanting to marry the first bloke's niece. Not, that is to say, if he has a nice sense of what is fitting, as the Woosters have.

'Oh, ah, yes. Thanks for reminding me.'

'Not at all.'

'I just thought I'd drop in and have a chat.'

'I see.'

What the thing wanted, of course, was edging into, and I found I had got the approach. I teed up with a certain access of confidence.

'Have you ever thought about love, Sir Watkyn?'

'I beg your pardon?'

'About love. Have you ever brooded on it to any extent?'

'You have not come here to discuss love?'

'Yes, I have. That's exactly it. I wonder if you have noticed a rather rummy thing about it – viz. that it is everywhere. You can't get away from it. Love, I mean. Wherever you go, there it is, buzzing along in every class of life. Quite remarkable. Take newts, for instance.'

'Are you quite well, Mr Wooster?'

'Oh, fine, thanks. Take newts, I was saying. You wouldn't think it, but Gussie Fink-Nottle tells me they get it right up their noses in the mating season. They stand in line by the hour, waggling their tails at the local belles. Starfish, too. Also undersea worms.'

'Mr Wooster –'

'And, according to Gussie, even ribbonlike seaweed. That surprises you, eh? It did me. But he assures me that it is so. Just where a bit of ribbonlike seaweed thinks it is going to get by pressing its suit is more than I can tell you, but at the time of the full moon it hears the voice of Love all right and is up and doing with the best of them. I suppose it builds on the hope that it will look good to other bits of ribbonlike seaweed, which, of course, would also be affected by the full moon. Well, be that as it may, what I'm working round to is that the moon is pretty full now, and if that's how it affects seaweed you can't very well blame a chap like me for feeling the impulse, can you?'

'I am afraid —'

'Well, can you?' I repeated, pressing him strongly. And I threw in an 'eh, what?' to clinch the thing.

But there was no answering spark of intelligence in his eye. He had been looking like a man who had missed the finer shades, and he still looked like a man who had missed the finer shades.

'I am afraid, Mr Wooster, that you will think me dense, but I have not the remotest notion what you are talking about.'

Now that the moment for letting him have it in the eyeball had arrived, I was pleased to find that the all-of-a-twitter feeling which had gripped me at the outset had ceased to function. I don't say that I had become exactly debonair and capable of flicking specks of dust from the irreproachable Mechlin lace at my wrists, but I felt perfectly calm.

What had soothed the system was the realization that in another half-jiffy I was about to slip a stick of dynamite under this old buster which would teach him that we are not put into the world for pleasure alone. When a magistrate has taken five quid off you for what, properly looked at, was a mere boyish peccadillo which would have been amply punished by a waggle of the forefinger and a brief 'Tut, tut!', it is always agreeable to make him jump like a pea on a hot shovel.

'I'm talking about me and Stiffy.'

'Stiffy?'

'Stephanie.'

'Stephanie? My niece?'

'That's right. Your niece. Sir Watkyn,' I said, remembering a good one, 'I have the honour to ask you for your niece's hand.'

'You — what?'

'I have the honour to ask you for your niece's hand.'

'I don't understand.'

'It's quite simple. I want to marry young Stiffy. She wants to marry me. Surely you've got it now? Take a line through that ribbonlike seaweed.'

There was no question as to its being value for money. On the cue 'niece's hand', he had come out of his chair like a rocketing pheasant. He now sank back, fanning himself with the pen. He seemed to have aged quite a lot.

'She wants to marry you?'

'That's the idea.'

'But I was not aware that you knew my niece.'

'Oh, rather. We two, if you care to put it that way, have plucked the gowans fine. Oh, yes, I know Stiffy, all right. Well, I mean to say, if I didn't, I shouldn't want to marry her, should I?'

He seemed to see the justice of this. He became silent, except for a soft, groaning noise. I remembered another good one.

'You will not be losing a niece. You will be gaining a nephew.'

'But I don't want a nephew, damn it!'

Well, there was that, of course.

He rose, and muttering something which sounded like 'Oh, dear! Oh, dear!' went to the fireplace and pressed the bell with a weak finger. Returning to his seat, he remained holding his head in his hands until the butler blew in.

'Butterfield,' he said in a low, hoarse voice, 'find Miss Stephanie and tell her that I wish to speak to her.'

A stage wait then occurred, but not such a long one as you might have expected. It was only about a minute before Stiffy appeared. I imagine she had been lurking in the offing, expectant of his summons. She tripped in, all merry and bright.

'You want to see me, Uncle Watkyn? Oh, hallo, Bertie.'

'Hallo.'

'I didn't know you were here. Have you and Uncle Watkyn been having a nice talk?'

Old Bassett, who had gone into a coma again, came out of it and uttered a sound like the death-rattle of a dying duck.

'"Nice",' he said, 'is not the adjective I would have selected.' He moistened his ashen lips. 'Mr Wooster has just informed me that he wishes to marry you.'

I must say that young Stiffy gave an extremely convincing performance. She stared at him. She stared at me. She clasped her hands. I rather think she blushed.

'Why Bertie!'

Old Bassett broke the pen. I had been wondering when he would.

'Oh, Bertie! You have made me very proud.'

'Proud?' I detected an incredulous note in old Bassett's voice. 'Did you say "proud"?'

'Well, it's the greatest compliment a man can pay a woman, you know. All the nibs are agreed on that. I'm tremendously flattered and grateful...and, well, all that sort of thing. But, Bertie dear, I'm terribly sorry. I'm afraid it's impossible.'

I hadn't supposed that there was anything in the world capable of jerking a man from the depths so effectively as one of those morning mixtures of Jeeves's, but these words acted on old Bassett with an even greater promptitude and zip. He had been sitting in his chair in a boneless, huddled sort of way, a broken man. He now started up, with gleaming eyes and twitching lips. You could see that hope had dawned.

'Impossible? Don't you want to marry him?'

'No.'

'He said you did.'

'He must have been thinking of a couple of other fellows. No, Bertie, darling, it cannot be. You see, I love somebody else.'

Old Bassett started.

'Eh? Who?'

'The most wonderful man in the world.'

'He has a name, I presume?'

'Harold Pinker.'

'Harold Pinker?...Pinker...The only Pinker I know is –'

'The curate. That's right. He's the chap.'

'You love the curate?'

'Ah!' said Stiffy, rolling her eyes up and looking like Aunt Dahlia when she had spoken of the merits of blackmail. 'We've been secretly engaged for weeks.'

It was plain from old Bassett's manner that he was not prepared to classify this under the heading of tidings of great joy. His brows were knitted, like those of some diner in a restaurant who, sailing into his dozen oysters, finds that the first one to pass his lips is a wrong 'un. I saw that Stiffy had shown a shrewd knowledge of human nature, if you could call his that, when she had told me that this man would have to be heavily sweetened before the news could be broken. You could see that he shared the almost universal opinion of parents and uncles that curates were nothing to start strewing roses out of a hat about.

'You know that vicarage that you have in your gift, Uncle Watkyn? What Harold and I were thinking was that you might give him that, and then we could get married at once. You see, apart from the increased dough, it would start him off on the road to higher things. Up till now, Harold has been working under wraps. As a curate, he has had no scope. But slip him a vicarage, and watch him let himself out. There is literally no eminence to which that boy will not rise, once he spits on his hands and starts in.'

She wriggled from base to apex with girlish enthusiasm, but there was no girlish enthusiasm in old Bassett's demeanour. Well, there wouldn't be, of course, but what I mean is there wasn't.

'Ridiculous!'

'Why?'

'I could not dream –'

'Why not?'

'In the first place, you are far too young –'

'What nonsense. Three of the girls I was at school with were married last year. I'm senile compared with some of the infants you see toddling up the aisle nowadays.'

Old Bassett thumped the desk – coming down, I was glad to see, on an upturned paper fastener. The bodily anguish induced by this lent vehemence to his tone.

'The whole thing is quite absurd and utterly out of the question. I refuse to consider the idea for an instant.'

'But what have you got against Harold?'

'I have nothing, as you put it, against him. He seems zealous in his duties and popular in the parish –'

'He's a baa-lamb.'

'No doubt.'

'He played football for England.'

'Very possibly.'

'And he's marvellous at tennis.'

'I dare say he is. But that is not a reason why he should marry my niece. What means has he, if any, beyond his stipend?'

'About five hundred a year.'

'Tchah!'

'Well, I don't call that bad. Five hundred's pretty good sugar, if you ask me. Besides, money doesn't matter.'

'It matters a great deal.'

'You really feel that, do you?'

'Certainly. You must be practical.'

'Right ho, I will. If you'd rather I married for money, I'll marry for money. Bertie, it's on. Start getting measured for the wedding trousers.'

Her words created what is known as a genuine sensation. Old Bassett's 'What!' and my 'Here, I say, dash it!' popped out neck and neck and collided in mid-air, my heart-cry having, perhaps, an even greater horse-power than his. I was frankly appalled. Experience has taught me that you never know with girls, and it might quite possibly happen, I felt, that she would go through with this frightful project as a gesture. Nobody could teach me anything about gestures. Brinkley Court in the preceding summer had crawled with them.

'Bertie is rolling in the stuff and, as you suggest, one might do worse than take a whack at the Wooster millions. Of course, Bertie dear, I am only marrying you to make you happy. I can never love you as I love Harold. But as Uncle Watkyn has taken this violent prejudice against him –'

Old Bassett hit the paper fastener again, but this time didn't seem to notice it.

'My dear child, don't talk such nonsense. You are quite mistaken. You must have completely misunderstood me. I have no prejudice against this young man Pinker. I like and respect him. If you really think your happiness lies in becoming his wife, I would be the last man to stand in your way. By all means, marry him. The alternative –'

He said no more, but gave me a long, shuddering look. Then, as if the sight of me were more than his frail strength could endure, he removed his gaze, only to bring it back again and give me a short quick one. He then closed his eyes and leaned back in his chair, breathing stertorously. And as there didn't seem anything to keep me, I sidled out. The last I saw of him, he was submitting without any great animation to a niece's embrace.

I suppose that when you have an uncle like Sir Watkyn Bassett on the receiving end, a niece's embrace is a thing you tend to make pretty snappy. It wasn't more than about a minute before Stiffy came out and immediately went into her dance.

'What a man! What a man! What a man! What a man! What a man!' she said, waving her arms and giving other indications of *bien-être*. 'Jeeves,' she explained, as if she supposed that I might imagine her to be alluding to the recent Bassett. 'Did he say it would work? He did. And was he right? He was. Bertie, could one kiss Jeeves?'

'Certainly not.'

'Shall I kiss you?'

'No, thank you. All I require from you, young Byng, is that notebook.'

'Well, I must kiss someone, and I'm dashed if I'm going to kiss Eustace Oates.'

She broke off. A graver look came into her dial.

'Eustace Oates!' she repeated meditatively. 'That reminds me. In the rush of recent events, I had forgotten him. I exchanged a few words with Eustace Oates just now, Bertie, while I was waiting on the stairs for the balloon to go up, and he was sinister to a degree.'

'Where's that notebook?'

'Never mind about the notebook. The subject under discussion is Eustace Oates and his sinisterness. He's on my trail about that helmet.'

'What!'

'Absolutely. I'm Suspect Number One. He told me that he reads a lot of detective stories, and he says that the first thing a detective makes a bee-line for is motive. After that, opportunity. And finally clues. Well, as he pointed out, with that high-handed behaviour of his about Bartholomew rankling in my bosom, I had a motive all right, and seeing that I was out and about at the time of the crime I had the opportunity, too. And as for clues, what do you think he had with him, when I saw him? One of my gloves! He had picked it up on the scene of the outrage – while measuring footprints or looking for cigar ash, I suppose. You remember when Harold brought me back my gloves, there was only one of them. The other he apparently dropped while scooping in the helmet.'

A sort of dull, bruised feeling weighed me down as I mused on this latest manifestation of Harold Pinker's goofiness, as if a strong hand had whanged me over the cupola with a blackjack. There was such a sort of hideous ingenuity in the way he thought up new methods of inviting ruin.

'He would!'

'What do you mean, he would?'

'Well, he did, didn't he?'

'That's not the same as saying he would – in a beastly sneering, supercilious tone, as if you were so frightfully hot yourself. I can't understand you, Bertie – the way you're always criticizing poor Harold. I thought you were so fond of him.'

'I love him like a b. But that doesn't alter my opinion that of all the pumpkin-headed foozlers who ever preached about Hivites and Jebusites, he is the foremost.'

'He isn't half as pumpkin-headed as you.'

'He is, at a conservative estimate, about twenty-seven times as pumpkin-headed as me. He begins where I leave off. It may be a strong thing to say, but he's more pumpkin-headed than Gussie.'

With a visible effort, she swallowed the rising choler.

'Well, never mind about that. The point is that Eustace Oates is on my trail, and I've got to look slippy and find a better safe-deposit vault for that helmet than my chest of drawers. Before I know where I am, the Ogpu will be searching my room. Where would be a good place, do you think?'

I dismissed the thing wearily.

'Oh dash it, use your own judgement. To return to the main issue, where is that notebook?'

'Oh, Bertie, you're a perfect bore about that notebook. Can't you talk of anything else?'

'No, I can't. Where is it?'

'You're going to laugh when I tell you.'

I gave her an austere look.

'It is possible that I may some day laugh again – when I have got well away from this house of terror, but there is a fat chance of my doing so at this early date. Where is that book?'

'Well, if you really must know, I hid it in the cow-creamer.'

Everyone, I imagine, has read stories in which things turned black and swam before people. As I heard these words, Stiffy turned black and swam before me. It was as if I had been looking at a flickering negress.

'You – what?'

'I hid it in the cow-creamer.'

'What on earth did you do that for?'

'Oh, I thought I would.'

'But how am I to get it?'

A slight smile curved the young pimple's mobile lips.

'Oh, dash it, use your own judgement,' she said. 'Well, see you soon, Bertie.'

She biffed off, and I leaned limply against the banisters, trying to rally from this frightful wallop. But the world still flickered, and a few moments later I became aware that I was being addressed by a flickering butler.

'Excuse me, sir. Miss Madeline desired me to say that she would be glad if you could spare her a moment.'

I gazed at the man dully, like someone in a prison cell when the jailer has stepped in at dawn to notify him that the firing squad is ready. I knew what this meant, of course. I had recognized this butler's voice for what it was – the voice of doom. There could be only one thing that Madeline Bassett would be glad if I could spare her a moment about.

'Oh, did she?'

'Yes, sir.'

'Where is Miss Bassett?'

'In the drawing room, sir.'

'Right ho.'

I braced myself with the old Wooster grit. Up came the chin, back went the shoulders.

'Lead on,' I said to the butler, and the butler led on.

THE SOUND of soft and wistful music percolating through the drawing-room door as I approached did nothing to brighten the general outlook: and when I went in and saw Madeline Bassett seated at the piano, drooping on her stem a goodish deal, the sight nearly caused me to turn and leg it. However, I fought down the impulse and started things off with a tentative 'What ho.'

The observation elicited no immediate response. She had risen, and for perhaps half a minute stood staring at me in a sad sort of way, like the Mona Lisa on one of the mornings when the sorrows of the world had been coming over the plate a bit too fast for her. Finally, just as I was thinking I had better try to fill in with something about the weather, she spoke.

'Bertie –'

It was, however, only a flash in the pan. She blew a fuse, and silence supervened again.

'Bertie –'

No good. Another wash-out.

I was beginning to feel the strain a bit. We had had one of these deaf-mutes-getting-together sessions before, at Brinkley Court, in the summer, but on that occasion I had been able to ease things along by working in a spot of stage business during the awkward gaps in the conversation. Our previous chat as you may or possibly may not recall, had taken place in the Brinkley dining room in the presence of a cold collation, and it had helped a lot being in a position to bound forward at intervals with a curried egg or a cheese straw. In the absence of these food stuffs, we were thrown back a good deal on straight staring, and this always tends to embarrass.

Her lips parted. I saw that something was coming to the surface. A couple of gulps, and she was off to a good start. 'Bertie, I wanted to see you...I asked you to come because I wanted to say...I wanted to tell you...Bertie, my engagement to Augustus is at an end.'

'Yes.'

'You knew?'

'Oh, rather. He told me.'

'Then you know why I asked you to come here. I wanted to say –'

'Yes.'

'That I am willing –'

'Yes.'

'To make you happy.'

She appeared to be held up for a moment by a slight return of the old tonsil trouble, but after another brace of gulps she got it out.

'I will be your wife, Bertie.'

I suppose that after this most chaps would have thought it scarcely worthwhile to struggle against the inev., but I had a dash at it. With such vital issues at stake, one would have felt a chump if one had left any stone unturned.

'Awfully decent of you,' I said civilly. 'Deeply sensible of the honour, and what not. But have you thought? Have you reflected? Don't you feel you're being a bit rough on poor old Gussie?'

'What! After what happened this evening?'

'Ah, I wanted to talk to you about that. I always think, don't you, that it is as well on these occasions, before doing anything drastic, to have a few words with a seasoned man of the world and get the real low-down. You wouldn't like later on to have to start wringing your hands and saying "Oh, if I had only known!" In my opinion, the whole thing should be re-examined with a view to threshing out. If you care to know what I think, you're wronging Gussie.'

'Wronging him? When I saw him with my own eyes –'

'Ah, but you haven't got the right angle. Let me explain.'

'There can be no explanation. We will not talk about it any more, Bertie. I have blotted Augustus from my life. Until tonight I saw him only through the golden mist of love, and thought him the perfect man. This evening he revealed himself as what he really is – a satyr.'

'But that's just what I'm driving at. That's just where you're making your bloomer. You see –'

'We will not talk about it any more.'

'But —'

'Please!'

I tuned out. You can't make any headway with that *tout comprendre, c'est tout pardonner* stuff if the girl won't listen.

She turned the bean away, no doubt to hide a silent tear, and there ensued a brief interval during which she swabbed the eyes with a pocket handkerchief and I, averting my gaze, dipped the beak into a jar of *pot-pourri* which stood on the piano.

Presently, she took the air again.

'It is useless, Bertie. I know, of course, why you are speaking like this. It is that sweet, generous nature of yours. There are no lengths to which you will not go to help a friend, even though it may mean the wrecking of your own happiness. But there is nothing you can say that will change me. I have finished with Augustus. From tonight he will be to me merely a memory – a memory that will grow fainter and fainter through the years as you and I draw ever closer together. You will help me to forget. With you beside me, I shall be able in time to exorcize Augustus's spell...And now I suppose I had better go and tell Daddy.'

I started. I could still see Pop Bassett's face when he had thought that he was going to draw me for a nephew. It would be a bit thick, I felt, while he was still quivering to the roots of the soul at the recollection of that hair's-breadth escape, to tell him that I was about to become his son-in-law. I was not fond of Pop Bassett, but one has one's humane instincts.

'Oh, my aunt!' I said. 'Don't do that!'

'But I must. He will have to know that I am to be your wife. He is expecting me to marry Augustus three weeks from tomorrow.'

I chewed this over. I saw what she meant, of course. You've got to keep a father posted about these things. You can't just let it all slide and have the poor old egg rolling up to the church in a topper and a buttonhole, to find that the wedding is off and nobody bothered to mention it to him.

'Well, don't tell him tonight,' I urged. 'Let him simmer a bit. He's just had a pretty testing shock.'

'A shock?'

'Yes. He's not quite himself.'

A concerned look came into her eyes, causing them to bulge a trifle.

'So I was right. I thought he was not himself, when I met him coming out of the library just now. He was wiping his forehead and making odd little gasping noises. And when I asked him if anything was the matter, he said that we all had our cross to bear in this world, but that he supposed he ought not to complain, because things were not so bad as they might have been. I couldn't think what he meant. He then said he was going to have a warm bath and take three aspirins and go to bed. What was it? What had happened?'

I saw that to reveal the full story would be to complicate an already fairly well complicated situation. I touched, accordingly, on only one aspect of it.

'Stiffy had just told him she wanted to marry the curate.'

'Stephanie? The curate? Mr Pinker?'

'That's right. Old Stinker Pinker. And it churned him up a good deal. He appears to be a bit allergic to curates.'

She was breathing emotionally, like the dog Bartholomew just after he had finished eating the candle.

'But...But...'

'Yes?'

'But does Stephanie love Mr Pinker?'

'Oh, rather. No question about that.'

'But then –'

I saw what was in her mind, and nipped in promptly.

'Then there can't be anything between her and Gussie, you were going to say? Exactly. This proves it, doesn't it? That's the very point I've been trying to work the conversation round to from the start.'

'But he –'

'Yes, I know he did. But his motives in doing so were as pure as the driven snow. Purer, if anything. I'll tell you all about it, and I am prepared to give you a hundred to eight that when I have finished you will admit that he was more to be pitied than censured.'

Give Bertram Wooster a good, clear story to unfold, and he can narrate it well. Starting at the beginning with Gussie's aghastness at the prospect of having to make a speech at the wedding breakfast, I took her step by step through the subsequent developments, and I may say that I was as limpid as dammit. By the time I had reached the final chapter, I had her a bit squiggle-eyed but definitely wavering on the edge of conviction.

'And you say Stephanie has hidden this notebook in Daddy's cow-creamer?'

'Plumb spang in the cow-creamer.'

'But I never heard such an extraordinary story in my life.'

'Bizarre, yes, but quite capable of being swallowed, don't you think? What you have got to take into consideration is the psychology of the individual. You may say that you wouldn't have a psychology like Stiffy's if you were paid for it, but it's hers all right.'

'Are you sure you are not making all this up, Bertie?'

'Why on earth?'

'I know your altruistic nature so well.'

'Oh, I see what you mean. No, rather not. This is the straight official stuff. Don't you believe it?'

'I shall, if I find the notebook where you say Stephanie put it. I think I had better go and look.'

'I would.'

'I will.'

'Fine.'

She hurried out, and I sat down at the piano and began to play 'Happy Days Are Here Again' with one finger. It was the only method of self-expression that seemed to present itself. I would have preferred to get outside a curried egg or two, for the strain had left me weak, but, as I have said, there were no curried eggs present.

I was profoundly braced. I felt like some Marathon runner who, after sweating himself to the bone for hours, at length breasts the tape. The only thing that kept my bracedness from being absolutely unmixed was the lurking thought that in this ill-omened house there was always the chance of something unforeseen suddenly popping up to mar the happy ending. I somehow couldn't see Totleigh Towers throwing in the towel quite so readily as it appeared to be doing. It must, I felt, have something up its sleeve.

Nor was I wrong. When Madeline Bassett returned a few minutes later, there was no notebook in her hand. She reported total inability to discover so much as a trace of a notebook in the spot indicated. And, I gathered from her remarks, she had ceased entirely to be a believer in that notebook's existence.

I don't know if you have ever had a bucket of cold water right in the mazzard. I received one once in my boyhood through the agency of a groom with whom I had had some difference of opinion. That same feeling of being knocked endways came over me now.

I was at a loss and nonplussed. As Constable Oates had said, the first move the knowledgeable bloke makes when rummy goings-on are in progress is to try to spot the motive, and what Stiffy's motive could be for saying the notebook was in the cow-creamer, when it wasn't, I was unable to fathom. With a firm hand this girl had pulled my leg, but why – that was the point that baffled – why had she pulled my leg?

I did my best.

'Are you sure you really looked?'

'Perfectly sure.'

'I mean, carefully.'

'Very carefully.'

'Stiffy certainly swore it was there.'

'Indeed?'

'How do you mean, indeed?'

'If you want to know what I mean, I do not believe there ever was a notebook.'

'You don't credit my story?'

'No, I do not.'

Well, after that, of course, there didn't seem much to say. I may have said 'Oh?' or something along those lines – I'm not sure – but if I did, that let me out. I edged to the door, and pushed off in a sort of daze, pondering.

You know how it is when you ponder. You become absorbed, concentrated. Outside phenomena do not register on the what-is-it. I suppose I was fully halfway along the passage leading to my bedroom before the beastly row that was going on there penetrated to my consciousness, causing me to stop, look and listen.

This row to which I refer was a kind of banging row, as if somebody were banging on something. And I had scarcely said to myself 'What ho, a banger!' when I saw who this banger was. It was Roderick Spode, and what he was banging on was the door of Gussie's bedroom. As I came up, he was in the act of delivering another buffet on the woodwork.

The spectacle had an immediate tranquillizing effect on my jangled nervous system. I felt a new man. And I'll tell you why.

Everyone, I suppose, has experienced the sensation of comfort and relief which comes when you are being given the run-around by forces beyond your control and suddenly discover someone on whom you can work off the pent-up feelings. The merchant prince, when things are going wrong, takes it out of the junior clerk. The junior clerk goes and ticks off the office boy. The office boy kicks the cat. The cat steps down the street to find a smaller cat, which in its turn, the interview concluded, starts scouring the countryside for a mouse.

It was so with me now. Snootered to bursting point by Pop Bassetts and Madeline Bassetts and Stiffy Byngs and what not, and hounded like the dickens by a remorseless Fate, I found solace in the thought that I could still slip it across Roderick Spode.

'Spode!' I cried sharply.

He paused with lifted fist and turned an inflamed face in my direction. Then, as he saw who had spoken, the red light died out of his eyes. He wilted obsequiously.

'Well, Spode, what is all this?'

'Oh, hullo, Wooster. Nice evening.'

I proceeded to work off the pent-up f's.

'Never mind what sort of an evening it is,' I said. 'Upon my word, Spode, this is too much. This is just that little bit above the odds which compels a man to take drastic steps.'

'But, Wooster –'

'What do you mean by disturbing the house with this abominable uproar? Have you forgotten already what I told you about checking this disposition of yours to run amok like a raging hippopotamus? I should have thought that after what I said you would have spent the remainder of the evening curled up with a good book. But no. I find you renewing your efforts to assault and batter my friends. I must warn you, Spode, that my patience is not inexhaustible.'

'But, Wooster, you don't understand.'

'What don't I understand?'

'You don't know the provocation I have received from this pop-eyed Fink-Nottle.' A wistful look came into his face. 'I must break his neck.'

'You are not going to break his neck.'

'Well, shake him like a rat.'

'Nor shake him like a rat.'

'But he says I'm a pompous ass.'

'When did Gussie say that to you?'

'He didn't exactly say it. He wrote it. Look. Here it is.'

Before my bulging eyes he produced from his pocket a small, brown, leather-covered notebook.

Harking back to Archimedes just once more, Jeeves's description of him discovering the principle of displacement, though brief, had made a deep impression on me, bringing before my eyes a very vivid picture of what must have happened on that occasion. I had been able to see the man testing the bath water with his toe…stepping in…immersing the frame. I had accompanied him in spirit through all the subsequent formalities – the soaping of the loofah, the shampooing of the head, the burst of song…

And then, abruptly, as he climbs towards the high note, there is a silence. His voice has died away. Through the streaming suds you can see that his eyes are glowing with a strange light. The loofah falls from his grasp, disregarded. He utters a triumphant cry. 'Got it! What ho! The principle of displacement!' And out he leaps, feeling like a million dollars.

In precisely the same manner did the miraculous appearance of this notebook affect me. There was that identical moment of stunned silence, followed by the triumphant cry. And I have no doubt that, as I stretched out a compelling hand, my eyes were glowing with a strange light.

'Give me that book, Spode!'

'Yes, I would like you to look at it, Wooster. Then you will see what I mean. I came upon this,' he said, 'in rather a remarkable way. The thought crossed my mind that Sir Watkyn might feel happier if I were to take charge of that cow-creamer of his. There have been a lot of burglaries in the neighbourhood,' he added hastily, 'a lot of burglaries, and those French windows are never really safe. So I – er – went to the collection-room, and took it out of its case. I was surprised to hear something bumping about inside it. I opened it, and found this book. Look,' he said, pointing a banana-like finger over my shoulder. 'There is what he says about the way I eat asparagus.'

I think Roderick Spode's idea was that we were going to pore over the pages together. When he saw me slip the volume into my pocket, I sensed the feeling of bereavement.

'Are you going to keep the book, Wooster?'

'I am.'

'But I wanted to show it to Sir Watkyn. There's a lot about him in it, too.'

'We will not cause Sir Watkyn needless pain, Spode.'

'Perhaps you're right. Then I'll be getting on with breaking this door down?'

'Certainly not,' I said sternly. 'All you do is pop off.'

'Pop off?'

'Pop off. Leave me, Spode. I would be alone.'

I watched him disappear round the bend, then rapped vigorously on the door.

'Gussie.'

No reply.

'Gussie, come out.'

'I'm dashed if I do.'

'Come out, you ass. Wooster speaking.'

But even this did not produce immediate results. He explained later that he was under the impression that it was Spode giving a cunning imitation of my voice. But eventually I convinced him that this was indeed the boyhood friend and no other, and there came the sound of furniture being dragged away, and presently the door opened and his head emerged cautiously, like that of a snail taking a look round after a thunderstorm.

Into the emotional scene which followed I need not go in detail. You will have witnessed much the same sort of thing in the pictures, when the United States Marines arrive in the nick of time to relieve the beleaguered garrison. I may sum it up by saying that he fawned upon me. He seemed to be under the impression that I had worsted Roderick Spode in personal combat and it wasn't worthwhile to correct it. Pressing the notebook into his hand, I sent him off to show it to Madeline Bassett, and proceeded to my room.

Jeeves was there, messing about at some professional task.

It had been my intention, on seeing this man again, to put him through it in no uncertain fashion for having subjected me to the tense nervous strain of my recent interview with Pop Bassett. But now I greeted him with the cordial smile rather than the acid glare. After all, I told myself, his scheme had dragged home the gravy, and in any case this was no moment for recriminations.

Wellington didn't go about ticking people off after the battle of Waterloo. He slapped their backs and stood them drinks.

'Aha, Jeeves! You're there, are you?'

'Yes, sir.'

'Well, Jeeves, you may start packing the effects.'

'Sir?'

'For the homeward trip. We leave tomorrow.'

'You are not proposing, then, sir, to extend your stay at Totleigh Towers?'

I laughed one of my gay, jolly ones.

'Don't ask foolish questions, Jeeves. Is Totleigh Towers a place where people extend their stays, if they haven't got to? And there is now no longer any necessity for me to linger on the premises. My work is done. We leave first thing tomorrow morning. Start packing, therefore, so that we shall be in a position to get off the mark without an instant's delay. It won't take you long?'

'No, sir. There are merely the two suitcases.'

He hauled them from beneath the bed, and, opening the larger of the brace, began to sling coats and things into it, while I, seating myself in the armchair, proceeded to put him abreast of recent events.

'Well, Jeeves, that plan of yours worked all right.'

'I am most gratified to hear it, sir.'

'I don't say that the scene won't haunt me in my dreams for some little time to come. I make no comment on your having let me in for such a thing. I merely state that it proved a winner. An uncle's blessing came popping out like a cork out of a champagne bottle, and Stiffy and Stinker are headed for the altar rails with no more fences ahead.'

'Extremely satisfactory, sir. Then Sir Watkyn's reactions were as we had anticipated?'

'If anything, more so. I don't know if you have ever seen a stout bark buffeted by the waves?'

'No, sir. My visits to the seaside have always been made in clement weather.'

'Well, that was what he resembled on being informed by me that I wanted to become his nephew by marriage. He looked and behaved like the Wreck of the *Hesperus*. You remember? It sailed the wintry sea, and the skipper had taken his little daughter to bear him company.'

'Yes, sir. Blue were her eyes as the fairy-flax, her cheeks like the dawn of day, and her bosom was white as the hawthorn buds that open in the month of May.'

'Quite. Well, as I was saying, he reeled beneath the blow and let water in at every seam. And when Stiffy appeared, and told him that it was all a mistake and that the *promesso sposo* was in reality old Stinker Pinker, his relief knew no bounds. He instantly gave his sanction to their union. Could hardly get the words out quick enough. But why am I wasting time telling you all this, Jeeves? A mere side issue. Here's the real front-page stuff. Here's the news that will shock the *chancelleries*. I've got that notebook.'

'Indeed, sir?'

'Yes, absolutely got it. I found Spode with it and took it away from him, and Gussie is even now showing it to Miss Bassett and clearing his name of the stigma that rested upon it. I shouldn't be surprised if at this very moment they were locked in a close embrace.'

'A consummation devoutly to be wished, sir.'

'You said it, Jeeves.'

'Then you have nothing to cause you further concern, sir.'

'Nothing. The relief is stupendous. I feel as if a great weight had been rolled from my shoulders. I could dance and sing. I think there can be no question that exhibiting that notebook will do the trick.'

'None, I should imagine, sir.'

'I say, Bertie,' said Gussie, trickling in at this juncture with the air of one who has been passed through a wringer, 'a most frightful thing has happened. The wedding's off.'

CHAPTER 11

I STARED at the man, clutching the brow and rocking on my base.

'Off?'

'Yes.'

'Your wedding?'

'Yes.'

'It's off?'

'Yes.'

'What — *off*?'

'Yes.'

I don't know what the Mona Lisa would have done in my place. Probably just what I did.

'Jeeves,' I said. 'Brandy!'

'Very good, sir.'

He rolled away on his errand of mercy, and I turned to Gussie, who was tacking about the room in a dazed manner, as if filling in the time before starting to pluck straws from his hair.

'I can't bear it!' I heard him mutter. 'Life without Madeline won't be worth living.'

It was an astounding attitude, of course, but you can't argue about fellows' tastes. One man's peach is another man's poison, and *vice versa*. Even my Aunt Agatha, I remembered, had roused the red-hot spark of pash in the late Spenser Gregson.

His wandering had taken him to the bed, and I saw that he was looking at the knotted sheet which lay there.

'I suppose,' he said, in an absent, soliloquizing voice, 'a chap could hang himself with that.'

I resolved to put a stopper on this trend of thought promptly. I had got more or less used by now to my bedroom being treated as a sort of meeting-place of the nations, but I was dashed if I was going to have it turned into the spot marked with an X. It was a point on which I felt strongly.

'You aren't going to hang yourself here.'

'I shall have to hang myself somewhere.'

'Well, you don't hang yourself in my bedroom.'

He raised his eyebrows.

'Have you any objection to my sitting in your armchair?'

'Go ahead.'

'Thanks.'

He seated himself, and stared before him with glazed eyes.

'Now, then, Gussie,' I said, 'I will take your statement. What is all this rot about the wedding being off?'

'It is off.'

'But didn't you show her the notebook?'

'Yes. I showed her the notebook.'

'Did she read its contents?'

'Yes.'

'Well, didn't she *tout comprendre*?'

'Yes.'

'And *tout pardonner*?'

'Yes.'

'Then you must have got your facts twisted. The wedding can't be off.'

'It is, I tell you. Do you think I don't know when a wedding's off and when it isn't? Sir Watkyn has forbidden it.'

This was an angle I had not foreseen.

'Why? Did you have a row or something?'

'Yes. About newts. He didn't like me putting them in the bath.'

'You put newts in the bath?'

'Yes.'

Like a keen cross-examining counsel, I swooped on the point.

'Why?'

His hand fluttered, as if about to reach for a straw.

'I broke the tank. The tank in my bedroom. The glass tank I keep my newts in. I broke the glass tank in my bedroom, and the bath was the only place to lodge the newts. The basin wasn't large enough. Newts need elbow-room. So I put them in the bath. Because I had broken the tank. The glass tank in my bedroom. The glass tank I keep my —'

I saw that if allowed to continue in this strain he might go on practically indefinitely, so I called him to order with a sharp rap of a china vase on the mantelpiece.

'I get the idea,' I said, brushing the fragments into the fireplace. 'Proceed. How does Pop Bassett come into the picture?'

'He went to take a bath. It never occurred to me that anyone would be taking a bath as late as this. And I was in the drawing room, when he burst in shouting: "Madeline, that blasted Fink-Nottle has been filling my bathtub with tadpoles!" And I lost my head a little, I'm afraid. I yelled: "Oh, my gosh, you silly old ass, be careful what you're doing with those newts. Don't touch them. I'm in the middle of a most important experiment."'

'I see. And then –'

'I went on to tell him how I wished to ascertain whether the full moon affected the love life of newts. And a strange look came into his face, and he quivered a bit, and then he told me that he had pulled out the plug and all my newts had gone down the waste pipe.'

I think he would have preferred at this point to fling himself on the bed and turn his face to the wall, but I headed him off. I was resolved to stick to the *res*.

'Upon which you did what?'

'I ticked him off properly. I called him every name I could think of. In fact, I called him names that I hadn't a notion I knew. They just seemed to come bubbling up from my subconsciousness. I was hampered a bit at first by the fact that Madeline was there, but it wasn't long before he told her to go to bed, and then I was really able to express myself. And when I finally paused for breath, he forbade the banns and pushed off. And I rang the bell and asked Butterfield to bring me a glass of orange juice.'

I started.

'Orange juice?'

'I wanted picking up.'

'But orange juice? At such a time?'

'It was what I felt I needed.'

I shrugged my shoulders.

'Oh, well,' I said.

Just another proof, of course, of what I often say – that it takes all sorts to make a world.

'As a matter of fact, I could do with a good long drink now.'

'The tooth-bottle is at your elbow.'

'Thanks…Ah! That's the stuff!'

'Have a go at the jug.'

'No, thanks. I know when to stop. Well, that's the position, Bertie. He won't let Madeline marry me, and I'm wondering if

THE CODE OF THE WOOSTERS

there is any possible way of bringing him round. I'm afraid there isn't. You see, it wasn't only that I called him names –'

'Such as?'

'Well, louse, I remember, was one of them. And skunk, I think. Yes, I'm pretty sure I called him a wall-eyed skunk. But he might forgive that. The real trouble is that I mocked at that cow-creamer of his.'

'Cow-creamer!'

I spoke sharply. He had started a train of thought. An idea had begun to burgeon. For some little time I had been calling on all the resources of the Wooster intellect to help me to solve this problem, and I don't often do that without something breaking loose. At this mention of the cow-creamer, the brain seemed suddenly to give itself a shake and start off across country with its nose to the ground.

'Yes. Knowing how much he loved and admired it, and searching for barbed words that would wound him, I told him it was Modern Dutch. I had gathered from his remarks at the dinner table last night that that was the last thing it ought to be. "You and your eighteenth-century cow-creamers!" I said. "Pah! Modern Dutch!" or words to that effect. The thrust got home. He turned purple, and broke off the wedding.'

'Listen, Gussie,' I said. 'I think I've got it.'

His face lit up. I could see that optimism had stirred and was shaking a leg. This Fink-Nottle has always been of an optimistic nature. Those who recall his address to the boys of Market Snodsbury Grammar School will remember that it was largely an appeal to the little blighters not to look on the dark side.

'Yes, I believe I see the way. What you have got to do, Gussie, is pinch that cow-creamer.'

His lips parted, and I thought an 'Eh, what?' was coming through, but it didn't. Just silence and a couple of bubbles.

'That is the first, essential step. Having secured the cow-creamer, you tell him it is in your possession and say: "Now, how about it?" I feel convinced that in order to recover that foul cow he would meet any terms you care to name. You know what collectors are like. Practically potty, every one of them. Why, my Uncle Tom wants the thing so badly that he is actually prepared to yield up his supreme cook, Anatole, in exchange for it.'

'Not the fellow who was functioning at Brinkley when I was there?'

'That's right.'

'The chap who dished up those *nonettes de poulet Agnes Sorel*?'

'That very artist.'

'You really mean that your uncle would consider Anatole well lost if he could secure this cow-creamer?'

'I have it from Aunt Dahlia's own lips.'

He drew a deep breath.

'Then you're right. This scheme of yours would certainly solve everything. Assuming, of course, that Sir Watkyn values the thing equally highly.'

'He does. Doesn't he, Jeeves?' I said, putting it up to him, as he trickled in with the brandy. 'Sir Watkyn Bassett has forbidden Gussie's wedding,' I explained, 'and I've been telling him that all he has to do in order to make him change his mind is to get hold of that cow-creamer and refuse to give it back until he coughs up a father's blessing. You concur?'

'Undoubtedly, sir. If Mr Fink-Nottle possesses himself of the *objet d'art* in question, he will be in a position to dictate. A very shrewd plan, sir.'

'Thank you, Jeeves. Yes, not bad, considering that I had to think on my feet and form my strategy at a moment's notice. If I were you, Gussie, I would put things in train immediately.'

'Excuse me, sir.'

'You spoke, Jeeves?'

'Yes, sir. I was about to say that before Mr Fink-Nottle can put the arrangements in operation there is an obstacle to be surmounted.'

'What's that?'

'In order to protect his interests, Sir Watkyn has posted Constable Oates on guard in the collection-room.'

'What!'

'Yes, sir.'

The sunshine died out of Gussie's face, and he uttered a stricken sound like a gramophone record running down.

'However, I think that with a little finesse it will be perfectly possible to eliminate this factor. I wonder if you recollect, sir, the occasion at Chufnell Hall, when Sir Roderick Glossop had become locked up in the potting-shed, and your efforts to release him appeared likely to be foiled by the fact that Police Constable Dobson had been stationed outside the door?'

'Vividly, Jeeves.'

'I ventured to suggest that it might be possible to induce him to leave his post by conveying word to him that the parlourmaid Mary, to whom he was betrothed, wished to confer with him in the raspberry bushes. The plan was put into effect and proved successful.'

'True, Jeeves. But,' I said dubiously, 'I don't see how anything like that could be worked here. Constable Dobson, you will recall, was young, ardent, romantic – just the sort of chap who would automatically go leaping into raspberry bushes if you told him there were girls there. Eustace Oates has none of the Dobson fire. He is well stricken in years and gives the impression of being a settled married man who would rather have a cup of tea.'

'Yes, sir, Constable Oates is, as you say, of a more sober temperament. But it is merely the principle of the thing which I would advocate applying to the present emergency. It would be necessary to provide a lure suited to the psychology of the individual. What I would suggest is that Mr Fink-Nottle should inform the officer that he has seen his helmet in your possession.'

'Egad, Jeeves!'

'Yes, sir.'

'I see the idea. Yes, very hot. Yes, that would do it.'

Gussie's glassy eye indicating that all this was failing to register, I explained.

'Earlier in the evening, Gussie, a hidden hand snitched this *gendarme*'s lid, cutting him to the quick. What Jeeves is saying is that a word from you to the effect that you have seen it in my room will bring him bounding up here like a tigress after its lost cub, thus leaving you a clear field in which to operate. That is your idea in essence, is it not, Jeeves?'

'Precisely, sir.'

Gussie brightened visibly.

'I see. It's a ruse.'

'That's right. One of the ruses, and not the worst of them. Nice work, Jeeves.'

'Thank you, sir.'

'That will do the trick, Gussie. Tell him I've got his helmet, wait while he bounds out, nip to the glass case and trouser the cow. A simple programme. A child could carry it out. My only regret, Jeeves, is that this appears to remove any chance Aunt Dahlia might have had of getting the thing. A pity there has been such a wide popular demand for it.'

'Yes, sir. But possibly Mrs Travers, feeling that Mr Fink-Nottle's need is greater than hers, will accept the disappointment philosophically.'

'Possibly. On the other hand, possibly not. Still, there it is. On these occasions when individual interests clash, somebody has got to draw the short straw.'

'Very true, sir.'

'You can't be expected to dish out happy endings all round – one per person, I mean.'

'No, sir.'

'The great thing is to get Gussie fixed. So buzz off, Gussie, and Heaven speed your efforts.'

I lit a cigarette.

'A very sound idea, that, Jeeves. How did you happen to think of it?'

'It was the officer himself who put it into my head, sir, when I was chatting with him not long ago. I gathered from what he said that he actually does suspect you of being the individual who purloined his helmet.'

'Me? Why on earth? Dash it, I scarcely know the man. I thought he suspected Stiffy.'

'Originally, yes, sir. And it is still his view that Miss Byng was the motivating force behind the theft. But he now believes that the young lady must have had a male accomplice, who did the rough work. Sir Watkyn, I understand, supports him in this theory.'

I suddenly remembered the opening passages of my interview with Pop Bassett in the library, and at last got on to what he had been driving at. Those remarks of his which had seemed to me then mere idle gossip had had, I now perceived, a sinister under-current of meaning. I had supposed that we were just two of the boys chewing over the latest bit of hot news, and all the time the thing had been a probe or quiz.

'But what makes them think that I was the male accomplice?'

'I gather that the officer was struck by the cordiality which he saw to exist between Miss Byng and yourself, when he encountered you in the road this afternoon, and his suspicions became strengthened when he found the young lady's glove on the scene of the outrage.'

'I don't get you, Jeeves.'

'He supposes you to be enamoured of Miss Byng, sir, and thinks that you were wearing her glove next your heart.'

'If it had been next my heart, how could I have dropped it?'

'His view is that you took it out to press to your lips, sir.'

'Come, come, Jeeves. Would I start pressing gloves to my lips at the moment when I was about to pinch a policeman's helmet?'

'Apparently Mr Pinker did, sir.'

I was on the point of explaining to him that what old Stinker would do in any given situation and what the ordinary, normal person with a couple of ounces more brain than a cuckoo clock would do were two vastly different things, when I was interrupted by the re-entrance of Gussie. I could see by the buoyancy of his demeanour that matters had been progressing well.

'Jeeves was right, Bertie,' he said. 'He read Eustace Oates like a book.'

'The information stirred him up?'

'I don't think I have ever seen a more thoroughly roused policeman. His first impulse was to drop everything and come dashing up here right away.'

'Why didn't he?'

'He couldn't quite bring himself to, in view of the fact that Sir Watkyn had told him to stay there.'

I followed the psychology. It was the same as that of the boy who stood on the burning deck, whence all but he had fled.

'Then the procedure, I take it, will be that he will send word to Pop Bassett, notifying him of the facts and asking permission to go ahead?'

'Yes. I expect you will have him with you in a few minutes.'

'Then you ought not to be here. You should be lurking in the hall.'

'I'm going there at once. I only came to report.'

'Be ready to slip in the moment he is gone.'

'I will. Trust me. There won't be a hitch. It was a wonderful idea of yours, Jeeves.'

'Thank you, sir.'

'You can imagine how relieved I'm feeling, knowing that in about five minutes everything will be all right. The only thing I'm a bit sorry for now,' said Gussie thoughtfully, 'is that I gave the old boy that notebook.'

He threw out this appalling statement so casually that it was a second or two before I got its import. When I did, a powerful shock permeated my system. It was as if I had been reclining in the electric chair and the authorities had turned on the juice.

'You gave him the notebook!'

'Yes. Just as he was leaving. I thought there might be some names in it which I had forgotten to call him.'

I supported myself with a trembling hand on the mantelpiece.

'Jeeves!'

'Sir?'

'More brandy!'

'Yes, sir.'

'And stop doling it out in those small glasses, as if it were radium. Bring the cask.'

Gussie was regarding me with a touch of surprise.

'Something the matter, Bertie?'

'Something the matter?' I let out a mirthless 'Ha! Well, this has torn it.'

'How do you mean? Why?'

'Can't you see what you've done, you poor chump? It's no use pinching that cow-creamer now. If old Bassett has read the contents of that notebook, nothing will bring him round.'

'Why not?'

'Well, you saw how they affected Spode. I don't suppose Pop Bassett is any fonder of reading home truths about himself than Spode is.'

'But he's had the home truths already. I told you how I ticked him off.'

'Yes, but you could have got away with that. Overlook it, please…spoken in hot blood…strangely forgot myself…all that sort of stuff. Coldly reasoned opinions, carefully inscribed day by day in a notebook, are a very different thing.'

I saw that it had penetrated at last. The greenish tinge was back in his face. His mouth opened and shut like that of a goldfish which sees another goldfish nip in and get away with the ant's egg which it had been earmarking for itself.

'Oh, gosh!'

'Yes.'

'What can I do?'

'I don't know.'

'Think, Bertie, think!'

I did so, tensely, and was rewarded with an idea.

'Tell me,' I said, 'what exactly occurred at the conclusion of the vulgar brawl? You handed him the book. Did he dip into it on the spot?'

'No. He shoved it away in his pocket.'

'And did you gather that he still intended to take a bath?'

'Yes.'

'Then answer me this. What pocket? I mean the pocket of what garment? What was he wearing?'

'A dressing gown.'

'Over – think carefully, Fink-Nottle, for everything hangs on this – over shirt and trousers and things?'

'Yes, he had his trousers on. I remember noticing.'

'Then there is still hope. After leaving you, he would have gone to his room to shed the upholstery. He was pretty steamed up, you say?'

'Yes, very much.'

'Good. My knowledge of human nature, Gussie, tells me that a steamed-up man does not loiter about feeling in his pocket for notebooks and steeping himself in their contents. He flings off the garments, and legs it to the *salle de bain*. The book must still be in the pocket of his dressing gown – which, no doubt, he flung on the bed or over a chair – and all you have to do is nip into his room and get it.'

I had anticipated that this clear thinking would produce the joyous cry and the heartfelt burst of thanks. Instead of which, he merely shuffled his feet dubiously.

'Nip into his room?'

'Yes.'

'But dash it!'

'Now, what?'

'You're sure there isn't some other way?'

'Of course there isn't.'

'I see…You wouldn't care to do it for me, Bertie?'

'No, I would not.'

'Many fellows would, to help an old school friend.'

'Many fellows are mugs.'

'Have you forgotten those days at the dear old school?'

'Yes.'

'You don't remember the time I shared my last bar of milk chocolate with you?'

'No.'

'Well, I did, and you told me then that if ever you had an opportunity of doing anything for me…However, if these obligations – sacred, some people might consider them – have no weight with you, I suppose there is nothing more to be said.'

He pottered about for a while, doing the old cat-in-an-adage stuff: then, taking from his breast pocket a cabinet photograph of Madeline Bassett, he gazed at it intently. It seemed to be the bracer he required. His eyes lit up. His face lost its fishlike look. He strode out, to return immediately, slamming the door behind him. 'I say, Bertie, Spode's out there!'

'What of it?'

'He made a grab at me.'

'Made a grab at you?'

I frowned. I am a patient man, but I can be pushed too far. It seemed incredible, after what I had said to him, that Roderick Spode's hat was still in the ring. I went to the door, and threw it open. It was even as Gussie had said. The man was lurking.

He sagged a bit, as he saw me. I addressed him with cold severity.

'Anything I can do for you, Spode?'

'No. No, nothing, thanks.'

'Push along, Gussie,' I said, and stood watching him with a protective eye as he sidled round the human gorilla and disappeared along the passage. Then I turned to Spode.

'Spode,' I said in a level voice, 'did I or did I not tell you to leave Gussie alone?'

He looked at me pleadingly.

'Couldn't you possibly see your way to letting me do something to him, Wooster? If it was only to kick his spine up through his hat?'

'Certainly not.'

'Well, just as you say, of course.' He scratched his cheek discontentedly. 'Did you read that notebook, Wooster?'

'No.'

'He says my moustache is like the faint discoloured smear left by a squashed blackbeetle on the side of a kitchen sink.'

'He always was a poetic sort of chap.'

'And that the way I eat asparagus alters one's whole conception of Man as Nature's last word.'

'Yes, he told me that, I remember. He's about right, too. I was noticing at dinner. What you want to do, Spode, in future is lower the vegetable gently into the abyss. Take it easy. Don't snap at it. Try to remember that you are a human being and not a shark.'

'Ha, ha! "A human being and not a shark." Cleverly put, Wooster. Most amusing.'

He was still chuckling, though not frightfully heartily I thought, when Jeeves came along with a decanter on a tray.

'The brandy, sir.'

'And about time, Jeeves.'

'Yes, sir. I must once more apologize for my delay. I was detained by Constable Oates.'

'Oh? Chatting with him again?'

'Not so much chatting, sir, as staunching the flow of blood.'

'Blood?'

'Yes, sir. The officer had met with an accident.'

My momentary pique vanished, and in its place there came a stern joy. Life at Totleigh Towers had hardened me, blunting the gentler emotions, and I derived nothing but gratification from the news that Constable Oates had been meeting with accidents. Only one thing, indeed, could have pleased me more – if I had been informed that Sir Watkyn Bassett had trodden on the soap and come a purler in the bath tub.

'How did that happen?'

'He was assaulted while endeavouring to recover Sir Watkyn's cow-creamer from a midnight marauder, sir.'

Spode uttered a cry.

'The cow-creamer has not been stolen?'

'Yes, sir.'

It was evident that Roderick Spode was deeply affected by the news. His attitude towards the cow-creamer had, if you remember, been fatherly from the first. Not lingering to hear more, he galloped off, and I accompanied Jeeves into the room, agog for details.

'What happened, Jeeves?'

'Well, sir, it was a little difficult to extract a coherent narrative from the officer, but I gather that he found himself restless and fidgety –'

'No doubt owing to his inability to get in touch with Pop Bassett, who, as we know, is in his bath, and receive permission to leave his post and come up here after his helmet.'

'No doubt, sir. And being restless, he experienced a strong desire to smoke a pipe. Reluctant, however, to run the risk of being found to have smoked while on duty – as might have been the case had he done so in an enclosed room, where the fumes would have lingered – he stepped out into the garden.'

'A quick thinker, this Oates.'

'He left the French window open behind him. And some little time later his attention was arrested by a sudden sound from within.'

'What sort of sound?'

'The sound of stealthy footsteps, sir.'

'Someone stepping stealthily, as it were?'

'Precisely, sir. Followed by the breaking of glass. He immediately hastened back to the room – which was, of course, in darkness.'

'Why?'

'Because he had turned the light out, sir.'

I nodded. I followed the idea.

'Sir Watkyn's instruction to him had been to keep his vigil in the dark, in order to convey to a marauder the impression that the room was unoccupied.'

I nodded again. It was a dirty trick, but one which would spring naturally to the mind of an ex-magistrate.

'He hurried to the case in which the cow-creamer had been deposited, and struck a match. This almost immediately went out, but not before he had been able to ascertain that the *objet d'art* had disappeared. And he was still in the process of endeavouring to adjust himself to the discovery, when he heard a movement and, turning, perceived a dim figure stealing out through the French window. He pursued it into the garden, and was overtaking it and might shortly have succeeded in effecting an arrest, when there sprang from the darkness a dim figure –'

'The same dim figure?'

'No, sir. Another one.'

'A big night for dim figures.'

'Yes, sir.'

'Better call them Pat and Mike, or we shall be getting mixed.'

'A and B perhaps, sir?'

'If you prefer it, Jeeves. He was overtaking dim figure A, you say, when dim figure B sprang from the darkness –'

'– and struck him upon the nose.'

I uttered an exclamash. The thing was a mystery no longer.

'Old Stinker!'

'Yes, sir. No doubt Miss Byng inadvertently forgot to apprise him that there had been a change in the evening's arrangements.'

'And he was lurking there, waiting for me.'

'So one would be disposed to imagine, sir.'

I inhaled deeply, my thoughts playing about the constable's injured beezer. There, I was feeling, but for whatever it is, went Bertram Wooster, as the fellow said.

'This assault diverted the officer's attention, and the object of his pursuit was enabled to escape.'

'What became of Stinker?'

'On becoming aware of the officer's identity, he apologized, sir. He then withdrew.'

'I don't blame him. A pretty good idea, at that. Well, I don't know what to make of this, Jeeves. This dim figure. I am referring to dim figure A. Who could it have been? Had Oates any views on the subject?'

'Very definite views, sir. He is convinced that it was you.'

I stared.

'Me? Why the dickens has everything that happens in this ghastly house got to be me?'

'And it is his intention, as soon as he is able to secure Sir Watkyn's co-operation, to proceed here and search your room.'

'He was going to do that, anyway, for the helmet.'

'Yes, sir.'

'This is going to be rather funny, Jeeves. It will be entertaining to watch these two blighters ferret about, feeling sillier and sillier asses as each moment goes by and they find nothing.'

'Most diverting, sir.'

'And when the search is over and they are standing there baffled, stammering out weak apologies, I shall get a bit of my own back. I shall fold my arms and draw myself up to my full height –'

There came from without the hoof beats of a galloping relative, and Aunt Dahlia whizzed in.

'Here, shove this away somewhere, young Bertie,' she panted, seeming touched in the wind.

And so saying, she thrust the cow-creamer into my hands.

IN MY recent picture of Sir Watkyn Bassett reeling beneath the blow of hearing that I wanted to marry into his family, I compared his garglings, if you remember, to the death rattle of a dying duck. I might now have been this duck's twin brother, equally stricken. For some moments I stood there, quacking feebly: then, with a powerful effort of the will, I pulled myself together and cheesed the bird imitation. I looked at Jeeves. He looked at me. I did not speak, save with the language of the eyes, but his trained senses enabled him to read my thoughts unerringly.

'Thank you, Jeeves.'

I took the tumbler from him, and lowered perhaps half an ounce of the raw spirit. Then, the dizzy spell overcome, I transferred my gaze to the aged relative, who was taking it easy in the armchair.

It is pretty generally admitted, both in the Drones Club and elsewhere, that Bertram Wooster in his dealings with the opposite sex invariably shows himself a man of the nicest chivalry – what you sometimes hear described as a *parfait gentil* knight. It is true that at the age of six, when the blood ran hot, I once gave my nurse a juicy one over the top knot with a porringer, but the lapse was merely a temporary one. Since then, though few men have been more sorely tried by the sex, I have never raised a hand against a woman. And I can give no better indication of my emotions at this moment than by saying that, *preux chevalier* though I am, I came within the veriest toucher of hauling off and letting a revered aunt have it on the side of the head with a *papier mâché* elephant – the only object on the mantelpiece which the fierce rush of life at Totleigh Towers had left still unbroken.

She, while this struggle was proceeding in my bosom, was at her chirpiest. Her breath recovered, she had begun to prattle with a carefree gaiety which cut me like a knife. It was obvious from her demeanour that, stringing along with the late Diamond, she little knew what she had done.

'As nice a run,' she was saying, 'as I have had since the last time I was out with the Berks and Bucks. Not a check from start to finish. Good clean British sport at its best. It was a close thing though, Bertie. I could feel that cop's hot breath on the back of my neck. If a posse of curates hadn't popped up out of a trap and lent a willing hand at precisely the right moment, he would have got me. Well, God bless the clergy, say I. A fine body of men. But what on earth were policemen doing on the premises? Nobody ever mentioned policemen to me.'

'That was Constable Oates, the vigilant guardian of the peace of Totleigh-in-the-Wold,' I replied, keeping a tight hold on myself lest I should howl like a banshee and shoot up to the ceiling. 'Sir Watkyn had stationed him in the room to watch over his belongings. He was lying in wait. I was the visitor he expected.'

'I'm glad you weren't the visitor he got. The situation would have been completely beyond you, my poor lamb. You would have lost your head and stood there like a stuffed wombat, to fall an easy prey. I don't mind telling you that when that man suddenly came in through the window, I myself was for a moment paralysed. Still, all's well that ends well.'

I shook a sombre head.

'You err, my misguided old object. This is not an end, but a beginning. Pop Bassett is about to spread a drag-net.'

'Let him.'

'And when he and the constable come and search this room?'

'They wouldn't do that.'

'They would and will. In the first place, they think the Oates helmet is here. In the second place, it is the officer's view, relayed to me by Jeeves, who had it from him first hand as he was staunching the flow of blood, that it was I whom he pursued.'

Her chirpiness waned. I had expected it would. She had been beaming. She beamed no longer. Eyeing her steadily, I saw that the native hue of resolution had become sicklied o'er with the pale cast of thought.

'H'm! This is awkward.'

'Most.'

'If they find the cow-creamer here, it may be a little difficult to explain.'

She rose, and broke the elephant thoughtfully.

'The great thing,' she said, 'is not to lose our heads. We must say to ourselves: "What would Napoleon have done?" He was the boy in a crisis. He knew his onions. We must do something very clever, very shrewd, which will completely baffle these bounders. Well, come on, I'm waiting for suggestions.'

'Mine is that you pop off without delay, taking that beastly cow with you.'

'And run into the search party on the stairs! Not if I know it. Have you any ideas, Jeeves?'

'Not at the moment, madam.'

'You can't produce a guilty secret of Sir Watkyn's out of the hat, as you did with Spode?'

'No, madam.'

'No, I suppose that's too much to ask. Then we've got to hide the thing somewhere. But where? It's the old problem, of course – the one that makes life so tough for murderers – what to do with the body. I suppose the old Purloined Letter stunt wouldn't work?'

'Mrs Travers is alluding to the well-known story by the late Edgar Allan Poe, sir,' said Jeeves, seeing that I was not abreast. 'It deals with the theft of an important document, and the character who had secured it foiled the police by placing it in full view in a letter-rack, his theory being that what is obvious is often over-looked. No doubt Mrs Travers wishes to suggest that we deposit the object on the mantelpiece.'

I laughed a hollow one.

'Take a look at the mantelpiece! It is as bare as a windswept prairie. Anything placed there would stick out like a sore thumb.'

'Yes, that's true,' Aunt Dahlia was forced to admit.

'Put the bally thing in the suitcase, Jeeves.'

'That's no good. They're bound to look there.'

'Merely as a palliative,' I explained. 'I can't stand the sight of it any longer. In with it, Jeeves.'

'Very good, sir.'

A silence ensued, and it was just after Aunt Dahlia had broken it to say how about barricading the door and standing a siege that there came from the passage the sound of approaching footsteps.

'Here they are,' I said.

'They seem in a hurry,' said Aunt Dahlia.

She was correct. These were running footsteps. Jeeves went to the door and looked out.

'It is Mr Fink-Nottle, sir.'

And the next moment Gussie entered, going strongly.

A single glance at him was enough to reveal to the discerning eye that he had not been running just for the sake of the exercise. His spectacles were glittering in a hunted sort of way, and there was more than a touch of the fretful porpentine about his hair.

'Do you mind if I hide here till the milk train goes, Bertie?' he said. 'Under the bed will do. I shan't be in your way.'

'What's the matter?'

'Or, still better, the knotted sheet. That's the stuff.'

A snort like a minute-gun showed that Aunt Dahlia was in no welcoming mood.

'Get out of here, you foul Spink-Bottle,' she said curtly. 'We're in conference. Bertie, if an aunt's wishes have any weight with you, you will stamp on this man with both feet and throw him out on his ear.'

I raised a hand.

'Wait! I want to get the strength of this. Stop messing about with those sheets, Gussie, and explain. Is Spode after you again? Because if so –'

'Not Spode. Sir Watkyn.'

Aunt Dahlia snorted again, like one giving an encore in response to a popular demand.

'Bertie –'

I raised another hand.

'Half a second, old ancestor. How do you mean Sir Watkyn? Why Sir Watkyn? What on earth is he chivvying you for?'

'He's read the notebook.'

'What!'

'Yes.'

'Bertie, I am only a weak woman –'

I raised a third hand. This was no time for listening to aunts.

'Go on, Gussie,' I said dully.

He took off his spectacles and wiped them with a trembling handkerchief. You could see that he was a man who had passed through the furnace.

'When I left you, I went to his room. The door was ajar, and I crept in. And when I had got in, I found that he hadn't gone to have a bath, after all. He was sitting on the bed in his underwear, reading the notebook. He looked up, and our eyes met. You've no notion what a frightful shock it gave me.'

'Yes, I have. I once had a very similar experience with the Rev. Aubrey Upjohn.'

'There was a long, dreadful pause. Then he uttered a sort of gurgling sound and rose, his face contorted. He made a leap in my direction. I pushed off. He followed. It was neck and neck down the stairs, but as we passed through the hall he stopped to get a hunting crop, and this enabled me to secure a good lead, which I –'

'Bertie,' said Aunt Dahlia, 'I am only a weak woman, but if you won't tread on this insect and throw the remains outside, I shall have to see what I can do. The most tremendous issues hanging in the balance…Our plan of action still to be decided on…Every second of priceless importance…and he comes in here, telling us the story of his life. Spink-Bottle, you ghastly goggle-eyed piece of gorgonzola, will you hop it or will you not?'

There is a compelling force about the old flesh and blood, when stirred, which generally gets her listened to. People have told me that in her hunting days she could make her wishes respected across two ploughed fields and a couple of spinneys. The word 'not' had left her lips like a high-powered shell, and Gussie, taking it between the eyes, rose some six inches into the air. When he returned to terra firma, his manner was apologetic and conciliatory.

'Yes, Mrs Travers. I'm just going, Mrs Travers. The moment we get the sheet working, Mrs Travers. If you and Jeeves will just hold this end, Bertie…'

'You want them to let you down from the window with a sheet?'

'Yes, Mrs Travers. Then I can borrow Bertie's car and drive to London.'

'It's a long drop.'

'Oh, not so very, Mrs Travers.'

'You may break your neck.'

'Oh, I don't think so, Mrs Travers.'

'But you may,' argued Aunt Dahlia. 'Come on, Bertie,' she said, speaking with real enthusiasm, 'hurry up. Let the man down with the sheet, can't you? What are you waiting for?'

I turned to Jeeves. 'Ready, Jeeves?'

'Yes, sir.' He coughed gently. 'And perhaps if Mr Fink-Nottle is driving your car to London, he might take your suitcase with him and leave it at the flat.'

I gasped. So did Aunt Dahlia. I stared at him. Aunt Dahlia the same. Our eyes met, and I saw in hers the same reverent awe which I have no doubt she viewed in mine.

I was overcome. A moment before, I had been dully conscious that nothing could save me from the soup. Already I had seemed to hear the beating of its wings. And now this!

Aunt Dahlia, speaking of Napoleon, had claimed that he was pretty hot in an emergency, but I was prepared to bet that not even Napoleon could have topped this superb effort. Once more, as so often in the past, the man had rung the bell and was entitled to the cigar or coconut.

'Yes, Jeeves,' I said, speaking with some difficulty, 'that is true. He might, mightn't he?'

'Yes, sir.'

'You won't mind taking my suitcase, Gussie? If you're borrowing the car, I shall have to go by train. I'm leaving in the morning myself. And it's a nuisance hauling about a lot of luggage.'

'Of course.'

'We'll just loose you down on the sheet and drop the suitcase after you. All set, Jeeves?'

'Yes, sir.'

'Then upsy-daisy!'

I don't think I have ever assisted at a ceremony which gave such universal pleasure to all concerned. The sheet didn't split, which pleased Gussie. Nobody came to interrupt us, which pleased me. And when I dropped the suitcase, it hit Gussie on the head, which delighted Aunt Dahlia. As for Jeeves, one could see that the faithful fellow was tickled pink at having been able to cluster round and save the young master in his hour of peril. His motto is 'Service'.

The stormy emotions through which I had been passing had not unnaturally left me weak, and I was glad when Aunt Dahlia, after a powerful speech in which she expressed her gratitude to our preserver in well-phrased terms, said that she would hop along and see what was going on in the enemy's camp. Her departure enabled me to sink into the armchair in which, had she remained, she would unquestionably have parked herself indefinitely. I flung myself on the cushioned seat and emitted a woof that came straight from the heart.

'So that's that, Jeeves!'

'Yes, sir.'

'Once again your swift thinking has averted disaster as it loomed.'

'It is very kind of you to say so, sir.'

'Not kind, Jeeves. I am merely saying what any thinking man would say. I didn't chip in while Aunt Dahlia was speaking, for I saw that she wished to have the floor, but you may take it that I was silently subscribing to every sentiment she uttered. You stand alone, Jeeves. What size hat do you take?'

'A number eight, sir.'

'I should have thought larger. Eleven or twelve.'

I helped myself to a spot of brandy, and sat rolling it round my tongue luxuriantly. It was delightful to relax after the strain and stress I had been through.

'Well, Jeeves, the going has been pretty tough, what?'

'Extremely, sir.'

'One begins to get some idea of how the skipper of the *Hesperus*'s little daughter must have felt. Still, I suppose these tests and trials are good for the character.'

'No doubt, sir.'

'Strengthening.'

'Yes, sir.'

'However, I can't say I'm sorry it's all over. Enough is always enough. And it is all over, one feels. Even this sinister house can surely have no further shocks to offer.'

'I imagine not, sir.'

'No, this is the finish. Totleigh Towers has shot its bolt, and at long last we are sitting pretty. Gratifying, Jeeves.'

'Most gratifying, sir.'

'You bet it is. Carry on with the packing. I want to get it done and go to bed.'

He opened the small suitcase, and I lit a cigarette and proceeded to stress the moral lesson to be learned from all this rannygazoo.

'Yes, Jeeves, "gratifying" is the word. A short while ago, the air was congested with V-shaped depressions, but now one looks north, south, east and west and descries not a single cloud on the horizon – except the fact that Gussie's wedding is still off, and that can't be helped. Well, this should certainly teach us, should it not, never to repine, never to despair, never to allow the upper lip to unstiffen, but always to remember that, no matter how dark the skies may be, the sun is shining somewhere and will eventually come smiling through.'

I paused. I perceived that I was not securing his attention. He was looking down with an intent, thoughtful expression on his face.

'Something the matter, Jeeves?'

'Sir?'

'You appear preoccupied.'

'Yes, sir. I have just discovered that there is a policeman's helmet in this suitcase.'

I HAD been right about the strengthening effect on the character of the vicissitudes to which I had been subjected since clocking in at the country residence of Sir Watkyn Bassett. Little by little, bit by bit, they had been moulding me, turning me from a sensitive clubman and *boulevardier* to a man of chilled steel. A novice to conditions in this pest house, abruptly handed the news item which I had just been handed, would, I imagine, have rolled up the eyeballs and swooned where he sat. But I, toughened and fortified by the routine of one damn thing after another which constituted life at Totleigh Towers, was enabled to keep my head and face the issue.

I don't say I didn't leave my chair like a jack-rabbit that has sat on a cactus, but having risen I wasted no time in fruitless twitterings. I went to the door and locked it. Then, tight-lipped and pale, I came back to Jeeves, who had now taken the helmet from the suitcase and was oscillating it meditatively by its strap.

His first words showed me that he had got the wrong angle on the situation.

'It would be wiser, sir,' he said with a faint reproach, 'to have selected some more adequate hiding place.'

I shook my head. I may even have smiled – wanly, of course. My swift intelligence had enabled me to probe to the bottom of this thing.

'Not me, Jeeves. Stiffy.'

'Sir?'

'The hand that placed that helmet there was not mine, but that of S. Byng. She had it in her room. She feared lest a search might be instituted, and when I last saw her was trying to think of a safer spot. This is her idea of one.'

I sighed.

'How do you imagine a girl gets a mind like Stiffy's, Jeeves?'

'Certainly the young lady is somewhat eccentric in her actions, sir.'

'Eccentric? She could step straight into Colney Hatch, and no questions asked. They would lay down the red carpet for her. The more the thoughts dwell on that young shrimp, the more the soul sickens in horror. One peers into the future, and shudders at what one sees there. One has to face it, Jeeves – Stiffy, who is pure padded cell from the foundations up, is about to marry the Rev. H. P. Pinker, himself about as pronounced a goop as ever broke bread, and there is no reason to suppose – one has to face this, too – that their union will not be blessed. There will, that is to say, ere long be little feet pattering about the home. And what one asks oneself is – Just how safe will human life be in the vicinity of those feet, assuming – as one is forced to assume – that they will inherit the combined loopiness of two such parents? It is with a sort of tender pity, Jeeves, that I think of the nurses, the governesses, the private-school masters and the public-school masters who will lightly take on the responsibility of looking after a blend of Stephanie Byng and Harold Pinker, little knowing that they are coming up against something hotter than mustard. However,' I went on, abandoning these speculations, 'all this, though of absorbing interest, is not really germane to the issue. Contemplating that helmet and bearing in mind the fact that the Oates–Bassett comedy duo will be arriving at any moment to start their search, what would you recommend?'

'It is a little difficult to say, sir. A really effective hiding place for so bulky an object does not readily present itself.'

'No. The damn thing seems to fill the room, doesn't it?'

'It unquestionably takes the eye, sir.'

'Yes. The authorities wrought well when they shaped this helmet for Constable Oates. They aimed to finish him off impressively, not to give him something which would balance on top of his head like a peanut, and they succeeded. You couldn't hide a lid like this in an impenetrable jungle. Ah, well,' I said, 'we will just have to see what tact and suavity will do. I wonder when these birds are going to arrive. I suppose we may expect them very shortly. Ah! That would be the hand of doom now, if I mistake not, Jeeves.'

But in assuming that the knocker who had just knocked on the door was Sir Watkyn Bassett, I had erred. It was Stiffy's voice that spoke.

'Bertie, let me in.'

There was nobody I was more anxious to see, but I did not immediately fling wide the gates. Prudence dictated a preliminary inquiry.

'Have you got that bally dog of yours with you?'

'No. He's being aired by the butler.'

'In that case, you may enter.'

When she did so, it was to find Bertram confronting her with folded arms and a hard look. She appeared, however, not to note my forbidding exterior.

'Bertie, darling –'

She broke off, checked by a fairly animal snarl from the Wooster lips.

'Not so much of the "Bertie, darling". I have just one thing to say to you, young Stiffy, and it is this: Was it you who put that helmet in my suitcase?'

'Of course it was. That's what I was coming to talk to you about. You remember I was trying to think of a good place. I racked the brain quite a bit, and then suddenly I got it.'

'And now I've got it.'

The acidity of my tone seemed to surprise her. She regarded me with girlish wonder – the wide-eyed kind.

'But you don't mind do you, Bertie, darling?'

'Ha!'

'But why? I thought you would be so glad to help me out.'

'Oh, yes?' I said, and I meant it to sting.

'I couldn't risk having Uncle Watkyn find it in my room.'

'You preferred to have him find it in mine?'

'But how can he? He can't come searching your room.'

'He can't, eh?'

'Of course not. You're his guest.'

'And you suppose that that will cause him to hold his hand?' I smiled one of those bitter, sardonic smiles. 'I think you are attributing to the old poison germ a niceness of feeling and a respect for the laws of hospitality which nothing in his record suggests that he possesses. You can take it from me that he definitely is going to search the room, and I imagine that the only reason he hasn't arrived already is that he is still scouring the house for Gussie.'

'Gussie?'

'He is at the moment chasing Gussie with a hunting crop. But a man cannot go on doing that indefinitely. Sooner or later he will give it up, and then we shall have him here, complete with magnifying glass and bloodhounds.'

The gravity of the situash had at last impressed itself upon her. She uttered a squeak of dismay, and her eyes became a bit soup-platey.

'Oh, Bertie! Then I'm afraid I've put you in rather a spot.'

'That covers the facts like a dust-sheet.'

'I'm sorry now I ever asked Harold to pinch the thing. It was a mistake. I admit it. Still, after all, even if Uncle Watkyn does come here and find it, it doesn't matter much, does it?'

'Did you hear that, Jeeves?'

'Yes, sir.'

'Thank you, Jeeves. What makes you suppose that I shall meekly assume the guilt and not blazon the truth forth to the world?'

I wouldn't have supposed that her eyes could have widened any more, but they did perceptibly. Another dismayed squeak escaped her. Indeed, such was its volume that it might perhaps be better to call it a squeal.

'But Bertie!'

'Well?'

'Bertie, listen!'

'I'm listening.'

'Surely you will take the rap? You can't let Harold get it in the neck. You were telling me this afternoon that he would be unfrocked. I won't have him unfrocked. Where is he going to get if they unfrock him? That sort of thing gives a curate a frightful black eye. Why can't you say you did it? All it would mean is that you would be kicked out of the house, and I don't suppose you're so anxious to stay on, are you?'

'Possibly you are not aware that your bally uncle is proposing to send the perpetrator of this outrage to chokey.'

'Oh, no. At the worst, just a fine.'

'Nothing of the kind. He specifically told me chokey.'

'He didn't mean it. I expect there was –'

'No, there was not a twinkle in his eye.'

'Then that settles it. I can't have my precious angel Harold doing a stretch.'

'How about your precious angel Bertram?'

'But Harold's sensitive.'

'So am I sensitive.'

'Not half so sensitive as Harold. Bertie, surely you aren't going to be difficult about this? You're much too good a sport. Didn't you tell me once that the Code of the Woosters was "Never let a pal down"?'

She had found the talking point. People who appeal to the Code of the Woosters rarely fail to touch a chord in Bertram. My iron front began to crumble.

'That's all very fine —'

'Bertie, darling!'

'Yes, I know, but, dash it all —'

'Bertie!'

'Oh, well!'

'You will take the rap?'

'I suppose so.'

She yodelled ecstatically, and I think that if I had not side-stepped she would have flung her arms about my neck. Certainly she came leaping forward with some such purpose apparently in view. Foiled by my agility, she began to tear off a few steps of that Spring dance to which she was so addicted.

'Thank you, Bertie, darling. I knew you would be sweet about it. I can't tell you how grateful I am, and how much I admire you. You remind me of Carter Paterson...no, that's not it...Nick Carter...no, not Nick Carter...Who does Mr Wooster remind me of, Jeeves?'

'Sydney Carton, miss.'

'That's right. Sydney Carton. But he was small-time stuff compared with you, Bertie. And, anyway, I expect we are getting the wind up quite unnecessarily. Why are we taking it for granted that Uncle Watkyn will find the helmet, if he comes and searches the room? There are a hundred places where you can hide it.'

And before I could say 'Name three!' she had pirouetted to the door and pirouetted out. I could hear her dying away in the distance with a song on the lips.

My own, as I turned to Jeeves, were twisted in a bitter smile.

'Women, Jeeves!'

'Yes, sir.'

'Well, Jeeves,' I said, my hand stealing towards the decanter, 'this is the end!'

'No, sir.'

I started with a violence that nearly unshipped my front uppers.

'Not the end?'

'No, sir.'

'You don't mean you have an idea?'

'Yes, sir.'

'But you told me just now you hadn't.'

'Yes, sir. But since then I have been giving the matter some thought, and am now in a position to say "Eureka!"'

'Say what?'

'Eureka, sir. Like Archimedes.'

'Did he say Eureka? I thought it was Shakespeare.'

'No, sir. Archimedes. What I would recommend is that you drop the helmet out of the window. It is most improbable that it will occur to Sir Watkyn to search the exterior of the premises, and we shall be able to recover it at our leisure.' He paused, and stood listening. 'Should this suggestion meet with your approval, sir, I feel that a certain haste would be advisable. I fancy I can hear the sound of approaching footsteps.'

He was right. The air was vibrant with their clumping. Assuming that a herd of bison was not making its way along the second-floor passage of Totleigh Towers, the enemy were upon us. With the nippiness of a lamb in the fold on observing the approach of Assyrians, I snatched up the helmet, bounded to the window and loosed the thing into the night. And scarcely had I done so, when the door opened, and through it came – in the order named – Aunt Dahlia, wearing an amused and indulgent look, as if she were joining in some game to please the children: Pop Bassett, in a purple dressing gown, and Police Constable Oates, who was dabbing at his nose with a pocket handkerchief.

'So sorry to disturb you, Bertie,' said the aged relative courteously.

'Not at all,' I replied with equal suavity. 'Is there something I can do for the multitude?'

'Sir Watkyn has got some extraordinary idea into his head about wanting to search your room.'

'Search my room?'

'I intend to search it from top to bottom,' said old Bassett, looking very Bosher Street-y.

I glanced at Aunt Dahlia, raising the eyebrows.

'I don't understand. What's all this about?'

She laughed indulgently.

'You will scarcely believe it, Bertie, but he thinks that cow-creamer is here.'

'Is it missing?'

'It's been stolen.'

'You don't say!'

'Yes.'

'Well, well, well!'

'He's very upset about it.'

'I don't wonder.'

'Most distressed.'

'Poor old bloke!'

I placed a kindly hand on Pop Bassett's shoulder. Probably the wrong thing to do, I can see, looking back, for it did not soothe.

'I can do without your condolences, Mr Wooster, and I should be glad if you would not refer to me as a bloke. I have every reason to believe that not only is my cow-creamer in your possession, but Constable Oates's helmet, as well.'

A cheery guffaw seemed in order. I uttered it.

'Ha, ha!'

Aunt Dahlia came across with another.

'Ha, ha!'

'How dashed absurd!'

'Perfectly ridiculous.'

'What on earth would I be doing with cow-creamers?'

'Or policemen's helmets?'

'Quite.'

'Did you ever hear such a weird idea?'

'Never. My dear old host,' I said, 'let us keep perfectly calm and cool and get all this straightened out. In the kindliest spirit, I must point out that you are on the verge – if not slightly past the verge – of making an ass of yourself. This sort of thing won't do, you know. You can't dash about accusing people of nameless crimes without a shadow of evidence.'

'I have all the evidence I require, Mr Wooster.'

'That's what you think. And that, I maintain, is where you are making the floater of a lifetime. When was this Modern Dutch gadget of yours abstracted?'

He quivered beneath the thrust, pinkening at the tip of the nose.

'It is not Modern Dutch!'

'Well, we can thresh that out later. The point is: when did it leave the premises?'

'It has not left the premises.'

'That, again, is what you think. Well, when was it stolen?'

'About twenty minutes ago.'

'Then there you are. Twenty minutes ago I was up here in my room.'

This rattled him. I had thought it would.

'You were in your room?'

'In my room.'

'Alone?'

'On the contrary. Jeeves was here.'

'Who is Jeeves?'

'Don't you know Jeeves? This is Jeeves. Jeeves...Sir Watkyn Bassett.'

'And who may you be, my man?'

'That's exactly what he is – my man. May I say my right-hand man?'

'Thank you, sir.'

'Not at all, Jeeves. Well-earned tribute.'

Pop Bassett's face was disfigured, if you could disfigure a face like his, by an ugly sneer.

'I regret, Mr Wooster, that I am not prepared to accept as conclusive evidence of your innocence the unsupported word of your manservant.'

'Unsupported, eh? Jeeves, go and page Mr Spode. Tell him I want him to come and put a bit of stuffing into my alibi.'

'Very good, sir.'

He shimmered away, and Pop Bassett seemed to swallow something hard and jagged.

'Was Roderick Spode with you?'

'Certainly he was. Perhaps you will believe him?'

'Yes, I would believe Roderick Spode.'

'Very well, then. He'll be here in a moment.'

He appeared to muse.

'I see. Well, apparently I was wrong, then, in supposing that you are concealing my cow-creamer. It must have been purloined by somebody else.'

'Outside job, if you ask me,' said Aunt Dahlia.

'Possibly the work of an international gang,' I hazarded.

'Very likely.'

'I expect it was all over the place that Sir Watkyn had bought the thing. You remember Uncle Tom had been counting on getting it, and no doubt he told all sorts of people where it had gone. It wouldn't take long for the news to filter through to the international gangs. They keep their ear to the ground.'

'Damn clever, those gangs,' assented the aged relative.

Pop Bassett had seemed to me to wince a trifle at the mention of Uncle Tom's name. Guilty conscience doing its stuff, no doubt – gnawing, as these guilty consciences do.

'Well, we need not discuss the matter further,' he said. 'As regards the cow-creamer, I admit that you have established your case. We will now turn to Constable Oates's helmet. That, Mr Wooster, I happen to know positively, is in your possession.'

'Oh, yes?'

'Yes. The constable received specific information on the point from an eyewitness. I will proceed, therefore, to search your room without delay.'

'You really feel you want to?'

'I do.'

I shrugged the shoulders.

'Very well,' I said, 'very well. If that is the spirit in which you interpret the duties of a host, carry on. We invite inspection. I can only say that you appear to have extraordinarily rummy views on making your guests comfortable over the weekend. Don't count on my coming here again.'

I had expressed the opinion to Jeeves that it would be entertaining to stand by and watch this blighter and his colleague ferret about, and so it proved. I don't know when I have extracted more solid amusement from anything. But all these good things have to come to an end at last. About ten minutes later, it was plain that the bloodhounds were planning to call it off and pack up.

To say that Pop Bassett was wry, as he desisted from his efforts and turned to me, would be to understate it.

'I appear to owe you an apology, Mr Wooster,' he said.

'Sir W. Bassett,' I rejoined, 'you never spoke a truer word.'

And folding my arms and drawing myself up to my full height, I let him have it.

The exact words of my harangue have, I am sorry to say, escaped my memory. It is a pity that there was nobody taking them down in shorthand, for I am not exaggerating when I say that I surpassed myself. Once or twice, when a bit lit at routs and revels, I have spoken with an eloquence which, rightly or wrongly, has won the plaudits of the Drones Club, but I don't think that I have ever quite reached the level to which I now soared. You could see the stuffing trickling out of old Bassett in great heaping handfuls.

But as I rounded into my peroration, I suddenly noticed that I was failing to grip. He had ceased to listen, and was staring past me at something out of my range of vision. And so worth looking at did this spectacle, judging from his expression, appear to be that I turned in order to take a dekko.

It was the butler who had so riveted Sir Watkyn Bassett's attention. He was standing in the doorway, holding in his right hand a silver salver. And on that salver was a policeman's helmet.

I REMEMBER old Stinker Pinker, who towards the end of his career at Oxford used to go in for social service in London's tougher districts, describing to me once in some detail the sensations he had experienced one afternoon, while spreading the light in Bethnal Green, on being unexpectedly kicked in the stomach by a costermonger. It gave him, he told me, a strange, dreamy feeling, together with an odd illusion of having walked into a thick fog. And the reason I mention it is that my own emotions at this moment were extraordinarily similar.

When I had last seen this butler, if you recollect, on the occasion when he had come to tell me that Madeline Bassett would be glad if I could spare her a moment, I mentioned that he had flickered. It was not so much at a flickering butler that I was gazing now as at a sort of heaving mist with a vague suggestion of something butlerine vibrating inside it. Then the scales fell from my eyes, and I was enabled to note the reactions of the rest of the company.

They were all taking it extremely big. Pop Bassett, like the chap in the poem which I had to write out fifty times at school for introducing a white mouse into the English Literature hour, was plainly feeling like some watcher of the skies when a new planet swims into his ken, while Aunt Dahlia and Constable Oates resembled respectively stout Cortez staring at the Pacific and all his men looking at each other with a wild surmise, silent upon a peak in Darien.

It was a goodish while before anybody stirred. Then, with a choking cry like that of a mother spotting her long-lost child in the offing, Constable Oates swooped forward and grabbed the lid, clasping it to his bosom with visible ecstasy.

The movement seemed to break the spell. Old Bassett came to life as if someone had pressed a button.

'Where — where did you get that, Butterfield?'

'I found it in a flowerbed, Sir Watkyn.'

'In a flowerbed?'

'Odd,' I said. 'Very strange.'

'Yes, sir. I was airing Miss Byng's dog, and, happening to be passing the side of the house, I observed Mr Wooster drop something from his window. It fell into the flowerbed beneath, and upon inspection proved to be this helmet.'

Old Bassett drew a deep breath.

'Thank you, Butterfield.'

The butler breezed off, and old B., revolving on his axis, faced me with gleaming pince-nez.

'So!' he said.

There is never very much you can do in the way of a telling comeback when a fellow says 'So!' to you. I preserved a judicious silence.

'Some mistake,' said Aunt Dahlia, taking the floor with an intrepidity which became her well. 'Probably came from one of the other windows. Easy to get confused on a dark night.'

'Tchah!'

'Or it may be that the man was lying. Yes, that seems a plausible explanation. I think I see it all. This Butterfield of yours is the guilty man. He stole the helmet, and knowing that the hunt was up and detection imminent, decided to play a bold game and try to shove it off on Bertie. Eh, Bertie?'

'I shouldn't wonder, Aunt Dahlia. I shouldn't wonder at all.'

'Yes, that is what must have happened. It becomes clearer every moment. You can't trust these saintly looking butlers an inch.'

'Not an inch.'

'I remember thinking the fellow had a furtive eye.'

'Me, too.'

'You noticed it yourself, did you?'

'Right away.'

'He reminds me of Murgatroyd. Do you remember Murgatroyd at Brinkley, Bertie?'

'The fellow before Pomeroy? Stoutish cove?'

'That's right. With a face like a more than usually respectable archbishop. Took us all in, that face. We trusted him implicitly. And what was the result? Fellow pinched a fish slice, put it up the spout and squandered the proceeds at the dog races. This Butterfield is another Murgatroyd.'

'Some relation, perhaps.'

'I shouldn't be surprised. Well, now that's all satisfactorily settled and Bertie dismissed without a stain on his character, how about all going to bed? It's getting late, and if I don't have my eight hours, I'm a rag.'

She had injected into the proceedings such a pleasant atmosphere of all-pals-together and hearty let's-say-no-more-about-it that it came quite as a shock to find that old Bassett was failing to see eye to eye. He proceeded immediately to strike the jarring note.

'With your theory that somebody is lying, Mrs Travers, I am in complete agreement. But when you assert that it is my butler, I must join issue with you. Mr Wooster has been exceedingly clever – most ingenious –'

'Oh, thanks.'

'– but I am afraid that I find myself unable to dismiss him, as you suggest, without a stain on his character. In fact, to be frank with you, I do not propose to dismiss him at all.'

He gave me the pince-nez in a cold and menacing manner. I can't remember when I've seen a man I liked the look of less.

'You may possibly recall, Mr Wooster, that in the course of our conversation in the library I informed you that I took the very gravest view of this affair. Your suggestion that I might be content with inflicting a fine of five pounds, as was the case when you appeared before me at Bosher Street convicted of a similar outrage, I declared myself unable to accept. I assured you that the perpetrator of this wanton assault on the person of Constable Oates would, when apprehended, serve a prison sentence. I see no reason to revise that decision.'

This statement had a mixed press. Eustace Oates obviously approved. He looked up from the helmet with a quick encouraging smile and but for the iron restraint of discipline would, I think, have said 'Hear, hear!' Aunt Dahlia and I, on the other hand, didn't like it.

'Here, come, I say now, Sir Watkyn, really, dash it,' she expostulated, always on her toes when the interests of the clan were threatened. 'You can't do that sort of thing.'

'Madam, I both can and will.' He twiddled a hand in the direction of Eustace Oates. 'Constable!'

He didn't add 'Arrest this man!' or 'Do your duty!' but the officer got the gist. He clumped forward zealously. I was rather expecting him to lay a hand on my shoulder or to produce the gyves and apply them to my wrists, but he didn't. He merely lined up beside me as if we were going to do a duet and stood there looking puff-faced.

Aunt Dahlia continued to plead and reason.

'But you can't invite a man to your house and the moment he steps inside the door calmly bung him into the coop. If that is Gloucestershire hospitality, then heaven help Gloucestershire.'

'Mr Wooster is not here on my invitation, but on my daughter's.'

'That makes no difference. You can't wriggle out of it like that. He is your guest. He has eaten your salt. And let me tell you, while we are on the subject, that there was a lot too much of it in the soup tonight.'

'Oh, would you say that?' I said. 'Just about right, it seemed to me.'

'No. Too salty.'

Pop Bassett intervened.

'I must apologize for the shortcomings of my cook. I may be making a change before long. Meanwhile, to return to the subject with which we were dealing, Mr Wooster is under arrest, and tomorrow I shall take the necessary steps to –'

'And what's going to happen to him tonight?'

'We maintain a small but serviceable police station in the village, presided over by Constable Oates. Oates will doubtless be able to find him accommodation.'

'You aren't proposing to lug the poor chap off to a police station at this time of night? You could at least let him doss in a decent bed.'

'Yes, I see no objection to that. One does not wish to be unduly harsh. You may remain in this room until tomorrow, Mr Wooster.'

'Oh, thanks.'

'I shall lock the door –'

'Oh, quite.'

'And take charge of the key –'

'Oh, rather.'

'And Constable Oates will patrol beneath the window for the remainder of the night.'

'Sir?'

'This will check Mr Wooster's known propensity for dropping things from windows. You had better take up your station at once, Oates.'

'Very good, sir.'

There was a note of quiet anguish in the officer's voice, and it was plain that the smug satisfaction with which he had been watching the progress of events had waned. His views on getting his eight hours were apparently the same as Aunt Dahlia's. Saluting sadly, he left the room in a depressed sort of way. He had his helmet again, but you could see that he was beginning to ask himself if helmets were everything.

'And now, Mrs Travers, I should like, if I may, to have a word with you in private.'

They oiled off, and I was alone.

I don't mind confessing that my emotions, as the key turned in the lock, were a bit poignant. On the one hand, it was nice to feel that I had got my bedroom to myself for a few minutes, but against that you had to put the fact that I was in what is known as durance vile and not likely to get out of it.

Of course, this was not new stuff to me, for I had heard the bars clang outside my cell door that time at Bosher Street. But on that occasion I had been able to buoy myself up with the reflection that the worst the aftermath was likely to provide was a rebuke from the bench or, as subsequently proved to be the case, a punch in the pocket-book. I was not faced, as I was faced now, by the prospect of waking on the morrow to begin serving a sentence of thirty days' duration in a prison where it was most improbable that I would be able to get my morning cup of tea.

Nor did the consciousness that I was innocent seem to help much. I drew no consolation from the fact that Stiffy Byng thought me like Sydney Carton. I had never met the chap, but I gathered that he was somebody who had taken it on the chin to oblige a girl, and to my mind this was enough to stamp him as a priceless ass. Sydney Carton and Bertram Wooster, I felt – nothing to choose between them. Sydney, one of the mugs – Bertram, the same.

I went to the window and looked out. Recalling the moody distaste which Constable Oates had exhibited at the suggestion that he should stand guard during the night hours, I had a faint hope that, once the eye of authority was removed, he might have ducked the assignment and gone off to get his beauty sleep. But no. There he was, padding up and down on the lawn, the picture of vigilance. And I had just gone to the wash-hand-stand to get a cake of soap to bung at him, feeling that this might soothe the bruised spirit a little, when I heard the door handle rattle.

I stepped across and put my lips to the woodwork.

'Hallo.'

'It is I, sir. Jeeves.'

'Oh, hallo, Jeeves.'

'The door appears to be locked, sir.'

'And you can take it from me, Jeeves, that appearances do not deceive. Pop Bassett locked it, and has trousered the key.'

'Sir?'

'I've been pinched.'

'Indeed, sir?'

'What was that?'

'I said "Indeed, sir?"'

'Oh, did you? Yes. Yes, indeed. And I'll tell you why.'

I gave him a *précis* of what had happened. It was not easy to hear, with a door between us, but I think the narrative elicited a spot of respectful tut-tutting.

'Unfortunate, sir.'

'Most. Well, Jeeves, what is your news?'

'I endeavoured to locate Mr Spode, sir, but he had gone for a walk in the grounds. No doubt he will be returning shortly.'

'Well, we shan't require him now. The rapid march of events has taken us far past the point where Spode could have been of service. Anything else been happening at your end?'

'I have had a word with Miss Byng, sir.'

'I should like a word with her myself. What had she to say?'

'The young lady was in considerable distress of mind, sir, her union with the Reverend Mr Pinker having been forbidden by Sir Watkyn.'

'Good Lord, Jeeves! Why?'

'Sir Watkyn appears to have taken umbrage at the part played by Mr Pinker in allowing the purloiner of the cow-creamer to effect his escape.'

'Why do you say "his"?'

'From motives of prudence, sir. Walls have ears.'

'I see what you mean. That's rather neat, Jeeves.'

'Thank you, sir.'

I mused a while on this latest development. There were certainly aching hearts in Gloucestershire all right this p.m. I was conscious of a pang of pity. Despite the fact that it was entirely owing to Stiffy that I found myself in my present predic., I wished the young loony well and mourned for her in her hour of disaster.

'So he has bunged a spanner into Stiffy's romance as well as Gussie's, has he? That old bird has certainly been throwing his weight about tonight, Jeeves.'

'Yes, sir.'

'And not a thing to be done about it, as far as I can see. Can you see anything to be done about it?'

'No, sir.'

'And switching to another aspect of the affair, you haven't any immediate plans for getting me out of this, I suppose?'

'Not adequately formulated, sir. I am turning over an idea in my mind.'

'Turn well, Jeeves. Spare no effort.'

'But it is at present merely nebulous.'

'It involves finesse, I presume?'

'Yes, sir.'

I shook my head. Waste of time really, of course, because he couldn't see me. Still, I shook it.

'It's no good trying to be subtle and snaky now, Jeeves. What is required is rapid action. And a thought has occurred to me. We were speaking not long since of the time when Sir Roderick Glossop was immured in the potting-shed, with Constable Dobson guarding every exit. Do you remember what old Pop Stoker's idea was for coping with the situation?'

'If I recollect rightly, sir, Mr Stoker advocated a physical assault upon the officer. "Bat him over the head with a shovel!" was, as I recall, his expression.'

'Correct, Jeeves. Those were his exact words. And though we scouted the idea at the time, it seems to me now that he displayed a considerable amount of rugged good sense. These practical, self-made men have a way of going straight to the point and avoiding side issues. Constable Oates is on sentry-go beneath my window. I still have the knotted sheets and they can readily be attached to the leg of the bed or something. So if you would just borrow a shovel somewhere and step down –'

'I fear, sir –'

'Come on, Jeeves. This is no time for *nolle prosequis*. I know you like finesse, but you must see that it won't help us now. The moment has arrived when only shovels can serve. You could go and engage him in conversation, keeping the instrument concealed behind your back, and waiting for the psychological –'

'Excuse me, sir. I think I hear somebody coming.'

'Well, ponder over what I have said. Who is coming?'

'It is Sir Watkyn and Mrs Travers, sir. I fancy they are about to call upon you.'

'I thought I shouldn't get this room to myself for long. Still, let them come. We Woosters keep open house.'

When the door was unlocked a few moments later, however, only the relative entered. She made for the old familiar armchair, and dumped herself heavily in it. Her demeanour was sombre, encouraging no hope that she had come to announce that Pop Bassett, wiser counsels having prevailed, had decided to set me free. And yet I'm dashed if that wasn't precisely what she had come to announce.

'Well, Bertie,' she said, having brooded in silence for a space, 'you can get on with your packing.'

'Eh?'

'He's called it off.'

'Called it off?'

'Yes. He isn't going to press the charge.'

'You mean I'm not headed for chokey?'

'No.'

'I'm as free as the air, as the expression is?'

'Yes.'

I was so busy rejoicing in spirit that it was some moments before I had leisure to observe that the buck-and-wing dance which I was performing was not being abetted by the old flesh and blood. She was still carrying on with her sombre sitting, and I looked at her with a touch of reproach.

'You don't seem very pleased.'

'Oh, I'm delighted.'

'I fail to detect the symptoms,' I said, rather coldly. 'I should have thought that a nephew's reprieve at the foot of the scaffold, as you might say, would have produced a bit of leaping and springing about.'

A deep sigh escaped her.

'Well, the trouble is, Bertie, there is a catch in it. The old buzzard has made a condition.'

'What is that?'

'He wants Anatole.'

I stared at her.

'Wants Anatole?'

'Yes. That is the price of your freedom. He says he will agree not to press the charge if I let him have Anatole. The darned old blackmailer!'

A spasm of anguish twisted her features. It was not so very long since she had been speaking in high terms of blackmail and giving it her hearty approval, but if you want to derive real satisfaction from blackmail, you have to be at the right end of it. Catching it coming, as it were, instead of going, this woman was suffering.

I wasn't feeling any too good myself. From time to time in the course of this narrative I have had occasion to indicate my sentiments regarding Anatole, that peerless artist, and you will remember that the relative's account of how Sir Watkyn Bassett had basely tried to snitch him from her employment during his visit to Brinkley Court had shocked me to my foundations.

It is difficult, of course, to convey to those who have not tasted this wizard's products the extraordinary importance which his roasts and boileds assume in the scheme of things to those who have. I can only say that once having bitten into one of his dishes you are left with the feeling that life will be deprived of all its poetry and meaning unless you are in a position to go on digging in. The thought that Aunt Dahlia was prepared to sacrifice this wonder man merely to save a nephew from the cooler was one that struck home and stirred.

I don't know when I have been so profoundly moved. It was with a melting eye that I gazed at her. She reminded me of Sydney Carton.

'You were actually contemplating giving up Anatole for my sake?' I gasped.

'Of course.'

'Of course jolly well not! I wouldn't hear of such a thing.'

'But you can't go to prison.'

'I certainly can, if my going means that that supreme maestro will continue working at the old stand. Don't dream of meeting old Bassett's demands.'

'Bertie! Do you mean this?'

'I should say so. What's a mere thirty days in the second division? A bagatelle. I can do it on my head. Let Bassett do his worst. And,' I added in a softer voice, 'when my time is up and I come out into the world once more a free man, let Anatole do his best. A month of bread and water or skilly or whatever they feed you on in these establishments will give me a rare appetite. On the night when I emerge, I shall expect a dinner that will live in legend and song.'

'You shall have it.'

'We might be sketching out the details now.'

'No time like the present. Start with caviare? Or *cantaloup*?'

'And *cantaloup*. Followed by a strengthening soup.'

'Thick or clear?'

'Clear.'

'You aren't forgetting Anatole's *Velouté aux fleurs de courgette*?'

'Not for a moment. But how about his *Consommé aux Pommes d'Amour*?'

'Perhaps you're right.'

'I think I am. I feel I am.'

'I'd better leave the ordering to you.'

'It might be wisest.'

I took pencil and paper, and some ten minutes later I was in a position to announce the result.

'This, then,' I said, 'subject to such additions as I may think out in my cell, is the menu as I see it.'

And I read as follows:

Le Diner

Caviar Frais
Cantaloup
Consommé aux Pommes d'Amour
Sylphides à la crème d'Écrevisses
Mignonette de poulet petit Duc
Points d'asperges à la Mistinguette
Suprême de fois gras au champagne
Neige aux Perles des Alpes
Timbale de ris de veau Toulousaine
Salade d'endive et de céleri
Le Plum Pudding

L'Étoile au Berger
Bénédictins Blancs
Bombe Néro
Friandises
Diablotins
Fruits

'That about covers it, Aunt Dahlia?'

'Yes, you don't seem to have missed out much.'

'Then let's have the man in and defy him. Bassett!' I cried.

'Bassett!' shouted Aunt Dahlia.

'Bassett!' I bawled, making the welkin ring.

It was still ringing when he popped in, looking annoyed.

'What the devil are you shouting at me like that for?'

'Oh, there you are, Bassett.' I wasted no time in getting down to the agenda. 'Bassett, we defy you.'

The man was plainly taken aback. He threw a questioning look at Aunt Dahlia. He seemed to be feeling that Bertram was speaking in riddles.

'He is alluding,' explained the relative, 'to that idiotic offer of yours to call the thing off if I let you have Anatole. Silliest idea I ever heard. We've been having a good laugh about it. Haven't we, Bertie?'

'Roaring our heads off,' I assented.

He seemed stunned.

'Do you mean that you refuse?'

'Of course we refuse. I might have known my nephew better than to suppose for an instant that he would consider bringing sorrow and bereavement to an aunt's home in order to save himself unpleasantness. The Woosters are not like that, are they, Bertie?'

'I should say not.'

'They don't put self first.'

'You bet they don't.'

'I ought never to have insulted him by mentioning the offer to him. I apologize, Bertie.'

'Quite all right, old flesh and blood.'

She wrung my hand.

'Good night, Bertie, and goodbye – or, rather *au revoir*. We shall meet again.'

'Absolutely. When the fields are white with daisies, if not sooner.'

'By the way, didn't you forget *Nomais de la Méditerranée au Fenouil?*'

'So I did. And *Selle d'Agneau aux laitues à la Grecque.* Shove them on the charge sheet, will you?'

Her departure, which was accompanied by a melting glance of admiration and esteem over her shoulder as she navigated across the threshold, was followed by a brief and, on my part, haughty silence. After a while, Pop Bassett spoke in a strained and nasty voice.

'Well, Mr Wooster, it seems that after all you will have to pay the penalty of your folly.'

'Quite.'

'I may say that I have changed my mind about allowing you to spend the night under my roof. You will go to the police station.'

'Vindictive, Bassett.'

'Not at all. I see no reason why Constable Oates should be deprived of his well-earned sleep merely to suit your convenience. I will send for him.' He opened the door. 'Here, you!'

It was a most improper way of addressing Jeeves, but the faithful fellow did not appear to resent it.

'Sir?'

'On the lawn outside the house you will find Constable Oates. Bring him here.'

'Very good, sir. I think Mr Spode wishes to speak to you, sir.'

'Eh?'

'Mr Spode, sir. He is coming along the passage now.'

Old Bassett came back into the room, seeming displeased.

'I wish Roderick would not interrupt me at a time like this,' he said querulously. 'I cannot imagine what reason he can have for wanting to see me.'

I laughed lightly. The irony of the thing amused me.

'He is coming – a bit late – to tell you that he was with me when the cow-creamer was pinched, thus clearing me of the guilt.'

'I see. Yes, as you say, he is somewhat late. I shall have to explain to him… Ah, Roderick.'

The massive frame of R. Spode had appeared in the doorway.

'Come in, Roderick, come in. But you need not have troubled, my dear fellow. Mr Wooster has made it quite evident that he had nothing to do with the theft of my cow-creamer. It was that that you wished to see me about, was it not?'

'Well – er – no,' said Roderick Spode.

There was an odd, strained look on the man's face. His eyes were glassy and, as far as a thing of that size was capable of being fingered, he was fingering his moustache. He seemed to be bracing himself for some unpleasant task.

'Well – er – no,' he said. 'The fact is, I hear there's been some trouble about that helmet I stole from Constable Oates.'

There was a stunned silence. Old Bassett goggled. I goggled. Roderick Spode continued to finger his moustache.

'It was a silly thing to do,' he said. 'I see that now. I – er – yielded to a uncontrollable impulse. One does sometimes, doesn't one? You remember I told you I once stole a policeman's helmet at Oxford. I was hoping I could keep quiet about it, but Wooster's man tells me that you have got the idea that Wooster did it, so of course I had to come and tell you. That's all. I think I'll go to bed,' said Roderick Spode. 'Good night.'

He edged off, and the stunned silence started functioning again.

I suppose there have been men who looked bigger asses than Sir Watkyn Bassett at this moment, but I have never seen one myself. The tip of his nose had gone bright scarlet, and his pince-nez were hanging limply to the parent nose at an angle of forty-five. Consistently though he had snootered me from the very inception of our relations, I felt almost sorry for the poor old blighter.

'H'rrmph!' he said at length.

He struggled with the vocal cords for a space. They seemed to have gone twisted on him.

'It appears that I owe you an apology, Mr Wooster.'

'Say no more about it, Bassett.'

'I am sorry that all this has occurred.'

'Don't mention it. My innocence is established. That is all that matters. I presume that I am now at liberty to depart?'

'Oh, certainly, certainly. Good night, Mr Wooster.'

'Good night, Bassett. I need scarcely say, I think, that I hope this will be a lesson to you.'

I dismissed him with a distant nod, and stood there wrapped in thought. I could make nothing of what had occurred. Following the old and tried Oates method of searching for the motive, I had to confess myself baffled. I could only suppose that this was the Sydney Carton spirit bobbing up again.

And then a sudden blinding light seemed to flash upon me.

'Jeeves!'

'Sir?'

'Were you behind this thing?'

'Sir?'

'Don't keep saying "Sir?" You know what I'm talking about. Was it you who egged Spode on to take the rap?'

I wouldn't say he smiled – he practically never does – but a muscle abaft the mouth did seem to quiver slightly for an instant.

'I did venture to suggest to Mr Spode that it would be a graceful act on his part to assume the blame, sir. My line of argument was that he would be saving you a great deal of unpleasantness, while running no risk himself. I pointed out to him that Sir Watkyn, being engaged to marry his aunt, would hardly be likely to inflict upon him the sentence which he had contemplated inflicting upon you. One does not send gentlemen to prison if one is betrothed to their aunts.'

'Profoundly true, Jeeves. But I still don't get it. Do you mean he just right-hoed? Without a murmur?'

'Not precisely without a murmur, sir. At first, I must confess, he betrayed a certain reluctance. I think I may have influenced his decision by informing him that I knew all about –'

I uttered a cry.

'Eulalie?'

'Yes, sir.'

A passionate desire to get to the bottom of this Eulalie thing swept over me.

'Jeeves, tell me. What did Spode actually do to the girl? Murder her?'

'I fear I am not at liberty to say, sir.'

'Come on, Jeeves.'

'I fear not, sir.'

I gave it up.

'Oh, well!'

I started shedding the garments. I climbed into the pyjamas. I slid into bed. The sheets being inextricably knotted, it would be necessary, I saw, to nestle between the blankets, but I was prepared to rough it for one night.

The rapid surge of events had left me pensive. I sat with my arms round my knees, meditating on Fortune's swift changes.

'An odd thing, life, Jeeves.'

'Very odd, sir.'

'You never know where you are with it, do you? To take a simple instance, I little thought half an hour ago that I would be sitting here in carefree pyjamas, watching you pack for the getaway. A very different future seemed to confront me.'

'Yes, sir.'

'One would have said that a curse had come upon me.'

'One would, indeed, sir.'

'But now my troubles, as you might say, have vanished like the dew on the what-is-it. Thanks to you.'

'I am delighted to have been able to be of service, sir.'

'You have delivered the goods as seldom before. And yet, Jeeves, there is always a snag.'

'Sir?'

'I wish you wouldn't keep saying "Sir?" What I mean is, Jeeves, loving hearts have been sundered in this vicinity and are still sundered. I may be all right – I am – but Gussie isn't all right. Nor is Stiffy all right. That is the fly in the ointment.'

'Yes, sir.'

'Though, pursuant on that, I never could see why flies shouldn't be in ointment. What harm do they do?'

'I wonder, sir –'

'Yes, Jeeves?'

'I was merely about to inquire if it is your intention to bring an action against Sir Watkyn for wrongful arrest and defamation of character before witnesses.'

'I hadn't thought of that. You think an action would lie?'

'There can be no question about it, sir. Both Mrs Travers and I could offer overwhelming testimony. You are undoubtedly in a position to mulct Sir Watkyn in heavy damages.'

'Yes, I suppose you're right. No doubt that was why he went up in the air to such an extent when Spode did his act.'

'Yes, sir. His trained legal mind would have envisaged the peril.'

'I don't think I ever saw a man go so red in the nose. Did you?'

'No, sir.'

'Still, it seems a shame to harry him further. I don't know that I want actually to grind the old bird into the dust.'

'I was merely thinking, sir, that were you to threaten such an action, Sir Watkyn, in order to avoid unpleasantness, might see his way to ratifying the betrothals of Miss Bassett and Mr Fink-Nottle and Miss Byng and the Reverend Mr Pinker.'

'Golly, Jeeves! Put the bite on him, what?'

'Precisely, sir.'

'The thing shall be put in train immediately.'

I sprang from the bed and nipped to the door.

'Bassett!' I yelled.

There was no immediate response. The man had presumably gone to earth. But after I had persevered for some minutes, shouting 'Bassett!' at regular intervals with increasing volume, I heard the distant sound of pattering feet, and along he came, in a very different spirit from that which he had exhibited on the previous occasion. This time it was more like some eager waiter answering the bell.

'Yes, Mr Wooster?'

I led the way back into the room, and hopped into bed again.

'There is something you wish to say to me, Mr Wooster?'

'There are about a dozen things I wish to say to you, Bassett, but the one we will touch on at the moment is this. Are you aware that your headstrong conduct in sticking police officers on to pinch me and locking me in my room has laid you open to an action for – what was it, Jeeves?'

'Wrongful arrest and defamation of character before witnesses, sir.'

'That's the baby. I could soak you for millions. What are you going to do about it?'

He writhed like an electric fan.

'I'll tell you what you are going to do about it,' I proceeded. 'You are going to issue your OK on the union of your daughter Madeline and Augustus Fink-Nottle and also on that of your niece Stephanie and the Rev. H. P. Pinker. And you will do it now.'

A short struggle seemed to take place in him. It might have lasted longer, if he hadn't caught my eye.

'Very well, Mr Wooster.'

'And touching that cow-creamer. It is highly probable that the international gang that got away with it will sell it to my Uncle Tom. Their system of underground information will have told them that he is in the market. Not a yip out of you, Bassett, if at some future date you see that cow-creamer in his collection.'

'Very well, Mr Wooster.'

'And one other thing. You owe me a fiver.'

'I beg your pardon?'

'In repayment of the one you took off me at Bosher Street. I shall want that before I leave.'

'I will write you a cheque in the morning.'

'I shall expect it on the breakfast tray. Good night, Bassett.'

'Good night, Mr Wooster. Is that brandy I see over there? I think I should like a glass, if I may.'

'Jeeves, a snootful for Sir Watkyn Bassett.'

'Very good, sir.'

He drained the beaker gratefully, and tottered out. Probably quite a nice chap, if you knew him.

Jeeves broke the silence.

'I have finished the packing, sir.'

'Good. Then I think I'll curl up. Open the windows, will you?'

'Very good, sir.'

'What sort of a night is it?'

'Unsettled, sir. It has begun to rain with some violence.'

The sound of a sneeze came to my ears.

'Hallo, who's that, Jeeves? Somebody out there?'

'Constable Oates, sir.'

'You don't mean he hasn't gone off duty?'

'No, sir. I imagine that in his preoccupation with other matters it escaped Sir Watkyn's mind to send word to him that there was no longer any necessity to keep his vigil.'

I sighed contentedly. It needed but this to complete my day. The thought of Constable Oates prowling in the rain like the troops of Midian, when he could have been snug in bed toasting his pink toes on the hot-water bottle, gave me a curiously mellowing sense of happiness.

'This is the end of a perfect day, Jeeves. What's that thing of yours about larks?'

'Sir?'

'And, I rather think, snails.'

'Oh, yes, sir. "The year's at the Spring, the day's at the morn, morning's at seven, the hill-side's dew-pearled —"'

'But the larks, Jeeves? The snails? I'm pretty sure larks and snails entered into it.'

'I am coming to the larks and snails, sir. "The lark's on the wing, the snail's on the thorn –"'

'Now you're talking. And the tab line?'

'"God's in His heaven, all's right with the world."'

'That's it in a nutshell. I couldn't have put it better myself. And yet, Jeeves, there is just one thing. I do wish you would give me the inside facts about Eulalie.'

'I fear, sir –'

'I would keep it dark. You know me – the silent tomb.'

'The rules of the Junior Ganymede are extremely strict, sir.'

'I know. But you might stretch a point.'

'I am sorry, sir –'

I made the great decision.

'Jeeves,' I said, 'give me the low-down, and I'll come on that World Cruise of yours.'

He wavered.

'Well, in the strictest confidence, sir –'

'Of course.'

'Mr Spode designs ladies' underclothing, sir. He has a considerable talent in that direction, and has indulged it secretly for some years. He is the founder and proprietor of the emporium in Bond Street known as Eulalie *Sœurs.*'

'You don't mean that?'

'Yes, sir.'

'Good Lord, Jeeves! No wonder he didn't want a thing like that to come out.'

'No, sir. It would unquestionably jeopardize his authority over his followers.'

'You can't be a successful Dictator and design women's underclothing.'

'No, sir.'

'One or the other. Not both.'

'Precisely, sir.'

I mused.

'Well, it was worth it, Jeeves. I couldn't have slept, wondering about it. Perhaps that cruise won't be so very foul, after all?'

'Most gentlemen find them enjoyable, sir.'

'Do they?'

'Yes, sir. Seeing new faces.'

'That's true. I hadn't thought of that. The faces will be new, won't they? Thousands and thousands of people, but no Stiffy.'

'Exactly, sir.'

'You had better get the tickets tomorrow.'

'I have already procured them, sir. Good night, sir.'

The door closed. I switched off the light. For some moments I lay there listening to the measured tramp of Constable Oates's feet and thinking of Gussie and Madeline Bassett and of Stiffy and old Stinker Pinker, and of the hotsy-totsiness which now prevailed in their love lives. I also thought of Uncle Tom being handed the cow-creamer and of Aunt Dahlia seizing the psychological moment and nicking him for a fat cheque for *Milady's Boudoir*. Jeeves was right, I felt. The snail was on the wing and the lark on the thorn – or, rather, the other way round – and God was in His heaven and all right with the world.

And presently the eyes closed, the muscles relaxed, the breathing became soft and regular, and sleep, which does something which has slipped my mind to the something sleeve of care, poured over me in a healing wave.

SHORT STORIES

JEEVES TAKES CHARGE

NOW, TOUCHING this business of old Jeeves – my man, you know – how do we stand? Lots of people think I'm much too dependent on him. My Aunt Agatha, in fact, has even gone so far as to call him my keeper. Well, what I say is: Why not? The man's a genius. From the collar upward he stands alone. I gave up trying to run my own affairs within a week of his coming to me. That was about half a dozen years ago, directly after the rather rummy business of Florence Craye, my Uncle Willoughby's book, and Edwin, the Boy Scout.

The thing really began when I got back to Easeby, my uncle's place in Shropshire. I was spending a week or so there, as I generally did in the summer; and I had had to break my visit to come back to London to get a new valet. I had found Meadowes, the fellow I had taken to Easeby with me, sneaking my silk socks, a thing no bloke of spirit could stick at any price. It transpiring, moreover, that he had looted a lot of other things here and there about the place, I was reluctantly compelled to hand the misguided blighter the mitten and go to London to ask the registry office to dig up another specimen for my approval. They sent me Jeeves.

I shall always remember the morning he came. It so happened that the night before I had been present at a rather cheery little supper, and I was feeling pretty rocky. On top of this I was trying to read a book Florence Craye had given me. She had been one of the house-party at Easeby, and two or three days before I left we had got engaged. I was due back at the end of the week, and I knew she would expect me to have finished the book by then. You see, she was particularly keen on boosting me up a bit nearer her own plane of intellect. She was a girl with a wonderful profile, but steeped to the gills in serious purpose. I can't give you a better idea of the way things stood than by telling you that the book she'd given me to read was called 'Types of Ethical Theory', and that when I opened it at random I struck a page beginning: –

'The postulate or common understanding involved in speech is certainly co-extensive, in the obligation it carries, with the social organism of which language is the instrument, and the ends of which it is an effort to subserve.'

All perfectly true, no doubt; but not the sort of thing to spring on a lad with a morning head.

I was doing my best to skim through this bright little volume when the bell rang. I crawled off the sofa and opened the door. A kind of darkish sort of respectful Johnnie stood without.

'I was sent by the agency, sir,' he said. 'I was given to understand that you required a valet.'

I'd have preferred an undertaker; but I told him to stagger in, and he floated noiselessly through the doorway like a healing zephyr. That impressed me from the start. Meadowes had had flat feet and used to clump. This fellow didn't seem to have any feet at all. He just streamed in. He had a grave, sympathetic face, as if he, too, knew what it was to sup with the lads.

'Excuse me, sir,' he said gently.

Then he seemed to flicker, and wasn't there any longer. I heard him moving about in the kitchen, and presently he came back with a glass on a tray.

'If you would drink this, sir,' he said, with a kind of bedside manner, rather like the royal doctor shooting the bracer into the sick prince. 'It is a little preparation of my own invention. It is the Worcester Sauce that gives it its colour. The raw egg makes it nutritious. The red pepper gives it its bite. Gentlemen have told me they have found it extremely invigorating after a late evening.'

I would have clutched at anything that looked like a life-line that morning. I swallowed the stuff. For a moment I felt as if somebody had touched off a bomb inside the old bean and was strolling down my throat with a lighted torch, and then everything seemed suddenly to get all right. The sun shone in through the window; birds twittered in the tree-tops; and, generally speaking, hope dawned once more.

'You're engaged!' I said, as soon as I could say anything.

I perceived clearly that this cove was one of the world's workers, the sort no home should be without.

'Thank you, sir. My name is Jeeves.'

'You can start in at once?'

'Immediately, sir.'

'Because I'm due down at Easeby, in Shropshire, the day after tomorrow.'

'Very good, sir.' He looked past me at the mantelpiece. 'That is an excellent likeness of Lady Florence Craye, sir. It is two years since I saw her ladyship. I was at one time in Lord Worplesdon's employment. I tendered my resignation because I could not see eye to eye with his lordship in his desire to dine in dress trousers, a flannel shirt, and a shooting coat.'

He couldn't tell me anything I didn't know about the old boy's eccentricity. This Lord Worplesdon was Florence's father. He was the old buster who, a few years later, came down to breakfast one morning, lifted the first cover he saw, said 'Eggs! Eggs! Eggs! Damn all eggs!' in an overwrought sort of voice, and instantly legged it for France, never to return to the bosom of his family. This, mind you, being a bit of luck for the bosom of the family, for old Worplesdon had the worst temper in the county.

I had known the family ever since I was a kid, and from boyhood up this old boy had put the fear of death into me. Time, the great healer, could never remove from my memory the occasion when he found me – then a stripling of fifteen – smoking one of his special cigars in the stables. He got after me with a hunting-crop just at the moment when I was beginning to realize that what I wanted most on earth was solitude and repose, and chased me more than a mile across difficult country. If there was a flaw, so to speak, in the pure joy of being engaged to Florence, it was the fact that she rather took after her father, and one was never certain when she might erupt. She had a wonderful profile, though.

'Lady Florence and I are engaged, Jeeves,' I said.

'Indeed, sir?'

You know, there was a kind of rummy something about his manner. Perfectly all right and all that, but not what you'd call chirpy. It somehow gave me the impression that he wasn't keen on Florence. Well, of course, it wasn't my business. I supposed that while he had been valeting old Worplesdon she must have trodden on his toes in some way. Florence was a dear girl, and, seen sideways, most awfully good-looking; but if she had a fault it was a tendency to be a bit imperious with the domestic staff.

At this point in the proceedings there was another ring at the front door. Jeeves shimmered out and came back with a telegram. I opened it. It ran:

> *Return immediately. Extremely urgent. Catch first train. Florence.*

'Rum!' I said.

'Sir?'

'Oh, nothing!'

It shows how little I knew Jeeves in those days that I didn't go a bit deeper into the matter with him. Nowadays I would never dream of reading a rummy communication without asking him what he thought of it. And this one was devilish odd. What I mean is, Florence knew I was going back to Easeby the day after to-morrow, anyway; so why the hurry call? Something must have happened, of course; but I couldn't see what on earth it could be.

'Jeeves,' I said, 'we shall be going down to Easeby this afternoon. Can you manage it?'

'Certainly, sir.'

'You can get your packing done and all that?'

'Without any difficulty, sir. Which suit will you wear for the journey?'

'This one.'

I had on a rather sprightly young check that morning, to which I was a good deal attached; I fancied it, in fact, more than a little. It was perhaps rather sudden till you got used to it, but, nevertheless, an extremely sound effort, which many lads at the club and elsewhere had admired unrestrainedly.

'Very good, sir.'

Again there was that kind of rummy something in his manner. It was the way he said it, don't you know. He didn't like the suit. I pulled myself together to assert myself. Something seemed to tell me that, unless I was jolly careful and nipped this lad in the bud, he would be starting to boss me. He had the aspect of a distinctly resolute blighter.

Well, I wasn't going to have any of that sort of thing, by Jove! I'd seen so many cases of fellows who had become perfect slaves to their valets. I remember poor old Aubrey Fothergill telling me – with absolute tears in his eyes, poor chap! – one night at the club, that he had been compelled to give up a favourite pair of brown shoes simply because Meekyn, his man, disapproved of them. You have to keep these fellows in their place, don't you know. You have to work the good old iron-hand-in-the-velvet-glove wheeze. If you give them a what's-its-name, they take a thingummy.

'Don't you like this suit, Jeeves?' I said coldly.

'Oh, yes, sir.'

'Well, what don't you like about it?'

'It is a very nice suit, sir.'

'Well, what's wrong with it? Out with it, dash it!'

'If I might make the suggestion, sir, a simple brown or blue, with a hint of some quiet twill—'

'What absolute rot!'

'Very good, sir.'

'Perfectly blithering, my dear man!'

'As you say, sir.'

I felt as if I had stepped on the place where the last stair ought to have been, but wasn't. I felt defiant, if you know what I mean, and there didn't seem anything to defy.

'All right, then,' I said.

'Yes, sir.'

And then he went away to collect his kit, while I started in again on 'Types of Ethical Theory' and took a stab at a chapter headed 'Idiopsychological Ethics'.

Most of the way down in the train that afternoon, I was wondering what could be up at the other end. I simply couldn't see what could have happened. Easeby wasn't one of those country houses you read about in the society novels, where young girls are lured on to play baccarat and then skinned to the bone of their jewellery, and so on. The house-party I had left had consisted entirely of law-abiding birds like myself.

Besides, my uncle wouldn't have let anything of that kind go on in his house. He was a rather stiff, precise sort of old boy, who liked a quiet life. He was just finishing a history of the family or something, which he had been working on for the last year, and didn't stir much from the library. He was rather a good instance of what they say about its being a good scheme for a fellow to sow his wild oats. I'd been told that in his youth Uncle Willoughby had been a bit of a rounder. You would never have thought it to look at him now.

When I got to the house, Oakshott, the butler, told me that Florence was in her room, watching her maid pack. Apparently there was a dance on at a house about twenty miles away that night, and she was motoring over with some of the Easeby lot and would be away some nights. Oakshott said she had told him to tell her the moment I arrived; so I trickled into the smoking-room and waited, and presently in she came. A glance showed me that she was perturbed, and even peeved. Her eyes had a goggly look, and altogether she appeared considerably pipped.

'Darling!' I said, and attempted the good old embrace; but she side-stepped like a bantam weight.

'Don't!'

'What's the matter?'

'Everything's the matter! Bertie, you remember asking me, when you left, to make myself pleasant to your uncle?'

'Yes.'

The idea being, of course, that as at that time I was more or less dependent on Uncle Willoughby I couldn't very well marry without his approval. And though I knew he wouldn't have any objection to Florence, having known her father since they were at Oxford together, I hadn't wanted to take any chances; so I had told her to make an effort to fascinate the old boy.

'You told me it would please him particularly if I asked him to read me some of his history of the family.'

'Wasn't he pleased?'

'He was delighted. He finished writing the thing yesterday afternoon, and read me nearly all of it last night. I have never had such a shock in my life. The book is an outrage. It is impossible. It is horrible!'

'But, dash it, the family weren't so bad as all that.'

'It is not a history of the family at all. Your uncle has written his reminiscences! He calls them "Recollections of a Long Life"!'

I began to understand. As I say, Uncle Willoughby had been somewhat on the tabasco side as a young man, and it began to look as if he might have turned out something pretty fruity if he had started recollecting his long life.

'If half of what he has written is true,' said Florence, 'your uncle's youth must have been perfectly appalling. The moment we began to read he plunged straight into a most scandalous story of how he and my father were thrown out of a music-hall in 1887!'

'Why?'

'I decline to tell you why.'

It must have been something pretty bad. It took a lot to make them chuck people out of music-halls in 1887.

'Your uncle specifically states that father had drunk a quart and a half of champagne before beginning the evening,' she went on. 'The book is full of stories like that. There is a dreadful one about Lord Emsworth.'

'Lord Emsworth? Not the one we know? Not the one at Blandings?'

A most respectable old Johnnie, don't you know. Doesn't do a thing nowadays but dig in the garden with a spud.

'The very same. That is what makes the book so unspeakable. It is full of stories about people one knows who are the essence of propriety today, but who seem to have behaved, when they were in London in the 'eighties, in a manner that would not have been tolerated in the fo'c'sle of a whaler. Your uncle seems to remember everything disgraceful that happened to anybody when he was in his early twenties. There is a story about Sir Stanley Gervase-Gervase at Rosherville Gardens which is ghastly in its perfection of detail. It seems that Sir Stanley – but I can't tell you!'

'Have a dash!'

'No!'

'Oh, well, I shouldn't worry. No publisher will print the book if it's as bad as all that.'

'On the contrary, your uncle told me that all negotiations are settled with Riggs and Ballinger, and he's sending off the manuscript tomorrow for immediate publication. They make a special thing of that sort of book. They published Lady Carnaby's "Memories of Eighty Interesting Years".'

'I read 'em!'

'Well, then, when I tell you that Lady Carnaby's Memories are simply not to be compared with your uncle's Recollections, you will understand my state of mind. And father appears in nearly every story in the book! I am horrified at the things he did when he was a young man!'

'What's to be done?'

'The manuscript must be intercepted before it reaches Riggs and Ballinger, and destroyed!'

I sat up.

This sounded rather sporting.

'How are you going to do it?' I inquired.

'How can I do it? Didn't I tell you the parcel goes off tomorrow? I am going to the Murgatroyds' dance tonight and shall not be back till Monday. You must do it. That is why I telegraphed to you.'

'What!'

She gave me a look.

'Do you mean to say you refuse to help me, Bertie?'

'No; but – I say!'

'It's quite simple.'

'But even if I— What I mean is— Of course, anything I can do – but – if you know what I mean—'

'You say you want to marry me, Bertie?'

'Yes, of course; but still—'

For a moment she looked exactly like her old father.

'I will never marry you if those Recollections are published.'

'But, Florence, old thing!'

'I mean it. You may look on it as a test, Bertie. If you have the resource and courage to carry this thing through, I will take it as evidence that you are not the vapid and shiftless person most people think you. If you fail, I shall know that your Aunt Agatha was right when she called you a spineless invertebrate and advised me strongly not to marry you. It will be perfectly simple for you to intercept the manuscript, Bertie. It only requires a little resolution.'

'But suppose Uncle Willoughby catches me at it? He'd cut me off with a bob.'

'If you care more for your uncle's money than for me—'

'No, no! Rather not!'

'Very well, then. The parcel containing the manuscript will, of course, be placed on the hall table tomorrow for Oakshott to take to the village with the letters. All you have to do is to take it away and destroy it. Then your uncle will think it has been lost in the post.'

It sounded thin to me.

'Hasn't he got a copy of it?'

'No; it has not been typed. He is sending the manuscript just as he wrote it.'

'But he could write it over again.'

'As if he would have the energy!'

'But—'

'If you are going to do nothing but make absurd objections, Bertie—'

'I was only pointing things out.'

'Well, don't! Once and for all, will you do me this quite simple act of kindness?'

The way she put it gave me an idea.

'Why not get Edwin to do it? Keep it in the family, kind of, don't you know. Besides, it would be a boon to the kid.'

A jolly bright idea it seemed to me. Edwin was her young brother, who was spending his holidays at Easeby. He was a ferret-faced kid, whom I had disliked since birth. As a matter of fact, talking of Recollections and Memories, it was young blighted Edwin who, nine years before, had led his father to where I was smoking his cigar and caused all the unpleasantness. He was fourteen now and had just joined the Boy Scouts. He was one of those thorough kids, and took his responsibilities pretty seriously. He was always in a sort of fever because he was dropping behind schedule with his daily acts of kindness. However hard he tried, he'd fall behind; and then you would find him prowling about the house, setting such a clip to try and catch up with himself that Easeby was rapidly becoming a perfect hell for man and beast.

The idea didn't seem to strike Florence.

'I shall do nothing of the kind, Bertie. I wonder you can't appreciate the compliment I am paying you – trusting you like this.'

'Oh, I see that all right, but what I mean is, Edwin would do it so much better than I would. These Boy Scouts are up to all sorts of dodges. They spoor, don't you know, and take cover and creep about, and what not.'

'Bertie, will you or will you not do this perfectly trivial thing for me? If not, say so now, and let us end this farce of pretending that you care a snap of the fingers for me.'

'Dear old soul, I love you devotedly!'

'Then will you or will you not—'

'Oh, all right,' I said. 'All right! All right! All right!'

And then I tottered forth to think it over. I met Jeeves in the passage just outside.

'I beg your pardon, sir. I was endeavouring to find you.'

'What's the matter?'

'I felt that I should tell you, sir, that somebody has been putting black polish on our brown walking shoes.'

'What! Who? Why?'

'I could not say, sir.'

'Can anything be done with them?'

'Nothing, sir.'

'Damn!'

'Very good, sir.'

I've often wondered since then how these murderer fellows manage to keep in shape while they're contemplating their next effort. I had a much simpler sort of job on hand, and the thought of it rattled me to such an extent in the night watches that I was a perfect wreck next day. Dark circles under the eyes – I give you my word! I had to call on Jeeves to rally round with one of those life-savers of his.

From breakfast on I felt like a bag-snatcher at a railway station. I had to hang about waiting for the parcel to be put on the hall table, and it wasn't put. Uncle Willoughby was a fixture in the library, adding the finishing touches to the great work, I supposed, and the more I thought the thing over the less I liked it. The chances against my pulling it off seemed about three to two, and the thought of what would happen if I didn't gave me cold shivers down the spine. Uncle Willoughby was a pretty mild sort of old boy, as a rule, but I've known him to cut up rough, and, by Jove, he was scheduled to extend himself if he caught me trying to get away with his life work.

It wasn't till nearly four that he toddled out of the library with the parcel under his arm, put it on the table, and toddled off again. I was hiding a bit to the south-east at the moment, behind a suit of armour. I bounded out and legged it for the table. Then I nipped upstairs to hide the swag. I charged in like a mustang and nearly stubbed my toe on young blighted Edwin, the Boy Scout. He was standing at the chest of drawers, confound him, messing about with my ties.

'Hallo!' he said.

'What are you doing here?'

'I'm tidying your room. It's my last Saturday's act of kind-ness.'

'Last Saturday's.'

'I'm five days behind. I was six till last night, but I polished your shoes.'

'Was it you—'

'Yes. Did you see them? I just happened to think of it. I was in here, looking round. Mr Berkeley had this room while you were away. He left this morning. I thought perhaps he might have left something in it that I could have sent on. I've often done acts of kindness that way.'

'You must be a comfort to one and all!'

It became more and more apparent to me that this infernal kid must somehow be turned out eftsoons or right speedily. I had hidden the parcel behind my back, and I didn't think he had seen it; but I wanted to get at that chest of drawers quick, before anyone else came along.

'I shouldn't bother about tidying the room,' I said.

'I like tidying it. It's not a bit of trouble – really.'

'But it's quite tidy now.'

'Not so tidy as I shall make it.'

This was getting perfectly rotten. I didn't want to murder the kid, and yet there didn't seem any other way of shifting him. I pressed down the mental accelerator. The old lemon throbbed fiercely. I got an idea.

'There's something much kinder than that which you could do,' I said. 'You see that box of cigars? Take it down to the smoking-room and snip off the ends for me. That would save me no end of trouble. Stagger along, laddie.'

He seemed a bit doubtful; but he staggered. I shoved the parcel into a drawer, locked it, trousered the key, and felt better. I might be a chump, but, dash it, I could out-general a mere kid with a face like a ferret. I went downstairs again. Just as I was passing the smoking-room door out curveted Edwin. It seemed to me that if he wanted to do a real act of kindness he would commit suicide.

'I'm snipping them,' he said.

'Snip on! Snip on!'

'Do you like them snipped much, or only a bit?'

'Medium.'

'All right. I'll be getting on, then.'

'I should.'

And we parted.

Fellows who know all about that sort of thing – detectives, and so on – will tell you that the most difficult thing in the world is to get rid of the body. I remember, as a kid, having to learn by heart a poem about a bird by the name of Eugene Aram, who had the deuce of a job in this respect. All I can recall of the actual poetry is the bit that goes:

> 'Tum-tum, tum-tum, tum-tumty-tum,
>   I slew him, tum-tum tum!'

But I recollect that the poor blighter spent much of his valuable time dumping the corpse into ponds and burying it, and what not, only to have it pop out at him again. It was about an hour after I had shoved the parcel into the drawer when I realized that I had let myself in for just the same sort of thing.

Florence had talked in an airy sort of way about destroying the manuscript; but when one came down to it, how the deuce can a chap destroy a great chunky mass of paper in somebody else's house in the middle of summer? I couldn't ask to have a fire in my bedroom, with the thermometer in the eighties. And if I didn't burn the thing, how else could I get rid of it? Fellows on the battle-field eat dispatches to keep them from falling into the hands of the enemy, but it would have taken me a year to eat Uncle Willoughby's Recollections.

I'm bound to say the problem absolutely baffled me. The only thing seemed to be to leave the parcel in the drawer and hope for the best.

I don't know whether you have ever experienced it, but it's a dashed unpleasant thing having a crime on one's conscience. Towards the end of the day the mere sight of the drawer began to depress me. I found myself getting all on edge; and once when Uncle Willoughby trickled silently into the smoking-room when I was alone there and spoke to me before I knew he was there, I broke the record for the sitting high jump.

I was wondering all the time when Uncle Willoughby would sit up and take notice. I didn't think he would have time to suspect that anything had gone wrong till Saturday morning, when he would be expecting, of course, to get the acknowledgement of the manuscript from the publishers. But early on Friday evening he came out of the library as I was passing and asked me to step in. He was looking considerably rattled.

'Bertie,' he said – he always spoke in a precise sort of pompous kind of way – 'an exceedingly disturbing thing has happened. As you know, I dispatched the manuscript of my book to Messrs Riggs and Ballinger, the publishers, yesterday afternoon. It should have reached them by the first post this morning. Why I should have been uneasy I cannot say, but my mind was not altogether at rest respecting the safety of the parcel. I therefore telephoned to Messrs Riggs and Ballinger a few moments back to make inquiries. To my consternation they informed me that they were not yet in receipt of my manuscript.'

'Very rum!'

'I recollect distinctly placing it myself on the hall table in good time to be taken to the village. But here is a sinister thing. I have spoken to Oakshott, who took the rest of the letters to the post office, and he cannot recall seeing it there. He is, indeed, unswerving in his assertions that when he went to the hall to collect the letters there was no parcel among them.'

'Sounds funny!'

'Bertie, shall I tell you what I suspect?'

'What's that?'

'The suspicion will no doubt sound to you incredible, but it alone seems to fit the facts as we know them. I incline to the belief that the parcel has been stolen.'

'Oh, I say! Surely not!'

'Wait! Hear me out. Though I have said nothing to you before, or to anyone else, concerning the matter, the fact remains that during the past few weeks a number of objects – some valuable, others not – have disappeared in this house. The conclusion to which one is irresistibly impelled is that we have a kleptomaniac in our midst. It is a peculiarity of kleptomania, as you are no doubt aware, that the subject is unable to differentiate between the intrinsic values of objects. He will purloin an old coat as readily as a diamond ring, or a tobacco pipe costing but a few shillings with the same eagerness as a purse of gold. The fact that this manuscript of mine could be of no possible value to any outside person convinces me that—'

'But, uncle, one moment; I know all about those things that were stolen. It was Meadowes, my man, who pinched them. I caught him snaffling my silk socks. Right in the act, by Jove!'

He was tremendously impressed.

'You amaze me, Bertie! Send for the man at once and question him.'

'But he isn't here. You see, directly I found that he was a sock-sneaker I gave him the boot. That's why I went to London – to get a new man.'

'Then, if the man Meadowes is no longer in the house it could not be he who purloined my manuscript. The whole thing is inexplicable.'

After which we brooded for a bit. Uncle Willoughby pottered about the room, registering baffledness, while I sat sucking at a cigarette, feeling rather like a chappie I'd once read about in a book, who murdered another cove and hid the body under the dining-room table, and then had to be the life and soul of a dinner party, with it there all the time. My guilty secret oppressed me to such an extent that after a while I couldn't stick it any longer. I lit another cigarette and started for a stroll in the grounds, by way of cooling off.

It was one of those still evenings you get in the summer, when you can hear a snail clear its throat a mile away. The sun was sinking over the hills and the gnats were fooling about all over the place, and everything smelled rather topping – what with the falling dew and so on – and I was just beginning to feel a little soothed by the peace of it all when suddenly I heard my name spoken.

'It's about Bertie.'

It was the loathsome voice of young blighted Edwin! For a moment I couldn't locate it. Then I realized that it came from the library. My stroll had taken me within a few yards of the open window.

I had often wondered how those Johnnies in books did it – I mean the fellows with whom it was the work of a moment to do about a dozen things that ought to have taken them about ten minutes. But, as a matter of fact, it was the work of a moment with me to chuck away my cigarette, swear a bit, leap about ten yards, dive into a bush that stood near the library window, and stand there with my ears flapping. I was as certain as I've ever been of anything that all sorts of rotten things were in the offing.

'About Bertie?' I heard Uncle Willoughby say.

'About Bertie and your parcel. I heard you talking to him just now. I believe he's got it.'

When I tell you that just as I heard these frightful words a fairly substantial beetle of sorts dropped from the bush down the back of my neck, and I couldn't even stir to squash the same, you will understand that I felt pretty rotten. Everything seemed against me.

'What do you mean, boy? I was discussing the disappearance of my manuscript with Bertie only a moment back, and he professed himself as perplexed by the mystery as myself.'

'Well, I was in his room yesterday afternoon, doing him an act of kindness, and he came in with a parcel. I could see it, though he tried to keep it behind his back. And then he asked me to go to the smoking-room and snip some cigars for him; and about two minutes afterwards he came down – and he wasn't carrying anything. So it must be in his room.'

I understand they deliberately teach these dashed Boy Scouts to cultivate their powers of observation and deduction and what not. Devilish thoughtless and inconsiderate of them, I call it. Look at the trouble it causes.

'It sounds incredible,' said Uncle Willoughby, thereby bucking me up a trifle.

'Shall I go and look in his room?' asked young blighted Edwin. 'I'm sure the parcel's there.'

'But what could be his motive for perpetrating this extraordinary theft?'

'Perhaps he's a – what you said just now.'

'A kleptomaniac? Impossible!'

'It might have been Bertie who took all those things from the very start,' suggested the little brute hopefully. 'He may be like Raffles.'

'Raffles?'

'He's a chap in a book who went about pinching things.'

'I cannot believe that Bertie would – ah – go about pinching things.'

'Well, I'm sure he's got the parcel. I'll tell you what you might do. You might say that Mr Berkeley wired that he had left something here. He had Bertie's room, you know. You might say you wanted to look for it.'

'That would be possible. I—'

I didn't wait to hear any more. Things were getting too hot. I sneaked softly out of my bush and raced for the front door. I sprinted up to my room and made for the drawer where I had put the parcel. And then I found I hadn't the key. It wasn't for the deuce of a time that I recollected I had shifted it to my evening trousers the night before and must have forgotten to take it out again.

Where the dickens were my evening things? I had looked all over the place before I remembered that Jeeves must have taken them away to brush. To leap at the bell and ring it was, with me, the work of a moment. I had just rung it when there was a footstep outside, and in came Uncle Willoughby.

'Oh, Bertie,' he said, without a blush, 'I have – ah – received a telegram from Berkeley, who occupied this room in your absence, asking me to forward him his – er – his cigarette-case, which, it would appear, he inadvertently omitted to take with him when he left the house. I cannot find it downstairs; and it has, therefore, occurred to me that he may have left it in this room. I will – er – just take a look round.'

It was one of the most disgusting spectacles I've ever seen – this white-haired old man, who should have been thinking of the hereafter, standing there lying like an actor.

'I haven't seen it anywhere,' I said.

'Nevertheless, I will search. I must – ah – spare no effort.'

'I should have seen it if it had been here – what?'

'It may have escaped your notice. It is – er – possibly in one of the drawers.'

He began to nose about. He pulled out drawer after drawer, pottering round like an old bloodhound, and babbling from time to time about Berkeley and his cigarette-case in a way that struck me as perfectly ghastly. I just stood there, losing weight every moment.

Then he came to the drawer where the parcel was.

'This appears to be locked,' he said, rattling the handle.

'Yes; I shouldn't bother about that one. It – it's – er – locked, and all that sort of thing.'

'You have not the key?'

A soft, respectful voice spoke behind me.

'I fancy, sir, that this must be the key you require. It was in the pocket of your evening trousers.'

It was Jeeves. He had shimmered in, carrying my evening things, and was standing there holding out the key. I could have massacred the man.

'Thank you,' said my uncle.

'Not at all, sir.'

The next moment Uncle Willoughby had opened the drawer. I shut my eyes.

'No,' said Uncle Willoughby, 'there is nothing here. The drawer is empty. Thank you, Bertie. I hope I have not disturbed you. I fancy – er – Berkeley must have taken his case with him after all.'

When he had gone I shut the door carefully. Then I turned to Jeeves. The man was putting my evening things out on a chair.

'Er – Jeeves!'

'Sir?'

'Oh, nothing.'

It was deuced difficult to know how to begin.

'Er – Jeeves!'

'Sir?'

'Did you— Was there— Have you by chance—'

'I removed the parcel this morning, sir.'

'Oh – ah – why?'

'I considered it more prudent, sir.'

I mused for a while.

'Of course, I suppose all this seems tolerably rummy to you, Jeeves?'

'Not at all, sir. I chanced to overhear you and Lady Florence speaking of the matter the other evening, sir.'

'Did you, by Jove?'

'Yes, sir.'

'Well – er – Jeeves, I think that, on the whole, if you were to – as it were – freeze on to that parcel until we get back to London—'

'Exactly, sir.'

'And then we might – er – so to speak – chuck it away somewhere – what?'

'Precisely, sir.'

'I'll leave it in your hands.'

'Entirely, sir.'

'You know, Jeeves, you're by way of being rather a topper.'

'I endeavour to give satisfaction, sir.'

'One in a million, by Jove!'

'It is very kind of you to say so, sir.'

'Well, that's about all, then, I think.'

'Very good, sir.'

Florence came back on Monday. I didn't see her till we were all having tea in the hall. It wasn't till the crowd had cleared away a bit that we got a chance of having a word together.

'Well, Bertie?' she said.

'It's all right.'

'You have destroyed the manuscript?'

'Not exactly; but—'

'What do you mean?'

'I mean I haven't absolutely—'

'Bertie, your manner is furtive!'

'It's all right. It's this way—'

And I was just going to explain how things stood when out of the library came leaping Uncle Willoughby, looking as braced as a two-year-old. The old boy was a changed man.

'A most remarkable thing, Bertie! I have just been speaking with Mr Riggs on the telephone, and he tells me he received my manuscript by the first post this morning. I cannot imagine what can have caused the delay. Our postal facilities are extremely inadequate in the rural districts. I shall write to headquarters about it. It is insufferable if valuable parcels are to be delayed in this fashion.'

I happened to be looking at Florence's profile at the moment, and at this juncture she swung round and gave me a look that went right through me like a knife. Uncle Willoughby meandered back to the library, and there was a silence that you could have dug bits out of with a spoon.

'I can't understand it,' I said at last. 'I can't understand it, by Jove!'

'I can. I can understand it perfectly, Bertie. Your heart failed you. Rather than risk offending your uncle you—'

'No, no! Absolutely!'

'You preferred to lose me rather than risk losing the money. Perhaps you did not think I meant what I said. I meant every word. Our engagement is ended.'

'But – I say!'

'Not another word!'

'But, Florence, old thing!'

'I do not wish to hear any more. I see now that your Aunt Agatha was perfectly right. I consider that I have had a very lucky escape. There was a time when I thought that, with patience, you might be moulded into something worth while. I see now that you are impossible!'

And she popped off, leaving me to pick up the pieces. When I had collected the *débris* to some extent I went to my room and rang for Jeeves. He came in looking as if nothing had happened or was ever going to happen. He was the calmest thing in captivity.

'Jeeves!' I yelled. 'Jeeves, that parcel has arrived in London!'

'Yes, sir?'

'Did you send it?'

'Yes, sir. I acted for the best, sir. I think that both you and Lady Florence overestimated the danger of people being offended at being mentioned in Sir Willoughby's Recollections. It has been my experience, sir, that the normal person enjoys seeing his or her name in print, irrespective of what is said about them. I have an aunt, sir, who a few years ago was a martyr to swollen limbs. She tried Walkinshaw's Supreme Ointment and obtained considerable relief – so much so that she sent them an unsolicited testimonial. Her pride at seeing her photograph in the daily papers in connection with descriptions of her lower limbs before taking, which were nothing less than revolting, was so intense that it led me to believe that publicity, of whatever sort, is what nearly everybody desires. Moreover, if you have ever studied psychology, sir, you will know that respectable old gentlemen are by no means averse to having it advertised that they were extremely wild in their youth. I have an uncle—'

I cursed his aunts and his uncles and him and all the rest of the family.

'Do you know that Lady Florence has broken off her engagement with me?'

'Indeed, sir?'

Not a bit of sympathy! I might have been telling him it was a fine day.

'You're sacked!'

'Very good, sir.'

He coughed gently.

'As I am no longer in your employment, sir, I can speak freely without appearing to take a liberty. In my opinion you and Lady Florence were quite unsuitably matched. Her ladyship is of a highly determined and arbitrary temperament, quite opposed to your own. I was in Lord Worplesdon's service for nearly a year, during which time I had ample opportunities of studying her ladyship. The opinion of the servants' hall was far from favourable to her. Her ladyship's temper caused a good deal of adverse comment among us. It was at times quite impossible. You would not have been happy, sir!'

'Get out!'

'I think you would also have found her educational methods a little trying, sir. I have glanced at the book her ladyship gave you – it has been lying on your table since our arrival – and it is, in my opinion, quite unsuitable. You would not have enjoyed it. And I have it from her ladyship's own maid, who happened to overhear a conversation between her ladyship and one of the gentlemen staying here – Mr Maxwell, who is employed in an editorial capacity by one of the reviews – that it was her intention to start you almost immediately upon Nietzsche. You would not enjoy Nietzsche, sir. He is fundamentally unsound.'

'Get out!'

'Very good, sir.'

It's rummy how sleeping on a thing often makes you feel quite different about it. It's happened to me over and over again. Somehow or other, when I woke next morning the old heart didn't feel half so broken as it had done. It was a perfectly topping day, and there was something about the way the sun came in at the window and the row the birds were kicking up in the ivy that made me half wonder whether Jeeves wasn't right. After all, though she had a wonderful profile, was it such a catch being engaged to Florence Craye as the casual observer might imagine? Wasn't there something in what Jeeves had said about her character? I began to realize that my ideal wife was something quite different, something a lot more clinging and drooping and prattling, and what not.

I had got as far as this in thinking the thing out when that 'Types of Ethical Theory' caught my eye. I opened it, and I give you my honest word this was what hit me:

Of the two antithetic terms in the Greek philosophy one only was real and self-subsisting; and that one was Ideal Thought as opposed to that which it has to penetrate and mould. The other, corresponding to our Nature, was in itself phenomenal, unreal, without any permanent footing, having no predicates that held true for two moments together; in short, redeemed from negation only by including indwelling realities appearing through.

Well – I mean to say – what? And Nietzsche, from all accounts, a lot worse than that!

'Jeeves,' I said, when he came in with my morning tea, 'I've been thinking it over. You're engaged again.'

'Thank you, sir.'

I sucked down a cheerful mouthful. A great respect for this bloke's judgement began to soak through me.

'Oh, Jeeves,' I said; 'about that check suit.'

'Yes, sir?'

'Is it really a frost?'

'A trifle too bizarre, sir, in my opinion.'

'But lots of fellows have asked me who my tailor is.'

'Doubtless in order to avoid him, sir.'

'He's supposed to be one of the best men in London.'

'I am saying nothing against his moral character, sir.'

I hesitated a bit. I had a feeling that I was passing into this chappie's clutches, and that if I gave in now I should become just like poor old Aubrey Fothergill, unable to call my soul my own. On the other hand, this was obviously a cove of rare intelligence, and it would be a comfort in a lot of ways to have him doing the thinking for me. I made up my mind.

'All right, Jeeves,' I said. 'You know! Give the bally thing away to somebody!'

He looked down at me like a father gazing tenderly at the wayward child.

'Thank you, sir. I gave it to the under-gardener last night. A little more tea, sir?'

JEEVES AND THE IMPENDING DOOM

IT WAS the morning of the day on which I was slated to pop down to my Aunt Agatha's place at Woollam Chersey in the county of Herts for a visit of three solid weeks; and, as I seated myself at the breakfast table, I don't mind confessing that the heart was singularly heavy. We Woosters are men of iron, but beneath my intrepid exterior at that moment there lurked a nameless dread.

'Jeeves,' I said, 'I am not the old merry self this morning.'

'Indeed, sir?'

'No, Jeeves. Far from it. Far from the old merry self.'

'I am sorry to hear that, sir.'

He uncovered the fragrant eggs and b., and I pronged a moody forkful.

'Why – this is what I keep asking myself, Jeeves – why has my Aunt Agatha invited me to her country seat?'

'I could not say, sir.'

'Not because she is fond of me.'

'No, sir.'

'It is a well-established fact that I give her a pain in the neck. How it happens I cannot say, but every time our paths cross, so to speak, it seems to be a mere matter of time before I perpetrate some ghastly floater and have her hopping after me with her hatchet. The result being that she regards me as a worm and an outcast. Am I right or wrong, Jeeves?'

'Perfectly correct, sir.'

'And yet now she has absolutely insisted on my scratching all previous engagements and buzzing down to Woollam Chersey. She must have some sinister reason of which we know nothing. Can you blame me, Jeeves, if the heart is heavy?'

'No, sir. Excuse me, sir, I fancy I heard the front-door bell.'

He shimmered out, and I took another listless stab at the e. and bacon.

'A telegram, sir,' said Jeeves, re-entering the presence.

'Open it, Jeeves, and read contents. Who is it from?'

'It is unsigned, sir.'

'You mean there's no name at the end of it?'

'That is precisely what I was endeavouring to convey, sir.'

'Let's have a look.'

I scanned the thing. It was a rummy communication. Rummy. No other word.

As follows:

Remember when you come here absolutely vital meet perfect strangers.

We Woosters are not very strong in the head, particularly at breakfast-time; and I was conscious of a dull ache between the eyebrows.

'What does it mean, Jeeves?'

'I could not say, sir.'

'It says "come here". Where's here?'

'You will notice that the message was handed in at Woollam Chersey, sir.'

'You're absolutely right. At Woollam, as you very cleverly spotted, Chersey. This tells us something, Jeeves.'

'What, sir?'

'I don't know. It couldn't be from my Aunt Agatha, do you think?'

'Hardly, sir.'

'No; you're right again. Then all we can say is that some person unknown, resident at Woollam Chersey, considers it absolutely vital for me to meet perfect strangers. But why should I meet perfect strangers, Jeeves?'

'I could not say, sir.'

'And yet, looking at it from another angle, why shouldn't I?'

'Precisely, sir.'

'Then what it comes to is that the thing is a mystery which time alone can solve. We must wait and see, Jeeves.'

'The very expression I was about to employ, sir.'

I hit Woollam Chersey at about four o'clock, and found Aunt Agatha in her lair, writing letters. And, from what I know of her, probably offensive letters, with nasty postscripts. She regarded me with not a fearful lot of joy.

'Oh, there you are, Bertie.'

'Yes, here I am.'

'There's a smut on your nose.'

I plied the handkerchief.

'I am glad you have arrived so early. I want to have a word with you before you meet Mr Filmer.'

'Who?'

'Mr Filmer, the Cabinet Minister. He is staying in the house. Surely even you must have heard of Mr Filmer?'

'Oh, rather,' I said, though as a matter of fact the bird was completely unknown to me. What with one thing and another, I'm not frightfully up in the personnel of the political world.

'I particularly wish you to make a good impression on Mr Filmer.'

'Right-ho.'

'Don't speak in that casual way, as if you supposed that it was perfectly natural that you would make a good impression upon him. Mr Filmer is a serious-minded man of high character and purpose, and you are just the type of vapid and frivolous wastrel against which he is most likely to be prejudiced.'

Hard words, of course, from one's own flesh and blood, but well in keeping with past form.

'You will endeavour, therefore, while you are here not to display yourself in the *rôle* of a vapid and frivolous wastrel. In the first place, you will give up smoking during your visit.'

'Oh, I say!'

'Mr Filmer is president of the Anti-Tobacco League. Nor will you drink alcoholic stimulants.'

'Oh, dash it!'

'And you will kindly exclude from your conversation all that is suggestive of the bar, the billiard-room, and the stage-door. Mr Filmer will judge you largely by your conversation.'

I rose to a point of order.

'Yes, but why have I got to make an impression on this – on Mr Filmer?'

'Because,' said the old relative, giving me the eye, 'I particularly wish it.'

Not, perhaps, a notably snappy come-back as come-backs go; but it was enough to show me that that was more or less that; and I beetled out with an aching heart.

I headed for the garden, and I'm dashed if the first person I saw wasn't young Bingo Little.

Bingo Little and I have been pals practically from birth. Born in the same village within a couple of days of one another, we went through kindergarten, Eton, and Oxford together; and, grown to riper years we have enjoyed in the old metrop. full many a first-class binge in each other's society. If there was one fellow in the world, I felt, who could alleviate the horrors of this blighted visit of mine, that bloke was young Bingo Little.

But how he came to be there was more than I could understand. Some time before, you see, he had married the celebrated authoress, Rosie M. Banks; and the last I had seen of him he had been on the point of accompanying her to America on a lecture tour. I distinctly remembered him cursing rather freely because the trip would mean his missing Ascot.

Still, rummy as it might seem, here he was. And aching for the sight of a friendly face, I gave tongue like a bloodhound.

'Bingo!'

He spun round; and, by Jove, his face wasn't friendly after all. It was what they call contorted. He waved his arms at me like a semaphore.

''Sh!' he hissed. 'Would you ruin me?'

'Eh?'

'Didn't you get my telegram?'

'Was that *your* telegram?'

'Of course it was my telegram.'

'Then why didn't you sign it?'

'I did sign it.'

'No, you didn't. I couldn't make out what it was all about.'

'Well, you got my letter.'

'What letter?'

'My letter.'

'I didn't get any letter.'

'Then I must have forgotten to post it. It was to tell you that I was down here tutoring your Cousin Thomas, and that it was essential that, when we met, you should treat me as a perfect stranger.'

'But why?'

'Because, if your aunt supposed that I was a pal of yours, she would naturally sack me on the spot.'

'Why?'

Bingo raised his eyebrows.

'Why? Be reasonable, Bertie. If you were your aunt, and you knew the sort of chap you were, would you let a fellow you knew to be your best pal tutor your son?'

This made the old head swim a bit, but I got his meaning after awhile, and I had to admit that there was much rugged good sense in what he said. Still, he hadn't explained what you might call the nub or gist of the mystery.

'I thought you were in America,' I said.

'Well, I'm not.'

'Why not?'

'Never mind why not. I'm not.'

'But why have you taken a tutoring job?'

'Never mind why. I have my reasons. And I want you to get it into your head, Bertie – to get it right through the concrete – that you and I must not be seen hobnobbing. Your foul cousin was caught smoking in the shrubbery the day before yesterday, and that has made my position pretty tottery, because your aunt said that, if I had exercised an adequate surveillance over him, it couldn't have happened. If, after that, she finds out I'm a friend of yours, nothing can save me from being shot out. And it is vital that I am not shot out.'

'Why?'

'Never mind why.'

At this point he seemed to think he heard somebody coming, for he suddenly leaped with incredible agility into a laurel bush. And I toddled along to consult Jeeves about these rummy happenings.

'Jeeves,' I said, repairing to the bedroom, where he was unpacking my things, 'you remember that telegram?'

'Yes, sir.'

'It was from Mr Little. He's here, tutoring my young Cousin Thomas.'

'Indeed, sir?'

'I can't understand it. He appears to be a free agent, if you know what I mean; and yet would any man who was a free agent wantonly come to a house which contained my Aunt Agatha?'

'It seems peculiar, sir.'

'Moreover, would anybody of his own free-will and as a mere pleasure-seeker tutor my Cousin Thomas, who is notoriously a tough egg and a fiend in human shape?'

'Most improbable, sir.'

'These are deep waters, Jeeves.'

'Precisely, sir.'

'And the ghastly part of it all is that he seems to consider it necessary, in order to keep his job, to treat me like a long-lost leper. Thus killing my only chance of having anything approaching a decent time in this abode of desolation. For do you realize, Jeeves, that my aunt says I mustn't smoke while I'm here?'

'Indeed, sir?'

'Nor drink.'

'Why is this, sir?'

'Because she wants me – for some dark and furtive reason which she will not explain – to impress a fellow named Filmer.'

'Too bad, sir. However, many doctors, I understand, advocate such abstinence as the secret of health. They say it promotes a freer circulation of the blood and insures the arteries against premature hardening.'

'Oh, do they? Well, you can tell them next time you see them that they are silly asses.'

'Very good, sir.'

And so began what, looking back along a fairly eventful career, I think I can confidently say was the scaliest visit I have ever experienced in the course of my life. What with the agony of missing the life-giving cocktail before dinner; the painful necessity of being obliged, every time I wanted a quiet cigarette, to lie on the floor in my bedroom and puff the smoke up the chimney; the constant discomfort of meeting Aunt Agatha round unexpected corners; and the fearful strain on the morale of having to chum with the Right Hon. A. B. Filmer, it was not long before Bertram was up against it to an extent hitherto undreamed of.

I played golf with the Right Hon. every day, and it was only by biting the Wooster lip and clenching the fists till the knuckles stood out white under the strain that I managed to pull through. The Right Hon. punctuated some of the ghastliest golf I have ever seen with a flow of conversation which, as far as I was concerned, went completely over the top; and, all in all, I was beginning to feel pretty sorry for myself when, one night as I was in my room listlessly donning the soup-and-fish in preparation for the evening meal, in trickled young Bingo and took my mind off my own troubles.

For when it is a question of a pal being in the soup, we Woosters no longer think of self; and that poor old Bingo was knee-deep in the bisque was made plain by his mere appearance – which was that of a cat which has just been struck by a half-brick and is expecting another shortly.

'Bertie,' said Bingo, having sat down on the bed and diffused silent gloom for a moment, 'how is Jeeves's brain these days?'

'Fairly strong on the wing, I fancy. How is the grey matter, Jeeves? Surging about pretty freely?'

'Yes, sir.'

'Thank Heaven for that,' said young Bingo, 'for I require your soundest counsel. Unless right-thinking people take strong steps through the proper channels, my name will be mud.'

'What's wrong, old thing?' I asked, sympathetically.

Bingo plucked at the coverlet.

'I will tell you,' he said. 'I will also now reveal why I am staying in this pest-house, tutoring a kid who requires not education in the Greek and Latin languages but a swift slosh on the base of the skull with a black-jack. I came here, Bertie, because it was the only thing I could do. At the last moment before she sailed to America, Rosie decided that I had better stay behind and look after the Peke. She left me a couple of hundred quid to see me through till her return. This sum, judiciously expended over the period of her absence, would have been enough to keep Peke and self in moderate affluence. But you know how it is.'

'How what is?'

'When someone comes slinking up to you in the club and tells you that some cripple of a horse can't help winning even if it develops lumbago and the botts ten yards from the starting-post. I tell you, I regarded the thing as a cautious and conservative investment.'

'You mean you planked the entire capital on a horse?'

Bingo laughed bitterly.

'If you could call the thing a horse. If it hadn't shown a flash of speed in the straight, it would have got mixed up with the next race. It came in last, putting me in a dashed delicate position. Somehow or other I had to find the funds to keep me going, so that I could win through till Rosie's return without her knowing what had occurred. Rosie is the dearest girl in the world; but if you were a married man, Bertie, you would be aware that the best of wives is apt to cut up rough if she finds that her husband has dropped six weeks' housekeeping money on a single race. Isn't that so, Jeeves?'

'Yes, sir. Women are odd in that respect.'

'It was a moment for swift thinking. There was enough left from the wreck to board the Peke out at a comfortable home. I signed him up for six weeks at the Kosy Komfort Kennels at Kingsbridge, Kent, and tottered out, a broken man, to a tutoring job. I landed the kid Thomas. And here I am.'

It was a sad story, of course, but it seemed to me that, awful as it might be to be in constant association with my Aunt Agatha and young Thos, he had got rather well out of a tight place.

'All you have to do,' I said, 'is to carry on here for a few weeks more, and everything will be oojah-cum-spiff.'

Bingo barked bleakly.

'A few weeks more! I shall be lucky if I stay two days. You remember I told you that your aunt's faith in me as a guardian of her blighted son was shaken a few days ago by the fact that he was caught smoking. I now find that the person who caught him smoking was the man Filmer. And ten minutes ago young Thomas told me that he was proposing to inflict some hideous revenge on Filmer for having reported him to your aunt. I don't know what he is going to do, but if he does it, out I inevitably go on my left ear. Your aunt thinks the world of Filmer, and would sack me on the spot. And three weeks before Rosie gets back!'

I saw all.

'Jeeves,' I said.

'Sir?'

'I see all. Do you see all?'

'Yes, sir.'

'Then flock round.'

'I fear, sir—'

Bingo gave a low moan.

'Don't tell me, Jeeves,' he said, brokenly, 'that nothing suggests itself.'

'Nothing at the moment, I regret to say, sir.'

Bingo uttered a stricken woofle like a bull-dog that has been refused cake.

'Well, then, the only thing I can do, I suppose,' he said sombrely, 'is not to let the pie-faced little thug out of my sight for a second.'

'Absolutely,' I said. 'Ceaseless vigilance, eh, Jeeves?'

'Precisely, sir.'

'But meanwhile, Jeeves,' said Bingo in a low, earnest voice, 'you will be devoting your best thought to the matter, won't you?'

'Most certainly, sir.'

'Thank you, Jeeves.'

'Not at all, sir.'

I will say for young Bingo that, once the need for action arrived, he behaved with an energy and determination which compelled respect. I suppose there was not a minute during the next two days when the kid Thos was able to say to himself, 'Alone at last!' But on the evening of the second day Aunt Agatha announced that some people were coming over on the morrow for a spot of tennis, and I feared that the worst must now befall.

Young Bingo, you see, is one of those fellows who, once their fingers close over the handle of a tennis racket, fall into a sort of trance in which nothing outside the radius of the lawn exists for them. If you came up to Bingo in the middle of a set and told him that panthers were devouring his best friend in the kitchen garden, he would look at you and say, 'Oh, ah?' or words to that effect. I knew that he would not give a thought to young Thomas and the Right Hon. till the last ball had bounced, and, as I dressed for dinner that night, I was conscious of an impending doom.

'Jeeves,' I said, 'have you ever pondered on Life?'

'From time to time, sir, in my leisure moments.'

'Grim, isn't it, what?'

'Grim, sir?'

'I mean to say, the difference between things as they look and things as they are.'

'The trousers perhaps a half-inch higher, sir. A very slight adjustment of the braces will effect the necessary alteration. You were saying, sir?'

'I mean, here at Woollam Chersey we have apparently a happy, care-free country-house party. But beneath the glittering surface, Jeeves, dark currents are running. One gazes at the Right Hon. wrapping himself round the salmon mayonnaise at lunch, and he seems a man without a care in the world. Yet all the while a dreadful fate is hanging over him, creeping nearer and nearer. What exact steps do you think the kid Thomas intends to take?'

'In the course of an informal conversation which I had with the young gentleman this afternoon, sir, he informed me that he had been reading a romance entitled *Treasure Island*, and had been much struck by the character and actions of a certain Captain Flint. I gathered that he was weighing the advisability of modelling his own conduct on that of the Captain.'

'But, good heavens, Jeeves! If I remember *Treasure Island*, Flint was the bird who went about hitting people with a cutlass. You don't think young Thomas would bean Mr Filmer with a cutlass?'

'Possibly he does not possess a cutlass, sir.'

'Well, with anything.'

'We can but wait and see, sir. The tie, if I might suggest it, sir, a shade more tightly knotted. One aims at the perfect butterfly effect. If you will permit me—'

'What do ties matter, Jeeves, at a time like this? Do you realize that Mr Little's domestic happiness is hanging in the scale?'

'There is no time, sir, at which ties do not matter.'

I could see the man was pained, but I did not try to heal the wound. What's the word I want? Preoccupied. I was too preoccupied, don't you know. And distrait. Not to say careworn.

I was still careworn when, next day at half-past two, the revels commenced on the tennis lawn. It was one of those close, baking days, with thunder rumbling just round the corner; and it seemed to me that there was a brooding menace in the air.

'Bingo,' I said, as we pushed forth to do our bit in the first doubles, 'I wonder what young Thos will be up to this afternoon, with the eye of authority no longer on him?'

'Eh?' said Bingo, absently. Already the tennis look had come into his face, and his eye was glazed. He swung his racket and snorted a little.

'I don't see him anywhere,' I said.

'You don't what?'

'See him.'

'Who?'

'Young Thos.'

'What about him?'

I let it go.

The only consolation I had in the black period of the opening of the tourney was the fact that the Right Hon. had taken a seat among the spectators and was wedged in between a couple of females with parasols. Reason told me that even a kid so steeped in sin as young Thomas would hardly perpetrate any outrage on a man in such a strong strategic position. Considerably relieved, I gave myself up to the game; and was in the act of putting it across the local curate with a good deal of vim when there was a roll of thunder and the rain started to come down in buckets.

We all stampeded for the house, and had gathered in the drawing-room for tea, when suddenly Aunt Agatha, looking up from a cucumber-sandwich, said:

'Has anybody seen Mr Filmer?'

It was one of the nastiest jars I have ever experienced. What with my fast serve zipping sweetly over the net and the man of God utterly unable to cope with my slow bending return down the centre-line, I had for some little time been living, as it were, in another world. I now came down to earth with a bang: and my slice of cake, slipping from my nerveless fingers, fell to the ground and was wolfed by Aunt Agatha's spaniel, Robert. Once more I seemed to become conscious of an impending doom.

For this man Filmer, you must understand, was not one of those men who are lightly kept from the tea-table. A hearty trencherman, and particularly fond of his five o'clock couple of cups and bite of muffin, he had until this afternoon always been well up among the leaders in the race for the food-trough. If one thing was certain, it was that only the machinations of some enemy could be keeping him from being in the drawing-room now, complete with nose-bag.

'He must have got caught in the rain and be sheltering some-where in the grounds,' said Aunt Agatha. 'Bertie, go out and find him. Take a raincoat to him.'

'Right-ho!' I said. My only desire in life now was to find the Right Hon. And I hoped it wouldn't be merely his body.

I put on a raincoat and tucked another under my arm, and was sallying forth, when in the hall I ran into Jeeves.

'Jeeves,' I said, 'I fear the worst. Mr Filmer is missing.'

'Yes, sir.'

'I am about to scour the grounds in search of him.'

'I can save you the trouble, sir. Mr Filmer is on the island in the middle of the lake.'

'In this rain? Why doesn't the chump row back?'

'He has no boat, sir.'

'Then how can he be on the island?'

'He rowed there, sir. But Master Thomas rowed after him and set his boat adrift. He was informing me of the circumstances a moment ago, sir. It appears that Captain Flint was in the habit of marooning people on islands, and Master Thomas felt that he could pursue no more judicious course than to follow his example.'

'But, good Lord, Jeeves! The man must be getting soaked.'

'Yes, sir. Master Thomas commented upon that aspect of the matter.'

It was a time for action.

'Come with me, Jeeves!'

'Very good, sir.'

I buzzed for the boathouse.

My Aunt Agatha's husband, Spenser Gregson, who is on the Stock Exchange, had recently cleaned up to an amazing extent in Sumatra Rubber; and Aunt Agatha, in selecting a country estate, had lashed out on an impressive scale. There were miles of what they call rolling parkland, trees in considerable profusion well provided with doves and what not cooing in no uncertain voice, gardens full of roses, and also stables, outhouses, and messuages, the whole forming a rather fruity *tout ensemble*. But the feature of the place was the lake.

It stood to the east of the house, beyond the rose garden, and covered several acres. In the middle of it was an island. In the middle of the island was a building known as the Octagon. And in the middle of the Octagon, seated on the roof and spouting water like a public fountain, was the Right Hon. A. B. Filmer. As we drew nearer, striking a fast clip with self at the oars and Jeeves handling the tiller-ropes, we heard cries of gradually increasing volume, if that's the expression I want; and presently, up aloft, looking from a distance as if he were perched on top of the bushes, I located the Right Hon. It seemed to me that even a Cabinet Minister ought to have had more sense than to stay right out in the open like that when there were trees to shelter under.

'A little more to the right, Jeeves.'

'Very good, sir.'

I made a neat landing.

'Wait here, Jeeves.'

'Very good, sir. The head gardener was informing me this morning, sir, that one of the swans had recently nested on this island.'

'This is no time for natural history gossip, Jeeves,' I said, a little severely, for the rain was coming down harder than ever and the Wooster trouser-legs were already considerably moistened.

'Very good, sir.'

I pushed my way through the bushes. The going was sticky and took about eight and elevenpence off the value of my Sure-Grip tennis shoes in the first two yards: but I persevered, and presently came out in the open and found myself in a sort of clearing facing the Octagon.

This building was run up somewhere in the last century, I have been told, to enable the grandfather of the late owner to have some quiet place out of earshot of the house where he could practise the fiddle. From what I know of fiddlers, I should imagine that he had produced some fairly frightful sounds there in his time: but they can have been nothing to the ones that were coming from the roof of the place now. The Right Hon., not having spotted the arrival of the rescue-party, was apparently trying to make his voice carry across the waste of waters to the house; and I'm not saying it was not a good sporting effort. He had one of those highish tenors, and his yowls seemed to screech over my head like shells.

I thought it about time to slip him the glad news that assistance had arrived, before he strained a vocal cord.

'Hi!' I shouted, waiting for a lull.

He poked his head over the edge.

'Hi!' he bellowed, looking in every direction but the right one, of course.

'Hi!'

'Hi!'

'Hi!'

'Hi!'

'Oh!' he said, spotting me at last.

'What-ho!' I replied, sort of clinching the thing. I suppose the conversation can't be said to have touched a frightfully high level up to this moment; but probably we should have got a good deal brainier very shortly – only just then, at the very instant when I was getting ready to say something good, there was a hissing noise like a tyre bursting in a nest of cobras, and out of the bushes to my left there popped something so large and white and active that, thinking quicker than I have ever done in my puff, I rose like a rocketing pheasant, and, before I knew what I was doing, had begun to climb for life. Something slapped against the wall about an inch below my right ankle, and any doubts I may have had about remaining below vanished. The lad who bore 'mid snow and ice the banner with the strange device 'Excelsior!' was the model for Bertram.

'Be careful!' yipped the Right Hon.

I was.

Whoever built the Octagon might have constructed it especially for this sort of crisis. Its walls had grooves at regular intervals which were just right for the hands and feet, and it wasn't very long before I was parked up on the roof beside the Right Hon., gazing down at one of the largest and shortest-tempered swans I had ever seen. It was standing below, stretching up a neck like a hosepipe, just where a bit of brick, judiciously bunged, would catch it amidships.

I bunged the brick and scored a bull's-eye.

The Right Hon. didn't seem any too well pleased.

'Don't tease it!' he said.

'It teased me,' I said.

The swan extended another eight feet of neck and gave an imitation of steam escaping from a leaky pipe. The rain continued to lash down with what you might call indescribable fury, and I was sorry that in the agitation inseparable from shinning up a stone wall at practically a second's notice I had dropped the raincoat which I had been bringing with me for my fellow-rooster. For a moment I thought of offering him mine, but wiser counsels prevailed.

'How near did it come to getting you?' I asked.

'Within an ace,' replied my companion, gazing down with a look of marked dislike. 'I had to make a very rapid spring.'

The Right Hon. was a tubby little chap who looked as if he had been poured into his clothes and had forgotten to say 'When!' and the picture he conjured up, if you know what I mean, was rather pleasing.

'It is no laughing matter,' he said, shifting the look of dislike to me.

'Sorry.'

'I might have been seriously injured.'

'Would you consider bunging another brick at the bird?'

'Do nothing of the sort. It will only annoy him.'

'Well, why not annoy him? He hasn't shown such a dashed lot of consideration for our feelings.'

The Right Hon. now turned to another aspect of the matter.

'I cannot understand how my boat, which I fastened securely to the stump of a willow-tree, can have drifted away.'

'Dashed mysterious.'

'I begin to suspect that it was deliberately set loose by some mischievous person.'

'Oh, I say, no, hardly likely, that. You'd have seen them doing it.'

'No, Mr Wooster. For the bushes form an effective screen. Moreover, rendered drowsy by the unusual warmth of the afternoon, I dozed off for some little time almost immediately I reached the island.'

This wasn't the sort of thing I wanted his mind dwelling on, so I changed the subject.

'Wet, isn't it, what?' I said.

'I had already observed it,' said the Right Hon. in one of those nasty, bitter voices. 'I thank you, however, for drawing the matter to my attention.'

Chit-chat about the weather hadn't gone with much of a bang, I perceived. I had a shot at Bird Life in the Home Counties.

'Have you ever noticed,' I said, 'how a swan's eyebrows sort of meet in the middle?'

'I have had every opportunity of observing all that there is to observe about swans.'

'Gives them a sort of peevish look, what?'

'The look to which you allude has not escaped me.'

'Rummy,' I said, rather warming to my subject, 'how bad an effect family life has on a swan's disposition.'

'I wish you would select some other topic of conversation than swans.'

'No, but, really, it's rather interesting. I mean to say, our old pal down there is probably a perfect ray of sunshine in normal circumstances. Quite the domestic pet, don't you know. But purely and simply because the little woman happens to be nesting—'

I paused. You will scarcely believe me, but until this moment, what with all the recent bustle and activity, I had clean forgotten that, while we were treed up on the roof like this, there lurked all the time in the background one whose giant brain, if notified of the emergency and requested to flock round, would probably be able to think up half-a-dozen schemes for solving our little difficulties in a couple of minutes.

'Jeeves!' I shouted.

'Sir?' came a faint respectful voice from the great open spaces.

'My man,' I explained to the Right Hon. 'A fellow of infinite resource and sagacity. He'll have us out of this in a minute. Jeeves!'

'Sir?'

'I'm sitting on the roof.'

'Very good, sir.'

'Don't say "Very good". Come and help us. Mr Filmer and I are treed, Jeeves.'

'Very good, sir.'

'Don't keep saying "Very good". It's nothing of the kind. The place is alive with swans.'

'I will attend to the matter immediately, sir.'

I turned to the Right Hon. I even went so far as to pat him on the back. It was like slapping a wet sponge.

'All is well,' I said. 'Jeeves is coming.'

'What can he do?'

I frowned a trifle. The man's tone had been peevish, and I didn't like it.

'That,' I replied with a touch of stiffness, 'we cannot say until we see him in action. He may pursue one course, or he may pursue another. But on one thing you can rely with the utmost confidence – Jeeves will find a way. See, here he comes stealing through the undergrowth, his face shining with the light of pure intelligence. There are no limits to Jeeves's brain-power. He virtually lives on fish.'

I bent over the edge and peered into the abyss.

'Look out for the swan, Jeeves.'

'I have the bird under close observation, sir.'

The swan had been uncoiling a further supply of neck in our direction; but now he whipped round. The sound of a voice speaking in his rear seemed to affect him powerfully. He subjected Jeeves to a short, keen scrutiny; and then, taking in some breath for hissing purposes, gave a sort of jump and charged ahead.

'Look out, Jeeves!'

'Very good, sir.'

Well, I could have told that swan it was no use. As swans go, he may have been well up in the ranks of the intelligentsia; but, when it came to pitting his brains against Jeeves, he was simply wasting his time. He might just as well have gone home at once.

Every young man starting life ought to know how to cope with an angry swan, so I will briefly relate the proper procedure. You begin by picking up the raincoat which somebody has dropped; and then, judging the distance to a nicety, you simply shove the raincoat over the bird's head; and, taking the boat-hook which you have prudently brought with you, you insert it underneath the swan and heave. The swan goes into a bush and starts trying to unscramble itself; and you saunter back to your boat, taking with you any friends who may happen at the moment to be sitting on roofs in the vicinity. That was Jeeves's method, and I cannot see how it could have been improved upon.

The Right Hon. showing a turn of speed of which I would not have believed him capable, we were in the boat in considerably under two ticks.

'You behaved very intelligently, my man,' said the Right Hon. as we pushed away from the shore.

'I endeavour to give satisfaction, sir.'

The Right Hon. appeared to have said his say for the time being. From that moment he seemed to sort of huddle up and meditate. Dashed absorbed he was. Even when I caught a crab and shot about a pint of water down his neck he didn't seem to notice it.

It was only when we were landing that he came to life again.

'Mr Wooster.'

'Oh, ah?'

'I have been thinking of that matter of which I spoke to you some time back – the problem of how my boat can have got adrift.'

I didn't like this.

'The dickens of a problem,' I said. 'Better not bother about it any more. You'll never solve it.'

'On the contrary, I have arrived at a solution, and one which I think is the only feasible solution. I am convinced that my boat was set adrift by the boy Thomas, my hostess's son.'

'Oh, I say, no! Why?'

'He had a grudge against me. And it is the sort of thing only a boy, or one who is practically an imbecile, would have thought of doing.'

He legged it for the house; and I turned to Jeeves, aghast. Yes, you might say aghast.

'You heard, Jeeves?'

'Yes, sir.'

'What's to be done?'

'Perhaps Mr Filmer, on thinking the matter over, will decide that his suspicions are unjust.'

'But they aren't unjust.'

'No, sir.'

'Then what's to be done?'

'I could not say, sir.'

I pushed off rather smartly to the house and reported to Aunt Agatha that the Right Hon. had been salved; and then I toddled upstairs to have a hot bath, being considerably soaked from stem to stern as the result of my rambles. While I was enjoying the grateful warmth, a knock came at the door.

It was Purvis, Aunt Agatha's butler.

'Mrs Gregson desires me to say, sir, that she would be glad to see you as soon as you are ready.'

'But she has seen me.'

'I gather that she wishes to see you again, sir.'

'Oh, right-ho.'

I lay beneath the surface for another few minutes; then, having dried the frame, went along the corridor to my room. Jeeves was there, fiddling about with underclothing.

'Oh, Jeeves,' I said, 'I've just been thinking. Oughtn't somebody to go and give Mr Filmer a spot of quinine or something? Errand of mercy, what?'

'I have already done so, sir.'

'Good. I wouldn't say I like the man frightfully, but I don't want him to get a cold in the head.' I shoved on a sock. 'Jeeves,' I said, 'I suppose you know that we've got to think of something pretty quick? I mean to say, you realize the position? Mr Filmer suspects young Thomas of doing exactly what he did do, and if he brings home the charge Aunt Agatha will undoubtedly fire Mr Little, and then Mrs Little will find out what Mr Little has been up to, and what will be the upshot and outcome, Jeeves? I will tell you. It will mean that Mrs Little will get the goods on Mr Little to an extent to which, though only a bachelor myself, I should say that no wife ought to get the goods on her husband if the proper give and take of married life – what you might call the essential balance, as it were – is to be preserved. Women bring these things up, Jeeves. They do not forget and forgive.'

'Very true, sir.'

'Then how about it?'

'I have already attended to the matter, sir.'

'You have?'

'Yes, sir. I had scarcely left you when the solution of the affair presented itself to me. It was a remark of Mr Filmer's that gave me the idea.'

'Jeeves, you're a marvel!'

'Thank you very much, sir.'

'What was the solution?'

'I conceived the notion of going to Mr Filmer and saying that it was you who had stolen his boat, sir.'

The man flickered before me. I clutched a sock in a feverish grip.

'Saying – what?'

'At first Mr Filmer was reluctant to credit my statement. But I pointed out to him that you had certainly known that he was on the island – a fact which he agreed was highly significant. I pointed out, furthermore, that you were a light-hearted young gentleman, sir, who might well do such a thing as a practical joke. I left him quite convinced, and there is now no danger of his attributing the action to Master Thomas.'

I gazed at the blighter spellbound.

'And that's what you consider a neat solution?' I said.

'Yes, sir. Mr Little will now retain his position as desired.'

'And what about me?'

'You are also benefited, sir.'

'Oh, I am, am I?'

'Yes, sir. I have ascertained that Mrs Gregson's motive in inviting you to this house was that she might present you to Mr Filmer with a view to your becoming his private secretary.'

'What!'

'Yes, sir. Purvis, the butler, chanced to overhear Mrs Gregson in conversation with Mr Filmer on the matter.'

'Secretary to that superfatted bore! Jeeves, I could never have survived it.'

'No, sir. I fancy you would not have found it agreeable. Mr Filmer is scarcely a congenial companion for you. Yet, had Mrs

Gregson secured the position for you, you might have found it embarrassing to decline to accept it.'

'Embarrassing is right!'

'Yes, sir.'

'But I say, Jeeves, there's just one point which you seem to have overlooked. Where exactly do I get off?'

'Sir?'

'I mean to say, Aunt Agatha sent word by Purvis just now that she wanted to see me. Probably she's polishing up her hatchet at this very moment.'

'It might be the most judicious plan not to meet her, sir.'

'But how can I help it?'

'There is a good, stout waterpipe running down the wall immediately outside this window, sir. And I could have the two-seater waiting outside the park gates in twenty minutes.'

I eyed him with reverence.

'Jeeves,' I said, 'you are always right. You couldn't make it five, could you?'

'Let us say ten, sir.'

'Ten it is. Lay out some raiment suitable for travel, and leave the rest to me. Where is this waterpipe of which you speak so highly?'

THE LOVE THAT PURIFIES

THERE IS a ghastly moment in the year, generally about the beginning of August, when Jeeves insists on taking a holiday, the slacker, and legs it off to some seaside resort for a couple of weeks, leaving me stranded. This moment had now arrived, and we were discussing what was to be done with the young master.

'I had gathered the impression, sir,' said Jeeves, 'that you were proposing to accept Mr Sipperley's invitation to join him at his Hampshire residence.'

I laughed. One of those bitter, rasping ones.

'Correct, Jeeves. I was. But mercifully I was enabled to discover young Sippy's foul plot in time. Do you know what?'

'No, sir.'

'My spies informed me that Sippy's fiancée, Miss Moon, was to be there. Also his fiancée's mother, Mrs Moon, and his fiancée's small brother, Master Moon. You see the hideous treachery lurking behind the invitation? You see the man's loathsome design? Obviously my job was to be the task of keeping Mrs Moon and little Sebastian Moon interested and amused while Sippy and his blighted girl went off for the day, roaming the pleasant woodlands and talking of this and that. I doubt if anyone has ever had a narrower escape. You remember little Sebastian?'

'Yes, sir.'

'His goggle eyes? His golden curls?'

'Yes, sir.'

'I don't know why it is, but I've never been able to bear with fortitude anything in the shape of a kid with golden curls. Confronted with one, I feel the urge to step on him or drop things on him from a height.'

'Many strong natures are affected in the same way, sir.'

'So no *chez* Sippy for me. Was that the front-door bell ringing?'

'Yes, sir.'

'Somebody stands without.'

'Yes, sir.'

'Better go and see who it is.'

'Yes, sir.'

He oozed off, to return a moment later bearing a telegram. I opened it, and a soft smile played about the lips.

'Amazing how often things happen as if on a cue, Jeeves. This is from my Aunt Dahlia, inviting me down to her place in Worcestershire.'

'Most satisfactory, sir.'

'Yes. How I came to overlook her when searching for a haven, I can't think. The ideal home from home. Picturesque surroundings. Company's own water, and the best cook in England. You have not forgotten Anatole?'

'No, sir.'

'And above all, Jeeves, at Aunt Dahlia's there should be an almost total shortage of blasted kids. True, there is her son Bonzo, who, I take it, will be home for the holidays, but I don't mind Bonzo. Buzz off and send a wire, accepting.'

'Yes, sir.'

'And then shove a few necessaries together, including golf-clubs and tennis racquet.'

'Very good, sir. I am glad that matters have been so happily adjusted.'

I think I have mentioned before that my Aunt Dahlia stands alone in the grim regiment of my aunts as a real good sort and a chirpy sportsman. She is the one, if you remember, who married old Tom Travers and, with the assistance of Jeeves, lured Mrs Bingo Little's French cook, Anatole, away from Mrs B. L. and into her own employment. To visit her is always a pleasure. She generally has some cheery birds staying with her, and there is none of that rot about getting up for breakfast which one is sadly apt to find at country-houses.

It was, accordingly, with unalloyed lightness of heart that I edged the two-seater into the garage at Brinkley Court, Worc., and strolled round to the house by way of the shrubbery and the tennis-lawn, to report arrival. I had just got across the lawn when a head poked itself out of the smoking-room window and beamed at me in an amiable sort of way.

'Ah, Mr Wooster,' it said. 'Ha, ha!'

'Ho, ho!' I replied, not to be outdone in the courtesies.

It had taken me a couple of seconds to place this head. I now perceived that it belonged to a rather moth-eaten septuagenarian of the name of Anstruther, an old friend of Aunt Dahlia's late father. I had met him at her house in London once or twice. An agreeable cove, but somewhat given to nervous breakdowns.

'Just arrived?' he asked, beaming as before.

'This minute,' I said, also beaming.

'I fancy you will find our good hostess in the drawing-room.'

'Right,' I said, and after a bit more beaming to and fro I pushed on.

Aunt Dahlia was in the drawing-room, and welcomed me with gratifying enthusiasm. She beamed, too. It was one of those big days for beamers.

'Hullo, ugly,' she said. 'So here you are. Thank heaven you were able to come.'

It was the right tone, and one I should be glad to hear in others of the family circle, notably my Aunt Agatha.

'Always a pleasure to enjoy your hosp., Aunt Dahlia,' I said cordially. 'I anticipate a delightful and restful visit. I see you've got Mr Anstruther staying here. Anybody else?'

'Do you know Lord Snettisham?'

'I've met him, racing.'

'He's here, and Lady Snettisham.'

'And Bonzo, of course?'

'Yes. And Thomas.'

'Uncle Thomas?'

'No, he's in Scotland. Your cousin Thomas.'

'You don't mean Aunt Agatha's loathly son?'

'Of course I do. How many cousin Thomases do you think you've got, fathead? Agatha has gone to Homburg and planted the child on me.'

I was visibly agitated.

'But, Aunt Dahlia! Do you realize what you've taken on? Have you an inkling of the sort of scourge you've introduced into your home? In the society of young Thos., strong men quail. He is England's premier fiend in human shape. There is no devilry beyond his scope.'

'That's what I have always gathered from the form book,' agreed the relative. 'But just now, curse him, he's behaving like something out of a Sunday School story. You see, poor old Mr Anstruther is very frail these days, and when he found he was in a house containing two small boys he acted promptly. He offered a prize of five pounds to whichever behaved best during his stay. The consequence is that, ever since, Thomas has had large white wings sprouting out of his shoulders.' A shadow seemed to pass across her face. She appeared embittered. 'Mercenary little brute!' she said. 'I never saw such a sickeningly well-behaved kid in my life. It's enough to make one despair of human nature.'

I couldn't follow her.

'But isn't that all to the good?'

'No, it's not.'

'I can't see why. Surely a smug, oily Thos. about the house is better than a Thos. raging hither and thither and being a menace to society? Stands to reason.'

'It doesn't stand to anything of the kind. You see, Bertie, this Good Conduct prize has made matters a bit complex. There are wheels within wheels. The thing stirred Jane Snettisham's sporting blood to such an extent that she insisted on having a bet on the result.'

A great light shone upon me. I got what she was driving at.

'Ah!' I said. 'Now I follow. Now I see. Now I comprehend. She's betting on Thos., is she?'

'Yes. And naturally, knowing him, I thought the thing was in the bag.'

'Of course.'

'I couldn't see myself losing. Heaven knows I have no illusions about my darling Bonzo. Bonzo is, and has been from the cradle, a pest. But to back him to win a Good Conduct contest with Thomas seemed to me simply money for jam.'

'Absolutely.'

'When it comes to devilry, Bonzo is just a good, ordinary selling-plater. Whereas Thomas is a classic yearling.'

'Exactly. I don't see that you have any cause to worry, Aunt Dahlia. Thos. can't last. He's bound to crack.'

'Yes. But before that the mischief may be done.'

'Mischief?'

'Yes. There is dirty work afoot, Bertie,' said Aunt Dahlia gravely. 'When I booked this bet, I reckoned without the hideous blackness of the Snettishams' souls. Only yesterday it came to my knowledge that Jack Snettisham had been urging Bonzo to climb on the roof and boo down Mr Anstruther's chimney.'

'No!'

'Yes. Mr Anstruther is very frail, poor old fellow, and it would have frightened him into a fit. On coming out of which, his first action would have been to disqualify Bonzo and declare Thomas the winner by default.'

'But Bonzo did not boo?'

'No,' said Aunt Dahlia, and a mother's pride rang in her voice. 'He firmly refused to boo. Mercifully, he is in love at the moment, and it has quite altered his nature. He scorned the tempter.'

'In love? Who with?'

'Lilian Gish. We had an old film of hers at the Bijou Dream in the village a week ago, and Bonzo saw her for the first time. He came out with a pale, set face, and ever since has been trying to lead a finer, better life. So the peril was averted.'

'That's good.'

'Yes. But now it's my turn. You don't suppose I am going to take a thing like that lying down, do you? Treat me right, and I am fairness itself: but try any of this nobbling of starters, and I can play that game, too. If this Good Conduct contest is to be run on rough lines, I can do my bit as well as anyone. Far too much hangs on the issue for me to handicap myself by remembering the lessons I learned at my mother's knee.'

'Lot of money involved?'

'Much more than mere money. I've betted Anatole against Jane Snettisham's kitchen-maid.'

'Great Scott! Uncle Thomas will have something to say if he comes back and finds Anatole gone.'

'And won't he say it!'

'Pretty long odds you gave her, didn't you? I mean, Anatole is famed far and wide as a hash-slinger without peer.'

'Well, Jane Snettisham's kitchen-maid is not to be sneezed at. She is very hot stuff, they tell me, and good kitchen-maids nowadays are about as rare as original Holbeins. Besides, I had to give her a shade the best of the odds. She stood out for it. Well, anyway, to get back to what I was saying, if the opposition are going to place temptations in Bonzo's path, they shall jolly well be placed in Thomas's path, too, and plenty of them. So ring for Jeeves and let him get his brain working.'

'But I haven't brought Jeeves.'

'You haven't brought Jeeves?'

'No. He always takes his holiday at this time of year. He's down at Bognor for the shrimping.'

Aunt Dahlia registered deep concern.

'Then send for him at once! What earthly use do you suppose you are without Jeeves, you poor ditherer?'

I drew myself up a trifle – in fact, to my full height. Nobody has a greater respect for Jeeves than I have, but the Wooster pride was stung.

'Jeeves isn't the only one with brains,' I said coldly. 'Leave this thing to me, Aunt Dahlia. By dinner-time tonight I shall hope to have a fully matured scheme to submit for your approval. If I can't thoroughly encompass this Thos., I'll eat my hat.'

'About all you'll get to eat if Anatole leaves,' said Aunt Dahlia in a pessimistic manner which I did not like to see.

I was brooding pretty tensely as I left the presence. I have always had a suspicion that Aunt Dahlia, while invariably matey and bonhomous and seeming to take pleasure in my society, has a lower opinion of my intelligence than I quite like. Too often it is her practice to address me as 'fathead', and if I put forward any little thought or idea or fancy in her hearing it is apt to be greeted with the affectionate but jarring guffaw. In our recent interview she had hinted quite plainly that she considered me negligible in a crisis which, like the present one, called for initiative and resource. It was my intention to show her how greatly she had underestimated me.

To let you see the sort of fellow I really am, I got a ripe, excellent idea before I had gone half-way down the corridor. I examined it for the space of one and a half cigarettes, and could see no flaw in it, provided – I say, provided old Mr Anstruther's notion of what constituted bad conduct squared with mine.

The great thing on these occasions, as Jeeves will tell you, is to get a toe-hold on the psychology of the individual. Study the individual, and you will bring home the bacon. Now, I had been studying young Thos. for years, and I knew his psychology from caviare to nuts. He is one of those kids who never let the sun go down on their wrath, if you know what I mean. I mean to say, do something to annoy or offend or upset this juvenile thug, and he will proceed at the earliest possible opp. to wreak a hideous vengeance upon you. Only the previous summer, for instance, it having been drawn to his attention that the latter had reported him for smoking, he had marooned a Cabinet Minister on an island in the lake, at Aunt Agatha's place in Hertfordshire – in the rain, mark you, and with no company but that of one of the nastiest-minded swans I have ever encountered. Well, I mean!

So now it seemed to me that a few well-chosen taunts, or jibes, directed at his more sensitive points, must infallibly induce in this Thos. a frame of mind which would lead to his working some sensational violence upon me. And, if you wonder that I was willing to sacrifice myself to this frightful extent in order to do Aunt Dahlia a bit of good, I can only say that we Woosters are like that.

The one point that seemed to me to want a spot of clearing up was this: viz., would old Mr Anstruther consider an outrage perpetrated on the person of Bertram Wooster a crime sufficiently black to cause him to rule Thos. out of the race? Or would he just give a senile chuckle and mumble something about boys being boys? Because, if the latter, the thing was off. I decided to have a word with the old boy and make sure.

He was still in the smoking-room, looking very frail over the morning *Times*. I got to the point at once.

'Oh, Mr Anstruther,' I said. 'What-ho!'

'I don't like the way the American market is shaping,' he said. 'I don't like this strong Bear movement.'

'No?' I said. 'Well, be that as it may, about this Good Conduct prize of yours?'

'Ah, you have heard of that, eh?'

'I don't quite understand how you are doing the judging.'

'No? It is very simple. I have a system of daily marks. At the beginning of each day I accord the two lads twenty marks apiece. These are subject to withdrawal either in small or large quantities according to the magnitude of the offence. To take a simple example, shouting outside my bedroom in the early morning would involve a loss of three marks – whistling two. The penalty for a more serious lapse would be correspondingly greater. Before retiring to rest at night I record the day's marks in my little book. Simple, but, I think, ingenious, Mr Wooster?'

'Absolutely.'

'So far the result has been extremely gratifying. Neither of the little fellows has lost a single mark, and my nervous system is acquiring a tone which, when I learned that two lads of immature years would be staying in the house during my visit, I confess I had not dared to anticipate.'

'I see,' I said. 'Great work. And how do you react to what I might call general moral turpitude?'

'I beg your pardon?'

'Well, I mean when the thing doesn't affect you personally. Suppose one of them did something to me, for instance? Set a booby-trap or something? Or, shall we say, put a toad or so in my bed?'

He seemed shocked at the very idea.

'I would certainly in such circumstances deprive the culprit of a full ten marks.'

'Only ten?'

'Fifteen, then.'

'Twenty is a nice, round number.'

'Well, possibly even twenty. I have a peculiar horror of practical joking.'

'Me, too.'

'You will not fail to advise me, Mr Wooster, should such an outrage occur?'

'You shall have the news before anyone,' I assured him.

And so out into the garden, ranging to and fro in quest of young Thos. I knew where I was now. Bertram's feet were on solid ground.

I hadn't been hunting long before I found him in the summer-house, reading an improving book.

'Hullo,' he said, smiling a saintlike smile.

This scourge of humanity was a chunky kid whom a too indulgent public had allowed to infest the country for a matter of fourteen years. His nose was snub, his eyes green, his general aspect that of one studying to be a gangster. I had never liked his looks much, and with a saintlike smile added to them they became ghastly to a degree.

I ran over in my mind a few assorted taunts.

'Well, young Thos.,' I said. 'So there you are. You're getting as fat as a pig.'

It seemed as good an opening as any other. Experience had taught me that if there was a subject on which he was unlikely to accept persiflage in a spirit of amused geniality it was this matter of his bulging tum. On the last occasion when I made a remark of this nature, he had replied to me, child though he was, in terms which I would have been proud to have had in my own vocabulary. But now, though a sort of wistful gleam did flit for a moment into his eyes, he merely smiled in a more saintlike manner than ever.

'Yes, I think I have been putting on a little weight,' he said gently. 'I must try and exercise a lot while I'm here. Won't you sit down, Bertie?' he asked, rising. 'You must be tired after your journey. I'll get you a cushion. Have you cigarettes? And matches? I could bring you some from the smoking-room. Would you like me to fetch you something to drink?'

It is not too much to say that I felt baffled. In spite of what Aunt Dahlia had told me, I don't think that until this moment I had really believed there could have been anything in the nature of a genuinely sensational change in this young plugugly's attitude towards his fellows. But now, hearing him talk as if he were a combination of Boy Scout and delivery wagon, I felt definitely baffled. However, I stuck at it in the old bull-dog way.

'Are you still at that rotten kids' school of yours?' I asked.

He might have been proof against jibes at his *embonpoint*, but it seemed to me incredible that he could have sold himself for gold so completely as to lie down under taunts directed at his school. I was wrong. The money-lust evidently held him in its grip. He merely shook his head.

'I left this term. I'm going to Pevenhurst next term.'

'They wear mortar-boards there, don't they?'

'Yes.'

'With pink tassels?'

'Yes.'

'What a priceless ass you'll look!' I said, but without much hope. And I laughed heartily.

'I expect I shall,' he said, and laughed still more heartily.

'Mortar-boards!'

'Ha, ha!'

'Pink tassels!'

'Ha, ha!'

I gave the thing up.

'Well, teuf-teuf,' I said moodily, and withdrew.

A couple of days later I realized that the virus had gone even deeper than I had thought. The kid was irredeemably sordid.

It was old Mr Anstruther who sprang the bad news.

'Oh, Mr Wooster,' he said, meeting me on the stairs as I came down after a refreshing breakfast. 'You were good enough to express an interest in this little prize for Good Conduct which I am offering.'

'Oh, ah?'

'I explained to you my system of marking, I believe. Well, this morning I was impelled to vary it somewhat. The circumstances seemed to me to demand it. I happened to encounter our hostess's nephew, the boy Thomas, returning to the house, his aspect somewhat weary, it appeared to me, and travel-stained. I inquired of him where he had been at that early hour – it was not yet breakfast-time – and he replied that he had heard you mention overnight a regret that you had omitted to order the *Sporting Times* to be sent to you before leaving London, and he had actually walked all the way to the railway-station, a distance of more than three miles, to procure it for you.'

The old boy swam before my eyes. He looked like two old Mr Anstruthers, both flickering at the edges.

'What!'

'I can understand your emotion, Mr Wooster. I can appreciate it. It is indeed rarely that one encounters such unselfish kindliness in a lad of his age. So genuinely touched was I by the goodness of heart which the episode showed that I have deviated from my original system and awarded the little fellow a bonus of fifteen marks.'

'Fifteen!'

'On second thoughts, I shall make it twenty. That, as you yourself suggested, is a nice, round number.'

He doddered away, and I bounded off to find Aunt Dahlia.

'Aunt Dahlia,' I said, 'matters have taken a sinister turn.'

'You bet your Sunday spats they have,' agreed Aunt Dahlia emphatically. 'Do you know what happened just now? That crook Snettisham, who ought to be warned off the turf and hounded out of his clubs, offered Bonzo ten shillings if he would burst a paper bag behind Mr Anstruther's chair at breakfast. Thank heaven the love of a good woman triumphed again. My sweet Bonzo merely looked at him and walked away in a marked manner. But it just shows you what we are up against.'

'We are up against worse than that, Aunt Dahlia,' I said. And I told her what had happened.

She was stunned. Aghast, you might call it.

'*Thomas* did that?'

'Thos. in person.'

'Walked six miles to get you a paper?'

'Six miles and a bit.'

'The young hound! Good heavens, Bertie, do you realize that he may go on doing these Acts of Kindness daily – perhaps twice a day? Is there no way of stopping him?'

'None that I can think of. No, Aunt Dahlia, I must confess it. I am baffled. There is only one thing to do. We must send for Jeeves.'

'And about time,' said the relative churlishly. 'He ought to have been here from the start. Wire him this morning.'

There is good stuff in Jeeves. His heart is in the right place. The acid test does not find him wanting. Many men in his position, summoned back by telegram in the middle of their annual vacation, might have cut up rough a bit. But not Jeeves. On the following afternoon in he blew, looking bronzed and fit, and I gave him the scenario without delay.

'So there you have it, Jeeves,' I said, having sketched out the facts. 'The problem is one that will exercise your intelligence to the utmost. Rest now, and tonight, after a light repast, withdraw to some solitary place and get down to it. Is there any particularly stimulating food or beverage you would like for dinner? Anything that you feel would give the old brain just that extra fillip? If so, name it.'

'Thank you very much, sir, but I have already hit upon a plan which should, I fancy, prove effective.'

I gazed at the man with some awe.

'Already?'

'Yes, sir.'

'Not *already*?'

'Yes, sir.'

'Something to do with the psychology of the individual?'

'Precisely, sir.'

I shook my head, a bit discouraged. Doubts had begun to creep in.

'Well, spring it, Jeeves,' I said. 'But I have not much hope. Having only just arrived, you cannot possibly be aware of the frightful change that has taken place in young Thos. You are probably building on your knowledge of him, when last seen. Useless, Jeeves. Stirred by the prospect of getting his hooks on five of the best, this blighted boy has become so dashed virtuous that his armour seems to contain no chink. I mocked at his waistline and sneered at his school and he merely smiled in a pale, dying-duck sort of way. Well, that'll show you. However, let us hear what you have to suggest.'

'It occurred to me, sir, that the most judicious plan in the circumstances would be for you to request Mrs Travers to invite Master Sebastian Moon here for a short visit.'

I shook the onion again. The scheme sounded to me like apple sauce, and Grade A apple sauce, at that.

'What earthly good would that do?' I asked, not without a touch of asperity. 'Why Sebastian Moon?'

'He has golden curls, sir.'

'What of it?'

'The strongest natures are sometimes not proof against long golden curls.'

Well, it was a thought, of course. But I can't say I was leaping about to any great extent. It might be that the sight of Sebastian Moon would break down Thos.'s iron self-control to the extent of causing him to inflict mayhem on the person, but I wasn't any too hopeful.

'It may be so, Jeeves.'

'I do not think I am too sanguine, sir. You must remember that Master Moon, apart from his curls, has a personality which is not uniformly pleasing. He is apt to express himself with a breezy candour which I fancy Master Thomas might feel inclined to resent in one some years his junior.'

I had had a feeling all along that there was a flaw somewhere, and now it seemed to me that I had spotted it.

'But, Jeeves. Granted that little Sebastian is the pot of poison you indicate, why won't he act just as forcibly on young Bonzo as on Thos.? Pretty silly we should look if our nominee started

putting it across him. Never forget that already Bonzo is twenty
marks down and falling back in the betting.'

'I do not anticipate any such contingency, sir. Master Travers
is in love, and love is a very powerful restraining influence at
the age of thirteen.'

'H'm.' I mused. 'Well, we can but try, Jeeves.'

'Yes, sir.'

'I'll get Aunt Dahlia to write to Sippy tonight.'

I'm bound to say that the spectacle of little Sebastian when
he arrived two days later did much to remove pessimism from
my outlook. If ever there was a kid whose whole appearance
seemed to call aloud to any right-minded boy to lure him into a
quiet spot and inflict violence upon him, that kid was undeniably
Sebastian Moon. He reminded me strongly of Little Lord Fauntleroy. I marked young Thos.'s demeanour closely at the moment
of their meeting and, unless I was much mistaken, there came into
his eyes the sort of look which would come into those of an Indian
chief – Chinchagook, let us say, or Sitting Bull – just before he
started reaching for his scalping-knife. He had the air of one who
is about ready to begin.

True, his manner as he shook hands was guarded. Only a keen
observer could have detected that he was stirred to his depths. But
I had seen, and I summoned Jeeves forthwith.

'Jeeves,' I said, 'if I appeared to think poorly of that scheme
of yours, I now withdraw my remarks. I believe you have found
the way. I was noticing Thos. at the moment of impact. His eyes
had a strange gleam.'

'Indeed, sir?'

'He shifted uneasily on his feet and his ears wiggled. He had,
in short, the appearance of a boy who was holding himself in with
an effort almost too great for his frail body.'

'Yes, sir?'

'Yes, Jeeves. I received a distinct impression of something being
on the point of exploding. Tomorrow I shall ask Aunt Dahlia to
take the two warts for a country ramble, to lose them in some
sequestered spot, and to leave the rest to Nature.'

'It is a good idea, sir.'

'It is more than a good idea, Jeeves,' I said. 'It is a pip.'

* * *

You know, the older I get the more firmly do I become convinced that there is no such thing as a pip in existence. Again and again have I seen the apparently sure thing go phut, and now it is rarely indeed that I can be lured from my aloof scepticism. Fellows come sidling up to me at the Drones and elsewhere, urging me to invest on some horse that can't lose even if it gets struck by lightning at the starting-post, but Bertram Wooster shakes his head. He has seen too much of life to be certain of anything.

If anyone had told me that my Cousin Thos., left alone for an extended period of time with a kid of the superlative foulness of Sebastian Moon, would not only refrain from cutting off his curls with a pocket-knife and chasing him across country into a muddy pond but would actually return home carrying the gruesome kid on his back because he had got a blister on his foot, I would have laughed scornfully. I knew Thos. I knew his work. I had seen him in action. And I was convinced that not even the prospect of collecting five pounds would be enough to give him pause.

And yet what happened? In the quiet evenfall, when the little birds were singing their sweetest and all Nature seemed to whisper of hope and happiness, the blow fell. I was chatting with old Mr Anstruther on the terrace when suddenly round a bend in the drive the two kids hove in view. Sebastian, seated on Thos.'s back, his hat off and his golden curls floating on the breeze, was singing as much as he could remember of a comic song, and Thos., bowed down by the burden but carrying on gamely, was trudging along, smiling that bally saintlike smile of his. He parked the kid on the front steps and came across to us.

'Sebastian got a nail in his shoe,' he said in a low, virtuous voice. 'It hurt him to walk, so I gave him a piggy-back.'

I heard old Mr Anstruther draw in his breath sharply.

'All the way home?'

'Yes, sir.'

'In this hot sunshine?'

'Yes, sir.'

'But was he not very heavy?'

'He was a little, sir,' said Thos., uncorking the saintlike once more. 'But it would have hurt him awfully to walk.'

I pushed off. I had had enough. If ever a septuagenarian looked on the point of handing out another bonus, that septuagenarian was old Mr Anstruther. He had the unmistakable bonus glitter in his eye. I withdrew, and found Jeeves in my bedroom messing about with ties and things.

He pursed the lips a bit on hearing the news.

'Serious, sir.'

'Very serious, Jeeves.'

'I had feared this, sir.'

'Had you? I hadn't. I was convinced Thos. would have massacred young Sebastian. I banked on it. It just shows what the greed for money will do. This is a commercial age, Jeeves. When I was a boy, I would cheerfully have forfeited five quid in order to deal faithfully with a kid like Sebastian. I would have considered it money well spent.'

'You are mistaken, sir, in your estimate of the motives actuating Master Thomas. It was not a mere desire to win five pounds that caused him to curb his natural impulses.'

'Eh?'

'I have ascertained the true reason for his change of heart, sir.'

I felt fogged.

'Religion, Jeeves?'

'No, sir. Love.'

'Love?'

'Yes, sir. The young gentleman confided in me during a brief conversation in the hall shortly after luncheon. We had been speaking for a while on neutral subjects, when he suddenly turned a deeper shade of pink and after some slight hesitation inquired of me if I did not think Miss Greta Garbo the most beautiful woman at present in existence.'

I clutched the brow.

'Jeeves! Don't tell me Thos. is in love with Greta Garbo?'

'Yes, sir. Unfortunately such is the case. He gave me to understand that it had been coming on for some time, and her last picture settled the issue. His voice shook with an emotion which it was impossible to misread. I gathered from his observations, sir, that he proposes to spend the remainder of his life trying to make himself worthy of her.'

It was a knock-out. This was the end.

'This is the end, Jeeves,' I said. 'Bonzo must be a good forty marks behind by now. Only some sensational and spectacular outrage upon the public weal on the part of young Thos. could have enabled him to wipe out the lead. And of that there is now, apparently, no chance.'

'The eventuality does appear remote, sir.'

I brooded.

'Uncle Thomas will have a fit when he comes back and finds Anatole gone.'

'Yes, sir.'

'Aunt Dahlia will drain the bitter cup to the dregs.'

'Yes, sir.'

'And, speaking from a purely selfish point of view, the finest cooking I have ever bitten will pass out of my life for ever, unless the Snettishams invite me in some night to take pot luck. And that eventuality is also remote.'

'Yes, sir.'

'Then the only thing I can do is square the shoulders and face the inevitable.'

'Yes, sir.'

'Like some aristocrat of the French Revolution popping into the tumbril, what? The brave smile. The stiff upper lip.'

'Yes, sir.'

'Right-ho, then. Is the shirt studded?'

'Yes, sir.'

'The tie chosen?'

'Yes, sir.'

'The collar and evening underwear all in order?'

'Yes, sir.'

'Then I'll have a bath and be with you in two ticks.'

It is all very well to talk about the brave smile and the stiff upper lip, but my experience – and I daresay others have found the same – is that they are a dashed sight easier to talk about than actually to fix on the face. For the next few days, I'm bound to admit, I found myself, in spite of every effort, registering gloom pretty consistently. For, as if to make things tougher than they might have been, Anatole at this juncture suddenly developed a cooking streak which put all his previous efforts in the shade.

Night after night we sat at the dinner-table, the food melting in our mouths, and Aunt Dahlia would look at me and I would look at Aunt Dahlia, and the male Snettisham would ask the female Snettisham in a ghastly, gloating sort of way if she had ever tasted such cooking and the female Snettisham would smirk at the male Snettisham and say she never had in all her puff, and I would look at Aunt Dahlia and Aunt Dahlia would look at me and our eyes would be full of unshed tears, if you know what I mean.

And all the time old Mr Anstruther's visit drawing to a close.

The sands running out, so to speak.

And then, on the very last afternoon of his stay, the thing happened.

It was one of those warm, drowsy, peaceful afternoons. I was up in my bedroom, getting off a spot of correspondence which I had neglected of late, and from where I sat I looked down on the shady lawn, fringed with its gay flower-beds. There was a bird or two hopping about, a butterfly or so fluttering to and fro, and an assortment of bees buzzing hither and thither. In a garden-chair sat old Mr Anstruther, getting his eight hours. It was a sight which, had I had less on my mind, would no doubt have soothed the old soul a bit. The only blot on the landscape was Lady Snettisham, walking among the flower-beds and probably sketching out future menus, curse her.

And so for a time everything carried on. The birds hopped, the butterflies fluttered, the bees buzzed, and old Mr Anstruther snored – all in accordance with the programme. And I worked through a letter to my tailor to the point where I proposed to say something pretty strong about the way the right sleeve of my last coat bagged.

There was a tap on the door, and Jeeves entered, bringing the second post. I laid the letters listlessly on the table beside me.

'Well, Jeeves,' I said sombrely.

'Sir?'

'Mr Anstruther leaves tomorrow.'

'Yes, sir.'

I gazed down at the sleeping septuagenarian.

'In my young days, Jeeves,' I said, 'however much I might have been in love, I could never have resisted the spectacle of an old gentleman asleep like that in a deck-chair. I would have done *something* to him, no matter what the cost.'

'Indeed, sir?'

'Yes. Probably with a pea-shooter. But the modern boy is degenerate. He has lost his vim. I suppose Thos. is indoors on this lovely afternoon, showing Sebastian his stamp-album or something. Ha!' I said, and I said it rather nastily.

'I fancy Master Thomas and Master Sebastian are playing in the stable-yard, sir. I encountered Master Sebastian not long back and he informed me he was on his way thither.'

'The motion-pictures, Jeeves,' I said, 'are the curse of the age. But for them, if Thos. had found himself alone in a stable-yard with a kid like Sebastian—'

I broke off. From some point to the south-west, out of my line of vision, there had proceeded a piercing squeal.

It cut through the air like a knife, and old Mr Anstruther leaped up as if it had run into the fleshy part of his leg. And the next moment little Sebastian appeared, going well and followed at a short interval by Thos., who was going even better. In spite of the fact that he was hampered in his movements by a large stable-bucket which he bore in his right hand, Thos. was running a great race. He had almost come up with Sebastian, when the latter, with great presence of mind, dodged behind Mr Anstruther, and there for a moment the matter rested.

But only for a moment. Thos., for some reason plainly stirred to the depths of his being, moved adroitly to one side and, poising the bucket for an instant, discharged its contents. And Mr Anstruther, who had just moved to the same side, received, as far as I could gather from a distance, the entire consignment. In one second, without any previous training or upbringing, he had become the wettest man in Worcestershire.

'Jeeves!' I cried.

'Yes, indeed, sir,' said Jeeves, and seemed to me to put the whole thing in a nutshell.

Down below, things were hotting up nicely. Old Mr Anstruther may have been frail, but he undoubtedly had his moments. I have rarely seen a man of his years conduct himself with such a lissom abandon. There was a stick lying beside the chair, and with this in hand he went into action like a two-year-old. A moment later, he and Thos. had passed out of the picture round the side of the house, Thos. cutting out a rare pace but, judging from the sounds of anguish, not quite good enough to distance the field.

The tumult and the shouting died; and, after gazing for a while with considerable satisfaction at the Snettisham, who was standing there with a sand-bagged look watching her nominee pass right out of the betting, I turned to Jeeves. I felt quietly triumphant. It is not often that I score off him, but now I had scored in no uncertain manner.

'You see, Jeeves,' I said, 'I was right and you were wrong. Blood will tell. Once a Thos., always a Thos. Can the leopard change his spots or the Ethiopian his what-not? What was that thing they used to teach us at school about expelling Nature?'

'You may expel Nature with a pitchfork, sir, but she will always return? In the original Latin—'

'Never mind about the original Latin. The point is that I told you Thos. could not resist those curls, and he couldn't. You would have it that he could.'

'I do not fancy it was the curls that caused the upheaval, sir.'

'Must have been.'

'No, sir. I think Master Sebastian had been speaking disparagingly of Miss Garbo.'

'Eh? Why would he do that?'

'I suggested that he should do so, sir, not long ago when I encountered him on his way to the stable-yard. It was a move which he was very willing to take, as he informed me that in his opinion Miss Garbo was definitely inferior both in beauty and talent to Miss Clara Bow, for whom he has long nourished a deep regard. From what we have just witnessed, sir, I imagine that Master Sebastian must have introduced the topic into the conversation at an early point.'

I sank into a chair. The Wooster system can stand just so much.

'Jeeves!'

'Sir?'

'You tell me that Sebastian Moon, a stripling of such tender years that he can go about the place with long curls without causing mob violence, is in love with Clara Bow?'

'And has been for some little time, he gave me to understand, sir.'

'Jeeves, this Younger Generation is hot stuff.'

'Yes, sir.'

'Were you like that in your day?'

'No, sir.'

'Nor I, Jeeves. At the age of fourteen I once wrote to Marie Lloyd for her autograph, but apart from that my private life could bear the strictest investigation. However, that is not the point.

The point is, Jeeves, that once more I must pay you a marked tribute.'

'Thank you very much, sir.'

'Once more you have stepped forward like the great man you are and spread sweetness and light in no uncertain measure.'

'I am glad to have given satisfaction, sir. Would you be requiring my services any further?'

'You mean you wish to return to Bognor and its shrimps? Do so, Jeeves, and stay there another fortnight, if you wish. And may success attend your net.'

'Thank you very much, sir.'

I eyed the man fixedly. His head stuck out at the back, and his eyes sparkled with the light of pure intelligence.

'I am sorry for the shrimp that tries to pit its feeble cunning against you, Jeeves,' I said.

And I meant it.

THE LETTER arrived on the morning of the sixteenth. I was pushing a bit of breakfast into the Wooster face at the moment and, feeling fairly well-fortified with coffee and kippers, I decided to break the news to Jeeves without delay. As Shakespeare says, if you're going to do a thing you might just as well pop right at it and get it over. The man would be disappointed, of course, and possibly even chagrined: but, dash it all, a splash of disappointment here and there does a fellow good. Makes him realize that life is stern and life is earnest.

'Oh, Jeeves,' I said.

'Sir?'

'We have here a communication from Lady Wickham. She has written inviting me to Skeldings for the festivities. So you will see about bunging the necessaries together. We repair thither on the twenty-third. Plenty of white ties, Jeeves, also a few hearty country suits for use in the daytime. We shall be there some little time, I expect.'

There was a pause. I could feel he was directing a frosty gaze at me, but I dug into the marmalade and refused to meet it.

'I thought I understood you to say, sir, that you proposed to visit Monte Carlo immediately after Christmas.'

'I know. But that's all off. Plans changed.'

'Very good, sir.'

At this point the telephone bell rang, tiding over very nicely what had threatened to be an awkward moment. Jeeves unhooked the receiver.

'Yes?... Yes, madam... Very good, madam. Here is Mr Wooster.' He handed me the instrument. 'Mrs Spenser Gregson, sir.'

You know, every now and then I can't help feeling that Jeeves is losing his grip. In his prime it would have been with him the work of a moment to have told Aunt Agatha that I was not at home. I gave him one of those reproachful glances, and took the machine.

'Hullo?' I said. 'Yes? Hullo? Hullo? Bertie speaking. Hullo? Hullo? Hullo?'

'Don't keep on saying Hullo,' yipped the old relative in her customary curt manner. 'You're not a parrot. Sometimes I wish you were, because then you might have a little sense.'

Quite the wrong sort of tone to adopt towards a fellow in the early morning, of course, but what can one do?

'Bertie, Lady Wickham tells me she has invited you to Skeldings for Christmas. Are you going?'

'Rather!'

'Well, mind you behave yourself. Lady Wickham is an old friend of mine.'

I was in no mood for this sort of thing over the telephone. Face to face, I'm not saying, but at the end of a wire, no.

'I shall naturally endeavour, Aunt Agatha,' I replied stiffly, 'to conduct myself in a manner befitting an English gentleman paying a visit—'

'What did you say? Speak up. I can't hear.'

'I said Right-ho.'

'Oh? Well, mind you do. And there's another reason why I particularly wish you to be as little of an imbecile as you can manage while at Skeldings. Sir Roderick Glossop will be there.'

'What!'

'Don't bellow like that. You nearly deafened me.'

'Did you say Sir Roderick Glossop?'

'I did.'

'You don't mean Tuppy Glossop?'

'I mean Sir Roderick Glossop. Which was my reason for saying Sir Roderick Glossop. Now, Bertie, I want you to listen to me attentively. Are you there?'

'Yes. Still here.'

'Well, then, listen. I have at last succeeded, after incredible difficulty, and in face of all the evidence, in almost persuading Sir Roderick that you are not actually insane. He is prepared to suspend judgement until he has seen you once more. On your behaviour at Skeldings, therefore—'

But I had hung up the receiver. Shaken. That's what I was. S. to the core.

Stop me if I've told you this before: but, in case you don't know, let me just mention the facts in the matter of this Glossop.

He was a formidable old bird with a bald head and out-size eye-brows, by profession a loony-doctor. How it happened, I couldn't tell you to this day, but I once got engaged to his daughter, Honoria, a ghastly dynamic exhibit who read Nietzsche and had a laugh like waves breaking on a stern and rock-bound coast. The fixture was scratched owing to events occurring which convinced the old boy that I was off my napper; and since then he has always had my name at the top of his list of 'Loonies I have Lunched With'.

It seemed to me that even at Christmas time, with all the peace on earth and goodwill towards men that there is knocking about at that season, a reunion with this bloke was likely to be tough going. If I hadn't had more than one particularly good reason for wanting to go to Skeldings, I'd have called the thing off.

'Jeeves,' I said, all of a twitter, 'do you know what? Sir Roderick Glossop is going to be at Lady Wickham's.'

'Very good, sir. If you have finished breakfast, I will clear away.'

Cold and haughty. No symp. None of the rallying-round spirit which one likes to see. As I had anticipated, the information that we were not going to Monte Carlo had got in amongst him. There is a keen sporting streak in Jeeves, and I knew he had been looking forward to a little flutter at the tables.

We Woosters can wear the mask. I ignored his lack of decent feeling.

'Do so, Jeeves,' I said proudly, 'and with all convenient speed.'

Relations continued pretty fairly strained all through the rest of the week. There was a frigid detachment in the way the man brought me my dollop of tea in the mornings. Going down to Skeldings in the car on the afternoon of the twenty-third, he was aloof and reserved. And before dinner on the first night of my visit he put the studs in my dress-shirt in what I can only call a marked manner. The whole thing was extremely painful, and it seemed to me, as I lay in bed on the morning of the twenty-fourth, that the only step to take was to put the whole facts of the case before him and trust to his native good sense to effect an understanding.

I was feeling considerably in the pink that morning. Everything had gone like a breeze. My hostess, Lady Wickham, was a beaky female built far too closely on the lines of my Aunt Agatha for comfort, but she had seemed matey enough on my arrival. Her daughter, Roberta, had welcomed me with a warmth which, I'm bound to say, had set the old heart-strings fluttering a bit. And Sir Roderick, in the brief moment we had had together, appeared to have let the Yule Tide Spirit soak into him to the most amazing extent. When he saw me, his mouth sort of flickered at one corner, which I took to be his idea of smiling, and he said 'Ha, young man!' Not particularly chummily, but he said it: and my view was that it practically amounted to the lion lying down with the lamb.

So, all in all, life at this juncture seemed pretty well all to the mustard, and I decided to tell Jeeves exactly how matters stood.

'Jeeves,' I said, as he appeared with the steaming.

'Sir?'

'Touching on this business of our being here, I would like to say a few words of explanation. I consider that you have a right to the facts.'

'Sir?'

'I'm afraid scratching that Monte Carlo trip has been a bit of a jar for you, Jeeves.'

'Not at all, sir.'

'Oh, yes, it has. The heart was set on wintering in the world's good old Plague Spot, I know. I saw your eye light up when I said we were due for a visit there. You snorted a bit and your fingers twitched. I know, I know. And now that there has been a change of programme the iron has entered into your soul.'

'Not at all, sir.'

'Oh, yes, it has. I've seen it. Very well, then, what I wish to impress upon you, Jeeves, is that I have not been actuated in this matter by any mere idle whim. It was through no light and airy caprice that I accepted this invitation to Lady Wickham's. I have been angling for it for weeks, prompted by many considerations. In the first place, does one get the Yule-tide spirit at a spot like Monte Carlo?'

'Does one desire the Yule-tide spirit, sir?'

'Certainly one does. I am all for it. Well, that's one thing. Now here's another. It was imperative that I should come to Skeldings for Christmas, Jeeves, because I knew that young Tuppy Glossop was going to be here.'

'Sir Roderick Glossop, sir?'

'His nephew. You may have observed hanging about the place a fellow with light hair and a Cheshire-cat grin. That is Tuppy, and I have been anxious for some time to get to grips with him. I have it in for that man of wrath. Listen to the facts, Jeeves, and tell me if I am not justified in planning a hideous vengeance.' I took a sip of tea, for the mere memory of my wrongs had shaken me. 'In spite of the fact that young Tuppy is the nephew of Sir Roderick Glossop, at whose hands, Jeeves, as you are aware, I have suffered much, I fraternized with him freely, both at the Drones Club and elsewhere. I said to myself that a man is not to be blamed for his relations, and that I would hate to have my pals hold my Aunt Agatha, for instance, against me. Broad-minded, Jeeves, I think?'

'Extremely, sir.'

'Well, then, as I say, I sought this Tuppy out, Jeeves, and hobnobbed, and what do you think he did?'

'I could not say, sir.'

'I will tell you. One night after dinner at the Drones he betted me I wouldn't swing myself across the swimming-bath by the ropes and rings. I took him on and was buzzing along in great style until I came to the last ring. And then I found that this fiend in human shape had looped it back against the rail, thus leaving me hanging in the void with no means of getting ashore to my home and loved ones. There was nothing for it but to drop into the water. He told me that he had often caught fellows that way: and what I maintain, Jeeves, is that, if I can't get back at him somehow at Skeldings – with all the vast resources which a country-house affords at my disposal – I am not the man I was.'

'I see, sir.'

There was still something in his manner which told me that even now he lacked complete sympathy and understanding, so, delicate though the subject was, I decided to put all my cards on the table.

'And now, Jeeves, we come to the most important reason why I had to spend Christmas at Skeldings. Jeeves,' I said, diving into the old cup once more for a moment and bringing myself out wreathed in blushes, 'the fact of the matter is, I'm in love.'

'Indeed, sir?'

'You've seen Miss Roberta Wickham?'

'Yes, sir.'

'Very well, then.'

There was a pause, while I let it sink in.

'During your stay here, Jeeves,' I said, 'you will, no doubt, be thrown a good deal together with Miss Wickham's maid. On such occasions, pitch it strong.'

'Sir?'

'You know what I mean. Tell her I'm rather a good chap. Mention my hidden depths. These things get round. Dwell on the fact that I have a kind heart and was runner-up in the Squash Handicap at the Drones this year. A boost is never wasted, Jeeves.'

'Very good, sir. But—'

'But what?'

'Well, sir—'

'I wish you wouldn't say "Well, sir" in that soupy tone of voice. I have had to speak of this before. The habit is one that is growing upon you. Check it. What's on your mind?'

'I hardly like to take the liberty—'

'Carry on, Jeeves. We are always glad to hear from you, always.'

'What I was about to remark, if you will excuse me, sir, was that I would scarcely have thought Miss Wickham a suitable—'

'Jeeves,' I said coldly, 'if you have anything to say against that lady, it had better not be said in my presence.'

'Very good, sir.'

'Or anywhere else, for that matter. What is your kick against Miss Wickham?'

'Oh, really, sir!'

'Jeeves, I insist. This is a time for plain speaking. You have beefed about Miss Wickham. I wish to know why.'

'It merely crossed my mind, sir, that for a gentleman of your description Miss Wickham is not a suitable mate.'

'What do you mean by a gentleman of my description?'

'Well, sir—'

'Jeeves!'

'I beg your pardon, sir. The expression escaped me inadvertently. I was about to observe that I can only asseverate—'

'Only what?'

'I can only say that, as you have invited my opinion—'

'But I didn't.'

'I was under the impression that you desired to canvass my views on the matter, sir.'

'Oh? Well, let's have them, anyway.'

'Very good, sir. Then briefly, if I may say so, sir, though Miss Wickham is a charming young lady—'

'There, Jeeves, you spoke an imperial quart. What eyes!'

'Yes, sir.'

'What hair!'

'Very true, sir.'

'And what *espièglerie*, if that's the word I want.'

'The exact word, sir.'

'All right, then. Carry on.'

'I grant Miss Wickham the possession of all these desirable qualities, sir. Nevertheless, considered as a matrimonial prospect for a gentleman of your description, I cannot look upon her as suitable. In my opinion Miss Wickham lacks seriousness, sir. She is too volatile and frivolous. To qualify as Miss Wickham's husband, a gentleman would need to possess a commanding personality and considerable strength of character.'

'Exactly!'

'I would always hesitate to recommend as a life's companion a young lady with quite such a vivid shade of red hair. Red hair, sir, in my opinion, is dangerous.'

I eyed the blighter squarely.

'Jeeves,' I said, 'you're talking rot.'

'Very good, sir.'

'Absolute drivel.'

'Very good, sir.'

'Pure mashed potatoes.'

'Very good, sir.'

'Very good, sir – I mean very good Jeeves, that will be all,' I said.

And I drank a modicum of tea, with a good deal of hauteur.

It isn't often that I find myself able to prove Jeeves in the wrong, but by dinner-time that night I was in a position to do so, and I did it without delay.

'Touching on that matter we were touching on, Jeeves,' I said, coming in from the bath and tackling him as he studied the shirt,

'I should be glad if you would give me your careful attention for a moment. I warn you that what I am about to say is going to make you look pretty silly.'

'Indeed, sir?'

'Yes, Jeeves. Pretty dashed silly it's going to make you look. It may lead you to be rather more careful in future about broadcasting these estimates of yours of people's characters. This morning, if I remember rightly, you stated that Miss Wickham was volatile, frivolous and lacking in seriousness. Am I correct?'

'Quite correct, sir.'

'Then what I have to tell you may cause you to alter that opinion. I went for a walk with Miss Wickham this afternoon: and, as we walked, I told her about what young Tuppy Glossop did to me in the swimming-bath at the Drones. She hung upon my words, Jeeves, and was full of sympathy.'

'Indeed, sir?'

'Dripping with it. And that's not all. Almost before I had finished, she was suggesting the ripest, fruitiest, brainiest scheme for bringing young Tuppy's grey hairs in sorrow to the grave that anyone could possibly imagine.'

'That is very gratifying, sir.'

'Gratifying is the word. It appears that at the girls' school where Miss Wickham was educated, Jeeves, it used to become necessary from time to time for the right-thinking element of the community to slip it across certain of the baser sort. Do you know what they did, Jeeves?'

'No, sir.'

'They took a long stick, Jeeves, and – follow me closely here – they tied a darning-needle to the end of it. Then at dead of night, it appears, they sneaked privily into the party of the second part's cubicle and shoved the needle through the bed-clothes and punctured her hot-water bottle. Girls are much subtler in these matters than boys, Jeeves. At my old school one would occasionally heave a jug of water over another bloke during the night-watches, but we never thought of effecting the same result in this particularly neat and scientific manner. Well, Jeeves, that was the scheme which Miss Wickham suggested I should work on young Tuppy, and that is the girl you call frivolous and lacking in seriousness. Any girl who can think up a wheeze like that is my idea of a helpmeet. I shall be glad, Jeeves, if by the time I come to bed tonight you have waiting for me in this room a stout stick with a good sharp darning needle attached.'

'Well, sir—'

I raised my hand.

'Jeeves,' I said. 'Not another word. Stick, one, and needle, darning, good, sharp, one, without fail in this room at eleven-thirty tonight.'

'Very good, sir.'

'Have you any idea where young Tuppy sleeps?'

'I could ascertain, sir.'

'Do so, Jeeves.'

In a few minutes he was back with the necessary informash.

'Mr Glossop is established in the Moat Room, sir.'

'Where's that?'

'The second door on the floor below this, sir.'

'Right ho, Jeeves. Are the studs in my shirt?'

'Yes, sir.'

'And the links also?'

'Yes, sir.'

'Then push me into it.'

The more I thought about this enterprise which a sense of duty and good citizenship had thrust upon me, the better it seemed to me. I am not a vindictive man, but I felt, as anybody would have felt in my place, that if fellows like young Tuppy are allowed to get away with it the whole fabric of Society and Civilization must inevitably crumble. The task to which I had set myself was one that involved hardship and discomfort, for it meant sitting up till well into the small hours and then padding down a cold corridor, but I did not shrink from it. After all, there is a lot to be said for family tradition. We Woosters did our bit in the Crusades.

It being Christmas Eve, there was, as I had foreseen, a good deal of revelry and what not. First, the village choir surged round and sang carols outside the front door, and then somebody suggested a dance, and after that we hung around chatting of this and that, so that it wasn't till past one that I got to my room. Allowing for everything, it didn't seem that it was going to be safe to start my little expedition till half-past two at the earliest: and I'm bound to say that it was only the utmost resolution that kept me from snuggling into the sheets and calling it a day. I'm not much of a lad now for late hours.

However, by half-past two everything appeared to be quiet. I shook off the mists of sleep, grabbed the good old stick-and-needle and toddled off along the corridor. And presently, pausing outside the Moat Room, I turned the handle, found the door wasn't locked, and went in.

I suppose a burglar – I mean a real professional who works at the job six nights a week all the year round – gets so that finding himself standing in the dark in somebody else's bedroom means absolutely nothing to him. But for a bird like me, who has had no previous experience, there's a lot to be said in favour of washing the whole thing out and closing the door gently and popping back to bed again. It was only by summoning up all the old bull-dog courage of the Woosters, and reminding myself that, if I let this opportunity slip another might never occur, that I managed to stick out what you might call the initial minute of the binge. Then the weakness passed, and Bertram was himself again.

At first when I beetled in, the room had seemed as black as a coal-cellar: but after a bit things began to lighten. The curtains weren't quite drawn over the window and I could see a trifle of the scenery here and there. The bed was opposite the window, with the head against the wall and the end where the feet were jutting out towards where I stood, thus rendering it possible after one had sown the seed, so to speak, to make a quick getaway. There only remained now the rather tricky problem of locating the old hot-water bottle. I mean to say, the one thing you can't do if you want to carry a job like this through with secrecy and dispatch is to stand at the end of a fellow's bed, jabbing the blankets at random with a darning-needle. Before proceeding to anything in the nature of definite steps, it is imperative that you locate the bot.

I was a good deal cheered at this juncture to hear a fruity snore from the direction of the pillows. Reason told me that a bloke who could snore like that wasn't going to be awakened by a trifle. I edged forward and ran a hand in a gingerly sort of way over the coverlet. A moment later I had found the bulge. I steered the good old darning-needle on to it, gripped the stick, and shoved. Then, pulling out the weapon, I sidled towards the door, and in another moment would have been outside, buzzing for home and the good night's rest, when suddenly there was a crash that sent my spine shooting up through the top of my head and the contents of the bed sat up like a jack-in-the-box and said:

'Who's that?'

It just shows how your most careful strategic moves can be the very ones that dish your campaign. In order to facilitate the orderly retreat according to plan I had left the door open, and the beastly thing had slammed like a bomb.

But I wasn't giving much thought to the causes of the explosion, having other things to occupy my mind. What was disturbing me was the discovery that, whoever else the bloke in the bed might be, he was not young Tuppy. Tuppy has one of those high, squeaky voices that sound like the tenor of the village choir failing to hit a high note. This one was something in between the last Trump and a tiger calling for breakfast after being on a diet for a day or two. It was the sort of nasty, rasping voice you hear shouting 'Fore!' when you're one of a slow foursome on the links and are holding up a couple of retired colonels. Among the qualities it lacked were kindliness, suavity and that sort of dove-like cooing note which makes a fellow feel he has found a friend.

I did not linger. Getting swiftly off the mark, I dived for the door-handle and was off and away, banging the door behind me. I may be a chump in many ways, as my Aunt Agatha will freely attest, but I know when and when not to be among those present.

And I was just about to do the stretch of corridor leading to the stairs in a split second under the record time for the course, when something brought me up with a sudden jerk. One moment, I was all dash and fire and speed; the next, an irresistible force had checked me in my stride and was holding me straining at the leash, as it were.

You know, sometimes it seems to me as if Fate were going out of its way to such an extent to snooter you that you wonder if it's worth while continuing to struggle. The night being a trifle chillier than the dickens, I had donned for this expedition a dressing-gown. It was the tail of this infernal garment that had caught in the door and pipped me at the eleventh hour.

The next moment the door had opened, light was streaming through it, and the bloke with the voice had grabbed me by the arm.

It was Sir Roderick Glossop.

*   *   *

The next thing that happened was a bit of a lull in the proceedings. For about three and a quarter seconds or possibly more we just stood there, drinking each other in, so to speak, the old boy still attached with a limpet-like grip to my elbow. If I hadn't been in a dressing-gown and he in pink pyjamas with a blue stripe, and if he hadn't been glaring quite so much as if he were shortly going to commit a murder, the tableau would have looked rather like one of those advertisements you see in the magazines, where the experienced elder is patting the young man's arm, and saying to him, 'My boy, if you subscribe to the Mutt-Jeff Correspondence School of Oswego, Kan., as I did, you may some day, like me, become Third Assistant Vice-President of the Schenectady Consolidated Nail-File and Eyebrow Tweezer Corporation.'

'You!' said Sir Roderick finally. And in this connection I want to state that it's all rot to say you can't hiss a word that hasn't an 's' in it. The way he pushed out that 'You!' sounded like an angry cobra, and I am betraying no secrets when I mention that it did me no good whatsoever.

By rights, I suppose, at this point I ought to have said something. The best I could manage, however, was a faint, soft bleating sound. Even on ordinary social occasions, when meeting this bloke as man to man and with a clear conscience, I could never be completely at my ease: and now those eyebrows seemed to pierce me like a knife.

'Come in here,' he said, lugging me into the room. 'We don't want to wake the whole house. Now,' he said, depositing me on the carpet and closing the door and doing a bit of eyebrow work, 'kindly inform me what is this latest manifestation of insanity?'

It seemed to me that a light and cheery laugh might help the thing along. So I had a pop at one.

'Don't gibber!' said my genial host. And I'm bound to admit that the light and cheery hadn't come out quite as I'd intended.

I pulled myself together with a strong effort.

'Awfully sorry about all this,' I said in a hearty sort of voice. 'The fact is, I thought you were Tuppy.'

'Kindly refrain from inflicting your idiotic slang on me. What do you mean by the adjective "tuppy"?'

'It isn't so much an adjective, don't you know. More of a noun, I should think, if you examine it squarely. What I mean to say is, I thought you were your nephew.'

'You thought I was my nephew? Why should I be my nephew?'

'What I'm driving at is, I thought this was his room.'

'My nephew and I changed rooms. I have a great dislike for sleeping on an upper floor. I am nervous about fire.'

For the first time since this interview had started, I braced up a trifle. The injustice of the whole thing stirred me to such an extent that for a moment I lost that sense of being a toad under the harrow which had been cramping my style up till now. I even went so far as to eye this pink-pyjamaed poltroon with a good deal of contempt and loathing. Just because he had this craven fear of fire and this selfish preference for letting Tuppy be cooked instead of himself should the emergency occur, my nicely reasoned plans had gone up the spout. I gave him a look, and I think I may even have snorted a bit.

'I should have thought that your man-servant would have informed you,' said Sir Roderick, 'that we contemplated making this change. I met him shortly before luncheon and told him to tell you.'

I reeled. Yes, it is not too much to say that I reeled. This extraordinary statement had taken me amidships without any preparation, and it staggered me. That Jeeves had been aware all along that this old crumb would be the occupant of the bed which I was proposing to prod with darning-needles and had let me rush upon my doom without a word of warning was almost beyond belief. You might say I was aghast. Yes, practically aghast.

'You told Jeeves that you were going to sleep in this room?' I gasped.

'I did. I was aware that you and my nephew were on terms of intimacy, and I wished to spare myself the possibility of a visit from you. I confess that it never occurred to me that such a visit was to be anticipated at three o'clock in the morning. What the devil do you mean,' he barked, suddenly hotting up, 'by prowling about the house at this hour? And what is that thing in your hand?'

I looked down, and found that I was still grasping the stick. I give you my honest word that, what with the maelstrom of emotions into which his revelation about Jeeves had cast me, the discovery came as an absolute surprise.

'This?' I said. 'Oh, yes.'

'What do you mean, "Oh, yes"? What is it?'

'Well, it's a long story—'

'We have the night before us.'

'It's this way. I will ask you to picture me some weeks ago, perfectly peaceful and inoffensive, after dinner at the Drones, smoking a thoughtful cigarette and—'

I broke off. The man wasn't listening. He was goggling in a rapt sort of way at the end of the bed, from which there had now begun to drip on to the carpet a series of drops.

'Good heavens!'

'—thoughtful cigarette and chatting pleasantly of this and that—'

I broke off again. He had lifted the sheets and was gazing at the corpse of the hot-water bottle.

'Did you do this?' he said in a low, strangled sort of voice.

'Er – yes. As a matter of fact, yes. I was just going to tell you—'

'And your aunt tried to persuade me that you were not insane!'

'I'm not. Absolutely not. If you'll just let me explain.'

'I will do nothing of the kind.'

'It all began—'

'Silence!'

'Right-ho.'

He did some deep-breathing exercises through the nose.

'My bed is drenched!'

'The way it all began—'

'Be quiet!' He heaved somewhat for awhile. 'You wretched, miserable idiot,' he said, 'kindly inform me which bedroom you are supposed to be occupying?'

'It's on the floor above. The Clock Room.'

'Thank you. I will find it.'

He gave me the eyebrow.

'I propose,' he said, 'to pass the remainder of the night in your room, where, I presume, there is a bed in a condition to be slept in. You may bestow yourself as comfortably as you can here. I will wish you good-night.'

He buzzed off, leaving me flat.

Well, we Woosters are old campaigners. We can take the rough with the smooth. But to say that I liked the prospect now before me would be paltering with the truth. One glance at the bed told me that any idea of sleeping there was out. A goldfish could have done it, but not Bertram. After a bit of a look round, I decided that the best chance of getting a sort of night's rest was to doss as well as

I could in the arm-chair. I pinched a couple of pillows off the bed, shoved the hearth-rug over my knees, and sat down and started counting sheep.

But it wasn't any good. The old lemon was sizzling much too much to admit of anything in the nature of slumber. This hideous revelation of the blackness of Jeeves's treachery kept coming back to me every time I nearly succeeded in dropping off: and, what's more, it seemed to get colder and colder as the long night wore on. I was just wondering if I would ever get to sleep again in this world when a voice at my elbow said 'Good-morning, sir,' and I sat up with a jerk.

I could have sworn I hadn't so much as dozed off for even a minute, but apparently I had. For the curtains were drawn back and daylight was coming in through the window and there was Jeeves standing beside me with a cup of tea on a tray.

'Merry Christmas, sir!'

I reached out a feeble hand for the restoring brew. I swallowed a mouthful or two, and felt a little better. I was aching in every limb and the dome felt like lead, but I was now able to think with a certain amount of clearness, and I fixed the man with a stony eye and prepared to let him have it.

'You think so, do you?' I said. 'Much, let me tell you, depends on what you mean by the adjective "merry". If, moreover, you suppose that it is going to be merry for you, correct that impression. Jeeves,' I said, taking another half-oz of tea and speaking in a cold, measured voice, 'I wish to ask you one question. Did you or did you not know that Sir Roderick Glossop was sleeping in this room last night?'

'Yes, sir.'

'You admit it!'

'Yes, sir.'

'And you didn't tell me!'

'No, sir. I thought it would be more judicious not to do so.'

'Jeeves—'

'If you will allow me to explain, sir.'

'Explain!'

'I was aware that my silence might lead to something in the nature of an embarrassing contretemps, sir—'

'You thought that, did you?'

'Yes, sir.'

'You were a good guesser,' I said, sucking down further Bohea.

'But it seemed to me, sir, that whatever might occur was all for the best.'

I would have put in a crisp word or two here, but he carried on without giving me the opp.

'I thought that possibly, on reflection, sir, your views being what they are, you would prefer your relations with Sir Roderick Glossop and his family to be distant rather than cordial.'

'My views? What do you mean, my views?'

'As regards a matrimonial alliance with Miss Honoria Glossop, sir.'

Something like an electric shock seemed to zip through me. The man had opened up a new line of thought. I suddenly saw what he was driving at, and realized all in a flash that I had been wronging this faithful fellow. All the while I supposed he had been landing me in the soup, he had really been steering me away from it. It was like those stories one used to read as a kid about the traveller going along on a dark night and his dog grabs him by the leg of his trousers and he says 'Down, sir! What are you doing, Rover?' and the dog hangs on and he gets rather hot under the collar and curses a bit but the dog won't let him go and then suddenly the moon shines through the clouds and he finds he's been standing on the edge of a precipice and one more step would have— well, anyway, you get the idea: and what I'm driving at is that much the same sort of thing seemed to have been happening now.

It's perfectly amazing how a fellow will let himself get off his guard and ignore the perils which surround him. I give you my honest word, it had never struck me till this moment that my Aunt Agatha had been scheming to get me in right with Sir Roderick so that I should eventually be received back into the fold, if you see what I mean, and subsequently pushed off on Honoria.

'My God, Jeeves!' I said, paling.

'Precisely, sir.'

'You think there was a risk?'

'I do, sir. A very grave risk.'

A disturbing thought struck me.

'But, Jeeves, on calm reflection won't Sir Roderick have gathered by now that my objective was young Tuppy and that puncturing his hot-water bottle was just one of those things that occur when the Yule-tide spirit is abroad – one of those things that have to be overlooked and taken with the indulgent smile and the fatherly shake of the head? I mean to say, Young Blood and all that sort of thing? What I mean is he'll realize that I wasn't trying to snooter him, and then all the good work will have been wasted.'

'No, sir. I fancy not. That might possibly have been Sir Roderick's mental reaction, had it not been for the second incident.'

'The second incident?'

'During the night, sir, while Sir Roderick was occupying your bed, somebody entered the room, pierced his hot-water bottle with some sharp instrument, and vanished in the darkness.'

I could make nothing of this.

'What! Do you think I walked in my sleep?'

'No, sir. It was young Mr Glossop who did it. I encountered him this morning, sir, shortly before I came here. He was in cheerful spirits and enquired of me how you were feeling about the incident. Not being aware that his victim had been Sir Roderick.'

'But, Jeeves, what an amazing coincidence!'

'Sir?'

'Why, young Tuppy getting exactly the same idea as I did. Or, rather, as Miss Wickham did. You can't say that's not rummy. A miracle, I call it.'

'Not altogether, sir. It appears that he received the suggestion from the young lady.'

'From Miss Wickham?'

'Yes, sir.'

'You mean to say that, after she had put me up to the scheme of puncturing Tuppy's hot-water bottle, she went away and tipped Tuppy off to puncturing mine?'

'Precisely, sir. She is a young lady with a keen sense of humour, sir.'

I sat there, you might say stunned. When I thought how near I had come to offering the heart and hand to a girl capable of double-crossing a strong man's honest love like that, I shivered.

'Are you cold, sir?'

'No, Jeeves. Just shuddering.'

'The occurrence, if I may take the liberty of saying so, sir, will perhaps lend colour to the view which I put forward yesterday that Miss Wickham, though in many respects a charming young lady—'

I raised the hand.

'Say no more, Jeeves,' I replied. 'Love is dead.'

'Very good, sir.'

I brooded for a while.

'You've seen Sir Roderick this morning, then?'

'Yes, sir.'

'How did he seem?'

'A trifle feverish, sir.'

'Feverish?'

'A little emotional, sir. He expressed a strong desire to meet you, sir.'

'What would you advise?'

'If you were to slip out by the back entrance as soon as you are dressed, sir, it would be possible for you to make your way across the field without being observed and reach the village, where you could hire an automobile to take you to London. I could bring on your effects later in your own car.'

'But London, Jeeves? Is any man safe? My Aunt Agatha is in London.'

'Yes, sir.'

'Well, then?'

He regarded me for a moment with a fathomless eye.

'I think the best plan, sir, would be for you to leave England, which is not pleasant at this time of the year, for some little while. I would not take the liberty of dictating your movements, sir, but as you already have accommodation engaged on the Blue Train for Monte Carlo for the day after tomorrow—'

'But you cancelled the booking?'

'No, sir.'

'I thought you had.'

'No, sir.'

'I told you to.'

'Yes, sir. It was remiss of me, but the matter slipped my mind.'

'Oh?'

'Yes, sir.'

'All right, Jeeves. Monte Carlo ho, then.'

'Very good, sir.'

'It's lucky, as things have turned out, that you forgot to cancel that booking.'

'Very fortunate indeed, sir. If you will wait here, sir, I will return to your room and procure a suit of clothes.'

THE GREAT SERMON HANDICAP

YOU CAN always rely on Jeeves. Just as I was wiping the brow and gasping like a stranded goldfish, in he drifted, merry and bright, with the good old tissue-restorers on a tray.

'Jeeves,' I said, 'it's beastly hot.'

'The weather *is* oppressive, sir.'

'Not all the soda, Jeeves.'

'No, sir.'

'London in August,' I said, quaffing deeply of the flowing b., 'rather tends to give me the pip. All my pals are away, most of the theatres are shut, and they're taking up Piccadilly in large spadefuls. The world is empty and smells of burning asphalt. Shift-ho, I think, Jeeves, what?'

'Just as you say, sir. There is a letter on the tray, sir.'

'By Jove, Jeeves, that was practically poetry. Rhymed, did you notice?' I opened the letter. 'I say, this is rather extraordinary.'

'Sir?'

'You know Twing Hall?'

'Yes, sir.'

'Well, Mr Little is there.'

'Indeed, sir?'

'Absolutely in the flesh. He's had to take another of those tutoring jobs.'

I don't know if you remember, but immediately after that fearful mix-up at Goodwood, young Bingo Little, a broken man, had touched me for a tenner and whizzed silently off into the unknown. I had been all over the place ever since, asking mutual friends if they had heard anything of him, but nobody had. And all the time he had been at Twing Hall. Rummy. And I'll tell you why it was rummy. Twing Hall belongs to old Lord Wickhammersley, a great pal of my guv'nor's when he was alive, and I have a standing invitation to pop down there when I like. I generally put in a week or two some time in the summer, and I was thinking of going there before I read the letter.

'And, what's more, Jeeves, my cousin Claude and my cousin Eustace – you remember them?'

'Very vividly, sir.'

'Well, they're down there, too, reading for some exam. or other with the vicar. I used to read with him myself at one time. He's known far and wide as a pretty hot coach for those of fairly feeble intellect. Well, when I tell you he got *me* through Smalls, you'll gather that he's a bit of a hummer. I call this most extraordinary.'

I read the letter again. It was from Eustace. Claude and Eustace are twins, and more or less generally admitted to be the curse of the human race.

'The Vicarage,
'Twing, Glos.

'Dear Bertie,

Do you want to make a bit of money? I hear you had a bad Goodwood, so you probably do. Well, come down here quick and get in on the biggest sporting event of the season. I'll explain when I see you, but you can take it from me it's all right.

'Claude and I are with a reading-party at old Heppenstall's. There are nine of us, not counting your pal Bingo Little, who is tutoring the kid up at the Hall.

'Don't miss this golden opportunity, which may never occur again. Come and join us.

'Yours,
'Eustace.'

I handed this to Jeeves. He studied it thoughtfully.

'What do you make of it? A rummy communication, what?'

'Very high-spirited young gentlemen, sir, Mr Claude and Mr Eustace. Up to some game, I should be disposed to imagine.'

'Yes. But what game, do you think?'

'It is impossible to say, sir. Did you observe that the letter continues over the page?'

'Eh, what?' I grabbed the thing. This was what was on the other side of the last page:

SERMON HANDICAP
RUNNERS AND BETTING
PROBABLE STARTERS.

Rev. Joseph Tucker (Badgwick), scratch.

Rev. Leonard Starkie (Stapleton), scratch.

Rev. Alexander Jones (Upper Bingley), receives three minutes.

Rev. W. Dix (Little Clickton-in-the-Wold), receives five minutes.

Rev. Francis Heppenstall (Twing), receives eight minutes.

Rev. Cuthbert Dibble (Boustead Parva), receives nine minutes.

Rev. Orlo Hough (Boustead Magna), receives nine minutes.

Rev. J. J. Roberts (Fale-by-the-Water), receives ten minutes.

Rev. G. Hayward (Lower Bingley), receives twelve minutes.

Rev. James Bates (Gandle-by-the-Hill), receives fifteen minutes.

The above have arrived.

Prices: 5–2, Tucker, Starkie; 3–1, Jones; 9–2, Dix; 6–1, Heppenstall, Dibble, Hough; 100–8 any other.

It baffled me.

'Do you understand it, Jeeves?'

'No, sir.'

'Well, I think we ought to have a look into it, anyway, what?'

'Undoubtedly, sir.'

'Right-o, then. Pack our spare dickey and a toothbrush in a neat brown-paper parcel, send a wire to Lord Wickhammersley to say we're coming, and buy two tickets on the five-ten at Paddington tomorrow.'

The five-ten was late as usual, and everybody was dressing for dinner when I arrived at the Hall. It was only by getting into my evening things in record time and taking the stairs to the dining-room in a couple of bounds that I managed to dead-heat with the soup. I slid into the vacant chair, and found that I was sitting next to old Wickhammersley's youngest daughter, Cynthia.

'Oh, hallo, old thing,' I said.

Great pals we've always been. In fact there was a time when I had an idea I was in love with Cynthia. However, it blew over. A dashed pretty and lively and attractive girl, mind you, but full of ideals and all that. I may be wronging her, but I have an idea that she's the sort of girl who would want a fellow to carve out a career and what not. I know I've heard her speak favourably of Napoleon. So what with one thing and another the jolly old frenzy sort of petered out, and now we're just pals. I think she's a topper, and she thinks me next door to a looney, so everything's nice and matey.

'Well, Bertie, so you've arrived?'

'Oh, yes, I've arrived. Yes, here I am. I say, I seem to have plunged into the middle of quite a young dinner-party. Who are all these coves?'

'Oh, just people from round about. You know most of them. You remember Colonel Willis, and the Spencers—'

'Of course, yes. And there's old Heppenstall. Who's the other clergyman next to Mrs Spencer?'

'Mr Hayward, from Lower Bingley.'

'What an amazing lot of clergymen there are round here. Why, there's another, next to Mrs Willis.'

'That's Mr Bates, Mr Heppenstall's nephew. He's an assistant-master at Eton. He's down here during the summer holidays, acting as locum tenens for Mr Spettigue, the rector of Gandle-by-the-Hill.'

'I thought I knew his face. He was in his fourth year at Oxford when I was a fresher. Rather a blood. Got his rowing-blue and all that.'

I took another look round the table, and spotted young Bingo.

'Ah, there he is,' I said. 'There's the old egg.'

'There's who?'

'Young Bingo Little. Great pal of mine. He's tutoring your brother, you know.'

'Good gracious! Is he a friend of yours?'

'Rather! Known him all my life.'

'Then tell me, Bertie, is he at all weak in the head?'

'Weak in the head?'

'I don't mean simply because he's a friend of yours. But he's so strange in his manner.'

'How do you mean?'

'Well, he keeps looking at me so oddly.'

'Oddly? How? Give an imitation.'

'I can't in front of all these people.'

'Yes, you can. I'll hold my napkin up.'

'All right, then. Quick. There!'

Considering that she had only about a second and a half to do it in, I must say it was a jolly fine exhibition. She opened her mouth and eyes pretty wide and let her jaw drop sideways, and managed to look so like a dyspeptic calf that I recognized the symptoms immediately.

'Oh, that's all right,' I said. 'No need to be alarmed. He's simply in love with you.'

'In love with me? Don't be absurd.'

'My dear old thing, you don't know young Bingo. He can fall in love with *anybody*.'

'Thank you!'

'Oh, I didn't mean it that way, you know. I don't wonder at his taking to you. Why, I was in love with you myself once.'

'Once? Ah! And all that remains now are the cold ashes? This isn't one of your tactful evenings, Bertie.'

'Well, my dear sweet thing, dash it all, considering that you gave me the bird and nearly laughed yourself into a permanent state of hiccoughs when I asked you—'

'Oh, I'm not reproaching you. No doubt there were faults on both sides. He's very good-looking, isn't he?'

'Good-looking? Bingo? Bingo good-looking? No, I say, come now, really!'

'I mean, compared with some people,' said Cynthia.

Some time after this, Lady Wickhammersley gave the signal for the females of the species to leg it, and they duly stampeded. I didn't get a chance of talking to young Bingo when they'd gone, and later, in the drawing-room, he didn't show up. I found him eventually in his room, lying on the bed with his feet on the rail, smoking a toofah. There was a notebook on the counterpane beside him.

'Hallo, old scream,' I said.

'Hallo, Bertie,' he replied, in what seemed to me rather a moody, distrait sort of manner.

'Rummy finding you down here. I take it your uncle cut off your allowance after that Goodwood binge and you had to take this tutoring job to keep the wolf from the door?'

'Correct,' said young Bingo, tersely.

'Well, you might have let your pals know where you were.'

He frowned darkly.

'I didn't want them to know where I was. I wanted to creep away and hide myself. I've been through a bad time, Bertie, these last weeks. The sun ceased to shine—'

'That's curious. We've had gorgeous weather in London.'

'The birds ceased to sing—'

'What birds?'

'What the devil does it matter what birds?' said young Bingo, with some asperity. 'Any birds. The birds round about here. You don't expect me to specify them by their pet names, do you? I tell you, Bertie, it hit me hard at first, very hard.'

'What hit you?' I simply couldn't follow the blighter.

'Charlotte's calculated callousness.'

'Oh, ah!' I've seen poor old Bingo through so many unsuccessful love-affairs that I'd almost forgotten there was a girl mixed up with that Goodwood business. Of course! Charlotte Corday Rowbotham. And she had given him the raspberry, I remembered now, and gone off with Comrade Butt.

'I went through torments. Recently, however, I've— er— bucked up a bit. Tell me, Bertie, what are you doing down here? I didn't know you knew these people.'

'Me? Why, I've known them since I was a kid.'

Young Bingo put his feet down with a thud.

'Do you mean to say you've known Lady Cynthia all that time?'

'Rather! She can't have been seven when I met her first.'

'Good Lord!' said young Bingo. He looked at me for the first time as though I amounted to something, and swallowed a mouthful of smoke the wrong way. 'I love that girl, Bertie,' he went on, when he'd finished coughing.

'Yes? Nice girl, of course.'

He eyed me with pretty deep loathing.

'Don't speak of her in that horrible casual way. She's an angel. An angel! Was she talking about me at all at dinner, Bertie?'

'Oh, yes.'

'What did she say?'

'I remember one thing. She said she thought you good-looking.'

Young Bingo closed his eyes in a sort of ecstasy. Then he picked up the notebook.

'Pop off now, old man, there's a good chap,' he said, in a hushed, far-away voice. 'I've got a bit of writing to do.'

'Writing?'

'Poetry, if you must know. I wish the dickens,' said young Bingo, not without some bitterness, 'she had been christened something except Cynthia. There isn't a damn word in the language it rhymes with. Ye gods, how I could have spread myself if she had only been called Jane!'

* * *

Bright and early next morning, as I lay in bed blinking at the sunlight on the dressing-table and wondering when Jeeves was going to show up with the cup of tea, a heavy weight descended on my toes, and the voice of young Bingo polluted the air. The blighter had apparently risen with the lark.

'Leave me,' I said, 'I would be alone. I can't see anybody till I've had my tea.'

'When Cynthia smiles,' said young Bingo, 'the skies are blue; the world takes on a roseate hue; birds in the garden trill and sing, and Joy is king of everything, when Cynthia smiles.' He coughed, changing gears. 'When Cynthia frowns—'

'What the devil are you talking about?'

'I'm reading you my poem. The one I wrote to Cynthia last night. I'll go on, shall I?'

'No!'

'No?'

'No. I haven't had my tea.'

At this moment Jeeves came in with the good old beverage, and I sprang on it with a glad cry. After a couple of sips things looked a bit brighter. Even young Bingo didn't offend the eye to quite such an extent. By the time I'd finished the first cup I was a new man, so much so that I not only permitted but encouraged the poor fish to read the rest of the bally thing, and even went so far as to criticize the scansion of the fourth line of the fifth verse. We were still arguing the point when the door burst open and in blew Claude and Eustace. One of the things which discourage me about rural life is the frightful earliness with which events begin to break loose. I've stayed at places in the country where they've jerked me out of the dreamless at about six-thirty to go for a jolly swim in the lake. At Twing, thank heaven, they know me, and let me breakfast in bed.

The twins seemed pleased to see me.

'Good old Bertie!' said Claude.

'Stout fellow!' said Eustace. 'The Rev. told us you had arrived. I thought that letter of mine would fetch you.'

'You can always bank on Bertie,' said Claude. 'A sportsman to the finger-tips. Well, has Bingo told you about it?'

'Not a word. He's been—'

'We've been talking,' said Bingo, hastily, 'of other matters.'

Claude pinched the last slice of thin bread-and-butter, and Eustace poured himself out a cup of tea.

'It's like this, Bertie,' said Eustace, settling down cosily. 'As I told you in my letter, there are nine of us marooned in this desert spot, reading with old Heppenstall. Well, of course, nothing is jollier than sweating up the Classics when it's a hundred in the shade, but there does come a time when you begin to feel the need of a little relaxation; and, by Jove, there are absolutely no facilities for relaxation in this place whatever. And then Steggles got this idea. Steggles is one of our reading-party, and, between ourselves, rather a worm as a general thing. Still, you have to give him credit for getting this idea.'

'What idea?'

'Well, you know how many parsons there are round about here. There are about a dozen hamlets within a radius of six miles, and each hamlet has a church and each church has a parson and each parson preaches a sermon every Sunday. Tomorrow week – Sunday the twenty-third – we're running off the great Sermon Handicap. Steggles is making the book. Each parson is to be clocked by a reliable steward of the course, and the one that preaches the longest sermon wins. Did you study the race-card I sent you?'

'I couldn't understand what it was all about.'

'Why, you chump, it gives the handicaps and the current odds on each starter. I've got another one here, in case you've lost yours. Take a careful look at it. It gives you the thing in a nutshell. Jeeves, old son, do you want a sporting flutter?'

'Sir?' said Jeeves, who had just meandered in with my breakfast.

Claude explained the scheme. Amazing the way Jeeves grasped it right off. But he merely smiled in a paternal sort of way.

'Thank you, sir, I think not.'

'Well, you're with us, Bertie, aren't you?' said Claude, sneaking a roll and a slice of bacon. 'Have you studied that card? Well, tell me, does anything strike you about it?'

Of course it did. It had struck me the moment I looked at it.

'Why, it's a sitter for old Heppenstall,' I said. 'He's got the event sewed up in a parcel. There isn't a parson in the land who could give him eight minutes. Your pal Steggles must be an ass, giving him a handicap like that. Why, in the days when I was with him, old Heppenstall never used to preach under half an hour, and there was one sermon of his on Brotherly Love which lasted forty-five minutes if it lasted a second. Has he lost his vim lately, or what is it?'

'Not a bit of it,' said Eustace. 'Tell him what happened, Claude.'

'Why,' said Claude, 'the first Sunday we were here, we all went to Twing church, and old Heppenstall preached a sermon that was well under twenty minutes. This is what happened. Steggles didn't notice it, and the Rev. didn't notice it himself, but Eustace and I both spotted that he had dropped a chunk of at least half-a-dozen pages out of his sermon-case as he was walking up to the pulpit. He sort of flickered when he got to the gap in the manuscript, but carried on all right, and Steggles went away with the impression that twenty minutes or a bit under was his usual form. The next Sunday we heard Tucker and Starkie, and they both went well over the thirty-five minutes, so Steggles arranged the handicapping as you see on the card. You must come into this, Bertie. You see, the trouble is that I haven't a bean, and Eustace hasn't a bean, and Bingo Little hasn't a bean, so you'll have to finance the syndicate. Don't weaken! It's just putting money in all our pockets. Well, we'll have to be getting back now. Think the thing over, and 'phone me later in the day. And, if you let us down, Bertie, may a cousin's curse— Come on, Claude, old thing.'

The more I studied the scheme, the better it looked.

'How about it, Jeeves?' I said.

Jeeves smiled gently, and drifted out.

'Jeeves has no sporting blood,' said Bingo.

'Well, I have. I'm coming into this. Claude's quite right. It's like finding money by the wayside.'

'Good man!' said Bingo. 'Now I can see daylight. Say I have a tenner on Heppenstall, and cop; that'll give me a bit in hand to back Pink Pill with in the two o'clock at Gatwick the week after next: cop on that, put the pile on Musk-Rat for the one-thirty at Lewes, and there I am with a nice little sum to take to Alexandra Park on September the tenth, when I've got a tip straight from the stable.'

It sounded like a bit out of 'Smiles's Self-Help'.

'And then,' said young Bingo, 'I'll be in a position to go to my uncle and beard him in his lair somewhat. He's quite a bit of a snob, you know, and when he hears that I'm going to marry the daughter of an earl—'

'I say, old man,' I couldn't help saying, 'aren't you looking ahead rather far?'

'Oh, that's all right. It's true nothing's actually settled yet, but she practically told me the other day she was fond of me.'

'What!'

'Well she said that the sort of man she liked was the self-reliant, manly man with strength, good looks, character, ambition, and initiative.'

'Leave me, laddie,' I said. 'Leave me to my fried egg.'

Directly I'd got up I went to the 'phone, snatched Eustace away from his morning's work, and instructed him to put a tenner on the Twing flier at current odds for each of the syndicate; and after lunch Eustace rang me up to say that he had done business at a snappy seven-to-one, the odds having lengthened owing to a rumour in knowledgeable circles that the Rev. was subject to hay-fever and was taking big chances strolling in the paddock behind the Vicarage in the early mornings. And it was dashed lucky, I thought next day, that we had managed to get the money on in time, for on the Sunday morning old Heppenstall fairly took the bit between his teeth, and gave us thirty-six solid minutes on Certain Popular Superstitions. I was sitting next to Steggles in the pew, and I saw him blench visibly. He was a little, rat-faced fellow, with shifty eyes and a suspicious nature. The first thing he did when we emerged into the open air was to announce, formally, that anyone who fancied the Rev. could now be accommodated at fifteen-to-eight on, and he added, in a rather nasty manner, that if he had his way, this sort of in-and-out running would be brought to the attention of the Jockey Club, but that he supposed that there was nothing to be done about it. This ruinous price checked the punters at once, and there was little money in sight. And so matters stood till just after lunch on Tuesday afternoon, when, as I was strolling up and down in front of the house with a cigarette, Claude and Eustace came bursting up the drive on bicycles, dripping with momentous news.

'Bertie,' said Claude, deeply agitated, 'unless we take immediate action and do a bit of quick thinking, we're in the cart.'

'What's the matter?'

'G. Hayward's the matter,' said Eustace, morosely. 'The Lower Bingley starter.'

'We never even considered him,' said Claude. 'Somehow or other, he got overlooked. It's always the way. Steggles overlooked him. We all overlooked him. But Eustace and I happened by the merest fluke to be riding through Lower Bingley this morning, and there was a wedding on at the church, and it suddenly struck us that it wouldn't be a bad move to get a line on G. Hayward's form, in case he might be a dark horse.'

'And it was jolly lucky we did,' said Eustace. 'He delivered an address of twenty-six minutes by Claude's stop-watch. At a village wedding, mark you! What'll he do when he really extends himself!'

'There's only one thing to be done, Bertie,' said Claude. 'You must spring some more funds, so that we can hedge on Hayward and save ourselves.'

'But—'

'Well, it's the only way out.'

'But I say, you know, I hate the idea of all that money we put on Heppenstall being chucked away.'

'What else can you suggest? You don't suppose the Rev. can give this absolute marvel a handicap and win, do you?'

'I've got it!' I said.

'What?'

'I see a way by which we can make it safe for our nominee. I'll pop over this afternoon, and ask him as a personal favour to preach that sermon of his on Brotherly Love on Sunday.'

Claude and Eustace looked at each other, like those chappies in the poem, with a wild surmise.

'It's a scheme,' said Claude.

'A jolly brainy scheme,' said Eustace. 'I didn't think you had it in you, Bertie.'

'But even so,' said Claude, 'fizzer as that sermon no doubt is, will it be good enough in the face of a four-minute handicap?'

'Rather!' I said. 'When I told you it lasted forty-five minutes, I was probably understating it. I should call it – from my recollection of the thing – nearer fifty.'

'Then carry on,' said Claude.

I toddled over in the evening and fixed the thing up. Old Heppenstall was most decent about the whole affair. He seemed pleased and touched that I should have remembered the sermon all these years, and said he had once or twice had an idea of preaching it again, only it had seemed to him, on reflection, that it was perhaps a trifle long for a rustic congregation.

'And in these restless times, my dear Wooster,' he said, 'I fear that brevity in the pulpit is becoming more and more desiderated by even the bucolic church-goer, who one might have supposed would be less afflicted with the spirit of hurry and impatience than his metropolitan brother. I have had many arguments on the subject with my nephew, young Bates, who is taking my old friend Spettigue's cure over at Gandle-by-the-Hill. His view is that a sermon nowadays should be a bright, brisk, straight-from-the-shoulder address, never lasting more than ten or twelve minutes.'

'Long?' I said. 'Why, my goodness! you don't call that Brotherly Love sermon of yours *long*, do you?'

'It takes fully fifty minutes to deliver.'

'Surely not?'

'Your incredulity, my dear Wooster, is extremely flattering – far more flattering, of course, than I deserve. Nevertheless, the facts are as I have stated. You are sure that I would not be well advised to make certain excisions and eliminations? You do not think it would be a good thing to cut, to prune? I might, for example, delete the rather exhaustive excursus into the family life of the early Assyrians?'

'Don't touch a word of it, or you'll spoil the whole thing,' I said earnestly.

'I am delighted to hear you say so, and I shall preach the sermon without fail next Sunday morning.'

What I have always said, and what I always shall say, is that this ante-post betting is a mistake, an error, and a mug's game. You never can tell what's going to happen. If fellows would only stick to the good old S.P. there would be fewer young men go wrong. I'd hardly finished my breakfast on the Saturday morning, when Jeeves came to my bedside to say that Eustace wanted me on the telephone.

'Good Lord, Jeeves, what's the matter, do you think?'

I'm bound to say I was beginning to get a bit jumpy by this time.

'Mr Eustace did not confide in me, sir.'

'Has he got the wind up?'

'Somewhat vertically, sir, to judge by his voice.'

'Do you know what I think, Jeeves? Something's gone wrong with the favourite.'

'Which is the favourite, sir?'

'Mr Heppenstall. He's gone to odds on. He was intending to preach a sermon on Brotherly Love which would have brought him home by lengths. I wonder if anything's happened to him.'

'You could ascertain, sir, by speaking to Mr Eustace on the telephone. He is holding the wire.'

'By Jove, yes!'

I shoved on a dressing-gown, and flew downstairs like a mighty, rushing wind. The moment I heard Eustace's voice I knew we were for it. It had a croak of agony in it.

'Bertie?'

'Here I am.'

'Deuce of a time you've been. Bertie, we're sunk. The favourite's blown up.'

'No!'

'Yes. Coughing in his stable all last night.'

'What!'

'Absolutely! Hay-fever.'

'Oh, my sainted aunt!'

'The doctor is with him now, and it's only a question of minutes before he's officially scratched. That means the curate will show up at the post instead, and he's no good at all. He is being offered at a hundred-to-six, but no takers. What shall we do?'

I had to grapple with the thing for a moment in silence.

'Eustace.'

'Hallo?'

'What can you get on G. Hayward?'

'Only four-to-one now. I think there's been a leak, and Steggles has heard something. The odds shortened late last night in a significant manner.'

'Well, four-to-one will clear us. Put another fiver all round on G. Hayward for the syndicate. That'll bring us out on the right side of the ledger.'

'If he wins.'

'What do you mean? I thought you considered him a cert., bar Heppenstall.'

'I'm beginning to wonder,' said Eustace, gloomily, 'if there's such a thing as a cert. in this world. I'm told the Rev. Joseph Tucker did an extraordinarily fine trial gallop at a mothers' meeting over at Badgwick yesterday. However, it seems our only chance. So-long.'

Not being one of the official stewards, I had my choice of churches next morning, and naturally I didn't hesitate. The only drawback to going to Lower Bingley was that it was ten miles away, which meant an early start, but I borrowed a bicycle from one of the grooms and tooled off. I had only Eustace's word for it that G. Hayward was such a stayer, and it might have been that he had showed too flattering form at that wedding where the twins had heard him preach; but any misgivings I may have had disappeared the moment he got into the pulpit. Eustace had been right. The man was a trier. He was a tall, rangy-looking greybeard, and he went off from the start with a nice, easy action, pausing and clearing his throat at the end of each sentence, and it wasn't five minutes before I realized that here was the winner. His habit of stopping dead and looking round the church at intervals was worth minutes to us, and in the home stretch we gained no little advantage owing to his dropping his pince-nez and having to grope for them. At the twenty-minute mark he had merely settled down. Twenty-five minutes saw him going strong. And when he finally finished with a good burst, the clock showed thirty-five minutes fourteen seconds. With the handicap which he had been given, this seemed to me to make the event easy for him, and it was with much *bonhomie* and good-will to all men that I hopped on to the old bike and started back to the Hall for lunch.

Bingo was talking on the 'phone when I arrived.

'Fine! Splendid! Topping!' he was saying. 'Eh? Oh, we needn't worry about him. Right-o, I'll tell Bertie.' He hung up the receiver and caught sight of me. 'Oh, hallo, Bertie; I was just talking to Eustace. It's all right, old man. The report from Lower Bingley has just got in. G. Hayward romps home.'

'I knew he would. I've just come from there.'

'Oh, were you there? I went to Badgwick. Tucker ran a splendid race, but the handicap was too much for him. Starkie had a sore throat and was nowhere. Roberts, of Fale-by-the-Water, ran third. Good old G. Hayward!' said Bingo, affectionately, and we strolled out on to the terrace.

'Are all the returns in, then?' I asked.

'All except Gandle-by-the-Hill. But we needn't worry about Bates. He never had a chance. By the way, poor old Jeeves loses his tenner. Silly ass!'

'Jeeves? How do you mean?'

'He came to me this morning, just after you had left, and asked me to put a tenner on Bates for him. I told him he was a chump and begged him not to throw his money away, but he would do it.'

'I beg your pardon, sir. This note arrived for you just after you had left the house this morning.'

Jeeves had materialized from nowhere, and was standing at my elbow.

'Eh? What? Note?'

'The Reverend Mr Heppenstall's butler brought it over from the Vicarage, sir. It came too late to be delivered to you at the moment.'

Young Bingo was talking to Jeeves like a father on the subject of betting against the form-book. The yell I gave made him bite his tongue in the middle of a sentence.

'What the dickens is the matter?' he asked, not a little peeved.

'We're dished! Listen to this!'

I read him the note:

> 'The Vicarage,
> 'Twing, Glos.

'My dear Wooster,

As you may have heard, circumstances over which I have no control will prevent my preaching the sermon on Brotherly Love for which you made such a flattering request. I am unwilling, however, that you shall be disappointed, so, if you will attend divine service at Gandle-by-the-Hill this morning, you will hear my sermon preached by young Bates, my nephew. I have lent him the manuscript at his urgent desire, for, between ourselves, there are wheels within wheels. My nephew is one of the candidates for the headmastership of a well-known public school, and the choice has narrowed down between him and one rival.

'Late yesterday evening James received private information that the head of the Board of Governors of the school proposed to sit under him this Sunday in order to judge of the merits of his preaching, a most important item in swaying the Board's choice. I acceded to his plea that I lend him my sermon on

Brotherly Love, of which, like you, he apparently retains a vivid recollection. It would have been too late for him to compose a sermon of suitable length in place of the brief address which – mistakenly, in my opinion – he had designed to deliver to his rustic flock, and I wished to help the boy.

'Trusting that his preaching of the sermon will supply you with as pleasant memories as you say you have of mine, I remain,

'Cordially yours,

'F. Heppenstall.

'P.S. The hay-fever has rendered my eyes unpleasantly weak for the time being, so I am dictating this letter to my butler, Brookfield, who will convey it to you.'

I don't know when I've experienced a more massive silence than the one that followed my reading of this cheery epistle. Young Bingo gulped once or twice, and practically every known emotion came and went on his face. Jeeves coughed one soft, low, gentle cough like a sheep with a blade of grass stuck in its throat, and then stood gazing serenely at the landscape. Finally young Bingo spoke.

'Great Scot!' he whispered, hoarsely. 'An S.P. job!'

'I believe that is the technical term, sir,' said Jeeves.

'So you had inside information, dash it!' said young Bingo.

'Why, yes, sir,' said Jeeves. 'Brookfield happened to mention the contents of the note to me when he brought it. We are old friends.'

Bingo registered grief, anguish, rage, despair, and resentment.

'Well, all I can say,' he cried, 'is that it's a bit thick! Preaching another man's sermon! Do you call that honest? Do you call that playing the game?'

'Well, my dear old thing,' I said, 'be fair. It's quite within the rules. Clergymen do it all the time. They aren't expected always to make up the sermons they preach.'

Jeeves coughed again, and fixed me with an expressionless eye.

'And in the present case, sir, if I may be permitted to take the liberty of making the observation, I think we should make allowances. We should remember that the securing of this headmastership meant everything to the young couple.'

'Young couple! What young couple?'

'The Reverend James Bates, sir, and Lady Cynthia. I am informed by her ladyship's maid that they have been engaged to be married for some weeks – provisionally, so to speak; and his lordship made his consent conditional on Mr Bates securing a really important and remunerative position.'

Young Bingo turned a light green.

'Engaged to be married!'

'Yes, sir.'

There was a silence.

'I think I'll go for a walk,' said Bingo.

'But, my dear old thing,' I said, 'it's just lunch-time. The gong will be going any minute now.'

'I don't want any lunch!' said Bingo.

UNCLE FRED FLITS BY

IN ORDER that they might enjoy their afternoon luncheon coffee in peace, the Crumpet had taken the guest whom he was entertaining at the Drones Club to the smaller and less frequented of the two smoking-rooms. In the other, he explained, though the conversation always touched an exceptionally high level of brilliance, there was apt to be a good deal of sugar thrown about.

The guest said he understood.

'Young blood, eh?'

'That's right. Young blood.'

'And animal spirits.'

'And animal, as you say, spirits,' agreed the Crumpet. 'We get a fairish amount of those here.'

'The complaint, however, is not, I observe, universal.'

'Eh?'

The other drew his host's attention to the doorway, where a young man in form-fitting tweeds had just appeared. The aspect of this young man was haggard. His eyes glared wildly and he sucked at an empty cigarette-holder. If he had a mind, there was something on it. When the Crumpet called to him to come and join the party, he merely shook his head in a distraught sort of way and disappeared, looking like a character out of a Greek tragedy pursued by the Fates.

The Crumpet sighed. 'Poor old Pongo!'

'Pongo?'

'That was Pongo Twistleton. He's all broken up about his Uncle Fred.'

'Dead?'

'No such luck. Coming up to London again tomorrow. Pongo had a wire this morning.'

'And that upsets him?'

'Naturally. After what happened last time.'

'What was that?'

'Ah!' said the Crumpet.

'What happened last time?'

'You may well ask.'

'I do ask.'

'Ah!' said the Crumpet.

Poor old Pongo (said the Crumpet) has often discussed his Uncle Fred with me, and if there weren't tears in his eyes when he did so, I don't know a tear in the eye when I see one. In round numbers the Earl of Ickenham, of Ickenham Hall, Ickenham, Hants, he lives in the country most of the year, but from time to time has a nasty way of slipping his collar and getting loose and descending upon Pongo at his flat in the Albany. And every time he does so, the unhappy young blighter is subjected to some soul-testing experience. Because the trouble with this uncle is that, though sixty if a day, he becomes on arriving in the metropolis as young as he feels – which is, apparently, a youngish twenty-two. I don't know if you happen to know what the word 'excesses' means, but those are what Pongo's Uncle Fred from the country, when in London, invariably commits.

It wouldn't so much matter, mind you, if he would confine his activities to the club premises. We're pretty broad-minded here, and if you stop short of smashing the piano, there isn't much that you can do at the Drones that will cause the raised eyebrow and the sharp intake of breath. The snag is that he will insist on lugging Pongo out in the open and there, right in the public eye, proceeding to step high, wide and plentiful.

So when, on the occasion to which I allude, he stood pink and genial on Pongo's hearth-rug, bulging with Pongo's lunch and wreathed in the smoke of one of Pongo's cigars, and said: 'And now, my boy, for a pleasant and instructive afternoon,' you will readily understand why the unfortunate young clam gazed at him as he would have gazed at two-penn'orth of dynamite, had he discovered it lighting up in his presence.

'A what?' he said, giving at the knees and paling beneath the tan a bit.

'A pleasant and instructive afternoon,' repeated Lord Ickenham, rolling the words round his tongue. 'I propose that you place yourself in my hands and leave the programme entirely to me.'

Now, owing to Pongo's circumstances being such as to neces-sitate his getting into the aged relative's ribs at intervals and shaking him down for an occasional much-needed tenner or what not, he isn't in a position to use the iron hand with the old buster. But at these words he displayed a manly firmness.

'You aren't going to get me to the dog races again.'

'No, no.'

'You remember what happened last June.'

'Quite,' said Lord Ickenham, 'quite. Though I still think that a wiser magistrate would have been content with a mere reprimand.'

'And I won't—'

'Certainly not. Nothing of that kind at all. What I propose to do this afternoon is to take you to visit the home of your ancestors.'

Pongo did not get this.

'I thought Ickenham was the home of my ancestors.'

'It is one of the homes of your ancestors. They also resided rather nearer the heart of things, at a place called Mitching Hill.'

'Down in the suburbs, do you mean?'

'The neighbourhood is now suburban, true. It is many years since the meadows where I sported as a child were sold and cut up into building lots. But when I was a boy Mitching Hill was open country. It was a vast, rolling estate belonging to your great-uncle, Marmaduke, a man with whiskers of a nature which you with your pure mind would scarcely credit, and I have long felt a sentimental urge to see what the hell the old place looks like now. Perfectly foul, I expect. Still, I think we should make the pious pilgrimage.'

Pongo absolutely-ed heartily. He was all for the scheme. A great weight seemed to have rolled off his mind. The way he looked at it was that even an uncle within a short jump of the loony bin couldn't very well get into much trouble in a suburb. I mean, you know what suburbs are. They don't, as it were, offer the scope. One follows his reasoning, of course.

'Fine!' he said. 'Splendid! Topping!'

'Then put on your hat and rompers, my boy,' said Lord Ickenham, 'and let us be off. I fancy one gets there by omnibuses and things.'

Well, Pongo hadn't expected much in the way of mental uplift from the sight of Mitching Hill, and he didn't get it. Alighting from the bus, he tells me, you found yourself in the middle of rows and rows of semi-detached villas, all looking exactly alike, and you went on and you came to more semi-detached villas, and those all looked exactly alike, too. Nevertheless, he did not repine. It was one of those early spring days which suddenly change to mid-winter and he had come out without his overcoat, and it looked like rain and he hadn't an umbrella, but despite this his mood was one of sober ecstasy. The hours were passing and his uncle had not yet made a goat of himself. At the Dog Races the other had been in the hands of the constabulary in the first ten minutes.

It began to seem to Pongo that with any luck he might be able to keep the old blister pottering harmlessly about here till nightfall, when he could shoot a bit of dinner into him and put him to bed. And as Lord Ickenham had specifically stated that his wife, Pongo's Aunt Jane, had expressed her intention of scalping him with a blunt knife if he wasn't back at the Hall by lunch time on the morrow, it really looked as if he might get through this visit without perpetrating a single major outrage on the public weal. It is rather interesting to note that as he thought this Pongo smiled, because it was the last time he smiled that day.

All this while, I should mention, Lord Ickenham had been stopping at intervals like a pointing dog and saying that it must have been just about here that he plugged the gardener in the trousers seat with his bow and arrow and that over there he had been sick after his first cigar, and he now paused in front of a villa which for some unknown reason called itself The Cedars. His face was tender and wistful.

'On this very spot, if I am not mistaken,' he said, heaving a bit of a sigh, 'on this very spot, fifty years ago come Lammas Eve, I…Oh, blast it!'

The concluding remark had been caused by the fact that the rain, which had held off until now, suddenly began to buzz down like a shower-bath. With no further words, they leaped into the porch of the villa and there took shelter, exchanging glances with a grey parrot which hung in a cage in the window.

Not that you could really call it shelter. They were protected from above all right, but the moisture was now falling with a sort of swivel action, whipping in through the sides of the porch and tickling them up properly. And it was just after Pongo had turned up his collar and was huddling against the door that the door gave way. From the fact that a female of general-servant aspect was standing there he gathered that his uncle must have rung the bell.

This female wore a long mackintosh, and Lord Ickenham beamed upon her with a fairish spot of suavity.

'Good afternoon,' he said.

The female said good afternoon.

'The Cedars?'

The female said yes, it was The Cedars.

'Are the old folks at home?'

The female said there was nobody at home.

'Ah? Well, never mind. I have come,' said Lord Ickenham, edging in, 'to clip the parrot's claws. My assistant, Mr Walkinshaw, who applies the anaesthetic,' he added, indicating Pongo with a gesture.

'Are you from the bird shop?'

'A very happy guess.'

'Nobody told me you were coming.'

'They keep things from you, do they?' said Lord Ickenham, sympathetically. 'Too bad.'

Continuing to edge, he had got into the parlour by now, Pongo following in a sort of dream and the female following Pongo.

'Well, I suppose it's all right,' she said. 'I was just going out. It's my afternoon.'

'Go out,' said Lord Ickenham cordially. 'By all means go out. We will leave everything in order.'

And presently the female, though still a bit on the dubious side, pushed off, and Lord Ickenham lit the gas-fire and drew a chair up.

'So here we are, my boy,' he said. 'A little tact, a little address, and here we are, snug and cosy and not catching our deaths of cold. You'll never go far wrong if you leave things to me.'

'But, dash it, we can't stop here,' said Pongo.

Lord Ickenham raised his eyebrows.

'Not stop here? Are you suggesting that we go out into that rain? My dear lad, you are not aware of the grave issues involved. This morning, as I was leaving home, I had a rather painful disagreement with your aunt. She said the weather was treacherous and wished me to take my woolly muffler. I replied that the weather was not treacherous and that I would be dashed if I took my woolly muffler. Eventually, by the exercise of an iron will, I had my way, and I ask you, my dear boy, to envisage what will happen if I return with a cold in the head. I shall sink to the level of a fifth-class power. Next time I came to London, it would be with a liver pad and a respirator. No! I shall remain here, toasting my toes at this really excellent fire. I had no idea that a gas-fire radiated such warmth. I feel all in a glow.'

So did Pongo. His brow was wet with honest sweat. He is reading for the Bar, and while he would be the first to admit that he hasn't yet got a complete toe-hold on the Law of Great Britain he had a sort of notion that oiling into a perfect stranger's semi-detached villa on the pretext of pruning the parrot was a tort or misdemeanour, if not actual barratry or soccage in fief or something like that. And apart from the legal aspect of the matter there was the embarrassment of the thing. Nobody is more of a whale on correctness and not doing what's not done than Pongo, and the situation in which he now found himself caused him to chew the lower lip and, as I say, perspire a goodish deal.

'But suppose the blighter who owns this ghastly house comes back?' he asked. 'Talking of envisaging things, try that one over on your pianola.'

And, sure enough, as he spoke, the front door bell rang.

'There!' said Pongo.

'Don't say "There!" my boy,' said Lord Ickenham reprovingly. 'It's the sort of thing your aunt says. I see no reason for alarm. Obviously this is some casual caller. A ratepayer would have used his latchkey. Glance cautiously out of the window and see if you can see anybody.'

'It's a pink chap,' said Pongo, having done so.

'How pink?'

'Pretty pink.'

'Well, there you are, then. I told you so. It can't be the big chief. The sort of fellows who own houses like this are pale and sallow, owing to working in offices all day. Go and see what he wants.'

'You go and see what he wants.'

'We'll both go and see what he wants,' said Lord Ickenham.

So they went and opened the front door, and there, as Pongo had said, was a pink chap. A small young pink chap, a bit moist about the shoulder-blades.

'Pardon me,' said this pink chap, 'is Mr Roddis in?'

'No,' said Pongo.

'Yes,' said Lord Ickenham. 'Don't be silly, Douglas — of course I'm in. I am Mr Roddis,' he said to the pink chap. 'This, such as he is, is my son Douglas. And you?'

'Name of Robinson.'

'What about it?'

'My name's Robinson.'

'Oh, *your* name's Robinson? Now we've got it straight. Delighted to see you, Mr Robinson. Come right in and take your boots off.'

They all trickled back to the parlour, Lord Ickenham pointing out objects of interest by the wayside to the chap, Pongo gulping for air a bit and trying to get himself abreast of this new twist in the scenario. His heart was becoming more and more bowed down with weight of woe. He hadn't liked being Mr Walkinshaw, the anaesthetist, and he didn't like it any better being Roddis Junior. In brief, he feared the worst. It was only too plain to him by now that his uncle had got it thoroughly up his nose and had settled down to one of his big afternoons, and he was asking himself, as he had so often asked himself before, what would the harvest be?

Arrived in the parlour, the pink chap proceeded to stand on one leg and look coy.

'Is Julia here?' he asked, simpering a bit, Pongo says.

'Is she?' said Lord Ickenham to Pongo.

'No,' said Pongo.

'No,' said Lord Ickenham.

'She wired me she was coming here today.'

'Ah, then we shall have a bridge four.'

The pink chap stood on the other leg.

'I don't suppose you've ever met Julia. Bit of trouble in the family, she gave me to understand.'

'It is often the way.'

'The Julia I mean is your niece Julia Parker. Or, rather, your wife's niece Julia Parker.'

'Any niece of my wife is a niece of mine,' said Lord Ickenham heartily. 'We share and share alike.'

'Julia and I want to get married.'

'Well, go ahead.'

'But they won't let us.'

'Who won't?'

'Her mother and father. And Uncle Charlie Parker and Uncle Henry Parker and the rest of them. They don't think I'm good enough.'

'The morality of the modern young man is notoriously lax.'

'Class enough, I mean. They're a haughty lot.'

'What makes them haughty? Are they earls?'

'No, they aren't earls.'

'Then why the devil,' said Lord Ickenham warmly, 'are they haughty? Only earls have a right to be haughty. Earls are hot stuff. When you get an earl, you've got something.'

'Besides, we've had words. Me and her father. One thing led to another, and in the end I called him a perishing old— Coo!' said the pink chap, breaking off suddenly.

He had been standing by the window, and he now leaped lissomely into the middle of the room, causing Pongo, whose nervous system was by this time definitely down among the wines and spirits and who hadn't been expecting this *adagio* stuff, to bite his tongue with some severity.

'They're on the doorstep! Julia and her mother and father. I didn't know they were all coming.'

'You do not wish to meet them?'

'No, I don't!'

'Then duck behind the settee, Mr Robinson,' said Lord Ickenham, and the pink chap, weighing the advice and finding it good, did so. And as he disappeared the door bell rang.

Once more, Lord Ickenham led Pongo out into the hall.

'I say!' said Pongo, and a close observer might have noted that he was quivering like an aspen.

'Say on, my dear boy.'

'I mean to say, what?'

'What?'

'You aren't going to let these bounders in, are you?'

'Certainly,' said Lord Ickenham. 'We Roddises keep open house. And as they are presumably aware that Mr Roddis has no son, I think we had better return to the old layout. You are the local vet, my boy, come to minister to my parrot. When I return, I should like to find you by the cage, staring at the bird in a scientific manner. Tap your teeth from time to time with a pencil and try to smell of iodoform. It will help to add conviction.'

So Pongo shifted back to the parrot's cage and stared so earnestly that it was only when a voice said 'Well!' that he became aware that there was anybody in the room. Turning, he perceived that Hampshire's leading curse had come back, bringing the gang.

It consisted of a stern, thin, middle-aged woman, a middle-aged man and a girl.

You can generally accept Pongo's estimate of girls, and when he says that this one was a pippin one knows that he uses the term in its most exact sense. She was about nineteen, he thinks, and she wore a black beret, a dark-green leather coat, a shortish tweed skirt, silk stockings and high-heeled shoes. Her eyes were large and lustrous and her face like a dewy rosebud at daybreak on a June morning. So Pongo tells me. Not that I suppose he has ever seen a rosebud at daybreak on a June morning, because it's generally as much as you can do to lug him out of bed in time for nine-thirty breakfast. Still, one gets the idea.

'Well,' said the woman, 'you don't know who I am, I'll be bound. I'm Laura's sister Connie. This is Claude, my husband. And this is my daughter Julia. Is Laura in?'

'I regret to say, no,' said Lord Ickenham.

The woman was looking at him as if he didn't come up to her specifications.

'I thought you were younger,' she said.

'Younger than what?' said Lord Ickenham.

'Younger than you are.'

'You can't be younger than you are, worse luck,' said Lord Ickenham. 'Still, one does one's best, and I am bound to say that of recent years I have made a pretty good go of it.'

The woman caught sight of Pongo, and he didn't seem to please her, either.

'Who's that?'

'The local vet, clustering round my parrot.'

'I can't talk in front of him.'

'It is quite all right,' Lord Ickenham assured her. 'The poor fellow is stone deaf.'

And with an imperious gesture at Pongo, as much as to bid him stare less at girls and more at parrots, he got the company seated.

'Now, then,' he said.

There was silence for a moment, then a sort of muffled sob, which Pongo thinks proceeded from the girl. He couldn't see, of course, because his back was turned and he was looking at the parrot, which looked back at him – most offensively, he says, as parrots will, using one eye only for the purpose. It also asked him to have a nut.

The woman came into action again.

'Although,' she said, 'Laura never did me the honour to invite me to her wedding, for which reason I have not communicated with her for five years, necessity compels me to cross her threshold today. There comes a time when differences must be forgotten and relatives must stand shoulder to shoulder.'

'I see what you mean,' said Lord Ickenham. 'Like the boys of the old brigade.'

'What I say is, let bygones be bygones. I would not have intruded on you, but needs must. I disregard the past and appeal to your sense of pity.'

The thing began to look to Pongo like a touch, and he is convinced that the parrot thought so, too, for it winked and cleared its throat. But they were both wrong. The woman went on.

'I want you and Laura to take Julia into your home for a week or so, until I can make other arrangements for her. Julia is studying the piano, and she sits for her examination in two weeks' time, so until then she must remain in London. The trouble is, she has fallen in love. Or thinks she has.'

'I know I have,' said Julia.

Her voice was so attractive that Pongo was compelled to slew round and take another look at her. Her eyes, he says, were shining like twin stars and there was a sort of Soul's Awakening expression on her face, and what the dickens there was in a pink chap like the pink chap, who even as pink chaps go wasn't much of a pink chap, to make her look like that, was frankly, Pongo says, more than he could understand. The thing baffled him. He sought in vain for a solution.

'Yesterday, Claude and I arrived in London from our Bexhill home to give Julia a pleasant surprise. We stayed, naturally, in the boarding-house where she has been living for the past six weeks. And what do you think we discovered?'

'Insects.'

'Not insects. A letter. From a young man. I found to my horror that a young man of whom I knew nothing was arranging to marry my daughter. I sent for him immediately, and found him to be quite impossible. He jellies eels!'

'Does what?'

'He is an assistant at a jellied eel shop.'

'But surely,' said Lord Ickenham, 'that speaks well for him. The capacity to jelly an eel seems to me to argue intelligence of a high order. It isn't everybody who can do it, by any means. I know if someone came to me and said "Jelly this eel!" I should be non-plussed. And so, or I am very much mistaken, would Ramsay MacDonald and Winston Churchill.'

The woman did not seem to see eye to eye.

'Tchah!' she said. 'What do you suppose my husband's brother Charlie Parker would say if I allowed his niece to marry a man who jellies eels?'

'Ah!' said Claude, who, before we go any further, was a tall, drooping bird with a red soup-strainer moustache.

'Or my husband's brother, Henry Parker.'

'Ah!' said Claude. 'Or Cousin Alf Robbins, for that matter.'

'Exactly. Cousin Alfred would die of shame.'

The girl Julia hiccoughed passionately, so much so that Pongo says it was all he could do to stop himself nipping across and taking her hand in his and patting it.

'I've told you a hundred times, mother, that Wilberforce is only jellying eels till he finds something better.'

'What is better than an eel?' asked Lord Ickenham, who had been following this discussion with the close attention it deserved. 'For jellying purposes, I mean.'

'He is ambitious. It won't be long,' said the girl, 'before Wilberforce suddenly rises in the world.'

She never spoke a truer word. At this very moment, up he came from behind the settee like a leaping salmon.

'Julia!' he cried.

'Wilby!' yipped the girl.

And Pongo says he never saw anything more sickening in his life than the way she flung herself into the blighter's arms and clung there like the ivy on the old garden wall. It wasn't that he had anything specific against the pink chap, but this girl had made a deep impression on him and he resented her glueing herself to another in this manner.

Julia's mother, after just that brief moment which a woman needs in which to recover from her natural surprise at seeing eel-jelliers pop up from behind sofas, got moving and plucked her away like a referee breaking a couple of welter-weights.

'Julia Parker,' she said, 'I'm ashamed of you!'

'So am I,' said Claude.

'I blush for you.'

'Me, too,' said Claude. 'Hugging and kissing a man who called your father a perishing old bottle-nosed Gawd-help-us.'

'I think,' said Lord Ickenham, shoving his oar in, 'that before proceeding any further we ought to go into that point. If he called you a perishing old bottle-nosed Gawd-help-us, it seems to me that the first thing to do is to decide whether he was right, and frankly, in my opinion…'

'Wilberforce will apologize.'

'Certainly I'll apologize. It isn't fair to hold a remark passed in the heat of the moment against a chap…'

'Mr Robinson,' said the woman, 'you know perfectly well that whatever remarks you may have seen fit to pass don't matter one way or the other. If you were listening to what I was saying you will understand…'

'Oh, I know, I know. Uncle Charlie Parker and Uncle Henry Parker and Cousin Alf Robbins and all that. Pack of snobs!'

'What!'

'Haughty, stuck-up snobs. Them and their class distinction. Think themselves everybody just because they've got money. I'd like to know how they got it.'

'What do you mean by that?'

'Never mind what I mean.'

'If you are insinuating—'

'Well, of course, you know, Connie,' said Lord Ickenham mildly, 'he's quite right. You can't get away from that.'

I don't know if you have ever seen a bull-terrier embarking on a scrap with an Airedale and just as it was getting down nicely to its work suddenly having an unexpected Kerry Blue sneak up behind it and bite it in the rear quarters. When this happens, it lets go of the Airedale and swivels round and fixes the butting-in animal with a pretty nasty eye. It was exactly the same with the woman Connie when Lord Ickenham spoke these words.

'What!'

'I was only wondering if you had forgotten how Charlie Parker made his pile.'

'What are you talking about?'

'I know it is painful,' said Lord Ickenham, 'and one doesn't mention it as a rule, but, as we are on the subject, you must admit that lending money at two hundred and fifty per cent interest is not done in the best circles. The judge, if you remember, said so at the trial.'

'I never knew that!' cried the girl Julia.

'Ah,' said Lord Ickenham. 'You kept it from the child? Quite right, quite right.'

'It's a lie!'

'And when Henry Parker had all that fuss with the bank it was touch and go they didn't send him to prison. Between ourselves, Connie, has a bank official, even a brother of your husband, any right to sneak fifty pounds from the till in order to put it on a hundred to one shot for the Grand National? Not quite playing the game, Connie. Not the straight bat. Henry, I grant you, won five thousand of the best and never looked back afterwards, but, though we applaud his judgement of form, we must surely look askance at his financial methods. As for Cousin Alf Robbins...'

The woman was making rummy stuttering sounds. Pongo tells me he once had a Pommery Seven which used to express itself in much the same way if you tried to get it to take a hill on high. A sort of mixture of gurgles and explosions.

'There is not a word of truth in this,' she gasped at length, having managed to get the vocal cords disentangled. 'Not a single word. I think you must have gone mad.'

Lord Ickenham shrugged his shoulders.

'Have it your own way, Connie. I was only going to say that, while the jury were probably compelled on the evidence submitted to them to give Cousin Alf Robbins the benefit of the doubt when charged with smuggling dope, everybody knew that he had been doing it for years. I am not blaming him, mind you. If a man can smuggle cocaine and get away with it, good luck to him, say I. The only point I am trying to make is that we are hardly a family that can afford to put on dog and sneer at honest suitors for our daughters' hands. Speaking for myself, I consider that we are very lucky to have the chance of marrying even into eel-jellying circles.'

'So do I,' said Julia firmly.

'You don't believe what this man is saying?'

'I believe every word.'

'So do I,' said the pink chap.

The woman snorted. She seemed overwrought.

'Well,' she said, 'goodness knows I have never liked Laura, but I would never have wished her a husband like you!'

'Husband?' said Lord Ickenham, puzzled. 'What gives you the impression that Laura and I are married?'

There was a weighty silence, during which the parrot threw out a general invitation to join it in a nut. Then the girl Julia spoke.

'You'll have to let me marry Wilberforce now,' she said. 'He knows too much about us.'

'I was rather thinking that myself,' said Lord Ickenham. 'Seal his lips, I say.'

'You wouldn't mind marrying into a low family, would you, darling?' asked the girl, with a touch of anxiety.

'No family could be too low for me, dearest, if it was yours,' said the pink chap.

'After all, we needn't see them.'

'That's right.'

'It isn't one's relations that matter: it's oneselves.'

'That's right, too.'

'Wilby!'

'Julia!'

They repeated the old ivy on the garden wall act. Pongo says he didn't like it any better than the first time, but his distaste wasn't in it with the woman Connie's.

'And what, may I ask,' she said, 'do you propose to marry on?'

This seemed to cast a damper. They came apart. They looked at each other. The girl looked at the pink chap, and the pink chap looked at the girl. You could see that a jarring note had been struck.

'Wilberforce is going to be a very rich man some day.'

'Some day!'

'If I had a hundred pounds,' said the pink chap, 'I could buy a half-share in one of the best milk walks in South London tomorrow.'

'If!' said the woman.

'Ah!' said Claude.

'Where are you going to get it?'

'Ah!' said Claude.

'Where,' repeated the woman, plainly pleased with the snappy crack and loath to let it ride without an encore, 'are you going to get it?'

'That,' said Claude, 'is the point. Where are you going to get a hundred pounds?'

'Why, bless my soul,' said Lord Ickenham jovially, 'from me, of course. Where else?'

And before Pongo's bulging eyes he fished out from the recesses of his costume a crackling bundle of notes and handed it over. And the agony of realizing that the old bounder had had all that stuff on him all this time and that he hadn't touched him for so much as a tithe of it was so keen, Pongo says, that before he knew what he was doing he had let out a sharp, whinnying cry which rang through the room like the yowl of a stepped-on puppy.

'Ah,' said Lord Ickenham. 'The vet wishes to speak to me. Yes, vet?'

This seemed to puzzle the cerise bloke a bit.

'I thought you said this chap was your son.'

'If I had a son,' said Lord Ickenham, a little hurt, 'he would be a good deal better-looking than that. No, this is the local veterinary surgeon. I may have said I *looked* on him as a son. Perhaps that was what confused you.'

He shifted across to Pongo and twiddled his hands enquiringly. Pongo gaped at him, and it was not until one of the hands caught him smartly in the lower ribs that he remembered he was deaf and started to twiddle back. Considering that he wasn't supposed to be dumb, I can't see why he should have twiddled, but no doubt there are moments when twiddling is about all a fellow feels himself equal to. For what seemed to him at least ten hours Pongo had been undergoing great mental stress, and one can't blame him for not being chatty. Anyway, be that as it may, he twiddled.

'I cannot quite understand what he says,' announced Lord Ickenham at length, 'because he sprained a finger this morning and that makes him stammer. But I gather that he wishes to have a word with me in private. Possibly my parrot has got something the matter with it which he is reluctant to mention even in sign language in front of a young unmarried girl. You know what parrots are. We will step outside.'

'*We* will step outside,' said Wilberforce.

'Yes,' said the girl Julia. 'I feel like a walk.'

'And you,' said Lord Ickenham to the woman Connie, who was looking like a female Napoleon at Moscow. 'Do you join the hikers?'

'I shall remain and make myself a cup of tea. You will not grudge us a cup of tea, I hope?'

'Far from it,' said Lord Ickenham cordially. 'This is Liberty Hall. Stick around and mop it up till your eyes bubble.'

Outside, the girl, looking more like a dewy rosebud than ever, fawned on the old buster pretty considerably.

'I don't know how to thank you!' she said. And the pink chap said he didn't, either.

'Not at all, my dear, not at all,' said Lord Ickenham.

'I think you're simply wonderful.'

'No, no.'

'You are. Perfectly marvellous.'

'Tut, tut,' said Lord Ickenham. 'Don't give the matter another thought.'

He kissed her on both cheeks, the chin, the forehead, the right eyebrow, and the tip of the nose, Pongo looking on the while in a baffled and discontented manner. Everybody seemed to be kissing this girl except him.

Eventually the degrading spectacle ceased and the girl and the pink chap shoved off, and Pongo was enabled to take up the matter of that hundred quid.

'Where,' he asked, 'did you get all that money?'

'Now, where did I?' mused Lord Ickenham. 'I know your aunt gave it to me for some purpose. But what? To pay some bill or other, I rather fancy.'

This cheered Pongo up slightly.

'She'll give you the devil when you get back,' he said, with not a little relish. 'I wouldn't be in your shoes for something. When you tell Aunt Jane,' he said, with confidence, for he knew his Aunt Jane's emotional nature, 'that you slipped her entire roll to a girl, and explain, as you will have to explain, that she was an extraordinarily pretty girl – a girl, in fine, who looked like something out of a beauty chorus of the better sort, I should think she would pluck down one of the ancestral battle-axes from the wall and jolly well strike you on the mazzard.'

'Have no anxiety, my dear boy,' said Lord Ickenham. 'It is like your kind heart to be so concerned, but have no anxiety. I shall tell her that I was compelled to give the money to you to enable you to buy back some compromising letters from a Spanish *demi-mondaine*. She will scarcely be able to blame me for rescuing a fondly loved nephew from the clutches of an adventuress. It may be that she will feel a little vexed with you for a while, and that you may have to allow a certain time to elapse before you visit Ickenham again, but then I shan't be wanting you at Ickenham till the ratting season starts, so all is well.'

At this moment, there came toddling up to the gate of The Cedars a large red-faced man. He was just going in when Lord Ickenham hailed him.

'Mr Roddis?'

'Hey?'

'Am I addressing Mr Roddis?'

'That's me.'

'I am Mr J. G. Bulstrode from down the road,' said Lord Ickenham. 'This is my sister's husband's brother, Percy Frensham, in the lard and imported-butter business.'

The red-faced bird said he was pleased to meet them. He asked Pongo if things were brisk in the lard and imported-butter business, and Pongo said they were all right, and the red-faced bird said he was glad to hear it.

'We have never met, Mr Roddis,' said Lord Ickenham, 'but I think it would be only neighbourly to inform you that a short while ago I observed two suspicious-looking persons in your house.'

'In my house? How on earth did they get there?'

'No doubt through a window at the back. They looked to me like cat burglars. If you creep up, you may be able to see them.'

The red-faced bird crept, and came back not exactly foaming at the mouth but with the air of a man who for two pins would so foam.

'You're perfectly right. They're sitting in my parlour as cool as dammit, swigging my tea and buttered toast.'

'I thought as much.'

'And they've opened a pot of my raspberry jam.'

'Ah, then you will be able to catch them red-handed. I should fetch a policeman.'

'I will. Thank you, Mr Bulstrode.'

'Only too glad to have been able to render you this little service, Mr Roddis,' said Lord Ickenham. 'Well, I must be moving. I have an appointment. Pleasant after the rain, is it not? Come, Percy.'

He lugged Pongo off.

'So that,' he said, with satisfaction, 'is that. On these visits of mine to the metropolis, my boy, I always make it my aim, if possible, to spread sweetness and light. I look about me, even in a foul hole like Mitching Hill, and I ask myself – How can I leave this foul hole a better and happier foul hole than I found it? And if I see a chance, I grab it. Here is our omnibus. Spring aboard, my boy, and on our way home we will be sketching out rough plans for the evening. If the old Leicester Grill is still in existence, we might look in there. It must be fully thirty-five years since I was last thrown out of the Leicester Grill. I wonder who is the bouncer there now.'

Such (concluded the Crumpet) is Pongo Twistleton's Uncle Fred from the country, and you will have gathered by now a rough notion of why it is that when a telegram comes announcing his impending arrival in the great city Pongo blenches to the core and calls for a couple of quick ones.

The whole situation, Pongo says, is very complex. Looking at it from one angle, it is fine that the man lives in the country most of the year. If he didn't, he would have him in his midst all the time. On the other hand, by living in the country he generates, as it were, a store of loopiness which expends itself with frightful violence on his rare visits to the centre of things.

What it boils down to is this – Is it better to have a loopy uncle whose loopiness is perpetually on tap but spread out thin, so to speak, or one who lies low in distant Hants for three hundred and sixty days in the year and does himself proud in London for the other five? Dashed moot, of course, and Pongo has never been able to make up his mind on the point.

Naturally, the ideal thing would be if someone would chain the old hound up permanently and keep him from Jan. One to Dec. Thirty-one where he wouldn't do any harm – viz. among the spuds and tenantry. But this, Pongo admits, is a Utopian dream. Nobody could work harder to that end than his Aunt Jane, and she has never been able to manage it.

THE CRIME WAVE AT BLANDINGS

THE DAY on which Lawlessness reared its ugly head at Blandings Castle was one of singular beauty. The sun shone down from a sky of cornflower blue, and what one would really like would be to describe in leisurely detail the ancient battlements, the smooth green lawns, the rolling parkland, the majestic trees, the well-bred bees and the gentlemanly birds on which it shone.

But those who read thrillers are an impatient race. They chafe at scenic rhapsodies and want to get on to the rough stuff. When, they ask, did the dirty work start? Who were mixed up in it? Was there blood, and, if so, how much? And – most particularly – where was everybody and what was everybody doing at whatever time it was? The chronicler who wishes to grip must supply this information at the earliest possible moment.

The wave of crime, then, which was to rock one of Shropshire's stateliest homes to its foundations broke out towards the middle of a fine summer afternoon, and the persons involved in it were disposed as follows:

Clarence, ninth Earl of Emsworth, the castle's owner and overlord, was down in the potting-shed, in conference with Angus McAllister, his head gardener, on the subject of sweet peas.

His sister, Lady Constance, was strolling on the terrace with a swarthy young man in spectacles, whose name was Rupert Baxter and who had at one time been Lord Emsworth's private secretary.

Beach, the butler, was in a deck-chair outside the back premises of the house, smoking a cigar and reading Chapter Sixteen of *The Man With The Missing Toe*.

George, Lord Emsworth's grandson, was prowling through the shrubbery with the airgun which was his constant companion.

Jane, his lordship's niece, was in the summer-house by the lake.

And the sun shone serenely down – on, as we say, the lawns, the battlements, the trees, the bees, the best type of bird and the rolling parkland.

* * *

Presently Lord Emsworth left the potting-shed and started to wander towards the house. He had never felt happier. All day his mood had been one of perfect contentment and tranquillity, and for once in a way Angus McAllister had done nothing to disturb it. Too often, when you tried to reason with that human mule, he had a way of saying 'Mph' and looking Scotch and then saying 'Grmph' and looking Scotch again, and after that just fingering his beard and looking Scotch without speaking, which was intensely irritating to a sensitive employer. But this afternoon Hollywood yes-men could have taken his correspondence course, and Lord Emsworth had none of that uneasy feeling, which usually came to him on these occasions, that the moment his back was turned his own sound, statesmanlike policies would be shelved and some sort of sweet pea New Deal put into practice as if he had never spoken a word.

He was humming as he approached the terrace. He had his programme all mapped out. For perhaps an hour, till the day had cooled off a little, he would read a Pig book in the library. After that he would go and take a sniff at a rose or two and possibly do a bit of snailing. These mild pleasures were all his simple soul demanded. He wanted nothing more. Just the quiet life, with nobody to fuss him.

And now that Baxter had left, he reflected buoyantly, nobody did fuss him. There had, he dimly recalled, been some sort of trouble a week or so back – something about some man his niece Jane wanted to marry and his sister Constance didn't want her to marry – but that had apparently all blown over. And even when the thing had been at its height, even when the air had been shrill with women's voices and Connie had kept popping out at him and saying 'Do *listen*, Clarence!' he had always been able to reflect that, though all this was pretty unpleasant, there was nevertheless a bright side. He had ceased to be the employer of Rupert Baxter.

There is a breed of granite-faced, strong-jawed business man to whom Lord Emsworth's attitude towards Rupert Baxter would have seemed frankly inexplicable. To these Titans a private secretary is simply a Hey-you, a Hi-there, a mere puppet to be ordered hither and thither at will. The trouble with Lord Emsworth was that it was he and not his secretary who had been the puppet. Their respective relations had always been those of a mild reigning monarch and the pushing young devil who has taken on the

dictatorship. For years, until he had mercifully tendered his resignation to join an American named Jevons, Baxter had worried
Lord Emsworth, bossed him, bustled him, had always been after
him to do things and remember things and sign things. Never a
moment's peace. Yes, it was certainly delightful to think that
Baxter had departed for ever. His going had relieved this Garden
of Eden of its one resident snake.

Still humming, Lord Emsworth reached the terrace. A moment later, the melody had died on his lips and he was rocking
back on his heels as if he had received a solid punch on the nose.

'God bless my soul!' he ejaculated, shaken to the core.

His pince-nez, as always happened when he was emotionally
stirred, had leaped from their moorings. He recovered them and
put them on again, hoping feebly that the ghastly sight he had seen
would prove to have been an optical illusion. But no. However
much he blinked, he could not blink away the fact that the man
over there talking to his sister Constance was Rupert Baxter in
person. He stood gaping at him with a horror which would have
been almost excessive if the other had returned from the tomb.

Lady Constance was smiling brightly, as women so often do
when they are in the process of slipping something raw over on
their nearest and dearest.

'Here is Mr Baxter, Clarence.'

'Ah,' said Lord Emsworth.

'He is touring England on his motor-bicycle, and finding
himself in these parts, of course, he looked us up.'

'Ah,' said Lord Emsworth.

He spoke dully, for his soul was heavy with foreboding. It was
all very well for Connie to say that Baxter was touring England, thus
giving the idea that in about five minutes the man would leap on
his motor-bicycle and dash off to some spot a hundred miles away.
He knew his sister. She was plotting. Always ardently pro-Baxter,
she was going to try to get Blandings Castle's leading incubus back
into office again. Lord Emsworth would have been prepared to
lay the odds on this in the most liberal spirit. So he said 'Ah.'

The monosyllable, taken in conjunction with the sagging of
her brother's jaw and the glare of agony behind his pince-nez,
caused Lady Constance's lips to tighten. A disciplinary light came
into her fine eyes. She looked like a female lion-tamer about to
assert her personality with one of the troupe.

'Clarence!' she said sharply. She turned to her companion. 'Would you excuse me for a moment, Mr Baxter. There is something I want to talk to Lord Emsworth about.'

She drew the pallid peer aside, and spoke with sharp rebuke.

'Just like a stuck pig!'

'Eh?' said Lord Emsworth. His mind had been wandering, as it so often did. The magic word brought it back. 'Pigs? What about pigs?'

'I was saying that you were looking like a stuck pig. You might at least have asked Mr Baxter how he was.'

'I could see how he was. What's he doing here?'

'I told you what he was doing here.'

'But how does he come to be touring England on motor-bicycles? I thought he was working for an American fellow named something or other.'

'He has left Mr Jevons.'

'What!'

'Yes. Mr Jevons had to return to America, and Mr Baxter did not want to leave England.'

Lord Emsworth reeled. Jevons had been his sheet anchor. He had never met that genial Chicagoan, but he had always thought kindly and gratefully of him, as one does of some great doctor who has succeeded in insulating and confining a disease germ.

'You mean the chap's out of a job?' he cried aghast.

'Yes. And it could not have happened at a more fortunate time, because something has got to be done about George.'

'Who's George?'

'You have a grandson of that name,' explained Lady Constance with the sweet, frozen patience which she so often used when conversing with her brother. 'Your heir, Bosham, if you recollect, has two sons, James and George. George, the younger, is spending his summer holidays here. You may have noticed him about. A boy of twelve with auburn hair and freckles.'

'Oh, George? You mean George? Yes, I know George. He's my grandson. What about him?'

'He is completely out of hand. Only yesterday he broke another window with that airgun of his.'

'He needs a mother's care.' Lord Emsworth was vague, but he had an idea that that was the right thing to say.

'He needs a tutor's care, and I am glad to say that Mr Baxter has very kindly consented to accept the position.'

'What!'

'Yes. It is all settled. His things are at the Emsworth Arms, and I am sending down for them.'

Lord Emsworth sought feverishly for arguments which would quash this frightful scheme.

'But he can't be a tutor if he's galumphing all over England on a motor-bicycle.'

'I had not overlooked that point. He will stop galumphing over England on a motor-bicycle.'

'But—'

'It will be a wonderful solution of a problem which was becoming more difficult every day. Mr Baxter will keep George in order. He is so firm.'

She turned away, and Lord Emsworth resumed his progress towards the library.

It was a black moment for the ninth Earl. His worst fears had been realized. He knew just what all this meant. On one of his rare visits to London he had once heard an extraordinarily vivid phrase which had made a deep impression upon him. He had been taking his after-luncheon coffee at the Senior Conservative Club and some fellows in an adjoining nest of arm-chairs had started a political discussion, and one of them had said about something or other that, mark his words, it was the 'thin end of the wedge'. He recognized what was happening now as the thin end of the wedge. From Baxter as a temporary tutor to Baxter as a permanent secretary would, he felt, be so short a step that the contemplation of it chilled him to the bone.

A short-sighted man whose pince-nez have gone astray at the very moment when vultures are gnawing at his bosom seldom guides his steps carefully. Anyone watching Lord Emsworth totter blindly across the terrace would have foreseen that he would shortly collide with something, the only point open to speculation being with what he would collide. This proved to be a small boy with ginger hair and freckles who emerged abruptly from the shrubbery carrying an airgun.

'Coo!' said the small boy. 'Sorry, grandpapa.'

Lord Emsworth recovered his pince-nez and, having adjusted them on the old spot, glared balefully.

'George! Why the dooce don't you look where you're going?'

'Sorry, grandpapa.'

'You might have injured me severely.'

'Sorry, grandpapa.'

'Be more careful another time.'

'Okay, big boy.'

'And don't call me "big boy".'

'Right ho, grandpapa. I say,' said George, shelving the topic, 'who's the bird talking to Aunt Connie?'

He pointed – a vulgarism which a good tutor would have corrected – and Lord Emsworth, following the finger, winced as his eye rested once more upon Rupert Baxter. The secretary – already Lord Emsworth had mentally abandoned the qualifying 'ex' – was gazing out over the rolling parkland, and it seemed to his lordship that his gaze was proprietorial. Rupert Baxter, flashing his spectacles over the grounds of Blandings Castle, wore – or so it appeared to Lord Emsworth – the smug air of some ruthless monarch of old surveying conquered territory.

'That is Mr Baxter,' he replied.

'Looks a bit of a blister,' said George critically.

The expression was new to Lord Emsworth, but he recognized it at once as the ideal description of Rupert Baxter. His heart warmed to the little fellow, and he might quite easily at this moment have given him sixpence.

'Do you think so?' he said lovingly.

'What's he doing here?'

Lord Emsworth felt a pang. It seemed brutal to dash the sunshine from the life of this admirable boy. Yet somebody had got to tell him.

'He is going to be your tutor.'

'Tutor?'

The word was a cry of agony forced from the depths of the boy's soul. A stunned sense that all the fundamental decencies of life were being outraged had swept over George. His voice was thick with emotion.

'Tutor?' he cried. '*Tew*-tor? Ter-YEW-tor? In the middle of the summer holidays? What have I got to have a tutor for in the middle of the summer holidays? I do call this a bit off. I mean, in the middle of the summer holidays. Why do I want a tutor? I mean to say, in the middle of…'

He would have spoken at greater length, for he had much to say on the subject, but at this point Lady Constance's voice, musical but imperious, interrupted his flow of speech.

'Gee-orge.'

'Coo! Right in the middle—'

'Come here, George. I want you to meet Mr Baxter.'

'Coo!' muttered the stricken child again and, frowning darkly, slouched across the terrace. Lord Emsworth proceeded to the library, a tender pity in his heart for this boy who by his crisp summing-up of Rupert Baxter had revealed himself so kindred a spirit. He knew just how George felt. It was not always easy to get anything into Lord Emsworth's head, but he had grasped the substance of his grandson's complaint unerringly. George, about to have a tutor in the middle of the summer holidays, did not want one.

Sighing a little, Lord Emsworth reached the library and found his book.

There were not many books which at a time like this could have diverted Lord Emsworth's mind from what weighed upon it, but this one did. It was Whiffle on *The Care Of The Pig* and, buried in its pages, he forgot everything. The chapter he was reading was that noble one about swill and bran-mash, and it took him completely out of the world, so much so that when some twenty minutes later the door suddenly burst open it was as if a bomb had been exploded under his nose. He dropped Whiffle and sat panting. Then, although his pince-nez had followed routine by flying off, he was able by some subtle instinct to sense that the intruder was his sister Constance, and an observation beginning with the words 'Good God, Connie!' had begun to leave his lips, when she cut it short.

'Clarence,' she said, and it was plain that her nervous system, like his, was much shaken, 'the most dreadful thing has happened!'

'Eh?'

'That man is here.'

'What man?'

'That man of Jane's. The man I told you about.'

'What man did you tell me about?'

Lady Constance seated herself. She would have preferred to have been able to do without tedious explanations, but long association with her brother had taught her that his was a memory that had to be refreshed. She embarked, accordingly, on these explanations, speaking wearily, like a schoolmistress to one of the duller members of her class.

'The man I told you about – certainly not less than a hundred times – was a man Jane met in the spring, when she went to stay with her friends the Leighs in Devonshire. She had a silly flirtation with him, which, of course, she insisted on magnifying into a great romance. She kept saying they were engaged. And he hasn't a penny. Nor prospects. Nor, so I gathered from Jane, a position.'

Lord Emsworth interrupted at this point to put a question.

'Who,' he asked courteously, 'is Jane?'

Lady Constance quivered a little.

'Oh, Clarence! Your niece Jane.'

'Oh, my *niece* Jane? Ah! Yes. Yes, of course. My niece Jane. Yes, of course, to be sure. My—'

'Clarence, please! For pity's sake! Do stop doddering and listen to me. For once in your life I want you to be firm.'

'Be what?'

'Firm. Put your foot down.'

'How do you mean?'

'About Jane. I had been hoping that she had got over this ridiculous infatuation – she has seemed perfectly happy and contented all this time – but no. Apparently they have been corresponding regularly, and now the man is here.'

'Here?'

'Yes.'

'Where?' asked Lord Emsworth, gazing in an interested manner about the room.

'He arrived last night and is staying in the village. I found out by the merest accident. I happened to ask George if he had seen Jane, because I wanted Mr Baxter to meet her, and he said he had met her going towards the lake. So I went down to the lake, and there I discovered her with a young man in a tweed coat and flannel knickerbockers. They were kissing one another in the summer-house.'

Lord Emsworth clicked his tongue.

'Ought to have been out in the sunshine,' he said, disapprovingly.

Lady Constance raised her foot quickly, but instead of kicking her brother on the shin merely tapped the carpet with it. Blood will tell.

'Jane was defiant. I think she must be off her head. She insisted that she was going to marry this man. And, as I say, not only has he not a penny, but he is apparently out of work.'

'What sort of work does he do?'

'I gather that he has been a land-agent on an estate in Devonshire.'

'It all comes back to me,' said Lord Emsworth. 'I remember now. This must be the man Jane was speaking to me about yesterday. Of course, yes. She asked me to give him Simmons's job. Simmons is retiring next month. Good fellow,' said Lord Emsworth sentimentally. 'Been here for years and years. I shall be sorry to lose him. Bless my soul, it won't seem like the same place without old Simmons. Still,' he said, brightening, for he was a man who could make the best of things, 'no doubt this new chap will turn out all right. Jane seems to think highly of him.'

Lady Constance had risen slowly from her chair. There was incredulous horror on her face.

'Clarence! You are not telling me that you have promised this man Simmons's place?'

'Eh? Yes, I have. Why not?'

'Why not! Do you realize that directly he gets it he will marry Jane?'

'Well, why shouldn't he? Very nice girl. Probably make him a good wife.'

Lady Constance struggled with her feelings for a space.

'Clarence,' she said, 'I am going out now to find Jane. I shall tell her that you have thought it over and changed your mind.'

'What about?'

'Giving this man Simmons's place.'

'But I haven't.'

'Yes, you have.'

And so, Lord Emsworth discovered as he met her eye, he had. It often happened that way after he and Connie had talked a thing over. But he was not pleased about it.

'But, Connie, dash it all—'

'We will not discuss it any more, Clarence.'

Her eye played upon him. Then she moved to the door and was gone.

Alone at last, Lord Emsworth took up his Whiffle on *The Care Of The Pig* in the hope that it might, as had happened before, bring calm to the troubled spirit. It did, and he was absorbed in it when the door opened once more.

His niece Jane stood on the threshold.

Lord Emsworth's niece Jane was the third prettiest girl in Shropshire. In her general appearance she resembled a dewy rose, and it might have been thought that Lord Emsworth, who yielded to none in his appreciation of roses, would have felt his heart leap up at the sight of her.

This was not the case. His heart did leap, but not up. He was a man with certain definite views about roses. He preferred them without quite such tight lips and determined chins. And he did not like them to look at him as if he were something slimy and horrible which they had found under a flat stone.

The wretched man was now fully conscious of his position. Under the magic spell of Whiffle he had been able to thrust from his mind for awhile the thought of what Jane was going to say when she heard the bad news; but now, as she started to advance slowly into the room in that sinister, purposeful way characteristic of so many of his female relations, he realized what he was in for, and his soul shrank into itself like a salted snail.

Jane, he could not but remember, was the daughter of his sister Charlotte, and many good judges considered Lady Charlotte a tougher egg even than Lady Constance, or her younger sister, Lady Julia. He still quivered at some of the things Charlotte had said to him in her time; and, eyeing Jane apprehensively, he saw no reason for supposing that she had not inherited quite a good deal of the maternal fire.

The girl came straight to the point. Her mother, Lord Emsworth recalled, had always done the same.

'I should like an explanation, Uncle Clarence.'

Lord Emsworth cleared his throat unhappily.

'Explanation, my dear?'

'Explanation was what I said.'

'Oh, explanation? Ah, yes. Er – what about?'

'You know jolly well what about. That agent job. Aunt Constance says you've changed your mind. Have you?'

'Er…Ah…Well…'

'Have you?'

'Ah…Well…Er…'

'HAVE you?'

'Well...Er...Ah...Yes.'

'Worm!' said Jane. 'Miserable, crawling, cringing, gelatine-backboned worm!'

Lord Emsworth, though he had been expecting something along these lines, quivered as if he had been harpooned.

'That,' he said, attempting a dignity which he was far from feeling, 'is not a very nice thing to say...'

'If you only knew the things I would like to say! I'm holding myself in. So you've changed your mind, have you? Ha! Does a sacred promise mean nothing to you, Uncle Clarence? Does a girl's whole life's happiness mean nothing to you? I never would have believed that you could have been such a blighter.'

'I am not a blighter.'

'Yes, you are. You're a life-blighter. You're trying to blight my life. Well, you aren't going to do it. Whatever happens, I mean to marry George.'

Lord Emsworth was genuinely surprised.

'Marry George? But Connie told me you were in love with this fellow you met in Devonshire.'

'His name is George Abercrombie.'

'Oh, ah?' said Lord Emsworth, enlightened. 'Bless my soul, I thought you meant my grandson George, and it puzzled me. Because you couldn't marry him, of course. He's your brother or cousin or something. Besides, he's too young for you. What would George be? Ten? Eleven?'

He broke off. A reproachful look had hit him like a shell.

'Uncle Clarence!'

'My dear?'

'Is this a time for drivelling?'

'My dear!'

'Well, is it? Look in your heart and ask yourself. Here I am, with everybody spitting on their hands and dashing about trying to ruin my life's whole happiness, and instead of being kind and under-standing and sympathetic you start talking rot about young George.'

'I was only saying—'

'I heard what you were saying, and it made me sick. You really must be the most callous man that ever lived. I can't understand you of all people behaving like this, Uncle Clarence. I always thought you were fond of me.'

'I am fond of you.'

'It doesn't look like it. Flinging yourself into this foul conspiracy to wreck my life.'

Lord Emsworth remembered a good one.

'I have your best interests at heart, my dear.'

It did not go very well. A distinct sheet of flame shot from the girl's eyes.

'What do you mean, my best interests? The way Aunt Constance talks, and the way you are backing her up, anyone would think that George was someone in a straw hat and a scarlet cummerbund that I'd picked up on the pier at Blackpool. The Abercrombies are one of the oldest families in Devonshire. They date back to the Conquest, and they practically ran the Crusades. When your ancestors were staying at home on the plea of war work of national importance and wangling jobs at the base, the Abercrombies were out fighting the Paynim.'

'I was at school with a boy named Abercrombie,' said Lord Emsworth musingly.

'I hope he kicked you. No, no, I don't mean that. I'm sorry. The one thing I'm trying to do is to keep this little talk free of – what's the word?'

Lord Emsworth said he did not know.

'Acrimony. I want to be calm and cool and sensible. Honestly, Uncle Clarence, you would love George. You'll be a sap if you give him the bird without seeing him. He's the most wonderful man on earth. He got into the last eight at Wimbledon this year.'

'Did he, indeed? Last eight what?'

'And there isn't anything he doesn't know about running an estate. The very first thing he said when he came into the park was that a lot of the timber wanted seeing to badly.'

'Blast his impertinence,' said Lord Emsworth warmly. 'My timber is in excellent condition.'

'Not if George says it isn't. George knows timber.'

'So do I know timber.'

'Not so well as George does. But never mind about that. Let's get back to this loathsome plot to ruin my life's whole happiness. Why can't you be a sport, Uncle Clarence, and stand up for me? Can't you understand what this means to me? Weren't you ever in love?'

'Certainly I was in love. Dozens of times. I'll tell you a very funny story—'

'I don't want to hear funny stories.'

'No, no. Quite. Exactly.'

'All I want is to hear you saying that you will give George Mr Simmons's job, so that we can get married.'

'But your aunt seems to feel so strongly—'

'I know what she feels strongly. She wants me to marry that ass Roegate.'

'Does she?'

'Yes, and I'm not going to. You can tell her from me that I wouldn't marry Bertie Roegate if he were the only man in the world—'

'There's a song of that name,' said Lord Emsworth, interested. 'They sang it during the War. No, it wasn't "man". It was "girl". If you were the only...How did it go? Ah, yes. "If you were the only girl in the world and I was the only boy"...'

'Uncle Clarence!'

'My dear?'

'Please don't sing. You're not in the tap-room of the Emsworth Arms now.'

'I have never been in the tap-room of the Emsworth Arms.'

'Or at a smoking-concert. Really, you seem to have the most extraordinary idea of the sort of attitude that's fitting when you're talking to a girl whose life's happiness everybody is sprinting about trying to ruin. First you talk rot about young George, then you start trying to tell funny stories, and now you sing comic songs.'

'It wasn't a comic song.'

'It was, the way you sang it. Well?'

'Eh?'

'Have you decided what you are going to do about this?'

'About what?'

The girl was silent for a moment, during which moment she looked so like her mother that Lord Emsworth shuddered.

'Uncle Clarence,' she said in a low, trembling voice, 'you are not going to pretend that you don't know what we've been talking about all this time? Are you or are you not going to give George that job?'

'Well—'

'Well?'

'Well—'

'We can't stay here for ever, saying "Well" at one another. Are you or are you not?'

'My dear, I don't see how I can. Your aunt seems to feel so very strongly…'

He spoke mumblingly, avoiding his companion's eye, and he had paused, searching for words, when from the drive outside there arose a sudden babble of noise. Raised voices were proceeding from the great open spaces. He recognized his sister Constance's penetrating soprano, and mingling with it his grandson George's treble 'Coo.' Competing with both, there came the throaty baritone of Rupert Baxter. Delighted with the opportunity of changing the subject, he hurried to the window.

'Bless my soul! What's all that?'

The battle, whatever it may have been about, had apparently rolled away in some unknown direction, for he could see nothing from the window but Rupert Baxter, who was smoking a cigarette in what seemed a rather overwrought manner. He turned back, and with infinite relief discovered that he was alone. His niece had disappeared. He took up Whiffle on *The Care Of The Pig* and had just started to savour once more the perfect prose of that chapter about swill and bran-mash, when the door opened. Jane was back. She stood on the threshold, eyeing her uncle coldly.

'Reading, Uncle Clarence?'

'Eh? Oh, ah, yes. I was just glancing at Whiffle on *The Care Of The Pig*!'

'So you actually have the heart to read at a time like this? Well, well! Do you ever read Western novels, Uncle Clarence?'

'Eh? Western novels? No. No, never.'

'I'm sorry. I was reading one the other day, and I hoped that you might be able to explain something that puzzled me. What one cowboy said to another cowboy.'

'Oh, yes?'

'This cowboy – the first cowboy – said to the other cowboy – the second cowboy – "Gol dern ye, Hank Spivis, for a sneaking, ornery, low-down, double-crossing, hornswoggling skunk." Can you tell me what a sneaking, ornery, low-down, double-crossing, hornswoggling skunk is, Uncle Clarence?'

'I'm afraid I can't, my dear.'

'I thought you might know.'

'No.'

'Oh.'

She passed from the room, and Lord Emsworth resumed his Whiffle.

But it was not long before the volume was resting on his knee while he stared before him with a sombre gaze. He was reviewing the recent scene and wishing that he had come better out of it. He was a vague man, but not so vague as to be unaware that he might have shown up in a more heroic light.

How long he sat brooding, he could not have said. Some little time, undoubtedly, for the shadows on the terrace had, he observed as he glanced out of the window, lengthened quite a good deal since he had seen them last. He was about to rise and seek consolation from a ramble among the flowers in the garden below, when the door opened – it seemed to Lord Emsworth, who was now feeling a little morbid, that that blasted door had never stopped opening since he had come to the library to be alone – and Beach, the butler, entered.

He was carrying an airgun in one hand and in the other a silver salver with a box of ammunition on it.

Beach was a man who invested all his actions with something of the impressiveness of a high priest conducting an intricate service at some romantic altar. It is not easy to be impressive when you are carrying an airgun in one hand and a silver salver with a box of ammunition on it in the other, but Beach managed it. Many butlers in such a position would have looked like sportsmen setting out for a day with the birds, but Beach still looked like a high priest. He advanced to the table at Lord Emsworth's side and laid his cargo upon it as if the gun and the box of ammunition had been a smoked offering and his lordship a tribal god.

Lord Emsworth eyed his faithful servitor sourly. His manner was that of a tribal god who considers the smoked offering not up to sample.

'What the devil's all this?'

'It is an airgun, m'lord.'

'I can see that, dash it. What are you bringing it here for?'

'Her ladyship instructed me to convey it to your lordship – I gathered for safe keeping, m'lord. The weapon was until recently the property of Master George.'

'Why the dooce are they taking his airgun away from the poor boy?' demanded Lord Emsworth hotly. Ever since the lad had called Rupert Baxter a blister he had been feeling a strong affection for his grandson.

'Her ladyship did not confide in me on that point, m'lord. I was merely instructed to convey the weapon to your lordship.'

At this moment, Lady Constance came sailing in to throw light on the mystery.

'Ah, I see Beach has brought it to you. I want you to lock that gun up somewhere, Clarence. George is not to be allowed to have it any more.'

'Why not?'

'Because he is not to be trusted with it. Do you know what happened? He shot Mr Baxter!'

'What!'

'Yes. Out on the drive just now. I noticed that the boy's manner was sullen when I introduced him to Mr Baxter, and said that he was going to be his tutor. He disappeared into the shrubbery, and just now, as Mr Baxter was standing on the drive, George shot him from behind a bush.'

'Good!' cried Lord Emsworth, then prudently added the word 'gracious'.

There was a pause. Lord Emsworth took up the gun and handled it curiously.

'Bang!' he said, pointing it at a bust of Aristotle which stood on a bracket by the book-shelves.

'Please don't wave the thing about like that, Clarence. It may be loaded.'

'Not if George has just shot Baxter with it. No,' said Lord Emsworth, pulling the trigger, 'it's not loaded.' He mused awhile. An odd, nostalgic feeling was creeping over him. Far-off memories of his hot boyhood had begun to stir within him. 'Bless my soul,' he said. 'I haven't had one of these things in my hand since I was a child. Did you ever have one of these things, Beach?'

'Yes, m'lord, when a small lad.'

'Bless my soul, I remember my sister Julia borrowing mine to shoot her governess. You remember Julia shooting the governess, Connie?'

'Don't be absurd, Clarence.'

'It's not absurd. She did shoot her. Fortunately women wore bustles in those days. Beach, don't you remember my sister Julia shooting the governess?'

'The incident would, no doubt, have occurred before my arrival at the castle, m'lord.'

'That will do, Beach,' said Lady Constance. 'I do wish, Clarence,' she continued as the door closed, 'that you would not say that sort of thing in front of Beach.'

'Julia did shoot the governess.'

'If she did, there is no need to make your butler a confidant.'

'Now, what was that governess's name? I have an idea it began with—'

'Never mind what her name was or what it began with. Tell me about Jane. I saw her coming out of the library. Had you been speaking to her?'

'Yes. Oh, yes. I spoke to her.'

'I hope you were firm.'

'Oh, very firm. I said "Jane..." But listen, Connie, damn it, aren't we being a little hard on the girl? One doesn't want to ruin her whole life's happiness, dash it.'

'I knew she would get round you. But you are not to give way an inch.'

'But this fellow seems to be a most suitable fellow. One of the Abercrombies and all that. Did well in the Crusades.'

'I am not going to have my niece throwing herself away on a man without a penny.'

'She isn't going to marry Roegate, you know. Nothing will induce her. She said she wouldn't marry Roegate if she were the only girl in the world and he was the only boy.'

'I don't care what she said. And I don't want to discuss the matter any longer. I am now going to send George in, for you to give him a good talking-to.'

'I haven't time.'

'You have time.'

'I haven't. I'm going to look at my flowers.'

'You are not. You are going to talk to George. I want you to make him see quite clearly what a wicked thing he has done. Mr Baxter was furious.'

'It all comes back to me,' cried Lord Emsworth. 'Mapleton!'

'What *are* you talking about?'

'Her name was Mapleton. Julia's governess.'

'Do stop about Julia's governess. Will you talk to George?'

'Oh, all right, all right.'

'Good. I'll go and send him to you.'

And presently George entered. For a boy who had just stained the escutcheon of a proud family by shooting tutors with airguns, he seemed remarkably cheerful. His manner was that of one getting together with an old crony for a cosy chat.

'Hullo, grandpapa,' he said breezily.

'Hullo, my boy,' replied Lord Emsworth, with equal affability.

'Aunt Connie said you wanted to see me.'

'Eh? Ah! Oh! Yes.' Lord Emsworth pulled himself together. 'Yes, that's right. Yes, to be sure. Certainly I want to see you. What's all this, my boy, eh? Eh, what? What's all this?'

'What's all what, grandpapa?'

'Shooting people and all that sort of thing. Shooting Baxter and all that sort of thing. Mustn't do that, you know. Can't have that. It's very wrong and – er – very dangerous to shoot at people with a dashed great gun. Don't you know that, hey? Might put their eye out, dash it.'

'Oh, I couldn't have hit him in the eye, grandpapa. His back was turned and he was bending over, tying his shoelace.'

Lord Emsworth started.

'What! Did you get Baxter in the seat of the trousers?'

'Yes, grandpapa.'

'Ha, ha…I mean, disgraceful…I – er – I expect he jumped?'

'Oh, yes, grandpapa. He jumped like billy-o.'

'Did he, indeed? How this reminds me of Julia's governess. Your Aunt Julia once shot her governess under precisely similar conditions. She was tying her shoelace.'

'Coo! Did *she* jump?'

'She certainly did, my boy.'

'Ha, ha!'

'Ha, ha!'

'Ha, ha!'

'Ha, h – … Ah… Er – well, just so,' said Lord Emsworth, a belated doubt assailing him as to whether this was quite the tone. 'Well, George, I shall of course impound this – er – instrument.'

'Right ho, grandpapa,' said George, with the easy amiability of a boy conscious of having two catapults in his drawer upstairs.

'Can't have you going about the place shooting people.'

'Okay, Chief.'

Lord Emsworth fondled the gun. That nostalgic feeling was growing.

'Do you know, young man, I used to have one of these things when I was a boy.'

'Coo! Were guns invented then?'

'Yes, I had one when I was your age.'

'Ever hit anything, grandpapa?'

Lord Emsworth drew himself up a little haughtily.

'Certainly I did. I hit all sorts of things. Rats and things. I had a very accurate aim. But now I wouldn't even know how to load the dashed affair.'

'This is how you load it, grandpapa. You open it like this and shove the slug in here and snap it together again like that and there you are.'

'Indeed? Really? I see. Yes. Yes, of course, I remember now.'

'You can't kill anything much with it,' said George, with a wistfulness which betrayed an aspiration to higher things. 'Still, it's awfully useful for tickling up cows.'

'And Baxter.'

'Yes.'

'Ha, ha!'

'Ha, ha!'

Once more, Lord Emsworth forced himself to concentrate on the right tone.

'We mustn't laugh about it, my boy. It's no joking matter. It's very wrong to shoot Mr Baxter.'

'But he's a blister.'

'He is a blister,' agreed Lord Emsworth, always fairminded. 'Nevertheless....Remember, he is your tutor.'

'Well, I don't see why I've got to have a tutor right in the middle of the summer holidays. I sweat like the dickens all through the term at school,' said George, his voice vibrant with self-pity, 'and then plumb spang in the middle of the holidays they slosh a tutor on me. I call it a bit thick.'

Lord Emsworth might have told the little fellow that thicker things than that were going on in Blandings Castle, but he refrained. He dismissed him with a kindly, sympathetic smile and resumed his fondling of the airgun.

Like so many men advancing into the sere and yellow of life, Lord Emsworth had an eccentric memory. It was not to be trusted an inch as far as the events of yesterday or the day before were concerned. Even in the small matter of assisting him to find a hat which he had laid down somewhere five minutes ago it was nearly always useless. But by way of compensation for this it was a perfect encyclopædia on the remote past. It rendered his boyhood an open book to him.

Lord Emsworth mused on his boyhood. Happy days, happy days. He could recall the exact uncle who had given him the weapon, so similar to this one, with which Julia had shot her governess. He could recall brave, windswept mornings when he had gone prowling through the stable yard in the hope of getting a rat – and many a fine head had he secured. Odd that the passage of time should remove the desire to go and pop at things with an airgun....

Or did it?

With a curious thrill that set his pince-nez rocking gently on his nose, Lord Emsworth suddenly became aware that it did not. All that the passage of time did was to remove the desire to pop temporarily – say for forty years or so. Dormant for a short while – well, call it fifty years – that desire, he perceived, still lurked unquenched. Little by little it began to stir within him now. Slowly but surely, as he sat there fondling the gun, he was once more becoming a potential popper.

At this point, the gun suddenly went off and broke the bust of Aristotle.

It was enough. The old killer instinct had awakened. Reloading with the swift efficiency of some hunter of the woods, Lord Emsworth went to the window. He was a little uncertain as to what he intended to do when he got there, except that he had a very clear determination to loose off at something. There flitted into his mind what his grandson George had said about tickling up cows, and this served to some extent to crystallize his aims. True, cows were not plentiful on the terrace of Blandings Castle. Still, one might have wandered there. You never knew with cows.

There were no cows. Only Rupert Baxter. The ex-secretary was in the act of throwing away a cigarette.

Most men are careless in the matter of throwing away cigarettes. The world is their ashtray. But Rupert Baxter had a tidy soul. He allowed the thing to fall to the ground like any ordinary young man, it is true, but immediately he had done so his better self awakened. He stooped to pick up the object that disfigured the smooth flagged stones, and the invitation of that beckoning trousers' seat would have been too powerful for a stronger man than Lord Emsworth to resist.

He pulled the trigger, and Rupert Baxter sprang into the air with a sharp cry. Lord Emsworth reseated himself and took up Whiffle on *The Care Of The Pig*.

Everybody is interested nowadays in the psychology of the criminal. The chronicler, therefore, feels that he runs no risk of losing his grip on the reader if he pauses at this point to examine and analyse the workings of Lord Emsworth's mind after the perpetration of the black act which has just been recorded.

At first, then, all that he felt as he sat turning the pages of his Whiffle was a sort of soft warm glow, a kind of tremulous joy such as he might have experienced if he had just been receiving the thanks of the nation for some great public service.

It was not merely the fact that he had caused his late employee to skip like the high hills that induced this glow. What pleased him so particularly was that it had been such a magnificent shot. He was a sensitive man, and though in his conversation with his grandson George he had tried to wear the mask, he had not been able completely to hide his annoyance at the boy's careless assumption that in his airgun days he had been an indifferent marksman.

'Did you ever hit anything, grandpapa?' Boys say these things with no wish to wound, but nevertheless they pierce the armour. 'Did you ever hit anything, grandpapa?' forsooth! He would have liked to see George stop putting finger to trigger for forty-seven years and then, first crack out of the box, pick off a medium-sized secretary at a distance like that! In rather a bad light, too.

But after he had sat for awhile, silently glowing, his mood underwent a change. A gunman's complacency after getting his man can never remain for long an unmixed complacency. Sooner or later there creeps in the thought of Retribution. It did with Lord Emsworth. Quite suddenly, whispering in his ear, he heard the voice of Conscience say:

'What if your sister Constance learns of this?'

A moment before this voice spoke, Lord Emsworth had been smirking. He now congealed, and the smile passed from his lips like breath off a razor blade, to be succeeded by a tense look of anxiety and alarm.

Nor was this alarm unjustified. When he reflected how scathing and terrible his sister Constance could be when he committed even so venial a misdemeanour as coming down to dinner with a brass paper-fastener in his shirt front instead of the more conventional stud, his imagination boggled at the thought of what she would do in a case like this. He was appalled. Whiffle on *The Care Of The Pig* fell from his nerveless hand, and he sat looking like a dying duck. And Lady Constance, who now entered, noted the expression and was curious as to its cause.

'What is the matter, Clarence?'

'Matter?'

'Why are you looking like a dying duck?'

'I am not looking like a dying duck,' retorted Lord Emsworth with what spirit he could muster.

'Well,' said Lady Constance, waiving the point, 'have you spoken to George?'

'Certainly. Yes, of course I've spoken to George. He was in here just now and I – er – spoke to him.'

'What did you say?'

'I said' – Lord Emsworth wanted to make this very clear – 'I said that I wouldn't even know how to load one of those things.'

'Didn't you give him a good talking-to?'

'Of course I did. A very good talking-to. I said "Er – George, you know how to load those things and I don't, but that's no reason why you should go about shooting Baxter."'

'Was that all you said?'

'No. That was just how I began. I—'

Lord Emsworth paused. He could not have finished the sentence if large rewards had been offered to him to do so. For, as he spoke, Rupert Baxter appeared in the doorway, and he shrank back in his chair like some Big Shot cornered by G-men.

The secretary came forward limping slightly. His eyes behind their spectacles were wild and his manner emotional. Lady Constance gazed at him wonderingly.

'Is something the matter, Mr Baxter?'

'Matter?' Rupert Baxter's voice was taut and he quivered in every limb. He had lost his customary suavity and was plainly in no frame of mind to mince his words. 'Matter? Do you know what has happened? That infernal boy has shot me *again*!'

'What!'

'Only a few minutes ago. Out on the terrace.'

Lord Emsworth shook off his palsy.

'I expect you imagined it,' he said.

'Imagined it!' Rupert Baxter shook from spectacles to shoes. 'I tell you I was on the terrace, stooping to pick up my cigarette, when something hit me on the...something hit me.'

'Probably a wasp,' said Lord Emsworth. 'They are very plentiful this year. I wonder,' he said chattily, 'if either of you are aware that wasps serve a very useful purpose. They keep down the leather–jackets, which, as you know, inflict serious injury upon—'

Lady Constance's concern became mixed with perplexity.

'But it could not have been George, Mr Baxter. The moment you told me of what he had done, I confiscated his airgun. Look, there it is on the table now.'

'Right there on the table,' said Lord Emsworth, pointing helpfully. 'If you come over here, you can see it clearly. Must have been a wasp.'

'You have not left the room, Clarence?'

'No. Been here all the time.'

'Then it would have been impossible for George to have shot you, Mr Baxter.'

'Quite,' said Lord Emsworth. 'A wasp, undoubtedly. Unless, as I say, you imagined the whole thing.'

The secretary stiffened.

'I am not subject to hallucinations, Lord Emsworth.'

'But you are, my dear fellow. I expect it comes from exerting your brain too much. You're always getting them.'

'Clarence!'

'Well, he is. You know that as well as I do. Look at that time he went grubbing about in a lot of flower-pots because he thought you had put your necklace there.'

'I did not—'

'You did, my dear fellow. I dare say you've forgotten it, but you did. And then, for some reason best known to yourself, you threw the flower-pots at me through my bedroom window.'

Baxter turned to Lady Constance, flushing darkly. The episode to which his former employer had alluded was one of which he never cared to be reminded.

'Lord Emsworth is referring to the occasion when your diamond necklace was stolen, Lady Constance. I was led to believe that the thief had hidden it in a flower-pot.'

'Of course, Mr Baxter.'

'Well, have it your own way,' said Lord Emsworth agreeably. 'But bless my soul, I shall never forget waking up and finding all those flower-pots pouring in through the window and then looking out and seeing Baxter on the lawn in lemon-coloured pyjamas with a wild glare in his—'

'Clarence!'

'Oh, all right. I merely mentioned it. Hallucinations – he gets them all the time,' he said stoutly, though in an undertone.

Lady Constance was cooing to the secretary like a mother to her child.

'It really is impossible that George should have done this, Mr Baxter. The gun has never left this—'

She broke off. Her handsome face seemed to turn suddenly to stone. When she spoke again the coo had gone out of her voice and it had become metallic.

'Clarence!'

'My dear?'

Lady Constance drew in her breath sharply.

'Mr Baxter, I wonder if you would mind leaving us for a moment. I wish to speak to Lord Emsworth.'

The closing of the door was followed by a silence, followed in its turn by an odd, whining noise like gas escaping from a pipe. It was Lord Emsworth trying to hum carelessly.

'Clarence!'

'Yes? Yes, my dear?'

The stoniness of Lady Constance's expression had become more marked with each succeeding moment. What had caused it in the first place was the recollection, coming to her like a flash, that when she had entered this room she had found her brother looking like a dying duck. Honest men, she felt, do not look like dying ducks. The only man whom an impartial observer could possibly mistake for one of these birds *in extremis* is the man with crime upon his soul.

'Clarence, was it you who shot Mr Baxter?'

Fortunately there had been that in her manner which led Lord Emsworth to expect the question. He was ready for it.

'Me? Who, me? Shoot Baxter? What the dooce would I want to shoot Baxter for?'

'We can go into your motives later. What I am asking you now is – Did you?'

'Of course I didn't.'

'The gun has not left the room.'

'Shoot Baxter, indeed! Never heard anything so dashed absurd in my life.'

'And you have been here all the time.'

'Well, what of it? Suppose I have? Suppose I had wanted to shoot Baxter? Suppose every fibre in my being had egged me on, dash it, to shoot the feller? How could I have done it, not even knowing how to load the contrivance?'

'You used to know how to load an airgun.'

'I used to know a lot of things.'

'It's quite easy to load an airgun. I could do it myself.'

'Well, I didn't.'

'Then how do you account for the fact that Mr Baxter was shot by an airgun which had never left the room you were in?'

Lord Emsworth raised pleading hands to heaven.

'How do you know he was shot with this airgun? God bless my soul, the way women jump to conclusions is enough to.... How do you know there wasn't another airgun? How do you know the place isn't bristling with airguns? How do you know Beach hasn't an airgun? Or anybody?'

'I scarcely imagine that Beach would shoot Mr Baxter.'

'How do you know he wouldn't? He used to have an airgun when he was a small lad. He said so. I'd watch the man closely.'

'Please don't be ridiculous, Clarence.'

'I'm not being half as ridiculous as you are. Saying I shoot people with airguns. Why should I shoot people with airguns? And how do you suppose I could have potted Baxter at that distance?'

'What distance?'

'He was standing on the terrace, wasn't he? He specifically stated that he was standing on the terrace. And I was up here. It would take a most expert marksman to pot the fellow at a distance like that. Who do you think I am? One of those chaps who shoot apples off their sons' heads?'

The reasoning was undeniably specious. It shook Lady Constance. She frowned undecidedly.

'Well, it's very strange that Mr Baxter should be so convinced that he was shot.'

'Nothing strange about it at all. There wouldn't be anything strange if Baxter was convinced that he was a turnip and had been bitten by a white rabbit with pink eyes. You know perfectly well, though you won't admit it, that the fellow's a raving lunatic.'

'Clarence!'

'It's no good saying "Clarence!" The fellow's potty to the core, and always has been. Haven't I seen him on the lawn at five o'clock in the morning in lemon-coloured pyjamas, throwing flower-pots in at my window? Pooh! Obviously, the whole thing is the outcome of the man's diseased imagination. Shot, indeed! Never heard such nonsense. And now,' said Lord Emsworth, rising firmly, 'I'm going out to have a look at my roses. I came to this room to enjoy a little quiet reading and meditation, and ever since I got here there's been a constant stream of people in and out, telling me they're going to marry men named Abercrombie and saying they've been shot and saying I shot them and so on and so forth....Bless my soul, one might as well try to read and meditate in the middle of Piccadilly Circus. Tchah!' said Lord Emsworth, who had now got near enough to the door to feel safe in uttering this unpleasant exclamation. 'Tchah!' he said, and adding 'Pah!' for good measure made a quick exit.

But even now his troubled spirit was not to know peace. To reach the great outdoors at Blandings Castle, if you start from the library and come down the main staircase, you have to pass through the hall. To the left of this hall there is a small writing-room. And outside this writing-room Lord Emsworth's niece Jane was standing.

'Yoo-hoo,' she cried. 'Uncle Clarence.'

Lord Emsworth was in no mood for yoo-hooing nieces. George Abercrombie might enjoy chatting with this girl. So might Herbert, Lord Roegate. But he wanted solitude. In the course of the afternoon he had had so much female society thrust upon him that if Helen of Troy had appeared in the doorway of the writing-room and yoo-hooed at him, he would merely have accelerated his pace.

He accelerated it now.

'Can't stop, my dear, can't stop.'

'Oh, yes you can, old Sure-Shot,' said Jane, and Lord Emsworth found that he could. He stopped so abruptly that he nearly dislocated his spine. His jaw had fallen and his pince-nez were dancing on their string like leaves in the wind.

'Two-Gun Thomas, the Marksman of the Prairie – He never misses. Kindly step this way, Uncle Clarence,' said Jane, 'I would like a word with you.'

Lord Emsworth stepped that way. He followed the girl into the writing-room and closed the door carefully behind him.

'You – you didn't see me?' he quavered.

'I certainly did see you,' said Jane. 'I was an interested eye-witness of the whole thing from start to finish.'

Lord Emsworth tottered to a chair and sank into it, staring glassily at his niece. Any Chicago business man of the modern school would have understood what he was feeling and would have sympathized with him.

The thing that poisons life for gunmen and sometimes makes them wonder moodily if it is worth-while going on is this tendency of the outside public to butt in at inconvenient moments. Whenever you settle some business dispute with a commercial competitor by means of your sub-machine gun, it always turns out that there was some officious witness passing at the time, and there you are, with a new problem confronting you.

And Lord Emsworth was in worse case than his spiritual brother of Chicago would have been, for the latter could always have solved his perplexities by rubbing out the witness. To him this melancholy pleasure was denied. A prominent Shropshire landowner, with a position to keep up in the county, cannot rub out his nieces. All he can do, when they reveal that they have seen him wallowing in crime, is to stare glassily at them.

'I had a front seat for the entire performance,' proceeded Jane. 'When I left you, I went into the shrubbery to cry my eyes out because of your frightful cruelty and inhumanity. And while I was crying my eyes out, I suddenly saw you creep to the window of the library with a hideous look of low cunning on your face and young George's airgun in your hand. And I was just wondering if I couldn't find a stone and bung it at you, because it seemed to me that something along those lines was what you had been asking for from the start, when you raised the gun and I saw that you were taking aim. The next moment there was a shot, a cry, and Baxter weltering in his blood on the terrace. And as I stood there, a thought floated into my mind. It was – What will Aunt Constance have to say about this when I tell her?'

Lord Emsworth emitted a low, gargling sound, like the death rattle of that dying duck to which his sister had compared him.

'You – you aren't going to tell her?'

'Why not?'

An aguelike convulsion shook Lord Emsworth.

'I implore you not to tell her, my dear. You know what she's like. I should never hear the end of it.'

'She would give you the devil, you think?'

'I do.'

'So do I. And you thoroughly deserve it.'

'My dear!'

'Well, don't you? Look at the way you've been behaving. Working like a beaver to ruin my life's happiness.'

'I don't want to ruin your life's happiness.'

'You don't? Then sit down at this desk and dash off a short letter to George, giving him that job.'

'But—'

'What did you say?'

'I only said, "But—"'

'Don't say it again. What I want from you, Uncle Clarence, is prompt and cheerful service. Are you ready? "Dear Mr Abercrombie…"'

'I don't know how to spell it,' said Lord Emsworth, with the air of a man who has found a way out satisfactory to all parties.

'I'll attend to the spelling. A–b, ab; e–r, er; c–r–o–m, crom; b–i–e, bie. The whole constituting the word "Abercrombie", which is the name of the man I love. Got it?'

'Yes,' said Lord Emsworth sepulchrally. 'I've got it.'

'Then carry on. "Dear Mr Abercrombie. Pursuant" – One p., two u's – spread 'em about a bit, an r., an s., and an ant – "Pursuant on our recent conversation—"'

'But I've never spoken to the man in my life.'

'It doesn't matter. It's just a form. "Pursuant on our recent conversation, I have much pleasure in offering you the post of land-agent at Blandings Castle, and shall be glad if you will take up your duties immediately. Yours faithfully Emsworth." E-m-s-w-o-r-t-h.'

Jane took the letter, pressed it lovingly on the blotting-pad and placed it in the recesses of her costume. 'Fine,' she said. 'That's that. Thanks most awfully, Uncle Clarence. This has squared you nicely for your recent foul behaviour in trying to ruin my life's happiness. You made a rocky start, but you've come through magnificently at the finish.'

Kissing him affectionately, she passed from the room, and Lord Emsworth, slumped in his chair, tried not to look at the vision of his sister Constance which was rising before his eyes. What Connie was going to say when she learned that in defiance of her direct commands he had given this young man...

He mused on Lady Constance, and wondered if there were any other men in the world so sister-pecked as he. It was weak of him, he knew, to curl up into an apologetic ball when assailed by a mere sister. Most men reserved such craven conduct for their wives. But it had always been so, right back to those boyhood days which he remembered so well. And too late to alter it now, he supposed.

The only consolation he was able to enjoy in this dark hour was the reflection that, though things were bad, they were unquestionably less bad than they might have been. At the least, his fearful secret was safe. That rash moment of recovered boyhood would never now be brought up against him. Connie would never know whose hand it was that had pulled the fatal trigger. She might suspect, but she could never know. Nor could Baxter ever know. Baxter would grow into an old, white-haired, spectacled pantaloon, and always this thing would remain an insoluble mystery to him.

Dashed lucky, felt Lord Emsworth, that the fellow had not been listening at the door during the recent conversation....

It was at this moment that a sound behind him caused him to turn and, having turned, to spring from his chair with a convulsive leap that nearly injured him internally. Over the sill of the open window, like those of a corpse emerging from the tomb to confront its murderer, the head and shoulders of Rupert Baxter were slowly rising. The evening sun fell upon his spectacles, and they seemed to Lord Emsworth to gleam like the eyes of a dragon.

Rupert Baxter had not been listening at the door. There had been no necessity for him to do so. Immediately outside the writing-room window at Blandings Castle there stands a rustic garden seat, and on this he had been sitting from beginning to end of the interview which has just been recorded. If he had been actually in the room, he might have heard a little better, but not much.

When two men stand face to face, one of whom has recently shot the other with an airgun and the second of whom has just discovered who it was that did it, it is rarely that conversation flows briskly from the start. One senses a certain awkwardness – what the French call *gêne*. In the first half-minute of this encounter the only thing that happened in a vocal way was that Lord Emsworth cleared his throat, immediately afterwards becoming silent again. And it is possible that his silence might have prolonged itself for some considerable time, had not Baxter made a movement as if about to withdraw. All this while he had been staring at his former employer, his face an open book in which it was easy for the least discerning eye to read a number of disconcerting emotions. He now took a step backwards, and Lord Emsworth's asphasia left him.

'Baxter!'

There was urgent appeal in the ninth Earl's voice. It was not often that he wanted Rupert Baxter to stop and talk to him, but he was most earnestly desirous of detaining him now. He wished to soothe, to apologize, to explain. He was even prepared, should it be necessary, to offer the man his old post of private secretary as the price of his silence.

'Baxter! My dear fellow!'

A high tenor voice, raised almost to A in Alt by agony of soul, has a compelling quality which it is difficult even for a man in Rupert Baxter's mental condition to resist. Rupert Baxter had not intended to halt his backward movement, but he did so, and Lord Emsworth, reaching the window and thrusting his head out, was relieved to see that he was still within range of the honeyed word.

'Er – Baxter,' he said, 'could you spare me a moment?'

The secretary's spectacles flashed coldly.

'You wish to speak to me, Lord Emsworth?'

'That's exactly it,' assented his lordship, as if he thought it a very happy way of putting the thing. 'Yes, I wish to speak to you.' He paused, and cleared his throat again. 'Tell me, Baxter – tell me, my dear fellow – were you – er – were you sitting on that seat just now?'

'I was.'

'Did you, by any chance, overhear my niece and myself talking?'

'I did.'

'Then I expect – I fancy – perhaps – possibly – no doubt you were surprised at what you heard?'

'I was astounded,' said Rupert Baxter, who was not going to be fobbed off with any weak verbs at a moment like this.

Lord Emsworth cleared his throat for the third time.

'I want to tell you all about that,' he said.

'Oh?' said Rupert Baxter.

'Yes. I – ah – welcome this opportunity of telling you all about it,' said Lord Emsworth, though with less pleasure in his voice than might have been expected from a man welcoming an opportunity of telling somebody all about something. 'I fancy that my niece's remarks may – er – possibly have misled you.'

'Not at all.'

'They may have put you on the wrong track.'

'On the contrary.'

'But, if I remember correctly, she gave the impression – by what she said – my niece gave the impression by what she said – anybody overhearing what my niece said would have received the impression that I took deliberate aim at you with that gun.'

'Precisely.'

'She was quite mistaken,' said Lord Emsworth warmly. 'She had got hold of the wrong end of the stick completely. Girls say such dashed silly things…cause a lot of trouble…upset people. They ought to be more careful. What actually happened, my dear fellow, was that I was glancing out of the library window…with the gun in my hand…and without knowing it I must have placed my finger on the trigger…for suddenly…without the slightest warning…you could have knocked me down with a feather… the dashed thing went off. By accident.'

'Indeed?'

'Purely by accident. I should not like you to think that I was aiming at you.'

'Indeed?'

'And I should not like you to tell – er – anybody about the unfortunate occurrence in a way that would give her...I mean them...the impression that I aimed at you.'

'Indeed?'

Lord Emsworth could not persuade himself that his companion's manner was encouraging. He had a feeling that he was not making headway.

'That's how it was,' he said, after a pause.

'I see.'

'Pure accident. Nobody more surprised than myself.'

'I see.'

So did Lord Emsworth. He saw that the time had come to play his last card. It was no moment for shrinking back and counting the cost. He must proceed to that last fearful extremity which he had contemplated.

'Tell me, Baxter,' he said, 'are you doing anything just now, Baxter?'

'Yes,' replied the other, with no trace of hesitation. 'I am going to look for Lady Constance.'

A convulsive gulp prevented Lord Emsworth from speaking for an instant.

'I mean,' he quavered, when the spasm had spent itself, 'I gathered from my sister that you were at liberty at the moment – that you had left that fellow what's-his-name – the American fellow – and I was hoping, my dear Baxter,' said Lord Emsworth, speaking thickly, as if the words choked him, 'that I might be able to persuade you to take up – to resume – in fact, I was going to ask you if you would care to become my secretary again.'

He paused and, reaching for his handkerchief, feebly mopped his brow. The dreadful speech was out, and its emergence had left him feeling spent and weak.

'You were?' cried Rupert Baxter.

'I was,' said Lord Emsworth hollowly.

A great change for the better had come over Rupert Baxter. It was as if those words had been a magic formula, filling with sweetness and light one who until that moment had been more like a spectacled thunder-cloud than anything human. He ceased to lower darkly. His air of being on the point of shooting out forked lightning left him. He even went so far as to smile. And if the smile was a smile that made Lord Emsworth feel as if his vital organs were being churned up with an egg-whisk, that was not his fault. He was trying to smile sunnily.

'Thank you,' he said. 'I shall be delighted.'

Lord Emsworth did not speak.

'I was always happy at the Castle.'

Lord Emsworth did not speak.

'Thank you very much,' said Rupert Baxter. 'What a beautiful evening.'

He passed from view, and Lord Emsworth examined the evening. As Baxter had said, it was beautiful, but it did not bring the balm which beautiful evenings usually brought to him. A blight seemed to hang over it. The setting sun shone bravely on the formal garden over which he looked, but it was the lengthening shadows rather than the sunshine that impressed themselves upon Lord Emsworth.

His heart was bowed down with weight of woe. Oh, says the poet, what a tangled web we weave when first we practise to deceive, and it was precisely the same, Lord Emsworth realized, when first we practise to shoot airguns. Just one careless, offhand pop at a bending Baxter, and what a harvest, what a retribution! As a result of that single idle shot he had been compelled to augment his personal staff with a land-agent, which would infuriate his sister Constance, and a private secretary, which would make his life once again the inferno it had been in the old, bad Baxter days. He could scarcely have got himself into more trouble if he had gone blazing away with a machine gun.

It was with a slow and distrait shuffle that he eventually took himself from the writing-room and proceeded with his interrupted plan of going and sniffing at his roses. And so preoccupied was his mood that Beach, his faithful butler, who came to him after he had been sniffing at them for perhaps half an hour, was obliged to speak twice before he could induce him to remove his nose from a Gloire de Dijon.

'Eh?'

'A note for you, m'lord.'

'A note? Who from?'

'Mr Baxter, m'lord.'

If Lord Emsworth had been less careworn, he might have noticed that the butler's voice had not its customary fruity ring. It had a dullness, a lack of tone. It was the voice of a butler who has lost the blue bird. But, being in the depths and so in no frame of mind to analyse the voice-production of butlers, he merely took the envelope from its salver and opened it listlessly, wondering what Baxter was sending him notes about.

The communication was so brief that he was enabled to discover this at a glance.

'LORD EMSWORTH,

'After what has occurred, I must reconsider my decision to accept the post of secretary which you offered me.

'I am leaving the Castle immediately.

'R. BAXTER.'

Simply that, and nothing more.

Lord Emsworth stared at the thing. It is not enough to say that he was bewildered. He was nonplussed. If the Gloire de Dijon at which he had recently been sniffing had snapped at his nose and bitten the tip off, he could scarcely have been more taken aback. He could make nothing of this.

As in a dream, he became aware that Beach was speaking.

'Eh?'

'My month's notice, m'lord.'

'Your what?'

'My month's notice, m'lord.'

'What about it?'

'I was saying that I wish to give my month's notice, m'lord.'

A weak irritation at all this chattering came upon Lord Emsworth. Here he was, trying to grapple with this frightful thing which had come upon him, and Beach would insist on weakening his concentration by babbling.

'Yes, yes, yes,' he said. 'I see. All right. Yes, yes.'

'Very good, m'lord.'

Left alone, Lord Emsworth faced the facts. He understood now what had happened. The note was no longer mystic. What it meant was that for some reason that trump card of his had proved useless. He had thought to stop Baxter's mouth with bribes, and he had failed. The man had seemed to accept the olive branch, but later there must have come some sharp revulsion of feeling, causing him to change his mind. No doubt a sudden twinge of pain in the wounded area had brought the memory of his wrongs flooding back upon him, so that he found himself preferring vengeance to material prosperity. And now he was going to blow the gaff. Even now the whole facts in the case might have been placed before Lady Constance. And even now, Lord Emsworth felt with a shiver, Connie might be looking for him.

The sight of a female form coming through the rose bushes brought him the sharpest shudder of the day, and for an instant he stood pointing like a dog. But it was not his sister Constance. It was his niece Jane.

Jane was in excellent spirits.

'Hullo, Uncle Clarence,' she said. 'Having a look at the roses? I've sent that letter off to George, Uncle Clarence. I got the boy who cleans the knives and boots to take it. Nice chap. His name is Cyril.'

'Jane,' said Lord Emsworth, 'a terrible, a ghastly thing has happened. Baxter was outside the window of the writing-room when we were talking, and he heard everything.'

'Golly! He didn't?'

'He did. Every word. And he means to tell your aunt.'

'How do you know?'

'Read this.'

Jane took the note.

'H'm,' she said, having scanned it. 'Well, it looks to me, Uncle Clarence, as if there was only one thing for you to do. You must assert yourself.'

'Assert myself?'

'You know what I mean. Get tough. When Aunt Constance comes trying to bully you, stick your elbows out and put your head on one side and talk back at her out of the corner of your mouth.'

'But what shall I say?'

'Good heavens, there are a hundred things you can say. "Oh, yeah?" "Is zat so?" "Hey, just a minute," "Listen baby," "Scram"...'

'Scram?'

'It means "Get the hell outa here."'

'But I can't tell Connie to get the hell outa here.'

'Why not? Aren't you master in your own house?'

'No,' said Lord Emsworth.

Jane reflected.

'Then I'll tell you what to do. Deny the whole thing.'

'Could I, do you think?'

'Of course you could. And then Aunt Constance will ask me, and I'll deny the whole thing. Categorically. We'll both deny it categorically. She'll have to believe us. We'll be two to one. Don't you worry, Uncle Clarence. Everything'll be all right.'

She spoke with the easy optimism of Youth, and when she passed on a few moments later seemed to be feeling that she was leaving an uncle with his mind at rest. Lord Emsworth could hear her singing a gay song.

He felt no disposition to join in the chorus. He could not bring himself to share her sunny outlook. He looked into the future and still found it dark.

There was only one way of taking his mind off this dark future, only one means of achieving a momentary forgetfulness of what lay in store. Five minutes later, Lord Emsworth was in the library, reading Whiffle on *The Care Of The Pig*.

But there is a point beyond which the magic of the noblest writer ceases to function. Whiffle was good – no question about that – but he was not good enough to purge from the mind such a load of care as was weighing upon Lord Emsworth's. To expect him to do so was trying him too high. It was like asking Whiffle to divert and entertain a man stretched upon the rack.

Lord Emsworth was already beginning to find a difficulty in concentrating on that perfect prose, when any chance he might have had of doing so was removed. Lady Constance appeared in the doorway.

'Oh, here you are, Clarence,' said Lady Constance.

'Yes,' said Lord Emsworth in a low, strained voice.

A close observer would have noted about Lady Constance's manner, as she came into the room, something a little nervous and apprehensive, something almost diffident, but to Lord Emsworth, who was not a close observer, she seemed pretty much as usual, and he remained gazing at her like a man confronted with a ticking bomb. A dazed sensation had come upon him. It was in an almost detached way that he found himself speculating as to which of his crimes was about to be brought up for discussion. Had she met Jane and learned of the fatal letter? Or had she come straight from an interview with Rupert Baxter in which that injured man had told all?

He was so certain that it must be one of these two topics that she had come to broach that her manner as she opened the conversation filled him with amazement. Not only did it lack ferocity, it was absolutely chummy. It was as if a lion had come into the library and started bleating like a lamb.

'All alone, Clarence?'

Lord Emsworth hitched up his lower jaw, and said Yes, he was all alone.

'What are you doing? Reading?'

Lord Emsworth said Yes, he was reading.

'I'm not disturbing you, am I?'

Lord Emsworth, though astonishment nearly robbed him of speech, contrived to say that she was not disturbing him. Lady Constance walked to the window and looked out.

'What a lovely evening.'

'Yes.'

'I wonder you aren't out of doors.'

'I was out of doors. I came in.'

'Yes. I saw you in the rose garden.' Lady Constance traced a pattern on the window-sill with her finger. 'You were speaking to Beach.'

'Yes.'

'Yes, I saw Beach come up and speak to you.'

There was a pause. Lord Emsworth was about to break it by asking his visitor if she felt quite well, when Lady Constance spoke again. That apprehension in her manner, that nervousness, was now well marked. She traced another pattern on the window-sill.

'Was it important?'

'Was what important?'

'I mean, did he want anything?'

'Who?'

'Beach.'

'Beach?'

'Yes. I was wondering what he wanted to see you about.'

Quite suddenly there flashed upon Lord Emsworth the recollection that Beach had done more than merely hand him Baxter's note. With it – dash it, yes, it all came back to him – with it he had given his month's notice. And it just showed, Lord Emsworth felt, what a morass of trouble he was engulfed in that the fact of this superb butler handing in his resignation had made almost no impression upon him. If such a thing had happened only as recently as yesterday, it would have constituted a major crisis. He would have felt that the foundations of his world were rocking. And he had scarcely listened. 'Yes, yes,' he had said, if he remembered correctly. 'Yes, yes, yes. All right.' Or words to that effect.

Bending his mind now on the disaster, Lord Emsworth sat stunned. He was appalled. Almost since the beginning of time, this super-butler had been at the Castle, and now he was about to melt away like snow in the sunshine — or as much like snow in the sunshine as was within the scope of a man who weighed sixteen stone in the buff. It was frightful. The thing was a nightmare. He couldn't get on without Beach. Life without Beach would be insupportable.

He gave tongue, his voice sharp and anguished.

'Connie! Do you know what's happened? Beach has given notice!'

'What!'

'Yes! His month's notice. He's given it. Beach has. And not a word of explanation. No reason. No—'

Lord Emsworth broke off. His face suddenly hardened. What seemed the only possible solution of the mystery had struck him. Connie was at the bottom of this. Connie must have been coming the *grande dame* on the butler, wounding his sensibilities.

Yes, that must be it. It was just the sort of thing she would do. If he had caught her being the Old English Aristocrat once, he had caught her a hundred times. That way of hers of pursing the lips and raising the eyebrows and generally doing the daughter-of-a-hundred-earls stuff. Naturally no butler would stand it.

'Connie,' he cried, adjusting his pince-nez and staring keenly and accusingly, 'what have you been doing to Beach?'

Something that was almost a sob burst from Lady Constance's lips. Her lovely complexion had paled, and in some odd way she seemed to have shrunk.

'I shot him,' she whispered.

Lord Emsworth was a little hard of hearing.

'You did what?'

'I shot him.'

'Shot him?'

'Yes.'

'You mean, *shot* him?'

'Yes, yes, yes! I shot him with George's airgun.'

A whistling sigh escaped Lord Emsworth. He leaned back in his chair, and the library seemed to be dancing old country dances before his eyes. To say that he felt weak with relief would be to understate the effect of this extraordinary communication. His relief was so intense that he felt absolutely boneless. Not once but many times during the past quarter of an hour he had said to himself that only a miracle could save him from the consequences of his sins, and now the miracle had happened. No one was more alive than he to the fact that women are abundantly possessed of crust, but after this surely even Connie could not have the crust to reproach him for what he had done.

'Shot him?' he said, recovering speech.

A fleeting touch of the old imperiousness returned to Lady Constance.

'Do stop saying "Shot him?" Clarence! Isn't it bad enough to have done a perfectly mad thing, without having to listen to you talking like a parrot? Oh, dear! Oh, dear!'

'But what did you do it for?'

'I don't know. I tell you I don't know. Something seemed suddenly to come over me. It was as if I had been bewitched. After you went out, I thought I would take the gun to Beach—'

'Why?'

'I…I…. Well, I thought it would be safer with him than lying about in the library. So I took it down to his pantry. And all the way there I kept remembering what a wonderful shot I had been as a child—'

'What?' Lord Emsworth could not let this pass. 'What do you mean, you were a wonderful shot as a child? You've never shot in your life.'

'I have. Clarence, you were talking about Julia shooting Miss Mapleton. It wasn't Julia – it was I. She had made me stay in and do my rivers of Europe over again, so I shot her. I was a splendid shot in those days.'

'I bet you weren't as good as me,' said Lord Emsworth, piqued. 'I used to shoot rats.'

'So used I to shoot rats.'

'How many rats did you ever shoot?'

'Oh, Clarence, Clarence! Never mind about the rats.'

'No,' said Lord Emsworth, called to order. 'No, dash it. Never mind about the rats. Tell me about this Beach business.'

'Well, when I got to the pantry, it was empty, and I saw Beach outside by the laurel bush, reading in a deck-chair—'

'How far away?'

'I don't know. What does it matter? About six feet, I suppose.'

'Six feet? Ha!'

'And I shot him. I couldn't resist it. It was like some horrible obsession. There was a sort of hideous picture in my mind of how he would jump. So I shot him.'

'How do you know you did? I expect you missed him.'

'No. Because he sprang up. And then he saw me at the window and came in, and I said "Oh, Beach, I want you to take this airgun and keep it," and he said, "Very good, m'lady."'

'He didn't say anything about your shooting him?'

'No. And I have been hoping and hoping that he had not realized what had happened. I have been in an agony of suspense. But now you tell me that he has given his notice, so he must have done. Clarence,' cried Lady Constance, clasping her hands like a persecuted heroine, 'you see the awful position, don't you? If he leaves us, he will spread the story all over the county and people will think I'm mad. I shall never be able to live it down. You must persuade him to withdraw his notice. Offer him double wages. Offer him anything. He must not be allowed to leave. If he does, I shall never...S'h!'

'What do you mean, S'...Oh, ah,' said Lord Emsworth, at last observing that the door was opening.

It was his niece Jane who entered.

'Oh, hullo, Aunt Constance,' she said. 'I was wondering if you were in here. Mr Baxter's looking for you.'

Lady Constance was distrait.

'Mr Baxter?'

'Yes. I heard him asking Beach where you were. I think he wants to see you about something,' said Jane.

She directed at Lord Emsworth a swift glance, accompanied by a fleeting wink. 'Remember!' said the glance. 'Categorically!' said the wink.

Footsteps sounded outside. Rupert Baxter strode into the room.

At an earlier point in this chronicle, we have compared the aspect of Rupert Baxter, when burning with resentment, to a thunder-cloud, and it is possible that the reader may have formed a mental picture of just an ordinary thunder-cloud, the kind that rumbles a bit but does not really amount to anything very much. It was not this kind of cloud that the secretary resembled now, but one of those which burst over cities in the Tropics, inundating countrysides while thousands flee. He moved darkly towards Lady Constance, his hand outstretched. Lord Emsworth he ignored.

'I have come to say good-bye, Lady Constance,' he said.

There were not many statements that could have roused Lady Constance from her preoccupation, but this one did. She ceased to be the sports-woman brooding on memories of shikari, and stared aghast.

'Good-bye?'

'Good-bye.'

'But, Mr Baxter, you are not leaving us?'

'Precisely.'

For the first time, Rupert Baxter deigned to recognize that the ninth Earl was present.

'I am not prepared,' he said bitterly, 'to remain in a house where my chief duty appears to be to act as a target for Lord Emsworth and his airgun.'

'What!'

'Exactly.'

In the silence which followed these words, Jane once more gave her uncle that glance of encouragement and stimulation – that glance which said 'Be firm!' To her astonishment, she perceived that it was not needed. Lord Emsworth was firm already. His face was calm, his eye steady, and his pince-nez were not even quivering.

'The fellow's potty,' said Lord Emsworth in a clear, resonant voice. 'Absolutely potty. Always told you he was. Target for my airgun? Pooh! Pah! What's he talking about?'

Rupert Baxter quivered. His spectacles flashed fire.

'Do you deny that you shot me, Lord Emsworth?'

'Certainly I do.'

'Perhaps you will deny admitting to this lady here in the writing-room that you shot me?'

'Certainly I do.'

'Did you tell me that you had shot Mr Baxter, Uncle Clarence?' said Jane. 'I didn't hear you.'

'Of course I didn't.'

'I thought you hadn't. I should have remembered it.'

Rupert Baxter's hands shot ceilingwards, as if he were calling upon heaven to see justice done.

'You admitted it to me personally. You begged me not to tell anyone. You tried to put matters right by engaging me as your secretary, and I accepted the position. At that time I was perfectly willing to forget the entire affair. But when, not half an hour later…'

Lord Emsworth raised his eyebrows. Jane raised hers.

'How very extraordinary,' said Jane.

'Most,' said Lord Emsworth.

He removed his pince-nez and began to polish them, speaking soothingly the while. But his manner, though soothing, was very resolute.

'Baxter, my dear fellow,' he said, 'there's only one explanation of all this. It's just what I was telling you. You've been having these hallucinations of yours again. I never said a word to you about shooting you. I never said a word to my niece about shooting you. Why should I, when I hadn't? And, as for what you say about engaging you as my secretary, the absurdity of the thing is manifest on the very face of it. There is nothing on earth that would induce me to have you as my secretary. I don't want to hurt your feelings, but I'd rather be dead in a ditch. Now, listen, my dear Baxter, I'll tell you what to do. You just jump on that motor-bicycle of yours and go on touring England where you left off. And soon you will find that the fresh air will do wonders for that pottiness of yours. In a day or two you won't know…'

Rupert Baxter turned and stalked from the room.

'Mr Baxter!' cried Lady Constance.

Her intention of going after the fellow and pleading with him to continue inflicting his beastly presence on the quiet home life of Blandings Castle was so plain that Lord Emsworth did not hesitate.

'Connie!'

'But, Clarence!'

'Constance, you will remain where you are. You will not stir a step.'

'But, Clarence!'

'Not a dashed step. You hear me? Let him scram!'

Lady Constance halted, irresolute. Then suddenly she met the full force of the pince-nez and it was as if she – like Rupert Baxter – had been struck by a bullet. She collapsed into a chair and sat there twisting her rings forlornly.

'Oh, and, by the way, Connie,' said Lord Emsworth, 'I've been meaning to tell you. I've given that fellow Abercrombie that job he was asking for. I thought it all over carefully, and decided to drop him a line saying that pursuant on our recent conversation I was offering him Simmons's place. I've been making inquiries, and I find he's a capital fellow.'

'He's a baa-lamb,' said Jane.

'You hear? Jane says he's a baa-lamb. Just the sort of chap we want about the place.'

'So now we're going to get married.'

'So now they're going to get married. An excellent match, don't you think, Connie?'

Lady Constance did not speak. Lord Emsworth raised his voice a little.

'DON'T YOU, CONNIE?'

Lady Constance leaped in her seat as if she had heard the Last Trump.

'Very,' she said. 'Oh, very.'

'Right,' said Lord Emsworth. 'And now I'll go and talk to Beach.'

In the pantry, gazing sadly out on the stable yard, Beach the butler sat sipping a glass of port. In moments of mental stress, port was to Beach what Whiffle was to his employer, or, as we must now ruefully put it, his late employer. He flew to it when Life had got him down, and never before had Life got him down as it had now.

Sitting there in his pantry, that pantry which so soon would know him no more, Beach was in the depths. He mourned like some fallen monarch about to say good-bye to all his greatness and pass into exile. The die was cast. The end had come. Eighteen years, eighteen happy years, he had been in service at Blandings Castle, and now he must go forth, never to return. Little wonder that he sipped port. A weaker man would have swigged brandy.

Something tempestuous burst open the door, and he perceived that his privacy had been invaded by Lord Emsworth. He rose, and stood staring. In all the eighteen years during which he had held office, his employer had never before paid a visit to the pantry.

But it was not simply the other's presence that caused his gooseberry eyes to dilate to their full width, remarkable though that was. The mystery went deeper than that. For this was a strange, unfamiliar Lord Emsworth, a Lord Emsworth who glared where once he had blinked, who spurned the floor like a mettlesome charger, who banged tables and spilled port.

'Beach,' thundered this changeling, 'what the dooce is all this dashed nonsense?'

'M'lord?'

'You know what I mean. About leaving me. Have you gone off your head?'

A sigh shook the butler's massive frame.

'I fear that in the circumstances it is inevitable, m'lord.'

'Why? What are you talking about? Don't be an ass, Beach. Inevitable, indeed! Never heard such nonsense in my life. Why is it inevitable? Look me in the face and answer me that.'

'I feel it is better to tender my resignation than to be dismissed, m'lord.'

It was Lord Emsworth's turn to stare.

'Dismissed?'

'Yes, m'lord.'

'Beach, you're tight.'

'No, m'lord. Has not Mr Baxter spoken to you, m'lord?'

'Of course he's spoken to me. He's been gassing away half the afternoon. What's that got to do with it?'

Another sigh, seeming to start at the soles of his flat feet, set the butler's waistcoat rippling like corn in the wind.

'I see that Mr Baxter has not yet informed you, m'lord. I assumed that he would have done so before this. But it is a mere matter of time, I fear, before he makes his report.'

'Informed me of what?'

'I regret to say, m'lord, that in a moment of uncontrollable impulse I shot Mr Baxter.'

Lord Emsworth's pince-nez flew from his nose. Without them he could see only indistinctly, but he continued to stare at the butler, and in his eyes there appeared an expression which was a blend of several emotions. Amazement would have been the chief of these, had it not been exceeded by affection. He did not speak, but his eyes said 'My brother!'

'With Master George's airgun, m'lord, which her ladyship left in my custody. I regret to say, m'lord, that upon receipt of the weapon I went out into the grounds and came upon Mr Baxter walking near the shrubbery. I tried to resist the temptation, m'lord, but it was too keen. I was seized with an urge which I have not experienced since I was a small lad, and, in short, I—'

'Plugged him?'

'Yes, m'lord.'

Lord Emsworth could put two and two together.

'So that's what he was talking about in the library. That's what made him change his mind and send me that note.... How far was he away when you shot him?'

'A matter of a few feet, m'lord. I endeavoured to conceal myself behind a tree, but he turned very sharply, and I was so convinced that he had detected me that I felt I had no alternative but to resign my situation before he could make his report to you, m'lord.'

'And I thought you were leaving because my sister Connie shot you!'

'Her ladyship did not shoot me, m'lord. It is true that the weapon exploded accidentally in her ladyship's hand, but the bullet passed me harmlessly.'

Lord Emsworth snorted.

'And she said she was a good shot! Can't even hit a sitting butler at six feet. Listen to me, Beach. I want no more of this nonsense of you resigning. Bless my soul, how do you suppose I could get on without you? How long have you been here?'

'Eighteen years, m'lord.'

'Eighteen years! And you talk of resigning! Of all the dashed absurd ideas!'

'But I fear, m'lord, when her ladyship learns—'

'Her ladyship won't learn. Baxter won't tell her. Baxter's gone.'

'Gone, m'lord?'

'Gone for ever.'

'But I understood, m'lord—'

'Never mind what you understood. He's gone. A few feet away, did you say?'

'M'lord?'

'Did you say Baxter was only a few feet away when you got him?'

'Yes, m'lord.'

'Ah!' said Lord Emsworth.

He took the gun absently from the table and absently slipped a slug into the breach. He was feeling pleased and proud, as champions do whose pre-eminence is undisputed. Connie had missed a mark like Beach – practically a haystack – at six feet. Beach had plugged Baxter – true – and so had young George – but only with the muzzle of the gun almost touching the fellow. It had been left for him, Clarence, ninth Earl of Emsworth, to do the real shooting....

A damping thought came to diminish his complacency. It was as if a voice had whispered in his ear the word 'Fluke!' His jaw dropped a little, and he stood for awhile, brooding. He felt flattened and discouraged.

Had it been merely a fluke, that superb shot from the library window? Had he been mistaken in supposing that the ancient skill still lingered? Would he – which was what the voice was hinting – under similar conditions miss nine times out of ten?

A stuttering, sputtering noise broke in upon his reverie. He raised his eyes to the window. Out in the stable yard, Rupert Baxter was starting up his motor-bicycle.

'Mr Baxter, m'lord.'

'I see him.'

An overwhelming desire came upon Lord Emsworth to put this thing to the test, to silence for ever that taunting voice.

'How far away would you say he was, Beach?'

'Fully twenty yards, m'lord.'

'Watch!' said Lord Emsworth.

Into the sputtering of the bicycle there cut a soft pop. It was followed by a sharp howl. Rupert Baxter, who had been leaning on the handle-bars, rose six inches with his hand to his thigh.

'There!' said Lord Emsworth.

Baxter had ceased to rub his thigh. He was a man of intelligence, and he realized that anyone on the premises of Blandings Castle who wasted time hanging about and rubbing thighs was simply asking for it. To one trapped in this inferno of a Blandings Castle instant flight was the only way of winning to safety. The sputtering rose in a crescendo, diminished, died away altogether. Rupert Baxter had gone on, touring England.

Lord Emsworth was still gazing out of the window, raptly, as if looking at the X which marked the spot. For a long moment Beach stood staring reverently at his turned back. Then, as if performing some symbolic rite in keeping with the dignity of the scene, he reached for his glass of port and raised it in a silent toast.

Peace reigned in the butler's pantry. The sweet air of the summer evening poured in through the open window. It was as if Nature had blown the All Clear.

Blandings Castle was itself again.

A BEAN was in a nursing-home with a broken leg as the result of trying to drive his sports-model Poppenheim through the Marble Arch instead of round it, and a kindly Crumpet had looked in to give him the gossip of the town. He found him playing halma with the nurse, and he sat down on the bed and took a grape, and the Bean asked what was going on in the great world.

'Well,' said the Crumpet, taking another grape, 'the finest minds in the Drones are still wrestling with the great Hat mystery.'

'What's that?'

'You don't mean you haven't heard about it?'

'Not a word.'

The Crumpet was astounded. He swallowed two grapes at once in his surprise.

'Why, London's seething with it. The general consensus of opinion is that it has something to do with the Fourth Dimension. You know how things go. I mean to say, something rummy occurs and you consult some big-brained bird and he wags his head and says "Ah! The Fourth Dimension!" Extraordinary nobody's told you about the great Hat mystery.'

'You're the first visitor I've had. What is it, anyway? What hat?'

'Well, there were two hats. Reading from left to right, Percy Wimbolt's and Nelson Cork's.'

The Bean nodded intelligently.

'I see what you mean. Percy had one, and Nelson had the other.'

'Exactly. Two hats in all. Top hats.'

'What was mysterious about them?'

'Why, Elizabeth Bottsworth and Diana Punter said they didn't fit.'

'Well, hats don't sometimes.'

'But these came from Bodmin's.'

The Bean shot up in bed. 'What?'

'You mustn't excite the patient,' said the nurse, who up to this point had taken no part in the conversation.

'But, dash it, nurse,' cried the Bean, 'you can't have caught what he said. If we are to give credence to his story, Percy Wimbolt and Nelson Cork bought a couple of hats at Bodmin's – at *Bodmin's*, I'll trouble you – and they didn't fit. It isn't possible.'

He spoke with strong emotion, and the Crumpet nodded understandingly. People can say what they please about the modern young man believing in nothing nowadays, but there is one thing every right-minded young man believes in, and that is the infallibility of Bodmin's hats. It is one of the eternal verities. Once admit that it is possible for a Bodmin hat not to fit, and you leave the door open for Doubt, Schism, and Chaos generally.

'That's exactly how Percy and Nelson felt, and it was for that reason that they were compelled to take the strong line they did with E. Bottsworth and D. Punter.'

'They took a strong line, did they?'

'A very strong line.'

'Won't you tell us the whole story from the beginning?' said the nurse.

'Right ho,' said the Crumpet, taking a grape. 'It'll make your head swim.'

'So mysterious?'

'So absolutely dashed uncanny from start to finish.'

You must know, to begin with, my dear old nurse (said the Crumpet), that these two blokes, Percy Wimbolt and Nelson Cork, are fellows who have to exercise the most watchful care about their lids, because they are so situated that in their case there can be none of that business of just charging into any old hattery and grabbing the first thing in sight. Percy is one of those large, stout, outsize chaps with a head like a water-melon, while Nelson is built more on the lines of a minor jockey and has a head like a peanut.

You will readily appreciate, therefore, that it requires an artist hand to fit them properly and that is why they have always gone to Bodmin. I have heard Percy say that his trust in Bodmin is like the unspotted faith of a young curate in his Bishop and I have no doubt that Nelson would have said the same, if he had thought of it.

It was at Bodmin's door that they ran into each other on the morning when my story begins.

'Hullo,' said Percy. 'You come to buy a hat?'

'Yes,' said Nelson. 'You come to buy a hat?'

'Yes.' Percy glanced cautiously about him, saw that he was alone (except for Nelson, of course) and unobserved, and drew closer and lowered his voice. 'There's a reason!'

'That's rummy,' said Nelson. He, also, spoke in a hushed tone. 'I have a special reason, too.'

Percy looked warily about, and lowered his voice another notch.

'Nelson,' he said, 'you know Elizabeth Bottsworth?'

'Intimately,' said Nelson.

'Rather a sound young potato, what?'

'Very much so.'

'Pretty.'

'I've often noticed it.'

'Me, too. She is so small, so sweet, so dainty, so lively, so viv— what's-the-word? – that a fellow wouldn't be far out in calling her an angel in human shape.'

'Aren't all angels in human shape?'

'Are they?' said Percy, who was a bit foggy on angels. 'Well, be that as it may,' he went on, his cheeks suffused to a certain extent, 'I love that girl, Nelson, and she's coming with me to the first day of Ascot, and I'm relying on this new hat of mine to do just that extra bit that's needed in the way of making her reciprocate my passion. Having only met her so far at country-houses, I've never yet flashed upon her in a topper.'

Nelson Cork was staring.

'Well, if that isn't the most remarkable coincidence I ever came across in my puff!' he exclaimed, amazed. 'I'm buying my new hat for exactly the same reason.'

A convulsive start shook Percy's massive frame. His eyes bulged.

'To fascinate Elizabeth Bottsworth?' he cried, beginning to writhe.

'No, no,' said Nelson, soothingly. 'Of course not. Elizabeth and I have always been great friends, but nothing more. What I meant was that I, like you, am counting on this forthcoming topper of mine to put me across with the girl I love.'

Percy stopped writhing.

'Who is she?' he asked, interested.

'Diana Punter, the niece of my godmother, old Ma Punter. It's an odd thing, I've known her all my life – brought up as kids together and so forth – but it's only recently that passion has burgeoned. I now worship that girl, Percy, from the top of her head to the soles of her divine feet.'

Percy looked dubious.

'That's a pretty longish distance, isn't it? Diana Punter is one of my closest friends, and a charming girl in every respect, but isn't she a bit tall for you, old man?'

'My dear chap, that's just what I admire so much about her, her superb statuesqueness. More like a Greek goddess than anything I've struck for years. Besides, she isn't any taller for me than you are for Elizabeth Bottsworth.'

'True,' admitted Percy.

'And, anyway, I love her, blast it, and I don't propose to argue the point. I love her, I love her, I love her, and we are lunching together the first day of Ascot.'

'At Ascot?'

'No. She isn't keen on racing, so I shall have to give Ascot a miss.'

'That's Love,' said Percy, awed.

'The binge will take place at my godmother's house in Berkeley Square, and it won't be long after that, I feel, before you see an interesting announcement in the *Morning Post*.'

Percy extended his hand. Nelson grasped it warmly.

'These new hats are pretty well bound to do the trick, I should say, wouldn't you?'

'Infallibly. Where girls are concerned, there is nothing that brings home the gravy like a well-fitting topper.'

'Bodmin must extend himself as never before,' said Percy.

'He certainly must,' said Nelson.

They entered the shop. And Bodmin, having measured them with his own hands, promised that two of his very finest efforts should be at their respective addresses in the course of the next few days.

Now, Percy Wimbolt isn't a chap you would suspect of having nerves, but there is no doubt that in the interval which elapsed before Bodmin was scheduled to deliver he got pretty twittery. He kept having awful visions of some great disaster happening to his new hat: and, as things turned out, these visions came jolly near being fulfilled. It has made Percy feel that he is psychic.

What occurred was this. Owing to these jitters of his, he hadn't been sleeping any too well, and on the morning before Ascot he was up as early as ten-thirty, and he went to his sitting-room window to see what sort of a day it was, and the sight he beheld from that window absolutely froze the blood in his veins.

For there below him, strutting up and down the pavement, were a uniformed little blighter whom he recognized as Bodmin's errand-boy and an equally foul kid in mufti. And balanced on each child's loathsome head was a top hat. Against the railings were leaning a couple of cardboard hat-boxes.

Now, considering that Percy had only just woken from a dream in which he had been standing outside the Guildhall in his new hat, receiving the Freedom of the City from the Lord Mayor, and the Lord Mayor had suddenly taken a terrific swipe at the hat with his mace, knocking it into hash, you might have supposed that he would have been hardened to anything. But he wasn't. His reaction was terrific. There was a moment of sort of paralysis, during which he was telling himself that he had always suspected this beastly little boy of Bodmin's of having a low and frivolous outlook and being temperamentally unfitted for his high office: and then he came alive with a jerk and let out probably the juiciest yell the neighbourhood had heard for years.

It stopped the striplings like a high-powered shell. One moment, they had been swanking up and down in a mincing and affected sort of way: the next, the second kid had legged it like a streak and Bodmin's boy was shoving the hats back in the boxes and trying to do it quickly enough to enable him to be elsewhere when Percy should arrive.

And in this he was successful. By the time Percy had got to the front door and opened it, there was nothing to be seen but a hat-box standing on the steps. He took it up to his flat and removed the contents with a gingerly and reverent hand, holding his breath for fear the nap should have got rubbed the wrong way or a dent of any nature been made in the gleaming surface; but apparently all was well. Bodmin's boy might sink to taking hats out of their boxes and fooling about with them, but at least he hadn't gone to the last awful extreme of dropping them.

The lid was OK absolutely: and on the following morning Percy, having spent the interval polishing it with stout, assembled the boots, the spats, the trousers, the coat, the flowered waistcoat, the collar, the shirt, the quiet grey tie, and the good old gardenia, and set off in a taxi for the house where Elizabeth was staying. And presently he was ringing the bell and being told she would be down in a minute, and eventually down she came, looking perfectly marvellous.

'What ho, what ho!' said Percy.

'Hullo, Percy,' said Elizabeth.

Now, naturally, up to this moment Percy had been standing with bared head. At this point, he put the hat on. He wanted her to get the full effect suddenly in a good light. And very strategic, too. I mean to say, it would have been the act of a juggins to have waited till they were in the taxi, because in a taxi all toppers look much alike.

So Percy popped the hat on his head with a meaning glance and stood waiting for the uncontrollable round of applause.

And instead of clapping her little hands in girlish ecstasy and doing Spring dances round him, this young Bottsworth gave a sort of gurgling scream not unlike a coloratura soprano choking on a fish-bone.

Then she blinked and became calmer.

'It's all right,' she said. 'The momentary weakness has passed. Tell me, Percy, when do you open?'

'Open?' said Percy, not having the remotest.

'On the Halls. Aren't you going to sing comic songs on the Music Halls?'

Percy's perplexity deepened.

'Me? No. How? Why? What do you mean?'

'I thought that hat must be part of the make-up and that you were trying it on the dog. I couldn't think of any other reason why you should wear one six sizes too small.'

Percy gasped. 'You aren't suggesting this hat doesn't fit me?'

'It doesn't fit you by a mile.'

'But it's a Bodmin.'

'Call it that if you like. I call it a public outrage.'

Percy was appalled. I mean, naturally. A nice thing for a chap to give his heart to a girl and then find her talking in this hideous, flippant way of sacred subjects.

Then it occurred to him that, living all the time in the country, she might not have learned to appreciate the holy significance of the name Bodmin.

'Listen,' he said gently. 'Let me explain. This hat was made by Bodmin, the world-famous hatter of Vigo Street. He measured me in person and guaranteed a fit.'

'And I nearly had one.'

'And if Bodmin guarantees that a hat shall fit,' proceeded Percy, trying to fight against a sickening sort of feeling that he had been all wrong about this girl, 'it fits. I mean, saying a Bodmin hat doesn't fit is like saying…well, I can't think of anything awful enough.'

'That hat's awful enough. It's like something out of a two-reel comedy. Pure Chas. Chaplin. I know a joke's a joke, Percy, and I'm as fond of a laugh as anyone, but there is such a thing as cruelty to animals. Imagine the feelings of the horses at Ascot when they see that hat.'

Poets and other literary blokes talk a lot about falling in love at first sight, but it's equally possible to fall out of love just as quickly. One moment, this girl was the be-all and the end-all, as you might say, of Percy Wimbolt's life. The next, she was just a regrettable young blister with whom he wished to hold no further communication. He could stand a good deal from the sex. Insults directed at himself left him unmoved. But he was not prepared to countenance destructive criticism of a Bodmin hat.

'Possibly,' he said, coldly, 'you would prefer to go to this bally race-meeting alone?'

'You bet I'm going alone. You don't suppose I mean to be seen in broad daylight in the paddock at Ascot with a hat like that?'

Percy stepped back and bowed formally.

'Drive on, driver,' he said to the driver, and the driver drove on.

Now, you would say that that was rummy enough. A full-sized mystery in itself, you might call it. But wait. Mark the sequel. You haven't heard anything yet.

We now turn to Nelson Cork. Shortly before one-thirty, Nelson had shoved over to Berkeley Square and had lunch with his godmother and Diana Punter, and Diana's manner and deportment had been absolutely all that could have been desired. In fact, so chummy had she been over the cutlets and fruit salad that it seemed to Nelson that, if she was like this now, imagination boggled at the thought of how utterly all over him she would be when he sprang his new hat on her.

So when the meal was concluded and coffee had been drunk and old Lady Punter had gone up to her boudoir with a digestive tablet and a sex-novel, he thought it would be a sound move to invite her to come for a stroll along Bond Street. There was the chance, of course, that she would fall into his arms right in the middle of the pavement: but if that happened, he told himself, they could always get into a cab. So he mooted the saunter, and she checked up, and presently they started off.

And you will scarcely believe this, but they hadn't gone more than half-way along Bruton Street when she suddenly stopped and looked at him in an odd manner.

'I don't want to be personal, Nelson,' she said, 'but really I do think you ought to take the trouble to get measured for your hats.'

If a gas main had exploded beneath Nelson's feet, he could hardly have been more taken aback.

'M-m-m-m...' he gasped. He could scarcely believe that he had heard aright.

'It's the only way with a head like yours. I know it's a temptation for a lazy man to go into a shop and take just whatever is offered him, but the result is so sloppy. That thing you're wearing now looks like an extinguisher.'

Nelson was telling himself that he must be strong.

'Are you endeavouring to intimate that this hat does not fit?'

'Can't you feel that it doesn't fit?'

'But it's a Bodmin.'

'I don't know what you mean. It's just an ordinary silk hat.'

'Not at all. It's a Bodmin.'

'I don't know what you are talking about.'

'The point I am trying to drive home,' said Nelson, stiffly, 'is that this hat was constructed under the personal auspices of Jno. Bodmin of Vigo Street.'

'Well, it's too big.'

'It is not too big.'

'I say it is too big.'

'And I say a Bodmin hat cannot be too big.'

'Well, I've got eyes, and I say it is.'

Nelson controlled himself with an effort.

'I would be the last person,' he said, 'to criticize your eyesight, but on the present occasion you will permit me to say that it has let you down with a considerable bump. Myopia is indicated. Allow me,' said Nelson, hot under the collar, but still dignified, 'to tell you something about Jno. Bodmin, as the name appears new to you. Jno. is the last of a long line of Bodmins, all of whom have made hats assiduously for the nobility and gentry all their lives. Hats are in Jno. Bodmin's blood.'

'I don't…'

Nelson held up a restraining hand.

'Over the door of his emporium in Vigo Street the passers-by may read a significant legend. It runs: "Bespoke Hatter To The Royal Family". That means, in simple language adapted to the lay intelligence, that if the King wants a new topper he simply ankles round to Bodmin's and says: "Good morning, Bodmin, we want a topper." He does not ask if it will fit. He takes it for granted that it will fit. He has bespoken Jno. Bodmin, and he trusts him blindly. You don't suppose His Gracious Majesty would bespeak a hatter whose hats did not fit. The whole essence of being a hatter is to make hats that fit, and it is to this end that Jno. Bodmin has strained every nerve for years. And that is why I say again – simply and without heat – This hat is a Bodmin.'

Diana was beginning to get a bit peeved. The blood of the Punters is hot, and very little is required to steam it up. She tapped Bruton Street with a testy foot.

'You always were an obstinate, pig-headed little fiend, Nelson, even as a child. I tell you once more, for the last time, that that hat is too big. If it were not for the fact that I can see a pair of boots and part of a pair of trousers, I should not know that there was a human being under it. I don't care how much you argue, I still think you ought to be ashamed of yourself for coming out in the thing. Even if you didn't mind for your own sake, you might have considered the feelings of the pedestrians and traffic.'

Nelson quivered.

'You do, do you?'

'Yes, I do.'

'Oh, you do?'

'I said I did. Didn't you hear me? No, I suppose you could hardly be expected to, with an enormous great hat coming down over your ears.'

'You say this hat comes down over my ears?'

'Right over your ears. It's a mystery to me why you think it worth while to deny it.'

I fear that what follows does not show Nelson Cork in the role of a parfait gentil knight, but in extenuation of his behaviour I must remind you that he and Diana Punter had been brought up as children together, and a dispute between a couple who have shared the same nursery is always liable to degenerate into an exchange of personalities and innuendos. What starts as an academic discussion on hats turns only too swiftly into a raking-up of old scores and a grand parade of family skeletons.

It was so in this case. At the word 'mystery', Nelson uttered a nasty laugh.

'A mystery, eh? As much a mystery, I suppose, as why your uncle George suddenly left England in the year 1920 without stopping to pack up?'

Diana's eyes flashed. Her foot struck the pavement another shrewd wallop.

'Uncle George,' she said haughtily, 'went abroad for his health.'

'You bet he did,' retorted Nelson. 'He knew what was good for him.'

'Anyway, he wouldn't have worn a hat like that.'

'Where they would have put him if he hadn't been off like a scalded kitten, he wouldn't have worn a hat at all.'

A small groove was now beginning to appear in the paving-stone on which Diana Punter stood.

'Well, Uncle George escaped one thing by going abroad, at any rate,' she said. 'He missed the big scandal about your aunt Clarissa in 1922.'

Nelson clenched his fists. 'The jury gave Aunt Clarissa the benefit of the doubt,' he said hoarsely.

'Well, we all know what that means. It was accompanied, if you recollect, by some very strong remarks from the Bench.'

There was a pause.

'I may be wrong,' said Nelson, 'but I should have thought it ill beseemed a girl whose brother Cyril was warned off the Turf in 1924 to haul up her slacks about other people's Aunt Clarissas.'

'Passing lightly over my brother Cyril in 1924,' rejoined Diana, 'what price your cousin Fred in 1927?'

They glared at one another in silence for a space, each realizing with a pang that the supply of erring relatives had now given out. Diana was still pawing the paving-stone, and Nelson was wondering what on earth he could ever have seen in a girl who, in addition to talking subversive drivel about hats, was eight feet tall and ungainly, to boot.

'While as for your brother-in-law's niece's sister-in-law Muriel…' began Diana, suddenly brightening.

Nelson checked her with a gesture.

'I prefer not to continue this discussion,' he said, frigidly.

'It is no pleasure to me,' replied Diana, with equal coldness, 'to have to listen to your vapid gibberings. That's the worst of a man who wears his hat over his mouth – he will talk through it.'

'I bid you a very hearty good afternoon, Miss Punter,' said Nelson.

He strode off without a backward glance.

Now, one advantage of having a row with a girl in Bruton Street is that the Drones is only just round the corner, so that you can pop in and restore the old nervous system with the minimum of trouble. Nelson was round there in what practically amounted to a trice, and the first person he saw was Percy, hunched up over a double and splash.

'Hullo,' said Percy.

'Hullo,' said Nelson.

There was a silence, broken only by the sound of Nelson ordering a mixed vermouth. Percy continued to stare before him like a man who has drained the wine-cup of life to its lees, only to discover a dead mouse at the bottom.

'Nelson,' he said at length, 'what are your views on the Modern Girl?'

'I think she's a mess.'

'I thoroughly agree with you,' said Percy. 'Of course, Diana Punter is a rare exception, but, apart from Diana, I wouldn't give you twopence for the modern girl. She lacks depth and reverence and has no sense of what is fitting. Hats, for example.'

'Exactly. But what do you mean Diana Punter is an exception? She's one of the ringleaders – the spearhead of the movement, if you like to put it that way. Think,' said Nelson, sipping his vermouth, 'of all the unpleasant qualities of the Modern Girl, add them up, double them, and what have you got? Diana Punter. Let me tell you what took place between me and this Punter only a few minutes ago.'

'No,' said Percy. 'Let me tell you what transpired between me and Elizabeth Bottsworth this morning. Nelson, old man, she said my hat – my Bodmin hat – was too small.'

'You don't mean that?'

'Those were her very words.'

'Well, I'm dashed. Listen. Diana Punter told me my equally Bodmin hat was too large.'

They stared at one another.

'It's the Spirit of something,' said Nelson. 'I don't know what, quite, but of something. You see it on all sides. Something very serious has gone wrong with girls nowadays. There is lawlessness and licence abroad.'

'And here in England, too.'

'Well, naturally, you silly ass,' said Nelson, with some asperity. 'When I said abroad, I didn't mean abroad, I meant abroad.'

He mused for a moment.

'I must say, though,' he continued, 'I am surprised at what you tell me about Elizabeth Bottsworth, and am inclined to think there must have been some mistake. I have always been a warm admirer of Elizabeth.'

'And I have always thought Diana one of the best, and I find it hard to believe that she should have shown up in such a dubious light as you suggest. Probably there was a misunderstanding of some kind.'

'Well, I ticked her off properly, anyway.'

Percy Wimbolt shook his head.

'You shouldn't have done that, Nelson. You may have wounded her feelings. In my case, of course, I had no alternative but to be pretty crisp with Elizabeth.'

Nelson Cork clicked his tongue.

'A pity,' he said. 'Elizabeth is sensitive.'

'So is Diana.'

'Not so sensitive as Elizabeth.'

'I should say, at a venture, about five times as sensitive as Elizabeth. However, we must not quarrel about a point like that, old man. The fact that emerges is that we seem both to have been dashed badly treated. I think I shall toddle home and take an aspirin.'

'Me, too.'

They went off to the cloak-room, where their hats were, and Percy put his on.

'Surely,' he said, 'nobody but a half-witted little pipsqueak who can't see straight would say this was too small?'

'It isn't a bit too small,' said Nelson. 'And take a look at this one. Am I not right in supposing that only a female giantess with straws in her hair and astigmatism in both eyes could say it was too large?'

'It's a lovely fit.'

And the cloak-room waiter, a knowledgeable chap of the name of Robinson, said the same.

'So there you are,' said Nelson.

'Ah, well,' said Percy.

They left the club, and parted at the top of Dover Street.

Now, though he had not said so in so many words, Nelson Cork's heart had bled for Percy Wimbolt. He knew the other's fine sensibilities and he could guess how deeply they must have been gashed by this unfortunate breaking-off of diplomatic relations with the girl he loved. For, whatever might have happened, however sorely he might have been wounded, the way Nelson Cork looked at it was that Percy loved Elizabeth Bottsworth in spite of everything. What was required here, felt Nelson, was a tactful mediator — a kindly, sensible friend of both parties who would hitch up his socks and plunge in and heal the breach.

So the moment he had got rid of Percy outside the club he hared round to the house where Elizabeth was staying and was lucky enough to catch her on the front door steps. For, naturally, Elizabeth hadn't gone off to Ascot by herself. Directly Percy was out of sight, she had told the taxi-man to drive her home, and she had been occupying the interval since the painful scene in thinking of things she wished she had said to him and taking her hostess's dog for a run — a Pekingese called Clarkson.

She seemed very pleased to see Nelson, and started to prattle of this and that, her whole demeanour that of a girl who, after having been compelled to associate for a while with the Underworld, has at last found a kindred soul. And the more he listened, the more he wanted to go on listening. And the more he looked at her, the more he felt that a lifetime spent in gazing at Elizabeth Bottsworth would be a lifetime dashed well spent.

There was something about the girl's exquisite petiteness and fragility that appealed to Nelson Cork's depths. After having wasted so much time looking at a female Carnera like Diana Punter, it was a genuine treat to him to be privileged to feast the eyes on one so small and dainty. And, what with one thing and another, he found the most extraordinary difficulty in lugging Percy into the conversation.

They strolled along, chatting. And, mark you, Elizabeth Bottsworth was a girl a fellow could chat with without getting a crick in the neck from goggling up at her, the way you had to do when you took the air with Diana Punter. Nelson realized now that talking to Diana Punter had been like trying to exchange thoughts with a flag-pole sitter. He was surprised that this had never occurred to him before.

'You know, you're looking perfectly ripping, Elizabeth,' he said.

'How funny!' said the girl. 'I was just going to say the same thing about you.'

'Not really?'

'Yes, I was. After some of the gargoyles I've seen today – Percy Wimbolt is an example that springs to the mind – it's such a relief to be with a man who really knows how to turn himself out.'

Now that the Percy *motif* had been introduced, it should have been a simple task for Nelson to turn the talk to the subject of his absent friend. But somehow he didn't. Instead, he just simpered a bit and said: 'Oh no, I say, really, do you mean that?'

'I do, indeed,' said Elizabeth earnestly. 'It's your hat, principally, I think. I don't know why it is, but ever since a child I have been intensely sensitive to hats, and it has always been a pleasure to me to remember that at the age of five I dropped a pot of jam out of the nursery window on to my Uncle Alexander when he came to visit us in a deer-stalker cap with ear-flaps, as worn by Sherlock Holmes. I consider the hat the final test of a man. Now, yours is perfect. I never saw such a beautiful fit. I can't tell you how much I admire that hat. It gives you quite an ambassadorial look.'

Nelson Cork drew a deep breath. He was tingling from head to foot. It was as if the scales had fallen from his eyes and a new life begun for him.

'I say,' he said, trembling with emotion, 'I wonder if you would mind if I pressed your little hand?'

'Do,' said Elizabeth cordially.

'I will,' said Nelson, and did so. 'And now,' he went on, clinging to the fin like glue and hiccoughing a bit, 'how about buzzing off somewhere for a quiet cup of tea? I have a feeling that we have much to say to one another.'

It is odd how often it happens in this world that when there are two chaps and one chap's heart is bleeding for the other chap you find that all the while the second chap's heart is bleeding just as much for the first chap. Both bleeding, I mean to say, not only one. It was so in the case of Nelson Cork and Percy Wimbolt. The moment he had left Nelson, Percy charged straight off in search of Diana Punter with the intention of putting everything right with a few well-chosen words.

Because what he felt was that, though at the actual moment of going to press pique might be putting Nelson off Diana, this would pass off and love come into its own again. All that was required, he considered, was a suave go-between, a genial mutual pal who would pour oil on the troubled w.'s and generally fix things up.

He found Diana walking round and round Berkeley Square with her chin up, breathing tensely through the nostrils. He drew up alongside and what-hoed, and as she beheld him the cold, hard gleam in her eyes changed to a light of cordiality. She appeared charmed to see him and at once embarked on an animated conversation. And with every word she spoke his conviction deepened that of all the ways of passing a summer afternoon there was none fruitier than having a friendly hike with Diana Punter.

And it was not only her talk that enchanted him. He was equally fascinated by that wonderful physique of hers. When he considered that he had actually wasted several valuable minutes that day conversing with a young shrimp like Elizabeth Bottsworth, he could have kicked himself.

Here, he reflected, as they walked round the square, was a girl whose ear was more or less on a level with a fellow's mouth, so that such observations as he might make were enabled to get from point to point with the least possible delay. Talking to Elizabeth Bottsworth had always been like bellowing down a well in the hope of attracting the attention of one of the smaller infusoria at the bottom. It surprised him that he had been so long in coming to this conclusion.

He was awakened from this reverie by hearing his companion utter the name of Nelson Cork.

'I beg your pardon?' he said.

'I was saying,' said Diana, 'that Nelson Cork is a wretched little undersized blob who, if he were not too lazy to work, would long since have signed up with some good troupe of midgets.'

'Oh, would you say that?'

'I would say more than that,' said Diana firmly. 'I tell you, Percy, that what makes life so ghastly for girls, what causes girls to get grey hair and go into convents, is the fact that it is not always possible for them to avoid being seen in public with men like Nelson Cork. I trust I am not uncharitable. I try to view these things in a broad-minded way, saying to myself that if a man looks like something that has come out from under a flat stone it is his misfortune rather than his fault and that he is more to be pitied than censured. But on one thing I do insist, that such a man does not wantonly aggravate the natural unpleasantness of his appearance by prancing about London in a hat that reaches down to his ankles. I cannot and will not endure being escorted along Bruton Street by a sort of human bacillus the brim of whose hat bumps on the pavement with every step he takes. What I have always said and what I shall always say is that the hat is the acid test. A man who cannot buy the right-sized hat is a man one could never like or trust. Your hat, now, Percy, is exactly right. I have seen a good many hats in my time, but I really do not think that I have ever come across a more perfect specimen of all that a hat should be. Not too large, not too small, fitting snugly to the head like the skin on a sausage. And you have just the kind of head that a silk hat shows off. It gives you a sort of look…how shall I describe it?…it conveys the idea of a master of men. Leonine is the word I want. There is something about the way it rests on the brow and the almost imperceptible tilt towards the south-east…'

Percy Wimbolt was quivering like an Oriental muscle-dancer. Soft music seemed to be playing from the direction of Hay Hill, and Berkeley Square had begun to skip round him on one foot.

He drew a deep breath.

'I say,' he said, 'stop me if you've heard this before, but what I feel we ought to do at this juncture is to dash off somewhere where it's quiet and there aren't so many houses dancing the "Blue Danube" and shove some tea into ourselves. And over the pot and muffins I shall have something very important to say to you.'

'So that,' concluded the Crumpet, taking a grape, 'is how the thing stands; and, in a sense, of course, you could say that it is a satisfactory ending.

'The announcement of Elizabeth's engagement to Nelson Cork appeared in the Press on the same day as that of Diana's projected hitching-up with Percy Wimbolt: and it is pleasant that the happy couples should be so well matched as regards size.

'I mean to say, there will be none of that business of a six-foot girl tripping down the aisle with a five-foot-four man, or a six-foot-two man trying to keep step along the sacred edifice with a four-foot-three girl. This is always good for a laugh from the ringside pews, but it does not make for wedded bliss.

'No, as far as the principals are concerned, we may say that all has ended well. But that doesn't seem to me the important point. What seems to me the important point is this extraordinary, baffling mystery of those hats.'

'Absolutely,' said the Bean.

'I mean to say, if Percy's hat really didn't fit, as Elizabeth Bottsworth contended, why should it have registered as a winner with Diana Punter?'

'Absolutely,' said the Bean.

'And, conversely, if Nelson's hat was the total loss which Diana Punter considered it, why, only a brief while later, was it going like a breeze with Elizabeth Bottsworth?'

'Absolutely,' said the Bean.

'The whole thing is utterly inscrutable.'

It was at this point that the nurse gave signs of wishing to catch the Speaker's eye.

'Shall I tell you what I think?'

'Say on, my dear young pillow-smoother.'

'I believe Bodmin's boy must have got those hats mixed. When he was putting them back in the boxes, I mean.'

The Crumpet shook his head, and took a grape.

'And then at the club they got the right ones again.'

The Crumpet smiled indulgently.

'Ingenious,' he said, taking a grape. 'Quite ingenious. But a little far-fetched. No, I prefer to think the whole thing, as I say, has something to do with the Fourth Dimension. I am convinced that that is the true explanation, if our minds could only grasp it.'

'Absolutely,' said the Bean.

'DO YOU believe in ghosts?' asked Mr Mulliner abruptly.

I weighed the question thoughtfully. I was a little surprised, for nothing in our previous conversation had suggested the topic.

'Well,' I replied, 'I don't like them, if that's what you mean. I was once butted by one as a child.'

'Ghosts. Not goats.'

'Oh, ghosts? Do I believe in ghosts?'

'Exactly.'

'Well, yes – and no.'

'Let me put it another way,' said Mr Mulliner, patiently. 'Do you believe in haunted houses? Do you believe that it is possible for a malign influence to envelop a place and work a spell on all who come within its radius?'

I hesitated.

'Well, no – and yes.'

Mr Mulliner sighed a little. He seemed to be wondering if I was always as bright as this.

'Of course,' I went on, 'one has read stories. Henry James's *Turn of the Screw*...'

'I am not talking about fiction.'

'Well, in real life— Well, look here, I once, as a matter of fact, did meet a man who knew a fellow—'

'My distant cousin James Rodman spent some weeks in a haunted house,' said Mr Mulliner, who, if he has a fault, is not a very good listener. 'It cost him five thousand pounds. That is to say, he sacrificed five thousand pounds by not remaining there. Did you ever,' he asked, wandering, it seemed to me, from the subject, 'hear of Leila J. Pinckney?'

Naturally I had heard of Leila J. Pinckney. Her death some years ago has diminished her vogue, but at one time it was impossible to pass a book-shop or a railway bookstall without seeing a long row of her novels. I had never myself actually read any of them, but I knew that in her particular line of literature, the

Squashily Sentimental, she had always been regarded by those entitled to judge as pre-eminent. The critics usually headed their reviews of her stories with the words:–

ANOTHER PINCKNEY

or sometimes, more offensively:–

ANOTHER PINCKNEY!!!

And once, dealing with, I think, *The Love Which Prevails*, the literary expert of the *Scrutinizer* had compressed his entire critique into the single phrase 'Oh, God!'

'Of course,' I said. 'But what about her?'

'She was James Rodman's aunt.'

'Yes?'

'And when she died James found that she had left him five thousand pounds and the house in the country where she had lived for the last twenty years of her life.'

'A very nice little legacy.'

'Twenty years,' repeated Mr Mulliner. 'Grasp that, for it has a vital bearing on what follows. Twenty years, mind you, and Miss Pinckney turned out two novels and twelve short stories regularly every year, besides a monthly page of Advice to Young Girls in one of the magazines. That is to say, forty of her novels and no fewer than two hundred and forty of her short stories were written under the roof of Honeysuckle Cottage.'

'A pretty name.'

'A nasty, sloppy name,' said Mr Mulliner severely, 'which should have warned my distant cousin James from the start. Have you a pencil and a piece of paper?' He scribbled for a while, poring frowningly over columns of figures. 'Yes,' he said, looking up, 'if my calculations are correct, Leila J. Pinckney wrote in all a matter of nine million one hundred and forty thousand words of glutinous sentimentality at Honeysuckle Cottage, and it was a condition of her will that James should reside there for six months in every year. Failing to do this, he was to forfeit the five thousand pounds.'

'It must be great fun making a freak will,' I mused. 'I often wish I was rich enough to do it.'

'This was not a freak will. The conditions are perfectly understandable. James Rodman was a writer of sensational mystery stories, and his aunt Leila had always disapproved of his work. She was a great believer in the influence of environment, and the reason why she inserted that clause in her will was that she wished to compel James to move from London to the country. She considered that living in London hardened him and made his outlook on life sordid. She often asked him if he thought it quite nice to harp so much on sudden death and blackmailers with squints. Surely, she said, there were enough squinting blackmailers in the world without writing about them.

'The fact that Literature meant such different things to these two had, I believe, caused something of a coolness between them, and James had never dreamed that he would be remembered in his aunt's will. For he had never concealed his opinion that Leila J. Pinckney's style of writing revolted him, however dear it might be to her enormous public. He held rigid views on the art of the novel, and always maintained that an artist with a true reverence for his craft should not descend to goo-ey love stories, but should stick austerely to revolvers, cries in the night, missing papers, mysterious Chinamen and dead bodies – with or without gash in throat. And not even the thought that his aunt had dandled him on her knee as a baby could induce him to stifle his literary conscience to the extent of pretending to enjoy her work. First, last and all the time, James Rodman had held the opinion – and voiced it fearlessly – that Leila J. Pinckney wrote bilge.

'It was a surprise to him, therefore, to find that he had been left this legacy. A pleasant surprise, of course. James was making quite a decent income out of the three novels and eighteen short stories which he produced annually, but an author can always find a use for five thousand pounds. And, as for the cottage, he had actually been looking about for a little place in the country at the very moment when he received the lawyer's letter. In less than a week he was installed at his new residence.'

James's first impressions of Honeysuckle Cottage were, he tells me, wholly favourable. He was delighted with the place. It was a low, rambling, picturesque old house with funny little chimneys and a red roof, placed in the middle of the most charming country. With its oak beams, its trim garden, its trilling birds and its rose-hung porch, it was the ideal spot for a writer. It was just the sort of place, he reflected whimsically, which his aunt had loved to write about in her books. Even the apple-cheeked old housekeeper who attended to his needs might have stepped straight out of one of them.

It seemed to James that his lot had been cast in pleasant places. He had brought down his books, his pipes and his golf-clubs, and was hard at work finishing the best thing he had ever done. *The Secret Nine* was the title of it; and on the beautiful summer afternoon on which this story opens he was in the study, hammering away at his typewriter, at peace with the world. The machine was running sweetly, the new tobacco he had bought the day before was proving admirable, and he was moving on all six cylinders to the end of a chapter.

He shoved in a fresh sheet of paper, chewed his pipe thoughtfully for a moment, then wrote rapidly:

'For an instant Lester Gage thought that he must have been mistaken. Then the noise came again, faint but unmistakable – a soft scratching on the outer panel.

'His mouth set in a grim line. Silently, like a panther, he made one quick step to the desk, noiselessly opened a drawer, drew out his automatic. After that affair of the poisoned needle, he was taking no chances. Still in dead silence, he tiptoed to the door; then, flinging it suddenly open, he stood there, his weapon poised.

'On the mat stood the most beautiful girl he had ever beheld. A veritable child of Faërie. She eyed him for a moment with a saucy smile; then with a pretty, roguish look of reproof shook a dainty fore-finger at him.

' "I believe you've forgotten me, Mr Gage!" she fluted with a mock severity which her eyes belied.'

James stared at the paper dumbly. He was utterly perplexed. He had not had the slightest intention of writing anything like this. To begin with, it was a rule with him, and one which he never broke, to allow no girls to appear in his stories. Sinister landladies, yes, and naturally any amount of adventuresses with foreign accents, but never under any pretext what may be broadly described as girls. A detective story, he maintained, should have no heroine. Heroines only held up the action and tried to flirt with the hero when he should have been busy looking for clues, and then went and let the villain kidnap them by some childishly simple trick. In his writing, James was positively monastic.

And yet here was this creature with her saucy smile and her dainty fore-finger horning in at the most important point in the story. It was uncanny.

He looked once more at his scenario. No, the scenario was all right.

In perfectly plain words it stated that what happened when the door opened was that a dying man fell in and after gasping, 'The beetle! Tell Scotland Yard that the blue beetle is—' expired on the hearth-rug, leaving Lester Gage not unnaturally somewhat mystified. Nothing whatever about any beautiful girls.

In a curious mood of irritation, James scratched out the offending passage, wrote in the necessary corrections and put the cover on the machine. It was at this point that he heard William whining.

The only blot on this paradise which James had so far been able to discover was the infernal dog, William. Belonging nominally to the gardener, on the very first morning he had adopted James by acclamation, and he maddened and infuriated James. He had a habit of coming and whining under the window when James was at work. The latter would ignore this as long as he could; then, when the thing became insupportable, would bound out of his chair, to see the animal standing on the gravel, gazing expectantly up at him with a stone in his mouth. William had a weak-minded passion for chasing stones; and on the first day James, in a rash spirit of camaraderie, had flung one for him. Since then James had thrown no more stones; but he had thrown any number of other solids, and the garden was littered with objects ranging from match boxes to a plaster statuette of the young Joseph prophesying before Pharaoh. And still William came and whined, an optimist to the last.

The whining, coming now at a moment when he felt irritable and unsettled, acted on James much as the scratching on the door had acted on Lester Gage. Silently, like a panther, he made one quick step to the mantelpiece, removed from it a china mug bearing the legend A Present from Clacton-on-Sea, and crept to the window.

And as he did so a voice outside said, 'Go away, sir, go away!' and there followed a short, high-pitched bark which was certainly not William's. William was a mixture of Airedale, setter, bull terrier, and mastiff; and when in vocal mood, favoured the mastiff side of his family.

James peered out. There on the porch stood a girl in blue. She held in her arms a small fluffy white dog, and she was endeavouring to foil the upward movement toward this of the blackguard William. William's mentality had been arrested some years before at the point where he imagined that everything in the world had been created for him to eat. A bone, a boot, a steak, the back wheel of a bicycle – it was all one to William. If it was there he tried to eat it. He had even made a plucky attempt to devour the remains of the young Joseph prophesying before Pharaoh. And it was perfectly plain now that he regarded the curious wriggling object in the girl's arms purely in the light of a snack to keep body and soul together till dinner-time.

'William!' bellowed James.

William looked courteously over his shoulder with eyes that beamed with the pure light of a life's devotion, wagged the whiplike tail which he had inherited from his bull-terrier ancestor and resumed his intent scrutiny of the fluffy dog.

'Oh, please!' cried the girl. 'This great rough dog is frightening poor Toto.'

The man of letters and the man of action do not always go hand in hand, but practice had made James perfect in handling with a swift efficiency any situation that involved William. A moment later that canine moron, having received the present from Clacton in the short ribs, was scuttling round the corner of the house, and James had jumped through the window and was facing the girl.

She was an extraordinarily pretty girl. Very sweet and fragile she looked as she stood there under the honeysuckle with the breeze ruffling a tendril of golden hair that strayed from beneath her coquettish little hat. Her eyes were very big and very blue, her rose-tinted face becomingly flushed. All wasted on James, though. He disliked all girls, and particularly the sweet, droopy type.

'Did you want to see somebody?' he asked stiffly.

'Just the house,' said the girl, 'if it wouldn't be giving any trouble. I do so want to see the room where Miss Pinckney wrote her books. This is where Leila J. Pinckney used to live, isn't it?'

'Yes; I am her nephew. My name is James Rodman.'

'Mine is Rose Maynard.'

James led the way into the house, and she stopped with a cry of delight on the threshold of the morning-room.

'Oh, how too perfect!' she cried. 'So this was her study?'

'Yes.'

'What a wonderful place it would be for you to think in if you were a writer too.'

James held no high opinion of women's literary taste, but nevertheless he was conscious of an unpleasant shock.

'I am a writer,' he said coldly. 'I write detective stories.'

'I – I'm afraid' – she blushed – 'I'm afraid I don't often read detective stories.'

'You no doubt prefer,' said James, still more coldly, 'the sort of thing my aunt used to write.'

'Oh, I love her stories!' cried the girl, clasping her hands ecstatically. 'Don't you?'

'I cannot say that I do.'

'What?'

'They are pure apple sauce,' said James sternly; 'just nasty blobs of sentimentality, thoroughly untrue to life.'

The girl stared.

'Why, that's just what's so wonderful about them, their true-ness to life! You feel they might all have happened. I don't understand what you mean.'

They were walking down the garden now. James held the gate open for her and she passed through into the road.

'Well, for one thing,' he said, 'I decline to believe that a marriage between two young people is invariably preceded by some violent and sensational experience in which they both share.'

'Are you thinking of *Scent o' the Blossom*, where Edgar saves Maud from drowning?'

'I am thinking of every single one of my aunt's books.' He looked at her curiously. He had just got the solution of a mystery which had been puzzling him for some time. Almost from the moment he had set eyes on her she had seemed somehow strangely familiar. It now suddenly came to him why it was that he disliked her so much. 'Do you know,' he said, 'you might be one of my aunt's heroines yourself? You're just the sort of girl she used to love to write about.'

Her face lit up.

'Oh, do you really think so?' She hesitated. 'Do you know what I have been feeling ever since I came here? I've been feeling that you are exactly like one of Miss Pinckney's heroes.'

'No, I say, really!' said James, revolted.

'Oh, but you are! When you jumped through that window it gave me quite a start. You were so exactly like Claude Masterson in *Heather o' the Hills*.'

'I have not read *Heather o' the Hills*,' said James, with a shudder.

'He was very strong and quiet, with deep, dark, sad eyes.'

James did not explain that his eyes were sad because her society gave him a pain in the neck. He merely laughed scornfully.

'So now, I suppose,' he said, 'a car will come and knock you down and I shall carry you gently into the house and lay you— Look out!' he cried.

It was too late. She was lying in a little huddled heap at his feet. Round the corner a large automobile had come bowling, keeping with an almost affected precision to the wrong side of the road. It was now receding into the distance, the occupant of the tonneau, a stout red-faced gentleman in a fur coat, leaning out over the back. He had bared his head – not, one fears, as a pretty gesture of respect and regret, but because he was using his hat to hide the number plate.

The dog Toto was unfortunately uninjured.

James carried the girl gently into the house and laid her on the sofa in the morning-room. He rang the bell and the apple-cheeked housekeeper appeared.

'Send for the doctor,' said James. 'There has been an accident.'

The housekeeper bent over the girl.

'Eh, dearie, dearie!' she said. 'Bless her sweet pretty face!'

The gardener, he who technically owned William, was routed out from among the young lettuces and told to fetch Doctor Brady. He separated his bicycle from William, who was making a light meal off the left pedal, and departed on his mission. Doctor Brady arrived and in due course he made his report.

'No bones broken, but a number of nasty bruises. And, of course, the shock. She will have to stay here for some time, Rodman. Can't be moved.'

'Stay here! But she can't! It isn't proper.'

'Your housekeeper will act as a chaperone.'

The doctor sighed. He was a stolid-looking man of middle age with side-whiskers.

'A beautiful girl, that, Rodman,' he said.

'I suppose so,' said James.

'A sweet, beautiful girl. An elfin child.'

'A what?' cried James, starting.

This imagery was very foreign to Doctor Brady as he knew him. On the only previous occasion on which they had had any extended conversation, the doctor had talked exclusively about the effect of too much protein on the gastric juices.

'An elfin child; a tender, fairy creature. When I was looking at her just now, Rodman, I nearly broke down. Her little hand on the coverlet like some white lily floating on the surface of a still pool, and her dear, trusting eyes gazed up at me.'

He pottered off down the garden, still babbling, and James stood staring after him blankly. And slowly, like some cloud athwart a summer sky, there crept over James's heart the chill shadow of a nameless fear.

It was about a week later that Mr Andrew McKinnon, the senior partner in the well-known firm of literary agents, McKinnon & Gooch, sat in his office in Chancery Lane, frowning thoughtfully over a telegram. He rang the bell.

'Ask Mr Gooch to step in here.' He resumed his study of the telegram. 'Oh, Gooch,' he said when his partner appeared, 'I've just had a curious wire from young Rodman. He seems to want to see me very urgently.'

Mr Gooch read the telegram.

'Written under the influence of some strong mental excitement,' he agreed. 'I wonder why he doesn't come to the office if he wants to see you so badly.'

'He's working very hard, finishing that novel for Prodder & Wiggs. Can't leave it, I suppose. Well, it's a nice day. If you will look after things here I think I'll motor down and let him give me lunch.'

As Mr McKinnon's car reached the crossroads a mile from Honeysuckle Cottage, he was aware of a gesticulating figure by the hedge. He stopped the car.

'Morning, Rodman.'

'Thank God, you've come!' said James. It seemed to Mr McKinnon that the young man looked paler and thinner. 'Would you mind walking the rest of the way? There's something I want to speak to you about.'

Mr McKinnon alighted; and James, as he glanced at him, felt cheered and encouraged by the very sight of the man. The literary agent was a grim, hard-bitten person, to whom, when he called at their offices to arrange terms, editors kept their faces turned so that they might at least retain their back collar studs. There was no sentiment in Andrew McKinnon. Editresses of society papers practised their blandishments on him in vain, and many a publisher had waked screaming in the night, dreaming that he was signing a McKinnon contract.

'Well, Rodman,' he said, 'Prodder & Wiggs have agreed to our terms. I was writing to tell you so when your wire arrived. I had a lot of trouble with them, but it's fixed at 20 per cent., rising to 25, and two hundred pounds advance royalties on day of publication.'

'Good!' said James absently. 'Good! McKinnon, do you remember my aunt, Leila J. Pinckney?'

'Remember her? Why, I was her agent all her life.'

'Of course. Then you know the sort of tripe she wrote.'

'No author,' said Mr McKinnon reprovingly, 'who pulls down a steady twenty thousand pounds a year writes tripe.'

'Well anyway, you know her stuff.'

'Who better?'

'When she died she left me five thousand pounds and her house, Honeysuckle Cottage. I'm living there now. McKinnon, do you believe in haunted houses?'

'No.'

'Yet I tell you solemnly that Honeysuckle Cottage is haunted!'

'By your aunt?' said Mr McKinnon, surprised.

'By her influence. There's a malignant spell over the place; a sort of miasma of sentimentalism. Everybody who enters it succumbs.'

'Tut-tut! You mustn't have these fancies.'

'They aren't fancies.'

'You aren't seriously meaning to tell me—'

'Well, how do you account for this? That book you were speaking about, which Prodder & Wiggs are to publish – *The Secret Nine*. Every time I sit down to write it a girl keeps trying to sneak in.'

'Into the room?'

'Into the story.'

'You don't want a love interest in your sort of book,' said Mr McKinnon, shaking his head. 'It delays the action.'

'I know it does. And every day I have to keep shooing this infernal female out. An awful girl, McKinnon. A soppy, soupy, treacly, drooping girl with a roguish smile. This morning she tried to butt in on the scene where Lester Gage is trapped in the den of the mysterious leper.'

'No!'

'She did, I assure you. I had to rewrite three pages before I could get her out of it. And that's not the worst. Do you know, McKinnon, that at this moment I am actually living the plot of a typical Leila May Pinckney novel in just the setting she always used! And I can see the happy ending coming nearer every day! A week ago a girl was knocked down by a car at my door and I've had to put her up, and every day I realize more clearly that sooner or later I shall ask her to marry me.'

'Don't do it,' said Mr McKinnon, a stout bachelor. 'You're too young to marry.'

'So was Methuselah,' said James, a stouter. 'But all the same I know I'm going to do it. It's the influence of this awful house weighing upon me. I feel like an eggshell in a maelstrom. I am being sucked in by a force too strong for me to resist. This morning I found myself kissing her dog!'

'No!'

'I did! And I loathe the little beast. Yesterday I got up at dawn and plucked a nosegay of flowers for her, wet with the dew.'

'Rodman!'

'It's a fact. I laid them at her door and went downstairs kicking myself all the way. And there in the hall was the apple-cheeked housekeeper regarding me archly. If she didn't murmur "Bless their sweet young hearts!" my ears deceived me.'

'Why don't you pack up and leave?'

'If I do I lose the five thousand pounds.'

'Ah!' said Mr McKinnon.

'I can understand what has happened. It's the same with all haunted houses. My aunt's subliminal ether vibrations have woven themselves into the texture of the place, creating an atmosphere which forces the ego of all who come in contact with it to attune themselves to it. It's either that or something to do with the fourth dimension.'

Mr McKinnon laughed scornfully.

'Tut-tut!' he said again. 'This is pure imagination. What has happened is that you've been working too hard. You'll see this precious atmosphere of yours will have no effect on me.'

'That's exactly why I asked you to come down. I hoped you might break the spell.'

'I will that,' said Mr McKinnon jovially.

The fact that the literary agent spoke little at lunch caused James no apprehension. Mr McKinnon was ever a silent trencherman. From time to time James caught him stealing a glance at the girl, who was well enough to come down to meals now, limping pathetically; but he could read nothing in his face. And yet the mere look of his face was a consolation. It was so solid, so matter of fact, so exactly like an unemotional coconut.

'You've done me good,' said James with a sigh of relief, as he escorted the agent down the garden to his car after lunch. 'I felt all along that I could rely on your rugged common sense. The whole atmosphere of the place seems different now.'

Mr McKinnon did not speak for a moment. He seemed to be plunged in thought.

'Rodman,' he said, as he got into his car, 'I've been thinking over that suggestion of yours of putting a love interest into *The Secret Nine*. I think you're wise. The story needs it. After all, what is there greater in the world than love? Love – love – aye, it's the sweetest word in the language. Put in a heroine and let her marry Lester Gage.'

'If,' said James grimly, 'she does succeed in worming her way in she'll jolly well marry the mysterious leper. But look here, I don't understand—'

'It was seeing that girl that changed me,' proceeded Mr McKinnon. And as James stared at him aghast, tears suddenly filled his hard-boiled eyes. He openly snuffled. 'Aye, seeing her sitting there under the roses, with all that smell of honeysuckle and all. And the birdies singing so sweet in the garden and the sun lighting up her bonny face. The puir wee lass!' he muttered, dabbing at his eyes. 'The puir bonny wee lass! Rodman,' he said, his voice quivering, 'I've decided that we're being hard on Prodder & Wiggs. Wiggs has had sickness in his home lately. We mustn't be hard on a man who's had sickness in his home, hey, laddie? No, no! I'm going to take back that contract and alter it to a flat 12 per cent. and no advance royalties.'

'What!'

'But you shan't lose by it, Rodman. No, no, you shan't lose by it, my manny. I am going to waive my commission. The puir bonny wee lass!'

The car rolled off down the road. Mr McKinnon, seated in the back, was blowing his nose violently.

'This is the end!' said James.

It is necessary at this point to pause and examine James Rodman's position with an unbiased eye. The average man, unless he puts himself in James's place, will be unable to appreciate it. James, he will feel, was making a lot of fuss about nothing. Here he was, drawing daily closer and closer to a charming girl with big blue eyes, and surely rather to be envied than pitied.

But we must remember that James was one of Nature's bachelors. And no ordinary man, looking forward dreamily to a little home of his own with a loving wife putting out his slippers and changing the gramophone records, can realize the intensity of the instinct for self-preservation which animates Nature's bachelors in times of peril.

James Rodman had a congenital horror of matrimony. Though a young man, he had allowed himself to develop a great many habits which were as the breath of life to him; and these habits, he knew instinctively, a wife would shoot to pieces within a week of the end of the honeymoon.

James liked to breakfast in bed; and, having breakfasted, to smoke in bed and knock the ashes out on the carpet. What wife would tolerate this practice?

James liked to pass his days in a tennis shirt, grey flannel trousers and slippers. What wife ever rests until she has inclosed her husband in a stiff collar, tight boots and a morning suit and taken him with her to *thés musicales*?

These and a thousand other thoughts of the same kind flashed through the unfortunate young man's mind as the days went by, and every day that passed seemed to draw him nearer to the brink of the chasm. Fate appeared to be taking a malicious pleasure in making things as difficult for him as possible. Now that the girl was well enough to leave her bed, she spent her time sitting in a chair on the sun-sprinkled porch, and James had to read to her – and poetry, at that; and not the jolly, wholesome sort of poetry the boys are turning out nowadays, either – good, honest stuff about sin and gas works and decaying corpses – but the old-fashioned kind with rhymes in it, dealing almost exclusively with love. The weather, moreover, continued superb. The honeysuckle cast its sweet scent on the gentle breeze; the roses over the porch stirred and nodded; the flowers in the garden were lovelier than ever; the birds sang their little throats sore. And every evening there was a magnificent sunset. It was almost as if Nature were doing it on purpose.

At last James intercepted Doctor Brady as he was leaving after one of his visits and put the thing to him squarely:

'When is that girl going?'

The doctor patted him on the arm.

'Not yet, Rodman,' he said in a low, understanding voice. 'No need to worry yourself about that. Mustn't be moved for days and days and days – I might almost say weeks and weeks and weeks.'

'Weeks and weeks!' cried James.

'And weeks,' said Doctor Brady. He prodded James roguishly in the abdomen. 'Good luck to you, my boy, good luck to you,' he said.

It was some small consolation to James that the mushy physician immediately afterward tripped over William on his way down the path and broke his stethoscope. When a man is up against it like James every little helps.

He was walking dismally back to the house after this conversation when he was met by the apple-cheeked housekeeper.

'The little lady would like to speak to you, sir,' said the apple-cheeked exhibit, rubbing her hands.

'Would she?' said James hollowly.

'So sweet and pretty she looks, sir – oh, sir, you wouldn't believe! Like a blessed angel sitting there with her dear eyes all a-shining.'

'Don't do it!' cried James with extraordinary vehemence. 'Don't do it!'

He found the girl propped up on the cushions and thought once again how singularly he disliked her. And yet, even as he thought this, some force against which he had to fight madly was whispering to him, 'Go to her and take that little hand! Breathe into that little ear the burning words that will make that little face turn away crimsoned with blushes!' He wiped a bead of perspiration from his forehead and sat down.

'Mrs Stick-in-the-Mud – what's her name? – says you want to see me.'

The girl nodded.

'I've had a letter from Uncle Henry. I wrote to him as soon as I was better and told him what had happened, and he is coming here tomorrow morning.'

'Uncle Henry?'

'That's what I call him, but he's really no relation. He is my guardian. He and daddy were officers in the same regiment, and when daddy was killed, fighting on the Afghan frontier, he died in Uncle Henry's arms and with his last breath begged him to take care of me.'

James started. A sudden wild hope had waked in his heart. Years ago, he remembered, he had read a book of his aunt's entitled *Rupert's Legacy*, and in that book—

'I'm engaged to marry him,' said the girl quietly.

'Wow!' shouted James.

'What?' asked the girl, startled.

'Touch of cramp,' said James. He was thrilling all over. That wild hope had been realized.

'It was daddy's dying wish that we should marry,' said the girl.

'And dashed sensible of him, too; dashed sensible,' said James warmly.

'And yet,' she went on, a little wistfully, 'I sometimes wonder—'

'Don't!' said James. 'Don't! You must respect daddy's dying wish. There's nothing like daddy's dying wish; you can't beat it. So he's coming here tomorrow, is he? Capital, capital! To lunch, I suppose? Excellent! I'll run down and tell Mrs Who-Is-It to lay in another chop.'

It was with a gay and uplifted heart that James strolled the garden and smoked his pipe next morning. A great cloud seemed to have rolled itself away from him. Everything was for the best in the best of all possible worlds. He had finished *The Secret Nine* and shipped it off to Mr McKinnon, and now as he strolled there was shaping itself in his mind a corking plot about a man with only half a face who lived in a secret den and terrorized London with a series of shocking murders. And what made them so shocking was the fact that each of the victims, when discovered, was found to have only half a face too. The rest had been chipped off, presumably by some blunt instrument.

The thing was coming out magnificently, when suddenly his attention was diverted by a piercing scream. Out of the bushes fringing the river that ran beside the garden burst the apple-cheeked housekeeper.

'Oh, sir! Oh, sir! Oh, sir!'

'What is it?' demanded James irritably.

'Oh, sir! Oh, sir! Oh, sir!'

'Yes, and then what?'

'The little dog, sir! He's in the river!'

'Well, whistle him to come out.'

'Oh, sir, do come quick! He'll be drowned!'

James followed her through the bushes, taking off his coat as he went. He was saying to himself, 'I will not rescue this dog. I do not like the dog. It is high time he had a bath, and in any case it would be much simpler to stand on the bank and fish for him with a rake. Only an ass out of a Leila J. Pinckney book would dive into a beastly river to save—'

At this point he dived. Toto, alarmed by the splash, swam rapidly for the bank, but James was too quick for him. Grasping him firmly by the neck, he scrambled ashore and ran for the house, followed by the housekeeper.

The girl was seated on the porch. Over her there bent the tall soldierly figure of a man with keen eyes and greying hair. The housekeeper raced up.

'Oh, miss! Toto! In the river! He saved him! He plunged in and saved him!'

The girl drew a quick breath.

'Gallant, damme! By Jove! By gad! Yes, gallant, by George!' exclaimed the soldierly man.

The girl seemed to wake from a reverie.

'Uncle Henry, this is Mr Rodman. Mr Rodman, my guardian, Colonel Carteret.'

'Proud to meet you, sir,' said the colonel, his honest blue eyes glowing as he fingered his short crisp moustache. 'As fine a thing as I ever heard of, damme!'

'Yes, you are brave – brave,' the girl whispered.

'I am wet – wet,' said James, and went upstairs to change his clothes.

When he came down for lunch, he found to his relief that the girl had decided not to join them, and Colonel Carteret was silent and preoccupied. James, exerting himself in his capacity of host, tried him with the weather, golf, India, the Government, the high cost of living, first-class cricket, the modern dancing craze, and murderers he had met, but the other still preserved that strange, absent-minded silence. It was only when the meal was concluded and James had produced cigarettes that he came abruptly out of his trance.

'Rodman,' he said, 'I should like to speak to you.'

'Yes?' said James, thinking it was about time.

'Rodman,' said Colonel Carteret, 'or rather, George – I may call you George?' he added, with a sort of wistful diffidence that had a singular charm.

'Certainly,' replied James, 'if you wish it. Though my name is James.'

'James, eh? Well, well, it amounts to the same thing, eh, what, damme, by gad?' said the colonel with a momentary return of his bluff soldierly manner. 'Well, then, James, I have something that I wish to say to you. Did Miss Maynard – did Rose happen to tell you anything about myself in – er – in connection with herself?'

'She mentioned that you and she were engaged to be married.'

The colonel's tightly drawn lips quivered.

'No longer,' he said.

'What?'

'No, John, my boy.'

'James.'

'No, James, my boy, no longer. While you were upstairs changing your clothes she told me – breaking down, poor child, as she spoke – that she wished our engagement to be at an end.'

James half rose from the table, his cheeks blanched.

'You don't mean that!' he gasped.

Colonel Carteret nodded. He was staring out of the window, his fine eyes set in a look of pain.

'But this is nonsense!' cried James. 'This is absurd! She – she mustn't be allowed to chop and change like this. I mean to say, it – it isn't fair—'

'Don't think of me, my boy.'

'I'm not – I mean, did she give any reason?'

'Her eyes did.'

'Her eyes did?'

'Her eyes, when she looked at you on the porch, as you stood there – young, heroic – having just saved the life of the dog she loves. It is you who won that tender heart, my boy.'

'Now listen,' protested James, 'you aren't going to sit there and tell me that a girl falls in love with a man just because he saves her dog from drowning?'

'Why, surely,' said Colonel Carteret, surprised. 'What better reason could she have?' He sighed. 'It is the old, old story, my boy. Youth to youth. I am an old man. I should have known – I should have foreseen – yes, youth to youth.'

'You aren't a bit old.'

'Yes, yes.'

'No, no.'

'Yes, yes.'

'Don't keep on saying yes, yes!' cried James, clutching at his hair. 'Besides, she wants a steady old buffer – a steady, sensible man of medium age – to look after her.'

Colonel Carteret shook his head with a gentle smile.

'This is mere quixotry, my boy. It is splendid of you to take this attitude; but no, no.'

'Yes, yes.'

'No, no.' He gripped James's hand for an instant, then rose and walked to the door. 'That is all I wished to say, Tom.'

'James.'

'James. I just thought that you ought to know how matters stood. Go to her, my boy, go to her, and don't let any thought of an old man's broken dream keep you from pouring out what is in your heart. I am an old soldier, lad, an old soldier. I have learned to take the rough with the smooth. But I think – I think I will leave you now. I – I should – should like to be alone for a while. If you need me you will find me in the raspberry bushes.'

He had scarcely gone when James also left the room. He took his hat and stick and walked blindly out of the garden, he knew not whither. His brain was numbed. Then, as his powers of reasoning returned, he told himself that he should have foreseen this ghastly thing. If there was one type of character over which Leila J. Pinckney had been wont to spread herself, it was the pathetic guardian who loves his ward but relinquishes her to the younger man. No wonder the girl had broken off the engagement. Any elderly guardian who allowed himself to come within a mile of Honeysuckle Cottage was simply asking for it. And then, as he turned to walk back, a sort of dull defiance gripped James. Why, he asked, should he be put upon in this manner? If the girl liked to throw over this man, why should he be the goat?

He saw his way clearly now. He just wouldn't do it, that was all. And if they didn't like it they could lump it.

Full of a new fortitude, he strode in at the gate. A tall, soldierly figure emerged from the raspberry bushes and came to meet him.

'Well?' said Colonel Carteret.

'Well?' said James defiantly.

'Am I to congratulate you?'

James caught his keen blue eye and hesitated. It was not going to be so simple as he had supposed.

'Well – er—' he said.

Into the keen blue eyes there came a look that James had not seen there before. It was the stern, hard look which – probably – had caused men to bestow upon this old soldier the name of Cold-Steel Carteret.

'You have not asked Rose to marry you?'

'Er – no; not yet.'

The keen blue eyes grew keener and bluer.

'Rodman,' said Colonel Carteret in a strange, quiet voice, 'I have known that little girl since she was a tiny child. For years she has been all in all to me. Her father died in my arms and with his last breath bade me see that no harm came to his darling. I have nursed her through mumps, measles – aye, and chicken pox – and I live but for her happiness.' He paused, with a significance that made James's toes curl. 'Rodman,' he said, 'do you know what I would do to any man who trifled with that little girl's affections?' He reached in his hip pocket and an ugly-looking revolver glittered in the sunlight. 'I would shoot him like a dog.'

'Like a dog?' faltered James.

'Like a dog,' said Colonel Carteret. He took James's arm and turned him toward the house. 'She is on the porch. Go to her. And if—' He broke off. 'But tut!' he said in a kindlier tone. 'I am doing you an injustice, my boy. I know it.'

'Oh, you are,' said James fervently.

'Your heart is in the right place.'

'Oh, absolutely,' said James.

'Then go to her, my boy. Later on you may have something to tell me. You will find me in the strawberry beds.'

It was very cool and fragrant on the porch. Overhead, little breezes played and laughed among the roses. Somewhere in the distance sheep bells tinkled, and in the shrubbery a thrush was singing its even-song.

Seated in her chair behind a wicker table laden with tea things, Rose Maynard watched James as he shambled up the path.

'Tea's ready,' she called gaily. 'Where is Uncle Henry?' A look of pity and distress flitted for a moment over her flower-like face. 'Oh, I – I forgot,' she whispered.

'He is in the strawberry beds,' said James in a low voice.

She nodded unhappily.

'Of course, of course. Oh, why is life like this?' James heard her whisper.

He sat down. He looked at the girl. She was leaning back with closed eyes, and he thought he had never seen such a little squirt in his life. The idea of passing his remaining days in her society revolted him. He was stoutly opposed to the idea of marrying anyone; but if, as happens to the best of us, he ever were compelled to perform the wedding glide, he had always hoped it would be with some lady golf champion who would help him with his putting, and thus, by bringing his handicap down a notch or two, enable him to save something from the wreck, so to speak. But to link his lot with a girl who read his aunt's books and liked them; a girl who could tolerate the presence of the dog Toto; a girl who clasped her hands in pretty, childish joy when she saw a nasturtium in bloom – it was too much. Nevertheless, he took her hand and began to speak.

'Miss Maynard – Rose—'

She opened her eyes and cast them down. A flush had come into her cheeks. The dog Toto at her side sat up and begged for cake, disregarded.

'Let me tell you a story. Once upon a time there was a lonely man who lived in a cottage all by himself—'

He stopped. Was it James Rodman who was talking this bilge?

'Yes?' whispered the girl.

'– but one day there came to him out of nowhere a little fairy princess. She—'

He stopped again, but this time not because of the sheer shame of listening to his own voice. What caused him to interrupt his tale was the fact that at this moment the tea table suddenly began to rise slowly in the air, tilting as it did so a considerable quantity of hot tea on to the knees of his trousers.

'Ouch!' cried James, leaping.

The table continued to rise, and then fell sideways, revealing the homely countenance of William, who, concealed by the cloth, had been taking a nap beneath it. He moved slowly forward, his eyes on Toto. For many a long day William had been desirous of putting to the test, once and for all, the problem of whether Toto was edible or not. Sometimes he thought yes, at other times no. Now seemed an admirable opportunity for a definite decision. He advanced on the object of his experiment, making a low whistling noise through his nostrils, not unlike a boiling kettle. And Toto, after one long look of incredulous horror, tucked his shapely tail between his legs and, turning, raced for safety. He had laid a course in a bee line for the open garden gate, and William, shaking a dish of marmalade off his head a little petulantly, galloped ponderously after him. Rose Maynard staggered to her feet.

'Oh, save him!' she cried.

Without a word James added himself to the procession. His interest in Toto was but tepid. What he wanted was to get near enough to William to discuss with him that matter of the tea on his trousers. He reached the road and found that the order of the runners had not changed. For so small a dog, Toto was moving magnificently. A cloud of dust rose as he skidded round the corner. William followed. James followed William.

And so they passed Farmer Birkett's barn, Farmer Giles' cow shed, the place where Farmer Willetts' pigsty used to be before the big fire, and the Bunch of Grapes public house, Jno Biggs propr., licensed to sell tobacco, wines and spirits. And it was as they were turning down the lane that leads past Farmer Robinson's chicken run that Toto, thinking swiftly, bolted abruptly into a small drain pipe.

'William!' roared James, coming up at a canter. He stopped to pluck a branch from the hedge and swooped darkly on.

William had been crouching before the pipe, making a noise like a bassoon into its interior; but now he rose and came beamingly to James. His eyes were aglow with chumminess and affection; and placing his forefeet on James's chest, he licked him three times on the face in rapid succession. And as he did so, something seemed to snap in James. The scales seemed to fall from James's eyes. For the first time he saw William as he really was, the authentic type of dog that saves his master from a frightful peril. A wave of emotion swept over him.

'William!' he muttered. 'William!'

William was making an early supper off a half brick he had found in the road. James stooped and patted him fondly.

'William,' he whispered, 'you knew when the time had come to change the conversation, didn't you, old boy!' He straightened himself. 'Come, William,' he said. 'Another four miles and we reach Meadowsweet Junction. Make it snappy and we shall just catch the up express, first stop London.'

William looked up into his face and it seemed to James that he gave a brief nod of comprehension and approval. James turned. Through the trees to the east he could see the red roof of Honeysuckle Cottage, lurking like some evil dragon in ambush.

Then, together, man and dog passed silently into the sunset.

That (concluded Mr Mulliner) is the story of my distant cousin James Rodman. As to whether it is true, that, of course, is an open question. I, personally, am of opinion that it is. There is no doubt that James did go to live at Honeysuckle Cottage and, while there, underwent some experience which has left an ineradicable mark upon him. His eyes today have that unmistakable look which is to be seen only in the eyes of confirmed bachelors whose feet have been dragged to the very brink of the pit and who have gazed at close range into the naked face of matrimony.

And, if further proof be needed, there is William. He is now James's inseparable companion. Would any man be habitually seen in public with a dog like William unless he had some solid cause to be grateful to him – unless they were linked together by some deep and imperishable memory? I think not. Myself, when I observe William coming along the street, I cross the road and look into a shop window till he has passed. I am not a snob, but I dare not risk my position in Society by being seen talking to that curious compound.

Nor is the precaution an unnecessary one. There is about William a shameless absence of appreciation of class distinctions which recalls the worst excesses of the French Revolution. I have seen him with these eyes chivvy a pomeranian belonging to a Baroness in her own right from near the Achilles Statue to within a few yards of the Marble Arch.

And yet James walks daily with him in Piccadilly. It is surely significant.

UKRIDGE ROUNDS A NASTY CORNER

THE LATE Sir Rupert Lakenheath, KCMG, CB, MVO, was one of those men at whom their countries point with pride. Until his retirement on a pension in the year 1906, he had been Governor of various insanitary outposts of the British Empire situated around the equator, and as such had won respect and esteem from all. A kindly editor of my acquaintance secured for me the job of assisting the widow of this great administrator to prepare his memoirs for publication; and on a certain summer afternoon I had just finished arraying myself suitably for my first call on her at her residence in Thurloe Square, South Kensington, when there was a knock at the door, and Bowles, my landlord, entered, bearing gifts.

These consisted of a bottle with a staring label and a large cardboard hat-box. I gazed at them blankly, for they held no message for me.

Bowles, in his ambassadorial manner, condescended to explain.

'Mr Ukridge,' he said, with the ring of paternal affection in his voice which always crept into it when speaking of that menace to civilization, 'called a moment ago, sir, and desired me to hand you these.'

Having now approached the table on which he had placed the objects, I was enabled to solve the mystery of the bottle. It was one of those fat, bulging bottles, and it bore across its diaphragm in red letters the single word 'PEPPO'. Beneath this, in black letters, ran the legend, 'It Bucks You Up'. I had not seen Ukridge for more than two weeks, but at our last meeting, I remembered, he had spoken of some foul patent medicine of which he had somehow secured the agency. This, apparently, was it.

'But what's in the hat-box?' I asked.

'I could not say, sir,' replied Bowles.

At this point the hat-box, which had hitherto not spoken, uttered a crisp, sailorly oath, and followed it up by singing the opening bars of 'Annie Laurie'. It then relapsed into its former moody silence.

A few doses of Peppo would, no doubt, have enabled me to endure this remarkable happening with fortitude and phlegm. Not having taken that specific, the thing had a devastating effect upon my nervous centres. I bounded back and upset a chair, while Bowles, his dignity laid aside, leaped silently towards the ceiling. It was the first time I had ever seen him lay off the mask, and even in that trying moment I could not help being gratified by the spectacle. It gave me one of those thrills that come once in a lifetime.

'For Gord's sake!' ejaculated Bowles.

'Have a nut,' observed the hat-box, hospitably. 'Have a nut.'

Bowles's panic subsided.

'It's a bird, sir. A parrot!'

'What the deuce does Ukridge mean,' I cried, becoming the outraged householder, 'by cluttering up my rooms with his beastly parrots? I'd like that man to know –'

The mention of Ukridge's name seemed to act on Bowles like a soothing draught. He recovered his poise.

'I have no doubt, sir,' he said, a touch of coldness in his voice that rebuked my outburst, 'that Mr Ukridge has good reasons for depositing the bird in our custody. I fancy he must wish you to take charge of it for him.'

'He may wish it –' I was beginning, when my eye fell on the clock. If I did not want to alienate my employer by keeping her waiting, I must be on my way immediately.

'Put that hat-box in the other room, Bowles,' I said. 'And I suppose you had better give the bird something to eat.'

'Very good, sir. You may leave the matter in my hands with complete confidence.'

The drawing-room into which I was shown on arriving at Thurloe Square was filled with many mementoes of the late Sir Rupert's gubernatorial career. In addition the room contained a small and bewilderingly pretty girl in a blue dress, who smiled upon me pleasantly.

'My aunt will be down in a moment,' she said, and for a few moments we exchanged commonplaces. Then the door opened and Lady Lakenheath appeared.

The widow of the Administrator was tall, angular, and thin, with a sun-tanned face of a cast so determined as to make it seem a tenable theory that in the years previous to 1906 she had done at least her share of the administrating. Her whole appearance was that of a woman designed by Nature to instil law and order into the bosoms of boisterous cannibal kings. She surveyed me with an appraising glance, and then, as if reconciled to the fact that, poor specimen though I might be, I was probably as good as anything else that could be got for the money, received me into the fold by pressing the bell and ordering tea.

Tea had arrived, and I was trying to combine bright dialogue with the difficult feat of balancing my cup on the smallest saucer I had ever seen, when my hostess, happening to glance out of the window into the street below, uttered something midway between a sigh and a click of the tongue.

'Oh, dear! That extraordinary man again!'

The girl in the blue dress, who had declined tea and was sewing in a distant corner, bent a little closer over her work.

'Millie!' said the administratess, plaintively, as if desiring sympathy in her trouble.

'Yes, Aunt Elizabeth?'

'That man is calling again!'

There was a short but perceptible pause. A delicate pink appeared in the girl's cheeks.

'Yes, Aunt Elizabeth?' she said.

'Mr Ukridge,' announced the maid at the door.

It seemed to me that if this sort of thing was to continue, if existence was to become a mere series of shocks and surprises, Peppo would have to be installed as an essential factor in my life. I stared speechlessly at Ukridge as he breezed in with the unmistakable air of sunny confidence which a man shows on familiar ground. Even if I had not had Lady Lakenheath's words as evidence, his manner would have been enough to tell me that he was a frequent visitor in her drawing-room; and how he had come to be on calling terms with a lady so pre-eminently respectable it was beyond me to imagine. I awoke from my stupor to find that we were being introduced, and that Ukridge, for some reason clear, no doubt, to his own tortuous mind but inexplicable to me, was treating me as a complete stranger. He nodded courteously but distantly, and I, falling in with his unspoken wishes, nodded back. Plainly relieved, he turned to Lady Lakenheath and plunged forthwith into the talk of intimacy.

'I've got good news for you,' he said. 'News about Leonard.'

The alteration in our hostess's manner at these words was remarkable. Her somewhat forbidding manner softened in an instant to quite a tremulous fluttering. Gone was the hauteur which had caused her but a moment back to allude to him as 'that extraordinary man'. She pressed tea upon him, and scones.

'Oh, Mr Ukridge!' she cried.

'I don't want to rouse false hopes and all that sort of thing laddie – I mean, Lady Lakenheath, but, upon my Sam, I really believe I am on the track. I have been making the most assiduous inquiries.'

'How very kind of you!'

'No, no,' said Ukridge, modestly.

'I have been so worried,' said Lady Lakenheath, 'that I have scarcely been able to rest.'

'Too bad!'

'Last night I had a return of my wretched malaria.'

At these words, as if he had been given a cue, Ukridge reached under his chair and produced from his hat, like some conjuror, a bottle that was own brother to the one he had left in my rooms. Even from where I sat I could read those magic words of cheer on its flaunting label.

'Then I've got the very stuff for you,' he boomed. 'This is what you want. Glowing reports on all sides. Two doses, and cripples fling away their crutches and join the Beauty Chorus.'

'I am scarcely a cripple, Mr Ukridge,' said Lady Lakenheath, with a return of her earlier bleakness.

'No, no! Good heavens, no! But you can't go wrong by taking Peppo.'

'Peppo?' said Lady Lakenheath, doubtfully.

'It bucks you up.'

'You think it might do me good?' asked the sufferer, wavering. There was a glitter in her eye that betrayed the hypochondriac, the woman who will try anything once.

'Can't fail.'

'Well, it is most kind and thoughtful of you to have brought it. What with worrying over Leonard –'

'I know, I know,' murmured Ukridge, in a positively bedside manner.

'It seems so strange,' said Lady Lakenheath, 'that, after I had advertised in all the papers, someone did not find him.'

'Perhaps someone did find him!' said Ukridge, darkly.

'You think he must have been stolen?'

'I am convinced of it. A beautiful parrot like Leonard, able to talk in six languages –'

'And sing,' murmured Lady Lakenheath.

'– *and* sing,' added Ukridge, 'is worth a lot of money. But don't you worry, old – er – don't you worry. If the investigations which I am conducting now are successful, you will have Leonard back safe and sound tomorrow.'

'Tomorrow?'

'Absolutely tomorrow. Now tell me all about your malaria.'

I felt that the time had come for me to leave. It was not merely that the conversation had taken a purely medical turn and that I was practically excluded from it; what was really driving me away was the imperative necessity of getting out in the open somewhere and thinking. My brain was whirling. The world seemed to have become suddenly full of significant and disturbing parrots. I seized my hat and rose. My hostess was able to take only an absent-minded interest in my departure. The last thing I saw as the door closed was Ukridge's look of big-hearted tenderness as he leaned forward so as not to miss a syllable of his companion's clinical revelations. He was not actually patting Lady Lakenheath's hand and telling her to be a brave little woman, but short of that he appeared to be doing everything a man could do to show her that, rugged though his exterior might be, his heart was in the right place and aching for her troubles.

I walked back to my rooms. I walked slowly and pensively, bumping into lamp-posts and pedestrians. It was a relief, when I finally reached Ebury Street, to find Ukridge smoking on my sofa. I was resolved that before he left he should explain what this was all about, if I had to wrench the truth from him.

'Hallo, laddie!' he said. 'Upon my Sam, Corky, old horse, did you ever in your puff hear of anything so astounding as our meeting like that? Hope you didn't mind my pretending not to know you. The fact is my position in that house – What the dickens were you doing there, by the way?'

'I'm helping Lady Lakenheath prepare her husband's memoirs.'

'Of course, yes. I remember hearing her say she was going to rope in someone. But what a dashed extraordinary thing it should be you! However, where was I? Oh, yes. My position in the house, Corky, is so delicate that I simply didn't dare risk entering into any entangling alliances. What I mean to say is, if we had rushed into each other's arms, and you had been established in the old lady's eyes as a friend of mine, and then one of these days you had happened to make a bloomer of some kind – as you well might, laddie – and got heaved into the street on your left ear – well, you see where I would be. I should be involved in your downfall. And I solemnly assure you, laddie, that my whole existence is staked on keeping in with that female. I *must* get her consent!'

'Her what?'

'Her consent. To the marriage.'

'The marriage?'

Ukridge blew a cloud of smoke, and gazed through it sentimentally at the ceiling.

'Isn't she a perfect angel?' he breathed, softly.

'Do you mean Lady Lakenheath?' I asked, bewildered.

'Fool! No, Millie.'

'Millie? The girl in blue?'

Ukridge sighed dreamily.

'She was wearing that blue dress when I first met her, Corky. And a hat with thingummies. It was on the Underground. I gave her my seat, and, as I hung over her, suspended by a strap, I fell in love absolutely in a flash. I give you my honest word, laddie, I fell in love with her for all eternity between Sloane Square and South Kensington stations. She got out at South Kensington. So did I. I followed her to the house, rang the bell, got the maid to show me in, and, once I was in, put up a yarn about being misdirected and coming to the wrong address and all that sort of thing. I think they thought I was looney or trying to sell life insurance or something, but I didn't mind that. A few days later I called, and after that I hung about, keeping an eye on their movements, met 'em everywhere they went, and bowed and passed a word and generally made my presence felt, and – well, to cut a long story short, old horse, we're engaged. I happened to find out that Millie was in the habit of taking the dog for a run in Kensington Gardens every morning at eleven, and after that things began to move. It took a bit of doing, of course, getting up so early, but I was on the spot every day and we talked and bunged sticks for the dog, and – well, as I say, we're engaged. She is the most amazing, wonderful girl, laddie, that you ever encountered in your life.'

I had listened to this recital dumbly. The thing was too cataclysmal for my mind. It overwhelmed me.

'But –' I began.

'But,' said Ukridge, 'the news has yet to be broken to the old lady, and I am striving with every nerve in my body, with every fibre of my brain, old horse, to get in right with her. That is why I brought her that Peppo. Not much, you may say, but every little helps. Shows zeal. Nothing like zeal. But, of course, what I'm really relying on is the parrot. That's my ace of trumps.'

I passed a hand over my corrugated forehead.

'The parrot!' I said, feebly. 'Explain about the parrot.' Ukridge eyed me with honest astonishment.

'Do you mean to tell me you haven't got on to that? A man of your intelligence! Corky, you amaze me. Why, I pinched it, of course. Or, rather, Millie and I pinched it together. Millie – a girl in a million, laddie! – put the bird in a string-bag one night when her aunt was dining out and lowered it to me out of the drawing-room window. And I've been keeping it in the background till the moment was ripe for the spectacular return. Wouldn't have done to take it back at once. Bad strategy. Wiser to hold it in reserve for a few days and show zeal and work up the interest. Millie and I are building on the old lady's being so supremely bucked at having the bird restored to her that there will be nothing she won't be willing to do for me.'

'But what do you want to dump the thing in my rooms for?' I demanded, reminded of my grievance. 'I never got such a shock as when that damned hat-box began to back-chat at me.'

'I'm sorry, old man, but it had to be. I could never tell that the old lady might not take it into her head to come round to my rooms about something. I'd thrown out – mistakenly, I realize now – an occasional suggestion about tea there some afternoon. So I had to park the bird with you. I'll take it away tomorrow.'

'You'll take it away tonight!'

'Not tonight, old man,' pleaded Ukridge. 'First thing tomorrow. You won't find it any trouble. Just throw it a word or two every now and then and give it a bit of bread dipped in tea or something, and you won't have to worry about it at all. And I'll be round by noon at the latest to take it away. May Heaven reward you, laddie, for the way you have stood by me this day!'

For a man like myself, who finds at least eight hours of sleep essential if that schoolgirl complexion is to be preserved, it was unfortunate that Leonard the parrot should have proved to be a bird of high-strung temperament, easily upset. The experiences which he had undergone since leaving home had, I was to discover, jarred his nervous system. He was reasonably tranquil during the hours preceding bedtime, and had started his beauty-sleep before I myself turned in; but at two in the morning something in the nature of a nightmare must have attacked him, for I was wrenched from slumber by the sounds of a hoarse soliloquy in what I took to be some native dialect. This lasted without a break till two-fifteen, when he made a noise like a steam-riveter for some moments; after which, apparently soothed, he fell asleep again. I dropped off at about three, and at three-thirty was awakened by the strains of a deep-sea chanty. From then on our periods of sleep never seemed to coincide. It was a wearing night, and before I went out after breakfast, I left imperative instructions with Bowles for Ukridge, on arrival, to be informed that, if anything went wrong with his plans for removing my guest that day, the mortality statistics among parrots would take an up-curve. Returning to my rooms in the evening, I was pleased to see that this manifesto had been taken to heart. The hat-box was gone, and about six o'clock Ukridge appeared, so beaming and effervescent that I understood what had happened before he spoke. 'Corky, my boy,' he said, vehemently, 'this is the maddest, merriest day of all the glad New Year, and you can quote me as saying so!'

'Lady Lakenheath has given her consent?'

'Not merely given it, but bestowed it blithely, jubilantly.'

'It beats me,' I said.

'What beats you?' demanded Ukridge, sensitive to the jarring note.

'Well, I don't want to cast any aspersions, but I should have thought the first thing she would have done would be to make searching inquiries about your financial position.'

'My financial position? What's wrong with my financial position? I've got considerably over fifty quid in the bank, and I'm on the eve of making an enormous fortune out of this Peppo stuff.'

'And that satisfied Lady Lakenheath?' I said, incredulously.

Ukridge hesitated for a moment.

'Well, to be absolutely frank, laddie,' he admitted, 'I have an idea that she rather supposes that in the matter of financing the venture my aunt will rally round and keep things going till I am on my feet.'

'Your aunt! But your aunt has finally and definitely disowned you.'

'Yes, to be perfectly accurate, she has. But the old lady doesn't know that. In fact, I rather made a point of keeping it from her. You see, I found it necessary, as things turned out, to play my aunt as my ace of trumps.'

'You told me the parrot was your ace of trumps.'

'I know I did. But these things slip up at the last moment. She seethed with gratitude about the bird, but when I seized the opportunity to ask her for her blessing I was shocked to see that she put her ears back and jibbed. Got that nasty steely look in her eyes and began to talk about clandestine meetings and things being kept from her. It was an occasion for the swiftest thinking, laddie. I got an inspiration. I played up my aunt. It worked like magic. It seems the old lady has long been an admirer of her novels, and has always wanted to meet her. She went down and out for the full count the moment I introduced my aunt into the conversation, and I have had no trouble with her since.'

'Have you thought what is going to happen when they do meet? I can't see your aunt delivering a striking testimonial to your merits.'

'That's all right. The fact of the matter is, luck has stood by me in the most amazing way all through. It happens that my aunt is out of town. She's down at her cottage in Sussex finishing a novel, and on Saturday she sails for America on a lecturing tour.'

'How did you find that out?'

'Another bit of luck. I ran into her new secretary, a bloke named Wassick, at the Savage smoker last Saturday. There's no chance of their meeting. When my aunt's finishing a novel, she won't read letters or telegrams, so it's no good the old lady trying to get a communication through to her. It's Wednesday now, she sails on Saturday, she will be away six months – why, damme, by the time she hears of the thing I shall be an old married man.'

It had been arranged between my employer and myself during the preliminary negotiations that I should give up my afternoons to the memoirs and that the most convenient plan would be for

me to present myself at Thurloe Square daily at three o'clock.
I had just settled myself on the following day in the ground-floor
study when the girl Millie came in, carrying papers.

'My aunt asked me to give you these,' she said. 'They are
Uncle Rupert's letters home for the year 1889.'

I looked at her with interest and something bordering on awe.
This was the girl who had actually committed herself to the
appalling task of going through life as Mrs Stanley Featherstone-
haugh Ukridge – and, what is more, seemed to like the prospect.
Of such stuff are heroines made.

'Thank you,' I said, putting the papers on the desk. 'By the
way, may I – I hope you will – What I mean is, Ukridge told me all
about it. I hope you will be very happy.'

Her face lit up. She really was the most delightful girl to look
at I had ever met. I could not blame Ukridge for falling in love
with her.

'Thank you very much,' she said. She sat in the huge armchair,
looking very small. 'Stanley has been telling me what friends you
and he are. He is devoted to you.'

'Great chap!' I said, heartily. I would have said anything which
I thought would please her. She exercised a spell, this girl. 'We
were at school together.'

'I know. He is always talking about it.' She looked at me with
round eyes exactly like a Persian kitten's. 'I suppose you will be his
best man?' She bubbled with happy laughter. 'At one time I was
awfully afraid there wouldn't be any need for a best man. Do you
think it was very wrong of us to steal Aunt Elizabeth's parrot?'

'Wrong?' I said, stoutly. 'Not a bit of it. What an idea!'

'She was terribly worried,' argued the girl.

'Best thing in the world,' I assured her. 'Too much peace of
mind leads to premature old age.'

'All the same, I have never felt so wicked and ashamed of
myself. And I know Stanley felt just like that, too.'

'I bet he did!' I agreed, effusively. Such was the magic of this
Dresden china child that even her preposterous suggestion that
Ukridge possessed a conscience could not shake me.

'He's so wonderful and chivalrous and considerate.'

'The very words I should have used myself!'

'Why to show you what a beautiful nature he has, he's gone
out now with my aunt to help her do her shopping.'

'You don't say so!'

'Just to try to make it up to her, you see, for the anxiety we caused her.'

'It's noble! That's what it is. Absolutely noble!'

'And if there's one thing in the world he loathes it is carrying parcels.'

'The man,' I exclaimed, with fanatical enthusiasm, 'is a perfect Sir Galahad!'

'Isn't he! Why, only the other day –'

She was interrupted. Outside, the front door slammed. There came a pounding of large feet in the passage. The door of the study flew open and Sir Galahad himself charged in, his arms full of parcels.

'Corky!' he began. Then, perceiving his future wife, who had risen from the chair in alarm, he gazed at her with a wild pity in his eyes, as one who has bad news to spring. 'Millie, old girl,' he said, feverishly, 'we're in the soup!'

The girl clutched the table.

'Oh, Stanley, darling!'

'There is just one hope. It occurred to me as I was –'

'You don't mean that Aunt Elizabeth has changed her mind?'

'She hasn't yet. But,' said Ukridge, grimly, 'she's pretty soon going to, unless we move with the utmost dispatch.'

'But what has happened?'

Ukridge shed the parcels. The action seemed to make him calmer.

'We had just come out of Harrod's,' he said, 'and I was about to leg it home with these parcels, when she sprang it on me! Right out of the blue sky!'

'What, Stanley, dear? Sprang what?'

'This ghastly thing. This frightful news that she proposes to attend the dinner of the Pen and Ink Club on Friday night. I saw her talking to a pug-nosed female we met in the fruit, vegetable, birds, and pet dogs department, but I never guessed what they were talking about. She was inviting the old lady to that infernal dinner!'

'But, Stanley, why shouldn't Aunt Elizabeth go to the Pen and Ink Club dinner?'

'Because my aunt is coming up to town on Friday specially to speak at that dinner, and your aunt is going to make a point of introducing herself and having a long chat about me.'

We gazed at one another silently. There was no disguising the gravity of the news. Like the coming together of two uncongenial chemicals, this meeting of aunt with aunt must inevitably produce an explosion. And in that explosion would perish the hopes and dreams of two loving hearts.

'Oh, Stanley! What can we do?'

If the question had been directed at me, I should have been hard put to it to answer; but Ukridge, that man of resource, though he might be down, was never out.

'There is just one scheme. It occurred to me as I was sprinting along the Brompton Road. Laddie,' he proceeded, laying a heavy hand on my shoulder, 'it involves your cooperation.'

'Oh, how splendid!' cried Millie.

It was not quite the comment I would have made myself. She proceeded to explain.

'Mr Corcoran is so clever. I'm sure, if it's anything that can be done, he will do it.'

This ruled me out as a potential resister. Ukridge I might have been able to withstand, but so potently had this girl's spell worked upon me that in her hands I was as wax.

Ukridge sat down on the desk, and spoke with a tenseness befitting the occasion.

'It's rummy in this life, laddie,' he began in moralizing vein, 'how the rottenest times a fellow goes through may often do him a bit of good in the end. I don't suppose I have enjoyed any period of my existence less than those months I spent at my aunt's house in Wimbledon. But mark the sequel, old horse! It was while going through that ghastly experience that I gained a knowledge of her habits which is going to save us now. You remember Dora Mason?'

'Who is Dora Mason?' inquired Millie, quickly.

'A plain, elderly sort of female who used to be my aunt's secretary,' replied Ukridge, with equal promptness.

Personally I remembered Miss Mason as a rather unusually pretty and attractive girl, but I felt that it would be injudicious to say so. I contented myself with making a mental note to the effect that Ukridge, whatever his drawbacks as a husband, had at any rate that ready tact which is so helpful in the home.

'Miss Mason,' he proceeded, speaking, I thought, in a manner a shade more careful and measured, 'used to talk to me about her job from time to time. I was sorry for the poor old thing, you understand, because hers was a grey life, and I made rather a point of trying to cheer her up now and then.'

'How like you, dear!'

It was not I who spoke – it was Millie. She regarded her betrothed with shining and admiring eyes, and I could see that she was thinking that my description of him as a modern Galahad was altogether too tame.

'And one of the things she told me,' continued Ukridge, 'was that my aunt, though she's always speaking at these bally dinners, can't say a word unless she has her speech written for her and memorizes it. Miss Mason swore solemnly to me that she had written every word my aunt had spoken in public in the last two years. You begin to get on to the scheme, laddie? The long and the short of it is that we must get hold of that speech she's going to deliver at the Pen and Ink Club binge. We must intercept it, old horse, before it can reach her. We shall thus spike her guns. Collar that speech, Corky, old man, before she can get her hooks on it, and you can take it from me that she'll find she has a headache on Friday night and can't appear.'

There stole over me the sickening conviction that comes to those in peril that I was for it.

'But it may be too late,' I faltered, with a last feeble effort at self-preservation. 'She may have the speech already.'

'Not a chance. I know what she's like when she's finishing one of these beastly books. No distractions of any sort are permitted. Wassick, the secretary bloke, will have had instructions to send the thing to her by registered post to arrive Friday morning, so that she can study it in the train. Now, listen carefully, laddie, for I have thought this thing out to the last detail. My aunt is at her cottage at Market Deeping, in Sussex. I don't know how the trains go, but there's sure to be one that'll get me to Market Deeping tonight. Directly I arrive I shall send a wire to Wassick – signed "Ukridge",' said the schemer. 'I have a perfect right to sign telegrams "Ukridge",' he added, virtuously, 'in which I tell him to hand the speech over to a gentleman who will call for it as arrangements have been made for him to take it down to the cottage. All you have to do is to call at my aunt's house, see Wassick – a splendid fellow, and just the sort of chump who won't suspect a thing – get the manuscript, and biff off. Once round the corner, you dump it in the nearest garbage-box, and all is well.'

'Isn't he wonderful, Mr Corcoran?' cried Millie.

'I can rely on you, Corky? You will not let me down over your end of the business?'

'You *will* do this for us, Mr Corcoran, won't you?' pleaded Millie.

I gave one look at her. Her Persian kitten eyes beamed into mine – gaily, trustfully, confidently. I gulped.

'All right,' I said, huskily.

A leaden premonition of impending doom weighed me down next morning as I got into the cab which was to take me to Heath House, Wimbledon Common. I tried to correct this shuddering panic, by telling myself that it was simply due to my recollection of what I had suffered at my previous visit to the place, but it refused to leave me. A black devil of apprehension sat on my shoulder all the way, and as I rang the front-door bell it seemed to me that this imp emitted a chuckle more sinister than any that had gone before. And suddenly as I waited there I understood.

No wonder the imp had chuckled! Like a flash I perceived where the fatal flaw in this enterprise lay. It was just like Ukridge, poor impetuous, woollen-headed ass, not to have spotted it; but that I myself should have overlooked it was bitter indeed. The simple fact which had escaped our joint attention was this – that, as I had visited the house before, the butler would recognize me. I might succeed in purloining the speech, but it would be reported to the Woman Up Top that the mysterious visitor who had called for the manuscript was none other than the loathly Mr Corcoran of hideous memory – and what would happen then? Prosecution! Jail? Social ruin?

I was on the very point of retreating down the steps when the door was flung open, and there swept over me the most exquisite relief I have ever known.

It was a new butler who stood before me.

'Well?'

He did not actually speak the word, but he had a pair of those expressive, beetling eyebrows, and they said it for him. A most forbidding man, fully as grim and austere as his predecessor.

'I wish to see Mr Wassick,' I said, firmly.

The butler's manner betrayed no cordiality, but he evidently saw that I was not to be trifled with. He led the way down that familiar hall, and presently I was in the drawing-room, being inspected once more by the six Pekingese, who, as on that other occasion, left their baskets, smelt me, registered disappointment, and made for their baskets again.

'What name shall I say, sir?'

I was not to be had like that.

'Mr Wassick is expecting me,' I replied, coldly.

'Very good, sir.'

I strolled buoyantly about the room, inspecting this object and that. I hummed lightly. I spoke kindly to the Pekes.

'Hallo, you Pekes!' I said.

I sauntered over to the mantelpiece, over which was a mirror. I was gazing at myself and thinking that it was not such a bad sort of face – not handsome, perhaps, but with a sort of something about it – when of a sudden the mirror reflected something else.

That something was the figure of that popular novelist and well-known after-dinner speaker, Miss Julia Ukridge. 'Good morning,' she said.

It is curious how often the gods who make sport of us poor humans defeat their own ends by overdoing the thing. Any contretemps less awful than this, however slightly less awful, would undoubtedly have left me as limp as a sheet of carbon paper, rattled and stammering, in prime condition to be made sport of. But as it was I found myself strangely cool. I had a subconscious feeling that there would be a reaction later, and that the next time I looked in a mirror I should find my hair strangely whitened, but for the moment I was unnaturally composed, and my brain buzzed like a circular-saw in an ice-box.

'How do you do?' I heard myself say. My voice seemed to come from a long distance, but it was steady and even pleasing in timbre.

'You wished to see me, Mr Corcoran?'

'Yes.'

'Then why,' inquired Miss Ukridge, softly, 'did you ask for my secretary?'

There was that same acid sub-tinkle in her voice which had been there at our previous battle in the same ring. But that odd alertness stood by me well.

'I understood that you were out of town,' I said.

'Who told you that?'

'They were saying so at the Savage Club the other night.' This seemed to hold her.

'Why did you wish to see me?' she asked, baffled by my ready intelligence.

'I hoped to get a few facts concerning your proposed lecture tour in America.'

'How did you know that I was about to lecture in America?'

I raised my eyebrows. This was childish.

'They were saying so at the Savage Club,' I replied. Baffled again.

'I had an idea, Mr Corcoran,' she said, with a nasty gleam in her blue eyes, 'that you might be the person alluded to in my nephew Stanley's telegram.'

'Telegram?'

'Yes. I altered my plans and returned to London last night instead of waiting till this evening, and I had scarcely arrived when a telegram came, signed Ukridge, from the village where I had been staying. It instructed my secretary to hand over to a gentleman who would call this morning the draft of the speech which I am to deliver at the dinner of the Pen and Ink Club. I assume the thing to have been some obscure practical joke on the part of my nephew, Stanley. And I also assumed, Mr Corcoran, that you must be the gentleman alluded to.'

I could parry this sort of stuff all day.

'What an odd idea!' I said.

'You think it odd? Then why did you tell my butler that my secretary was expecting you?'

It was the worst one yet, but I blocked it.

'The man must have misunderstood me. He seemed,' I added loftily, 'an unintelligent sort of fellow.'

Our eyes met in silent conflict for a brief instant, but all was well. Julia Ukridge was a civilized woman, and this handicapped her in the contest. For people may say what they like about the artificialities of modern civilization and hold its hypocrisies up to scorn, but there is no denying that it has one outstanding merit. Whatever its defects, civilization prevents a gently bred lady of high standing in the literary world from calling a man a liar and punching him on the nose, however convinced she may be that he deserves it. Miss Ukridge's hands twitched, her lips tightened, and her eyes gleamed bluely – but she restrained herself. She shrugged her shoulders.

'What do you wish to know about my lecture tour?' she said.
It was the white flag.

Ukridge and I had arranged to dine together at the Regent
Grill Room that night and celebrate the happy ending of his
troubles. I was first at the tryst, and my heart bled for my poor
friend as I noted the care-free way in which he ambled up the aisle
to our table. I broke the bad news as gently as I could, and the
man sagged like a filleted fish. It was not a cheery meal. I extended
myself as host, plying him with rich foods and spirited young wines,
but he would not be comforted. The only remark he contributed
to the conversation, outside of scattered monosyllables, occurred as
the waiter retired with the cigar-box.

'What's the time, Corky, old man?'

I looked at my watch.

'Just on half-past nine.'

'About now,' said Ukridge, dully, 'my aunt is starting to give
the old lady an earful!'

Lady Lakenheath was never, even at the best of times, what
I should call a sparkling woman, but it seemed to me, as I sat with
her at tea on the following afternoon, that her manner was more
sombre than usual. She had all the earmarks of a woman who has
had disturbing news. She looked, in fact, exactly like a woman who
has been told by the aunt of the man who is endeavouring to marry
into her respectable family the true character of that individual.

It was not easy in the circumstances to keep the ball rolling on
the subject of the 'Mgomo-'Mgomos, but I was struggling bravely,
when the last thing happened which I should have predicted.

'Mr Ukridge,' announced the maid.

That Ukridge should be here at all was astounding: but that he
should bustle in, as he did, with that same air of being the household pet which had marked his demeanour at our first meeting in
this drawing-room, soared into the very empyrean of the inexplicable. So acutely was I affected by the spectacle of this man, whom
I had left on the previous night a broken hulk, behaving with the
ebullience of an honoured member of the family, that I did what
I had been on the verge of doing every time I had partaken of Lady
Lakenheath's hospitality – upset my tea.

'I wonder,' said Ukridge, plunging into speech with the same
old breezy abruptness, 'if this stuff would be any good, Aunt
Elizabeth.'

I had got my cup balanced again as he started speaking, but at the sound of this affectionate address over it went again. Only a juggler of long experience could have manipulated Lady Lakenheath's miniature cups and saucers successfully under the stress of emotions such as I was experiencing.

'What is it, Stanley?' asked Lady Lakenheath, with a flicker of interest.

They were bending their heads over a bottle which Ukridge had pulled out of his pocket.

'It's some new stuff, Aunt Elizabeth. Just put on the market. Said to be excellent for parrots. Might be worth trying.'

'It is exceedingly thoughtful of you, Stanley, to have brought it,' said Lady Lakenheath, warmly. 'And I shall certainly try the effect of a dose if Leonard has another seizure. Fortunately, he seems almost himself again this afternoon.'

'Splendid!'

'My parrot,' said Lady Lakenheath, including me in the conversation, 'had a most peculiar attack last night. I cannot account for it. His health has always been so particularly good. I was dressing for dinner at the time, and so was not present at the outset of the seizure, but my niece, who was an eye-witness of what occurred, tells me he behaved in a most unusual way. Quite suddenly, it appears, he started to sing very excitedly; then, after a while, he stopped in the middle of a bar and appeared to be suffering. My niece, who is a most warm-hearted girl, was naturally exceedingly alarmed. She ran to fetch me, and when I came down poor Leonard was leaning against the side of his cage in an attitude of complete exhaustion, and all he would say was, "Have a nut!" He repeated this several times in a low voice, and then closed his eyes and tumbled off his perch. I was up half the night with him, but now he seems mercifully to have turned the corner. This afternoon he is almost his old bright self again, and has been talking in Swahili, always a sign that he is feeling cheerful.'

I murmured my condolences and congratulations.

'It was particularly unfortunate,' observed Ukridge, sympathetically, 'that the thing should have happened last night, because it prevented Aunt Elizabeth going to the Pen and Ink Club dinner.'

'What!' Fortunately I had set down my cup by this time.

'Yes,' said Lady Lakenheath, regretfully. 'And I had been so looking forward to meeting Stanley's aunt there. Miss Julia

Ukridge, the novelist. I have been an admirer of hers for many years. But, with Leonard in this terrible state, naturally I could not stir from the house. His claims were paramount. I shall have to wait till Miss Ukridge returns from America.'

'Next April,' murmured Ukridge, softly.

'I think, if you will excuse me now, Mr Corcoran, I will just run up and see how Leonard is.'

The door closed.

'Laddie,' said Ukridge, solemnly, 'doesn't this just show –'

I gazed at him accusingly.

'Did you poison that parrot?'

'Me? Poison the parrot? Of course I didn't poison the parrot. The whole thing was due to an act of mistaken kindness carried out in a spirit of the purest altruism. And, as I was saying, doesn't it just show that no little act of kindness, however trivial, is ever wasted in the great scheme of things? One might have supposed that when I brought the old lady that bottle of Peppo the thing would have begun and ended there with a few conventional words of thanks. But mark, laddie, how all things work together for good. Millie, who, between ourselves, is absolutely a girl in a million, happened to think the bird was looking a bit off colour last night, and with a kindly anxiety to do him a bit of good, gave him a slice of bread soaked in Peppo. Thought it might brace him up. Now, what they put in that stuff, old man, I don't know, but the fact remains that the bird almost instantly became perfectly pie-eyed. You have heard the old lady's account of the affair, but, believe me, she doesn't know one half of it. Millie informs me that Leonard's behaviour had to be seen to be believed. When the old lady came down he was practically in a drunken stupor, and all today he has been suffering from a shocking head. If he's really sitting up and taking notice again, it simply means that he has worked off one of the finest hang-overs of the age. Let this be a lesson to you, laddie, never to let a day go by without its act of kindness. What's the time, old horse?'

'Getting on for five.'

Ukridge seemed to muse for a moment, and a happy smile irradiated his face.

'About now,' he said, complacently, 'my aunt is out in the Channel somewhere. And I see by the morning paper that there is a nasty gale blowing up from the south-east!'

'LIFE, LADDIE,' said Ukridge, 'is very rum.'

He had been lying for some time silent on the sofa, his face towards the ceiling; and I had supposed that he was asleep. But now it appeared that it was thought, not slumber, that had caused his unwonted quietude.

'Very, very rum,' said Ukridge.

He heaved himself up and stared out of the window. The sitting-room window of the cottage which I had taken in the country looked upon a stretch of lawn, backed by a little spinney; and now there stole in through it from the waking world outside that first cool breeze which heralds the dawning of a summer day.

'Great Scott!' I said, looking at my watch. 'Do you realize you've kept me up talking all night?'

Ukridge did not answer. There was a curious, far-away look on his face, and he uttered a sound like the last gurgle of an expiring soda-water siphon; which I took to be his idea of a sigh. I saw what had happened. There is a certain hour at the day's beginning which brings with it a strange magic, tapping wells of sentiment in the most hard-boiled. In this hour, with the sun pinking the eastern sky and the early bird chirping over its worm, Stanley Featherstone-haugh Ukridge, that battered man of wrath, had become maudlin; and, instead of being allowed to go to bed, I was in for some story of his murky past.

'Extraordinarily rum,' said Ukridge. 'So is Fate. It's curious to think, Corky, old horse, that if things had not happened as they did I might now be a man of tremendous importance, looked up to and respected by all in Singapore.'

'Why should anyone respect you in Singapore?'

'Rolling in money,' proceeded Ukridge wistfully.

'You?'

'Yes, me. Did you ever hear of one of those blokes out East who didn't amass a huge fortune? Of course you didn't. Well, think what I should have done, with my brain and vision. Mabel's father made a perfect pot of money in Singapore, and I don't suppose he had any vision whatever.'

'Who was Mabel?'

'Haven't I ever spoken to you of Mabel?'

'No. Mabel who?'

'I won't mention names.'

'I hate stories without names.'

'You'll have this story without names – and like it,' said Ukridge with spirit. He sighed again. A most unpleasant sound. 'Corky, my boy,' he said, 'do you realize on what slender threads our lives hang? Do you realize how trifling can be the snags on which we stub our toes as we go through this world? Do you realize –'

'Get on with it.'

'In my case it was a top-hat.'

'What was a top-hat?'

'The snag.'

'You stubbed your toe on a top-hat?'

'Figuratively, yes. It was a top-hat which altered the whole course of my life.'

'You never had a top-hat.'

'Yes, I did have a top-hat. It's absurd for you to pretend that I never had a top-hat. You know perfectly well that when I go to live with my Aunt Julia in Wimbledon I roll in top-hats – literally roll.'

'Oh, yes, when you go to live with your aunt.'

'Well, it was when I was living with her that I met Mabel. The affair of the top-hat happened –'

I looked at my watch again.

'I can give you half an hour,' I said. 'After that I'm going to bed. If you can condense Mabel into a thirty-minute sketch, carry on.'

'This is not quite the sympathetic attitude I should like to see in an old friend, Corky.'

'It's the only attitude I'm capable of at half-past three in the morning. Snap into it.'

Ukridge pondered.

'It's difficult to know where to begin.'

'Well, to start with, who was she?'

'She was the daughter of a bloke who ran some sort of im-mensely wealthy business in Singapore.'

'Where did she live?'

'In Onslow Square.'

'Where were you living?'

'With my aunt in Wimbledon.'

'Where did you meet her?'

'At a dinner-party at my aunt's.'

'You fell in love with her at first sight?'

'Yes.'

'For a while it seemed that she might return your love?'

'Exactly.'

'And then one day she saw you in a top-hat and the whole thing was off. There you are. The entire story in two minutes fifteen seconds. Now let's go to bed.'

Ukridge shook his head.

'You've got it wrong, old horse. Nothing like that at all. You'd better let me tell the whole thing from the beginning.'

The first thing I did after that dinner (said Ukridge) was to go and call at Onslow Square. As a matter of fact, I called about three times in the first week; and it seemed to me that everything was going like a breeze. You know what I'm like when I'm staying with my Aunt Julia, Corky. Dapper is the word. Debonair. Perfectly groomed. Mind you, I don't say I enjoy dressing the way she makes me dress when I'm with her, but there's no getting away from it that it gives me an air. Seeing me strolling along the street with the gloves, the cane, the spats, the shoes, and the old top-hat, you might wonder if I was a marquess or a duke, but you would be pretty sure I was one of the two.

These things count with a girl. They count still more with her mother. By the end of the second week you wouldn't be far wrong in saying that I was the popular pet at Onslow Square. And then, rolling in one afternoon for a dish of tea, I was shocked to perceive nestling in my favourite chair, with all the appearance of a cove who is absolutely at home, another bloke. Mabel's mother was fussing over him as if he were the long-lost son. Mabel seemed to like him a good deal. And the nastiest shock of all came when I discovered that the fellow was a baronet.

Now, you know as well as I do, Corky, that for the ordinary workaday bloke Barts are tough birds to go up against. There is something about Barts that appeals to the most soulful girl. And as for the average mother, she eats them alive. Even an elderly Bart with two chins and a bald head is bad enough, and this was a young and juicy specimen. He had a clean-cut, slightly pimply, patrician face; and, what was worse, he was in the Coldstream Guards. And you will bear me out, Corky, when I say that, while an ordinary civilian Bart is bad enough, a Bart who is also a Guardee is a rival the stoutest-hearted cove might well shudder at.

And when you consider that practically all I had to put up against this serious menace was honest worth and a happy disposition, you will understand why the brow was a good deal wrinkled as I sat sipping my tea and listening to the rest of the company talking about people I'd never heard of and entertainments where I hadn't been among those we also noticed.

After a while the conversation turned to Ascot.

'Are you going to Ascot, Mr Ukridge?' said Mabel's mother, apparently feeling that it was time to include me in the chit-chat.

'Wouldn't miss it for worlds,' I said.

Though, as a matter of fact, until that moment I had rather intended to give it the go-by. Fond as I am of the sport of kings, to my mind a race meeting where you've got to go in a morning coat and a top-hat – with the thermometer probably in the nineties – lacks fascination. I'm all for being the young duke when occasion requires, but races and toppers don't seem to me to go together.

'That's splendid,' said Mabel, and I'm bound to say these kind words cheered me up a good deal. 'We shall meet there.'

'Sir Aubrey,' said Mabel's mother, 'has invited us to his house-party.'

'Taken a place for the week down there,' explained the Bart.

'Ah!' I said. And, mark you, that was about all there was to say. For the sickening realization that this Guardee Bart, in addition to being a Bart and a Guardee, also possessed enough cash to take country houses for Ascot Week in that careless, off-hand manner seemed to go all over me like nettle-rash. I was rattled, Corky. Your old friend was rattled. I did some pretty tense thinking on my way back to Wimbledon.

When I got there, I found my aunt in the drawing-room. And suddenly something in her attitude seemed to smite me like a blow. I don't know if you have ever had that rummy feeling which seems to whisper in your ear that Hell's foundations are about to quiver, but I got it the moment I caught sight of her. She was sitting bolt upright in a chair, and as I came in she looked at me. You know her, Corky, and you know just how she shoots her eyes at you without turning her head, as if she were a basilisk with a stiff neck. Well, that's how she looked at me now.

'Good evening,' she said.

'Good evening,' I said.

'So you've come in,' she said.

'Yes,' I said.

'Well, then, you can go straight out again,' she said.

'Eh,' I said.

'And never come back,' she said.

I goggled at her. Mark you, I had been heaved out of the old home by my Aunt Julia many a time before, so it wasn't as if I wasn't used to it; but I had never got the boot quite so suddenly before and so completely out of a blue sky. Usually, when Aunt Julia bungs me out on my ear, it is possible to see it coming days ahead.

'I might have guessed that something like this would happen,' she said.

And then all things were made plain. She had found out about the clock. And it shows what love can do to a fellow, Corky, when I tell you that I had clean forgotten all about it.

You know the position of affairs when I go to live with my Aunt Julia. She feeds me and buys me clothes, but for some reason best known to her own distorted mind it is impossible to induce her to part with a little ready cash. The consequence was that, falling in love with Mabel as I had done and needing a quid or two for current expenses, I had had to rely on my native ingenuity and resource. It was absolutely imperative that I should give the girl a few flowers and chocolates from time to time, and this runs into money. So, seeing a rather juicy clock doing nothing on the mantelpiece of the spare bedroom, I had sneaked it off under my coat and put it up the spout at the local pawnbroker's. And now, apparently, in some devious and underhand manner she had discovered this.

Well, it was no good arguing. When my Aunt Julia is standing over you with her sleeves rolled up preparatory to getting a grip on the scruff of your neck and the seat of your trousers, it has always been my experience that words are useless. The only thing to do is to drift away and trust to Time, the great healer. Some forty minutes later, therefore, a solitary figure might have been observed legging it to the station with a suit-case. I was out in the great world once more.

* * *

However, you know me, Corky. The Old Campaigner. It takes more than a knock like that to crush your old friend. I took a bed-sitting-room in Arundel Street and sat down to envisage the situation.

Undeniably things had taken a nasty twist, and many a man lacking my vision and enterprise might have turned his face to the wall and said: 'This is the end!' But I am made of sterner stuff. It seemed to me that all was not yet over. I had packed the morning coat, the waistcoat, the trousers, the shoes, the spats, and the gloves, and had gone away wearing the old top-hat; so, from a purely ornamental point of view, I was in precisely the position I had been before. That is to say, I could still continue to call at Onslow Square; and, what is more, if I could touch George Tupper for a fiver – which I intended to do without delay – I should have the funds to go to Ascot.

The sun, it appeared to me, therefore, was still shining. How true it is, Corky, that, no matter how the tempests lower, there is always sunshine somewhere! How true it is – Oh, all right, I was only mentioning it.

Well, George Tupper, splendid fellow, parted without a murmur. Well, no, not – to be absolutely accurate – without a murmur. Still, he parted. And the position of affairs was now as follows. Cash in hand, five pounds. Price of admission to grandstand and paddock at Ascot for first day of meeting, two pounds. Time to elapse before Ascot, ten days. Net result – three quid in my kick to keep me going till then and pay my fare down and buy flowers and so on. It all looked very rosy.

But note, Corky, how Fate plays with us. Two days before Ascot, as I was coming back from having tea at Onslow Square – not a little preoccupied, for the Bart had been very strong on the wing that afternoon – there happened what seemed at first sight an irremediable disaster.

The weather, which had been fair and warm until that evening, had suddenly broken, and a rather nippy wind had sprung up from the east. Now, if I had not been so tensely occupied with my thoughts, brooding on the Bart, I should of course have exercised reasonable precautions; but, as it was, I turned the corner into the Fulham Road in what you might call a brown study; and the first thing I knew my top-hat had been whisked off my head and was tooling along briskly in the direction of Putney.

Well, you know what the Fulham Road's like. A top-hat has about as much chance in it as a rabbit at a dog-show. I dashed after the thing with all possible speed, but what was the use? A taxi-cab knocked it sideways towards a 'bus; and the 'bus, curse it, did the rest. By the time the traffic had cleared a bit, I caught sight of the ruins and turned away with a silent groan. The thing wasn't worth picking up.

So there I was, dished.

Or, rather, what the casual observer who didn't know my enterprise and resource would have called dished. For a man like me, Corky, may be down, but he is never out. So swift were my mental processes that the time that elapsed between the sight of that ruined hat and my decision to pop round to the Foreign Office and touch George Tupper for another fiver was not more than fifty seconds. It is in the crises of life that brains really tell.

You can't accumulate if you don't speculate. So, though funds were running a bit low by this time, I invested a couple of bob in a cab. It was better to be two shillings out than to risk getting to the Foreign Office and finding that Tuppy had left.

Well, late though it was, he was still there. That's one of the things I like about George Tupper, one of the reasons why I always maintain that he will rise to impressive heights in his country's service – he does not shirk; he is not a clock-watcher. Many civil servants are apt to call it a day at five o'clock, but not George Tupper. That is why one of these days, Corky, when you are still struggling along turning out articles for *Interesting Bits* and writing footling short stories about girls who turn out to be the missing heiress, Tuppy will be Sir George Tupper, KCMG and a devil of a fellow among the Chancelleries.

I found him up to his eyes in official-looking papers, and I came to the point with all speed. I knew that he was probably busy declaring war on Montenegro or somewhere and wouldn't want a lot of idle chatter.

'Tuppy, old horse,' I said, 'it is imperative that I have a fiver immediately.'

'A what?' said Tuppy.

'A tenner,' I said.

It was at this point that I was horrified to observe in the man's eye that rather cold, forbidding look which you sometimes see in blokes' eyes on these occasions.

'I lent you five pounds only a week ago,' he said.

'And may Heaven reward you, old horse,' I replied courteously.

'What do you want any more for?'

I was just about to tell him the whole circumstances when it was as if a voice whispered to me: 'Don't do it!' Something told me that Tuppy was in a nasty frame of mind and was going to turn me down – yes, me, an old schoolfellow, who had known him since he was in Eton collars. And at the same time I suddenly perceived, lying on a chair by the door, Tuppy's topper. For Tuppy is not one of those civil servants who lounge into Whitehall in flannels and a straw hat. He is a correct dresser, and I honour him for it.

'What on earth,' said Tuppy, 'do you need money for?'

'Personal expenses, laddie,' I replied. 'The cost of living is very high these days.'

'What you want,' said Tuppy, 'is work.'

'What I want,' I reminded him – if old Tuppy has a fault, it is that he will not stick to the point – 'is a fiver.'

He shook his head in a way I did not like to see.

'It's very bad for you, all this messing about on borrowed money. It's not that I grudge it to you,' said Tuppy; and I knew, when I heard him talk in that pompous, Foreign Official way, that something had gone wrong that day in the country's service. Probably the draft treaty with Switzerland had been pinched by a foreign adventuress. That sort of thing is happening all the time in the Foreign Office. Mysterious veiled women blow in on old Tuppy and engage him in conversation, and when he turns round he finds the long blue envelope with the important papers in it gone.

'It's not that I grudge you the money,' said Tuppy, 'but you really ought to be in some regular job. I must think,' said Tuppy, 'I must think. I must have a look round.'

'And meanwhile,' I said, 'the fiver?'

'No. I'm not going to give it to you.'

'Only five pounds,' I urged. 'Five little pounds, Tuppy, old horse.'

'No.'

'You can chalk it up in the books to Office Expenses and throw the burden on the taxpayer.'

'No.'

'Will nothing move you?'

'No. And I'm awfully sorry, old man, but I must ask you to clear out now. I'm terribly busy.'

'Oh, right ho,' I said.

He burrowed down into the documents again; and I moved to the door, scooped up the top-hat from the chair, and passed out.

Next morning, when I was having a bit of breakfast, in rolled old Tuppy.

'I say,' said Tuppy.

'Say on, laddie.'

'You know when you came to see me yesterday?'

'Yes. You've come to tell me you've changed your mind about that fiver?'

'No, I haven't come to tell you I've changed my mind about that fiver. I was going to say that, when I started to leave the office, I found my top-hat had gone.'

'Too bad,' I said.

Tuppy gave me a piercing glance.

'You didn't take it, I suppose?'

'Who, me? What would I want with a top-hat?'

'Well, it's very mysterious.'

'I expect you'll find it was pinched by an international spy or something.'

Tuppy brooded for some moments.

'It's all very odd,' he said. 'I've never had it happen to me before.'

'One gets new experiences.'

'Well, never mind about that. What I really came about was to tell you that I think I have got you a job.'

'You don't mean that!'

'I met a man at the club last night who wants a secretary. It's more a matter with him of having somebody to keep his papers in order and all that sort of thing, so typing and shorthand are not essential. You can't do shorthand, I suppose?'

'I don't know. I've never tried.'

'Well, you're to go and see him tomorrow morning at ten. His name's Bulstrode, and you'll find him at my club. It's a good chance, so for Heaven's sake don't be lounging in bed at ten.'

'I won't. I'll be up and ready, with a heart for any fate.'

'Well, mind you are.'

'And I am deeply grateful, Tuppy, old horse, for these esteemed favours.'

'That's all right,' said Tuppy. He paused at the door. 'It's a mystery about that hat.'

'Insoluble, I should say. I shouldn't worry any more about it.'

'One moment it was there, and the next it had gone.'

'How like life!' I said. 'Makes one think a bit, that sort of thing.'

He pushed off, and I was just finishing my breakfast when Mrs Beale, my landlady, came in with a letter.

It was from Mabel, reminding me to be sure to come to Ascot. I read it three times while I was consuming a fried egg; and I am not ashamed to say, Corky, that tears filled my eyes. To think of her caring so much that she should send special letters urging me to be there made me tremble like a leaf. It looked to me as though the Bart's number was up. Yes, at that moment, Corky, I felt positively sorry for the Bart, who was in his way quite a good chap, though pimply.

That night I made my final preparations. I counted the cash in hand. I had just enough to pay my fare to Ascot and back, my entrance fee to the grandstand and paddock, with a matter of fifteen bob over for lunch and general expenses and a thoughtful ten bob to do a bit of betting with. Financially, I was on velvet.

Nor was there much wrong with the costume department. I dug out the trousers, the morning coat, the waistcoat, the shoes and the spats, and I tried on Tuppy's topper again. And for the twentieth time I wished that old Tuppy, a man of sterling qualities in every other respect, had had a slightly bigger head. It's a curious thing about old George Tupper. There's a man who you might say is practically directing the destinies of a great nation – at any rate, he's in the Foreign Office and extremely well thought of by the Nibs – and yet his size in hats is a small seven. I don't know if you've ever noticed that Tuppy's head goes up to a sort of point. Mine, on the other hand, is shaped more like a mangel-wurzel, and this made the whole thing rather complex and unpleasant.

As I stood looking in the glass, giving myself a final inspection, I couldn't help feeling what a difference a hat makes to a man. Bare-headed, I was perfect in every detail; but with a hat on I looked a good deal like a bloke about to go on and do a comic song at one of the halls. Still, there it was, and it was no good worrying about it. I put the trousers under the mattress, to ensure an adequate crease; and I rang the bell for Mrs Beale and gave her the coat to press with a hot iron. I also gave her the hat and instructed her to rub stout on it. This, as you doubtless know, gives a topper the deuce of a gloss; and when a fellow is up against a Bart, he can't afford to neglect the smallest detail.

And so to bed.

I didn't sleep very well. At about one in the morning it started to rain in buckets, and the thought suddenly struck me: what the deuce was I going to do if it rained during the day? To buy an umbrella would simply dislocate the budget beyond repair. The consequence was that I tossed pretty restlessly on my pillow.

But all was well. When I woke at eight o'clock the sun was pouring into the room, and the last snag seemed to have been removed from my path. I had breakfast, and then I dug the trouserings out from under the mattress, slipped into them, put on the shoes, buckled the spats, and rang the bell for Mrs Beale. I was feeling debonair to a degree. The crease in the trousers was perfect.

'Oh, Mrs Beale,' I said. 'The coat and the hat, please. What a lovely morning!'

Now, this Beale woman, I must tell you, was a slightly sinister sort of female, with eyes that reminded me a good deal of my Aunt Julia. And I was now somewhat rattled to perceive that she was looking at me in a rather meaning kind of manner. I also perceived that she held in her hand a paper or document. And there shot through me, Corky, a nameless fear.

It's a kind of instinct, I suppose. A man who has been up against it as frequently as I have comes to shudder automatically when he sees a landlady holding a sheet of paper and looking at him in a meaning manner.

A moment later it was plain that my sixth sense had not deceived me.

'I've brought your little account, Mr Ukridge,' said this fearful female.

'Right!' I said, heartily. 'Just shove it on the table, will you? And bring the coat and hat.'

She looked more like my Aunt Julia than ever.

'I must ask you for the money now,' she said. 'Being a week overdue.'

All this was taking the sunshine out of the morning, but I remained debonair.

'Yes, yes,' I said. 'I quite understand. We'll have a good long talk about that later. The hat and coat, please, Mrs Beale.'

'I must ask you –' she was beginning again, but I checked her with one of my looks. If there's one thing I bar in this world, Corky, it's sordidness.

'Yes, yes,' I said testily. 'Some other time. I want the hat and coat, please.'

At this moment, by the greatest bad luck, her vampire gaze fell on the mantelpiece. You know how it is when you are dressing with unusual care – you fill your pockets last thing. And I had most unfortunately placed my little capital on the mantelpiece. Too late I saw that she had spotted it. Take the advice of a man who has seen something of life, Corky, and never leave your money lying about. It's bound to start a disagreeable train of thought in the mind of anyone who sees it.

'You've got the money there,' said Mrs Beale.

I leaped for the mantelpiece and trousered the cash.

'No, no,' I said, hastily. 'You can't have that. I need that.'

'Ho?' she said. 'So do I.'

'Now listen, Mrs Beale,' I said. 'You know as well as I do –'

'I know as well as you do that you owe me two pounds three and sixpence ha'penny.'

'And in God's good time,' I said, 'you shall have it. But just for the moment you must be patient. Why, dash it, Mrs Beale,' I said warmly, 'you know as well as I do that in all financial transactions a certain amount of credit is an understood thing. Credit is the lifeblood of commerce. So bring the hat and coat, and later on we will thresh this matter out thoroughly.'

And then this woman showed a baseness of soul, a horrible low cunning, which, I like to think, is rarely seen in the female sex.

'I'll either have the money,' she said, 'or I'll keep the coat and hat.' And words cannot express, Corky, the hideous malignity in her voice. 'They ought to fetch a bit.'

I stared at her, appalled.

'But I can't go to Ascot without a top-hat.'

'Then you'd better not go to Ascot.'

'Be reasonable!' I begged. 'Reflect!'

It was no good. She stood firm on her demand for two pounds three and sixpence ha'penny, and nothing that I could say would shift her. I offered her double the sum at some future date, but no business was done. The curse of landladies as a class, Corky, and the reason why they never rise to ease and opulence, is that they have no vision. They do not understand high finance. They lack the big, broad, flexible outlook which wins to wealth. The deadlock continued, and finally she went off, leaving me dished once more.

It is only when you are in a situation like that, Corky, that you really begin to be able to appreciate the true hollowness of the world. It is only then that the absolute silliness and futility of human institutions comes home to you. This Ascot business, for instance. Why in the name of Heaven, if you are going to hold a race meeting, should you make a foolish regulation about the sort of costume people must wear if they want to attend it? Why should it be necessary to wear a top-hat at Ascot, when you can go to all the other races in anything you like?

Here was I perfectly equipped for Hurst Park, Sandown, Gatwick, Ally Pally, Lingfield, or any other meeting you care to name; and, simply because a ghoul of a landlady had pinched my topper, I was utterly debarred from going to Ascot, though the price of admission was bulging in my pocket. It's just that sort of thing that makes a fellow chafe at our modern civilization and wonder if, after all, Man can be Nature's last word.

Such, Corky, were my meditations as I stood at the window and gazed bleakly out at the sunshine. And then suddenly, as I gazed, I observed a bloke approaching up the street.

I eyed him with interest. He was an elderly, prosperous bloke with a yellowish face and a white moustache, and he was looking at the numbers on the doors, as if he were trying to spot a destination. And at this moment he halted outside the front door of my house, squinted up at the number, and then trotted up the steps and rang the bell. And I realized at once that this must be Tuppy's secretary man, the fellow I was due to go and see at the club in another half-hour. For a moment it seemed odd that he should have come to call on me instead of waiting for me to call on him; and then I reflected that this was just the sort of thing that the energetic, world's-worker type of man that Tuppy chummed up with at his club would be likely to do. Time is money with these coves, and no doubt he had remembered some other appointment which he couldn't make if he waited at his club till ten.

Anyway, here he was, and I peered down at him with a beating heart. For what sent a thrill through me, Corky, was the fact that he was much about my build and was brightly clad in correct

morning costume with top-hat complete. And though it was hard
to tell exactly at such a distance and elevation, the thought flashed
across me like an inspiration from above that that top-hat would
fit me a dashed sight better than Tuppy's had done.

In another minute there was a knock on the door, and he
came in.

Seeing him at close range, I perceived that I had not misjudged
this man. He was shortish, but his shoulders were just about the
same size as mine, and his head was large and round. If ever, in a
word, a bloke might have been designed by Providence to wear a
coat and hat that would fit me, this bloke was that bloke. I gazed at
him with a gleaming eye.

'Mr Ukridge?'

'Yes,' I said. 'Come in. Awfully good of you to call.'

'Not at all.'

And now, Corky, as you will no doubt have divined, I was, so
to speak, at the cross-roads. The finger-post of Prudence pointed
one way, that of Love another. Prudence whispered to me to
conciliate this bloke, to speak him fair, to comport myself towards
him as towards one who held my destinies in his hand and who
could, if well disposed, give me a job which would keep the wolf
from the door while I was looking round for something bigger
and more attuned to my vision and abilities.

Love, on the other hand, was shouting to me to pinch his coat
and leg it for the open spaces.

It was the deuce of a dilemma.

'I have called –' began the bloke.

I made up my mind. Love got the decision.

'I say,' I said. 'I think you've got something on the back of your
coat.'

'Eh?' said the bloke, trying to squint round and look between
his shoulder-blades – silly ass.

'It's a squashed tomato or something.'

'A squashed tomato?'

'Or something.'

'How would I get a squashed tomato on my coat?'

'Ah!' I said, giving him to understand with a wave of the hand
that these were deep matters.

'Very curious,' said the bloke.

'Very,' I said. 'Slip off your hat and let's have a look at it.'

He slid out of the coat, and I was on it like a knife. You have to move quick on these occasions, and I moved quick. I had the coat out of his hand and the top-hat off the table where he had put it, and was out of the door and dashing down the stairs before he could utter a yip.

I put on the coat, and it fitted like a glove. I slapped the top-hat on to my head, and it might have been made for me. And then I went out into the sunshine, as natty a specimen as ever paced down Piccadilly.

I was passing down the front steps when I heard a sort of bellow from above. There was the bloke, protruding from the window; and, strong man though I am, Corky, I admit that for an instant I quailed at the sight of the hideous fury that distorted his countenance.

'Come back!' shouted the bloke.

Well, it wasn't a time for standing and making explanations and generally exchanging idle chatter. When a man is leaning out of a window in his shirt-sleeves, making the amount of noise that this cove was making, it doesn't take long for a crowd to gather. And my experience has been that, when a crowd gathers, it isn't much longer before some infernal officious policeman rolls round as well. Nothing was farther from my wishes than to have this little purely private affair between the bloke and myself sifted by a policeman in front of a large crowd.

So I didn't linger. I waved my hand as much as to say that all would come right in the future, and then I nipped at a fairly high rate of speed round the corner and hailed a taxi. It had been no part of my plans to incur the expense of a taxi, I having earmarked twopence for a ride on the Tube to Waterloo; but there are times when economy is false prudence.

Once in the cab, whizzing along and putting more distance between the bloke and myself with every revolution of the wheels, I perked up amazingly. I had been, I confess, a trifle apprehensive until now; but from this moment everything seemed splendid. I forgot to mention it before, but this final top-hat which now nestled so snugly on the brow was a grey top-hat; and, if there is one thing that really lends a zip and a sort of devilish fascination to a fellow's appearance, it is one of those grey toppers. As I looked at myself in the glass and then gazed out of the window at the gay sunshine, it seemed to me that God was in His Heaven and all was right with the world.

The general excellence of things continued. I had a pleasant journey; and when I got to Ascot I planked my ten bob on a horse I heard some fellows talking about in the train, and, by Jove, it ambled home at a crisp ten to one. So there I was, five quid ahead of the game almost, you might say, before I strolled off to the paddock to have a look at the multitude and try to find Mabel. And I had hardly emerged from that tunnel thing that you have to walk through to get from the stand to the paddock when I ran into old Tuppy.

My first feeling on observing the dear old chap was one of relief that I wasn't wearing his hat. Old Tuppy is one of the best, but little things are apt to upset him, and I was in no mood for a painful scene. I passed the time of day genially.

'Ah, Tuppy!' I said.

George Tupper is a man with a heart of gold, but he is deficient in tact.

'How the deuce did you get here?' he asked.

'In the ordinary way, laddie,' I said.

'I mean, what are you doing here, dressed up to the nines like this?'

'Naturally,' I replied, with a touch of stiffness, 'when I come to Ascot, I wear the accepted morning costume of the well-dressed Englishman.'

'You look as if you had come into a fortune.'

'Yes?' I said, rather wishing he would change the subject. In spite of what you might call the perfect *alibi* of the grey topper, I did not want to discuss hats and clothes with Tuppy so soon after his recent bereavement. I could see that the hat he had on was a brand-new one and must have set him back at least a couple of quid.

'I suppose you've gone back to your aunt?' said Tuppy, jumping at a plausible solution. 'Well, I'm awfully glad, old man, because I'm afraid that secretary job is off. I was going to write to you tonight.'

'Off?' I said. Having had the advantage of seeing the bloke's face as he hung out of the window at the moment of our parting, I knew it was off; but I couldn't see how Tuppy could know.

'He rang me up last night, to tell me that he was afraid you wouldn't do, as he had thought it over and decided that he must have a secretary who knew shorthand.'

'Oh?' I said. 'Oh, did he? Then I'm dashed glad,' I said warmly, 'that I pinched his hat. It will be a sharp lesson to him not to raise people's hopes and shilly-shally in this manner.'

'Pinched his hat? What do you mean?'

I perceived that there was need for caution. Tuppy was looking at me in an odd manner, and I could see that the turn the conversation had taken was once more wakening in him suspicions which he ought to have known better than to entertain of an old school friend.

'It was like this, Tuppy,' I said. 'When you came to me and told me about that international spy sneaking your hat from the Foreign Office, it gave me an idea. I had been wanting to come to Ascot, but I had no topper. Of course, if I had pinched yours, as you imagined for a moment I had done, I should have had one; but, not having pinched yours, of course I hadn't one. So when your friend Bulstrode called on me this morning I collared his. And now that you have revealed to me what a fickle, changeable character he is, I'm very glad I did.'

Tuppy gaped slightly.

'Bulstrode called on you this morning, did you say?'

'This morning at about half-past nine.'

'He couldn't have done.'

'Then how do you account for my having his hat? Pull yourself together, Tuppy, old horse.'

'The man who came to see you couldn't have been Bulstrode.'

'Why not?'

'He left for Paris last night.'

'What!'

'He 'phoned me from the station just before his train started. He had had to change his plans.'

'Then who was the bloke?' I said.

The thing seemed to me to have the makings of one of those great historic mysteries you read about. I saw no reason why posterity should not discuss for ever the problem of the bloke in the grey topper as keenly as they do the man in the iron mask. 'The facts,' I said, 'are precisely as I have stated. At nine-thirty this morning a bird, gaily apparelled in morning coat, sponge-bag trousers, and grey top-hat, presented himself at my rooms and –'

At this moment a voice spoke behind me.

'Oh, hullo!'

I turned, and observed the Bart.

'Hullo!' I said.

I introduced Tuppy. The Bart nodded courteously.

'I say,' said the Bart, 'where's the old man?'

'What old man?'

'Mabel's father. Didn't he catch you?'

I stared at the man. He appeared to me to be gibbering. And a gibbering Bart is a nasty thing to have hanging about you before you have strengthened yourself with a bit of lunch.

'Mabel's father's in Singapore,' I said.

'No, he isn't,' said the Bart. 'He got home yesterday, and Mabel sent him round to your place to pick you up and bring you down here in the car. Had you left before he arrived?'

Well, that's where the story ends, Corky. From the moment that pimply Baronet uttered those words, you might say that I faded out of the picture. I never went near Onslow Square again. Nobody can say that I lack nerve, but I hadn't nerve enough to creep into the family circle and resume acquaintance with that fearsome bloke. There are some men, no doubt, with whom I might have been able to pass the whole thing off with a light laugh, but that glimpse I had had of him as he bellowed out of the window told me that he was not one of them. I faded away, Corky, old horse, just faded away. And about a couple of months later I read in the paper that Mabel had married the Bart.

Ukridge sighed another sigh and heaved himself up from the sofa. Outside the world was blue-grey with the growing dawn, and even the later birds were busy among the worms.

'You might make a story out of that, Corky,' said Ukridge.

'I might,' I said.

'All profits to be shared on a strict fifty-fifty basis, of course.'

'Of course.'

Ukridge brooded.

'Though it really wants a bigger man to do it justice and tell it properly, bringing out all the fine shades of the tragedy. It wants somebody like Thomas Hardy or Kipling, or somebody.'

'Better let me have a shot at it.'

'All right,' said Ukridge. 'And, as regards a title, I should call it "His Lost Romance", or something like that. Or would you suggest simply something terse and telling, like "Fate" or "Destiny"?'

'I'll think of a title,' I said.

THE EDITOR REGRETS

WHEN BINGO Little's wife, the well-known female novelist Rosie M. Banks, exerted her pull and secured for Bingo the editorship of *Wee Tots*, that popular and influential organ which has done so much to mould thought in the nursery, a sort of literary renaissance swept the Drones Club. Scarcely an Egg, Bean, Pieface or Crumpet on the list of members but took pen in hand with the feeling that here was where he cashed in and got back some of the stuff that had gone down the drain at Ally Pally and Kempton Park.

It was a painful shock to the intelligentsia, accordingly, when they discovered that their old friend was not going to prove the geyser of easy money they had anticipated. In quick succession he turned down the Egg who wanted to do Racing Notes, the Bean with the inside stuff on Night Clubs, and the Pieface who suggested that he should be given a sort of roving commission to potter round the south of France and contribute gossipy articles of human interest from such centres as Cannes and Monte Carlo. Even a Crumpet who had known him since they were in sailor suits had his thoughtful piece on Some Little Known Cocktails declined with thanks.

'On the plea,' said the Crumpet, 'that his proprietor wouldn't like it.'

'That's what he told me,' said the Egg. 'Who is this bally proprietor of Bingo's?'

'A man named Purkiss. It was through her life-long friendship with Mrs Purkiss that Mrs Bingo was able to get Bingo the job.'

'Then Purkiss can have no red blood in him,' said the Egg.

'Purkiss lacks vision,' said the Bean.

'Purkiss is an ass,' said the Pieface.

The Crumpet shook his head.

'I'm not so sure,' he said. 'My belief is that Bingo merely uses Purkiss as a blind or screen. I think the man is drunk with a sense of power and definitely enjoys rejecting contributions from outside talent. And one of these days he is going to get himself into serious trouble by coming the heavy editor like this. In fact, not long ago he very nearly did so. Only the luck of the Littles saved him from taking a toss which threatened to jar his fat trouser-seat clean out of the editorial chair, never to return. I allude, of course, to the Bella Mae Jobson affair.'

The Bean asked what the Bella Mae Jobson affair was, and the Crumpet, expressing surprise that he had not heard of it, said that it was the affair of Bella Mae Jobson.

The American authoress, he explained. Scarcely known in this country, she has for some years past been holding American childhood spellbound with her tales of Willie Walrus, Charlie Chipmunk, and other fauna. Purkiss, who had been paying a visit to New York, met her on the boat coming back, and she lent him *Charlie Chipmunk Up the Orinoco*. A single glance was enough to tell him that here was the circulation-building stuff for which *Wee Tots* had been waiting and he entered into tentative negotiations for her whole output, asking her on arriving in London to look in at the office and fix things up with his editor – viz., Bingo.

Now, unfortunately, Purkiss's absence from the centre of things had caused Bingo to get it up his nose a bit. When on the spot, the other had a way of making criticisms and suggestions, and an editor, he tells me, feels shackled when a proprietor with bronchial catarrh keeps popping in all the time trying to dictate the policy of the 'Uncle Joe to His Chickabiddies' page. All through these last weeks of freedom, therefore, he had been getting more and more above himself, with the result that, when informed per desk telephone that a Miss Jobson waited without he just tapped his teeth with a pencil and said: 'Oh, she does, does she? Well, bung her out and tell her to write. We do not see callers without an appointment.'

He then returned to the 'What a Tiny Girlie Can Do to Help Mother' feature, and was still roughing it out when the door opened and in walked Purkiss, looking bronzed and fit. And after a bit of Well-here-I-am-back-again-ing and Oh-hullo-Mr-Purkiss-did-you-have-a-good-trip-ing, as is inevitable on these occasions, Purkiss said:

'By the way, Mr Little, a Miss Jobson will be calling shortly.'

Bingo gave a light laugh.

'Oh, jolly old Jobson?' he said airily. 'She's been and gone, leaving not a wrack behind. I gave her the air.'

'I beg your pardon?'

'Turfed her out,' explained Bingo.

Purkiss reeled.

'You mean…you refused to see her?'

'That's right,' said Bingo. 'Busy. Busy, busy, busy. Much too busy to talk to females. I told her to write, stating her business legibly on one side of the paper only.'

I don't know if any of you happened to see that picture, *The Hurricane*, that was on not long ago. Briefly, the plot of it was that there was a bevy of unfortunate blighters on a South Sea island and the dickens of a howling tempest came along and blew them cross-eyed. I bring this up because Bingo tells me that very much the same sort of thing happened now. For some moments, he says, all he was conscious of was a vast atmospheric disturbance, with him swaying in the middle of it, and then gradually, Purkiss's remarks becoming clearer, he gathered that he had made something of a floater, and that this bird Jobson was a bird who should have been conciliated, sucked up to, given the old oil and generally made to feel that she was among friends and admirers.

'Well, I'm sorry,' he said, feeling that something in the nature of an apology was indicated. 'I deeply regret the whole unfortunate occurrence. I was the victim of a misunderstanding. It never crossed my mind that the above was a sweet ginger specializing in chipmunks. The impression I received was of somebody trying to sell richly illustrated sets of Dumas on the easy payment plan.'

Then, seeing that Purkiss had buried his face in his hands and hearing him mutter something about 'God's gift to the nursery' and 'ruin', he stepped across and gave him a kindly pat on the shoulder.

'Cheer up,' he said. 'You still have me.'

'No, I haven't,' said Purkiss. 'You're fired.'

And in words whose meaning there was no mistaking he informed Bingo that the end of the month would see his finish as Ye Ed., and that it was his, Purkiss's, dearest hope that when he, Bingo, finally left the premises, he would trip over the doormat and break his neck.

He, Purkiss, then withdrew.

* * *

His departure gave Bingo the opportunity for some intensive thinking. And as you will readily appreciate, intensive thinking was just what the situation could do with a spot of.

It was on Mrs Bingo's reactions that he found himself brooding for the most part. There were many reasons why it cut him to the quick to be forced to relinquish his grasp on the tiller of *Wee Tots*. The salary, though small, had come under the head of manna from heaven, and the holding of the post had filled him with a spiritual pride such as he had not experienced since he won the Woolly-Mat-Tatting Prize at his first kindergarten. But what really got in amongst him was the thought of what Mrs Bingo was going to say on hearing the news.

The Bingo *ménage*, as you are no doubt aware, is one that has been conducted from its inception on one hundred per cent Romeo and Juliet lines. She is devoted to him, and his ingrowing love for her is such that you would be justified in comparing them to a couple of turtle doves. Nevertheless, he was ill at ease. Any male turtle dove will tell you that, if conditions are right, the female turtle dove can spit on her hands and throw her weight about like Donald Duck. And it needed no diagram to show Bingo that conditions here were just right. Mrs Bingo had taken a lot of trouble to get him his job, and when she found that through sheer fatheadedness he had chucked it away she would, something told him, have a lot of comment to make.

Little wonder, then, that the barometer of his soul pointed steadily to 'Stormy'. Out of the night that covered him, black as the pit from pole to pole, one solitary bit of goose presented itself – the fact that the head of the family was away at the moment, visiting friends in the country. This at least enabled him to postpone the springing of the bad tidings.

But the thought that the hour of that springing must inevitably come kept him in pretty much of a doodah, and to distract his mind he plunged into the life of pleasure. And it was at a bottle-party a couple of nights later that he found himself going like a breeze with a female of considerable attractions, and with indescribable emotion learned that her name was Jobson, Bella Mae.

It altered the whole outlook, enabling him to get an entirely new angle on the situation.

Until this moment, he had been feeling that his only chance of wangling a happy ending would be to put up a good, carefully constructed, plausible story. He had planned, accordingly, on Mrs Bingo's return, to inform her quite frankly that he had been relieved of his portfolio for giving Purkiss's girl-friend the raspberry, and then to go on to explain why he had taken this stand. He had felt, he would say, that he owed it to her not to allow himself to be closeted with strange women. Too often, he would tell her, female visitors pat editors on the knee or even straighten their tie, and his pure soul had shrunk from the thought of anything like that happening to a sober married man like himself. It might get by, or it might not get by. It was a straight, sporting venture.

But now he saw that he could do much better than this. He could obviate all necessity for such explanations by retaining his job.

When I said that he found himself going like a breeze with this chipmunk-fancier, I used the expression in its most exact sense. I don't know if any of you have ever seen Bingo when he was going really well, but I can testify that at such times he does his stuff like a master. Irresistible charm about sums it up. Think of Ronald Colman, and you have the idea. Well, you will under-stand what I mean when I tell you that as early as the second cocktail B. M. Jobson was saying how lonely she felt in this big, strange city, and he was saying 'There, there' and pointing out that this was a state of things that could be readily adjusted. They parted in a flurry of telephone numbers and good wishes, and he went home feeling that the thing was in the bag.

What he proposed to do, I need scarcely explain, was to keep after this tomato and bump up their ripening friendship to a point where she would be able to refuse him nothing. He would then tear off his whiskers and reveal himself as the editor of *Wee Tots*, whereupon she would let him have her frightful bilge on easy terms and he would go to Purkiss and say: 'Well, Purkiss, and now how about it?' Upon which, of course, Purkiss would immedi-ately fold him in a close embrace and issue a reprieve at the foot of the scaffold.

To this end, accordingly, he devoted all his energies. He took Bella Mae Jobson to the Zoo, the Tower of London, Madame Tussaud's, five matinées, seven lunches and four dinners. He also gave her a bunch of white heather, several packets of cigarettes, eleven lots of roses and a signed photograph. And came a day when she said she really must buy back. She was sailing for America on the following Wednesday, she said, and on Tuesday she was going to give a lovely luncheon-party at her hotel suite and he must be the guest of honour.

Bingo accepted effusively. The moment, he realized, had come. He had got the thing all worked out. He would stick on till the other guests had gone and then, while she still mellowed with lunch, spring his big scene. He didn't see how it could miss.

It was only when a telegram arrived from Mrs Bingo on the Monday morning, announcing that she would be returning that evening, that he began to appreciate that there might be complications which he had not foreseen.

In normal circs, the return of the wife of his b. after a longish absence would have been enough to send Bingo singing about the house. But now he didn't emit so much as a single bar, and it was with a drawn and thoughtful face that he met her at the station round about six-thirty.

'Well, well, well,' he said heartily, or as heartily as he could manage, embracing her on the platform. 'This is fine! This is great! This is terrific! And what a surprise, what? I thought you were planning to put in rather longer in the provinces.'

Mrs Bingo registered astonishment.

'What, miss our wedding anniversary?' she cried. She paused, and he became aware that she was eyeing him fairly narrowly. 'You hadn't forgotten that tomorrow was our wedding anniversary?'

Bingo, who had given a sharp, convulsive leap like a gaffed salmon, reassembled himself.

'Me?' he cried. 'I should say not. I've been ticking off the days on the calendar.'

'So have I,' said Mrs Bingo. 'Oh, Bingo, darling, we'll have lunch tomorrow at that little place near Charing Cross, where we had our wedding breakfast. And we'll pretend we've just been married. Won't it be fun!'

Bingo swallowed a couple of times. He was having trouble with his Adam's apple.

'Stupendous,' he said.

'Only it won't be quite the same, of course, because then you hadn't an important job to hurry back to.'

'No,' said Bingo.

'How is everything at the office, by the way?'

'Oh, fine.'

'Is Mr Purkiss still pleased with your work?'

'Fascinated,' said Bingo.

But he spoke absently, and it was with a heavy heart that he rose next morning and toyed listlessly with a fried egg and bacon. Nor was he any chirpier when he reached the editorial sanctum. He could see no daylight.

It would be possible, of course, to pop in on Bella Mae in the course of the afternoon, but he saw only too clearly that that would not be the same thing at all. The way he had had it planned out, he was to have been the life and soul of the gathering all through lunch, winning all hearts with his gay wit; and then, when the last guest had tottered away, holding his sides, and his hostess was thanking him brokenly for making her party such a success, he would have given her the works. It would be very different barging in on her at four o'clock and trying to swing the deal in cold blood.

And then, after he had been sitting for a goodish time with his head in his hands, exercising every cell in his brain to its utmost capacity, he received an inspiration and saw what Napoleon would have done. A moment later, he was on the telephone with Mrs Bingo's silvery voice are-you-there-ing at the other end.

'Hullo, darling,' he said.

'Hullo, angel,' said Mrs Bingo.

'Hullo, precious,' said Bingo.

'Hullo, sweetie-pie,' said Mrs Bingo.

'I say, moon of my delight,' said Bingo, 'listen. A rather awkward thing has happened, and I should like your advice as to how to act for the best. There's a most important *littérateuse* we are anxious to land for the old sheet, and the question has arisen of my taking her out to lunch today.'

'Oh, Bingo!'

'Now, my personal inclination is to tell her to go to blazes.'

'Oh, no, you mustn't do that.'

'Yes, I think I will. "Nuts to you, *littérateuse*," I shall say.'

'No, Bingo, please! Of course you must take her out to lunch.'

'But how about our binge?'

'We can have dinner instead.'

'Dinner?'

'Yes.'

Bingo allowed himself to be persuaded.

'Now, that's an idea,' he said. 'There, I rather think, you've got something.'

'Dinner will be just as good.'

'Better. More suited to unbridled revelry.'

'You won't have to hurry off after dinner.'

'That's right.'

'We'll go to a theatre and supper afterwards.'

'We will, indeed,' said Bingo, feeling how simple these things were, if only one used a bit of tact. 'That, as I see it, is the exact programme.'

'And, as a matter of fact,' said Mrs Bingo, 'it's really rather convenient, because now I shall be able to go to Miss Jobson's luncheon-party, after all.'

Bingo swayed like a jelly in a high wind.

'Miss who's luncheon-party?'

'Jobson. You wouldn't know her. An American writer named Bella Mae Jobson. Mrs Purkiss rang up a little while ago, saying she was going and could I come along, because Miss Jobson has long been an admirer of my work. Of course, I refused. But now it's all right, and I shall be able to go. She sails tomorrow, so this is our last chance of meeting. Well, good-bye, my poppet, I mustn't keep you from your work any longer.'

If Mrs Bingo supposed that Bingo, having hung up the receiver, immediately returned to the task of assembling wholesome literature for the kiddies, she was gravely in error. For possibly a quarter of an hour after she had rung off, he sat motionless in his chair, using up time which Purkiss was paying him for in staring sightlessly before him and breathing in quick jerks. His whole aspect was that of a man who has unexpectedly been struck by lightning.

This, it seemed to him, was the end. He couldn't possibly roll up to the Jobson lunch, if Mrs Bingo was going to be there. You see, in order not to divert her mind from the main issue, he had avoided informing Bella Mae that he was married. Rightly or wrongly, he had felt that better results were to be obtained by keeping this news item under his hat. And if she lugged Mrs Bingo up to him and said, 'Oh, Mr Little, I wonder if you know Miss

Rosie M. Banks?' and he replied, 'Oh, rather. She's my wife,' only embarrassment could ensue.

No, there was only one thing to be done. He must abandon all idea of retaining his job and go back to the plan he had originally sketched out, of explaining to Mrs Bingo why he had refused to see Bella Mae Jobson that day when she called at the office. This, he felt with the first stirring of optimism which so far had animated him, might go pretty well after the former had met the latter. For Bella Mae, as I have said, was a female of considerable personal attractions. She had a lissome form, surmounted by a map of elfin charm and platinum-blonde hair. Stranger things had happened than that Mrs Bingo might approve his prudence in declining to be cooped up with all that sex-appeal.

Feeling somewhat better, he went out and dispatched a telegram to the Jobson, regretting his inability to be present at the festivities. And he was about to return to the office, when a sudden thought struck him amidships and he had to clutch at a passing lamp-post to keep himself from falling in his tracks.

He had remembered that signed photograph.

The whole question of signed photographs is one that bulks largely in married life. When husbands bestow them on external females, wives want to know why. And the present case was complicated by the fact that in doing the signing Bingo – with the best motives – had rather spread himself. Mere cordiality would have been bad enough, and he had gone a shade beyond the cordial. And the finished product was probably standing on the Jobson's mantelpiece and would be the first thing that Mrs Bingo would see on entering the other's suite.

It was not an enterprise to which he in any sense of the phrase looked forward, but he saw that, if a major disaster was to be avoided and the solidity of the Bingo–Mrs Bingo axis to be maintained, he would have to get hold of that photograph well in advance of the luncheon hour and remove it.

I don't know if you have ever called at an hotel with a view to pinching a signed photograph from one of the suites. If not, I may tell you that technical difficulties present themselves at the very outset – notably the problem of how the hell to get in. Bingo, inquiring at the desk, learned that Miss Jobson was not at home, and was for a moment encouraged by the information. It was only after he had sneaked up the stairs and was standing outside the locked door that he realized that this was not an end but a beginning.

And then, just as he was feeling that he was a mere puppet in the grip of a remorseless fate and that it wasn't any use going on struggling, he saw a maid coming along the corridor, and remembered that maids have keys.

It was a moment for exerting that charm of his to the uttermost. He switched it on and allowed it to play upon the maid like a searchlight.

'Oh, hullo, maid,' he said. 'Good morning.'

'Good morning, sir,' said the maid.

'Gosh!' said Bingo. 'You have a nice, kind, open, tenderhearted face. I wonder if you would do something for me. First, however,' he said, shoving across a ten-bob note, 'take this.'

'Thank you, sir,' said the maid.

'The facts, briefly,' said Bingo, 'are these. I am lunching today with Miss Jobson.'

'She's out,' said the maid. 'I saw her go along the passage with the little dog.'

'Exactly,' said Bingo. 'And there you have put your finger on the nub. She's out, and I want to get in. I hate waiting in hotel lobbies. You know how it is. Bores come up and tell you their troubles. Cadgers come up and try to touch you. I shall be happier in Miss Jobson's suite. Could you possibly' – here he ladled out another currency bill – 'let me in?'

'Certainly, sir,' said the maid, and did so.

'Thanks,' said Bingo. 'Heaven bless you, my dear old maid. Lovely day.'

'Beautiful,' said the maid.

He had scarcely crossed the threshold before he perceived that he had done the shrewd thing in sweetening her. He was a quid down, and he could ill spare quids, but it had been worth every penny of the money. There, as he had anticipated, was the photograph, plumb spang in the middle of the mantelpiece where it could not have failed to catch the eye of an incoming wife. To snatch it up and trouser it was with him the work of a moment, and he was just turning to the door to make the quick getaway, when his attention was drawn to a row of bottles on the sideboard. There they stood, smiling up at him, and as he was feeling more than a little faint after his ordeal he decided to have one for the road before withdrawing.

So he sloshed some Italian vermouth into a glass, and sloshed some French vermouth on top of it, and was reaching for the gin, to start sloshing that, when his heart did three double somersaults and a swan-dive. There had come to his ears the rattle of a key in the door.

It is difficult to say what would really have been the right thing to do in the circumstances. Some chaps, I suppose, would just have stayed put and tried to pass it off with jovial breeziness. Others might have jumped out of the window. But he wasn't feeling equal to jovial breeziness and the suite was on the fourth floor, so he took a middle course. He cleared the sofa in a single bound, and had scarcely gone to earth behind it when the door opened.

It was not Bella Mae Jobson who entered, but his old pal the maid. She was escorting another early popper-in. Through the gap at the bottom of his zareba he could see the concluding portion of a pair of trousers and a pair of boots. And when the lips above these trousers spoke, he found that this was no stranger but a familiar acquaintance. The voice was the voice of Purkiss.

'Thank you, my dear,' said Purkiss.

'Thank *you*, sir,' said the maid, leading Bingo to suppose that once more money had passed into her possession. He found himself brooding on the irony of the thing. Such a big day for the maid, I mean, and such a rotten one for him.

Purkiss coughed.

'I seem to be early.'

'Yes, sir.'

'Then, perhaps, to fill in the time, I might be taking Miss Jobson's dog for a run.'

'Miss Jobson's out with the dog now, sir.'

'Oh?' said Purkiss.

There was a momentary silence, and then the maid said that that was funny, and Purkiss asked what was funny.

'There ought to be another gentleman here,' said the maid. 'But I don't see him. Oh yes,' she proceeded, as Bingo, who for some little while now had been inhaling fluff in rather large quantities, gave a hearty sneeze, 'there he is, behind the sofa.'

And the next moment Bingo was aware of an eye peering down at him from the upper regions. Purkiss's eye.

'Mr Little!' cried Purkiss.

Bingo rose, feeling that it was useless to dissemble further.

'Ah, Purkiss,' he said distantly, for they were not on good terms, and with what dignity he could muster, which was not much, he rose and made for the door.

'Hey!' cried Purkiss. 'Just a minute.'

Bingo carried on doorwards.

'If you wish to speak to me, Purkiss,' he said, 'you will find me in the bar.'

But it was not thither that he immediately proceeded. His need for a bracer was urgent, but even more than a bracer he wanted air. He had been under the sofa only about three minutes, but as nobody had swept there for nearly six years quite a lot of mixed substances had found their way into his lungs. He was, indeed, feeling more like a dustbin than a man. He passed through the lobby and stood outside the door of the hotel, drinking in great draughts of the life-giving, and after a while began to feel better.

The improvement in his condition, however, was purely physical. Spiritually, he continued in the depths. As he reviewed the position of affairs, his heart struck a new low. He had secured the photograph, yes, and that was good, as far as it went. But it did not, he perceived, go so dashed far. If Purkiss was to be one of the guests at the Jobson lunch, he was still waist-high in the soup and likely to sink without trace at any moment.

He could envisage just what would occur at the beano. His tortured mind threw the thing into a sort of dialogue scene.

The Apartment of B. M. Jobson. Afternoon. Discovered – B. M. Jobson and Purkiss. Enter Mrs Bingo.

MRS BINGO: Cheerio. I'm Rosie M. Banks.

JOBSON: Oh, what ho, Miss Banks. Do you know Mr Purkiss?

MRS BINGO: You betcher. He owns the paper my husband is editor of.

JOBSON: You're married, then?

MRS BINGO: Oh, rather. Name of Little.

JOBSON: Little? Odd. I know a bird named Little. In fact when I say 'know', that's understating it a bit. He's been giving me the rush of a lifetime. 'Bingo', mine calls himself. Some relation, perhaps.

MRS BINGO:

But he preferred not to sketch in Mrs Bingo's lines. He stood there groaning in spirit. And he had just groaned for about the fifteenth time, when a car drew up before him and through a sort of mist he saw Mrs Bingo seated at the steering-wheel.

'Oh, Bingo, darling!' cried Mrs Bingo. 'What luck finding you here. Is this where you're lunching with your writer? What an extraordinary coincidence.'

It seemed to Bingo that if he was going to put up any kind of a story, now was the time to put it up. In a few brief moments Mrs Bingo would be entering the presence of the Jobson, with results as already indicated, and her mind must be prepared.

But beyond a sort of mixed snort and gurgle he found himself unable to utter, and Mrs Bingo carried on.

'I can't stop a minute,' she said. 'I've got to rush back to Mrs Purkiss. She's in great distress. When I got to her house, to pick her up and drive her here, I found her in a terrible state. Apparently her dog has been lost. I just came here to tell Miss Jobson that we shan't be able to lunch. Will you be an angel and ring her up from the desk and explain?'

Bingo blinked. The hotel, though solidly built, seemed to be swaying above him.

'You...what was that you said? You won't be able to lunch with –'

'No. Mrs Purkiss wants me with her. She's gone to bed with a hot-water bottle. So will you ring Miss Jobson up? Then I can hurry off.'

Bingo drew a deep breath.

'Of course, of course, of course, of course, of course,' he said. 'Oh rather. Rather. Ring Miss Jobson up...tell her you and Mrs Purkiss will not be among those present...explain fully. A simple task. Leave it to me, light of my life.'

'Thank you, darling. Good-bye.'

'Good-bye,' said Bingo.

She drove off, and he stood there, his eyes closed and his lips moving silently. Only once in his life before had he been conscious of this awed sense of being the favourite son of a benevolent providence. That was at his private school, when the Rev. Aubrey Upjohn, his headmaster, in the very act of raising the cane to land him a juicy one on the old spot, had ricked his shoulder and had to postpone the ceremony indefinitely.

Presently, life returned to the rigid limbs and he tottered to the bar to have one quick one, followed by another rather slower. And the first person he saw there, sucking down something pink, was Purkiss. He gave him an austere look, and settled himself at the farther end of the counter. Later on, it would presumably be his nauseous task to step across and inform the man of the tragedy which had come upon his home, but the thought of holding speech with him after the way he had behaved was so revolting that he did not propose to do it until he had fortified himself with a couple of refreshers.

And he had had the first one and was waiting for the second, when he felt something pawing at his sleeve. He glanced round, and there was Purkiss with a pleading look in his eyes, like a spaniel trying to ingratiate itself with someone whom it knows to be allergic to dogs.

'Mr Little.'

'Well, Purkiss?'

'Mr Little, it is in your power to do me a great kindness.'

Well, I don't know what you would have replied to that, if you had been in Bingo's position – addressed in this fashion, I mean, by a man who had not only given you the push but in doing so called you at least six offensive names. Personally, I would have said 'Oh?' or possibly 'Ho!' and that may have been what Bingo was intending to say. But before he could get going, Purkiss proceeded.

'Mr Little, I am faced by a disaster so hideous that the mind reels, contemplating it, and only you can save me. At any moment now, my wife will be arriving here. We are lunching with Miss Jobson. Mr Little, I appeal to you. Will you think of some suitable story and go and stand at the door and intercept her and prevent her coming to this luncheon-party? My whole future happiness depends on this.'

At this juncture, Bingo's second refresher arrived and he sat sipping it thoughtfully. He could make nothing of all this, but is a pretty intelligent chap, and he was beginning to see that circumstances had arisen which might culminate in him doing a bit of good for himself.

'It is imperative that my wife does not enter Miss Jobson's suite.'

Bingo got outside the mixture, and laid the glass down.

'Tell me the whole story in your own words, Purkiss,' he said.

Purkiss had produced a handkerchief, and was mopping his forehead with it. With his other hand he continued to massage

Bingo's arm. His whole deportment was vastly different from what it had been when he had called Bingo those six offensive names.

'It was only late this morning,' he said, 'that Miss Jobson informed me on the telephone that she had invited my wife to be a guest at this luncheon-party – which, until then, I had supposed would be a *tête-à-tête* between her and myself. I may mention that I have concluded negotiations with Miss Jobson for the publication of her brilliant works. I had presumed that over the luncheon-table we would discuss such details as illustrations and general make-up.'

'Matters,' said Bingo coldly, 'more customarily left to the editor.'

'Quite, quite, but as…yes, quite. But the point is, Mr Little, that in order to secure this material from Miss Jobson I had been compelled to – ah – how shall I put it –'

'Bring a little pressure to bear?'

'Precisely. Yes, that is exactly what I did. It seemed to me that the end justified the means. *Wee Tots*, as I saw it, was standing at the cross-roads. Let me secure the works of Bella Mae Jobson, and the dear old paper would soar beyond reach of rival competition. Let her, on the other hand, go to any of my trade rivals, and it would sustain a blow from which it might not recover. So I left no stone unturned.'

'And avenues?'

'Avenues, too. I explored them all.'

Bingo pursed his lips.

'I have no wish to condemn you unheard, Purkiss,' he said, 'but all this begins to look a bit French. Did you kiss Miss Jobson?'

A violent start shook Purkiss from stem to stern.

'No, no, no, no!' he protested vehemently. 'Certainly not. Most decidedly not. Nothing of that nature whatsoever. From start to finish our relations have been conducted with the utmost circumspection on my part, complete maidenly dignity on hers. But I took her to the National Gallery, the British Museum, and a matinée at Sadlers Wells. And then, seeing that she was weakening, I…'

His voice faltered and died away. Recovering it, he asked the barman for another of those pink ones for himself and whatever Bingo desired for Bingo. Then, when the tissue-restorers had appeared and he had drained his at a gulp, he found strength to continue.

'I gave her my wife's Pekingese.'

'What!'

'Yes. She had admired the animal when visiting my house, and I smuggled it out in a hat-box when I left home this morning and brought it to this hotel. Ten minutes later she had signed the contract. An hour later she apparently decided to include my wife in her list of guests. Two hours after that, she was informing me of this fact on the telephone, and I hastened here in the hope of being able to purloin the animal.

'But it was not to be. She had taken it for a run. Consider my position, Mr Little. What am I to do if my wife enters Miss Jobson's suite and finds her in possession of this dog? There will be explanations. And what will be the harvest when those explanations have been made?' He broke off, quivering in every limb. 'But why are we wasting time? While we sit talking here, she may be arriving. Your post is at the door. Fly, Mr Little!'

Bingo eyed him coldly.

'It's all very well to say "Fly!",' he said, 'but the question that springs to the lips is, "What is there in this for me?" Really, Purkiss, after your recent behaviour I rather fail to see why I should sweat myself to the bone, lugging you out of messes. It is true,' he went on meditatively, 'that I have thought of a pippin of a story which cannot fail to head Mrs Purkiss off when she arrives, but why should I bother to dish it out? At the end of this week I cease to be in your employment. It would be a very different thing, of course, if I were continuing as editor of *Wee Tots* –'

'But you are, Mr Little, you are.'

'– at a considerably increased salary –'

'Your salary shall be doubled.'

Bingo reflected.

'H'm!' he said. 'And no more muscling in and trying to dictate the policy of the "Uncle Joe to His Chickabiddies" page?'

'None, none. From now on, none. You shall have a completely free hand.'

'Then, Purkiss, you may set your mind at rest. Mrs Purkiss will not be present at the luncheon-party.'

'You guarantee that?'

'I guarantee it,' said Bingo. 'Just step along with me to the writing-room and embody the terms of our new contract in a brief letter, and I will do the needful.'

THE HEART OF A GOOF

IT WAS a morning when all nature shouted 'Fore!' The breeze, as it blew gently up from the valley, seemed to bring a message of hope and cheer, whispering of chip-shots holed and brassies landing squarely on the meat. The fairway, as yet unscarred by the irons of a hundred clubs, smiled greenly up at the azure sky; and the sun, peeping above the trees, looked like a giant golf-ball perfectly lofted by the mashie of some unseen god and about to drop dead by the pin of the eighteenth. It was the day of the opening of the course after the long winter, and a crowd of considerable dimensions had collected at the first tee. Plus fours gleamed in the sunshine, and the air was charged with happy anticipation.

In all that gay throng there was but one sad face. It belonged to the man who was waggling his driver over the new ball perched on its little hill of sand. This man seemed careworn, hopeless. He gazed down the fairway, shifted his feet, waggled, gazed down the fairway again, shifted the dogs once more, and waggled afresh. He waggled as Hamlet might have waggled, moodily, irresolutely. Then, at last, he swung, and, taking from his caddie the niblick which the intelligent lad had been holding in readiness from the moment when he had walked on to the tee, trudged wearily off to play his second.

The Oldest Member, who had been observing the scene with a benevolent eye from his favourite chair on the terrace, sighed.

'Poor Jenkinson,' he said, 'does not improve.'

'No,' agreed his companion, a young man with open features and a handicap of six. 'And yet I happen to know that he has been taking lessons all the winter at one of those indoor places.'

'Futile, quite futile,' said the Sage with a shake of his snowy head. 'There is no wizard living who could make that man go round in an average of sevens. I keep advising him to give up the game.'

'You!' cried the young man, raising a shocked and startled face from the driver with which he was toying. '*You* told him to give up golf! Why I thought—'

'I understand and approve of your horror,' said the Oldest Member, gently. 'But you must bear in mind that Jenkinson's is not an ordinary case. You know and I know scores of men who have never broken a hundred and twenty in their lives, and yet contrive to be happy, useful members of society. However badly they may play, they are able to forget. But with Jenkinson it is different. He is not one of those who can take it or leave it alone. His only chance of happiness lies in complete abstinence. Jenkinson is a goof.'

'A what?'

'A goof,' repeated the Sage. 'One of those unfortunate beings who have allowed this noblest of sports to get too great a grip upon them, who have permitted it to eat into their souls, like some malignant growth. The goof, you must understand, is not like you and me. He broods. He becomes morbid. His goofery unfits him for the battles of life. Jenkinson, for example, was once a man with a glowing future in the hay, corn, and feed business, but a constant stream of hooks, tops, and slices gradually made him so diffident and mistrustful of himself, that he let opportunity after opportunity slip, with the result that other, sterner, hay, corn, and feed merchants passed him in the race. Every time he had the chance to carry through some big deal in hay, or to execute some flashing *coup* in corn and feed, the fatal diffidence generated by a hundred rotten rounds would undo him. I understand his bankruptcy may be expected at any moment.'

'My golly!' said the young man, deeply impressed. 'I hope I never become a goof. Do you mean to say there is really no cure except giving up the game?'

The Oldest Member was silent for a while.

'It is curious that you should have asked that question,' he said at last, 'for only this morning I was thinking of the one case in my experience where a goof was enabled to overcome his deplorable malady. It was owing to a girl, of course. The longer I live, the more I come to see that most things are. But you will, no doubt, wish to hear the story from the beginning.'

The young man rose with the startled haste of some wild creature, which, wandering through the undergrowth, perceives the trap in his path.

'I should love to,' he mumbled, 'only I shall be losing my place at the tee.'

'The goof in question,' said the Sage, attaching himself with quiet firmness to the youth's coat-button, 'was a man of about your age, by name Ferdinand Dibble. I knew him well. In fact, it was to me—'

'Some other time, eh?'

'It was to me,' proceeded the Sage, placidly, 'that he came for sympathy in the great crisis of his life, and I am not ashamed to say that when he had finished laying bare his soul to me there were tears in my eyes. My heart bled for the boy.'

'I bet it did. But—'

The Oldest Member pushed him gently back into his seat.

'Golf,' he said, 'is the Great Mystery. Like some capricious goddess—'

The young man, who had been exhibiting symptoms of feverishness, appeared to become resigned. He sighed softly.

'Did you ever read "The Ancient Mariner"?' he said.

'Many years ago,' said the Oldest Member. 'Why do you ask?'

'Oh, I don't know,' said the young man. 'It just occurred to me.'

Golf (resumed the Oldest Member) is the Great Mystery. Like some capricious goddess, it bestows its favours with what would appear an almost fat-headed lack of method and discrimination. On every side we see big two-fisted he-men floundering round in three figures, stopping every few minutes to let through little shrimps with knock knees and hollow cheeks, who are tearing off snappy seventy-fours. Giants of finance have to accept a stroke per from their junior clerks. Men capable of governing empires fail to control a small, white ball, which presents no difficulties whatever to others with one ounce more brain than a cuckoo-clock. Mysterious, but there it is. There was no apparent reason why Ferdinand Dibble should not have been a competent golfer. He had strong wrists and a good eye. Nevertheless, the fact remains that he was a dud. And on a certain evening in June I realized that he was also a goof. I found it out quite suddenly as the result of a conversation which we had on this very terrace.

I was sitting here that evening thinking of this and that, when by the corner of the club-house I observed young Dibble in conversation with a girl in white. I could not see who she was, for her back was turned. Presently they parted and Ferdinand came slowly across to where I sat. His air was dejected. He had

had the boots licked off him earlier in the afternoon by Jimmy Fothergill, and it was to this that I attributed his gloom. I was to find out in a few moments that I was partly but not entirely correct in this surmise. He took the next chair to mine, and for several minutes sat staring moodily down into the valley.

'I've just been talking to Barbara Medway,' he said, suddenly breaking the silence.

'Indeed?' I said. 'A delightful girl.'

'She's going away for the summer to Marvis Bay.'

'She will take the sunshine with her.'

'You bet she will!' said Ferdinand Dibble, with extraordinary warmth, and there was another long silence.

Presently Ferdinand uttered a hollow groan.

'I love her, dammit!' he muttered brokenly. 'Oh, golly, how I love her!'

I was not surprised at his making me the recipient of his confidences like this. Most of the young folk in the place brought their troubles to me sooner or later.

'And does she return your love?'

'I don't know. I haven't asked her.'

'Why not? I should have thought the point not without its interest for you.'

Ferdinand gnawed the handle of his putter distractedly.

'I haven't the nerve,' he burst out at length. 'I simply can't summon up the cold gall to ask a girl, least of all an angel like her, to marry me. You see, it's like this. Every time I work myself up to the point of having a dash at it, I go out and get trimmed by someone giving me a stroke a hole. Every time I feel I've mustered up enough pep to propose, I take ten on a bogey three. Every time I think I'm in good mid-season form for putting my fate to the test, to win or lose it all, something goes all blooey with my swing, and I slice into the rough at every tee. And then my self-confidence leaves me. I become nervous, tongue-tied, diffident. I wish to goodness I knew the man who invented this infernal game. I'd strangle him. But I suppose he's been dead for ages. Still, I could go and jump on his grave.'

It was at this point that I understood all, and the heart within me sank like lead. The truth was out. Ferdinand Dibble was a goof.

'Come, come, my boy,' I said, though feeling the uselessness of any words. 'Master this weakness.'

'I can't.'

'Try!'

'I have tried.'

He gnawed his putter again.

'She was asking me just now if I couldn't manage to come to Marvis Bay, too,' he said.

'That surely is encouraging? It suggests that she is not entirely indifferent to your society.'

'Yes, but what's the use? Do you know,' a gleam coming into his eyes for a moment, 'I have a feeling that if I could ever beat some really fairly good player – just once – I could bring the thing off.' The gleam faded. 'But what chance is there of that?'

It was a question which I did not care to answer. I merely patted his shoulder sympathetically, and after a little while he left me and walked away. I was still sitting there, thinking over his hard case, when Barbara Medway came out of the club-house.

She, too, seemed grave and pre-occupied, as if there was something on her mind. She took the chair which Ferdinand had vacated, and sighed wearily.

'Have you ever felt,' she asked, 'that you would like to bang a man on the head with something hard and heavy? With knobs on?'

I said I had sometimes experienced such a desire, and asked if she had any particular man in mind. She seemed to hesitate for a moment before replying, then, apparently, made up her mind to confide in me. My advanced years carry with them certain pleasant compensations, one of which is that nice girls often confide in me. I frequently find myself enrolled as a father-confessor on the most intimate matters by beautiful creatures from whom many a younger man would give his eye-teeth to get a friendly word. Besides, I had known Barbara since she was a child. Frequently – though not recently – I had given her her evening bath. These things form a bond.

'Why are men such chumps?' she exclaimed.

'You still have not told me who it is that has caused these harsh words. Do I know him?'

'Of course you do. You've just been talking to him.'

'Ferdinand Dibble? But why should you wish to bang Ferdinand Dibble on the head with something hard and heavy with knobs on?'

'Because he's such a goop.'

'You mean a goof?' I queried, wondering how she could have penetrated the unhappy man's secret.

'No, a goop. A goop is a man who's in love with a girl and won't tell her so. I am as certain as I am of anything that Ferdinand is fond of me.'

'Your instinct is unerring. He has just been confiding in me on that very point.'

'Well, why doesn't he confide in *me*, the poor fish?' cried the high-spirited girl, petulantly flicking a pebble at a passing grasshopper. 'I can't be expected to fling myself into his arms unless he gives some sort of a hint that he's ready to catch me.'

'Would it help if I were to repeat to him the substance of this conversation of ours?'

'If you breathe a word of it, I'll never speak to you again,' she cried. 'I'd rather die an awful death than have any man think I wanted him so badly that I had to send relays of messengers begging him to marry me.'

I saw her point.

'Then I fear,' I said, gravely, 'that there is nothing to be done. One can only wait and hope. It may be that in the years to come Ferdinand Dibble will acquire a nice lissom, wristy swing, with the head kept rigid and the right leg firmly braced and—'

'What are you talking about?'

'I was toying with the hope that some sunny day Ferdinand Dibble would cease to be a goof.'

'You mean a goop?'

'No, a goof. A goof is a man who—' And I went on to explain the peculiar psychological difficulties which lay in the way of any declaration of affection on Ferdinand's part.

'But I never heard of anything so ridiculous in my life,' she ejaculated. 'Do you mean to say that he is waiting till he is good at golf before he asks me to marry him?'

'It is not quite so simple as that,' I said sadly. 'Many bad golfers marry, feeling that a wife's loving solicitude may improve their game. But they are rugged, thick-skinned men, not sensitive and introspective, like Ferdinand. Ferdinand has allowed himself to become morbid. It is one of the chief merits of golf that non-success at the game induces a certain amount of decent humility, which keeps a man from pluming himself too much on any petty triumphs he may achieve in other walks of life; but in all things there is a happy mean, and with Ferdinand this humility has gone too far. It has taken all the spirit out of him. He feels crushed and worthless. He is grateful to caddies when they accept a tip instead of drawing themselves up to their full height and flinging the money in his face.'

'Then do you mean that things have got to go on like this for ever?'

I thought for a moment.

'It is a pity,' I said, 'that you could not have induced Ferdinand to go to Marvis Bay for a month or two.'

'Why?'

'Because it seems to me, thinking the thing over, that it is just possible that Marvis Bay might cure him. At the hotel there he would find collected a mob of golfers — I used the term in its broadest sense, to embrace the paralytics and the men who play left-handed — whom even he would be able to beat. When I was last at Marvis Bay, the hotel links were a sort of Sargasso Sea into which had drifted all the pitiful flotsam and jetsam of golf. I have seen things done on that course at which I shuddered and averted my eyes — and I am not a weak man. If Ferdinand can polish up his game so as to go round in a fairly steady hundred and five, I fancy there is hope. But I understand he is not going to Marvis Bay.'

'Oh yes, he is,' said the girl.

'Indeed! He did not tell me that when we were talking just now.'

'He didn't know it then. He will when I have had a few words with him.'

And she walked with firm steps back into the club-house.

It has been well said that there are many kinds of golf, beginning at the top with the golf of professionals and the best amateurs and working down through the golf of ossified men to that of Scotch University professors. Until recently this last was looked upon as the lowest possible depth; but nowadays, with the growing popularity of summer hotels, we are able to add a brand still lower, the golf you find at places like Marvis Bay.

To Ferdinand Dibble, coming from a club where the standard of play was rather unusually high, Marvis Bay was a revelation, and for some days after his arrival there he went about dazed, like a man who cannot believe it is really true. To go out on the links at this summer resort was like entering a new world. The hotel was full of stout, middle-aged men, who, after a mis-spent youth devoted to making money, had taken to a game at which real proficiency can only be acquired by those who start playing in their cradles and keep their weight down. Out on the course each morning you could see representatives of every nightmare style that was ever invented. There was the man who seemed to be attempting to deceive his ball and lull it into a false security by looking away from it and then making a lightning slash in the apparent hope of catching it off its guard. There was the man who wielded his mid-iron like one killing snakes. There was the man who addressed his ball as if he were stroking a cat, the man who drove as if he were cracking a whip, the man who brooded over each shot like one whose heart is bowed down by bad news from home, and the man who scooped with his mashie as if he were ladling soup. By the end of the first week Ferdinand Dibble was the acknowledged champion of the place. He had gone through the entire menagerie like a bullet through a cream puff.

First, scarcely daring to consider the possibility of success, he had taken on the man who tried to catch his ball off its guard and had beaten him five up and four to play. Then, with gradually growing confidence, he tackled in turn the Cat-Stroker, the Whip-Cracker, the Heart Bowed Down, and the Soup-Scooper, and walked all over their faces with spiked shoes. And as these were the leading local amateurs, whose prowess the octogenarians and the men who went round in bath-chairs vainly strove to emulate, Ferdinand Dibble was faced on the eighth morning of his visit by the startling fact that he had no more worlds to conquer. He was monarch of all he surveyed, and, what is more, had won his first trophy, the prize in the great medal-play handicap tournament, in which he had nosed in ahead of the field by two strokes, edging out his nearest rival, a venerable old gentleman, by means of a brilliant and unexpected four on the last hole. The prize was a handsome pewter mug, about the size of the old oaken bucket, and Ferdinand used to go to his room immediately after dinner to croon over it like a mother over her child.

You are wondering, no doubt, why, in these circumstances, he did not take advantage of the new spirit of exhilarated pride which had replaced his old humility and instantly propose to Barbara Medway. I will tell you. He did not propose to Barbara because Barbara was not there. At the last moment she had been detained at home to nurse a sick parent and had been compelled to postpone her visit for a couple of weeks. He could, no doubt, have proposed in one of the daily letters which he wrote to her, but somehow, once he started writing, he found that he used up so much space describing his best shots on the links that day that it was difficult to squeeze in a declaration of undying passion. After all, you can hardly cram that sort of thing into a postscript.

He decided, therefore, to wait till she arrived, and meanwhile pursued his conquering course. The longer he waited the better, in one way, for every morning and afternoon that passed was adding new layers to his self-esteem. Day by day in every way he grew chestier and chestier.

Meanwhile, however, dark clouds were gathering. Sullen mutterings were to be heard in corners of the hotel lounge, and the spirit of revolt was abroad. For Ferdinand's chestiness had not escaped the notice of his defeated rivals. There is nobody so chesty as a normally unchesty man who suddenly becomes chesty, and I am sorry to say that the chestiness which had come to Ferdinand was the aggressive type of chestiness which breeds enemies. He had developed a habit of holding the game up in order to give his opponent advice. The Whip-Cracker had not forgiven, and never would forgive, his well-meant but galling criticism of his backswing. The Scooper, who had always scooped since the day when, at the age of sixty-four, he subscribed to the Correspondence Course which was to teach him golf in twelve lessons by mail, resented being told by a snip of a boy that the mashie-stroke should be a smooth, unhurried swing. The Snake-Killer— But I need not weary you with a detailed recital of these men's grievances; it is enough to say that they all had it in for Ferdinand, and one night, after dinner, they met in the lounge to decide what was to be done about it.

A nasty spirit was displayed by all.

'A mere lad telling me how to use my mashie!' growled the Scooper. 'Smooth and unhurried my left eyeball! I get it up, don't I? Well, what more do you want?'

'I keep telling him that mine is the old, full St Andrews swing,' muttered the Whip-Cracker, between set teeth, 'but he won't listen to me.'

'He ought to be taken down a peg or two,' hissed the Snake-Killer. It is not easy to hiss a sentence without a single 's' in it, and the fact that he succeeded in doing so shows to what a pitch of emotion the man had been goaded by Ferdinand's maddening air of superiority.

'Yes, but what can we do?' queried an octogenarian, when this last remark had been passed on to him down his ear-trumpet.

'That's the trouble,' sighed the Scooper. 'What can we do?' And there was a sorrowful shaking of heads.

'I know!' exclaimed the Cat-Stroker, who had not hitherto spoken. He was a lawyer, and a man of subtle and sinister mind. 'I have it! There's a boy in my office – young Parsloe – who could beat this man Dibble hollow. I'll wire him to come down here and we'll spring him on this fellow and knock some of the conceit out of him.'

There was a chorus of approval.

'But are you sure he can beat him?' asked the Snake-Killer, anxiously. 'It would never do to make a mistake.'

'Of course I'm sure,' said the Cat-Stroker. 'George Parsloe once went round in ninety-four.'

'Many changes there have been since ninety-four,' said the octogenarian, nodding sagely. 'Ah, many, many changes. None of these motor-cars then, tearing about and killing—'

Kindly hands led him off to have an egg-and-milk, and the remaining conspirators returned to the point at issue with bent brows.

'Ninety-four?' said the Scooper, incredulously. 'Do you mean counting every stroke?'

'Counting every stroke.'

'Not conceding himself any putts?'

'Not one.'

'Wire him to come at once,' said the meeting with one voice.

That night the Cat-Stroker approached Ferdinand, smooth, subtle, lawyer-like.

'Oh, Dibble,' he said, 'just the man I wanted to see. Dibble, there's a young friend of mine coming down here who goes in for golf a little. George Parsloe is his name. I was wondering if you could spare time to give him a game. He is just a novice, you know.'

'I shall be delighted to play a round with him,' said Ferdinand, kindly.

'He might pick up a pointer or two from watching you,' said the Cat-Stroker.

'True, true,' said Ferdinand.

'Then I'll introduce you when he shows up.'

'Delighted,' said Ferdinand.

He was in excellent humour that night, for he had had a letter from Barbara saying that she was arriving on the next day but one.

It was Ferdinand's healthy custom of a morning to get up in good time and take a dip in the sea before breakfast. On the morning of the day of Barbara's arrival, he arose, as usual, donned his flannels, took a good look at the cup, and started out. It was a fine, fresh morning, and he glowed both externally and internally. As he crossed the links, for the nearest route to the water was through the fairway of the seventh, he was whistling happily and rehearsing in his mind the opening sentences of his proposal. For it was his firm resolve that night after dinner to ask Barbara to marry him. He was proceeding over the smooth turf without a care in the world, when there was a sudden cry of 'Fore!' and the next moment a golf ball, missing him by inches, sailed up the fairway and came to a rest fifty yards from where he stood. He looked round and observed a figure coming towards him from the tee.

The distance from the tee was fully a hundred and thirty yards. Add fifty to that, and you have a hundred and eighty yards. No such drive had been made on the Marvis Bay links since their foundation, and such is the generous spirit of the true golfer that Ferdinand's first emotion, after the not inexcusable spasm of panic caused by the hum of the ball past his ear, was one of cordial admiration. By some kindly miracle, he supposed, one of his hotel acquaintances had been permitted for once in his life to time a drive right. It was only when the other man came up that there began to steal over him a sickening apprehension. The faces of all those who hewed divots on the hotel course were familiar to him, and the fact that this fellow was a stranger seemed to point with dreadful certainty to his being the man he had agreed to play.

'Sorry,' said the man. He was a tall, strikingly handsome youth, with brown eyes and a dark moustache.

'Oh, that's all right,' said Ferdinand. 'Er – do you always drive like that?'

'Well, I generally get a bit longer ball, but I'm off my drive this morning. It's lucky I came out and got this practice. I'm playing a match tomorrow with a fellow named Dibble, who's a local champion, or something.'

'Me,' said Ferdinand, humbly.

'Eh? Oh, you?' Mr Parsloe eyed him appraisingly. 'Well, may the best man win.'

As this was precisely what Ferdinand was afraid was going to happen, he nodded in a sickly manner and tottered off to his bathe. The magic had gone out of the morning. The sun still shone, but in a silly, feeble way; and a cold and depressing wind had sprung up. For Ferdinand's inferiority complex, which had seemed cured for ever, was back again, doing business at the old stand.

How sad it is in this life that the moment to which we have looked forward with the most glowing anticipation so often turns out on arrival, flat, cold, and disappointing. For ten days Barbara Medway had been living for that meeting with Ferdinand, when, getting out of the train, she would see him popping about on the horizon with the love-light sparkling in his eyes and words of devotion trembling on his lips. The poor girl never doubted for an instant that he would unleash his pent-up emotions inside the first five minutes, and her only worry was lest he should give an embarrassing publicity to the sacred scene by falling on his knees on the station platform.

'Well, here I am at last,' she cried gaily.

'Hullo!' said Ferdinand, with a twisted smile.

The girl looked at him, chilled. How could she know that his peculiar manner was due entirely to the severe attack of cold feet resultant upon his meeting with George Parsloe that morning? The interpretation which she placed upon it was that he was not glad to see her. If he had behaved like this before, she would, of course, have put it down to ingrowing goofery, but now she had his written statements to prove that for the last ten days his golf had been one long series of triumphs.

'I got your letters,' she said, persevering bravely.

'I thought you would,' said Ferdinand, absently.

'You seem to have been doing wonders.'

'Yes.'

There was a silence.

'Have a nice journey?' said Ferdinand.

'Very,' said Barbara.

She spoke coldly, for she was madder than a wet hen. She saw it all now. In the ten days since they had parted, his love, she realized, had waned. Some other girl, met in the romantic surroundings of this picturesque resort, had supplanted her in his affections. She knew how quickly Cupid gets off the mark at a summer hotel, and for an instant she blamed herself for ever having been so ivory-skulled as to let him come to this place alone. Then regret was swallowed up in wrath, and she became so glacial that Ferdinand, who had been on the point of telling her the secret of his gloom, retired into his shell and conversation during the drive to the hotel never soared above a certain level. Ferdinand said the sunshine was nice and Barbara said yes, it was nice, and Ferdinand said it looked pretty on the water, and Barbara said yes, it did look pretty on the water, and Ferdinand said he hoped it was not going to rain, and Barbara said yes, it would be a pity if it rained. And then there was another lengthy silence.

'How is my uncle?' asked Barbara at last.

I omitted to mention that the individual to whom I have referred as the Cat-Stroker was Barbara's mother's brother, and her host at Marvis Bay.

'Your uncle?'

'His name is Tuttle. Have you met him?'

'Oh yes. I've seen a good deal of him. He has got a friend staying with him,' said Ferdinand, his mind returning to the matter nearest his heart. 'A fellow named Parsloe.'

'Oh, is George Parsloe here? How jolly!'

'Do you know him?' barked Ferdinand, hollowly. He would not have supposed that anything could have added to his existing depression, but he was conscious now of having slipped a few rungs farther down the ladder of gloom. There had been a horribly joyful ring in her voice. Ah, well, he reflected morosely, how like life it all was! We never know what the morrow may bring forth. We strike a good patch and are beginning to think pretty well of ourselves, and along comes a George Parsloe.

'Of course I do,' said Barbara. 'Why, there he is.'

The cab had drawn up at the door of the hotel, and on the porch George Parsloe was airing his graceful person. To Ferdinand's fevered eye he looked like a Greek god, and his inferiority complex began to exhibit symptoms of elephantiasis. How could he compete at love or golf with a fellow who looked as if he had stepped out of the movies and considered himself off his drive when he did a hundred and eighty yards?

'Geor-gee!' cried Barbara, blithely. 'Hullo, George!'

'Why, hullo, Barbara!'

They fell into pleasant conversation, while Ferdinand hung miserably about in the offing. And presently, feeling that his society was not essential to their happiness, he slunk away.

George Parsloe dined at the Cat-Stroker's table that night, and it was with George Parsloe that Barbara roamed in the moonlight after dinner. Ferdinand, after a profitless hour at the billiard-table, went early to his room. But not even the rays of the moon, glinting on his cup, could soothe the fever in his soul. He practised putting sombrely into his tooth-glass for a while; then, going to bed, fell at last into a troubled sleep.

Barbara slept late the next morning and breakfasted in her room. Coming down towards noon, she found a strange emptiness in the hotel. It was her experience of summer hotels that a really fine day like this one was the cue for half the inhabitants to collect in the lounge, shut all the windows, and talk about conditions in the jute industry. To her surprise, though the sun was streaming down from a cloudless sky, the only occupant of the lounge was the octogenarian with the ear-trumpet. She observed that he was chuckling to himself in a senile manner.

'Good morning,' she said, politely, for she had made his acquaintance on the previous evening.

'Hey?' said the octogenarian, suspending his chuckling and getting his trumpet into position.

'I said "Good morning!"' roared Barbara into the receiver.

'Hey?'

'Good morning!'

'Ah! Yes, it's a very fine morning, a very fine morning. If it wasn't for missing my bun and glass of milk at twelve sharp,' said the octogenarian, 'I'd be down on the links. That's where I'd be, down on the links. If it wasn't for missing my bun and glass of milk.'

This refreshment arriving at this moment, he dismantled the radio outfit and began to restore his tissues.

'Watching the match,' he explained, pausing for a moment in his bun-mangling.

'What match?'

The octogenarian sipped his milk.

'What match?' repeated Barbara.

'Hey?'

'What match?'

The octogenarian began to chuckle again and nearly swallowed a crumb the wrong way.

'Take some of the conceit out of him,' he gurgled.

'Out of who?' asked Barbara, knowing perfectly well that she should have said 'whom'.

'Yes,' said the octogenarian.

'Who is conceited?'

'Ah! This young fellow, Dibble. Very conceited. I saw it in his eye from the first, but nobody would listen to me. Mark my words, I said, that boy needs taking down a peg or two. Well, he's going to be this morning. Your uncle wired to young Parsloe to come down, and he's arranged a match between them. Dibble—' Here the octogenarian choked again and had to rinse himself out with milk, 'Dibble doesn't know that Parsloe once went round in ninety-four!'

'What?'

Everything seemed to go black to Barbara. Through a murky mist she appeared to be looking at a negro octogenarian, sipping ink. Then her eyes cleared, and she found herself clutching for support at the back of a chair. She understood now. She realized why Ferdinand had been so distrait, and her whole heart went out to him in a spasm of maternal pity. How she had wronged him!

'Take some of the conceit out of him,' the octogenarian was mumbling, and Barbara felt a sudden sharp loathing for the old man. For two pins she could have dropped a beetle in his milk. Then the need for action roused her. What action? She did not know. All she knew was that she must act.

'Oh!' she cried.

'Hey?' said the octogenarian, bringing his trumpet to the ready.

But Barbara had gone.

It was not far to the links, and Barbara covered the distance on flying feet. She reached the club-house, but the course was empty except for the Scooper, who was preparing to drive off the first tee. In spite of the fact that something seemed to tell her subconsciously that this was one of the sights she ought not to miss, the girl did not wait to watch. Assuming that the match had started soon after breakfast, it must by now have reached one of the holes on the second nine. She ran down the hill, looking to left and right, and was presently aware of a group of spectators clustered about a green in the distance. As she hurried towards them they moved away, and now she could see Ferdinand advancing to the next tee. With a thrill that shook her whole body she realized that he had the honour. So he must have won one hole, at any rate. Then she saw her uncle.

'How are they?' she gasped.

Mr Tuttle seemed moody. It was apparent that things were not going altogether to his liking.

'All square at the fifteenth,' he replied, gloomily.

'All square!'

'Yes. Young Parsloe,' said Mr Tuttle with a sour look in the direction of that lissom athlete, 'doesn't seem to be able to do a thing right on the greens. He has been putting like a sheep with the botts.'

From the foregoing remark of Mr Tuttle you will, no doubt, have gleaned at least a clue to the mystery of how Ferdinand Dibble had managed to hold his long-driving adversary up to the fifteenth green, but for all that you will probably consider that some further explanation of this amazing state of affairs is required. Mere bad putting on the part of George Parsloe is not, you feel, sufficient to cover the matter entirely. You are right. There was another very important factor in the situation – to wit, that by some extraordinary chance Ferdinand Dibble had started right off from the first tee, playing the game of a lifetime. Never had he made such drives, never chipped his chips so shrewdly.

About Ferdinand's driving there was as a general thing a fatal stiffness and over-caution which prevented success. And with his chip-shots he rarely achieved accuracy owing to his habit of rearing his head like the lion of the jungle just before the club struck the ball. But today he had been swinging with a careless freedom, and his chips had been true and clean. The thing had puzzled him all the way round. It had not elated him, for, owing to Barbara's aloofness and the way in which she had gambolled about George Parsloe, like a young lamb in the springtime, he was in too deep a state of dejection to be elated by anything. And now, suddenly, in a flash of clear vision, he perceived the reason why he had been playing so well today. It was just because he was not elated. It was simply because he was so profoundly miserable.

That was what Ferdinand told himself as he stepped off the sixteenth, after hitting a screamer down the centre of the fairway, and I am convinced that he was right. Like so many indifferent golfers, Ferdinand Dibble had always made the game hard for himself by thinking too much. He was a deep student of the works of the masters, and whenever he prepared to play a stroke he had a complete mental list of all the mistakes which it was possible to make. He would remember how Taylor had warned against dipping the right shoulder, how Vardon had inveighed against any movement of the head; he would recall how Ray had mentioned the tendency to snatch back the club, how Braid had spoken sadly of those who sin against their better selves by stiffening the muscles and heaving.

The consequence was that when, after waggling in a frozen manner till mere shame urged him to take some definite course of action, he eventually swung, he invariably proceeded to dip his right shoulder, stiffen his muscles, heave, and snatch back the club, at the same time raising his head sharply as in the illustrated plate ('Some Frequent Faults of Beginners – No. 3 – Lifting the Bean') facing page thirty-four of James Braid's *Golf Without Tears*. Today he had been so preoccupied with his broken heart that he had made his shots absently, almost carelessly, with the result that at least one in every three had been a lallapaloosa.

Meanwhile, George Parsloe had driven off and the match was progressing. George was feeling a little flustered by now. He had been given to understand that this bird Dibble was a hundred-at-his-best man, and all the way round the fellow had been reeling off fives in great profusion, and had once actually got a four. True, there had been an occasional six, and even a seven, but that did not alter the main fact that the man was making the dickens of a game of it. With the haughty spirit of one who had once done a ninety-four, George Parsloe had anticipated being at least three up at the turn. Instead of which he had been two down, and had had to fight strenuously to draw level.

Nevertheless, he drove steadily and well, and would certainly have won the hole had it not been for his weak and sinful putting.

The same defect caused him to halve the seventeenth, after being on in two, with Ferdinand wandering in the desert and only reaching the green with his fourth. Then, however, Ferdinand holed out from a distance of seven yards, getting a five; which George's three putts just enabled him to equal.

Barbara had watched the proceedings with a beating heart. At first she had looked on from afar; but now, drawn as by a magnet, she approached the tee. Ferdinand was driving off. She held her breath. Ferdinand held his breath. And all around one could see their respective breaths being held by George Parsloe, Mr Tuttle, and the enthralled crowd of spectators. It was a moment of the acutest tension, and it was broken by the crack of Ferdinand's driver as it met the ball and sent it hopping along the ground for a mere thirty yards. At this supreme crisis in the match Ferdinand Dibble had topped.

George Parsloe teed up his ball. There was a smile of quiet satisfaction on his face. He snuggled the driver in his hands, and gave it a preliminary swish. This, felt George Parsloe, was where the happy ending came. He could drive as he had never driven before. He would so drive that it would take his opponent at least three shots to catch up with him. He drew back his club with infinite caution, poised it at the top of the swing—

'I always wonder—' said a clear, girlish voice, ripping the silence like the explosion of a bomb.

George Parsloe started. His club wobbled. It descended. The ball trickled into the long grass in front of the tee. There was a grim pause.

'You were saying, Miss Medway—' said George Parsloe, in a small, flat voice.

'Oh, I'm so sorry,' said Barbara. 'I'm afraid I put you off.'

'A little, perhaps. Possibly the merest trifle. But you were saying you wondered about something. Can I be of any assistance?'

'I was only saying,' said Barbara, 'that I always wonder why tees are called tees.'

George Parsloe swallowed once or twice. He also blinked a little feverishly. His eyes had a dazed, staring expression.

'I am afraid I cannot tell you off-hand,' he said, 'but I will make a point of consulting some good encyclopædia at the earliest opportunity.'

'Thank you so much.'

'Not at all. It will be a pleasure. In case you were thinking of inquiring at the moment when I am putting why greens are called greens, may I venture the suggestion now that it is because they are green?'

And, so saying, George Parsloe stalked to his ball and found it nestling in the heart of some shrub of which, not being a botanist, I cannot give you the name. It was a close-knit, adhesive shrub, and it twined its tentacles so lovingly around George Parsloe's niblick that he missed his first shot altogether. His second made the ball rock, and his third dislodged it. Playing a full swing with his brassie and being by now a mere cauldron of seething emotions he missed his fourth. His fifth came to within a few inches of Ferdinand's drive, and he picked it up and hurled it from him into the rough as if it had been something venomous.

'Your hole and match,' said George Parsloe, thinly.

Ferdinand Dibble sat beside the glittering ocean. He had hurried off the course with swift strides the moment George Parsloe had spoken those bitter words. He wanted to be alone with his thoughts.

They were mixed thoughts. For a moment joy at the reflection that he had won a tough match came irresistibly to the surface, only to sink again as he remembered that life, whatever its triumphs, could hold nothing for him now that Barbara Medway loved another.

'Mr Dibble!'

He looked up. She was standing at his side. He gulped and rose to his feet.

'Yes?'

There was a silence.

'Doesn't the sun look pretty on the water?' said Barbara.

Ferdinand groaned. This was too much.

'Leave me,' he said, hollowly. 'Go back to your Parsloe, the man with whom you walked in the moonlight beside this same water.'

'Well, why shouldn't I walk with Mr Parsloe in the moonlight beside this same water?' demanded Barbara, with spirit.

'I never said,' replied Ferdinand, for he was a fair man at heart, 'that you shouldn't walk with Mr Parsloe beside this same water. I simply said you did walk with Mr Parsloe beside this same water.'

'I've a perfect right to walk with Mr Parsloe beside this same water,' persisted Barbara. 'He and I are old friends.'

Ferdinand groaned again.

'Exactly! There you are! As I suspected. Old friends. Played together as children, and what not, I shouldn't wonder.'

'No, we didn't. I've only known him five years. But he is engaged to be married to my greatest chum, so that draws us together.'

Ferdinand uttered a strangled cry.

'Parsloe engaged to be married!'

'Yes. The wedding takes place next month.'

'But look here.' Ferdinand's forehead was wrinkled. He was thinking tensely. 'Look here,' said Ferdinand, a close reasoner. 'If Parsloe's engaged to your greatest chum, he can't be in love with *you*.'

'No.'

'And you aren't in love with him?'

'No.'

'Then, by gad,' said Ferdinand, 'how about it?'

'What do you mean?'

'Will you marry me?' bellowed Ferdinand.

'Yes.'

'You will?'

'Of course I will.'

'Darling!' cried Ferdinand.

'There is only one thing that bothers me a bit,' said Ferdinand, thoughtfully, as they strolled together over the scented meadows, while in the trees above them a thousand birds trilled Mendelssohn's Wedding March.

'What is that?'

'Well, I'll tell you,' said Ferdinand. 'The fact is, I've just discovered the great secret of golf. You can't play a really hot game unless you're so miserable that you don't worry over your shots. Take the case of a chip-shot, for instance. If you're really wretched, you don't care where the ball is going and so you don't raise your head to see. Grief automatically prevents pressing and over-swinging. Look at the top-notchers. Have you ever seen a happy pro?'

'No. I don't think I have.'

'Well, then!'

'But pros are all Scotchmen,' argued Barbara.

'It doesn't matter. I'm sure I'm right. And the darned thing is that I'm going to be so infernally happy all the rest of my life that I suppose my handicap will go up to thirty or something.'

Barbara squeezed his hand lovingly. 'Don't worry, precious,' she said, soothingly. 'It will be all right. I am a woman, and, once we are married, I shall be able to think of at least a hundred ways of snootering you to such an extent that you'll be fit to win the Amateur Championship.'

'You will?' said Ferdinand, anxiously. 'You're sure?'

'Quite, quite sure, dearest,' said Barbara.

'My angel!' said Ferdinand.

He folded her in his arms, using the interlocking grip.

THE NODDER

THE PRESENTATION of the super film, 'Baby Boy', at the Bijou Dream in the High Street, had led to an animated discussion in the bar-parlour of the Angler's Rest. Several of our prominent first-nighters had dropped in there for a much-needed restorative after the performance, and the conversation had turned to the subject of child stars in the motion-pictures.

'I understand they're all midgets, really,' said a Rum and Milk.

'That's what I heard, too,' said a Whisky and Splash. 'Somebody told me that at every studio in Hollywood they have a special man who does nothing but go round the country, combing the circuses, and when he finds a good midget he signs him up.'

Almost automatically we looked at Mr Mulliner, as if seeking from that unfailing fount of wisdom an authoritative pronouncement on this difficult point. The Sage of the bar-parlour sipped his hot Scotch and lemon for a moment in thoughtful silence.

'The question you have raised,' he said at length, 'is one that has occupied the minds of thinking men ever since these little excrescences first became popular on the screen. Some argue that mere children could scarcely be so loathsome. Others maintain that a right-minded midget would hardly stoop to some of the things these child stars do. But, then, arising from that, we have to ask ourselves: Are midgets right-minded? The whole thing is very moot.'

'Well, this kid we saw tonight,' said the Rum and Milk. 'This Johnny Bingley. Nobody's going to tell me he's only eight years old.'

'In the case of Johnny Bingley,' assented Mr Mulliner, 'your intuition has not led you astray. I believe he is in the early forties. I happen to know all about him because it was he who played so important a part in the affairs of my distant connection, Wilmot.'

'Was your distant connection Wilmot a midget?'

'No. He was a Nodder.'

'A what?'

Mr Mulliner smiled.

'It is not easy to explain to the lay mind the extremely intricate ramifications of the personnel of a Hollywood motion-picture organization. Putting it as briefly as possible, a Nodder is something like a Yes-Man, only lower in the social scale. A Yes-Man's duty is to attend conferences and say "Yes." A Nodder's, as the name implies, is to nod. The chief executive throws out some statement of opinion, and looks about him expectantly. This is the cue for the senior Yes-Man to say yes. He is followed, in order of precedence, by the second Yes-Man – or Vice-Yesser, as he is sometimes called – and the junior Yes-Man. Only when all the Yes-Men have yessed, do the Nodders begin to function. They nod.'

A Pint of Half-and-Half said it didn't sound much of a job.

'Not very exalted,' agreed Mr Mulliner. 'It is a position which you might say, roughly, lies socially somewhere in between that of the man who works the wind-machine and that of a writer of additional dialogue. There is also a class of Untouchables who are know as Nodders' assistants, but this is a technicality with which I need not trouble you.'

At the time when my story begins (said Mr Mulliner), my distant connection Wilmot was a full Nodder. Yet, even so, there is no doubt that he was aiming a little high when he ventured to aspire to the hand of Mabel Potter, the private secretary of Mr Schnellenhamer, the head of the Perfecto-Zizzbaum Corporation.

Indeed, between a girl so placed and a man in my distant connection's position there could, in ordinary circumstances, scarcely have been anything in the nature of friendly intercourse. Wilmot owed his entry to her good graces to a combination of two facts – the first, that in his youth he had been brought up on a farm and so was familiar with the customs and habits of birds; the second, that before coming to Hollywood, Miss Potter had been a bird-imitator in vaudeville.

Too little has been written of vaudeville bird-imitators and their passionate devotion to their art: but everybody knows the saying, Once a Bird-Imitator, Always a Bird-Imitator. The Mabel Potter of today might be a mere lovely machine for taking notes and tapping out her employer's correspondence, but within her there still burned the steady flame of those high ideals which always animate a girl who has once been accustomed to render to packed houses the liquid notes of the cuckoo, the whip-poor-will, and other songsters who are familiar to you all.

That this was so was revealed to Wilmot one morning when, wandering past an outlying set, he heard raised voices within and, recognizing the silver tones of his adored one, paused to listen. Mabel Potter seemed to be having some kind of an argument with a director.

'Considering,' she was saying, 'that I only did it to oblige and that it is in no sense a part of my regular duties for which I draw my salary, I must say…'

'All right, all right,' said the director.

'…that you have a nerve calling me down on the subject of cuckoos. Let me tell you, Mr Murgatroyd, that I have made a lifelong study of cuckoos and know them from soup to nuts. I have imitated cuckoos in every theatre on every circuit in the land. Not to mention urgent offers from England, Australia and…'

'I know, I know,' said the director.

'…South Africa, which I was compelled to turn down because my dear mother, then living, disliked ocean travel. My cuckoo is world-famous. Give me time to go home and fetch it and I'll show you the clipping from the *St Louis Post-Democrat* where it says…'

'I know, I know, I know,' said the director, 'but, all the same, I think I'll have somebody do it who'll do it my way.'

The next moment Mabel Potter had swept out, and Wilmot addressed her with respectful tenderness.

'Is something the matter, Miss Potter? Is there anything I can do?'

Mabel Potter was shaking with dry sobs. Her self-esteem had been rudely bruised.

'Well, look,' she said. 'They ask me as a special favour to come and imitate the call of the cuckoo for this new picture, and when I do it Mr Murgatroyd says I've done it wrong.'

'The hound,' breathed Wilmot.

'He says a cuckoo goes Cuckoo, Cuckoo, when everybody who has studied the question knows that what it really goes is Wuckoo, Wuckoo.'

'Of course. Not a doubt about it. A distinct "W" sound.'

'As if it had got something wrong with the roof of its mouth.'

'Or had omitted to have its adenoids treated.'

'Wuckoo, Wuckoo…Like that.'

'Exactly like that,' said Wilmot.

The girl gazed at him with a new friendliness.

'I'll bet you've heard rafts of cuckoos.'

'Millions. I was brought up on a farm.'

'These know–it–all directors make me tired.'

'Me, too,' said Wilmot. Then, putting his fate to the touch, to win or lose it all, 'I wonder, Miss Potter, if you would care to step round to the commissary and join me in a small coffee?'

She accepted gratefully, and from that moment their intimacy may be said to have begun. Day after day, in the weeks that followed, at such times as their duties would permit, you would see them sitting together either in the commissary or on the steps of some Oriental palace on the outskirts of the lot; he gazing silently up into her face; she, an artist's enthusiasm in her beautiful eyes, filling the air with the liquid note of the Baltimore oriole or possibly the more strident cry of the African buzzard. While ever and anon, by special request, she would hitch up the muscles of the larynx and go 'Wuckoo, Wuckoo.'

But when at length Wilmot, emboldened, asked her to be his wife, she shook her head.

'No,' she said, 'I like you, Wilmot. Sometimes I even think that I love you. But I can never marry a mere serf.'

'A what was that?'

'A serf. A peon. A man who earns his living by nodding his head at Mr Schnellenhamer. A Yes-Man would be bad enough, but a Nodder!'

She paused, and Wilmot, from sheer force of habit, nodded.

'I am ambitious,' proceeded Mabel. 'The man I marry must be a king among men…well, what I mean, at least a supervisor. Rather than wed a Nodder, I would starve in the gutter.'

The objection to this as a practical policy was, of course, that, owing to the weather being so uniformly fine all the year round, there are no gutters in Hollywood. But Wilmot was too distressed to point this out. He uttered a heart-stricken cry not unlike the mating-call of the Alaskan wild duck and began to plead with her. But she was not to be moved.

'We will always be friends,' she said, 'but marry a Nodder, no.'

And with a brief 'Wuckoo' she turned away.

There is not much scope or variety of action open to a man whose heart has been shattered and whose romance has proved an empty dream. Practically speaking, only two courses lie before him. He can go out West and begin a new life, or he can drown his sorrow in drink. In Wilmot's case, the former of these alternatives was rendered impossible by the fact that he was out West already. Little wonder, then, that as he sat in his lonely lodging that night his thoughts turned ever more and more insistently to the second.

Like all the Mulliners, my distant connection Wilmot had always been a scrupulously temperate man. Had his love-life but run smoothly, he would have been amply contented with a nut sundae or a malted milk after the day's work. But now, with desolation staring him in the face, he felt a fierce urge toward something with a bit more kick in it.

About half-way down Hollywood Boulevard, he knew, there was a place where, if you knocked twice and whistled 'My Country, 'tis of thee', a grille opened and a whiskered face appeared. The Face said 'Well?' and you said 'Service and Co-operation', and then the door was unbarred and you saw before you the primrose path that led to perdition. And as this was precisely what, in his present mood, Wilmot most desired to locate, you will readily understand how it came about that, some hour and a half later, he was seated at a table in this establishment, feeling a good deal better.

How long it was before he realized that his table had another occupant he could not have said. But came a moment when, raising his glass, he found himself looking into the eyes of a small child in a Lord Fauntleroy costume, in whom he recognized none other than Little Johnny Bingley, the Idol of American Motherhood − the star of this picture, 'Baby Boy', which you, gentlemen, have just been witnessing at the Bijou Dream in the High Street.

To say that Wilmot was astonished at seeing this infant in such surroundings would be to overstate the case. After half an hour at this home-from-home the customer is seldom in a condition to be astonished at anything − not even a gamboge elephant in golfing costume. He was, however, sufficiently interested to say 'Hullo.'

'Hullo,' replied the child. 'Listen,' he went on, placing a cube of ice in his tumbler, 'don't tell old Schnellenhamer you saw me here. There's a morality clause in my contract.'

'Tell who?' said Wilmot.

'Schnellenhamer.'

'How do you spell it?'

'I don't know.'

'Nor do I,' said Wilmot. 'Nevertheless, be that as it may,' he continued, holding out his hand impulsively, 'he shall never learn from me.'

'Who won't?' said the child.

'He won't,' said Wilmot.

'Won't what?' asked the child.

'Learn from me,' said Wilmot.

'Learn what?' inquired the child.

'I've forgotten,' said Wilmot.

They sat for a space in silence, each busy with his own thoughts.

'You're Johnny Bingley, aren't you?' said Wilmot.

'Who is?' said the child.

'You are.'

'I'm what?'

'Listen,' said Wilmot. 'My name's Mulliner. That's what it is. Mulliner. And let them make the most of it.'

'Who?'

'I don't know,' said Wilmot.

He gazed at his companion affectionately. It was a little difficult to focus him, because he kept flickering, but Wilmot could take the big, broad view about that. If the heart is in the right place, he reasoned, what does it matter if the body flickers?

'You're a good chap, Bingley.'

'So are you, Mulliner.'

'Both good chaps?'

'Both good chaps.'

'Making two in all?' asked Wilmot, anxious to get this straight.

'That's how I work it out.'

'Yes, two,' agreed Wilmot, ceasing to twiddle his fingers. 'In fact, you might say both gentlemen.'

'Both gentlemen is correct.'

'Then let us see what we have got. Yes,' said Wilmot, as he laid down the pencil with which he had been writing figures on the table-cloth. 'Here are the final returns, as I get them. Two good chaps, two gentlemen. And yet,' he said, frowning in a puzzled way, 'that seems to make four, and there are only two of us.

However,' he went on, 'let that go. Immaterial. Not germane to the issue. The fact we have to face, Bingley, is that my heart is heavy.'

'You don't say!'

'I do say. Heavy, Hearty. My bing is heavy.'

'What's the trouble?'

Wilmot decided to confide in this singularly sympathetic infant. He felt he had never met a child he liked better.

'Well, it's like this.'

'What is?'

'This is.'

'Like what?'

'I'm telling you. The girl I love won't marry me.'

'She won't?'

'So she says.'

'Well, well,' said the child star commiseratingly. 'That's too bad. Spurned your love, did she?'

'You're dern tooting she spurned my love,' said Wilmot. 'Spurned it good and hard. Some spurning!'

'Well, that's how it goes,' said the child star. 'What a world!'

'You're right, what a world.'

'I shouldn't wonder if it didn't make your heart heavy.'

'You bet it makes my heart heavy,' said Wilmot, crying softly. He dried his eyes on the edge of the table-cloth. 'How can I shake off this awful depression?' he asked.

The child star reflected.

'Well, I'll tell you,' he said. 'I know a better place than this one. It's out Venice way. We might give it a try.'

'We certainly might,' said Wilmot.

'And then there's another one down at Santa Monica.'

'We'll go there, too,' said Wilmot. 'The great thing is to keep moving about and seeing new scenes and fresh faces.'

'The faces are always nice and fresh down at Venice.'

'Then let's go,' said Wilmot.

It was at eleven o'clock on the following morning that Mr Schnellenhamer burst in upon his fellow-executive, Mr Levitsky, with agitation written on every feature of his expressive face. The cigar trembled between his lips.

'Listen!' he said. 'Do you know what?'

'Listen!' said Mr Levitsky. 'What?'

'Johnny Bingley has just been in to see me.'

'If he wants a raise of salary, talk about the Depression.'

'Raise of salary? What's worrying me is how long is he going to be worth the salary he's getting.'

'Worth it?' Mr Levitsky stared. 'Johnny Bingley? The Child With The Tear Behind The Smile? The Idol Of American Motherhood?'

'Yes, and how long is he going to be the idol of American Motherhood after American Motherhood finds out he's a midget from Connolly's Circus, and an elderly, hard-boiled midget, at that?'

'Well, nobody knows that but you and me.'

'Is that so?' said Mr Schnellenhamer. 'Well, let me tell you, he was out on a toot last night with one of my Nodders, and he comes to me this morning and says he couldn't actually swear he told this guy he was a midget, but, on the other hand, he rather thinks he must have done. He says that between the time they were thrown out of Mike's Place and the time he stabbed the waiter with the pickle-fork there's a sort of gap in his memory, a kind of blur, and he thinks it may have been then, because by that time they had got pretty confidential and he doesn't think he would have had any secrets from him.'

All Mr Levitsky's nonchalance had vanished.

'But if this fellow – what's his name?'

'Mulliner.'

'If this fellow Mulliner sells this story to the Press Johnny Bingley won't be worth a nickel to us. And his contract calls for two more pictures at two hundred and fifty thousand each.'

'That's right.'

'But what are we to do?'

'You tell me.'

Mr Levitsky pondered.

'Well, first of all,' he said, 'we'll have to find out if this Mulliner really knows.'

'We can't ask him.'

'No, but we'll be able to tell by his manner. A fellow with a stranglehold on the Corporation like that isn't going to be able to go on acting same as he's always done. What sort of a fellow is he?'

'The ideal Nodder,' said Mr Schnellenhamer regretfully. 'I don't know when I've had a better. Always on his cues. Never tries to alibi himself by saying he had a stiff neck. Quiet …Respectful…What's that word that begins with a "d"?'

'Damn?'

'Deferential. And what's the word beginning with an "o"?'

'Oyster?'

'Obsequious. That's what he is. Quiet, respectful, deferential, and obsequious – that's Mulliner.'

'Well, then, it'll be easy to see. If we find him suddenly not being all what you said…if he suddenly ups and starts to throw his weight about, understand what I mean…why, then we'll know that he knows that Little Johnny Bingley is a midget.'

'And then?'

'Why, then we'll have to square him. And do it right, too. No half-measures.'

Mr Schnellenhamer tore at his hair. He seemed disappointed that he had no straws to stick in it.

'Yes,' he agreed, the brief spasm over, 'I suppose it's the only way. Well, it won't be long before we know. There's a story-conference in my office at noon, and he'll be there to nod.'

'We must watch him like a lynx.'

'Like a what?'

'Lynx. Sort of wild-cat. It watches things.'

'Ah,' said Mr Schnellenhamer, 'I get you now. What confused me at first was that I thought you meant golf-links.'

The fears of the two magnates, had they but known it, were quite without foundation. If Wilmot Mulliner had ever learned the fatal secret, he had certainly not remembered it next morning. He had woken that day with a confused sense of having passed through some soul-testing experience, but as regarded details his mind was a blank. His only thought as he entered Mr Schnellenhamer's office for the conference was a rooted conviction that, unless he kept very still, his head would come apart in the middle.

Nevertheless, Mr Schnellenhamer, alert for significant and sinister signs, plucked anxiously at Mr Levitsky's sleeve.

'Look!'

'Eh?'

'Did you see that?'

'See what?'

'That fellow Mulliner. He sort of quivered when he caught my eye, as if with unholy glee.'

'He did?'

'It seemed to me he did.'

As a matter of fact, what had happened was that Wilmot, suddenly sighting his employer, had been enable to restrain a quick shudder of agony. It seemed to him that somebody had been painting Mr Schnellenhamer yellow. Even at the best of times, the President of the Perfecto-Zizzbaum, considered as an object for the eye, was not everybody's money. Flickering at the rims and a dull orange in colour, as he appeared to be now, he had smitten Wilmot like a blow, causing him to wince like a salted snail.

Mr Levitsky was regarding the young man thoughtfully.

'I don't like his looks,' he said.

'Nor do I,' said Mr Schnellenhamer.

'There's a kind of horrid gloating in his manner.'

'I noticed it, too.'

'See how he's just buried his head in his hands, as if he were thinking out dreadful plots?'

'I believe he knows everything.'

'I shouldn't wonder if you weren't right. Well, let's start the conference and see what he does when the time comes for him to nod. That's when he'll break out, if he's going to.'

As a rule, these story-conferences were the part of his work which Wilmot most enjoyed. His own share in them was not exacting, and, as he often said, you met such interesting people.

Today, however, though there were eleven of the studio's weirdest authors present, each well worth more than a cursory inspection, he found himself unable to overcome the dull list-lessness which had been gripping him since he had first gone to the refrigerator that morning to put ice on his temples. As the poet Keats puts it in his 'Ode to a Nightingale', his head ached and a drowsy numbness pained his sense. And the sight of Mabel Potter, recalling to him those dreams of happiness which he had once dared to dream and which now could never come to fulfilment, plunged him still deeper into the despondency. If he had been a character in a Russian novel, he would have gone and hanged himself in the barn. As it was, he merely sat staring before him and keeping perfectly rigid.

Most people, eyeing him, would have been reminded of a corpse which had been several days in the water: but Mr Schnellenhamer thought he looked like a leopard about to spring, and he mentioned this to Mr Levitsky in an undertone.

'Bend down. I want to whisper.'

'What's the matter?'

'He looks to me just like a crouching leopard.'

'I beg your pardon,' said Mabel Potter, who, her duty being to take notes of the proceedings, was seated at her employer's side. 'Did you say "crouching leopard" or "grouchy shepherd"?'

Mr Schnellenhamer started. He had forgotten the risk of being overheard. He felt that he had been incautious.

'Don't put that down,' he said. 'It wasn't part of the conference. Well, now, come on, come on,' he proceeded, with a pitiful attempt at the bluffness which he used at conferences, 'let's get at it. Where did we leave off yesterday, Miss Potter?'

Mabel consulted her notes.

'Cabot Delancy, a scion of an old Boston family, has gone to try to reach the North Pole in a submarine, and he's on an iceberg, and the scenes of his youth are passing before his eyes.'

'What scenes?'

'You didn't get to what scenes.'

'Then that's where we begin,' said Mr Schnellenhamer. 'What scenes pass before this fellow's eyes?'

One of the authors, a weedy young man in spectacles, who had come to Hollywood to start a Gyffte Shoppe and had been scooped up in the studio's drag-net and forced into the writing-staff much against his will, said why not a scene where Cabot Delancy sees himself dressing his window with kewpie-dolls and fancy note-paper.

'Why kewpie-dolls?' asked Mr Schnellenhamer testily.

The author said they were a good selling line.

'Listen!' said Mr Schnellenhamer brusquely. 'This Delancy never sold anything in his life. He's a millionaire. What we want is something romantic.'

A diffident old gentleman suggested a polo-game.

'No good,' said Mr Schnellenhamer. 'Who cares anything about polo? When you're working on a picture you've got to bear in mind the small-town population of the Middle West. Aren't I right?'

'Yes,' said the senior Yes-Man.

'Yes,' said the Vice-Yesser.

'Yes,' said the junior Yes-Man.

And all the Nodders nodded. Wilmot, waking with a start to the realization that duty called, hurriedly inclined his throbbing head. The movement made him feel as if a red-hot spike had been thrust through it, and he winced. Mr Levitsky plucked at Mr Schnellenhamer's sleeve.

'He scowled!'

'I thought he scowled, too.'

'As it might be with sullen hate.'

'That's the way it struck me. Keep watching him.'

The conference proceeded. Each of the authors put forward a suggestion, but it was left for Mr Schnellenhamer to solve what had begun to seem an insoluble problem.

'I've got it,' said Mr Schnellenhamer. 'He sits on this iceberg and he seems to see himself – he's always been an athlete, you understand – he seems to see himself scoring the winning goal in one of these polo-games. Everybody's interested in polo nowadays. Aren't I right?'

'Yes,' said the senior Yes-Man.

'Yes,' said the Vice-Yesser.

'Yes,' said the junior Yes-Man.

Wilmot was quicker off the mark this time. A conscientious employee, he did not intend mere physical pain to cause him to fall short in his duty. He nodded quickly, and returned to the 'ready' a little surprised that his head was still attached to its moorings. He had felt so certain it was going to come off that time.

The effect of this quiet, respectful, deferential and obsequious nod on Mr Schnellenhamer was stupendous. The anxious look had passed from his eyes. He was convinced now that Wilmot knew nothing. The magnate's confidence mounted high. He proceeded briskly. There was a new strength in his voice.

'Well,' he said, 'that's set for one of the visions We want two, and the other's got to be something that'll pull in the women. Something touching and sweet and tender.'

The young author in spectacles thought it would be kind of touching and sweet and tender if Cabot Delancy remembered the time he was in his Gyffte Shoppe and a beautiful girl came in and their eyes met as he wrapped up her order of Indian bead-work.

Mr Schnellenhamer banged the desk.

'What is all this about Gyffte Shoppes and Indian beadwork? Don't I tell you this guy is a prominent clubman? Where would he get a Gyffte Shoppe? Bring a girl into it, yes – so far you're talking sense. And let him gaze into her eyes – certainly he can gaze into her eyes. But not in any Gyffte Shoppe. It's got to be a lovely, peaceful, old-world exterior set, with bees humming and doves cooing and trees waving in the breeze. Listen!' said Mr Schnellenhamer. 'It's spring, see, and all around is the beauty of Nature in the first shy sun-glow. The grass that waves. The buds that... what's the word?'

'Bud?' suggested Mr Levitsky.

'No, it's two syllables,' said Mr Schnellenhamer, speaking a little self-consciously, for he was modestly proud of knowing words of two syllables.

'Burgeon?' hazarded an author who looked like a trained seal.

'I beg your pardon,' said Mabel Potter. 'A burgeon's a sort of fish.'

'You're thinking of sturgeon,' said the author.

'Excuse it, please,' murmured Mabel. 'I'm not strong on fishes. Birds are what I'm best at.'

'We'll have birds, too,' said Mr Schnellenhamer jovially. 'All the birds you want. Especially the cuckoo. And I'll tell you why. It gives us a nice little comedy touch. This fellow's with this girl in this old-world garden where everything's burgeoning... and when I say burgeoning I mean burgeoning. That burgeoning's got to be done *right*, or somebody'll get fired... and they're locked in a close embrace. Hold as long as the Philadelphia censors'll let you, and then comes your nice little comedy touch. Just as these two young folks are kissing each other without a thought of anything else in the world, suddenly a cuckoo close by goes "Cuckoo! Cuckoo!" Meaning how goofy they are. That's good for a laugh, isn't it?'

'Yes,' said the senior Yes-Man.

'Yes,' said the Vice-Yesser.

'Yes,' said the junior Yes-Man.

And then, while the Nodders' heads – Wilmot's among them – were trembling on their stalks preparatory to the downward swoop, there spoke abruptly a clear female voice. It was the voice of Mabel Potter, and those nearest her were able to see that her face was flushed and her eyes gleaming with an almost fanatic light. All the bird-imitator in her had sprung to sudden life.

'I beg your purdon, Mr Schnellenhamer, that's wrong.'

A deadly stillness had fallen on the room. Eleven authors sat transfixed in their chairs, as if wondering if they could believe their twenty-two ears. Mr Schnellenhamer uttered a little gasp. Nothing like this had ever happened to him before in his long experience.

'What did you say?' he asked incredulously. 'Did you say that I... I... was wrong?'

Mabel met his gaze steadily. So might Joan of Arc have faced her inquisitors.

'The cuckoo,' she said, 'does not go "Cuckoo, cuckoo"... it goes "Wuckoo, wuckoo." A distinct "*W*" sound.'

A gasp at the girl's temerity ran through the room. In the eyes of several of those present there was something that was not far from a tear. She seemed so young, so fragile.

Mr Schnellenhamer's joviality had vanished. He breathed loudly through his nose. He was plainly mastering himself with a strong effort.

'So I don't know the low-down on cuckoos?'

'Wuckoos,' corrected Mabel.

'Cuckoos!'

'Wuckoos!'

'You're fired,' said Mr Schnellenhamer.

Mabel flushed to the roots of her hair.

'It's unfair and unjust,' she cried. 'I'm right, and anybody who's studied cuckoos will tell you I'm right. When it was a matter of burgeons, I was mistaken, and I admitted that I was mistaken, and apologized. But when it comes to cuckoos, let me tell you you're talking to somebody who has imitated the call of the cuckoo from the Palace, Portland, Oregon, to the Hippodrome, Sumquamset, Maine, and taken three bows after every performance. Yes, sir, I know my cuckoos! And if you don't believe me I'll put it up to Mr Mulliner there, who was born and bred on a farm and has heard more cuckoos in his time than a month of Sundays. Mr Mulliner, how about it? Does the cuckoo go "Cuckoo"?'

Wilmot Mulliner was on his feet, and his eyes met hers with the love-light in them. The spectacle of the girl he loved in distress and appealing to him for aid had brought my distant connection's better self to the surface as if it had been jerked up on the end of a pin. For one brief instant he had been about to seek safety in a cowardly cringing to the side of those in power. He loved Mabel Potter madly, desperately, he had told himself in that short, sickening moment of poltroonery, but Mr Schnellenhamer was the man who signed the cheques: and the thought of risking his displeasure and being summarily dismissed had appalled him. For there is no spiritual anguish like that of the man who, grown accustomed to opening the crackling envelope each Saturday morning, reaches out for it one day and finds that it is not there. The thought of the Perfecto-Zizzbaum cashier ceasing to be a fount of gold and becoming just a man with a walrus moustache had turned Wilmot's spine to Jell-o. And for an instant, as I say, he had been on the point of betraying this sweet girl's trust.

But now, gazing into her eyes, he was strong again. Come what might, he would stand by her to the end.

'No!' he thundered, and his voice rang through the room like a trumpet-blast. 'No, it does not go "Cuckoo." You have fallen into a popular error, Mr Schnellenhamer. The bird wooks, and, by heaven, I shall never cease to maintain that it wooks, no matter what offence I give to powerful vested interests. I endorse Miss Potter's view wholeheartedly and without compromise. I say the cuckoo does not cook. It wooks, so make the most of it!'

There was a sudden whirring noise. It was Mabel Potter shooting through the air into his arms.

'Oh, Wilmot!' she cried.

He glared over her back-hair at the magnate.

'"Wuckoo, wuckoo!"' he shouted, almost savagely.

He was surprised to observe that Mr Schnellenhamer and Mr Levitsky were hurriedly clearing the room. Authors had begun to stream through the door in a foaming torrent. Presently, he and Mabel were alone with the two directors of the destinies of the Perfecto-Zizzbaum Corporation, and Mr Levitsky was carefully closing the door, while Mr Schnellenhamer came towards him, a winning, if nervous, smile upon his face.

'There, there, Mulliner,' he said.

And Mr Levitsky said 'There, there,' too.

'I can understand your warmth, Mulliner,' said Mr Schnellenhamer. 'Nothing is more annoying to the man who knows than to have people making these silly mistakes. I consider the firm stand you have taken as striking evidence of your loyalty to the Corporation.'

'Me, too,' said Mr Levitsky. 'I was admiring it myself.'

'For you are loyal to the Corporation, Mulliner, I know. You would never do anything to prejudice its interests, would you?'

'Sure he wouldn't,' said Mr Levitsky.

'You would not reveal the Corporation's little secrets, thereby causing it alarm and despondency, would you, Mulliner?'

'Certainly he wouldn't,' said Mr Levitsky. 'Especially now that we're going to make him an executive.'

'An executive?' said Mr Schnellenhamer, starting.

'An executive,' repeated Mr Levitsky firmly. 'With brevet rank as a brother-in-law.'

Mr Schnellenhamer was silent for a moment. He seemed to be having a little trouble in adjusting his mind to this extremely drastic step. But he was a man of sterling sense, who realized that there are times when only the big gesture will suffice.

'That's right,' he said. 'I'll notify the legal department and have the contract drawn up right away.'

'That will be agreeable to you, Mulliner?' inquired Mr Levitsky anxiously. 'You will consent to become an executive?'

Wilmot Mulliner drew himself up. It was his moment. His head was still aching, and he would have been the last person to claim that he knew what all this was about: but this he did know – that Mabel was nestling in his arms and that his future was secure.

'I…'

Then words failed him, and he nodded.

UNCLE FRED IN THE SPRINGTIME

CHAPTER I

THE DOOR of the Drones Club swung open, and a young man in form-fitting tweeds came down the steps and started to walk westwards. An observant passer-by, scanning his face, would have fancied that he discerned on it a keen, tense look, like that of an African hunter stalking a hippopotamus. And he would have been right. Pongo Twistleton – for it was he – was on his way to try to touch Horace Pendlebury-Davenport for two hundred pounds.

To touch Horace Pendlebury-Davenport, if you are coming from the Drones, you go down Hay Hill, through Berkeley Square, along Mount Street and up Park Lane to the new block of luxury flats which they have built where Bloxham House used to be: and it did not take Pongo long to reach journey's end. It was perhaps ten minutes later that Webster, Horace's man, opened the door in answer to his ring.

'What ho, Webster. Mr Davenport in?'

'No, sir. He has stepped out to take a dancing lesson.'

'Well, he won't be long, I suppose, what? I'll come in, shall I?'

'Very good, sir. Perhaps you would not mind waiting in the library. The sitting-room is in some little disorder at the moment.'

'Spring cleaning?'

'No, sir. Mr Davenport has been entertaining his uncle, the Duke of Dunstable, to luncheon, and over the coffee His Grace broke most of the sitting-room furniture with the poker.'

To say that this information surprised Pongo would be correct. To say that he was astounded, however, would be going too far. His Uncle Alaric's eccentricities were a favourite theme of conversation with Horace Davenport, and in Pongo he had always found a sympathetic confidant, for Pongo had an eccentric uncle himself. Though hearing Horace speak of his Uncle Alaric and thinking of his own Uncle Fred, he felt like Noah listening to someone making a fuss about a drizzle.

'What made him do that?'

'I am inclined to think, sir, that something may have occurred to annoy His Grace.'

This seemed plausible, and in the absence of further data Pongo left it at that. He made his way to the small apartment dignified by the name of library, and wandering to the window stood looking out on Park Lane.

It was a cheerless prospect that met his eyes. Like all English springs, the one which had just come to London seemed totally unable to make up its fat-headed mind whether it was supposed to be that ethereal mildness of which the poet sings or something suitable for ski-ers left over from the winter. A few moments before, the sun had been shining with extraordinary brilliance, but now a sort of young blizzard was raging, and the spectacle had the effect of plunging Pongo into despondency.

Horace was engaged to marry his sister Valerie, but was it conceivable, he asked himself, that any man, even to oblige a future brother-in-law, would cough up the colossal sum of two hundred potatoes? The answer, he felt, was in the negative, and with a mournful sigh he turned away and began to pace the room.

If you pace the library of Number 52 Bloxham Mansions, starting at the window and going straight across country, your outward journey takes you past the writing-table. And as Pongo reached this writing-table, something there attracted his eye. From beneath the blotter the end of a paper was protruding, and on it were written the intriguing words:

Signed

CLAUDE POTT

(*Private Investigator*)

They brought him up with as round a turn as if he had seen a baronet lying on the floor with an Oriental paper-knife of antique design in his back. An overwhelming desire came upon him to see what all this was about. He was not in the habit of reading other people's letters, but here was one which a man of the nicest scruples could scarcely be expected to pass up.

The thing was cast in narrative form, being, he found on examination, a sort of saga in which the leading character – a star part, if ever there was one – was somebody referred to as The Subject. From the activities of this individual Claude Pott seemed unable to tear himself away.

The Subject, who appeared to be abroad somewhere, for there was frequent mention of a Casino, was evidently one of those people who live for pleasure alone. You didn't catch The Subject doing good to the poor or making a thoughtful study of local political conditions. When he – or she – was not entering Casino in comp. of friends (two male, one female) at 11.17 p.m., he – or she, for there was no clue as to whether this was a story with a hero or a heroine – was playing tenn., riding h's, out on the golf links, lunching with three f's, driving to Montreuil with one m., or dancing with party consisting of four m's, ditto f's, and in this latter case keeping it up into the small hours. Pongo was familiar with the expression 'living the life of Riley', and that it was a life of this nature that The Subject had been leading was manifest in the document's every sentence.

But what the idea behind the narrative could be he found himself unable to divine. Claude Pott had a nice, crisp style, but his work was marred by the same obscurity which has caused complaint in the case of the poet Browning.

He had begun to read it for the third time, hoping for enlightenment, when the click of a latchkey came to his ears, and as he hastily restored the paper to its place the door opened and there entered a young man of great height but lacking the width of shoulder and ruggedness of limb which make height impressive. Nature, stretching Horace Davenport out, had forgotten to stretch him sideways, and one could have pictured Euclid, had they met, nudging a friend and saying, 'Don't look now, but this chap coming along illustrates exactly what I was telling you about a straight line having length without breadth.'

Farthest north of this great expanse there appeared a tortoise-shell-rimmed-spectacled face of so much amiability of expression that Pongo, sighting it, found himself once again hoping for the best.

'What ho, Horace,' he said, almost exuberantly.

'Hullo, Pongo. You here? Has Webster told you about my uncle's latest?'

'He did just touch on it. His theory is that the old boy was annoyed about something. Does that seem to fit the facts?'

'Absolutely. He was annoyed about quite a number of things. In the first place, he was going off to the country today and he had been counting on that fellow Baxter, his secretary, to go with him. He always likes to have someone with him on a railway journey.'

'To dance before him, no doubt, and generally entertain him?'

'And at the last moment Baxter said he would have to stay on in London to do some work at the British Museum in connection with that Family History Uncle Alaric has been messing about with for years. This made him shirty, for a start. He seemed to think it came under the head of being thwarted.'

'A touch of thwarting about it, perhaps.'

'And before coming to me he had been to see my cousin Ricky, and Ricky had managed to put his back up about something. So he was in dangerous mood when he got here. And we had scarcely sat down to lunch, when up popped a *soufflé* looking like a diseased custard. This did not help to ease the strain. And when we had had our coffee, and the time came for him to catch his train and he told me to go to the station with him and I said I couldn't, that seemed to touch him off. He reached for the poker and started in.'

'Why wouldn't you go to the station with him?'

'I couldn't. I was late for my dancing lesson.'

'I was going to ask you about that. What's this idea of your suddenly taking dancing lessons?'

'Valerie insisted on it. She said I danced like a dromedary with the staggers.'

Pongo did not blame his sister. Indeed, in comparing her loved one to a dromedary with the staggers she had been, he thought, rather complimentary.

'How are you coming along?'

'I think I'm making progress. Polly assures me so. Polly says I shall be able to go to the Ball tomorrow night. The Bohemian Ball at the Albert Hall. I'm going as a Boy Scout. I want to take Valerie to it and surprise her. Polly thinks I can get by all right.'

'But isn't Val at Le Touquet?'

'She's flying back today.'

'Oh, I see. Tell me, who is this Polly who has crept into your conversation?'

'She's the girl who's teaching me. I met her through Ricky. She's a friend of his. Polly Pott. A nice, sympathetic sort of girl I'd always found her, so when this business of staggering dromedaries came up, I asked her if she would give me a few lessons.'

A pang of pity for this heroine shot through Pongo. He himself was reading for the Bar and had sometimes felt like cracking under the strain of it all, but he saw that compared with Polly Pott he was on velvet. Between trying to extract some meaning from the rambling writings of the Messrs Coke and Littleton and teaching dancing to Horace Davenport there was a substantial difference, and it was the person on whom life had thrust the latter task who must be considered to have drawn the short straw. The trouble was, he reflected, that Horace was so tall. A chap of that length didn't really get on to what his feet were doing till some minutes after it had happened. What you wanted, of course, was to slice him in half and have two Horaces.

'Polly Pott, eh? Any relation to Claude Pott, private investigator?'

'His daughter. What do you know about Claude Pott, private investigator?'

Pongo stirred uneasily. Too late, he saw that he had rather invited the question.

'Well, the fact is, old man, happening to pass the writing-table just now, and chancing inadvertently to catch sight of that document—'

'I wish you wouldn't read my letters.'

'Oh, I wouldn't. But I could see that this wasn't a letter. Just a document. So I ran my eye over it. I thought it might possibly be something with reference to which you were going to seek my advice, knowing me to be a bit of a nib in legal matters, and I felt that a lot of time would be saved if I had the *res* at my fingers' ends.'

'And now I suppose you'll go racing off to Valerie to tell her I had her watched by detectives while she was at Le Touquet.'

A blinding light flashed upon Pongo.

'Great Scott! Was that what the thing was about?'

He pursed his lips – not too tightly, for he was still hoping to float that loan, but tightly enough to indicate that the Twistletons had their pride and resented their sisters being tailed up by detectives. Horace read his thoughts correctly.

'Yes, I know, but you don't realize the position, Pongo. It was the Drones Club week-end at Le Touquet. The thought of the girl I loved surrounded by about eighty-seven members of the Drones in the lax atmosphere of a foreign pleasure resort while

I was far away was like a knife in my heart. Polly happened to mention that her father was a private investigator, never happier than when putting on a false nose and shadowing people, and the temptation was more than I could resist. Pongo, for Heaven's sake don't breathe a word about this to Valerie. If she has a fault, it is that she's touchy. The sweetest of her sex, but a bit apt to go in off the deep end, when stirred. I can trust you?'

Pongo unpursed his lips. He understood all and pardoned all.

'Of course, old man. She shall never learn from me. You don't suppose I would wreck the happiness of my best friend...my oldest friend...my dearest friend...Horace, old top,' said Pongo, for it was a Twistleton trait to recognize when the iron was hot, 'I wonder if...I wonder whether...I wonder if you could possibly....'

'Mr Claude Pott,' announced Webster at the door.

To Pongo Twistleton, whose idea of a private investigator was a hawk-faced man with keen, piercing eyes and the general deportment of a leopard, Claude Pott came as a complete surprise. Hawks have no chins. Claude Pott had two. Leopards pad. Pott waddled. And his eyes, so far from being keen and piercing, were dull and expressionless, seeming, as is so often the case with those who go through life endeavouring to conceal their thoughts from the world, to be covered with a sort of film or glaze.

He was a stout, round, bald, pursy little man of about fifty, who might have been taken for a Silver Ring bookie or a minor Shakespearian actor – and, oddly enough, in the course of a life in which he had played many parts, he had actually been both.

'Good afternoon, Mr D.,' said this gargoyle.

'Hullo, Mr Pott. When did you get back?'

'Last night, sir. And thinking it over in bed this morning it occurred to me that it might be best if I were to deliver the concluding portion of my report verbally, thus saving time.'

'Oh, there's some more?'

'Yes, sir. I will apprise you of the facts,' said Claude Pott, giving Pongo a rather hard stare, 'when you are at liberty.'

'Oh, that's all right. You may speak freely before Mr Twistleton. He knows all. This is Mr Twistleton, The Subject's brother.'

'Pongo to pals,' murmured that young man weakly. He was finding the hard stare trying.

The austerity of the investigator's manner relaxed.

'Mr Pongo Twistleton? Then you must be the nephew of the Earl of Ickenham that he used to talk about.'

'Yes, he's my uncle.'

'A splendid gentleman. One of the real old school. A sportsman to his fingertips.'

Pongo, though fond of his uncle, could not quite bring himself to share this wholehearted enthusiasm.

'Yes, Uncle Fred's all right, I suppose,' he said. 'Apart from being loopy to the tonsils. You know him, do you?'

'I do indeed, sir. It was he who most kindly advanced me the money to start in business as a private investigator. So The Subject is Lord I's niece, is she? How odd! That his lordship should have financed me in my venture, I mean, and before I know where I am, I'm following his niece and taking notes of her movements. Strange!' said Mr Pott. 'Queer!'

'Curious,' assented Pongo.

'Unusual,' said Claude Pott.

'Bizarre,' suggested Pongo.

'Most. Shows what a small world it is.'

'Dashed small.'

Horace, who had been listening to these philosophical exchanges with some impatience, intervened.

'You were going to make your report, Mr Pott.'

'Coo!' said Claude Pott, called to order. 'That's right, isn't it? Well then, Mr D., to put the thing in a nutshell, I regret to have to inform you that there's been what you might call a bit of an unfortunate occurrence. On the nineteenth Ap., which was yesterday, The Subject, having lunched at Hotel Picardy with party consisting of two females, three males, proceeded to the golf club, where she took out her hockey-knockers and started playing round with one associate, the junior professional, self following at a cautious distance. For some time nothing noteworthy transpired, but at the fourteenth hole ... I don't know if you happen to be familiar with the golf links at Le Touquet, sir?'

'Oh, rather.'

'Then you will be aware that as you pass from the fourteenth tee along the fairway you come opposite a house with a hedge in front of it. And just as The Subject came opposite this house, there appeared behind the hedge two males, one with cocktail shaker. They started yodelling to The Subject, evidently inviting her to

step along and have one, and The Subject, dismissing her associate, went through the gate in the hedge and by the time I came up
was lost to sight in the house.'

A soft groan broke from Horace Davenport. He had the air of a
man who was contemplating burying his face in his hands.

'Acting in your interests, I, too, passed through the gate and
crept to the window from behind which I could hear chat and
revelry in progress. And I was just stooping down to investigate
further, when a hand fell on my shoulder and, turning, I perceived
one male. And at the same moment The Subject, poking her
head out of the window, observed "Nice work, Barmy. That's
the blighter that's been following me about all the week. You
be knocking his head off, while Catsmeat phones for the
police. We'll have him sent to the guillotine for ingrowing
molestation." And I saw that there was only one course for me
to pursue.'

'I wouldn't have thought even that,' said Pongo, who had been
following the narrative with close attention.

'Yes, sir – one. I could clear myself by issuing a full statement.'

A sharp, agonized cry escaped Horace Davenport.

'Yes, sir. I'm sorry, but there was no alternative. I had no desire
to get embroiled with French rozzers. I issued my statement. While
the male, Barmy, was calling me a trailing arbutus and the male,
Catsmeat, was saying did anyone know the French for "police" and
The Subject was talking about horsewhips, I explained the situation fully. It took me some time to get the facts into their heads, but
I managed it finally and was permitted to depart, The Subject
saying that if she ever set eyes on me again—'

'Miss Twistleton,' announced Webster.

'Well, good-bye, all,' said Claude Pott.

A critic who had been disappointed by the absence of the leopard
note in Mr Pott's demeanour would have found nothing to
complain of in that of Pongo's sister Valerie. She was a tall,
handsome girl, who seemed to be running a temperature, and
her whole aspect, as she came into the room, was that of some
jungle creature advancing on its prey.

'Worm!' she said, opening the conversation.

'Valerie, darling, let me explain!'

'Let *me* explain,' said Pongo.

His sister directed at him a stare of a hardness far exceeding that of Mr Pott.

'Could you possibly keep your fat head out of this?'

'No, I couldn't keep my fat head out of it,' said Pongo. 'You don't think I'm going to stand supinely by and see a good man wronged, do you? Why should you barge in here, gnashing your bally teeth, just because Horace sicked Claude Pott, private investigator, on to you? If you had any sense, you would see that it was a compliment, really. Shows how much he loves you.'

'Oh, does it? Well—'

'Valerie, darling!'

The girl turned to Pongo.

'Would you,' she said formally, 'be good enough to ask your friend not to address me as "Valerie, darling". My name is Miss Twistleton.'

'Your name,' said Pongo, with brotherly sternness, 'will be mud if you pass up an excellent bet like good old Horace Davenport – the whitest man I know – simply because his great love made him want to keep an eye on you during Drones Club week-end.'

'I did not—'

'And as events have proved he was thoroughly justified in the course he took. You appear to have been cutting up like a glamour girl at a Hollywood party. What about those two males, one with cocktail shaker?'

'I did not—'

'And the m. you drove to Montreuil with?'

'Yes,' said Horace, for the first time perking up and showing a little of the Pendlebury-Davenport fire. 'What about the m. you drove to Montreuil with?'

Valerie Twistleton's face was cold and hard.

'If you will allow me to speak for a moment and not keep interrupting every time I open my mouth, I was about to say that I did not come here to argue. I merely came to inform you that our engagement is at an end, and that a notice to that effect will appear in *The Times* tomorrow morning. The only explanation I can think of that offers a particle of excuse for your conduct is that you have finally gone off your rocker. I've been expecting it for months. Look at your Uncle Alaric. Barmy to the back teeth.'

Horace Davenport was in the depths, but he could not let this pass.

'That's all right about my Uncle Alaric. What price your Uncle Fred?'

'What about him?'

'Loopy to the tonsils.'

'My Uncle Fred is not loopy to the tonsils.'

'Yes, he is. Pongo says so.'

'Pongo's an ass.'

Pongo raised his eyebrows.

'Cannot we,' he suggested coldly, 'preserve the decencies of debate?'

'This isn't a debate. As I told you before, I came here simply to inform Mr Davenport that our engagement is jolly well terminated.'

There was a set look on Horace's face. He took off his spectacles, and polished them with an ominous calm.

'So you're handing me the mitten?'

'Yes, I am.'

'You'll be sorry.'

'No, I shan't.'

'I shall go straight to the devil.'

'All right, trot along.'

'I shall plunge into a riot of reckless living.'

'Go ahead.'

'And my first step, I may mention, will be to take Polly Pott to that Bohemian Ball at the Albert Hall.'

'Poor soul! I hope you will do the square thing by her.'

'I fail to understand you.'

'Well, she'll need a pair of crutches next day. In common fairness you ought to pay for them.'

There was a silence. Only the sound of tense breathing could be heard – the breathing of a man with whom a woman has gone just too far.

'If you will be kind enough to buzz off,' said Horace icily, 'I will be ringing her up now.'

The door slammed. He went to the telephone.

Pongo cleared his throat. It was not precisely the moment he would have chosen for putting his fortune to the test, had he been free to choose, but his needs were immediate, the day was already well advanced and no business done, and he had gathered that Horace's time in the near future was likely to be rather fully occupied. So now he cleared his throat and, shooting his cuffs, called upon the splendid Twistleton courage to nerve him for his task.

'Horace, old man.'

'Hullo?'

'Horace, old chap.'

'Hullo? Polly?'

'Horace, old egg.'

'Half a minute. There's somebody talking. Well?'

'Horace, old top, you remember what we were starting to chat about when the recent Pott blew in. What I was going to say, when we were interrupted, was that owing to circumstances over which I had no – or very little – control. ...'

'Buck up. Don't take all day over it.'

Pongo saw that preambles would have to be dispensed with.

'Can you lend me two hundred quid?'

'No.'

'Oh? Right ho. Well, in that case,' said Pongo stiffly, 'tinkerty-tonk.'

He left the room and walked round to the garage where he kept his Buffy-Porson two-seater, and instructed the proprietor to have it in readiness for him on the morrow.

'Going far, sir?'

'To Ickenham, in Hampshire,' said Pongo.

He spoke moodily. He had not planned to reveal his financial difficulties to his Uncle Fred, but he could think of no other source of revenue.

CHAPTER 2

HAVING PUT the finishing touches to his nephew's sitting-room and removed himself from Bloxham Mansions in a cab, the Duke of Dunstable, feeling much better after his little bit of exercise, had driven to Paddington Station and caught the 2.45 train to Market Blandings in the county of Shropshire. For he had invited himself – he was a man of too impatient spirit to hang about waiting for other people to invite him – to spend an indefinite period as the guest of Clarence, ninth Earl of Emsworth, and his sister, Lady Constance Keeble, at that haunt of ancient peace, Blandings Castle.

The postcard which he had dispatched some days previously announcing his impending arrival and ordering an airy ground-floor bedroom with a southern exposure and a quiet sitting-room in which he could work with his secretary, Rupert Baxter, on his history of the family had had a mixed reception at the Blandings breakfast-table.

Lord Emsworth, frankly appalled, had received the bad news with a sharp 'Eh, what? Oh, I say, dash it!' He had disliked the Duke in a dreamy way for forty-seven years, and as for Rupert Baxter he had hoped never to be obliged to meet him again either in this world or the next. Until fairly recently that efficient young man had been his own secretary, and his attitude towards him was a little like that of some miraculously cured convalescent towards the hideous disease which has come within an ace of laying him low. It was true, of course, that this time the frightful fellow would be infesting the castle in the capacity of somebody else's employee, but he drew small comfort from that. The mere thought of being under the same roof with Rupert Baxter was revolting to him.

Lady Constance, on the other hand, was pleased. She was a devoted admirer of the efficient Baxter, and there had been a time, when the world was young, when she and the Duke of Dunstable had whispered together in dim conservatories and been the last couple to straggle home from picnics. And though nothing had come of it – it was long before he succeeded to the title, and they shipped him abroad at about that time to allow an England which he had made too hot for him to cool off a little – the memory lingered.

Lord Emsworth lodged a protest, though realizing as he did so that it was purely formal. He was, and always had been, a cipher in the home.

'It's only about a week since he was here last.'

'It is nearly seven months.'

'Can't you tell him we're full up?'

'Of course I can't.'

'The last time he was here,' said Lord Emsworth broodingly, 'he poked the Empress in the ribs with an umbrella.'

'Well, I am certainly not going to offend one of my oldest friends just because he poked your pig with an umbrella,' said Lady Constance. 'I shall write to Alaric and tell him that we shall be delighted to have him for as long as he cares to stay. I see that he says he must be on the ground floor, because he is nervous of fire. He had better have the Garden Suite.'

And so it was in that luxurious set of apartments that the Duke awoke on the morning following his luncheon-party at Bloxham Mansions. For some time he lay gazing at the sunlight that filtered through the curtains which covered the French windows opening on the lawn: then, ringing the bell, he instructed the footman to bring him toast, marmalade, a pot of China tea, two lightly boiled eggs and *The Times*. And it was perhaps twenty minutes later that Lady Constance, sunning herself on the terrace, was informed by Beach, her butler, that His Grace would be glad if she would step to his room for a moment.

Her immediate sensation, on receiving this summons, was one of apprehension and alarm. The story which the Duke had told at dinner on the previous night, at great length and with a ghoulish relish, of the lesson which he had taught his nephew Horace had made a deep impression on her, and she fully expected on reaching the Blue Room to find it – possibly owing to some lapse from the required standard in His Grace's breakfast – a devastated area. It was with profound relief that she saw that all was well. The ducal poker remained a potential threat in the background, but it had not been brought into operation as yet, and she looked at the mauve-pajamaed occupant of the bed with that quiet affection which hostesses feel towards guests who have not smashed their furniture – blended with the tenderness which a woman never quite loses for the man who has once breathed words of love down the back of her neck.

'Good morning, Alaric.'

''Morning, Connie. I say, who the devil's that whistling feller?'

'What do you mean?'

'I mean a whistling feller. A feller who whistles. There's been a blighter outside my window ever since I woke up, whistling the "Bonny Bonny Banks of Loch Lomond".'

'One of the gardeners, I expect.'

'Ah!' said the Duke quietly.

Pongo Twistleton had been surprised that a private investigator could look like Claude Pott, and he would have been equally surprised if he had been introduced to the Duke of Dunstable and informed that this was the notorious sitting-room-wrecker of whom he had heard so much. The Duke did not look a killer. Except for the Dunstable nose, always a little startling at first sight, there was nothing obviously formidable and intimidating about Horace's Uncle Alaric. A bald head...A cascade of white moustache...Prominent blue eyes...A rather nice old bird, you would have said.

'Was that what you wanted to see me about?'

'No. Have the car ready to take me to the station directly after lunch. I've got to go to London.'

'But you only came last night.'

'It doesn't matter what happened last night. It's what has happened this morning. I glance through my *Times*, and what do I see? My nephew Horace has gone and got his engagement broken off.'

'What!'

'You heard.'

'But why?'

'How the dickens should I know why? It's just because I don't know why that I've got to go and find out. When an engagement has been broken off *The Times* doesn't print long reports from its special correspondent. It simply says "The marriage arranged between George Tiddlypush and Amelia Stick-in-the-mud will not take place."'

'The girl was Lord Ickenham's niece, wasn't she?'

'Still is.'

'I know Lady Ickenham, but I have never met Lord Ickenham.'

'Nor have I. But she's his niece, just the same.'

'They say he is very eccentric.'

'He's potty. Everybody's potty nowadays, except a few people like myself. It's the spirit of the age. Look at Clarence. Ought to have been certified years ago.'

'Don't you think that it's simply that he is dreamy and absent-minded?'

'Absent-minded be blowed. He's potty. So's Horace. So's my other nephew, Ricky. You take my advice, Connie. Never have nephews.'

Lady Constance's sigh seemed to say that he spoke too late.

'I've got dozens, Alaric.'

'Potty?'

'I sometimes think so. They seem to do the most extraordinary things.'

'I'll bet they don't do such extraordinary things as mine.'

'My nephew Ronald married a chorus girl.'

'My nephew Ricky writes poetry.'

'My nephew Bosham once bought a gold brick from a man in the street.'

'And now he wants to sell soup.'

'Bosham?'

'Ricky. He wants to sell soup.'

'Sell soup?'

'Good God, Connie, don't repeat everything I say, as if you were an echo in the Swiss mountains. I tell you he wants to sell soup. I go and see him yesterday, and he has the impertinence, if you please, to ask me to give him five hundred pounds to buy an onion soup bar. I refused to give him a penny, of course. He was as sick as mud. Not so sick as Horace will be, though, when he's finished with me. I shall start by disembowelling him. Go and order that car.'

'Well, it does seem a shame that you should have to go to London on a lovely day like this.'

'You don't think I want to go, do you? I've got to go.'

'Couldn't you tell Mr Baxter to go and see Horace? He is still in London, isn't he?'

'Yes, he is, the shirking, skrimshanking, four-eyed young son of a what-not, and I'm quite convinced that he stayed there because he was planning to go on a toot the moment my back was turned. If I can bring it home to him, by George, I'll sack him as soon as he shows his ugly face here. No, I couldn't tell Baxter to go and see Horace. I'm not going to have my nephew, half-witted though he is, subjected to the inquisition of a dashed underling.'

There were several points in this speech, which, if it had not been for the thought of that poker which hung over Blandings Castle like a sword of Damocles, Lady Constance would have liked to criticize. She resented the suggestion that Rupert Baxter was a man capable of going on toots. She did not consider his face ugly. And it pained her to hear him described as a dashed underling. But there are times when the tongue must be curbed. She maintained a discreet silence, from which she emerged a few moments later with a suggestion.

'I know! Bosham is going to London this morning. Why couldn't Horace drive him back in his car? Then you could have your talk with him without any trouble or inconvenience.'

'The first sensible word you've spoken since you came into this room,' said the Duke approvingly. 'Yes, tell Bosham to rout him out and bring him back alive or dead. Well, I can't stay here talking to you all day, Connie. Got to get up, got to get up. Where's Clarence?'

'Down at the pig-sty, I suppose.'

'Don't tell me he's still mooning over that pig of his.'

'He's quite absurd about it.'

'Quite crazy, you mean. If you want to know what I think, Connie, it's that pig that's at the root of his whole trouble. It's a very bad influence in his life, and if something isn't done soon to remove it you'll find him suddenly sticking straws in his hair and saying he's a poached egg. Talking of eggs, send me up a dozen.'

'Eggs? But haven't you had your breakfast?'

'Of course I've had my breakfast.'

'I see. But you want some more,' said Lady Constance pacifically. 'How would you like them done?'

'I don't want them done at all. I don't want eating eggs. I want throwing eggs. I intend to give that whistling feller a sharp lesson. Hark! There he is again. Singing now.'

'Alaric,' said Lady Constance, a pleading note in her voice, 'must you throw eggs at the gardeners?'

'Yes.'

'Very well,' said Lady Constance resignedly, and went off to avert the threatened horror by removing the vocalist from the danger zone.

Her thoughts, as she went, were long, long thoughts.

Lord Emsworth, meanwhile, unaware of the solicitude which he was causing, was down in the meadow by the kitchen garden, drooping over the comfortable sty which housed his pre-eminent sow, Empress of Blandings, twice in successive years silver medal-list in the Fat Pigs' class at the Shropshire Agricultural Show. The noble animal, under his adoring eyes, was finishing a late breakfast.

The ninth Earl of Emsworth was a resilient man. It had not taken him long to get over the first sharp agony of the discovery that Rupert Baxter was about to re-enter his life. This morning, Baxter was forgotten, and he was experiencing that perfect happiness which comes from a clear conscience, absence of loved ones, congenial society and fine weather. For once in a way there was nothing which he was trying to conceal from his sister Constance, no disrupting influences had come to mar his communion with the Empress, and the weather, as almost always in this favoured spot, was wonderful. We have seen spring being whimsical and capricious in London, but it knew enough not to try anything of that sort on Blandings Castle.

The only concern Lord Emsworth had was a fear that this golden solitude could not last, and the apprehension was well founded. A raucous cry shattered the drowsy stillness and, turning, he perceived, as Claude Pott would have said, one male. His guest, the Duke, was crossing the meadow towards him.

''Morning, Clarence.'

'Good morning, Alaric.'

Lord Emsworth forced a welcoming smile to his lips. His breeding – and about fifteen thousand words from Lady Constance from time to time – had taught him that a host must wear the mask. He tried his hardest not to feel like a stag at bay.

'Seen Bosham anywhere?'

'No. No, I have not.'

'I want a word with him before he leaves. I'll wait here and intercept him on his way out. He's going to London today, to bring Horace here. His engagement has been broken off.'

This puzzled Lord Emsworth. His son and heir, Lord Bosham, who was visiting the castle for the Bridgeford races, had been, he felt pretty sure, for some years a married man. He mentioned this.

'Not Bosham's engagement. Horace's.'

Again Lord Emsworth was at a loss.

'Who is Horace?'

'My nephew.'

'And he is engaged?'

'He was. Ickenham's niece.'

'Who is?'

'The girl he was engaged to.'

'Who is Ickenham?'

'Her uncle.'

'Oh,' said Lord Emsworth, brightening. The name had struck a chord in his memory. 'Oh, Ickenham? Of course. Ickenham, to be sure. I know Ickenham. He is a friend of my brother Galahad. I think they used to be thrown out of night clubs together. I am glad Ickenham is coming here.'

'He isn't.'

'You said he was.'

'I didn't say he was. I said Horace was.'

The name was new to Lord Emsworth.

'Who,' he asked, 'is Horace?'

'I told you two seconds ago,' said the Duke, with the asperity which never left him for long, 'that he was my nephew. I have no reason to believe that conditions have altered since.'

'Oh?' said Lord Emsworth. 'Ah? Yes. Yes, to be sure. Your nephew. Well, we must try to make his stay pleasant. Perhaps he is interested in pigs. Are you interested in pigs, Alaric? You know my sow, Empress of Blandings, I think. I believe you met when you were here in the summer.'

He moved aside to allow his guest an uninterrupted view of the superb animal. The Duke advanced to the rail, and there followed a brief silence – on Lord Emsworth's side reverent, on that of the Duke austere. He had produced a large pair of spectacles from his breast pocket and through them was scrutinizing the silver medallist in a spirit only too plainly captious and disrespectful.

'Disgusting!' he said at length.

Lord Emsworth started violently. He could scarcely believe that he had heard aright.

'What!'

'That pig is too fat.'

'Too fat?'

'Much too fat. Look at her. Bulging.'

'But my dear Alaric, she is supposed to be fat.'

'Not as fat as that.'

'Yes, I assure you. She has already been given two medals for being fat.'

'Don't be silly, Clarence. What would a pig do with medals? It's no good trying to shirk the issue. There is only one word for that pig – gross. She reminds me of my Aunt Horatia, who died of apoplexy during Christmas dinner. Keeled over half-way through her second helping of plum pudding and never spoke again. This animal might be her double. And what do you expect? You stuff her and stuff her and stuff her, and I don't suppose she gets a lick of exercise from one week's end to another. What she wants is a cracking good gallop every morning, and no starchy foods. That would get her into shape.'

Lord Emsworth had recovered the pince-nez which emotion had caused, as it always did, to leap from his nose. He replaced them insecurely.

'Are you under the impression,' he said, for when deeply moved he could be terribly sarcastic, 'that I want to enter my pig for the Derby?'

The Duke had been musing. He had not liked that nonsense about pigs being given medals and he was thinking how sad all this was for poor Connie. But at these words he looked up sharply. An involuntary shudder shook him, and his manner took on a sort of bedside tenderness.

'I wouldn't, Clarence.'

'Wouldn't what?'

'Enter this pig for the Derby. She might not win, and then you would have had all your trouble for nothing. What you want is to get her out of your life. And I'll tell you what I'll do. Listen, my dear Clarence,' said the Duke, patting his host's shoulder, 'I'll take this pig over – lock, stock, and barrel. Yes, I mean it. Have her sent to my place – I'll wire them to expect her – and in a few weeks' time she will be a different creature. Keen, alert, eyes sparkling. And you'll be different, too. Brighter. Less potty. Improved out of all knowledge…Ah, there's Bosham. Hi, Bosham! Half a minute, Bosham, I want a word with you.'

For some moments after his companion had left him, Lord Emsworth remained leaning limply against the rail of the sty. The sun was bright. The sky was blue. A gentle breeze caressed the Empress's tail, as it wiggled over the trough. But to him the heavens seemed darkened by a murky mist, and there appeared to be an east wind blowing through the world. It was not for some time that he became aware that a voice was speaking his name, but he heard it at last and pulling together with a powerful effort, saw his sister Constance.

She was asking him if he was getting deaf. He said No, he was not getting deaf.

'Well, I've been shouting at you for ever so long. I wish you would listen to me sometimes. Clarence, I have come to have a talk about Alaric. I am very worried about him. He seems to have got so odd.'

'Odd? I should say he was odd. Do you know what, Connie? He came to me just now—'

'He was asking me to give him eggs to throw at the gardeners.'

At a less tense moment, her words would have shocked Lord Emsworth. An English landed proprietor of the better type comes to regard himself as *in loco parentis* to those in his employment, and if visitors start throwing eggs at them he resents it. But now he did not even lose his pince-nez.

'And do you know what he said to me?'

'He can't be sane, if he wants to throw eggs at gardeners.'

'He can't be sane, if he wants me to give him the Empress.'

'Does he?'

'Yes.'

'Then, of course,' said Lady Constance, 'you will have to.'

This time Lord Emsworth did lose his pince-nez, and lose them thoroughly. They flew at the end of their string like leaves in a storm. He stared incredulously.

'What!'

'You *are* getting deaf.'

'I am not getting deaf. When I said "What!" I didn't mean "What?" I meant "What!!"'

'What on earth are you talking about?'

'I'm talking about this extraordinary remark of yours. I tell you this frightful Duke wants me to give him the Empress, and instead of being appalled and horrified and – er – appalled you say "Of course you will have to!" Without turning an eyelash! God bless my soul, do you imagine for an instant—'

'And do you imagine for an instant that I am going to run the risk of having Alaric career through the castle with a poker? If he destroyed all the furniture in his nephew Horace's sitting-room just because Horace wouldn't go to the station and see him off, what do you think he would do in a case like this? I do not intend to have my home wrecked for the sake of a pig. Personally, I think it's a blessing that we are going to get rid of the miserable animal.'

'Did you say "miserable animal"?'

'Yes, I did say "miserable animal". Alaric was telling me that he thought it a very bad influence in your life.'

'Dash his impertinence!'

'And I quite agree with him. In any case, there is no use arguing about it. If he wants the pig, he must have it.'

'Oh, very well, very well, very well, very well,' said Lord Emsworth. 'I suppose the next thing he'll want will be the castle, and you'll give him that. Be sure to tell him not to be afraid to ask for it, if he takes a fancy to it. I think I will go and read a little in the library, before Alaric decides to have all my books packed up and shipped off.'

It was a good exit speech – mordant – bitter, satirical – but it brought no glow of satisfaction to Lord Emsworth as he uttered it. His heart was bowed down with weight of woe. The experience gained from a hundred battles had taught him that his sister Constance always got her way. One might bluster and one might struggle, one might raise hands to heaven and clench fists and shake them, but in the end the result was always the same – Connie got what she wanted.

As he sat some ten minutes later in the cloistered coolness of the library, vainly trying to concentrate his attention on *Whiffle On The Care Of The Pig*, a feeling of being alone and helpless in a hostile world came upon Lord Emsworth. What he needed above all else in this crisis which had come to blast his life was a friend ... an ally ... a sympathetic adviser. But who was there to whom he could turn? Bosham was useless. Beach, his butler, was sympathetic, but not a constructive thinker. And his brother Galahad, the only male member of the family capable of coping with that family's females, was away....

Lord Emsworth started. A thought had struck him. Musing on Galahad, he had suddenly remembered that friend of his, that redoubtable Lord Ickenham of whom the Duke had been talking just now.

The Hon. Galahad Threepwood was a man of high standards. He weighed people before stamping them with the seal of his approval, and picked his words before he spoke. If Galahad Threepwood said a man was hot stuff, he used the phrase not carelessly but in its deepest sense. And not once but many times had Lord Emsworth heard him bestow this accolade on Frederick, Earl of Ickenham.

His eyes gleamed behind their pince-nez with a new light. He was planning and scheming. Debrett's Peerage, standing over there on its shelf, would inform him of this wonder-man's address, and what more simple than to ring him up on the telephone and arrange a meeting and then pop up to London and place the facts before him and seek his advice. A man like that would have a hundred ideas for the saving of the Empress....

The gleam died away. In classing the act of popping up to London as simple, he saw that he had erred. While this ghastly Duke remained on the premises, there was not the slightest hope of Connie allowing him to get away, even for a night. Boys who stood on burning decks had a better chance of leaving their post than the master of Blandings Castle when there were visitors.

He was just reaching feebly for his *Whiffle*, which he had dropped in his anguish, hoping that its magic pages would act as an opiate, when Lady Constance burst into the room.

'Clarence!'

'Eh?'

'Clarence, did you tell Alaric you wanted to enter your pig for the Derby?'

'No, I told him I didn't.'

'Then he misunderstood you. He said you did. And he wants me to get a brain specialist down to observe you.'

'I like his dashed cheek!'

'So you must go to London immediately.'

Once more *Whiffle* fell from Lord Emsworth's limp hand.

'Go to London?'

'Now, please, Clarence, don't be difficult. There is no need for you to tell me how you dislike going to London. But this is vitally important. Ever since Alaric arrived, I have been feeling that he ought to be under the observation of some good brain specialist, but I couldn't think how it was to be managed without offending him. This has solved everything. Do you know Sir Roderick Glossop?'

'Never heard of him.'

'He is supposed to be quite the best man in that line. Lady Gimblett told me he had done wonders for her sister's problem child. I want you to go to London this afternoon and bring him back with you. Give him lunch at your club tomorrow and explain the whole situation to him. Assure him that expense is no object, and that he must come back with you. He will tell us what is the best thing to be done about poor Alaric. I am hopeful that some quite simple form of treatment may be all that is required. You must catch the two o'clock train.'

'Very well, Connie. If you say so.'

There was a strange look on Lord Emsworth's face as the door closed. It was the look of a man who has just found himself on the receiving end of a miracle. His knees were trembling a little as he rose and walked to the book-case, where the red and gold of *Debrett's Peerage* gleamed like the ray of a lighthouse guiding a storm-tossed mariner.

Beach, the butler, hearing the bell, presented himself at the library.

'M'lord?'

'Oh, Beach, I want you to put in a trunk telephone call for me. I don't know the number, but the address is Ickenham Hall, Ickenham, Hampshire. I want a personal call to Lord Ickenham.'

'Very good, m'lord.'

'And when you get it,' said Lord Emsworth, glancing nervously over his shoulder, 'have it put through to my bedroom.'

CHAPTER 3

IF YOUR Buffy-Porson is running well, the journey from London to Hampshire does not take long. Pongo Twistleton, making good time, arrived at Ickenham Hall a few minutes before noon – at about the moment, in fact, when Lord Emsworth in far-off Shropshire was sitting down in the library of Blandings Castle to his *Whiffle On The Care Of The Pig*.

Half-way up the drive, where the rhododendrons masked a sharp turning, he nearly collided with the Hall Rolls, proceeding in the opposite direction, and a glimpse of luggage on its grid caused him to fear that he might just have missed his uncle. But all was well. Reaching the house, he found him standing on the front steps.

Frederick Altamont Cornwallis Twistleton, fifth Earl of Ickenham, was a tall, slim, distinguished-looking man with a jaunty moustache and an alert and enterprising eye. In actual count of time, he was no longer in his first youth. The spring now enlivening England with its alternate sunshine and blizzards was one of many that had passed over his head, leaving it a becoming iron-grey. But just as the years had failed to deprive him of his slender figure, so had they been impotent to quench his indomitable spirit. Together with a juvenile waist-line, he still retained the bright enthusiasms and the fresh, unspoiled outlook of a slightly inebriated undergraduate – though to catch him at his best, as he would have been the first to admit, you had to catch him in London.

It was for this reason that Jane, Countess of Ickenham, had prudently decided that the evening of her husband's life should be spent exclusively at his rural seat, going so far as to inform him that if he ever tried to sneak up to London she would skin him with a blunt knife. And if, as he now stood on the steps, his agreeable face seemed to be alight with some inner glow, this was due to the reflection that she had just left for a distant spot where she proposed to remain for some considerable time. He was devoted to his helpmeet, never wavering in the opinion that she was the sweetest thing that had ever replied 'Yes' to a clergyman's 'Wilt thou?' but there was no gainsaying the fact that her absence would render it easier for him to get that breath of London air which keeps a man from growing rusty and puts him in touch with the latest developments of modern thought.

At the sight of his nephew, his cheerfulness increased. He was very fond of Pongo, in whose society many of his happiest and most instructive hours had been passed. A day which they had spent together at the Dog Races some months before still haunted the young man's dreams.

'Why, hullo, my boy,' he cried. 'Delighted to see you. Park the scooter and come in. What a morning! Warm, fragrant, balmy, yet with just that nip in the air that puts a fellow on his toes. I saw one of those Western pictures at our local cinema last night, in which a character described himself as being all spooked up with zip and vinegar. That is precisely how I feel. The yeast of spring is fermenting in my veins, and I am ready for anything. You've just missed the boss.'

'Was that Aunt Jane I saw going off in the car?'

'That was the Big White Chief.'

The information relieved Pongo. He respected and admired his aunt, but from boyhood days she had always inspired him with a certain fear, and he was glad that he had not got to meet her while he was passing through his present financial crisis. Like so many aunts, she was gifted with a sort of second sight and one glance at his face would almost certainly have told her that he was two hundred in the red. From that to the confession that his difficulties were due to unsuccessful speculations on the turf would have been the shortest of steps. He did not like to think what would happen if she discovered his recent activities.

'She's motoring to Dover to catch the afternoon boat. She is off to the South of France to nurse her mother, who is having one of her spells.'

'Then you're all alone?'

'Except for your sister Valerie.'

'Oh, my gosh. Is she here?'

'She arrived last night, breathing flame through her nostrils. You've heard about her broken engagement? Perhaps you have come here with the idea of comforting her in her distress?'

'Well, not absolutely. In fact, between you and me, I'm not any too keen on meeting her at the moment. I rather took Horace's side in the recent brawl, and our relations are distant.'

Lord Ickenham nodded.

'Yes, now that you mention it, I recollect her saying something about your being some offensive breed of insect. An emotional girl.'

'Yes.'

'But I can't understand her making such heavy weather over the thing. Everybody knows a broken engagement doesn't amount to anything. Your aunt, I remember, broke ours six times in all before making me the happiest man in the world. Bless her! The sweetest, truest wife man ever had. I hope her mother responds to treatment and that she will be back with me soon. But not too soon. You know, Pongo, it's an odd thing that the detective Horace commissioned to chase Valerie across the ice with blood-hounds should have been old Pott. Mustard Pott, we used to call him. I've known him for years.'

'Yes, he was telling me. You started him as a sleuth.'

'That's right. A versatile chap, Mustard. There aren't many things he hasn't done in his time. He was on the stage once, I believe. Then he took to Silver Ring bookeying. Then he ran a club. And I rather suspect him of being a defrocked butler. Though what Nature really intended him to be, I have always felt, was a confidence-trick man. Which, by the way, is a thing I've wanted to have a shot at all my life, but never seemed able to get round to somehow.'

'What rot.'

'It isn't rot. You shouldn't mock at an old man's daydreams. Every time I read one of those bits in the paper about Another Victim Of The Confidence Trick, I yearn to try it for myself, because I simply cannot bring myself to believe that there are people in the world mugs enough to fall for it. Well, young Pongo, how much?'

'Eh?'

'I can see in your eye that you've come to make a touch. What's the figure?'

Such ready intelligence on the part of an uncle should have pleased a nephew, but Pongo remained sombre. Now that the moment had come, his natural pessimism had asserted itself again.

'Well, it's rather a lot.'

'A fiver?'

'A bit more than that.'

'Ten?'

'Two hundred.'

'Two – *what*? How in the world did you manage to get in the hole for a sum like that?'

'I came a bit of a mucker at Lincoln, being led astray by my advisers, and when I tried to get it back at Hurst Park things came unstuck again, and the outcome and upshot is that I owe a bookie named George Budd two hundred quid. Do you know George Budd?'

'Since my time. When I was a prominent figure on the turf, George Budd was probably in his cradle, sucking his pink toes.'

'Well, he isn't sucking any pink toes now. He's a tough egg. Bingo Little had a bit on the slate with him last winter, and when he started trying to break it gently to him that he might not be able to pay up, this Budd said he did hope he would—'

'So the modern bookie feels like that, does he? The ones in my time always used to.'

'– because he said he knew it was silly to be superstitious but he had noticed that every time anyone did him down for money some nasty accident happened to them. He said it was like some sort of fate. And he summoned a great beefy brute called Erb and dangled him before Bingo's eyes. Erb called on me yesterday.'

'What did he say?'

'He didn't say anything. He seemed to be one of those strong, silent men. He just looked at me and nodded. So if you could possibly see your way, Uncle Fred, to advancing—'

Lord Ickenham shook his head regretfully.

'Alas, my boy, the ear which you are trying to bite, though not unresponsive, is helpless to assist. There has been a shake-up in the Treasury department here. Some little time ago, your aunt unfortunately decided to take over the family finances and administer them herself, leaving me with just that bit of spending money which a man requires for tobacco, self-respect, golf-balls and what not. My limit is a tenner.'

'Oh, my gosh! And Erb's going to call again on Wednesday.'

There was a wealth of sympathy and understanding in Lord Ickenham's eye, as he patted his nephew's shoulder. He was gazing back across the years and seeing himself, an ardent lad in the twenties, thoughtfully glueing a large black moustache above his lips, his motive being to deceive and frustrate a bygone turf commissioner doing business under the name of Jimmy Timms, the Safe Man.

'I know just how you must be feeling, my boy. We have all gone through it, from the Archbishop of Canterbury, I imagine, downwards. Thirty-six years ago, almost to this very day, I was climbing out of a window and shinning down a waterspout to avoid a muscular individual named Syd, employed by a bookie who was my creditor at the moment in very much the same executive capacity as this Erb of yours. I got away all right, I remember, though what I have always thought must have been an ormolu clock missed me by inches. There is only one thing to be done. You must touch Horace Davenport.'

A bitter smile wreathed Pongo's lips.

'Ha!' he said briefly.

'You mean you have already tried? And failed? Too bad. Still, I wouldn't despair. No doubt you went the wrong way to work. I fancy that we shall find that when tactfully approached by a man of my presence and dignity he will prove far more plastic. Leave it to me. I will get into his ribs for you. There are no limits, literally none, to what I can accomplish in the springtime.'

'But you can't come to London.'

'Can't come to London? I don't understand you.'

'Didn't Aunt Jane say she would skin you if you did?'

'In her whimsical way she did say something to that effect, true. But you appear to have forgotten that she is on her way to the South of France.'

'Yes – leaving Valerie here to keep an eye on you.'

'I see what you mean. Yes, now that you mention it, there may possibly have been some idea in her mind that Valerie would maintain an affectionate watch over my movements during her absence. But be of good cheer. Valerie is not making a long stay. She will be returning to London with you in your car.'

'What?'

'Yes. She does not know it yet – in fact, I understood her to say that she was proposing to remain some weeks – but I think you will find her at your side.'

'What do you mean? You can't chuck her out.'

'My dear boy!' said Lord Ickenham, shocked. 'Of course not. But one has one's methods. Ah, there she is,' he went on, as a girlish figure came round the corner of the house. 'Valerie, my dear, here's Pongo.'

Valerie Twistleton had paused to stare at a passing snail – coldly and forbiddingly, as if it had been Horace Davenport. Looking up, she transferred this cold stare to her brother.

'So I see,' she said distantly. 'What's he doing here?'

'He has come to take you back to London.'

'I have no intention whatsoever—'

'Nothing,' proceeded Lord Ickenham, 'could be more delightful than to have you with me to cheer my loneliness, but Pongo feels – and I must say I agree with him – that you are making a great mistake in running away like this.'

'Doing *what*?'

'I'm afraid that is the construction people will place on the fact of your leaving London after what has happened. You know what people are. They sneer. They jibe. They laugh behind the back. It will be different, of course, with your real friends. They will merely feel a tender pity. They will look on you as the wounded animal crawling to its lair, and will understand and sympathize. But I repeat that in my opinion you are making a mistake. We Twistletons have always rather prided ourselves on keeping the stiff upper lip in times of trouble, and I confess that if I were in your place my impulse would be to show myself in my usual haunts – gay, smiling, debonair...Yes, Coggs?'

The butler had appeared from the hall.

'A trunk call for you, m'lord.'

'I will come at once. Be thinking it over, my dear.'

For some moments there had been proceeding from Valerie Twistleton a soft noise like the escape of steam. It now ceased, and her teeth came together with a sharp, unpleasant click.

'Can you wait ten minutes while I pack, Pongo?' she said. 'I will try not to keep you longer.'

She passed into the house, and Pongo lit a reverent cigarette. He did not approve of his Uncle Fred, but he could not but admire his work.

Lord Ickenham returned, looking about him.

'Where's Valerie?'

'Upstairs, packing.'

'Ah, she decided to leave, then? I think she was wise. That was old Emsworth on the 'phone. I don't think you've met him, have you? Lives at Blandings Castle in Shropshire. I hardly know him myself, but he is the brother of a very old pal of mine. He wants me to lunch with him at his club tomorrow. It will fit in quite nicely. We'll get this business of Horace over with in the morning. I'll meet you at the Drones at about twelve. And now come in and have a quick one. Bless my soul, it's wonderful to think that tomorrow I shall be in London. I feel like a child about to be taken to the circus.'

Pongo's feelings, as he followed his uncle to the smoking-room, were more mixed. It was stimulating, of course, to think that by his arts the other might succeed in inducing Horace Davenport to join the Share-The-Wealth movement, but the picture of him loose in London was one that tended definitely to knit the brow. As always when Lord Ickenham proposed to share with him the bracing atmosphere of the metropolis, he found himself regarding with apprehension the shape of things to come.

A thoughtful member of the Drones had once put the thing in a nutshell.

'The trouble with Pongo's Uncle Fred,' he had said, and the Drones is about the only place nowadays where you hear sound, penetrating stuff like this, 'is that, though sixty if a day, he becomes on arriving in London as young as he feels – which is, apparently, a youngish twenty-two. He has a nasty way of lugging Pongo out into the open and there, right in the public eye, proceeding to step high, wide and plentiful. I don't know if you happen to know what the word "excesses" means, but those are what Pongo's Uncle Fred, when in London, invariably commits.'

The young man's face, as he sipped his cocktail, was a little drawn and anxious.

CHAPTER 4

HIS UNCLE Fred's theory that Horace Davenport, scientifically worked, would develop pay gold had impressed Pongo Twistleton a good deal both when he heard it and during the remainder of the day. Throughout the drive back to London it kept him in optimistic mood. But when he woke on the following morning the idea struck him as unsound and impractical.

It was hopeless, he felt, to expect to mace any one given person for a sum like two hundred pounds. The only possible solution of his financial worries was to open a subscription list and let the general public in on the thing. He decided to look in at the Drones immediately and test the sentiment of the investors. And having arrived there, he was gratified to note that all the indications seemed to point to a successful flotation.

The atmosphere in the smoking-room of the Drones Club on the return of its members from their annual week-end at Le Touquet was not always one of cheerfulness and gaiety – there had been years when you might have mistaken the place for the Wailing Wall of Jerusalem – but today a delightful spirit of happiness prevailed. The dingy gods who preside over the *chemin-de-fer* tables at Continental Casinos had, it appeared, been extraordinarily kind to many of the Eggs, Beans and Crumpets revelling at the bar. And Pongo, drinking in the tales of their exploits, had just decided to raise the assessment of several of those present another ten pounds, when through the haze of cigarette smoke he caught sight of a familiar face. On a chair at the far end of the room sat Claude Pott.

It was not merely curiosity as to what Mr Pott was doing there or a fear lest he might be feeling lonely in these unaccustomed surroundings that caused Pongo to go and engage him in conversation. At the sight of the private investigator, there had floated into his mind like drifting thistledown the thought that it might be possible to start the ball rolling by obtaining a small donation from him. He crossed the room with outstretched hand.

'Why, hullo, Mr Pott. What brings you here?'

'Good morning, sir. I came with Mr Davenport. He is at the moment in the telephone booth, telephoning.'

'I didn't know old Horace ever got up as early as this.'

'He has not retired to bed yet. He went to a dance last night.'

'Of course, yes. The Bohemian Ball at the Albert Hall. I remember. Well, it's nice seeing you again, Mr Pott. You left a bit hurriedly that time we met.'

'Yes,' said Claude Pott meditatively. 'How did you come out with The Subject?'

'Not too well. She threw her weight about a bit.'

'I had an idea she would.'

'You were better away.'

'That's what I thought.'

'Still,' said Pongo heartily, 'I was very sorry you had to go, very. I could see that we were a couple of chaps who were going to get along together. Will you have a drink or something?'

'No, thank you, Mr T.'

'A cigarette or something?'

'No, thank you.'

'A chair or something? Oh, you've got one. I say, Mr Pott,' said Pongo, 'I was wondering—'

The babble at the bar had risen in a sudden crescendo. Oofy Prosser, the club's tame millionaire, was repeating for the benefit of some new arrivals the story of how he had run his bank seven times, and there had come into Mr Pott's eyes a dull glow, like the phosphorescent gleam on the stomach of a dead fish.

'Coo!' he said, directing at Oofy the sort of look a thoughtful vulture in the Sahara casts at a dying camel. 'Seems to be a lot of money in here this morning.'

'Yes. And talking of money—'

'Now would be just the time to run the old Hat Stakes.'

'Hat Stakes?'

'Haven't you ever heard of the Hat Stakes? It sometimes seems to me they don't teach you boys nothing at your public schools. Here's the way it works. You take somebody, as it might be me, and he opens a book on the Hat Race, the finish to be wherever you like – call it that door over there. See what I mean? The punters would bet on what sort of hat the first bloke coming in through that door would be wearing. You, for instance, might feel like having a tenner—'

Pongo flicked a speck of dust from his companion's sleeve.

'Ah, but I haven't got a tenner,' he said. 'And that's precisely why I was saying that I wondered—'

'– on Top Hat. Then if a feller wearing a top hat was the first to come in, you'd cop.'

'Yes, I see the idea. Amusing. Ingenious.'

'But you can't play the Hat Stakes nowadays, with everybody wearing these Homburgs. There wouldn't be enough starters. Cor!'

'Cor!' agreed Pongo sympathetically. 'You'd have to make it clothes or something, what? But you were speaking of tenners, and while on that subject…Stop me if you've heard this before…'

Claude Pott, who had seemed about to sink into a brooding reverie, came out of his meditations with a start.

'What's that you said?'

'I was saying that while on the subject of tenners—'

'Clothes!' Mr Pott rose from his chair with a spasmodic leap, as if he had seen The Subject entering the room. 'Well, strike me pink!'

He shot for the door at a speed quite remarkable in a man of his build. A few moments later, he shot back again, and suddenly the Eggs, Beans and Crumpets assembled at the bar were shocked to discover that some bounder, contrary to all club etiquette, was making a speech.

'Gentlemen!'

The babble died away, to be succeeded by a stunned silence, through which there came the voice of Claude Pott, speaking with all the fervour and *brio* of his Silver Ring days.

'Gentlemen and sportsmen, if I may claim your kind indulgence for one instant! Gentlemen and sportsmen, I know gentlemen and sportsmen when I see them, and what I have been privileged to overhear of your conversation since entering this room has shown me that you are all gentlemen and sportsmen who are ready at all times to take part in a little sporting flutter.'

The words 'sporting flutter' were words which never failed to touch a chord in the members of the Drones Club. Something resembling warmth and sympathy began to creep into the atmosphere of cold disapproval. How this little blister had man-aged to worm his way into their smoking-room they were still at a loss to understand, but the initial impulse of those present to bung him out on his ear had softened into a more friendly desire to hear what he had to say.

'Pott is my name, gentlemen – a name at one time, I venture to assert, not unfamiliar to patrons of the sport of kings, and though I have retired from active business as a turf commission agent I am still willing to make a little book from time to time to entertain sportsmen and gentlemen, and there's no time like the present. Here we all are – you with the money, me with the book – so I say again, gentlemen, let's have a little flutter. Gentlemen all, the Clothes Stakes are about to be run.'

Few members of the Drones are at their brightest and alertest in the morning. There was a puzzled murmur. A Bean said, 'What did he say?' and a Crumpet whispered, 'The what Stakes?'

'I was explaining the how-you-do-it of the Hat Stakes to my friend Mr Twistleton over there, and the Clothes Stakes are run on precisely the same principle. There is at the present moment a gentleman in the telephone booth along the corridor, and I have just taken the precaution to instruct a page-boy to shove a wedge under the door, thus ensuring that he will remain there and so accord you all ample leisure in which to place your wagers. Coo!' said Claude Pott, struck by an unpleasant idea. 'Nobody's going to come along and let him out, are they?'

'Of course not!' cried his audience indignantly. The thought of anybody wantonly releasing a fellow member who had got stuck in the telephone booth, a thing that only happened once in a blue moon, was revolting to them.

'Then that's all right. Now then, gentlemen, the simple ques-tion you have to ask yourselves is – What is the gentleman in the telephone booth wearing? Or putting it another way – What's he got on? Hence the term Clothes Stakes. It might be one thing, or it might be another. He might be in his Sunday-go-to-meetings, or he might have been taking a dip in the Serpentine and be in his little bathing suit. Or he may have joined the Salvation Army. To give you a lead, I am offering nine to four against Blue Serge, four to one Pin-Striped Grey Tweed, ten to one Golf Coat and Plus Fours, a hundred to six Gymnasium Vest and Running Shorts, twenty to one Court Dress as worn at Buckingham Palace, nine to four the field. And perhaps you, sir,' said Mr Pott, addressing an adjacent Egg, 'would be good enough to officiate as my clerk.'

'That doesn't mean I can't have a bit on?'

'By no means, sir. Follow the dictates of your heart and fear nothing.'

'What are you giving Herringbone Cheviot Lounge?'

'Six to one Herringbone Cheviot Lounge, sir.'

'I'll have ten bob.'

'Right, sir. Six halves Herringbone Cheviot Lounge. Ready money, if you please, sir. It's not that I don't trust you, but I'm not allowed by law. Thank you, sir. Walk up, walk up, my noble sportsmen. Nine to four the field.'

The lead thus given them removed the last inhibitions of the company. Business became brisk, and it was not long before Mr Pott had vanished completely behind a mass of eager punters.

Among the first to invest had been Pongo Twistleton. Hastening to the hall porter's desk, he had written a cheque for his last ten pounds in the world, and he was now leaning against the bar, filled with the quiet satisfaction of the man who has spotted the winner and got his money down in good time.

For from the very inception of these proceedings it had been clear to Pongo that Fortune, hitherto capricious, had at last decided that it was no use trying to keep a good man down and had handed him something on a plate. To be a successful punter, what you need is information, and this he possessed in abundant measure. Alone of those present, he was aware of the identity of the gentleman in the telephone booth, and he had the additional advantage of knowing the inside facts about the latter's wardrobe.

You take a chap like – say – Catsmeat Potter-Pirbright, that modern Brummel, and you might guess for hours without hitting on the precise suit he would be wearing on any given morning. But with Horace Pendlebury-Davenport it was different. Horace had never been a vivacious dresser. He liked to stick to the old and tried till they came apart on him, and it was this idiosyncrasy of his which had caused his recent *fiancée*, just before her departure for Le Touquet, to take a drastic step.

Swooping down on Horace's flat, at a moment when Pongo was there chatting with its proprietor, and ignoring her loved one's protesting cries, Valerie Twistleton had scooped up virtually his entire outfit and borne it away in a cab, to be given to the deserving poor. She could not actually leave the unhappy man in the nude, so she had allowed him to retain the shabby grey flannel suit he stood up in and also the morning clothes which he was reserving for the wedding day. But she had got away with all the rest, and as no tailor could have delivered a fresh supply at this early date, Pongo had felt justified in plunging to the uttermost. The bulk of his fortune on Grey Flannel at ten to one and a small covering bet on Morning Suit, and there he was, sitting pretty.

And he was just sipping his cocktail and reflecting that while his winnings must necessarily fall far short of the stupendous sum which he owed to George Budd, they would at least constitute something on account and remove the dark shadow of Erb at any rate temporarily from his life, when like a blow on the base of the skull there came to him the realization that he had overlooked a vital point.

The opening words of his conversation with Claude Pott came back to him, and he remembered that Mr Pott, in addition to informing him that Horace was in the telephone booth, had stated that the latter had attended the Bohemian Ball at the Albert Hall and had not been to bed yet. And like the knell of a tolling bell there rang in his ears Horace's words: 'I am going as a Boy Scout.'

The smoking-room reeled before Pongo's eyes. He saw now why Claude Pott had leaped so enthusiastically at the idea of starting these Clothes Stakes. The man had known it would be a skinner for the book. The shrewdest and most imaginative Drone would never think of Boy Scouts in telephone booths at this hour of the morning.

He uttered a stricken cry. At the eleventh hour the road to wealth had been indicated to him, and owing to that ready-money clause he was not in a position to take advantage of the fact. And then he caught sight of Oofy Prosser at the other end of the bar, and saw how by swift, decisive action he might save his fortunes from the wreck.

The attitude of Oofy Prosser towards the Clothes Stake had been from the first contemptuous and supercilious, like that of a Wolf of Wall Street watching small boys scrambling for pennies. This Silver Ring stuff did not interest Oofy. He held himself aloof from it, and as the latter slid down the bar and accosted him he tried to hold himself aloof from Pongo. It was only by clutching his coat sleeve and holding on to it with a fevered grip that Pongo was able to keep him rooted to the spot.

'I say, Oofy—'

'No,' replied Oofy Prosser curtly. 'Not a penny!'

Pongo danced a few frantic dance steps. Already there was a lull over by the table where Mr Pott was conducting his business, and the closing of the book seemed imminent.

'But I want to put you on to a good thing!'

'Oh?'

'A cert.'

'Ah?'

'An absolute dashed cast-iron cert.'

Oofy Prosser sneered visibly.

'I'm not betting. What's the use of winning a couple of quid? Why, last Sunday at the big table at Le Touquet—'

Pongo sped towards Claude Pott, scattering Eggs, Beans and Crumpets from his path.

'Mr Pott!'

'Sir?'

'Any limit?'

'No, sir.'

'I've a friend here who wants to put on something big.'

'Ready money only, Mr T., may I remind you? It's the law.'

'Nonsense. This is Mr Prosser. You can take his cheque. You must have heard of Mr Prosser.'

'Oh, Mr Prosser? Yes, that's different. I don't mind breaking the law to oblige Mr Prosser.'

Pongo, bounding back to the bar, found there an Oofy no longer aloof and supercilious.

'Do you really know something, Pongo?'

'You bet I know something. Will you cut me in for fifty?'

'All right.'

'Then put your shirt on Boy Scout,' hissed Pongo. 'I have first-hand stable information that the bloke in the telephone booth is Horace Davenport, and I happen to know that he went to a fancy-dress dance last night as a Boy Scout and hasn't been home to change yet.'

'What! Is that right?'

'Absolutely official.'

'Then it's money for jam!'

'Money for pickles,' asserted Pongo enthusiastically. 'Follow me and fear nothing. And don't forget I'm in for the sum I mentioned.'

With a kindling eye he watched his financial backer force his way into the local Tattersall's, and it was at this tense moment that a page-boy came up and informed him that Lord Ickenham was waiting for him in the hall. He went floating out to meet him, his feet scarcely touching the carpet.

Lord Ickenham watched his approach with interest.

'Aha!' he said.

'Aha!' said Pongo, but absently, as one who has no time for formal greetings. 'Listen, Uncle Fred, slip me every bally cent you've got on you. I may just be able to get it down before the book closes. Your pal, Claude Pott, came here with Horace Davenport—'

'I wonder what Horace was doing, bringing Mustard to the Drones. Capital chap, of course, but quite the wrong person to let loose in a gathering of impressionable young men.'

Pongo's manner betrayed impatience.

'We haven't time to go into the ethics of the thing. Suffice it that Horace did bring him, and he shut Horace up in the telephone booth and started a book on what sort of clothes he had on. How much can you raise?'

'To wager against Mustard Pott?' Lord Ickenham smiled gently. 'Nothing, my dear boy, nothing. One of the hard lessons Life will teach you, as you grow to know him better, is that you can't make money out of Mustard. Hundreds have tried it, and hundreds have failed.'

Pongo shrugged his shoulders. He had done his best.

'Well, you're missing the chance of a lifetime. I happen to know that Horace went to a dance last night as a Boy Scout, and I have it from Pott's own lips that he hasn't been home to change. Oofy Prosser is carrying me for fifty.'

It was evident from his expression that Lord Ickenham was genuinely shocked.

'Horace Davenport went to a dance as a Boy Scout? What a ghastly sight he must have looked. I can't believe this. I must verify it. Bates,' said Lord Ickenham, walking over to the hall-porter's desk, 'were you here when Mr Davenport came in?'

'Yes, m'lord.'

'How did he look?'

'Terrible, m'lord.'

It seemed to Pongo that his uncle had wandered from the point.

'I concede,' he said, 'that a chap of Horace's height and skinniness ought to have been shrewder than to flaunt himself at a public dance in the costume of a Boy Scout. Involving as it does, knickerbockers and bare knees—'

'But he didn't, sir.'

'What!'

The hall porter was polite, but firm.

'Mr Davenport didn't go to no dance as no Boy ruddy Scout, if you'll pardon me contradicting you, sir. More like some sort of negroid character, it seemed to me. His face was all blacked up, and he had a spear with him. Gave me a nasty turn when he come through.'

Pongo clutched the desk. The hall-porter's seventeen stone seemed to be swaying before his eyes.

'Blacked up?'

A movement along the passage attracted their attention. Claude Pott, accompanied by a small committee, was proceeding to the telephone booth. He removed the wedge from beneath the door, and as he opened it there emerged a figure.

Nature hath framed strange fellows in her time, but few stranger than the one that now whizzed out of the telephone booth, whizzed down the corridor, whizzed past the little group at the desk and, bursting through the door of the club, whizzed down the steps and into a passing cab.

The face of this individual, as the hall porter had foreshadowed, was a rich black in colour. Its long body was draped in tights of the same sombre hue, surmounted by a leopard's skin. Towering above his head was a head-dress of ostrich feathers, and in its right hand it grasped an assegai. It was wearing tortoise-shell-rimmed spectacles.

Pongo, sliding back against the desk, found his arm gripped by a kindly hand.

'Shift ho, my boy, I think, eh?' said Lord Ickenham. 'There would appear to be nothing to keep you here, and a meeting with Oofy Prosser at this moment might be fraught with pain and embarrassment. Let us follow Horace – he seemed to be homing –

and hold an enquiry into this in-and-out running of his. Tell me, how much did you say Oofy Prosser was carrying you for? Fifty pounds?'

Pongo nodded bleakly.

'Then let us assemble the facts. Your assets are nil. You owe George Budd two hundred. You now owe Oofy fifty. If you don't pay Oofy, he will presumably report you to the committee and have you thrown into the street, where you will doubtless find Erb waiting for you with a knuckleduster. Well,' said Lord Ickenham, impressed, 'nobody can say you don't lead a full life. To a yokel like myself all this is very stimulating. One has the sense of being right at the pulsing heart of things.'

They came to Bloxham Mansions, and were informed by Webster that Mr Davenport was in his bath.

CHAPTER 5

THE HORACE who entered the library some ten minutes later in pyjamas and a dressing-gown was a far more prepossessing spectacle than the ghastly figure which had popped out of the Drones Club telephone booth, but he was still patently a man who had suffered. His face, scrubbed with butter and rinsed with soap and water, shone rosily, but it was a haggard face, and the eyes were dark with anguish.

Into these eyes, as he beheld the senior of his two visitors, there crept a look of alarm. Horace Davenport was not unfamiliar with stories in which the male relatives of injured girls called on young men with horsewhips.

Lord Ickenham's manner, however, was reassuring. Though considering him weak in the head, he had always liked Horace, and he was touched by the forlornness of his aspect.

'How are you, my dear fellow? I looked in earlier in the day, but you were out.'

'Yes, Webster told me.'

'And when I saw you at the Drones just now, you seemed pressed for time and not in the mood for conversation. I wanted to have a talk with you about this unfortunate rift between yourself and Valerie. She has given me a fairly comprehensive eyewitness's report of the facts.'

Horace seemed to swallow something jagged.

'Oh, has she?'

'Yes. I was chatting with her last night, and your name happened to come up.'

'Oh, did it?'

'Yes. In fact, she rather dwelt on you. Valerie – we must face it – is piqued.'

'Yes.'

'But don't let that worry you,' said Lord Ickenham cheerily. 'She'll come round. I'm convinced of it. When you reach my age, you will know that it is an excellent sign when a girl speaks of a man as a goggle-eyed nit-wit and says that her dearest wish is to dip him in boiling oil and watch him wriggle.'

'Did she say that?'

'Yes, she was most definite about it – showing, I feel, that love still lingers. My advice is – give her a day or two to cool off, and then start sending her flowers. She will tear them to shreds. Send some more. She will rend them to ribbons. Shoot in a further supply. And very soon, if you persevere, you will find that the little daily dose is having its effect. I anticipate a complete reconciliation somewhere about the first week in May.'

'I see,' said Horace moodily. 'Well, that's fine.'

Lord Ickenham felt a trifle ruffled.

'You don't seem pleased.'

'Oh, I am. Oh yes, rather.'

'Then why do you continue to look like a dead fish on a slab?'

'Well, the fact is, there's something else worrying me a bit at the moment.'

Pongo broke a silence which had lasted for some twenty minutes. Since entering the apartment he had been sitting with folded arms, as if hewn from the living rock.

'Oh, is there?' he cried. 'And there's something that's jolly well worrying me at the moment. Did you or did you not, you blighted Pendlebury-Davenport, definitely and specifically state to me that you were going to that Ball as a Boy Scout? Come on now. Did you or didn't you?'

'Yes, I did. I remember. But I changed my mind.'

'Changed your mind! Coo!' said Pongo, speaking through tightly clenched teeth and borrowing from the powerful vocabulary of Claude Pott to give emphasis to his words. 'He changed his mind! He changed his bally mind! Ha! Coo! Cor!'

'Why, what's up?'

'Oh, nothing. You have merely utterly and completely ruined me, that's all.'

'Yes, my dear Horace,' said Lord Ickenham, 'I'm afraid you have let Pongo down rather badly. When Pongo joins the Foreign Legion, the responsibility will be yours. You give him your solemn assurance that you are going to the Ball in one costume and actually attend it in another. Not very British.'

'But why does it matter?'

'There was some betting in the club smoking-room on what you were wearing, and Pongo, unhappy lad, plunging in the light of what he thought was inside knowledge on Boy Scout, took the knock.'

'Oh, I say! I'm frightfully sorry.'

'Too late to be sorry now.'

'The thing was, you see, that Polly thought it would be fun if I went as a Zulu warrior.'

'Evidently a girl of exotic and rather unwholesome tastes. The word "morbid" is one that springs to the lips. Who is this Polly?'

'Pott's daughter. She went to the Ball with me.'

Lord Ickenham uttered an exclamation.

'Not little Polly Pott? Good heavens, how time flies. Fancy Polly being old enough to go to dances. I knew her when she was a kid. She used to come and spend her holidays at Ickenham. A very jolly child she was, too, beloved by all. Quite grown up now, eh? Well, well, we're none of us getting younger. I was a boy in the early fifties when I saw her last. So you took Polly to the Ball, did you?'

'Yes. You see, the original idea was that Valerie was to have gone. But when she gave me the bird, I told her I would take Polly instead.'

'Your view being, of course, that that would learn her? A fine, defiant gesture. Did Pott go along?'

'No, he wasn't there.'

'Then what was he doing at the Drones with you?'

'Well, you see, he had come to Marlborough Street to pay my fine, and we sort of drifted on there afterwards. I suppose I had some idea of buying him a drink or something.'

A faint stir of interest ruffled the stone of Pongo's face.

'What do you mean, your fine? Were you pinched last night?'

'Yes. There was a bit of unpleasantness at the Ball, and they scooped me in. It was Ricky's fault.'

'Who,' asked Lord Ickenham, 'is Ricky?'

'My cousin. Alaric Gilpin.'

'Poet. Beefy chap with red hair. It was he who introduced this girl Polly to Horace,' interpolated Pongo, supplying additional footnotes. 'She was giving him dancing lessons.'

'And how did he come to mix you up in unpleasantness?'

'Well, it was like this. Ricky, though I didn't know it, is engaged to Polly. And another thing I didn't know was that he hadn't much liked the idea of her giving me dancing lessons and, when she told him I was taking her to the Ball, expressly forbade her to go. So when he found us together there...I say, he wasn't hanging about outside when you arrived, was he?'

'I saw no lurking figure.'

'He said he was going to look in today and break my neck.'

'I didn't know poets broke people's necks.'

'Ricky does. He once took on three simultaneous coster-mongers in Covent Garden and cleaned them up in five minutes. He had gone there to get inspiration for a pastoral, and they started chi-iking him, and he sailed in and knocked them base over apex into a pile of Brussels sprouts.'

'How different from the home life of the late Lord Tennyson. But you were telling us about this trouble at the Ball.'

Horace mused for a moment, his thoughts in the stormy past.

'Well, it was after the proceedings had been in progress for about a couple of hours that it started. Polly was off somewhere, hobnobbing with pals, and I was having a smoke and resting the ankles, when Ricky appeared and came up and joined me. He said a friend of his had given him a ticket at the last moment and he thought he might as well look in for a bit, so he hired a Little Lord Fauntleroy suit and came along. He was perfectly all right then – in fact, exceptionally affable. He sat down and tried to borrow five hundred pounds from me to buy an onion soup bar.'

Lord Ickenham shook his head.

'You are taking me out of my depth. We rustics who don't get up to London much are not in touch with the latest developments of modern civilization. What is an onion soup bar?'

'Place where you sell onion soup,' explained Pongo. 'There are lots of them round Piccadilly Circus way these days. You stay open all night and sell onion soup to the multitude as they reel out of the bottle-party places. Pots of money in it, I believe.'

'So Ricky said. A pal of his, an American, started one a couple of years ago in Coventry Street and, according to him, worked the profits up to about two thousand quid a year. But apparently he has got homesick and wants to sell out and go back to New York, and he's willing to let Ricky have the thing for five hundred. And Ricky wanted me to lend it to him. And he was just getting rather eloquent and convincing, when he suddenly broke off and I saw that he was glaring at something over my shoulder.'

'Don't tell me,' said Lord Ickenham. 'Let me guess. Polly?'

'In person. And then the whole aspect of affairs changed. He had just been stroking my arm and saying what pals we had always been and asking me if I remembered the days when we used to go ratting together at my father's place, and he cheesed it like a flash. He turned vermilion, and the next moment he had started kicking up a frightful row...cursing me...cursing Polly...showing quite a different side to his nature, I mean to say. Well, you know how it is when you do that sort of thing at a place like the Albert Hall. People began to cluster round, asking questions. And what with one thing and another, I got a bit rattled, and I suppose it was because I was rattled that I did it. It was a mistake, of course. I see that now.'

'Did what?'

'Jabbed him with my assegai. Mind you,' said Horace, 'I didn't mean to. It wasn't as if I had had any settled plans. I was just trying to hold him off. But I misjudged the distance, and the next thing I knew he was rubbing his stomach and coming for me with a nasty glint in his eyes. So I jabbed him again, and then things hotted up still further. And what really led to my getting arrested was that he managed to edge past the assegai and land me a juicy one on the jaw.'

Lord Ickenham found himself unable to reconcile cause and effect.

'But surely no policeman, however flat-footed, would take a man into custody for being landed a juicy one on the jaw. You have probably got your facts twisted. I expect we shall find, when we look into it, that it was Ricky who was taken to Marlborough Street.'

'No, you see what happened was this juicy one on the jaw made me a bit dizzy, and I didn't quite know what I was doing. Everything was a sort of blur, and I just jabbed wildly in the general direction of what I thought was the seat of the trouble. And after a while I discovered that I was jabbing a female dressed as Marie Antoinette. It came as a great surprise to me. As a matter of fact, I had been rather puzzled for some moments. You see, I could feel the assegai going into some yielding substance, and I was surprised that Ricky was so squashy and had such a high voice. And then, as I say, I found it wasn't Ricky, but this woman.'

'Embarrassing.'

'It was a bit. The man who was with the woman summoned the cops. And what made it still more awkward was that by that time Ricky was nowhere near. Almost at the start of the proceedings, it appeared, people had gripped him and bustled him off. So that when the policeman arrived and found me running amuck with an assegai apparently without provocation, it was rather difficult to convince him that I wasn't tight. In fact, I didn't convince him. The magistrate was a bit terse about it all this morning. I say, are you sure Ricky wasn't hanging about outside?'

'We saw no signs of him.'

'Then I'll get dressed and go round and see Polly.'

'With what motive?'

'Well, dash it, I want to tell her to go and explain to Ricky that my behaviour towards her throughout was scrupulously correct. At present, he's got the idea that I'm a kind of…Who was the chap who was such a devil with the other sex?…Donald something.'

'Donald Duck?'

'Don Juan. That's the fellow I mean. Unless I can convince Ricky immediately that I'm not a Don Juan and was not up to any funny business with Polly, the worst will happen. You've no notion what he was like last night. Absolutely frothing at the mouth. I must go and see her at once.'

'And if he comes in while you are there?'

Horace, half-way to the door, halted.

'I never thought of that.'

'No.'

'You think it would be better to telephone her?'

'I don't think anything of the sort. You can't conduct a delicate negotiation like this over the telephone. You need the language of the eye…those little appealing gestures of the hand…Obviously you must entrust the thing to an ambassador. And what better ambassador could you have than Pongo here?'

'Pongo?'

'A silver-tongued orator, if ever there was one. Oh, I know what you are thinking,' said Lord Ickenham. 'You feel that there may be a coolness on his side, due to the fact that you recently refused to lend him a bit of money. My dear boy, Pongo is too big and fine to be unwilling to help you out because of that. Besides, in return for his services you will of course naturally slip him the trifle he requires.'

'But he said he wanted two hundred pounds.'

'Two hundred and fifty. He doesn't always speak distinctly.'

'But that's a frightful lot.'

'To a man of your wealth as the price of your safety? You show a cheeseparing spirit which I do not like to see. Fight against it.'

'But, dash it, why does everybody come trying to touch *me*?'

'Because you've got the stuff, my boy. It is the penalty you pay for having an ancestress who couldn't say No to Charles the Second.'

Horace chewed a dubious lip.

'I don't see how I can manage—'

'Well, please yourself, of course. Tell me about this fellow Ricky, Pongo. A rather formidable chap, is he? Robust? Well-developed? Muscular? His strength is as the strength of ten?'

'Definitely, Uncle Fred.'

'And in addition to that he appears to be both jealous and quick-tempered. An unpleasant combination. One of those men, I imagine, who if he inflicted some serious injury on anyone, would be the first to regret it after he had calmed down, but would calm down about ten minutes too late. I've met the type. There was a chap named Bricky Bostock in my young days who laid a fellow out for weeks over some misunderstanding about a girl, and it was pitiful to see his remorse when he realized what he had done. Used to hang about outside the hospital all the time the man was in danger, trembling like a leaf. But, as I said to him, "What's the use of trembling like a leaf now? The time to have trembled like a leaf was when you had your hands on his throat and were starting to squeeze the juice out of him."'

'It'll be all right about that two-fifty, Pongo,' said Horace.

'Thanks, old man.'

'When can you go and see Polly?'

'The instant I've had a bit of lunch.'

'I'll give you her address. You will find her a most intelligent girl, quick to understand. But pitch it strong.'

'Leave it to me.'

'And impress upon her particularly that there is no time to waste. Full explanations should be made to Ricky by this evening at the latest. And now,' said Horace, 'I suppose I'd better go and dress.'

The door closed. Lord Ickenham glanced at his watch.

'Hullo,' he said. 'I must be off. I have to go to the Senior Conservative Club to meet old Emsworth. So good-bye, my dear boy, for the present. I am delighted that everything has come out so smoothly. We shall probably meet at Pott's. I am going to slip round there after lunch and see Polly. Give her my love, and don't let Mustard lure you into any card game. A dear, good chap, one of the best, but rather apt to try to get people to play something he calls Persian Monarchs. When he was running that club of his, I've known him to go through the place like a devouring flame, leaving ruin and desolation behind him on every side.'

CHAPTER 6

THE METHOD of Lord Emsworth, when telling a story, being to repeat all the unimportant parts several times and to diverge from the main stream of narrative at intervals in order to supply lengthy character studies of the various persons involved in it, luncheon was almost over before he was able to place his guest in full possession of the facts relating to the Empress of Blandings. When eventually he had succeeded in doing so, he adjusted his pince-nez and looked hopefully across the table.

'What do you advise, my dear Ickenham?'

Lord Ickenham ate a thoughtful cheese straw.

'Well, it is obvious that immediate steps must be taken through the proper channels, but the question that presents itself is "What steps?"'

'Exactly.'

'We have here,' said Lord Ickenham, illustrating by means of a knife, a radish and a piece of bread, 'one pig, one sister, one Duke.'

'Yes.'

'The Duke wants the pig.'

'Quite.'

'The sister says he's got to have it.'

'Precisely.'

'The pig, no doubt, would prefer to be dissociated from the affair altogether. Very well, then. To what conclusion do we come?'

'I don't know,' said Lord Emsworth.

'We come to the conclusion that the whole situation pivots on the pig. Eliminate the pig, and we see daylight. "What, no pig?" says the Duke, and after a little natural disappointment turns his thoughts to other things – I don't know what, but whatever things Dukes do turn their thoughts to. There must be dozens. This leaves us with the simple problem – How is the existing state of what I might call "plus pig" to be converted into a state of "minus pig"? There can be only one answer, my dear Emsworth. The pig must be smuggled away to a place of safety and kept under cover till the Duke has blown over.'

Lord Emsworth, as always when confronted with a problem, had allowed his lower jaw to sag restfully.

'How?' he asked.

Lord Ickenham regarded him with approval.

'I was expecting you to say that. I knew your razor-like brain would cut cleanly to the heart of the thing. Well, it ought not to be difficult. You creep out by night with an accomplice and – one shoving and one pulling – you load the animal into some vehicle and ship her off to my family seat, where she will be looked after like a favourite child till you are ready to receive her again. It is a long journey from Shropshire to Hampshire, of course, but she can stop off from time to time for a strengthening bran-mash or a quick acorn. The only point to be decided is who draws the job of accomplice. Who is there at Blandings that you can trust?'

'Nobody,' said Lord Emsworth promptly.

'Ah? That seems to constitute an obstacle.'

'I suppose you would not care to come down yourself?'

'I should love it, and it is what I would have suggested. But unfortunately I am under strict orders from my wife to remain at Ickenham. My wife, I should mention, is a woman who believes in a strong centralized government.'

'But you aren't at Ickenham.'

'No. The Boss being away, I am playing hookey at the moment. But I have often heard her mention her friend Lady Constance Keeble, and were I to come to Blandings Lady Constance would inevitably reveal the fact to her sooner or later. Some casual remark in a letter, perhaps, saying how delightful it had been to meet her old bit of trouble at last and how my visit had brightened up the place. You see what I mean?'

'Oh, quite. Yes, quite, dash it.'

'My prestige in the home is already low, and a substantiated charge of being AWOL would put a further crimp in it, from which it might never recover.'

'I see.'

'But I think,' said Lord Ickenham, helping himself to the radish which had been doing duty as Lady Constance, 'that I have got the solution. There is always a way. We must place the thing in the hands of Mustard Pott.'

'Who is Mustard Pott?'

'A very dear and valued friend of mine. I feel pretty sure that, if we stress the fact that there is a bit in it for him, he would be delighted to smuggle pigs. Mustard is always ready and anxious to add to his bank balance. I was intending to call upon him after lunch, to renew our old acquaintance. Would you care to come along and sound him?'

'It is a most admirable idea. Does he live far from here?'

'No, quite close. Down in the Sloane Square neighbourhood.'

'I ask because I have an appointment with Sir Roderick Glossop at three o'clock. Connie told me to ask him to lunch, but I was dashed if I was going to do that. Do you know Sir Roderick Glossop, the brain specialist?'

'Only to the extent of having sat next to him at a public dinner not long ago.'

'A talented man, I believe.'

'So he told me. He spoke very highly of himself.'

'Connie wants me to bring him to Blandings, to observe the Duke, and he made an appointment with me for three o'clock. But I am all anxiety to see this man Pott. Would there be time?'

'Oh, certainly. And I think we have found the right way out of the impasse. If it had been a question of introducing Mustard into the home, I might have hesitated. But in this case he will put up at the local inn and confine himself entirely to outside work. You won't even have to ask him to dinner. The only danger I can see is that he may get this pig of yours into a friendly game and take her last bit of potato peel off her. Still, that is a risk that must be faced.'

'Of course.'

'Nothing venture, nothing have, eh?'

'Precisely.'

'Then suppose we dispense with coffee and go round and see him. We shall probably find my nephew Pongo there. A nice boy. You will like him.'

Pongo Twistleton had arrived at Claude Pott's residence at about the time when Lord Emsworth and his guest were leaving the Senior Conservative Club, and had almost immediately tried to borrow ten pounds from him. For even though Horace Davenport had guaranteed in the event of his soothing Ricky Gilpin to underwrite his gambling losses, he could not forget that he was still fiscally crippled, and he felt that he owed it to himself to omit no word or act which might lead to the acquisition of a bit of the needful.

In the sleuth hound of 6, Wilbraham Place, Sloane Square, however, he speedily discovered that he had come up against one of the Untouchables, a man to whom even Oofy Prosser, that outstanding non-parter, would have felt compelled to raise his hat. Beginning by quoting from Polonius' speech to Laertes, which a surprising number of people whom you would not have suspected of familiarity with the writings of Shakespeare seem to know, Mr Pott had gone on to say that lending money always made him feel as if he were rubbing velvet the wrong way, and that in any case he would not lend it to Pongo, because he valued his friendship too highly. The surest method of creating a rift between two pals, explained Mr Pott, was for one pal to place the other pal under a financial obligation.

It was, in consequence, into an atmosphere of some slight strain that the Lords Emsworth and Ickenham entered a few moments later. And though the mutual courtesies of the latter and Claude Pott, getting together again after long separation, lightened the gloom temporarily, the clouds gathered once more when Mr Pott, having listened to Lord Emsworth's proposal, regretfully declined to have anything to do with removing the Empress from her sty and wafting her away to Ickenham Hall.

'I couldn't do it, Lord E.'

'Eh? Why not?'

'It wouldn't be in accordance with the dignity of the profession.'

Lord Ickenham resented this superior attitude.

'Don't stick on such beastly side, Mustard. You and your bally dignity! I never heard such swank.'

'One has one's self-respect.'

'What's self-respect got to do with it? There's nothing *infra dig* about snitching pigs. If I were differently situated, I'd do it like a shot. And I'm one of the haughtiest men in Hampshire.'

'Well, between you and me, Lord I,' said Claude Pott, discarding loftiness and coming clean, 'there's another reason. I was once bitten by a pig.'

'Not really?'

'Yes, sir. And ever since then I've had a horror of the animals.'

Lord Emsworth hastened to point out that the present was a special case.

'You can't be bitten by the Empress.'

'Oh, no? Who made that rule?'

'She's as gentle as a lamb.'

'I was once bitten by a lamb.'

Lord Ickenham was surprised.

'What an extraordinary past you seem to have had, Mustard. One whirl of excitement. One of these days you must look me up and tell me some of the things you haven't been bitten by. Well, if you won't take the job on, you won't, of course. But I'm disappointed in you.'

Mr Pott sighed slightly, but it was plain that he did not intend to recede from his attitude of civil disobedience.

'I suppose I shall now have to approach the matter from another angle. If you're seeing Glossop at three, Emsworth, you'd better be starting.'

'Eh? Oh, ah, yes. True.'

'You leaving us, Lord E?' said Mr Pott. 'Which way are you going?'

'I have an appointment in Harley Street.'

'I'll come with you,' said Mr Pott, who had marked down the dreamy peer as almost an ideal person with whom to play Persian Monarchs and wished to cement their acquaintanceship. 'I've got to see a man up in that direction. We could share a cab.'

He escorted Lord Emsworth lovingly to the door, and Lord Ickenham stood brooding.

'A set-back,' he said. 'An unquestionable set-back. I had been relying on Mustard. Still, if a fellow's been bitten by pigs I suppose his views on associating with them do get coloured. But how the devil does a man *get* bitten by a pig? I wouldn't have thought they would ever meet on that footing. Ah, well, there it is. And now what about Polly? There seems to be no sign of her. Is she out?'

Pongo roused himself from a brown study.

'She's in her room, Pott told me. Dressing or something, I take it.'

Lord Ickenham went to the door.

'Ahoy!' he shouted. 'Polly!'

There came in reply from somewhere in the distance a voice which even in his gloom Pongo was able to recognize as silvery.

'Hullo?'

'Come here. I want to see you.'

'Who's there?'

'Frederick Altamont Cornwallis Twistleton, fifth Earl of good old Ickenham. Have you forgotten your honorary uncle Fred?'

'Oo!' cried the silvery voice. There was a patter of feet in the passage, and a kimono-clad figure burst into the room.

'Uncle Fur-RED! Well, it is nice seeing you again!'

'Dashed mutual, I assure you, my dear. I say, you've grown.'

'Well, it's six years.'

'So it is, by Jove.'

'You're just as handsome as ever.'

'Handsomer, I should have said. And you're prettier than ever. But what's become of your legs?'

'They're still there.'

'Yes, but when I saw you last they were about eight feet long, like a colt's.'

'I was at the awkward age.'

'You aren't now, by George. How old are you, Polly?'

'Twenty-one.'

'Gol durn yuh, l'il gal, as my spooked-up-with-vinegar friend would say, you're a peach!'

Lord Ickenham patted her hand, put his arm about her waist and kissed her tenderly. Pongo wished he had thought of that himself. He reflected moodily that this was always the way. In the course of their previous adventures together, if there had ever been any kissing or hand-patting or waist-encircling to be done, it had always been his nimbler uncle who had nipped in ahead of him and attended to it. He coughed austerely.

'Oh, hullo! I'd forgotten you were there,' said Lord Ickenham, apologetically. 'Miss Polly Pott…My nephew – such as he is – Pongo Twistleton.'

'How do you do?'

'How do you do?' said Pongo.

He spoke a little huskily, for he had once more fallen in love at first sight. The heart of Pongo Twistleton had always been an open door with 'Welcome' clearly inscribed on the mat, and you never knew what would walk in next. At brief intervals during the past few years he had fallen in love at first sight with a mixed gaggle or assortment of females to the number of about twenty, but as he gazed at this girl like an ostrich goggling at a brass door-knob it seemed to him that here was the best yet. There was something about her that differentiated her from the other lodgers.

It was not the fact that she was small, though the troupe hitherto had tended to be on the tall and willowy side. It was not that her eyes were grey and soft, while his tastes previously had rather lain in the direction of the dark and bold and flashing. It was something about her personality – a matiness, a simplicity, an absence of that lipsticky sophistication to which the others had been so addicted. This was a cosy girl. A girl you could tell your troubles to. You could lay your head in her lap and ask her to stroke it.

Not that he did, of course. He merely lit a cigarette.

'Won't you … sit down?' he said.

'What I'd really like to do,' said Polly Pott, 'is to lie down – and go to sleep. I'm a wreck, Uncle Fred. I was up nearly all last night at a dance.'

'We know all about your last night's goings-on, my child,' said Lord Ickenham. 'That is why we are here. We have come on behalf of Horace Davenport, who is in a state of alarm and despondency on account of the unfriendly attitude of your young man.'

The girl laughed – the gay, wholehearted laugh of youth. Pongo remembered that he had laughed like that in the days before he had begun to see so much of his Uncle Fred.

'Ricky was marvellous last night. You ought to have seen him jumping about, trying to dodge Horace's spear.'

'He speaks of breaking Horace's neck.'

'Yes, I remember he said something about that. Ricky's got rather a way of wanting to break people's necks.'

'And we would like you to get in touch with him immediately and assure him that this will not be necessary, because Horace's behaviour towards you has always been gentlemanly, respectful – in short, *preux* to the last drop. I don't know if this public menace you're engaged to has ever heard of Sir Galahad but, if so, convey the idea that the heart of that stainless knight might have been even purer if he had taken a tip or two from Horace.'

'Oh, but everything is quite all right now. I've calmed Ricky down, and he has forgiven Horace. Has Horace been worrying?'

'That is not overstating it. Horace *has* been worrying.'

'I'll ring him up and tell him there's no need to, shall I?'

'On no account,' said Lord Ickenham. 'Pongo will handle the whole affair, acting as your agent. It would be tedious to go into the reasons for this, but you can take it from me that it is essential. You had better be toddling off, Pongo, and bringing the roses back to Horace's cheeks.'

'I will.'

'The sooner you get that cheque, the better. Run along. I will remain and pick up the threads with Polly. I feel that she owes me an explanation. The moment my back is turned, she appears to have gone and got engaged to a young plug-ugly who seems to possess all the less engaging qualities of a Borneo head-hunter. Tell me about this lad of yours, Polly,' said Lord Ickenham, as the door closed. 'You seem to like them tough. Where did you find him? On Devil's Island?'

'He brought Father home one night.'

'You mean Father brought him home.'

'No, I don't. Father couldn't walk very well, and Ricky was practically carrying him. Apparently Father had been set upon in the street by some men who had a grudge against him – I don't know why.'

Lord Ickenham thought he could guess. He was well aware that, given a pack of cards, Claude Pott could offend the mildest lamb. Indeed, it was a tenable theory that this might have been the cause of his once having been bitten by one.

'And Ricky happened to be passing, and he jumped in and rescued him.'

'How many men were there?'

'Thousands, I believe.'

'But he wouldn't mind that?'

'Oh, no.'

'He just broke their necks.'

'I expect so. He had a black eye. I put steak on it.'

'Romantic. Did you fall in love at first sight?'

'Oh, yes.'

'My nephew Pongo always does. Perhaps it's the best way. Saves time. Did he fall in love with you at first sight?'

'Oh, yes.'

'I begin to think better of this Borstal exhibit. He will probably wind up in Broadmoor, but he has taste.'

'You would never have thought so, though; he just sat and glared at me with his good eye, and growled when I spoke to him.'

'Uncouth young wart-hog.'

'He's nothing of the kind. He was shy. Later on, he got better.'

'And when he was better, was he good?'

'Yes.'

'I wish I could have heard him propose. The sort of chap who would be likely to think up something new.'

'He did, rather. He grabbed me by the wrist and nearly broke it and told me to marry him. I said I would.'

'Well, you know your own business best, of course. What does your father think of it?'

'He doesn't approve. He says Ricky isn't worthy of me.'

'What a judge!'

'And he's got an extraordinary idea into his head that if I'm encouraged I may marry Horace. He was encouraging me all this morning. It's just because Ricky hasn't any money, of course. But I don't care. He's sweet.'

'Would you call that the *mot juste*?'

'Yes, I would. Most of the time he's an absolute darling. He can't help being jealous.'

'Well, all right. I suppose I shall have to give my consent. Bless you, my children. And here is a piece of advice which you will find useful in your married life. Don't watch his eyes. Watch his knees. They will tell you when he is setting himself for a swing. And when he swings, roll with the punch.'

'But when am I going to get any married life? He makes practically nothing with his poetry.'

'Still, he may have a flair for selling onion soup.'

'But how are we going to find the money to buy the bar? And his friend won't hold the offer open for ever.'

'I see what you mean, and I wish I could help you, my dear. But I can't raise anything like the sum you need. Hasn't he any money at all?'

'There's a little bit his mother left him, but he can't get at the capital. He tried to borrow some from his uncle. Do you know the Duke of Dunstable?'

'Only from hearing Horace speak of him.'

'He seems an awful old man. When Ricky told him he wanted five hundred pounds to buy an onion soup bar, he was furious.'

'Did he say he wanted to get married?'

'No. He thought it would be better not to.'

'I don't agree with him. He should have told Dunstable all about it and shown him your photograph.'

'He didn't dare risk it.'

'Well, I think he missed a trick. The ideal thing, of course, would be if you could meet Dunstable without him knowing who you are and play upon him like a stringed instrument. Because you could, you know. You've no notion what a pretty, charming girl you are, Polly. You'd be surprised. When you came in just now, I was stunned. I would have given you anything you asked, even unto half my kingdom. And I see no reason why Dunstable's reactions should not be the same. Dukes are not above the softer emotions. If somehow we could work it so that you slid imperceptibly into his life....'

He looked up, annoyed. The door-bell had rung.

'Callers? Just when we need to be alone in order to concentrate. I'll tell them to go to blazes.'

He went down the passage. His nephew Pongo was standing on the mat.

CHAPTER 7

PONGO'S MANNER was marked by the extreme of agitation. His eyes were bulging, and he began to pour out his troubles almost before the door was open. There was nothing in his bearing of a young man who has just concluded a satisfactory financial deal.

'I say, Uncle Fred, he's not there! Horace, I mean. At his flat, I mean. He's gone, I mean.'

'Gone?'

'Webster told me he had just left in his car with a gentleman.'

Lord Ickenham, while appreciating his nephew's natural chagrin, was disposed to make light of the matter.

'A little after-luncheon spin through the park with a crony, no doubt. He will return.'

'But he won't, dash it!' cried Pongo, performing the opening steps of a sort of tarantella. 'That's the whole point. He took a lot of luggage with him. He may be away for weeks. And George Budd planning to unleash Erb on me if I don't pay up by Wednesday!'

Lord Ickenham perceived that the situation was more serious than he had supposed.

'Did Webster say where he was off to?'

'No. He didn't know.'

'Tell me the whole story in your own words, my boy, omitting no detail, however slight.'

Pongo marshalled his facts.

'Well, apparently the first thing that happened was that Horace, having lunched frugally off some tinned stuff, sent Webster out to take a look round and see if Ricky was hanging about, telling him – if he wasn't – to go round to the garage and get his car, as he thought he would take a drive in order to correct a slight headache. He said it caught him just above the eyebrows,' added Pongo, mindful of the injunction not to omit details.

'I see. And then?'

'Webster came back and reported that the car was outside but Ricky wasn't, and Horace said "Thanks". And Horace went to the front door and opened it, as a preliminary to making his get-away, and there on the mat, his hand just raised to press the bell, was this bloke.'

'What sort of bloke?'

'Webster describes him as a pink chap.'

'Park Lane seems to have been very much congested with pink chaps today. I had a chat there with one this morning. Some convention up in town, perhaps. What was his name?'

'No names were exchanged. Horace said "Oh, hullo!" and the chap said "Hullo!" and Horace said "Did you come to see me?" and the chap said "Yes", and Horace said "Step this way," or words to that effect, and they went into the library. Webster states that they were closeted there for some ten minutes, and then Horace rang for Webster and told him to pack his things and put them in the car. And Webster packed his things and put them in the car and came back to Horace and said "I have packed your things and put them in the car, sir," and Horace said "Right ho" and shot out, followed by the pink chap. Webster describes him as pale and anxious-looking, as if he were going to meet some doom.'

Lord Ickenham pondered. The story, admirably clear in its construction and delivery, left no room for doubt concerning the probability of an extended absence on the part of the young seigneur of 52, Bloxham Mansions.

'H'm!' he said. 'Well, it's a little awkward that this should have arisen just now, my boy, because I am not really at liberty to weigh the thing and decide what is to be done for the best. Just at the moment my brain is bespoke. I am immersed in a discussion of ways and means with Polly. She is in trouble, poor child.'

All that was fine and chivalrous in Pongo Twistleton rose to the surface. He had been expecting to reel for some time beneath the stunning blow of Horace's disappearance, but now he forgot self.

'Trouble?'

He was deeply concerned. As a rule, when he fell in love at first sight, his primary impulse was a desire to reach out for the adored object and start handling her like a sack of coals, but the love with which this girl inspired him was a tender, chivalrous love. Her appeal was to his finer side, not to the caveman who lurked in all the Twistletons. He wanted to shield her from a harsh world. He wanted to perform knightly services for her. She was the sort of girl he could see himself kissing gently on the forehead and then going out into the sunset. And the thought of her being in trouble gashed him like a knife.

'Trouble? Oh, I say! Why, what's the matter?'

'The old, old story. Like so many of us, she is in sore need of the ready, and does not see where she is going to get it. Her young man has this glittering opportunity of buying a lucrative onion-soupery, which would enable them to get married, but he seeks in vain for someone to come across with the purchase price. Owing to that unfortunate affair at the Ball, he failed to enlist Horace's sympathy. The Duke of Dunstable, whom he also approached, proved equally unresponsive. I was starting to tell Polly, when you arrived, that the only solution is for her to meet Dunstable and fascinate him, and we were wondering how this was to be contrived. Step along and join us. Your fresh young intelligence may be just what we require. Here is Pongo, Polly,' he said, rejoining the girl. 'It is possible that he may have an idea. He nearly had one about three years ago. At any rate, he wishes to espouse your cause. Eh, Pongo?'

'Oh, rather.'

'Well, then, as I was saying, Polly, the solution is for you to meet the Duke, but it must not be as Ricky's *fiancée*—'

'Why not?' asked Pongo, starting to display the fresh young intelligence.

'Because he wouldn't think me good enough,' said Polly.

'My dear,' Lord Ickenham assured her, patting her hand, 'if you are good enough for me, you are good enough for a blasted, pop-eyed Duke. But the trouble is that he is the one who has to be conciliated, and it would be fatal to make a bad start. You must meet him as a stranger. You must glide imperceptibly into his life and fascinate him before he knows who you are. We want to get him saying to himself "A charming girl, egad! Just the sort I could wish my nephew Ricky to marry." And then along comes the anthropoid ape to whom you have given your heart and says he thinks so, too. All that is quite straight. But how the dickens are you to glide imperceptibly into his life? How do you establish contact?'

Pongo bent himself frowningly to the problem. He was aware of a keen agony at the reflection that the cream of his brain was being given to thinking up ways of getting this girl married to another man, but together with the agony there was a comfortable glow, as he felt that the opportunity of helping her had been accorded him. He reminded himself of Cyrano de Bergerac.

'Difficult,' he said. 'For one thing, the Duke's away some-where. I remember Horace telling me that it was because he wouldn't go to the station and see him off that he broke up the sitting-room with the poker. Of course, he may just have been going home. He has a lair in Wiltshire, I believe.'

'No, I know where he's gone. He is at Blandings Castle.'

'Isn't that your pal Emsworth's place?'

'It is.'

'Well, then, there you are,' said Pongo, feeling how lucky it was that there was a trained legal mind present to solve all perplexities. 'You get Emsworth to invite Miss Pott down there.'

Lord Ickenham shook his head.

'It is not quite so simple as that, I fear. You have a rather inaccurate idea of Emsworth's position at Blandings. He was telling me about it at lunch and, broadly, what it amounts to is this. There may be men who are able to invite unattached and unexplained girls of great personal charm to their homes, but Emsworth is not one of them. He has a sister, Lady Constance Keeble, who holds revisionary powers over his visiting list.'

Pongo caught his drift. He remembered having heard his friend Ronnie Fish speak of Lady Constance Keeble in a critical spirit, and Ronnie's views had been endorsed by others of his circle who had encountered the lady.

'If Emsworth invited Polly to stay, Lady Constance would have her out of the place within five minutes of her arrival.'

'Yes, I understand she's more or less of a fiend in human shape,' assented Pongo. 'Never met her myself, but I have it from three separate sources – Ronnie Fish, Hugo Carmody and Monty Bodkin – that strong men run like rabbits to avoid meeting her.'

'Precisely. And so … Oh, my Lord, that bell again!'

'I'll go,' said Polly, and vanished in the direction of the front door.

Lord Ickenham took advantage of her absence to point out the fundamental difficulty of the position.

'You see, Pongo, the real trouble is old Mustard. If Polly had a presentable father, everything would be simple. Emsworth may not be able to issue invitations to unattached girls, but even he, I imagine, would be allowed to bring a friend and his daughter to stay. But with a father like hers this is not practicable. I wouldn't for the world say a word against Mustard – one of Nature's gentlemen – but his greatest admirer couldn't call him a social asset to a girl. Mustard – there is no getting away from it – looks just what he is – a retired Silver Ring bookie who for years has been doing himself too well on the starchy foods. And even if he were an Adonis, I would still be disinclined to let him loose in a refined English home. I say this in no derogatory sense, of course. One of my oldest pals. Still, there it is.'

Pongo felt that the moment had come to clear up a mystery. Voices could be heard in the passage, but there was just time to put the question which had been perplexing him ever since Polly Pott had glided imperceptibly into his life.

'I say, how does a chap like that come to be her father?'

'He married her mother. You understand the facts of life, don't you?'

'You mean she's his stepdaughter?'

'I was too elliptical. What I should have said was that he married the woman who subsequently became her mother. A delightful creature she was, too.'

'But why did a delightful creature marry Pott?'

'Why does anyone marry anybody? Why does Polly want to marry a modern poet of apparently homicidal tendencies? Why have you wanted to marry the last forty-six frightful girls you've met?…But hist!'

'Eh?'

'I said "Hist!"'

'Oh, hist?' said Pongo, once more catching his drift. The door had opened, and Polly was with them again.

She was accompanied by Lord Emsworth, not looking his best.

The ninth Earl of Emsworth was a man who in times of stress always tended to resemble the Aged Parent in an old-fashioned melodrama when informed that the villain intended to foreclose the mortgage. He wore now a disintegrated air, as if somebody had removed most of his interior organs. You see the same sort of thing in stuffed parrots when the sawdust has leaked out of them. His pince-nez were askew, and his collar had come off its stud.

'Could I have a glass of water?' he asked feebly, like a hart heated in the chase.

Polly hurried off solicitously, and Lord Ickenham regarded his brother Peer with growing interest.

'Something the matter?'

'My dear Ickenham, a disastrous thing has happened.'

'Tell me all.'

'What I am to say to Connie, I really do not know.'

'What about?'

'She will be furious.'

'Why?'

'And she is a woman who can make things so confoundedly uncomfortable about the place when she is annoyed. Ah, thank you, my dear.'

Lord Emsworth drained the contents of the glass gratefully, and became more lucid.

'You remember, my dear Ickenham, that I left you to keep an appointment with Sir Roderick Glossop, the brain specialist. My sister Constance, I think I told you, had given me the strictest instructions to bring him back to Blandings, to observe Dunstable. Dunstable's behaviour has been worrying her. He breaks furniture with pokers and throws eggs at gardeners. So Connie sent me to bring Glossop.'

'And—?'

'My dear fellow, he won't come!'

'But why should that upset you so much? Lady Constance surely can't blame you for not producing brain specialists, if they're too busy to leave London.'

Lord Emsworth moaned softly.

'He is not too busy to leave London. He refuses to come because he says I insulted him.'

'Did you?'

'Yes.'

'How?'

'Well, it started with my calling him "Pimples". He didn't like it.'

'I don't quite follow you.'

'Who do you think this Sir Roderick Glossop turned out to be, Ickenham? A boy whom I had known at school. A most unpleasant boy with a nasty, superior manner and an extraordinary number of spots on his face. I was shown in, and he said: "Well, it's a long time since we met, eh?" And I said: "Eh?" And he said:

"You don't remember me, eh?" And I said: "Eh?" And then I took a good look at him, and I said "God bless my soul! Why, it's Pimples!"'

'An affecting reunion.'

'I recall now that he seemed to flush, and his manner lost its cordiality. It took on that supercilious superiority which I had always so much resented, and he asked me brusquely to state my business. I told him all about Dunstable wanting the Empress, and he became most offensive. He said something about being a busy man and having no time to waste, and he sneered openly at what he called "this absurd fuss" that was being made about what he described as "a mere pig".'

Lord Emsworth's face darkened. It was plain that the wound still throbbed.

'Well, I wasn't going to stand that sort of thing from young Pimples. I told him not to be a conceited ass. And he, I think, called me a doddering old fool. Something of that general nature, at any rate. And one word led to another, and in the end I confess that I did become perhaps a little more outspoken than was prudent. I remembered that there had been a scandal connected with his name – something to do with overeating himself and being sick at the house supper – and rather injudiciously I brought this up. And shortly afterwards he was ringing the bell for me to be shown out and telling me that nothing would induce him to come to Blandings after what had occurred. And now I am wondering how I am to explain to Constance.'

Lord Ickenham nodded brightly. There had come into his eyes a gleam which Pongo had no difficulty in recognizing. He had observed it on several previous occasions, notably during that visit to the Dog Races just before his uncle's behaviour had attracted the attention of the police. He could read its message. It meant that some pleasing inspiration had floated into Lord Ickenham's mind, and it caused a strong shudder to pass through his frame, together with a wish that he were far away. When pleasing inspirations floated into Lord Ickenham's mind, the prudent man made for the nearest bomb-proof shelter.

'This is all most interesting.'

'It is a terrible state of affairs.'

'On the contrary, nothing more fortunate could have happened. I now see daylight.'

'Eh?'

'You were not here when we were holding our conference just now, my dear Emsworth, or your lightning mind would long ere this have leaped at my meaning. Briefly, the position is as follows. It is essential that young Polly… By the way, you don't know each other, do you? Miss Polly Pott, only daughter of Claude ("Mustard") Pott – Lord Emsworth.'

'How do you do?'

'It is essential, I was saying, that Polly goes to Blandings and there meets and fascinates Dunstable.'

'Why?'

'She desires his approval of her projected union with his nephew, a young thug named Ricky Gilpin.'

'Ah?'

'And the snag against which we had come up, when you arrived, was the problem of how to get her to Blandings. You, we felt, were scarcely in a position to invite her by herself and there are various reasons, into which I need not go, why old Mustard should not trail along. Everything is now simple. You are in urgent need of a Sir Roderick Glossop. She is in urgent need of an impressive father. I am prepared to play both roles. Tomorrow, by a suitable train, Sir Roderick Glossop will set out with you for Blandings Castle, accompanied by his daughter and secretary—'

'Hey!' said Pongo, speaking abruptly.

Lord Ickenham surveyed him with mild surprise.

'You are surely not proposing to remain in London, my dear boy? Didn't you tell me that you were expecting a visit from Erb on Wednesday?'

'Oh!'

'Exactly. You must obviously get away and lie low somewhere. And what better haven could you find than Blandings Castle? But perhaps you were thinking that you would rather go there as my valet?'

'No, I'm dashed if I was.'

'Very well, then. Secretary it shall be. You follow what I am driving at, Emsworth?'

'No,' said Lord Emsworth, who seldom followed what people were driving at.

'I will run through the agenda again.'

He did so, and this time a faint light of intelligence seemed to brighten Lord Emsworth's eye.

'Oh, ah, yes. Yes, I think I see what you mean. But can you—'

'Get away with it? My dear fellow! Pongo here will tell you that on one occasion last year, in the course of a single afternoon in the suburb of Valley Fields, I impersonated with complete success not only an official from the bird shop, come to clip the claws of the parrot at The Cedars, Mafeking Road, but Mr Roddis, owner of The Cedars, and a Mr J. G. Bulstrode, a resident of the same neighbourhood. And I have no doubt that, if called upon to do so, I could have done them a very good parrot, too. The present task will be a childishly simple one to a man of my gifts. When were you thinking of returning to Blandings?'

'I should like to catch the five o'clock train this afternoon.'

'That will fit in admirably with our plans. You will go down today on the five o'clock train and announce that Sir Roderick Glossop will be arriving tomorrow with his secretary, and that you have invited him to bring his charming daughter. What good trains have you? The two-forty-five? Excellent. We will catch that, and there we shall be. I don't think that even you, Pongo, can pick any holes in that scenario.'

'I can tell you this, if you care to hear it, that you're definitely cuckoo and that everything is jolly well bound to go wrong and land us in the soup.'

'Nothing of the kind. I hope he isn't frightening you, Polly.'

'He is.'

'Don't let him. When you get to know Pongo better,' said Lord Ickenham, 'you will realize that he is always like this – moody, sombre, full of doubts and misgivings. Shakespeare drew Hamlet from him. You will feel better, my boy, when you have had a drink. Let us nip round to my club and get a swift one.'

CHAPTER 8

THE TWO-FORTY-FIVE express – Paddington to Market Blandings, first stop Oxford – stood at its platform with that air of well-
bred reserve which is characteristic of Paddington trains, and
Pongo Twistleton and Lord Ickenham stood beside it, waiting
for Polly Pott. The clock over the bookstall pointed to thirty-eight
minutes after the hour.

Anyone ignorant of the difference between a pessimist and
an optimist would have been able to pick up a useful pointer or
two by scanning the faces of this nephew and this uncle. The
passage of time had done nothing to relieve Pongo's apprehen-
sions regarding the expedition on which he was about to embark,
and his mobile features indicated clearly the concern with which
he was viewing the future. As always when fate had linked his
movements with those of the head of the family, he was feeling
like a man floating over Niagara Falls in a barrel.

Lord Ickenham, on the other hand, was all that was jovial and
debonair. Tilting his hat at a jaunty angle, he gazed about him
with approval at the decorous station which has for so many years
echoed to the tread of county families.

'To one like myself,' he said, 'who, living in Hampshire, gets
out of the metropolis, when he is fortunate enough to get into
it, *via* Waterloo, there is something very soothing in the note of
refined calm which Paddington strikes. At Waterloo, all is hustle
and bustle, and the society tends to be mixed. Here a leisured
peace prevails, and you get only the best people – cultured men
accustomed to mingling with basset hounds and women in
tailored suits who look like horses. Note the chap next door. No
doubt some son of the ruling classes, returning after a quiet jaunt in
London to his huntin', shootin', and fishin'.'

The individual to whom he alluded was a swarthy young
man who was leaning out of the window of the adjoining compartment, surveying the Paddington scene through a pair of steel-
rimmed spectacles. Pongo, who thought he looked a bit of a blister,

said so, and the rancour of his tone caused Lord Ickenham to shoot a quick, reproachful glance at him. Feeling himself like a school-boy going home for Christmas, he wanted happy, smiling faces about him.

'I don't believe you're enjoying this, Pongo. I wish you would try to get the holiday spirit. That day down at Valley Fields you were the life and soul of the party. Don't you like spreading sweetness and light?'

'If by spreading sweetness and light, you mean gatecrashing a strange house and—'

'Not so loud,' said Lord Ickenham warningly, 'stations have ears.'

He led his nephew away down the platform, apologizing with a charming affability to the various travellers with whom the latter collided from time to time in his preoccupation. One of these, a portly man of imposing aspect, paused for an instant on seeing Lord Ickenham, as if wavering on the verge of recognition. Lord Ickenham passed on with a genial nod.

'Who was that?' asked Pongo dully.

'I haven't an idea,' said Lord Ickenham. 'I seem to have a vague recollection of having met him somewhere, but I can't place him and do not propose to institute enquiries. He would probably turn out to be someone who was at school with me, though some years my junior. When you reach my age, you learn to avoid these reunions. The last man I met who was at school with me, though some years my junior, had a long white beard and no teeth. It blurred the picture I had formed of myself as a sprightly young fellow on the threshold of life. Ah, here's Polly.'

He moved forward with elastic step and folded the girl in a warm embrace. It seemed to Pongo, not for the first time, that this man went out of his way to kiss girls. On the present occasion, a fatherly nod would amply have met the case.

'Well, my dear, so here you are. Did you have any trouble getting away?'

'Trouble?'

'I should have supposed that your father would have been curious as to where you were off to. But no doubt you told him some frank, straightforward story about visiting a school friend.'

'I told him I was going to stay with you for a few days. Of course, he may have thought I meant that I was going to Ickenham.'

'True. He may. But it wouldn't have done to have revealed the actual facts to him. He might have disapproved. There is an odd, Puritan streak in old Mustard. Well, everything seems to be working out capitally. You're looking wonderful, Polly. If this Duke has a spark of human feeling in him, he cannot fail to fall for you like a ton of bricks. You remind me of some radiant spirit of the Spring. Pongo, on the other hand, does not. There is something worrying Pongo, and I can't make out what it is.'

'Ha!'

'Don't say "Ha!" my boy. You ought to be jumping with joy at the thought of going to a delightful place like Blandings Castle.'

'I ought, ought I? How about Lady Constance?'

'What about her?'

'She's waiting for us at the other end, isn't she? And what a pill! Ronnie Fish says she has to be seen to be believed. Hugo Carmody paled beneath his tan as he spoke of her. Monty Bodkin strongly suspects that she conducts human sacrifices at the time of the full moon.'

'Nonsense. These boys exaggerate so. Probably a gentle, sweet-faced lady of the old school, with mittens. You must fight against this tendency of yours to take the sombre view. Where you get your streak of pessimism from, I can't imagine. Not from my side of the family. Nothing will go wrong. I feel it in my bones. I am convinced that this is going to be one of my major triumphs.'

'Like that day at the Dog Races.'

'I wish you would not keep harping on that day at the Dog Races. I have always maintained that the constable acted far too precipitately on that occasion. They are letting a rather neurotic type of man into the Force nowadays. Well, if we are going to Blandings Castle for a restful little holiday, I suppose we ought to be taking our seats. I notice an official down the platform fidgeting with a green flag.'

They entered their compartment. The young man in spectacles was still leaning out of the window. As they passed him, he eyed them keenly — so keenly, indeed, that one might have supposed that he had found in these three fellow-travellers something to view with suspicion. This, however, was not the case. Rupert Baxter, formerly secretary to Lord Emsworth and now secretary to the Duke of Dunstable, always eyed people keenly. It was pure routine.

All that he was actually feeling at the moment was that the elder of the two men looked a pleasant old buffer, that the younger seemed to have something on his mind, and that the girl was a pretty girl. He also had a nebulous idea that he had seen her before somewhere. But he did not follow up this train of thought. Substituting a travelling-cap for the rather forbidding black hat which he was wearing, he took his seat and leaned back with closed eyes. And presently Rupert Baxter slept.

In the next compartment, Lord Ickenham was attending to some minor details.

'A thing we have got to get settled before our arrival,' he said, 'is the question of names. Nothing is more difficult than to think of a good name on the spur of the moment. That day at the Dog Races, I remember, we were well on our way to the police station before I was able to select "George Robinson" for myself and to lean over to Pongo and whisper that he was Edwin Smith. And I felt all the while that, as names, they were poor stuff. They did not satisfy the artist in me. This time we must do much better. I, of course, automatically become Sir Roderick Glossop. You, Polly, had better be Gwendoline. "Polly" seems to me not quite dignified enough for one in your position. But what of Pongo?'

Pongo bared his teeth in a bitter smile.

'I wouldn't worry about me. What I am going to be called is "this man". "Ptarmigan", Lady Constance will say, addressing the butler—'

'Ptarmigan isn't a bad name.'

'"Ptarmigan, send for Charles and Herbert and throw this man out. And see that he lands on something sharp."'

'That pessimistic streak again! Think of some movie stars, Polly.'

'Fred Astaire?'

'No.'

'Warner Baxter?'

'Baxter would be excellent, but we can't use it. It is the name of the Duke's secretary. Emsworth was telling me about him. It would be confusing to have two Baxters about the place. Why, of course. I've got it. Glossop. Sir Roderick Glossop, as I see it, was one of two brothers and, as so often happens, the younger brother did not equal the elder's success in life. He became a curate, dreaming away the years in a country parish, and when he died, leaving only a copy of Hymns Ancient and Modern and a son called Basil, Sir Roderick found himself stuck with the latter. So with the idea of saving something out of the wreck he made him his secretary. That's what I call a nice, well-rounded story. Telling it will give you something to talk about to Lady Constance over the pipes and whisky in her boudoir. If you get to her boudoir, that is to say. I am not quite clear as to the social standing of secretaries. Do they mingle with the nobs or squash in with the domestic staff?'

A flicker of animation lit up Pongo's sombre eyes.

'I'll be dashed if I squash in with any domestic staff.'

'Well, we'll try you on the nobs,' said Lord Ickenham doubtfully. 'But don't blame me if it turns out that that's the wrong thing and Lady Constance takes her lorgnette to you. God bless my soul, though, you can't compare the lorgnettes of today with the ones I used to know as a boy. I remember walking one day in Grosvenor Square with my aunt Brenda and her pug dog Jabberwocky, and a policeman came up and said that the latter ought to be wearing a muzzle. My aunt made no verbal reply. She merely whipped her lorgnette from its holster and looked at the man, who gave one choking gasp and fell back against the railings, without a mark on him but with an awful look of horror in his staring eyes, as if he had seen some dreadful sight. A doctor was sent for, and they managed to bring him round, but he was never the same again. He had to leave the Force, and eventually drifted into the grocery business. And that is how Sir Thomas Lipton got his start.'

He broke off. During his remarks, a face had been peering in through the glass door of the compartment, and now entered a portly man of imposing aspect with a large, round head like the dome of St. Paul's. He stood framed in the doorway, his manner majestic but benevolent.

'Ah,' he said. 'So it was you, Ickenham. I thought I recognized you on the platform just now. You remember me?'

Now that he was seeing him without his hat, Lord Ickenham did, and seemed delighted at the happy chance that had brought them together again.

'Of course.'

'May I come in, or am I interrupting a private conversation?'

'Of course come in, my dear fellow. We were only talking about lorgnettes. I was saying that in the deepest and fullest sense of the word there are none nowadays. Where are you off to?'

'My immediate objective is an obscure station in Shropshire of the name of Market Blandings. One alights there, I understand, for Blandings Castle.'

'Blandings Castle?'

'The residence of Lord Emsworth. That is my ultimate destination. You know the place?'

'I have heard of it. By the way, you have not met my daughter and nephew. My daughter Gwendoline and my nephew Basil – Sir Roderick Glossop.'

Sir Roderick Glossop seated himself, shooting a keen glance at Polly and Pongo as he did so. Their demeanour had aroused his professional interest. From the young man, as Lord Ickenham performed the ceremony of introduction, there had proceeded a bubbling grunt like that of some strong swimmer in his agony, while the girl's eyes had become like saucers. She was now breathing in an odd, gasping sort of way. It was not Sir Roderick's place to drum up trade by suggesting it, but he found himself strongly of the opinion that these young folks would do well to place themselves in the care of a good nerve specialist.

Lord Ickenham, apparently oblivious to the seismic upheaval which had left his nephew a mere pile of ruins, had begun to prattle genially.

'Well, Glossop, it's extraordinarily nice, seeing you again. We haven't met since that dinner of the Loyal Sons of Hampshire, where you got so tight. How are all the loonies? It must be amazingly interesting work, sitting on people's heads and yelling to somebody to hurry up with the strait waistcoat.'

Sir Roderick Glossop, who had stiffened, relaxed. The monstrous suggestion that he had been intemperate at the annual banquet of the Loyal Sons of Hampshire had offended him deeply, nor had he liked that reference to sitting on people's heads. But he was a man who pined without conversation, and in order to carry on this particular conversation it appeared to be necessary to accept his companion's peculiar way of expressing himself.

'Yes,' he said, 'the work, though sometimes distressing, is as you say, full of interest.'

'And you're always at it, I suppose? You are going to Blandings Castle now, no doubt, to inspect some well-connected screwball?'

Sir Roderick pursed his lips.

'You are asking me to betray confidences, I fear, my dear Ickenham. However, I may perhaps gratify your curiosity to the extent of saying that my visit is a professional one. A friend of the family has been giving evidence of an over-excited nervous condition.'

'There is no need to be coy with me, Glossop. You are going to Blandings to put ice on the head of the chap with the egg-throwing urge.'

Sir Roderick started.

'You appear singularly well-informed.'

'I had that one straight from the stable. Emsworth told me.'

'Oh, you know Emsworth?'

'Intimately. I was lunching with him yesterday, and he went off to see you. But when I ran into him later in the day, he rather hinted that things had not gone too well between you, with the result that you had refused to interest yourself in this unbalanced egg-jerker.'

Sir Roderick flushed.

'You are perfectly correct. Emsworth's manner left me no alternative but to decline the commission. But this morning I received a letter from his sister, Lady Constance Keeble, so charming in its tone that I was constrained to change my mind. You know Lady Constance?'

'What, dear old Connie? I should say so! A lifelong friend. My nephew Basil there looks on her as a second mother.'

'Indeed? I have not yet met her myself.'

'You haven't? Capital!'

'I beg your pardon?'

'You still have that treat in store,' explained Lord Ickenham.

'Lady Constance expressed so strong a desire that I should go to Blandings that I decided to overlook Emsworth's discourtesy. The summons comes at a singularly inopportune time, unfortunately, for I have an important conference in London tomorrow after-noon. However, I have been looking up the trains, and I see that there is one that leaves Market Blandings at eight-twenty in the morning, arriving at Paddington shortly before noon, so I shall be able to make my examination and return in time.'

'Surely a single examination won't work the trick?'

'Oh, I think so.'

'I wish I had a brain like yours,' said Lord Ickenham. 'What an amazing thing. I suppose you could walk down a line of people, giving each of them a quick glance, and separate the sheep from the goats like shelling peas.... "Loony...not loony.... This one wants watching.... This one's all right.... Keep an eye on this chap. Don't let him get near the bread-knife...." Extraordinary. What do you do exactly? Ask questions? Start topics and observe reactions?'

'Yes, I suppose you might say – broadly – that that is the method I employ.'

'I see. You bring the conversation round to the subject of birds, for instance, and if the fellow says he's a canary and hops on to the mantelpiece and starts singing, you sense that there is something wrong. Yes, I understand. Well, it seems to me that, if it's as simple as that, you could save yourself a lot of trouble by making your examination now.'

'I do not understand you.'

'You're in luck, Glossop. The man Emsworth wants you to run the rule over is on the train. You'll find him in the compartment next door. A dark chap with spectacles. Emsworth asked me to keep an eye on him during the journey, but if you want my opinion – there's nothing wrong with the fellow at all. Connie was always such a nervous little soul, bless her. I suppose some chance remark of his about eggs gave her the idea that he had said he wanted to throw them, and she went all of a twitter. Why don't you go in and engage him in conversation and note the results? If there's anything wrong with him, that sixth sense of yours will enable you to spot it in a second. If he's all right, on the other hand, you could leave the train at Oxford and return to London in comfort.'

'It is a most admirable idea.'

'Don't mention my name, of course.'

'My dear Ickenham, you may trust me to exercise perfect discretion. The whole thing will be perfectly casual. I shall embark on our little talk quite simply and naturally by asking him if he can oblige me with a match.'

'Genius!' said Lord Ickenham.

The silence which followed Sir Roderick's departure was broken by a groan from Pongo.

'I knew something like this would happen,' he said.

'But my dear boy,' protested Lord Ickenham, 'what has happened, except that I have been refreshed by an intelligent chat with a fine mind, and have picked up some hints on deportment for brain specialists which should prove invaluable? The old Gawd-help-us will alight at Oxford—'

'So will I jolly well alight at Oxford!'

'And return to your flat? I wonder if you will find Erb waiting for you on the doorstep?'

'Oh, gosh!'

'Yes, I thought you had overlooked that point. Pull yourself together, my dear Pongo. Stiffen the sinews, summon up the blood. Everything is going to be all right. You seem thoughtful, Polly.'

'I was only wondering why Lord Emsworth called him Pimples.'

'You mean he hasn't any now? No, I noticed that,' said Lord Ickenham. 'It is so often the way. We start out in life with more pimples than we know what to do with, and in the careless arrogance of youth think they are going to last for ever. But comes a day when we suddenly find that we are down to our last half-dozen. And then those go. There is a lesson in this for all of us. Ah, Glossop, what news from the front?'

Sir Roderick Glossop radiated satisfaction.

'You were perfectly correct, my dear Ickenham. Absolutely nothing wrong. No indication whatsoever of any egg-fixation. There was no basis at all for Lady Constance's alarm. I should describe the man as exceptionally intelligent. But I was surprised to find him so young.'

'We all were once.'

'True. But I had imagined from Lady Constance's letter that he was far older. Whether she said so or not, I cannot recall, but the impression I gathered was that he was a contemporary of Emsworth's.'

'Probably looks younger than he is. The country air. Or as a child he may have been fed on Bevo.'

'Ah,' said Sir Roderick non-committally. 'Well, if I am to leave the train at Oxford, I must be getting back to my compartment and collecting my things. It has been a great pleasure meeting you again, Ickenham, and I am exceedingly obliged for that very thoughtful suggestion of yours. I confess that I was not looking forward to an early-morning journey. Good-bye.'

'Good-bye.'

'Good-bye,' said Polly.

'Good-bye,' said Pongo, speaking last and speaking with difficulty. He had been sitting for some moments in a deep silence,
broken only by an occasional sharp, whistling intake of breath.
Sir Roderick carried away with him an impression of a sombre
and introspective young man. He mentioned him later in a lecture
to the Mothers of West Kensington as an example of the tendency
of post-war youth towards a brooding melancholia.

Lord Ickenham, too, seemed to feel that he needed cheering
up, and for the remainder of the journey spared no effort to amuse
and entertain. All through the afternoon he maintained a high
level of sprightliness and gaiety, and it was only when they had
alighted at Market Blandings station that he found himself compelled to strike a jarring note.

Market Blandings station, never a congested area, was this
evening more than usually somnolent and deserted. Its only
occupants were a porter and a cat. The swarthy young man got
out and walked to the end of the train, where the porter was
extracting luggage from the van. Polly wandered off to fraternize
with the cat. And Lord Ickenham, having bought Pongo a penny-
worth of butterscotch from the slot machine, was just comment-
ing on the remissness of his host and hostess in not sending anyone
down to meet so distinguished a guest, when there came on to the
platform a solid man in the middle thirties. The afterglow of the
sunset lit up his face, and it was at this point that Lord Ickenham
struck the jarring note.

'I wonder if you remember, Pongo,' he said, 'that when you
looked in on me at Ickenham the day before yesterday
I mentioned that it had always been the ambition of my life to
play the confidence trick on someone? Owing to all the rush and
bustle of this Emsworth business, I quite forgot to tell you that
yesterday morning the opportunity arose.'

'What!'

'Yes. Before coming to the Drones, I went to call on Horace
Davenport, and finding him not at home, waited for a while in the
street outside his flat. And while I was doing so a pink chap came
along, and it seemed to me that if ever I was going to make the
experiment, now was the time. There was something about this
fellow that told me that I could never hope for a better subject.

And so it proved. He handed me over his wallet, and I walked off with it. The whole affair was a triumph of mind over matter, and I am modestly proud of it.'

It had always been an axiom with Pongo Twistleton that his Uncle Fred was one of those people who ought not to be allowed at large, but he had never suspected that the reasons for not allowing him at large were so solidly based as this. He clutched his brow.

As had happened that day at the Dog Races, this man seemed to have taken him into a strange nightmare world.

'I sent the wallet back, of course. My interest in the experiment was purely scientific. I had no thought of vulgar gain. The chap's card was inside, and I shipped it off by registered post. And the reason why I mention it now…Do you see the fellow coming along the platform?'

Pongo turned an ashen face.

'You don't mean—?'

'Yes,' said Lord Ickenham, with a breezy insouciance which cut his nephew like a knife, 'that's the chap.'

CHAPTER 9

'HIS NAME,' said Lord Ickenham, 'is Bosham. It was on the card I found in his wallet. But I distinctly remember that the address on the card was some place down in Hampshire, not far from my own little dosshouse, so it seems extremely odd that he should be here. It looks to me like one of those strained coincidences which are so inartistic. Unless he's a ghost.'

Pongo, who might have been taken for one himself by a short-sighted man, found speech. For some moments he had been squeaking and gibbering like the sheeted dead in the Roman streets a little ere the mightiest Julius fell.

'Bosham is Lord Emsworth's son,' he said hollowly.

'Is he, indeed? I am not very well up in the Peerage. I seldom read it except to get a laugh out of the names. Then that explains it,' said Lord Ickenham heartily. 'He must have been on a visit to Blandings, and when he ran up to London for the day to get his hair cut the Duke told him on no account to fail, while there, to go and slap his nephew Horace on the back and give him his best. It was perfectly natural that his pilgrimage to Bloxham Mansions should chance to synchronize with mine. How simple these apparently extraordinary things are, when you go into them.'

'He's coming this way.'

'He would be. I presume he is here to escort us to the castle.'

'But, dash it, what are you going to do?'

'Do? Why, nothing.'

'Well, I'll bet he will. Do you mean to tell me that if a chap has the confidence trick played on him by a chap, and meets the chap again, he isn't going to set about the chap?'

'My dear boy, for a young man who has enjoyed the advantage of having a refined uncle constantly at his elbow, you seem singularly ignorant of the manners and customs of good society. We bloods do not make scenes in public places.'

'You think he will wait till later before having you pinched?'

Lord Ickenham clicked his tongue.

'My dear Pongo, you have a gift for taking the dark view that amounts almost to genius. I should imagine that the prophet Isaiah as a young man must have been very like you. Tell me – I don't want to turn till I can see the whites of his eyes – where is our friend? Does he approach?'

'He's sort of backing and filling at the moment.'

'I quite understand. It is the decent diffidence of the English upper classes. All his life he has been brought up in the creed that there is nothing that is more beastly bad form than accosting a stranger, and he is wondering if I am indeed the Sir Roderick Glossop of whom he has heard so much. He shrinks from taking a chance. I think it must be your presence that is bothering him. No doubt Emsworth completely forgot to mention that I should be accompanied by my secretary, and this has made him confused. "It may be Glossop," he is saying to himself. "I wouldn't be prepared to bet it isn't Glossop. But if it is Glossop, who's the chap with him? There was nothing in my instructions about chaps-with-Glossop." And so he backs and fills. Well, this gives us time to go further into the matter we were discussing. What on earth leads you to suppose that this Bosham will denounce me for having played the confidence trick on him? The moment I say that I am Sir Roderick Glossop, the eagerly awaited guest, he will naturally assume that he was deceived by a chance resemblance. Where is he now?'

'Just abaft the try-your-weight machine.'

'Then watch me turn and nonplus him,' said Lord Ickenham, and pivoted gracefully. 'Excuse me, sir,' he said. 'I wonder if you could inform me if there is any possibility of my obtaining a vehicle of some sort here, to take me to Blandings Castle?'

He had not overestimated the effect of his manoeuvre. Lord Bosham halted as if he had walked into a lamp-post, and stood gaping.

The heir to the Earldom of Emsworth was a slow thinker, but he was not incapable of inductive reasoning. He had been told to meet an elderly gentleman who would arrive on the two-forty-five train en route for Blandings Castle. The only elderly gentleman who had arrived on the two-forty-five train en route for Blandings Castle was the elderly gentleman before him. This elderly gentle-man, therefore, must be that elderly gentleman. In which case, he was Sir Roderick Glossop, the eminent brain-specialist, and so could not be, as in that first instant of seeing his face he had been prepared to swear he was, the pleasant stranger who had relieved him of his wallet in Park Lane.

For Lord Bosham, though he lived a secluded life in a remote corner of Hampshire, was sufficiently in touch with things to know that eminent brain-specialists do not go about playing the confidence trick on people. Every young man starting out in the world, he was aware, has his choice. He can become an eminent brain-specialist, or he can become a confidence trickster. But not both.

'Are you Sir Roderick Glossop?' he asked, his round eyes drinking in those features that had seemed so familiar.

'That is my name.'

'Oh? Ah? Mine's Bosham. We – er – we haven't met before, by any chance?'

'Unfortunately, no. The loss,' said Lord Ickenham, courteously but inaccurately, 'was mine. But I have heard of you. When I saw him yesterday, Lord Emsworth spoke with a fatherly warmth of your many gifts.'

'Ah? Well, I tooled down in the car to meet you.'

'Vastly civil of you, my dear Bosham.'

'You've got some luggage in the van, I take it, what? I'll slide along and see to it.'

'Thank you, thank you.'

'Then we can tool up to the castle.'

'Precisely what I would have suggested myself. Is there a large party there?'

'Eh? Oh, no. Only my father and my aunt and the Duke and Horace Davenport.'

'Horace Davenport?'

'The Duke's nephew. Well, I'll be sliding along and seeing about that luggage.'

He slid, and Pongo resumed his imitation of the sheeted dead.

'Well?' he said, at length becoming coherent. 'Now what? On arrival at this ghastly castle, we shall immediately find ourselves cheek by jowl with a chap who knows you, knows Miss Pott and has been a close pal of mine for years. "Hullo, Pongo!" he will say, bounding up, as we stand chatting with Lady Constance. "Hullo, Lord Ickenham! Golly, Polly, isn't this jolly, here we all are, what?" If you have nothing else to do at the moment, you might be trying that one over on your bazooka.'

Lord Ickenham did not reply. He was looking down the platform. At the far end, a reunion seemed to be taking place between Lord Bosham and the swarthy young man who had occupied the adjoining compartment on the train. They had just shaken hands, and were now engaged in conversation.

'You were saying, my boy?' he asked, coming out of his thoughts.

Pongo repeated the substance of his remarks.

'Yes, I see what you mean,' agreed Lord Ickenham. 'You must always remember, however, that there is nothing either good or bad, but thinking makes it so. Still, in feeling that a problem has arisen I am not saying that you are not right. I confess that I had not anticipated Horace. Fate seems to have arranged that this shall be Old Home Week at Blandings Castle. We only need Mustard Pott and my dear wife to have what you might call a full hand.'

'Could we get hold of him before he spills the beans, and explain things to him and ask him to sit in?'

Lord Ickenham shook his head.

'I think not. Horace is a nice boy, but he would be a total loss as a conspirator.'

'Then what are we going to do?'

'Keep cool.'

'A fat lot of help keeping cool will be.'

'This is the pessimist in you speaking again. What I was about to say was that we must keep cool and level heads and deny our identity.'

'And you think he will swallow that? Ha!'

'I wish you wouldn't say "Ha!" Why shouldn't he swallow it? Who can say what limits, if any, there are to what Horace Davenport will swallow? With an uncle like his, if he is anything of a student of heredity, he must frequently have speculated on the possibility of his little grey cells suddenly turning blue on him. I imagine that he will think that it is this disaster that has happened. Still, I feel that we would do well to separate, so that we steal upon him little by little, as it were, instead of confronting him in a solid bunch. If the distance is not too great, I shall walk to the castle, allowing you and Polly to go on ahead in the car and pave the way.'

'Or we might all walk back to London.'

'My dear boy, do try to rid yourself of this horrible defeatist attitude. You have seen for yourself how stout denial of identity affected our friend Bosham. All you have to do, when you meet Horace, is to give him a cold stare and say that your name is Basil. That in itself should carry conviction, for who would say his name was Basil if he did not know that it could be proved against him? As for Polly, I have no misgivings. She will hold her end up. She is Mustard's daughter and must have been taught to tell the tale as soon as her infant lips could lisp. And if you don't think it's difficult to say "lips could lisp", try it yourself. You might step over and explain the situation to her. And now,' said Lord Ickenham, with relish, 'we come to another small difficulty.'

A sound like the dying gurgle of a siphon of soda water proceeded from Pongo.

'Oh, golly! Don't tell me there's something else?'

A happy smile was playing over Lord Ickenham's handsome face.

'Things are certainly being made somewhat intricate for us on this little expedition of ours,' he said contentedly. 'I had anticipated strolling in over the red carpet and being accepted without demur at my face value, but apparently this is not to be.'

'What the dickens has happened?'

'It is not so much what has happened as what is going to happen. If you glance along the platform, you will note that Bosham is returning, accompanied not only by a porter in a uniform much too tight for him but by our dark friend in the spectacles. Does it not occur to you that when Bosham introduces me to him, he may feel that Sir Roderick Glossop has changed a bit since he saw him last?'

'Oh, my aunt!'

'Yes, stimulating, isn't it?'

'Perhaps Glossop didn't tell him he was Glossop.'

'If you suppose that Glossop could be alone with anyone for two minutes without telling him he was Glossop, you are a very indifferent reader of character.'

'We must clear out of here at once!'

Lord Ickenham was shocked.

'Clear out? That is no way for a member of a proud family to talk. Did Twistletons clear out at Agincourt and Crecy? At Malplaquet and Blenheim? When the Old Guard made their last desperate charge up the blood-soaked slopes of Waterloo, do you suppose that Wellington, glancing over his shoulder, saw a Twistleton sneaking off with ill-assumed carelessness in the direction of Brussels? We Twistletons do not clear out, my boy. We stick around, generally long after we have outstayed our welcome. I feel sure that I shall be able to find some way of dealing with the matter. All it needs is a little thought, and my brain is at its brightest this evening. Run along and explain things to Polly, and I will have everything comfortably adjusted by the time you return.... Ah, Bosham, my dear fellow, I see that you have collected our impedimenta. Very good of you to have bothered.'

'Eh? Oh no, not a bit.'

'Tell me, Bosham, is it far to the castle?'

'About a couple of miles.'

'Then I think, if you don't mind, that I will walk. It would be pleasant to stretch my legs.'

Lord Bosham seemed relieved.

'Well, that's fine, if you'd like to. Might have been a bit of a squash in the car. I didn't know Baxter was turning up. This is Mr Baxter the Duke's secretary – Sir Roderick Glossop.'

'How do you do? I am very glad you did turn up, Mr Baxter,' said Lord Ickenham, beaming upon the dark young man, who was eyeing him with silent intentness. 'It gives me the opportunity of discussing that poor fellow on the train. I saw him go into your compartment, but I hesitated to intrude upon you and ask you what you made of him. One of my patients,' explained Lord Ickenham. 'He suffers from delusions – or did. I am hopeful that my treatment may have been effective. Certainly he seemed normal enough while he was talking to me. But in these cases a relapse often comes like a flash, and I know the presence of strangers excites him. Did he by any chance tell you he was Mussolini?'

'He did not.'

'Or Shirley Temple?'

'He told me that he was Sir Roderick Glossop.'

'Then I am in distinguished company. Not that it is anything to joke about, of course. The whole thing is terribly sad and disheartening. Evidently all my work has gone for nothing. It almost makes one lose confidence in oneself.'

'I should not have thought that you were a man who easily lost his self-confidence.'

'Kind of you to say so, my dear fellow. No, as a rule, I do not. But absolute failure like this.... Ah, well, one must keep one's flag flying, must one not? You humoured him, I hope? It is always the best and safest plan. Well, here are my daughter and my nephew Basil, who acts as my secretary. This is Lord Bosham, my dear, Lord Emsworth's son. And Mr Baxter. I was telling them that I thought I would walk to the castle. I am feeling a little cramped after the journey. We shall meet at Philippi.'

CHAPTER 10

TO REACH Blandings Castle from Market Blandings, you leave the latter, if you can bear to tear yourself away from one of the most picturesque little towns in England, by way of the High Street. This, ending in a flurry of old-world cottages, takes you to a broad highway, running between leafy hedges that border pasture land and barley fields, and you come eventually to the great stone gates by the main lodge and through these to a drive which winds uphill for some three-quarters of a mile. A testing bit, this last, for the indifferent pedestrian. Beach, the butler, who sometimes walked to Market Blandings and back to discipline his figure, always felt a sinking feeling as he approached it.

Lord Ickenham took it in his stride. The recent happenings on the station platform had left him pleasantly exhilarated, and he was all eagerness to get to his destination and see what further entertainment awaited him in the shape of obstacles and problems. Breasting the slope with a song on his lips, he had reached the last of the bends in the drive and was pausing to admire the grey bulk of the castle as it stood out against the saffron sky, when he observed coming towards him a man of his own age but much fatter and not half so beautiful.

'Hoy!' cried this person.

'Hoy!' responded Lord Ickenham civilly.

The fact that he had heard Horace Davenport speak of his uncle Alaric as a baldheaded old coot with a walrus moustache had enabled him to identify the newcomer without difficulty. Few coots could have had less hair than this man, and any walrus would have been proud to possess the moustache at which he was puffing.

'You the brain chap?'

Rightly concluding that this was a crisper and neater way of saying 'psychiatrist', Lord Ickenham replied that he was.

'The others are in the hall, having drinks and things. When I heard you were walking up, I thought I'd come along and meet you. Dunstable's my name. The Duke of Dunstable.'

They fell into step together. The Duke produced a bandanna handkerchief and mopped his forehead with it. The evening was warm, and he was not in the best of condition.

'I wanted a quiet talk——' he began.

'Speaking of Dukes,' said Lord Ickenham, 'did you ever hear the one about the Duke and the lady snake-charmer?'

It was a jocund little tale, slightly blue in spots, and he told it well. But though his companion was plainly amused, his chief emotion appeared to be perplexity.

'Are you really Sir Roderick Glossop?'

'Why do you ask?'

'Man at the club told me he was a pompous old ass. But you're not a pompous old ass.'

'Your friend probably met me in my professional capacity. You know how it is. One puts on a bit of dog in office hours, to impress the customers. I dare say you have done the same thing yourself in the House of Lords.'

'That's true.'

'But you were saying something about wanting a quiet talk.'

'Exactly. Before Connie could get hold of you and stuff you up with a lot of nonsense. Emsworth's sister, Lady Constance Keeble. She's like all women – won't face facts. The first thing she's going to do when she meets you is to try to pull the wool over your eyes and persuade you that he's as sane as I am. Quite understandable, no doubt. Her brother, and all that.'

'You are speaking of Lord Emsworth?'

'Yes. What did you make of him?'

'He seemed clean and sober.'

Again the Duke appeared a little puzzled.

'Why shouldn't he be sober?'

'Don't think I am complaining,' Lord Ickenham hastened to assure him. 'I was pleased.'

'Oh? Well, as I was saying, Connie will try to make you think that the whole thing has been much exaggerated and that he's simply dreamy and absent-minded. Don't let her fool you. The man's potty.'

'Indeed?'

'No question about it. The whole family's potty. You saw Bosham at the station. There's a loony for you. Goes up to London and lets a chap play the confidence trick on him. "Give me your wallet to show you trust me," says the chap. "Right ho," says Bosham. Just like that. Ever meet the other boy – Freddie Threepwood? Worse than Bosham. Sells dog-biscuits. So you can get a rough idea what Emsworth must be like. Man can't have two sons like that and be sane himself, I mean to say. You've got to start with that idea well in your head, or you'll never get anywhere. Shall I tell you about Emsworth?'

'Do.'

'Here are the facts. He's got a pig, and he's crazy about it.'

'The good man loves his pig.'

'Yes, but he doesn't want to run it in the Derby.'

'Does Emsworth?'

'Told me so himself.'

Lord Ickenham looked dubious.

'I doubt if the Stewards would accept a pig. You might starch its ears and enter it as a greyhound for the Waterloo Cup, but not the Derby.'

'Exactly. Well, that shows you.'

'It does, indeed.'

The Duke puffed at his moustache approvingly, so that it flew before him like a banner. It pleased him to find this expert in such complete agreement with his views. The man, he could see, knew his business, and he decided to abandon reserve and lay bare the skeleton in his own cupboard. He had not intended to draw attention to the dark shadow which had fallen on the house of Dunstable, but he saw now that it would be best to tell all. In the hall which he had just left, strange and disconcerting things had been happening, and he wanted a skilled opinion on them.

'A nice little place Emsworth has here,' said Lord Ickenham, as they reached the broad gravel sweep that flanked the terrace.

'Not so bad. Makes it all the sadder that he'll probably end his days in Colney Hatch. Unless you can cure him.'

'I seldom fail.'

'Then I wish,' said the Duke, coming out with it, 'that while you're here you would take a look at my nephew Horace.'

'Is he giving you cause for anxiety?'

'Acute anxiety.'

The Duke, about to unveil the Dunstable skeleton, checked himself abruptly and blew furiously at his moustache. From some spot hidden from them by thick shrubberies there had come the sound of a pleasant tenor voice. It was rendering the 'Bonny Bonny Banks of Loch Lomond', and putting a good deal of feeling into it.

'Gah! That whistling feller again!'

'I beg your pardon?'

'Chap who comes whistling and singing outside my window,' said the Duke, like the heroine of an old-fashioned novelette speaking of her lover. 'I've been trying to get to grips with him ever since I arrived, but he eludes me. Well I can wait. I've got a dozen best new-laid eggs in my room, and sooner or later…But I was telling you about Horace.'

'Yes, I want to hear all about Horace. Your nephew, you say?'

'One of them. My late brother's son. He's potty. The other's my late sister's son. He's potty, too. My late brother was potty. So was my late sister.'

'And where would you rank Horace in this galaxy of goofiness? Is he, in your opinion, above or below the family average?'

The Duke considered.

'Above. Decidedly above. After what happened in the hall just now, most emphatically above. Do you know what happened in the hall just now?'

'I'm sorry, no. I'm a stranger in these parts myself.'

'It shocked me profoundly.'

'What happened in the hall?'

'And always the "Bonny Bonny Banks of Loch Lomond",' said the Duke peevishly. 'A song I've hated all my life. Who wrote the beastly thing?'

'Burns, I believe. But you were going to tell me what happened in the hall.'

'Yes. So I was. It showed me that I had wronged that chap Baxter. I expect you met Baxter at the station. My secretary. He was on your train. He should have come down with me, but he insisted on remaining in London on the plea that he had work to do in connection with a history of my family that I'm writing. I didn't believe him. It seemed to me that he had a furtive look in his eye. My feeling all along was that he was planning to go on some toot. And when Horace told me this morning that he had seen him at some dance or other a couple of nights ago, leaping about all over the place in the costume of a Corsican brigand, I was all ready for him. The moment his foot crossed the threshold, I sacked him. And then this thing happened in the hall.'

'You were going to tell me about that, weren't you?'

'I am telling you about it. It was when we were in the hall. Connie had taken your daughter out to show her the portraits in the gallery, though why any girl should be supposed to be anxious to look at that collection of gargoyles is more than I can imagine. I should be vastly surprised to learn that there was an uglier lot of devils in the whole of England than Emsworth's ancestors. However, be that as it may, Connie had taken your daughter to see them, leaving Bosham and your nephew and myself in the hall. And in comes Horace. And no sooner had I directed his attention to your nephew than he gives a jump and says "Pongo!" See? "Pongo!" Like that. Your nephew looked taken aback, and said in a low voice that his name was Basil.'

'Brave lad!'

'What?'

'I said "Brave lad!"'

'Why?'

'Why not?' argued Lord Ickenham.

The Duke turned this over for a moment, and seemed to see justice in it.

'What had happened, you see, was that Horace had mistaken him for a friend of his. Well, all right. Nothing so very remarkable about that, you are saying. Sort of thing that might happen to anyone. Quite. But mark the sequel. If Burns thought "Loch Lomond" rhymes with "before ye",' said the Duke, with a return of his peevishness, 'he must have been a borderline case.'

'And the sequel, you were about to say?'

'Eh? Oh, the sequel. I'm coming to that. Not that there are many rhymes to "Loch Lomond". Got to be fair to the chap, I suppose. Yes, the sequel. Well, right on top of this, Connie comes back with your daughter. She's charming.'

'I have not met Lady Constance.'

'You daughter, I mean.'

'Oh, very. Her name is Gwendoline.'

'So she told us. But that didn't stop Horace from going up to her and calling her Polly.'

'Polly?'

'Polly. "Why, hullo, Polly!" were his exact words.'

Lord Ickenham reflected.

'The conclusion that suggests itself is that he had mistaken her for a girl called Polly.'

'Exactly. The very thought that flashed on me. Well, you can imagine that that made me realize that matters were grave. One bloomer of that sort – yes. But when it happens twice in two minutes, you begin to fear the worst. I've always been uneasy about Horace's mental condition, ever since he had measles as a boy and suddenly shot up to the height of about eight foot six. It stands to reason a chap's brain can't be all that way from his heart and still function normally. Look at the distance the blood's got to travel. Well, here we are,' said the Duke, as they passed through the great front door that stood hospitably open. 'Hullo, where's everybody? Dressing, I suppose. You'll be wanting to go to your room. I'll take you there. You're in the Red Room. The bathroom's at the end of the passage. What was I saying? Oh, yes. I said I began to fear the worst. I reasoned the whole thing out. A chap can't be eight foot six and the son of my late brother and expect to carry on as if nothing had happened. Something's bound to give. I remembered what he had told me about thinking he had seen Baxter at the Ball, and it suddenly struck me like a blow that he must have developed – I don't know what you call it, but I suppose there's some scientific term for it when a feller starts seeing things.'

'You mean a sublunary medulla oblongata diathesis.'

'Very possibly. I can see now why that girl broke off the engagement. She must have realized that he had got this – whatever it was you said, and decided it wasn't good enough. No girl wants a potty husband, though it's dashed hard not to get one nowadays. Here's your room. I wish you would see what you can do for the boy. Can't you examine him or something?'

'I shall be delighted to examine him. Just give me time to have a bath, and I will be at his disposal.'

'Then I'll send him to you. If there's anything to be done for him, I'd be glad if you would do it. What with him and Bosham and Emsworth and that whistling feller, I feel as if I were living in a private asylum, and I don't like it.'

The Duke stumped off, and Lord Ickenham, armed with his great sponge Joyeuse, made his way to the bathroom. He had just got back from a refreshing dip, when there was a knock at the door and Horace entered. And, having done so, he stood staring dumbly.

Horace Davenport's face had two features that called for attention. From his father he had inherited the spacious Dunstable nose; from his mother, a Hilsbury-Hepworth, the large, fawnlike eyes which distinguish that family. This nose, as he gazed at Lord Ickenham, was twitching like a rabbit's, and in the eyes behind their tortoiseshell-rimmed spectacles there was dawning slowly a look of incredulous horror. It was as if he had been cast for the part of Macbeth and was starting to run through the Banquo's ghost scene.

The events of the evening had come as a great shock to Horace. Firmly convinced for some time past that his Uncle Alaric was one of England's outstanding schizophrenic cases, a naturally nervous disposition had led him to look on the latter's mental condition as something which might at any moment spread to himself, like a cold in the head. The double hallucination which he had so recently experienced, coming on top of the delusion he had had about seeing Baxter at the Ball, had rendered him apprehensive in the last degree, and he had welcomed the suggestion that he should get together with Sir Roderick Glossop for a quiet talk.

And now, so all his senses told him, he was suffering yet another hallucination. In the bathrobed figure before him, he could have sworn that he was gazing at his late *fiancée*'s uncle, the Earl of Ickenham.

Yet this was the Red Room, and in the Red Room he had been specifically informed, Sir Roderick Glossop was to be found. Moreover, in the other's demeanour there was no suggestion of recognition, merely a courteous air of mild enquiry.

After what seemed an age-long pause, he managed to speak.

'Sir Roderick Glossop?'

'Yes.'

'Er – my name's Davenport.'

'Of course, yes. Come in, my dear fellow. You won't mind if I dress while we are talking? I haven't left myself too much time.'

Horace watched him with a dazed eye as he dived with boyish animation into a studded shirt. The grey head, popping out a moment later at shirt's end, gave him a renewed sense of shock, so intensely Ickenhamian was it in every respect.

A sudden feeble hope came to him that this time there might be a simple explanation. It might prove to be one of those cases of extraordinary physical resemblance of which you read in the papers.

'I – er – I say,' he asked, 'do you by any chance know a man named Lord Ickenham?'

'Lord Ickenham?' said Lord Ickenham, springing into dress trousers like a trained acrobat. 'Yes. I've met him.'

'You're amazingly like him, aren't you?'

Lord Ickenham did not reply for a moment. He was tying his tie, and on these occasions the conscientious man anxious to give of his best at the dinner-table rivets his attention on the task in hand. Presently the frown passed from his face, and he was his genial self again.

'I'm afraid I missed that. You were saying—'

'You and Lord Ickenham look exactly alike, don't you?'

His companion seemed surprised.

'Well, that's a thing nobody has ever said to me before. Considering that Lord Ickenham is tall and slender – while I am short and stout...'

'Short?'

'Quite short.'

'And stout?'

'Extremely stout.'

A low gulp escaped Horace Davenport. It might have been the expiring gurgle of that feeble hope. The sound caused his companion to look at him sharply, and as he did so his manner changed.

'You really must forgive me,' he said. 'I fear I missed the point of what you have been saying. Inexcusable of me, for your uncle gave me your case history. He told me how in the hall this evening you mistook my daughter and nephew for old acquaintances, and there was something about thinking that a man you saw at some Ball in London was his secretary Mr Baxter. Was that the first time this sort of thing happened?'

'Yes.'

'I see. The delusion metabolis came on quite suddenly, as it so often does. Can you suggest anything that might account for it?'

Horace hesitated. He shrank from putting his secret fears into words.

'Well, I was wondering…'

'Yes?'

'Is loopiness hereditary?'

'It can be, no doubt.'

'Noses are.'

'True.'

'This beezer of mine has come down through the ages.'

'Indeed?'

'So what I was wondering was, if a chap's got a dotty uncle, is he bound to catch it?'

'I would not say it was inevitable. Still…How dotty is your uncle?'

'Quite fairly dotty.'

'I see. Had your father any such structural weakness?'

'No. No, he was all right. He collected Japanese prints,' said Horace, with an afterthought.

'He didn't think he *was* a Japanese print?'

'Oh, no. Rather not.'

'Then that is all right. I feel sure that there need be no real anxiety. I am convinced that all that we are suffering from is some minor nervous lesion, brought about possibly by worry. Have we been worried lately?'

The question seemed to affect Horace Davenport much as it might have affected Job. He stared at his companion as at one who does not know the half of it.

'Have we!'

'We have?'

'You bet we have.'

'Then what we need is a long sea voyage.'

'But, dash it, we're a rotten sailor. Would you mind awfully if we got a second opinion?'

'By all means.'

'The other chap might simply tell us to go to Bournemouth or somewhere.'

'Bournemouth would be just as good. We came here in our car, did we not? Then directly after dinner I advise that we steal quietly off, without going through the strain of saying good-bye to anyone, and drive to London. Having reached London, we can pack anything that may be necessary and go to Bournemouth and stay there.'

'And you think that that will put us right?'

'Unquestionably.'

'And one other point. Would there be any medical objection to just one good, stiff, energetic binge in London? You see,' said Horace, with a touch of apology, 'we do rather feel, what with one thing and another, as if we wanted taking out of ourself at the moment.'

Lord Ickenham patted his shoulder.

'My dear boy, it is what any member of my profession would advise. Do we by any chance know a beverage called May Queen? Its full name is "Tomorrow'll be of all the year the maddest, merriest day, for I'm to be Queen of the May, mother, I'm to be Queen of the May". A clumsy title, generally shortened for purposes of ordinary conversation. Its foundation is any good, dry champagne, to which is added liqueur brandy, armagnac, kummel, yellow chartreuse and old stout, to taste. It is a good many years since I tried it myself, but I can thoroughly recommend it to alleviate the deepest despondency. Ah!' said Lord Ickenham, as a mellow booming rose from below. 'Dinner. Let us be going down. We do not want to be late for the trough our first night at a house, do we? Creates a bad impression.'

IT HAD been Lord Ickenham's intention, directly dinner was over, to seek out his nephew Pongo with a view to giving him a bracing pep talk. But a lengthy conference with his hostess delayed him in the drawing-room, and it was only after the subject of the Duke had been thoroughly threshed out between them that he was able to tear himself away. He found the young man eventually in the billiard-room, practising solitary cannons.

Pongo's demeanour at dinner had been such as to cause concern to an uncle and a fellow-conspirator. Solomon in all his glory, arrayed for the banquet, could not have surpassed him in splendour, but there is no question that he would have looked happier. Pongo's tie was right, and his shirt was right, and his socks were right, and the crease in his trousers was a genuine feast for the eye, but his resemblance to a fox with a pack of hounds and a bevy of the best people on its trail, which had been so noticeable all through the day, had become more pronounced than ever.

It was the cheerful, stimulating note, accordingly, that Lord Ickenham now set himself to strike. This wilting object before him was patently in need of all the cheer and stimulation he could get.

'Well, my young ray of sunshine,' he said, 'I can see by our expression that we are feeling that everything is going like a breeze. I hear you put it across Horace properly.'

Pongo brightened momentarily, as a veteran of Agincourt might have done at the mention of the name of Crispian.

'Yes, I put it across old H. all right.'

'You did indeed. You appear to have conducted yourself with admirable *sang-froid*. I am proud of you.'

'But what's the use?' said Pongo, subsiding into gloom once more. 'It can't last. Even a goop like Horace, though nonplussed for the moment, is bound to start figuring things out and arriving at the nub. Directly he sees you—'

'He has seen me.'

'Oh, my gosh! What happened?'

'We had a long and interesting conversation, and I am happy to be able to report that he is leaving immediately for Bournemouth, merely pausing in London on his way, like some butterfly alighting on a flower, in order to get pickled to the tonsils.'

Pongo, listening attentively to the *précis* of recent events, seemed grudgingly pleased.

'Well, that's something, I suppose,' he said. 'Getting Horace out of the place is better than nothing.'

His tone pained Lord Ickenham.

'You appear still moody,' he said reproachfully. 'I had supposed that my narrative would have had you dancing about the room, clapping your little hands. Is it possible that you are still finding Lady Constance a source of anxiety?'

'And that man Baxter.'

Lord Ickenham waved a cue in airy scorn of his hostess and the spectacled secretary.

'Why do you bother about Connie and Baxter? A gorilla could lick them both. What has she been doing to you?'

'She hasn't been doing anything, exactly. She's been quite matey, as a matter of fact. But my informants were right. She is the sort of woman who makes you feel that, no matter how suave her manner for the nonce, she is at heart a twenty-minute egg and may start functioning at any moment.'

Lord Ickenham nodded.

'I know what you mean. I have noticed the same thing in volcanoes, and the head mistress of my first kindergarten was just like that. It is several years, of course, since I graduated from the old place, but I can remember her vividly. The sweet, placid face... the cooing voice...but always, like some haunting strain in a piece of music, that underlying suggestion of the sudden whack over the knuckles with a ruler. Why did Baxter jar upon you?'

'He kept asking me questions about my methods of work.'

'Ah, the two secs getting together and swapping shop. I thought that might happen.'

'Then I wish you had warned me. That bird gives me the creeps.'

'He struck you as sinister, did he? I have felt the same thing myself. Our conversation on the platform left me not altogether satisfied in my mind about that young man. It seemed to me that during my explanations with reference to the poor fellow on the

train who thought he was Sir Roderick Glossop I detected a
certain dryness in his manner, a subtle something that suggested
that, lacking our friend Bosham's Norman blood, he was equally
deficient in that simple faith which the poet ranks even more
highly. If you ask me, my dear Pongo, Baxter suspects.'

'Then I'm jolly well going to get out of this!'

'Impossible. Have you forgotten that Polly has to fascinate the
Duke and will be lost without you beside her to stimulate and
encourage? Where's your chivalry? A nice figure you would have
cut at King Arthur's Round Table.'

He had found the talking point. Pongo said Yes, there was
something in that. Lord Ickenham said he had known that Pongo
would arrive at that conclusion, once he had really given his keen
brain to the thing.

'Yes,' he said, 'we have set our hands to the plough, and we
cannot sheathe the sword. Besides, I shall require your help in
snitching the pig. But I was forgetting. You are not abreast of that
side of our activities, are you? Emsworth has a pig. The Duke
wants it. Emsworth would like to defy him, but dare not, owing to
that twist in the other's character which leads him, when defied on
any premises, to give those premises the works with a poker. So, on
my advice, he is resorting to strategy. I have promised him that we
will remove the animal from its sty, and you will then drive it across
country to Ickenham, where it can lie low till the danger is past.'

It was not often that Pongo Twistleton disarranged his hair,
once he had brushed it for the evening, but he did so now. Such
was his emotion that he plunged both hands through those perfect
waves.

'Ha!'

'I keep asking you not to say "Ha!" my boy.'

'So that's the latest, is it? I'm to become a blasted pig's chauf-
feur, am I?'

'A brilliant summing-up of the situation. Flaubert could not
have put it better.'

'I absolutely and definitely refuse to have anything to do with
the bally scheme.'

'That is your last word?'

'Specifically.'

'I see. Well, it's a pity, for Emsworth would undoubtedly have
rewarded you with a purse of gold. Noblesse would have obliged.

He has the stuff in sackfuls, and this pig is the apple of his eye. And you could do with a purse of gold just now, could you not?'

Pongo started. He had missed this angle of the situation.

'Oh! I didn't think of that.'

'Start pondering on it now. And while you are doing so,' said Lord Ickenham, 'I will show you how billiards should be played. Watch this shot.'

He had begun to bend over the table, a bright eye fixed on the object ball, when he glanced round. The door had opened, and he was aware of something like a death ray playing about his person.

Rupert Baxter was there, staring at him through his spectacles.

To most people at whom the efficient Baxter directed that silent, steely, spectacled stare of his there was wont to come a sudden malaise, a disposition to shuffle the feet and explore the conscience guiltily: and even those whose consciences were clear generally quailed a little. Lord Ickenham, however, continued undisturbed.

'Ah, my dear Baxter. Looking for me?'

'I should be glad if you could spare me a moment.'

'Something you want to talk to me about?'

'If you have no objection.'

'You have not come to consult me in my professional capacity, I trust? We have not been suffering from delusions, have we?'

'I never suffer from delusions.'

'No, I should imagine not. Well, come on in. Push off, Basil.'

'He can remain,' said Baxter sombrely. 'What I have to say will interest him also.'

It seemed to Pongo, as he withdrew into the farthest corner of the room and ran a finger round the inside of his collar, that if ever he had heard the voice of doom speak, he had heard it then. To him there was something so menacing in the secretary's manner that he marvelled at his uncle's lack of emotion. Lord Ickenham, having scattered the red and spot balls carelessly about the table, was now preparing to execute a tricky shot.

'Lovely evening,' he said.

'Very. You had a pleasant walk, I hope?'

'That is understating it. Ecstatic,' said Lord Ickenham, making a dexterous cannon, 'would be a better word. What with the pure air, the majestic scenery, the old gypsy feeling of tramping along the high road and the Duke's conversation, I don't know when I have enjoyed a walk more. By the way, the Duke was telling me that there had been a little friction on your arrival. He said he had handed you the two weeks' notice because Horace Davenport told him that he had seen you at a Ball in London.'

'Yes.'

'Everything satisfactory now, I hope?'

'Quite. He discovered that he had been misinformed, and apologized. I am continuing in his employment.'

'I'm glad. You wouldn't want to lose a job like that. A man can stick on a lot of side about being secretary to a Duke. Practically as good as being a Duke himself. I am afraid Basil here has no such excuse for spiritual uplift. Just an ordinary secretary – Basil.'

'A very peculiar one, I should have said.'

'Peculiar? In what respect? In the words of the bridegroom of Antigua, is it manners you mean or do you refer to his figuah?'

'He seems ignorant of the very rudiments of his work.'

'Yes, I fear poor Basil would strike a man like you as something of an amateur. He has not had your wide experience. You were Lord Emsworth's secretary once, were you not?'

'I was.'

A flush deepened the swarthiness of Rupert Baxter's cheek. He had been Lord Emsworth's secretary several times, and on each occasion his employer, aided by the breaks, had succeeded in throwing him out. He did not care to be reminded of these flaws in a successful career.

'And before that?'

'I was with Sir Ralph Dillingworth, a Yorkshire baronet.'

'Yours has been a very steady rise in the social scale,' said Lord Ickenham admiringly. 'Starting at the bottom with a humble baronet – slumming, you might almost call it – you go on to an earl and then to a duke. It does you credit.'

'Thank you.'

'Not at all. I think I've heard of Dillingworth. Odd sort of fellow, isn't he?'

'Very.'

'There was some story about him shooting mice in the drawing-room with an elephant gun.'

'Yes.'

'Painful for the family. For the mice, too, of course.'

'Most.'

'They should have called me in.'

'They did.'

'I beg your pardon?'

'I say they did.'

'I don't remember it.'

'I am not surprised.'

Rupert Baxter was sitting back in his chair, tapping the tips of his fingers together. It seemed to Pongo, watching him pallidly from afar, that if he had had a different-shaped face and had not worn spectacles he would have looked like Sherlock Holmes.

'It was unfortunate for you that I should have met the real Sir Roderick. When I saw him on the train, he had forgotten me, of course, but I knew him immediately. He has altered very little!'

Lord Ickenham raised his eyebrows.

'Are you insinuating that I am not Sir Roderick Glossop?'

'I am.'

'I see. You accuse me of assuming another man's identity, do you, of abusing Lady Constance's hospitality by entering her house under false pretences? You deliberately assert that I am a fraud and an impostor?'

'I do.'

'And how right you are, my dear fellow!' said Lord Ickenham. 'How right you are.'

Rupert Baxter continued to tap his fingertips together and to project through his spectacles as stern a glare as they had ever been called upon to filter, but he was conscious as he did so of a certain sense of flatness. Unmasked Guilt, in his opinion, should have taken it rather bigger than this man before him appeared to be doing. Lord Ickenham was now peering at himself in the mirror and fiddling with his moustache. He may have been feeling as if the bottom of his world had dropped out, but he did not look it.

'I don't know who you are—'

'Call me Uncle Fred.'

'I will not call you Uncle Fred!' said Rupert Baxter violently.

He restored his composure with a glance at Pongo. There, he felt, was Unmasked Guilt looking as Unmasked Guilt should look.

'Well, there you are,' he resumed, becoming calmer. 'The risk you run, when you impersonate another man, is that you are apt to come up against somebody to whom his appearance is familiar.'

'Trite, but true. Do you like me with my moustache like that? Or like this?'

Rupert Baxter's impatient gesture seemed to say that he was Nemesis, not a judge in a male beauty contest.

'Perhaps it would interest you now,' he said, 'to hear about the local train service.'

'Is there a milk train?' asked Pongo, speaking for the first time.

'I expect so,' said Baxter, giving him a cold look, 'but probably you would prefer to take the eight-twenty in the morning.'

Lord Ickenham seemed puzzled.

'You speak as if you were under the impression that we were leaving.'

'That is my impression.'

'You are not going to respect our little secret, then?'

'I intend to expose you immediately.'

'Even if I assure you that we did not come here after the spoons, but rather to do two loving hearts a bit of good?'

'Your motives do not interest me.'

Lord Ickenham gave his moustache a thoughtful twirl.

'I see. You are a hard man, Baxter.'

'I do my duty.'

'Not always, surely? How about the toot in London?'

'I don't understand you.'

'So you won't talk? Still, you know you went to that Ball at the Albert Hall. Horace Davenport saw you there.'

'Horace!'

'Yes, I admit that at the moment what Horace says is not evidence. But why is it not evidence, Baxter? Simply because the Duke, after seeing him make what appeared to be two bad shots at identifying people this evening, assumes that he must also have been mistaken in thinking that he saw you at the Ball. He supposes that his young relative is suffering from hallucinations. But if you denounce me, my daughter and nephew will testify that they really are the persons he supposed them to be, and it will become clear to the Duke that Horace is not suffering from hallucinations and that when he says he saw you at the Ball he did see you at the Ball. Then where will you be?'

He paused, and in the background Pongo revived like a watered flower. During this admirably lucid exposition of the state of affairs, there had come into his eyes a look of worshipping admiration which was not always there when he gazed at his uncle.

'At-a-boy!' he said reverently. 'It's a dead stymie.'

'I think so.'

Rupert Baxter's was one of those strong, square jaws which do not readily fall, but it had undeniably wavered, as if its steely muscles were about to relax. And though he hitched it up, there was dismay in the eyes behind the spectacles.

'It doesn't follow at all!'

'Baxter, it must follow as the night the day.'

'I shall deny—'

'What's the use? I have not known the Duke long, but I have known him long enough to be able to recognize him as one of those sturdy, tenacious souls, the backbone of England, who when they have once got an idea into their fat heads are not to be induced to relinquish it by any denials. No, if you do not wish to imperil the cordial relations existing between your employer and yourself, I would reflect, Baxter.'

'Definitely,' said Pongo.

'I would consider.'

'Like billy-o.'

'If you do, you will perceive that we stand or fall together. You cannot unmask us without unmasking yourself. But whereas we, unmasked, merely suffer the passing embarrassment of being thrown out by strong-armed domestics, you lose that splendid post of yours and have to go back to mixing with baronets. And how do you know,' said Lord Ickenham, 'that next time it would even be a baronet? It might be some bounder of a knight.'

He placed a kindly hand on the secretary's arm, and led him to the door.

'I really think, my dear fellow,' he said, 'that we had better pursue a mutual policy of Live and Let Live. Let our motto be that of the great Roi Pausole – *Ne nuis pas à ton voisin*. It is the only way to get comfortably through life.'

He closed the door. Pongo drew a deep breath.

'Uncle Fred,' he said, 'there have been times, I don't mind admitting, when I have viewed you with concern—'

'You mean that afternoon down at Valley Fields?'

'I was thinking more of our day at the Dog Races.'

'Ah, yes. We did slip up a little there.'

'But this time you have saved my life.'

'My dear boy, you embarrass me. A mere nothing. It is always my aim to try to spread sweetness and light.'

'I should describe that bird as baffled, wouldn't you?'

'Baffled as few secretaries have ever been, I think. We can look upon him, I fancy, as a spent force. And now, my boy, if you will excuse me, I must leave you. I promised the Duke to drop in on him for a chat round about ten o'clock.'

IN SUPPOSING that their heart-to-heart talk would cause Rupert Baxter to abandon his intention of making a public exposure of his machinations, Lord Ickenham had been correct. In his assumption that he had rendered the man behind the steel-rimmed spectacles a spent force, however, he had erred. Baxter's hat was still in the ring. At Blandings Castle he had a staunch ally in whom he could always confide, and it was to her boudoir that he made his way within five minutes of leaving the billiard-room.

'Could I speak to you for a moment, Lady Constance?'

'Certainly, Mr Baxter.'

'Thank you,' said the secretary, and took a seat.

He had found Lady Constance in a mood of serene content-ment. In the drawing-room over the coffee she had had an extended interview with that eminent brain specialist, Sir Roderick Glossop, and his views regarding the Duke, she was pleased to find, were in complete accord with her own. He endorsed her opinion that steps must be taken immediately, but assured her that only the simplest form of treatment was required to render His Grace a man who, if you put an egg into his hand, would not know what to do with it.

And she had been running over in her mind a few of his most soothing pronouncements and thinking what a delightful man he was, when in came Baxter. And within a minute, for he was never a man to beat about the bush and break things gently, he had wrecked her peace of mind as thoroughly as if it had been a sitting-room and he her old friend with a whippy-shafted poker in his hand.

'Mr Baxter!' she cried.

From anyone else she would have received the extraordinary statement which he had just made with raised eyebrows and a shrivelling stare. But her faith in this man was the faith of a little child. The strength of his personality, though she had a strong personality herself, had always dominated her completely.

'Mr BAX-ter!'

The secretary had anticipated some such reaction on her part. This spasm of emotion was what is known in the motion-picture world as 'the quick take 'um', and in the circumstances he supposed that it was inevitable. He waited in stern silence for it to expend itself.

'Are you sure?'

A flash of steel-rimmed spectacles told her that Rupert Baxter was not a man who made statements without being sure.

'He admitted it to me personally.'

'But he is such a charming man.'

'Naturally. Charm is the chief stock-in-trade of persons of that type.'

Lady Constance's mind was beginning to adjust itself to the position of affairs. After all, she reflected, this was not the first time that impostors had insinuated themselves into Blandings Castle. Her nephew Ronald's chorus-girl, to name one instance, had arrived in the guise of an American heiress. And there had been other cases. Indeed, she might have felt justified in moments of depression in yielding to the gloomy view that her visiting list consisted almost exclusively of impostors. There appeared to be something about Blandings Castle that attracted impostors as cat-nip attracts cats.

'You say he admitted it?'

'He had no alternative.'

'Then I suppose he has left the house?'

Something of embarrassment crept into Rupert Baxter's manner. His spectacles seemed to flicker.

'Well, no,' he said.

'No?' cried Lady Constance, amazed. Impostors were tougher stuff than she had supposed.

'A difficulty has arisen.'

It is never pleasant for a proud man to have to confess that scoundrels have got him in cleft sticks, and in Rupert Baxter's manner as he told his tale there was nothing of relish. But painful though it was, he told it clearly.

'To make anything in the nature of an overt move is impossible. It would result in my losing my post, and my post is all important to me. It is my intention ultimately to become the Duke's man of affairs, in charge of all his interests. I hope I can rely on you to do nothing that will jeopardize my career.'

'Of course,' said Lady Constance. Not for an instant did she contemplate the idea of hindering this man's rise to the heights. Nevertheless, she chafed. 'But is there nothing to be done? Are we to allow this person to remain and loot the house at his leisure?'

On this point, Rupert Baxter felt that he was in a position to reassure her.

'He is not here with any motive of robbery. He has come in the hope of trapping Horace Davenport into marriage with that girl.'

'What!'

'He virtually said as much. When I told him that I knew him to be an impostor, he said something flippant about not having come after the spoons but because he was trying to do what he described as "a bit of good to two loving hearts". His meaning escaped me at the time, but I have now remembered something which had been hovering on the edge of my mind ever since I saw these people at Paddington. I had had one of those vague ideas one gets that I had seen this girl before somewhere. It has now come back to me. She was at that Ball with Horace Davenport. One sees the whole thing quite clearly. In London, presumably, she was unable to make him commit himself definitely, so she has followed him here in the hope of creating some situation which will compel him to marry her.'

The fiendish cunning of the scheme appalled Lady Constance.

'But what can we do?'

'I myself, as I have explained, can do nothing. But surely a hint from you to the Duke that his nephew is in danger of being lured into a disastrous marriage—'

'But he does not know it is a disastrous marriage.'

'You mean that he is under the impression that the girl is the daughter of Sir Roderick Glossop, the brain specialist? But even so. The Duke is a man acutely alive to the existence of class distinctions, and I think that as a wife for his nephew he would consider the daughter of a brain specialist hardly—'

'Oh, yes,' said Lady Constance, brightening. 'I see what you mean. Yes, Alaric is and always has been a perfect snob.'

'Quite,' said Baxter, glad to find his point taken. 'I feel sure that it will not be difficult for you to influence him. Then I will leave the matter in your hands.'

The initial emotion of Lady Constance, when she found herself alone, was relief, and for a while nothing came to weaken this relief. Rupert Baxter, as always, seemed in his efficient way to have put everything right and pointed out with masterly clearness the solution of the problem. There was, she felt, as she had so often felt, nobody like him.

But gradually, now that his magnetic personality was no longer there to sway her mind, there began to steal over her a growing uneasiness. Specious though the theory was which he had put forward, that the current instalment of impostors at Blandings Castle had no designs on the castle's many valuable contents but were bent simply on the task of getting Horace Davenport into a morning coat and sponge-bag trousers and leading him up the aisle, she found herself less and less able to credit it.

To Lady Constance's mind, impostors were not like that. Practical rather than romantic, as she saw it, they preferred jewellery to wedding bells. They might not actually disdain the 'Voice That Breathed O'er Eden', but in their scale of values it ran a very poor second to diamond necklaces.

She rose from her chair in agitation. She felt that something must be done, and done immediately. Even in her alarm, of course, she did not consider the idea of finding Rupert Baxter and trying to argue him out of his opinions. One did not argue with Rupert Baxter. What he said, he said, and you had to accept it. Her desire was to buttonhole some soothingly solid person who would listen to her and either allay her fears or suggest some way of staving off disaster. And it so happened that Blandings Castle housed at that moment perhaps the most solid person who had ever said 'Yoicks' to a foxhound.

In the hope that he would also prove soothing, she hurried from the room in quest of her nephew, Lord Bosham.

Rupert Baxter, meanwhile, feeling in need of fresh air after the mental strain to which he had been subjected, had left the house and was strolling under the stars. His wandering feet had taken him to that velvet lawn which lay outside the Garden Suite. There, pacing up and down, brow knitted and hands clasped behind back, he gave himself up to thought.

His admission to Lady Constance that there was nothing which he himself could do in this situation which called so imperiously for decisive action had irked Rupert Baxter and wounded his self-esteem. That remark of Pongo's, moreover, about a dead stymie still rankled in his bosom like a poisoned dart. He was not accustomed to being laid dead stymies by the dregs of the underworld. Was there, he asked himself, no method by which he could express his personality, no means whereby he could make his presence felt? He concentrated on the problem exercising his brain vigorously.

It often happens that great brains, when vigorously exercised, find a musical accompaniment of assistance to their activities. Or, putting it another way, thinkers, while thinking, frequently whistle. Rupert Baxter did, selecting for his purpose a melody which had always been a favourite of his – the 'Bonny Bonny Banks of Loch Lomond'.

If he had been less preoccupied, he would have observed that at about the fourth bar a certain liveliness had begun to manifest itself behind the French window which he was passing. It opened softly, and a white-moustached head peered furtively out. But he was preoccupied, and consequently did not observe it. He reached the end of the lawn, ground a heel into the immemorial turf and turned. Starting his measured walk anew, he once more approached the window.

He was now singing. He had a pleasant tenor voice.

> 'You take the high road
> And I'll take the low road,
> And I'll be in Scotland a-FORE ye.
> For I and my true love
> Will never meet again—'

The starlight gleamed on a white-moustached figure.

> 'On the bonny bonny BANKS of Loch LO—'

Something whizzed through the night air…crashed on Rupert Baxter's cheek…spread itself in sticky ruin…

And simultaneously there came from the Garden Suite the sudden, sharp cry of a strong man in pain.

It was perhaps half an hour after he had left it that Lord Ickenham returned to the billiard-room. He found Pongo still there, but no longer alone. He had been joined by Lord Bosham, who had suggested a hundred up, and Lord Ickenham found the game nearing its conclusion, with Pongo, exhilarated by recent happenings, performing prodigies with the cue. He took a seat, and with a decent respect for the amenities waited in silence until the struggle was over.

Lord Bosham resumed his coat.

'Jolly well played, sir,' he said handsomely, a gallant loser. 'Jolly good game. Very jolly, the whole thing.' He paused, and looked at Lord Ickenham enquiringly. The latter had clicked his tongue and was shaking his head with an air of rebuke. 'Eh?' he said.

'It was simply that the irony of the thing struck me,' explained Lord Ickenham. 'Tragedy has been stalking through this house: doctors have been telephoned for, sick rooms made ready, cool compresses prepared: and here are you two young men carelessly playing billiards. Fiddling while Rome burns is about what it amounts to.'

'Eh?' said Lord Bosham again, this time adding a 'What?' to lend the word greater weight. He found him cryptic.

'Somebody ill?' asked Pongo. 'Not Baxter?' he went on, a note of hope in his voice.

'I would not say that Baxter was actually ill,' said Lord Ickenham, 'though no doubt much bruised in spirit. He got an egg on the left cheek-bone. But soap and water will by now have put this right. Far more serious is the case of the Duke. It was he who threw the egg, and overestimating the limberness of what is known in America, I believe, as the old soup-bone, he put his shoulder out. I left him drinking barley-water with his arm in a sling.'

'I say!' said Lord Bosham. 'How dashed unpleasant for him.'

'Yes, he didn't seem too elated about it.'

'Still,' argued Pongo, pointing out the bright side, 'he got Baxter all right?'

'Oh, he got him squarely. I must confess that my respect for the Duke has become considerably enhanced by tonight's exhibition of marksmanship. Say what you will, there is something fine about our old aristocracy. I'll bet Trotsky couldn't hit a moving secretary with an egg on a dark night.'

A point occurred to Lord Bosham. His was rather a slow mind, but he had a way of getting down to essentials.

'Why did old Dunstable bung an egg at Baxter?'

'I thought you might want to know that. Events moved towards the big moment with the inevitability of Greek tragedy.

There appears to be a member of the gardening staff of Blandings
Castle who has a partiality for the "Bonny Bonny Banks of Loch
Lomond", and he whistles and sings it outside the Duke's window, with the result that the latter has for some time been lying in
wait for him with a basket of eggs. Tonight, for some reason
which I am unable to explain, Baxter put himself on as an understudy. The Duke and I were in the Garden Suite, chatting of this
and that, when he suddenly came on the air and the Duke, diving
into a cupboard like a performing seal, emerged with laden hands
and started to say it with eggs. I should have explained that he has a
rooted distaste for that particular song. I gather that his sensitive
ear is offended by that rather daring rhyme – "Loch Lomond" and
"afore ye". Still, if I had given the matter more thought, I would
have warned him. You can't throw eggs at his age without—'

The opening of the door caused him to suspend his remarks.
Lady Constance came in. Her sigh of relief as she saw Lord
Bosham died away as she perceived the low company he was
keeping.

'Oh!' she said, surveying his foul associates with unconcealed
dislike, and Pongo, on whom the first full force of her gaze had
been turned, shook like a jelly and fell backwards against the
billiard-table.

Lord Ickenham, as usual, remained suave and debonair.

'Ah, Lady Constance. I have just been telling the boys about
the Duke's unfortunate accident.'

'Yes,' said Lord Bosham. 'It's true, is it, that the old bird has
bust a flipper?'

'He has wrenched his shoulder most painfully,' assented Lady
Constance, with a happier choice of phrase. 'Have you finished
your game, Bosham? Then I would like to speak to you.'

She led her nephew out, and Lord Ickenham looked after her
thoughtfully.

'Odd,' he said. 'Surely her manner was frigid? Did you notice a
frigidity in her manner, Pongo?'

'I don't know about her manner. Her eye was piping hot,' said
Pongo, who was still quivering.

'Warm eye, cold manner. . . . This must mean something. Can
Baxter have been blowing the gaff, after all? But no, he wouldn't
dare. I suppose it was just a hostess's natural reaction to having her
guests wrench themselves asunder and involve her in a lot of fuss

with doctors. Let us dismiss her from our thoughts, for we have plenty of other things to talk about. To begin with, that pig-snitching scheme is off.'

'Eh?'

'You remember I outlined it to you? It was to have started with you driving Emsworth's pig to Ickenham and ended with him gratefully pressing purses of gold into your hand, but I'm afraid it is not to be. The Duke's stranglehold on Emsworth, you will recall, was the fact that if the latter did not obey his lightest word he would wreck the home with a poker. This accident, of course, has rendered him incapable of any serious poker-work for some time to come, and Emsworth, seizing his advantage like a master-strategist, has notified him that he cannot have the pig. So he no longer wishes it snitched.'

Pongo had listened to this exposition with mixed feelings. On the whole, relief prevailed. A purse of gold would undoubtedly have come in uncommonly handy, but better, he felt, to give it a miss than to pass a night of terror in a car with a pig. Like so many sensitive young men, he shrank from making himself conspicu-ous, and only a person wilfully blind to the realities of life could deny that you made yourself dashed conspicuous, driving pigs across England in cars.

'Well,' he said, having considered, 'I could have used a purse of gold, but I don't know that I'm sorry.'

'You may be.'

'What do you mean?'

'Another complication has arisen, which is going to make it a little difficult for us to linger here and look about at our leisure for ways of collecting cash.'

'Oh, my gosh, what's wrong now?'

'I would not say that there was anything *wrong*. This is just an additional obstacle, and one welcomes obstacles. They put one on one's mettle and bring out the best in one.'

Pongo danced a step or two.

'Can't you tell me what has happened?'

'I will tell you in a word. You know Polly's minstrel boy. The poet with a punch.'

'What about him?'

'He will shortly be with us.'

'What?'

'Yes, he's joining the troupe. When we were alone together, after the tumult and the shouting had died and the captains and kings – I allude to Emsworth, Connie and the doctor – had departed, the Duke confided in me that he was going to show Emsworth what was what. That pig, he said, had been definitely promised to him, and if Emsworth thought he could double-cross him, he was dashed well mistaken. He intends to steal the pig, and has sent for Ricky Gilpin to come and do it. In my presence, he dictated a long telegram to the young man, commanding his instant presence.'

'But if Ricky comes here and meets Miss Pott, we shall be dished. You can't fool a hardheaded bird like that the way we did Horace.'

'No. That is why I called it an obstacle. Still, he will not actually be in residence at the castle. The Duke's instructions to him were to take a room at the Emsworth Arms. He may not meet Polly.'

'A fat chance!'

'Pretty obese, I admit. Still, we must hope for the best. Pull yourself together, my dear Pongo. Square the shoulders and chuck out the chest. Sing like the birdies sing – Tweet, tweet-tweet, tweet-tweet.'

'If you're interested in my plans, I'm going to bed.'

'Yes, do, and get a nice rest.'

'Rest!'

'You think you may have some difficulty in dropping off? Count sheep.'

'Sheep! I shall count Baxters and Lady Constances and loony uncles. Ha!' said Pongo, withdrawing.

Lord Ickenham took up a cue and gave the white ball a pensive tap. He was a little perplexed. The reference to Baxter and Lady Constance he could understand. It was the allusion to loony uncles that puzzled him.

Lady Constance Keeble was a gifted *raconteuse*. She had the knack of telling a story in a way that left her audience, even when it consisted of a nephew who had to have the He-and-She jokes in the comic papers explained to him, with a clear grasp of what she was talking about. After a shaky start, Lord Bosham followed her like a bloodhound. Long before she had finished speaking, he had gathered that what Blandings Castle was overrun with was impostors, not mice.

His first words indicated this.

'What ho!' he said. 'Impostors!'

'Impostors!' said Lady Constance, driving it home.

'What ho, what ho!' said Lord Bosham, giving additional proof that he was alive to the gravity of the situation.

A silence followed. Furrows across his forehead and a tense look on his pink face showed that Lord Bosham was thinking.

'Then, by Jove,' he said, 'this bird is the bird, after all! I thought for a while,' he explained, 'that he couldn't be the bird, but now you've told me this it's quite clear he must be the bird. The bird in the flesh, by Jingo! Well, I'm dashed!'

Lady Constance was very seldom in the mood for this sort of thing, and tonight after the nervous strain to which she had been subjected she was less in the mood for it than ever.

'What *are* you talking about, George?'

'This bird,' said Lord Bosham, seeing that he had not made himself clear. 'It turns out he was the bird, after all.'

'Oh, George!' Lady Constance paused for an instant. It was a hard thing that she was going to say, but she felt she must say it. 'Really, there are times when you are exactly like your father!'

'The confidence-trick bird,' said Lord Bosham, annoyed at her slowness of comprehension. 'Dash it, you can't have forgotten me telling you about the suave bimbo who got away with my wallet in Park Lane.'

Lady Constance's fine eyes widened.

'You don't mean—?'

'Yes, I do. That's just what I do mean. Absolutely. When I met him at the station, the first thing I said to myself was "What ho, the bird!" Then I said to myself: "What ho, no, not the bird." Because you had told me he was a big bug in the medical world. But now you tell me he isn't a big bug in the medical world—'

Lady Constance brought her hand sharply down on the arm of her chair.

'This settles it! Mr Baxter was wrong.'

'Eh?'

'Mr Baxter thinks that the reason these people have come here is that they are trying to trap Horace Davenport into marrying the girl. I don't believe it. They are after my diamond necklace. George, we must act immediately!'

'How?' asked Lord Bosham, and for the second time since their conference had begun Lady Constance was struck by the resemblance of his thought-processes to those of a brother whom she had often wanted to hit over the head with a blunt instrument.

'There is only one thing to do. We must—'

'But half a jiffy. Aren't you missing the nub? If you know these bounders are wrong 'uns, why don't we just whistle up the local police force?'

'We can't. Do you suppose I did not think of that? It would mean that Mr Baxter would lose his position with Alaric.'

'Eh? Why? What? Which? Wherefore? Why would Baxter lose his posish?'

It irked Lady Constance to be obliged to waste valuable time in order to explain the position of affairs, but she did it.

'Oh, ah?' said Lord Bosham, enlightened. 'Yes, I see. But couldn't he get another job?'

'Of course he could. But he was emphatic about wishing to continue in Alaric's employment, so what you suggest is out of the question. We must—'

'I'll tell you one thing. I don't intend to be far away from my gun these next few days. This is official.'

Lady Constance stamped her foot. It was not an easy thing for a sitting woman to do impressively, but she did it in a way that effectually silenced a nephew who in his boyhood had frequently been spanked by her with the back of a hairbrush. Lord Bosham, who had intended to speak further of his gun, of which he was very fond, desisted.

'Will you please not keep interrupting me, George! I say there is only one thing to do. We must send for a detective to watch these people.'

'Why, of course!' Like his younger brother, Frederick Threepwood, now over in the United States of America selling the dog-biscuits manufactured by the father of his charming wife, Lord Bosham was a great reader of thrillers, and anything about detectives touched a ready chord in him. 'That's the stuff! And you know just the man, don't you?'

'I?'

'Wasn't there a detective here last summer?'

Lady Constance shuddered. The visit of the person to whom he alluded had not passed from her memory. Sometimes she thought it never would. Occasionally in the late afternoon, when the vitality is low and one tends to fall a prey to strange, morbid fancies, she had the illusion that she was still seeing that waxed moustache of his.

'Pilbeam!' she cried. 'I would rather be murdered in my bed than have that man Pilbeam in the house again. Don't you know any detectives?'

'Me? No. Why should I know any...By Jove, yes, I do, though,' said Lord Bosham, inspired. 'By Jingo, now I come to think of it, of course I do. That man of Horace's.'

'What man of Horace's?'

Lord Bosham dissembled. Belatedly, he had realized that he was on the verge of betraying confidences. Horace, he recalled, when unburdening his soul during their drive from London, had sworn him to the strictest secrecy on the subject of his activities as an employer of private investigators.

'Well, when I say he was a man of Horace's, of course, I'm sort of speaking loosely. He was a fellow Horace told me about that a friend of his engaged to – to – er – do something or other.'

'And did he do it?'

'Oh, yes, he did it.'

'He is competent, then?'

'Oh, most competent.'

'What is his name?'

'Pott. Claude Pott.'

'Do you know his address?'

'I expect it would be in the book.'

'Then go and speak to him now. Tell him to come down here immediately.'

'Right ho,' said Lord Bosham.

THE DUKE'S decision, on receiving Lord Emsworth's ultimatum regarding the Empress of Blandings, to mobilize his nephew Ricky and plunge immediately into power politics was one which would have occasioned no surprise to anybody acquainted with the militant traditions of his proud family. It was this man's father who had twice cut down the barbed wire fence separating the garden of his villa in the South of France from the local golf links. His grandfather, lunching at his club, had once rubbed the nose of a member of the committee in an unsatisfactory omelette. The Dukes of Dunstable had always been men of a high and haughty spirit, swift to resent affronts and institute reprisals – the last persons in the world, in short, from whom you could hope to withhold pigs with impunity.

His shoulder, thanks to the prompt treatment it had received, had soon ceased to pain him. Waking next morning, he found himself troubled physically by nothing worse than an uncomfortable stiffness. But there was no corresponding improvement in his spiritual condition. Far into the night he had lain brooding on Lord Emsworth's chicanery, and a new day brought no relief. The bitterness still persisted, and with it the grim determination to fight for his rights.

At lunch-time a telegram came from his nephew saying that he was catching the five o'clock train, and at ten o'clock on the following morning, after another wakeful night, he summoned his secretary, Rupert Baxter, and bade him commandeer a car from the castle garage and drive him to the Emsworth Arms. He arrived there at half-past ten precisely, and a red-haired, thickset, freckled young man came bounding across the lounge to greet him.

Between Horace Davenport and his cousin Alaric Gilpin there was nothing in the nature of a family resemblance. Each had inherited his physique from his father, and the father of Ricky Gilpin had been an outsize gentleman with a chest like an all-in-wrestler's. This chest he had handed down to his son, together with enough muscle to have fitted out two sons. Looking at Ricky, you might be a little surprised that he wrote poetry, but you had no difficulty in understanding how he was able to clean up costermongers in Covent Garden.

But though externally as intimidating as ever and continuing to give the impression of being a young man with whom no prudent person would walk down a dark alley, Ricky Gilpin on this April morning was feeling a sort of universal benevolence towards all created things. A child could have played with him, and the cat attached to the Emsworth Arms had actually done so. Outwardly tough, inwardly he was a Cheeryble Brother.

There is nothing that so braces a young man in love as a statement on the part of the girl of his dreams, after events have occurred which have made him think her ardour has begun to cool, that he is the only man for her, and that though she may have attended dances in the company of Zulu warriors the latter are to be looked on as the mere playthings of an idle hour. Polly Pott's assurance after that scene at the Bohemian Ball that Horace Davenport was a purely negligible factor in her life had affected Ricky profoundly. And on top of that had come his uncle's telegram.

That telegram, he considered, could mean only one thing. He was about to be afforded the opportunity of placing him under an obligation – of putting him in a position, in short, where he could scarcely fail to do the decent thing in return. The Duke's attitude in the matter of sympathy and support for that onion soup project would, he felt, be very different after he had been helped out of whatever difficulty it was that had caused him to start dispatching SOS's.

It was a buoyant and optimistic Ricky Gilpin who had caught the five o'clock train to Market Blandings on the previous afternoon, and it was a gay and effervescent Ricky Gilpin who now bounded forward with a hamlike hand outstretched. Only then did he observe that his relative's right arm was in a sling.

'Good Lord, Uncle Alaric,' he cried, in a voice vibrant with dismay and concern, 'have you hurt yourself? I'm so sorry. What a shame! How absolutely rotten! How did it happen?'

The Duke snorted.

'I put my shoulder out, throwing an egg at my secretary.'

Many young men, on receipt of this information, would have said the wrong thing. Ricky's manner, however, was perfect. He placed the blame in the right quarter.

'What the dickens was he doing, making you throw eggs at him?' he demanded indignantly. 'The man must be an ass. You ought to sack him.'

'I'm going to, directly we've had our talk. It was only this morning that I found out he was the feller. Ever since I came here,' explained the Duke, 'there's been a mystery man whistling the "Bonny Bonny Banks of Loch Lomond" day in and day out on the lawn outside my room. Got on my nerves. Beastly song.'

'Foul.'

'I wasn't going to stand it.'

'Quite right.'

'I laid in eggs.'

'Very sensible.'

'To throw at him.'

'Of course.'

'Last night, there he was again with his "You take the high road" and all the rest of it, and I loosed off. And this morning Connie comes to me and says I ought to be ashamed of myself for behaving like that to poor Mr Baxter.'

'What an absolutely imbecile thing to say! Who is this fathead?'

'Emsworth's sister. Lord Emsworth. Blandings Castle. I'm staying there. She's potty, of course.'

'Must be. Any balanced woman would have seen in a second that you had right on your side. It seems to me, Uncle Alaric,' said Ricky, with warmth, 'that you have been subjected to a campaign of deliberate and systematic persecution, and I'm not surprised that you decided to send for me. What do you want me to do? Throw some more eggs at this man Baxter? Say the word, and I start today.'

If his arm had not been in a sling, the Duke would have patted his nephew on the back. He was conscious of a keen remorse for having so misjudged him all these years. Ricky Gilpin might have his faults – one looked askance at that habit of his of writing poetry – but his heart was sound.

'No,' he said. 'After tonight there won't be any Baxter to throw eggs at. I sacked him a couple of days ago, and with foolish kindheartedness took him back, but this time it's final. What I've come to talk to you about is this pig.'

'What pig would that be?'

'Emsworth's. And there's another high-handed outrage!'

Ricky was not quite able to follow the trend of his uncle's remarks.

'They've been setting the pig on you?' he asked, groping.

'Emsworth promised to give it to me.'

'Oh, I see.'

'Nothing down in writing, of course, but a gentleman's agreement, thoroughly understood on both sides. And now he says he won't.'

'What!' Ricky had not thought that human nature could sink so low. 'You mean he intends to go back on his sacred word? The man must be a louse of the first water.'

The Duke was now quite certain that he had been all wrong about this splendid young man.

'That's how it strikes you, eh?'

'It is how it would strike any right-thinking person. After all, one has a certain code.'

'Exactly.'

'And one expects other people to live up to it.'

'Quite.'

'So I suppose you want me to pinch this pig for you?' said Ricky.

The Duke gasped. His admiration for his nephew had now reached boiling point. He had been expecting to have to spend long minutes in tedious explanation. It was not often, he felt, that you found in the youth of today such lightning intelligence combined with so fine a moral outlook.

'Precisely,' he said. 'When you're dealing with men like Emsworth, you can't be too nice in your methods.'

'I should say not. Anything goes. Well, how do I set about it? I shall require some pointers, you know.'

'Of course, of course, of course. You shall have them. I have been giving this matter a great deal of thought. I lay awake most of last night—'

'What a shame!'

'– and before I went to sleep I had my plan of campaign mapped out to the last detail. I examined it this morning, and it seems to me flawless. Have you a pencil and a piece of paper?'

'Here you are. I'll tear off the top page. It has a few rough notes for a ballade on it.'

'Thanks. Now then,' said the Duke, puffing at his moustache under the strain of artistic composition, 'I'll draw a map for you. Here's the castle. Here's my room. It's got a lawn outside it. Lawn,' he announced, having drawn something that looked like a clumsily fried egg.

'Lawn,' said Ricky, looking over his shoulder. 'I see.'

'Now along here, round the end of the lawn, curves the drive. It curves past a thick shrubbery – that's at the farther side of the lawn – and then curves past a meadow which adjoins the kitchen garden. In this meadow,' said the Duke, marking the spot with a cross, 'is the sty where the pig resides. You see the strategic significance of this?'

'No,' said Ricky.

'Nor did I,' admitted the Duke handsomely, 'till I was brushing my teeth this morning. Then it suddenly flashed on me.'

'You have an extraordinarily fine brain, Uncle Alaric. I've sometimes thought you would have made a great general.'

'Look at it for yourself. Anybody removing that pig from its sty could dive into the shrubbery with it, thus securing excellent cover, and the only time he would be in danger of being observed would be when he was crossing the lawn to my room. And I propose to select a moment for the operation when there will be no eyewitnesses.'

Ricky blinked.

'I don't quite follow that, Uncle Alaric. You aren't going to keep the animal in your room?'

'That is exactly what I am going to do. It's on the ground floor, with serviceable French windows. What simpler than to bring the pig in through these windows and lodge it in the bathroom?'

'What, and keep it there all night?'

'Who said anything about night? It enters the bathroom at two o'clock in the afternoon. Use your intelligence. At two o'clock in the afternoon everyone's at lunch. Butler, footmen and so forth, all in the dining-room. Maids of all descriptions, their work in the bedrooms completed during the morning, in the kitchen or the housekeeper's room or wherever they go. And the pig-man, I happen to know, off having his dinner. The coast is clear. A thousand men could steal a thousand pigs from the piggeries of Blandings Castle at two o'clock in the afternoon, and defy detection.'

Ricky was impressed. This was unquestionably GHQ stuff. 'Throughout the afternoon,' continued the Duke, 'the pig remains in the bathroom, and continues to do so till nightfall. Then—'

'But, Uncle Alaric, somebody's sure to go into the bathroom before that. Housemaids with clean towels....'

The Duke swelled belligerently.

'I'd like to see anybody go into my bathroom, after I've issued orders that they're not to. I shall stay in my room all through the day, refusing admittance to one and all. I shall have my dinner there on a tray. And if any dashed housemaid thinks she's going to muscle in with clean towels, she'll soon find herself sent off with a flea in her ear. And during dinner you will return. You will have a car waiting here' – he prodded the sketch map with a large thumb – 'where the road curves along the bushes at the end of the lawn. You will remove the pig, place it in the car and drive it to my house in Wiltshire. That is the plan I have evolved. Is there anything about it you don't understand?'

'Not a thing, Uncle Alaric!'

'And you think you can do it?'

'On my head, Uncle Alaric. It's in the bag. And may I say, Uncle Alaric, that I don't believe there's another man in England who could have thought all that out as you have done. It's genius.'

'Would you call it that?'

'I certainly would.'

'Perhaps you're right.'

'I know I'm right. It's the most extraordinary exhibition of sheer ice-cold brainwork that I've ever encountered. What did you do in the Great War, Uncle Alaric?'

'Oh, this and that. Work of national importance, you know.'

'I mean, they didn't put you on the Staff?'

'Oh, no. Nothing of that sort.'

'What waste! What criminal waste! Thank God we had a Navy.'

The most delightful atmosphere now prevailed in the lounge of the Emsworth Arms. The Duke said it was extremely kind of Ricky to be so flattering. Ricky said that 'flattering' was surely hardly the word, for he had merely given a frank opinion which would have been the opinion of anybody who recognized genius when they came across it. The Duke said would Ricky have a drink? Ricky, thanking him profusely, said it was a bit early. The Duke asked Ricky if he had been writing anything lately. Ricky said not just lately, but he had a sonnet coming out in the *Poetry Review* next month. Dashed interesting things, sonnets, said the Duke, and asked if Ricky had regular hours for sitting at his desk or did he wait for an inspiration. Ricky said he found the policy that suited him best was to lurk quietly till an idea came along and then jump out and land on the back of its neck with both feet. The Duke said that if somebody offered him a million pounds he himself would be incapable of writing a sonnet. Ricky said Oh, it was just a knack – not to be compared with work that took real, hard thinking, and gave as an instance of such work the planning out of campaigns for stealing pigs. To do that said Ricky, a fellow really had to have something.

There was, in fact, only one word to describe what was in progress in that dim lounge – the word 'Love-feast'. And it was a thousand pities, therefore, that Ricky should have proceeded, as he now did, to destroy the harmony.

Poets, as a class, are business men. Shakespeare describes the poet's eye as rolling in a fine frenzy from heaven to earth, from earth to heaven, and giving to airy nothing a local habitation and a name, but in practice you will find that one corner of that eye is generally glued on the royalty returns. Ricky was no exception. Like all poets, he had his times of dreaminess, but an editor who sent him a cheque for a pound instead of the guinea which had been agreed upon as the price of his latest *morceau* was very little older before he found a sharp letter on his desk or felt his ear burning at what was coming over the telephone wire. And now, having accepted this commission and discussed it in broad outline, he was anxious to get the terms settled.

'By the way, Uncle Alaric,' he said.

'Hey?' said the Duke, who had been interrupted in what promised to be rather a long story about a man he had known in South Africa who had once written a limerick.

Ricky, though feeling that this sort of negotiation would have been better placed in the hands of one's agent, was resolute.

'There's just one small point,' he said. 'Would you rather give me your cheque before I do the job, or after?'

The cosy glow which had been enveloping the Duke became shot through by a sudden chill. It was as if he had been luxuriating in a warm shower-bath, and some hidden hand had turned on the cold tap.

'My cheque? What do you mean, my cheque?'

'For two hundred and fifty pounds.'

The Duke shot back in his chair, and his moustache, foaming upwards as if a gale had struck it, broke like a wave on the stern and rockbound coast of the Dunstable nose. A lesser moustache, under the impact of that quick, agonized expulsion of breath, would have worked loose at the roots. His recent high opinion of his nephew had undergone a sharp revision. Though there were many points on which their souls would not have touched, he was at one with Mr Pott in his dislike of parting with money. Only a man of very exceptional charm could have retained his esteem after asking him for two hundred and fifty pounds.

'What the devil are you talking about?' he cried. Ricky was looking anxious, like one *vis-à-vis* with a tiger and not any too sure that the bars of the cage are to be depended on, but he continued resolute.

'I am taking it for granted that you will now let me have the money to buy that onion soup bar. You remember we discussed it in London a few days ago. At that time five hundred was the price, but the man has since come down to two hundred and fifty, provided the cash is in his hands by the end of the week. The most convenient thing for me, of course, would be if you would write out a cheque now. Then I could mail it to him this morning and he would get it first thing tomorrow. Still, suit yourself about that. Just so long as I get the money by Friday—'

'I never heard anything so dashed absurd in my life!'

'You mean you won't give me two hundred and fifty pounds?'

'Of course I mean I won't give you two hundred and fifty pounds,' said the Duke, recovering his moustache and starting to chew it. 'Gah!' he said, summing up.

The love-feast was over.

A tense silence fell upon the lounge of the Emsworth Arms.

'I thought I had heard the last of that silly nonsense,' said the Duke, breaking it. 'What on earth do you want with an onion soup bar?'

It was perhaps the memory of how close they had been to one another only a few brief minutes back – two of the boys kidding back and forth about the Sonnet question, as you might say – that decided Ricky to be frank with his uncle. He was conscious as he spoke that frankness is a quality that can be overdone and one

which in the present case might lead to disagreeable consequences, but some powerful argument had to be produced if
there was to be a change for the better in the other's attitude.
And there was just a chance – Mr Pott in his Silver Ring days
would probably have estimated it at 100–8 – that what he was
about to say would touch the man's heart. After all, the toughest
specimens were sometimes melted by a tale of true love.

'I want to get married,' he said.

If the Duke's heart was touched, his rugged exterior showed
no sign of it. His eyes came out of his head like a prawn's, and once
more his moustache foamed up against his breakwater of a nose.

'Married?' he cried. 'What do you mean, married? Don't be
an ass.'

Ricky had started the day with a tenderness towards all created
things, and this attitude he had hoped to be able to maintain. But
he could not help feeling that Providence, in creating his Uncle
Alaric, was trying him a little high.

'I never heard such nonsense in my life. How the devil can you
afford to get married? You've got about twopence a year which
your mother left you, and I don't suppose you make enough out
of those sonnets of yours to keep you in cigarettes.'

'That's why I want to buy this onion soup bar.'

'And a nice fool you would look, selling onion soup.'

With a strong effort, Ricky succeeded in making no comment
on this. It seemed to him that silence was best. Galling though it
was to allow his companion to score debating points, it was better
than to close all avenues leading to an appeasement with a blistering repartee. At the moment, moreover, he could not think of a
blistering repartee.

The Duke's moustache was rising and falling like seaweed on
an ebb tide.

'And a nice fool I'd look, going about trying to explain away a
nephew who dished soup out of a tureen. It's been bad enough
having to tell my friends you write poetry. "What's that nephew
of yours doing these days?"' the Duke proceeded, giving an
imitation of an enquiring friend with – for some reason – a falsetto
voice. '"The Guards? Diplomatic Service? Reading for the Bar?"
"No," I tell them. "He's writing poetry," and there's an awkward
silence. And now you want me to have to spread it about that
you've become a blasted soup-dispenser. Gah!'

A deep flush had spread itself over Ricky's face. His temper, always a little inclined to be up and doing, had begun to flex its muscles like an acrobat about to do a trick.

'As for this idea of yours of getting married ... Why do you want to get married? Hey? Why?'

'Oh, just to score off the girl. I dislike her.'

'What!'

'Why do you think I want to get married? Why do people usually want to get married? I want to get married because I've found the most wonderful girl in the world, and I love her.'

'You said you disliked her.'

'I was merely trying to be funny.'

The Duke took in a mouthful of moustache, chewed it for a moment, seemed dissatisfied with the flavour and expelled it again with another forceful puff.

'Who is she?'

'Nobody you know.'

'Well, who's her father?'

'Oh, nobody special.'

A sudden, sinister calm fell upon the Duke, causing his manner to resemble that of a volcano which is holding itself in by sheer will-power.

'You don't need to tell me any more. I see it all. The wench is a dashed outsider.'

'She is not!'

'Don't argue with me. Well, that settles it. Not a penny do you get from me.'

'All right. And not a pig do you get from me.'

'Hey?'

The Duke was taken aback. It was seldom that he found himself in the position of having to deal with open mutiny in the ranks. Indeed, the experience had never happened to him before, and for an instant he was at a loss. Then he recovered himself, and the old imperious glare returned to his bulging eyes.

'Don't take that tone with me, young man.'

'Not one single, solitary porker do you set your hands on,' said Ricky. 'My price for stealing pigs is two hundred and fifty pounds per pig per person, and if you don't wish to meet my terms, the deal is off. If, on the other hand, you consent to pay this absurdly moderate fee for a very difficult and exacting piece of work, I on my side am willing to overlook the offensive things you have said about a girl you ought to think yourself honoured to have the chance of welcoming into the family.'

'Stop talking like a damned fool. She's obviously the scum of the earth. The way a man's nephews get entangled with the dregs of the human species is enough to give one apoplexy. I absolutely forbid you to marry this female crossing-sweeper.'

Ricky drew a deep breath. His face was like a stormy sky, and his eyes bored into his uncle like bradawls.

'Uncle Alaric,' he said, 'your white hairs protect you. You are an old man on the brink of the tomb—'

The Duke started.

'What do you mean, on the brink of the tomb?'

'On the brink of the tomb,' repeated Ricky firmly. 'And I am not going to shove you into it by giving you the slosh on the jaw which you have been asking for with every word you have uttered. But I would just like to say this. You are without exception the worst tick and bounder that ever got fatty degeneration of the heart through half a century of gorging food and swilling wine wrenched from the lips of a starving proletariat. You make me sick. You poison the air. Good-bye, Uncle Alaric,' said Ricky, drawing away rather ostentatiously. 'I think that we had better terminate this interview, or I may become brusque.'

With a parting look of a kind which no nephew should have cast at an uncle, Ricky Gilpin strode to the door and was gone. The Duke remained where he sat. He felt himself for the moment incapable of rising.

It is bad enough for a man of imperious soul to be defied by a beardless boy, and his nephew's determination, in face of his opposition, to cling to the ballet girl or whatever she might be with whom he had become entangled would have been in itself enough to cause a temporary coma. But far more paralysing was the reflection that in alienating Ricky Gilpin he had alienated the one man who could secure the person of the Empress for him. Pig-kidnappers do not grow on every bush.

The Duke of Dunstable's mind was one of those which readily fall into the grip of obsessions, and though reason now strove to convince him that there were prizes in life worth striving for beside the acquisition of a pig, he still felt that only that way lay happiness and contentment. He was a man who wanted what he wanted when he wanted it, and what he wanted now was the Empress of Blandings.

A cold voice, speaking at his side, roused him from his reverie.

'Pardon me, your Grace.'

'Hey? What's the matter?'

Rupert Baxter continued to speak coldly. He was feeling bleakly hostile towards this old image. He disliked people who threw eggs at him. Nor was he the man to allow himself to be softened by any sportsmanlike admiration for a shot which had unquestionably been a very creditable one, showing great accuracy of aim under testing conditions.

'A policeman has just informed me that I must move the car from the inn door.'

'He has, has he? Well, tell him from me that he's a blasted officious jack-in-office.'

'With your Grace's permission, I propose to drive it round the corner.'

The Duke did not speak. A sudden, flaming inspiration had come to him.

'Hey, you,' he said. 'Sit down.'

Rupert Baxter sat down. The Duke eyed him closely, and felt that his inspiration had been sound. The secretary, he observed, had a strong, well-knit frame, admirably suited for the performance of such feats as the removal of pigs from their sties. A moment before, he had been feeling that, Ricky having failed him, he would seek in vain for an assistant to do the rough work. And now, it seemed, he had found him. From this quarter he anticipated no defiance. He was well aware of the high value which Rupert Baxter placed upon his job.

'Ever done any pig-stealing?' he asked.

'I have not,' said Rupert Baxter coldly.

'Well, you start today,' said the Duke.

IT WAS at about three o'clock that afternoon that the Market Blandings station cab (Ed. Robinson, propr.) turned in at the gates of Blandings Castle and started creakily up the long drive. And presently Mr Pott, seated in its smelly interior, was setting eyes for the first time on the historic home of the Earls of Emsworth.

His emotions, as he did so, differed a good deal from those of the ordinary visitor in such circumstances. Claude Pott was a realist, and this tended to colour his outlook. Where others, getting their initial glimpse of this last stronghold of an old order, usually admired the rolling parkland and the noble trees or thrilled with romantic awe as they thought of what sights those grey walls must have seen in the days when knights were bold, he merely felt that the owner of a place like this must unquestionably have what it takes to play Persian Monarchs.

Mr Pott, like Ricky, had arrived at Market Blandings in good spirits. Lord Bosham's telephone call, coming through just as he was dropping off to sleep, had at first inclined him to peevishness. But when he discovered that he was talking to a client, and not only to a client but a client who was inviting him to Blandings Castle, he had become sunny to a degree. And this sunniness still lingered.

Ever since he had made Lord Emsworth's acquaintance, Claude Pott had been sighing for a closer intimacy with one whom his experienced eye had classified immediately as the king of the mugs. There, he had felt, went one literally designed by Nature to be a good man's opponent at Persian Monarchs, and the thought that they had met and parted like ships that pass in the night was very bitter to him. And now he was being asked to come to Lord Emsworth's home and, what was more, was being paid for coming.

Little wonder that life looked rosy to Claude Pott. And he was still suffused with an optimistic glow, when the cab drew up at the front door and he was conducted by Beach, the butler, to the smoking-room, where he found a substantial, pink young man warming a solid trouser-seat in front of a cheerful fire.

'Mr Claude Pott, m'lord,' announced Beach, and withdrew with just that touch of aloofness in his manner which butlers exhibit when they would prefer not to be held responsible for peculiar visitors.

The pink young man, on the other hand, was cordiality itself.

'Hullo, Pott. So here you are, Pott, what? Fine. Splendid. Excellent. Capital. Take a seat, dear old clue-collector. My name's Bosham. I'm by way of being Lord Emsworth's son. To refresh your memory, I'm the bird who rang you up.'

Mr Pott found himself unable to speak. The sight of his employer had stirred him to his depths.

Up till now, he had regarded Lord Emsworth as the most promising claim that any prospector for ore could hope to stake out, but one glance at the latter's son told him that he had been mistaken. This was the mug of a good man's dreams. For a long instant he stood staring silently at Lord Bosham with the same undisguised interest which stout Cortez had once displayed when inspecting the Pacific. It is scarcely exaggerating to say that Mr Pott was feeling as if a new planet had swum into his ken.

Lord Bosham, too, after that opening speech of welcome, had fallen into a thoughtful silence. Like so many men who have done their business on the mail-order system, he was reflecting, now that the parcel had been unwrapped, that it would have been more prudent to have inspected the goods before purchasing. It seemed to him, as it had seemed to Pongo Twistleton on a former occasion, that if this rummy object before him was a detective, his whole ideas about detectives would have to be revised from the bottom up.

'You *are* the right Pott?' he said.

Mr Pott seemed to find a difficulty in helping him out. The question of the rightness or wrongness of Potts appeared to be one on which he was loth to set himself up as an authority.

'The private investigator, I mean. The bloodstain-and-magnifying-glass bloke.'

'My card,' said Pott, who had been through this sort of thing before.

Lord Bosham examined the card, and was convinced.

'Ah,' he said. 'Fine. Well, going back to what I was saying, here you are, what?'

'Yes, sir.'

'I was expecting you yesterday.'

'I'm sorry, Lord B. I'd have come if I could. But the boys at the Yard just wouldn't let me.'

'What yard would that be?'

'Scotland Yard.'

'Oh, ah, of course. You work for them, do you?' said Lord Bosham, feeling that this was more the stuff.

'When they get stuck, they generally call me in,' said Pott nonchalantly. 'This was a particularly tough job.'

'What was it?'

'I can't tell you that,' said Mr Pott, 'my lips being sealed by the Official Secrets Act, of which you have doubtless heard.'

Lord Bosham felt that his misgivings had been unworthy. He remembered now that quite a number of the hottest detectives on his library list had been handicapped – or possibly assisted – by a misleading appearance. Buxton Black in *Three Dead at Mistleigh Court* and Drake Denver in *The Blue Ribbon Murders* were instances that sprang to the mind. The former had looked like a prosperous solicitor, the latter like a pleasure-loving young man about town. What Mr Pott looked like he could not have said on the spur of the moment, but the point was that it didn't matter.

'Well, let's get down to it, shall we?'

'I should be glad to have a brief outline of the position of affairs.'

'Brief?' Lord Bosham looked dubious. 'I'm not so sure about that. As a matter of fact, bloodhound, it's rather a long and intricate story. But I'll cut it as short as I can. Do you know what impostors are?'

'Yes, sir.'

'Well, we've got them in the house. That's the nub of the thing. Three of them – count 'em! Three! – all imposting away like the dickens.'

'H'm.'

'You may well say "H'm." It's a most exasperating state of affairs, and I don't wonder my aunt's upset. Not nice for a woman, feeling that every time she goes to her room to fetch a handkerchief or what not she may find the place littered with bounders rifling her jewel-case.'

'Are these impostors male?'

'Two of them are. The third, in sharp contra-distinction, is female. And speaking of her brings us to what you will probably find it convenient to register in your mind as the Baxter Theory. Do you register things in your mind, or do you use a notebook?'

'Is Baxter an impostor?'

'No,' said Lord Bosham, with the air of one being fair. 'He's a gosh-awful tick with steel-rimmed spectacles, but he's not an impostor. He's the Duke's secretary, and his theory is that these blighters are here not for what they can pouch, but in order to lure the Duke into allowing his nephew to marry the girl. Ingenious, of course, but in my opinion there is nothing to it and you may dismiss it absolutely. They are after the swag. Well, when I tell you that one of them played the confidence trick on me a couple of days ago, you will be able to estimate the sort of hell-hounds they are. Write them down in your notebook, if you use a notebook, as men who will stick at nothing.'

Mr Pott was beginning to feel fogged. If anything emerged clearly from this narrative, it seemed to him that it was the fact that the entire household was fully aware of the moral character of these miscreants. And yet they were apparently being given the run of the house and encouraged to make themselves at home.

'But if you know that these individuals are here with criminal intent—'

'Why don't we have them led off with gyves upon their wrists? My dear old cigar-ash inspector, it's what I'd give my eye-teeth to do, but it can't be done. You wouldn't understand, if I explained for an hour, so just take it at this, that no − what's that word beginning with "o"?'

'What word beginning with "o"?'

'That's what I'm asking you. Opal? Oval? Ha! Got it! Overt. You must just accept the fact that no overt act can be contemplated, because it would lead to consequences which we don't want led to. When I say "we", I speak principally for my aunt. Personally, I don't care if Baxter loses his job tomorrow.'

Mr Pott gave it up.

'I don't follow you, Lord B.'

'I thought you wouldn't. Still, you've grasped the salient fact that the place is crawling with impostors?'

Mr Pott said he had.

'Then that's all right. That's all you really need to know. Your job is to keep an eye on them. See what I mean? You follow them about watchfully, and if you see them dipping into the till, you shout "Hoy!" and they cheese it. That's simple enough? Fine,' said Lord Bosham. 'Capital. Excellent. Splendid. Then you can start in at once. And, by the way, you'd like something in the nature of a retaining fee, what?'

Mr Pott said he would, and his employer suddenly began to spray bank-notes like a fountain. It was Lord Bosham's prudent practice, when he attended a rural meeting, as he proposed to do on the morrow, to have plenty of ready cash on his person.

'Call it a tenner?'

'Thank you, Lord B.'

'Here you are, then.'

Mr Pott's eyes were glistening a little, as he trousered the note.

'You've got a lot of money there, Lord B.'

'And I may need it before tomorrow's sun has set. It's the first day of the Bridgeford races, where I usually get skinned to the bone. Very hard to estimate form at these country meetings. You interested in racing?'

'I was at one time a turf commissioner, operating in the Silver Ring.'

'Good Lord! Were you really? My young brother Freddie was a partner in a bookie's firm once. His father-in-law made him give it up and go over to America and peddle dog-biscuits. Absorbing work.'

'Most.'

'I expect you miss it, don't you?'

'I do at times, Lord B.'

'What do you do for amusement these days?'

'I like a quiet little game of cards.'

'So do I.' Lord Bosham regarded this twin soul with a kindly eye. Deep had spoken to deep. 'Only the trouble is, it's a dashed difficult thing for a married man to get. You a married man?'

'A widower, Lord B.'

'I wish you wouldn't keep saying "Lord B". It sounds as if you had been starting to call me something improper and changed your mind. Where was I? Oh, yes. When I'm at home, I don't get a chance of little games of cards. My wife objects.'

'Some wives are like that.'

'All wives are like that. You start out in life a willing, eager sportsman, ready to take anybody on at anything, and then you meet a girl and fall in love, and when you come out of the ether you find not only that you are married but that you have signed on for a lifetime of bridge at threepence a hundred.'

'Too true,' sighed Mr Pott.

'No more friendly little games with nothing barred except biting and bottles.'

'Ah!' said Mr Pott.

'We could do far worse,' said Lord Bosham, 'while we're waiting for these impostors to get up steam, than have a friendly little game now.'

'As your lordship pleases.'

Lord Bosham winced.

'I wish you wouldn't use that expression. It was what counsel for the defence kept saying to the judge at my breach-of-promise case, every time the latter ticked him off for talking out of his turn. So don't do it, if you don't mind.'

'Very good, your lordship.'

'And don't call me "your lordship", either. I hate all this formality. I like your face … well, no, that's overstating it a bit … put it this way, I like your personality, bloodhound, and feel that we shall be friends. Call me Bosham.'

'Right ho, Bosham.'

'I'll ring for some cards, shall I?'

'Don't bother to do that, Bosham. I have some.'

The sudden appearance of a well-thumbed pack from the recesses of Mr Pott's costume seemed to interest Lord Bosham.

'Do you always go about with a pack of cards on you?'

'When I travel. I like to play solitaire in the train.'

'Do you play anything else?'

'I am fond of Snap.'

'Yes, Snap's a good game.'

'And Animal Grab.'

'That's not bad, either. But I can tell you something that's better than both.'

'Have—' said Mr Pott.

'Have you—' said Lord Bosham.

'Have you ever—' said Mr Pott.

'Have you ever,' concluded Lord Bosham, 'heard of a game called Persian Monarchs?'

Mr Pott's eyes rolled up to the ceiling, and for an instant he could not speak. His lips moved silently. He may have been praying.

'No,' he said, at length. 'What is it?'

'It's a thing I used to play a good deal at one time,' said Lord Bosham, 'though in recent years I've dropped it a bit. As I say, a married man of the right sort defers to his wife's wishes. If she's around. But now she isn't around, and it would be interesting to see if the old skill still lingers.'

'It's a pretty name,' said Mr Pott, still experiencing some trouble with his vocal cords. 'Is it difficult to learn?'

'I could teach it you in a minute. In its essentials it is not unlike Blind Hooky. Here's the way it goes. You cut a card, if you see what I mean, and the other fellow cuts a card, if you follow me. Then if the card you've cut is higher than the card the other fellow has cut, you win. While, conversely, if the card the other fellow's cut is higher than the card you've cut, he wins.'

He shot an anxious glance at Mr Pott, as if wondering if he had been too abstruse. But Mr Pott appeared to have followed him perfectly.

'I think I see the idea,' he said. 'Anyway, I'll pick it up as I go along. Come on, my noble sportsman. Follow the dictates of your heart and fear nothing. Roll, bowl or pitch! Ladies half-way and all bad nuts returned! If you don't speculate, you can't accumulate.'

'You have a rummy way of expressing yourself,' said Lord Bosham, 'but no doubt your heart is in the right place. Start ho, Pott?'

'Start ho, Bosham!'

Twilight had begun to fall, the soft mysterious twilight of an English spring evening, when a rotund figure came out of the front door of Blandings Castle and began to walk down the drive. It was Claude Pott, private investigator, on his way to the Emsworth Arms to have a couple. The beer, he knew, was admirable there. And if it should seem strange that one so recently arrived in Market Blandings was in possession of this local knowledge, it may be explained that his first act on alighting from the station cab had been to canvass Ed. Robinson's views on the matter.

Like some canny explorer in the wilds, Mr Pott, on coming to a strange place, always made sure of his drink supply before doing anything else.

Ed. Robinson, a perfect encyclopædia on the subject in hand, had been fluent and informative. But while he had spoken with a generous warmth of the Wheatsheaf, the Waggoner's Rest, the Beetle and Wedge, the Stitch in Time, the Blue Cow, the Blue Boar, the Blue Dragon and the Jolly Cricketers, for he was always a man to give credit where credit was due, he had made it quite clear where his heart lay, and it was thither that Mr Pott was now proceeding.

He walked slowly, with bowed head, for he was counting ten-pound notes. And it was because his head was bowed that he did not immediately observe the approach of his old friend Lord Ickenham, who was coming with springy steps along the drive towards him. It was only when he heard a surprised voice utter his name that he looked up.

Lord Ickenham had been for an afternoon ramble, in the course of which he had seen many interesting objects of the countryside, but here was one which he had not expected to see, and in his eyes as he saw it there was no welcoming glow. Claude Pott's advent, he could not but feel, added another complication to an already complicated situation. And even a man who holds that complications lend spice to life may legitimately consider that enough is enough.

'Mustard!'

'Coo! Lord I!'

'What on earth are you doing in the middle of Shropshire, Mustard?'

Mr Pott hesitated. For a moment, it seemed that professional caution was about to cause him to be evasive. Then he decided that so ancient a crony as his companion deserved to enjoy his confidence.

'Well, it's a secret, Lord I., but I know you won't let it go any further. I was sent for.'

'Sent for? By Polly?'

'Polly? She's not here?'

'Yes, she is.'

'I thought she was at your country seat.'

'No, she's at this country seat. Who sent for you?'

'A member of the aristocracy residing at Blandings Castle. Name of Bosham. He rang me up night before last, engaging my professional services. Seems there's impostors in the place, and he wants an eye kept on them.'

For the first time since George, Viscount Bosham, had come into his life, Lord Ickenham began to feel a grudging respect for that young man's intelligence stealing over him. It was clear that he had formed too low an estimate of this adversary. In lulling suspicion as he had done on the station platform by looking pink and letting his mouth hang open, while all the time he was planning to send for detectives, the other had acted, he was forced to confess, with a shrewdness amounting to the snaky.

'Does he, by Jove?' he said, giving his moustache a thoughtful twirl.

'Yes, I'm to take up my residence as an unsuspected guest and keep my eyes skinned to see that they don't walk off with the *objets d'art.*'

'I see. What did he tell you about these impostors? Did he go into details?'

'Not what you would call details. But he told me there was three of them – two *m*, one *f.*'

'Myself, my nephew Pongo and your daughter Polly.'

'Eh?'

'The impostors to whom Bosham refers are – reading from right to left – your daughter Polly, my nephew Pongo and myself.'

'You're pulling my leg, Lord I.'

'No.'

'Well, this beats me.'

'I thought it might. Perhaps I had better explain.'

Before starting to do so, however, Lord Ickenham paused for a moment in thought. He had just remembered that Mr Pott was not an admirer of Ricky Gilpin and did not approve of his daughter's desire to marry that ineligible young man. He also recalled that Polly had said that it was her father's hope that she would succumb to the charms of Horace Davenport. It seemed to him, therefore, that if Mr Pott's sympathy for and co-operation in their little venture was to be secured, it would be necessary to deviate slightly from the actual facts. So he deviated from them. He was a man who was always ready to deviate from facts when the cause was good.

'Polly,' he began, 'is in love with Horace Davenport.'

Mr Pott's eyes widened to saucerlike dimensions, and such was his emotion that he dropped a ten-pound note. Lord Ickenham picked it up, and looked at it with interest.

'Hullo! Somebody been leaving you a fortune, Mustard?'

Mr Pott smirked.

'Tantamount to that, Lord I. Young Bosham — and a nice young fellow he is — was teaching me to play Persian Monarchs.'

'You seem to have cleaned up.'

'I had beginner's luck,' said Mr Pott modestly.

'How much did you get away with?'

'Two hundred and fifty I make it. He had a system which involved doubling up when he lost.'

'That will make a nice little dowry for Polly. Help her to buy her trousseau.'

'Eh?'

'But I shall be coming back to that later. For the moment, I will be putting you *au courant* with the position of affairs at Blandings Castle. The key to the whole business, the thing you have to grasp at the outset, is that Polly is in love with Horace Davenport.'

'When you told me that, you could have knocked me down with a feather. I thought the one she was in love with was young Gilpin.'

'Oh, that? A mere passing flirtation. And even if it had been anything deeper, his behaviour at that Ball would have quenched love's spark.'

'Love's what?'

'Spark.'

'Oh, spark? Yes, that's right, too,' said Mr Pott, beginning to get the whole thing into perspective. 'Cursing and swearing and calling her names, all because she went to a dance with somebody, such as is happening in our midst every day. Seems he'd told her not to go. A nice way to carry on with a girl of spirit. What right has he to get bossy and tell my dear daughter what she can do and what she can't do? Who does he think he is? Ben Bolt?'

'Ben who?'

'Bolt. Bloke with the girl called Sweet-Alice-With-Hair-So-Brown who laughed with delight at his smile and trembled with fear at his frown. Does he expect my dear daughter to do that? Coo! Whoever heard of such a thing? Is this Greece?'

Lord Ickenham weighed the question.

'Not that I know of. Why?'

'I didn't mean Greece,' said Mr Pott, correcting himself with some annoyance. 'I meant Turkey, where women are kept in subjection and daren't call their souls their own. If Polly hadn't got a sweet nature, she'd have hit him with a bottle. But she's her mother's daughter.'

'Whose daughter did you expect her to be?'

'You don't apprehend my meaning, Lord I.,' said Mr Pott patiently. 'I meant that she takes after her dear mother in having a sweet nature. Her dear mother had the loving kindness of an angel or something, and so has Polly. That's what I meant. Her dear mother wouldn't hurt a fly, nor would Polly hurt a fly. I've seen her dear mother take a fly tenderly in her hand—'

Lord Ickenham interrupted. He would have liked to hear all about the late Mrs Pott and the insect kingdom, but time was getting on.

'Suppose we shelve the subject of flies for the moment, shall we, Mustard? Let us get back to Horace Davenport. As I was saying, he is the man Polly has got her eye on. And he loves her just as she loves him. He came down here the day after that dance, and we came the day after, following him.'

'Why?'

'It's quite simple. You know who Horace is, Mustard. The nephew and heir of the Duke of Dunstable.'

'Ah!' said Mr Pott, and seemed about to bare his head.

'And we have come here in the humble capacity of impostors because it is essential, if there is to be a happy ending, that Polly shall fascinate the Duke and set him thinking that she is the ideal girl to marry his nephew and heir. This Duke is tough, Mustard. He nails his collar to the back of his neck to save buying studs. Horace has been scared to death of him since infancy, and would never have the nerve to marry unless he first put up the All Right sign. Before Polly can walk up the aisle with Horace Davenport, the Duke has got to be worked on lovingly and patiently. And I cannot impress it upon you too emphatically that you must keep yourself in the background, Mustard. Polly is supposed to be my daughter.'

In a few well-chosen words Lord Ickenham sketched out the position of affairs. Mr Pott, when he had finished, seemed inclined to be critical.

'Seems a roundabout way of doing things,' he complained. 'Why couldn't she have come here as my daughter?'

'Well, it just happened to work out the other way,' said Lord Ickenham tactfully. 'Too late to do anything about it now. But you understand?'

'Oh, I understand.'

'I knew you would. Nobody has ever disparaged your intelligence, though I have known people to be a bit captious about that habit of yours of always cutting the ace. And that brings me back to what I was saying just now. This money you've taken off Bosham. Kiss it good-bye, Mustard.'

'I don't follow you, Lord I.'

'I want you to give me that money, my dear old friend—'

'What!'

'– and I will hand it over to Polly as her wedding portion. I know, I know,' said Lord Ickenham sympathetically. 'You've no need to tell me that it will be agony. I can see the thought searing your soul. But there comes a time in every man's life, Mustard, when he has to decide whether to do the fine, generous thing or be as the beasts that perish. Put yourself in Polly's place. The child must have her little bit of stuff, to make her feel that she is not going empty-handed to the man she loves. Her pride demands it.'

'Yes, but hoy—!'

'And think how you have always watched over her with a father's tender care. Did she have measles as a child?'

'Yes, she had measles, but that's not the point—'

'It is the point, Mustard. Throw your mind back to the picture of her lying there, flushed and feverish. You would have given all you possessed to help her then. I see your eyes are wet with tears.'

'No, they aren't.'

'Well, they ought to be.'

'I don't approve of a young girl having a lot of money. I wouldn't mind giving her a tenner.'

'Pah!'

'Yes, but two hundred and fifty—'

'A trifle compared with your peace of mind. If you fail her now, you will never have another happy moment. It would be criminal to allow a sensitive girl like Polly to get married without a penny in her pocket. You're a man of the world, Mustard. You know what buying a trousseau means. She will need two of everything. And can you subject her to the degradation of going and touching her future husband for those intimate articles of underclothing which a nice girl shrinks from naming when there are gentlemen present? Compel her to do so, and you leave a scar on her pure soul which the years may hide but which will always be there.'

Mr Pott shuffled his feet.

'She needn't tell him what she wants the money for.'

'For Heaven's sake, Mustard, don't try to evade the issue. Of course, she would have to tell him what she wanted the money for. A girl can't be whispering in the twilight with the man she loves and suddenly introduce a demand for two hundred and fifty pounds as a sort of side issue. She will have to get right down to it and speak of camisoles and slips. Are you going to force her to do that? It will not make very pleasant reading in your Biography, my dear chap. As I see it,' said Lord Ickenham gravely, 'you are standing at the cross-roads, Mustard. This way lies happiness for Polly, peace of mind for you ... that way, self-scorn for you, misery for her. Which road will you take? I seem to picture your late wife asking herself the same question. I can see her up there now ... watching ... waiting ... all agog ... wondering if you are going to do the square thing. Don't disappoint her, Mustard.'

Mr Pott continued to shuffle his feet. It was plain that in one sense he was touched, but not so certain that he intended to be in another.

'How about a nice twenty?'

'All or nothing, Mustard, all or nothing. Dash it, it's not as if the money would be lost. You can always take it off Horace at Persian Monarchs after the honeymoon.'

Mr Pott's face lit up with a sudden glow that made it for a moment almost beautiful.

'Coo! That's right, isn't it?'

'It seems to me to solve the whole difficulty.'

'Of course I can. Here you are, Lord I.'

'Thank you, Mustard. I knew you would not fail. And now, if you will excuse me, I will be going and taking a bath. In the course of my rambles I seem to have got quite a lot of Shropshire on my person. The moment I have removed it, I will find Polly and tell her the good news. You will never regret this, my dear fellow.'

In this prediction, Lord Ickenham was wrong. Mr Pott was regretting it rather keenly. He was not the man to see two hundred and fifty pounds pass from his possession without a pang, and already a doubt had begun to creep over him as to whether the transaction could, as his companion had so jauntily suggested, be looked on as merely a temporary loan. Long before he reached Market Blandings he had begun to wonder if he could really rely on Horace Davenport. It takes two to play Persian Monarchs, and it might be that Horace would prove to be one of those odd, unpleasant people who have no fondness for the game. He had sometimes met them on race trains.

However, there is always something stimulating in the doing of a good deed, and Claude Pott, as he entered the private bar of the Emsworth Arms, could have been written down as on the whole a reasonably happy man. He was at any rate sufficiently uplifted to be in a mood for conversation, and it was with the idea of initiating a feast of reason and a flow of soul that he addressed the only other occupant of the bar, a thick-set young man seated at its shadowy end.

'Nice day,' he said.

His fellow-customer turned, revealing himself as Ricky Gilpin.

CHAPTER 15

RICKY HAD come to the private bar in search of relief for his bruised soul, and he could have made no wiser move. Nothing can ever render the shattering of his hopes and the bringing of his dream castles to ruin about his ears really agreeable to a young man, but the beer purveyed by G. Ovens, proprietor of the Emsworth Arms, unquestionably does its best. The Ovens home-brewed is a liquid Pollyanna, for ever pointing out the bright side and indicating silver linings. It slips its little hand in yours, and whispers 'Cheer up!' If King Lear had had a tankard of it handy, we should have had far less of that 'Blow, winds, and crack your cheeks!' stuff.

On Ricky it acted like magic. Hours of brooding over that interview with his Uncle Alaric had brought him into the bar a broken man. At the moment of Mr Pott's entry, he was once more facing the future with something like fortitude.

Money, the beer pointed out, was not everything. 'Look at it this way,' it argued. 'It's absurd to say there aren't a hundred ways by which a smart and enterprising young fellow can get enough money to marry on. The essential thing about this marrying business is not money, but the girl. If the girl's all right, everything's all right. It's true that at the moment you're down among the wines and spirits a bit financially, but what of it? Polly's still there, loving you just as much as ever. And something is sure to turn up.'

And now Mr Pott had turned up. And at the sight of him it was as if the scales had suddenly fallen from Ricky Gilpin's eyes.

Until this moment, the idea of trying to secure the purchase price of the onion soup bar from Claude Pott had never occurred to him. But when you examined it, what an obvious solution it seemed. Mr Pott was Polly's father. He had once rescued Mr Pott from an infuriated mob. That Mr Pott should supply the money to ensure Polly's happiness and repay that old debt was one of the things that one recognizes as dramatically right.

'Why, hullo, Mr Pott!' he said.

The affection in his voice was quite untinged with surprise. A ready explanation of the other's presence here had presented itself. He assumed he had come for the Bridgeford races, of which he had been hearing so much since his arrival in Market Blandings. But if he was not surprised to see Mr Pott, Mr Pott was extremely surprised to see him.

'Young Gilpin! What are you doing here?'

'My uncle sent for me. He's staying at Blandings Castle, a couple of miles down the road. He wanted to see me on a business matter.'

Mr Pott was aghast.

'You mean you're going to the castle?'

'No. My uncle came down here this morning to discuss the thing, but it fell through. I'm leaving for London this evening.'

Mr Pott breathed again. The thought of this young man coming blundering into the delicate web of intrigue at Blandings Castle had appalled him.

'You're here for the races, of course?'

'That's right,' said Mr Pott, grateful for the suggestion.

'Where are you staying?'

'In the vicinity.'

'Have some of this beer. It's good.'

'Thanks,' said Mr Pott. 'Thanks.'

Until his guest had been supplied with the refreshment, Ricky did not speak again. All his life he had been sturdy and independent, and it embarrassed him to have to ask a comparative stranger for money. This diffidence, with an effort, he overcame. Stranger or no stranger, he reminded himself, Claude Pott would most certainly have spent several weeks in hospital but for the prowess of Alaric Gilpin.

'Mr Pott.'

'Sir?'

'There's something I would like a word with you about, Mr Pott.'

'Oh?'

'Are you fond of onion soup?'

'No.'

'Well, lots of people are. And in this connection I want to put a business proposition up to you.'

'Ah?'

Ricky took a sip of G. Ovens's home-brewed. It had not escaped him that his companion's manner was reserved. Mr Pott's eyes seemed always to be covered by a protective layer of film. Now, it was as if another layer had been superimposed.

'I don't know if Polly has happened to mention to you, Mr Pott, that I have the opportunity of buying one of these onion soup bars? You've probably noticed them round Piccadilly Circus way.'

'I seem to remember her talking about it.'

'Enthusiastically, I expect. They coin money. Gold mines, every one of them. The one I'm speaking of belongs to an American friend of mine. He has offered to let me have it for two hundred and fifty pounds.'

The mention of that exact sum caused Mr Pott to wince a little, as if an exposed nerve had been touched. He was still unable to make up his mind about Horace Davenport as a sportsman with a taste for Persian Monarchs. Sometimes he could see him reaching out to cut from the pack. Sometimes he could not. The future was wrapped in mist.

'That's a lot of money,' he said.

Ricky was amazed.

'A lot of money? For a going concern right in the heart of London's onion-soup-drinking belt? He's simply giving it away. But he's homesick for New York, and would like to sail to-morrow, if he could. Well, that's the position. He says I can have this going concern for two hundred and fifty, provided I give him the money by the end of the week. And let me tell you, Mr Pott, the potentialities of that bar are stupendous. I've stood there night after night and watched the bottle-party addicts rolling up with their tongues out. It was like a herd of buffaloes stampeding for a water-hole.'

'Then you'd better give him his two hundred and fifty.'

'I would, if I had it. That's exactly the point I was coming to. Can you lend me the money?'

'No.'

'You can have any interest you like.'

'No, sir. Include me out.'

'But you can't say you haven't got it.'

'I have got it, and more. I've got it in cash in my pocket now, on account of the Clothes Stakes I ran at the Drones Club Tuesday.'

'Then why—?'

Mr Pott drained the remains of his tankard, but the noble brew had no mellowing effect. He might have been full of lemonade.

'I'll tell you why. Because if I give it you, you'll go and talk my dear daughter into marrying you. Polly's easily led. She's like her mother. Anything to make people happy. You'd tell her the tale, and she'd act against her better judgement. And then,' said Mr Pott, 'the bitter awakening.'

'What do you mean, the bitter awakening? Polly loves me.'

'What makes you think that?'

'She told me so.'

'That was just being civil. Love you? Coo! What would she want to love you for? If I were a girl, I wouldn't give you one little rose from my hair.'

'You haven't got any hair.'

'There is no occasion to be personal,' said Mr Pott stiffly. 'And hair's not everything, let me tell you. There's been a lot of fellows that found themselves wishing they'd been more like me in that respect. Absolom, for one. And you're wilfully missing the point of my remarks, which is that if I was a girl and had hair and there was a rose in it and you asked me for that rose, I wouldn't give it to you. Because, after all, young G., what are you? Just a poet. Simply a ruddy ink-slinger, that's you. Polly can do better.'

'I'm sorry you dislike me—'

'It's not disliking. It's disapproving of in the capacity of a suitor for my dear daughter's hand. There's nothing fundamentally wrong with you, young G. – I'll admit you've got a sweet left hook – but you aren't an om seerioo. A French term,' explained Mr Pott, 'meaning a fellow that's going to get on in the world and be able to support a sweet girl as a sweet girl ought to be supported. If you were an om seerioo, you wouldn't be wasting your time messing about writing poetry.'

Ricky was telling himself that he must be calm. But calmness was a thing that did not come readily to him in trying circumstances.

'My dear daughter ought to marry a man of substance. This Horace Davenport, now....'

'Horace!'

'It's all very well to say "Horace!" in that tone of voice. He's the nephew of a Duke,' said Mr Pott reverently.

'Well, if we're being snobs, so am I the nephew of a Duke.'

'Ah, but your Ma hadn't the stuff, and Horace's Pa had. That's where the difference comes in. The way I got the story, your Ma married beneath her. Too late to regret it now, of course.'

'The thing I regret is that you won't listen to reason.'

'I haven't heard any yet.'

There was a silence. Mr Pott would have liked another tankard of home-brew, but the way things seemed to be shaping, it appeared probable that he would have to pay for it himself.

'Mr Pott,' said Ricky, 'I saved your life once.'

'And on that last awful day when we all have to render account it will be duly chalked up to you on the credit side. Though, as a matter of fact,' said Mr Pott nonchalantly, 'I've no doubt I could have handled those fellows all right myself.'

The muscles inherited from his robust father stood out on Ricky's cheek-bones.

'I hope you will have many more opportunities of doing so,' he said.

Mr Pott seemed wounded.

'That's a nasty thing to say.'

'It was meant to be. Because,' said Ricky, becoming frank, 'if ever there was a pot-bellied little human louse who needed to have the stuffing kicked out of him and his remains jumped on by strong men in hobnailed boots, it is you, Mr Pott. The next time I see a mob in the street setting on you, I shall offer to hold their coats and stand by and cheer.'

Mr Pott rose.

'Ho! If that's the sort of nasty mind you have, I don't wonder she prefers Horace.'

'May I ask where you got the idea that she prefers Horace?'

'I got it by seeing her that night he took her to the Ball. There was a look in her eyes that made me think right away that she was feeling he was her Prince Charming. And this has since been confirmed by a reliable source.'

Ricky laughed.

'Would it interest you to know,' he said, 'that Polly has promised me that she will never see Horace again?'

'It wouldn't interest me in the slightest degree,' retorted Mr Pott. 'Because I happen to know that she's seeing him regular.'

Whether it was excusable in the circumstances for Ricky at this point to tell Mr Pott that he was lying in his teeth, and that only the fact of his being an undersized little squirt whom no decent man would bring himself to touch with a barge pole saved him from having his neck wrung, is open to debate. Mr Pott, who thought not, drew himself up stiffly.

'Young G.,' he said, 'I will wish you a very good afternoon. After that crack, I must decline to hold any association with you. There is such a thing as going too far, and you have gone it. I will take my refreshment elsewhere.'

He went off to the Jolly Cricketers to do so, and for some moments Ricky continued to sit over his tankard. Now that the first spasm of indignation had spent itself, he was feeling more amused than wrathful. The lie had been so clumsy, so easily seen through. He blamed himself for ever having allowed it to annoy him.

If there was one thing certain in an uncertain world, it was that Polly was as straight as a die. How she came to be so with a father like that constituted one of the great mysteries, but there it was. The thought of Polly cheating was inconceivable.

With a glowing heart, Ricky Gilpin rose and walked down the passage that led to the back door of the inn. He felt he wanted air. After having had Mr Pott in it, the bar struck him as a little close.

The garden of the Emsworth Arms runs down to the river, and is a pleasant, scented place on a spring evening. Ricky wished that he could linger there, but he was intending to catch the late-afternoon express back to London, and he still had his packing to do. He turned regretfully, and he had just reached the inn, when from somewhere in its interior there came a disembodied voice.

'Hullo,' it was saying. 'Hullo.'

Ricky halted, amazed. There was only one man in the world who said 'Hullo' with just that lilting bleat.

'Hullo...Polly?'

Ricky Gilpin's heart seemed to leap straight up into the air twiddling its feet, like a Russian dancer. He had sometimes wondered how fellows in the electric chair must feel when the authorities turned on the juice. Now he knew.

'Hullo? Polly? Polly, old pet, this is Horace. Yes, I know. Never mind all that. I've got to see you immediately. Of course it's important. Matter of life and death. So drop everything like the sweet angel you are, and come along. Meet me at the castle gate, out in the road. I don't want anybody to see us. Eh? What? Yes. All right. I've got my car. I'll be there before you are.'

A red-haired bombshell burst into the lounge of the Emsworth Arms. There, in the corner near the window, stood the telephone, but the speaker had gone. And from outside in the street there came the sound of a car.

Ricky Gilpin leaped to the door. A rakish Bingley was moving off up the High Street, a long, thin, familiar figure at its wheel.

For an instant, he contemplated shouting. Then, perceiving that there was a better way, he ran, sprang and flung himself on to the Bingley's stern.

Horace Davenport, all unconscious that he had taken aboard a stowaway, pressed his foot on the accelerator and the Bingley gathered speed.

Lord Ickenham, much refreshed after his bath, had left his room, and begun to search through Blandings Castle for Polly. Unable to find her, he sought information from Pongo, whom he discovered in the smoking-room staring silently at nothing. The burden of life was weighing on Pongo Twistleton a good deal just now.

'Ah, my boy. Seen Polly anywhere?'

Pongo roused himself from his thoughts.

'Yes, I saw her...'

He broke off. His eyes had started from their sockets. He had just observed what it was that the other was holding in his hand.

'My gosh! Money?'

'Yes.'

'How much?'

'Two hundred and fifty pounds.'

'Oh, my golly! Where did you get it?'

'From – you will scarcely credit this – Mustard Pott.'

'What!'

'Yes. Mustard, it will astound you to hear, has just arrived at the castle in his professional capacity, sent for by Bosham to watch our movements. I seem to have dismissed Bosham as a force too lightly. He appears to have seen through my well-meant attempt to convince him that I was not the man who got away with his wallet and to have decided to seek assistance. A dashed deep young man. He took me in completely. What led him to select Mustard from London's myriad sleuths is more than I can tell you. I can only suppose that he must have heard of him from Horace.

At any rate, he's here, and he has not been idle. Within half an hour of his arrival, he took this nice round sum off Bosham at Persian Monarchs, and I, after wrestling with him as the angel wrestled with Jacob, have taken it off him.'

Pongo was quivering in every limb.

'But this is stupendous! This is definitely the happy ending, with the maker's name woven into every yard. I had a feeling all along that you would pull it off sooner or later. Good old Uncle Fred! You stand alone. There is none like you, none. Gimme!'

Lord Ickenham perceived that his nephew was labouring under a misapprehension. Regretfully he put him straight.

'Alas, my boy, this is not for you.'

'What do you mean?'

'It is earmarked for Polly. It is the purchase price of that onion soup bar, which will enable her to marry the man she loves. I'm sorry. I can appreciate what a blow this must be for you. All I can say by way of apology is that her need is greater than yours.'

There was the right stuff in Pongo Twistleton. It had seemed to him for an instant that the world was tumbling about him in rending chaos, but already his finer self had begun to take command of things. Yes, he felt – yes, it was better thus. Agony though it was to think that he was not going to get his hooks on the boodle, it was a not unpleasant agony. His great love demanded some such sacrifice.

'I see what you mean,' he said. 'Yes, something in that.'

'Where is she?'

'I think she's gone to Market Blandings.'

'What would she be going to Market Blandings for?'

'Ah, there you have me. But I was on the terrace having a cigarette not long ago and she came out, hatted and booted, and gave the impression, when questioned, that that was where she was heading.'

'Well, go after her and bring the sunlight into her life.'

The idea did not seem immediately attractive to Pongo.

'It's four miles there and back, you know.'

'Well, you're young and strong.'

'Why don't you go?'

'Because Age has its privileges, my boy. My ramble having left me a little drowsy, I propose to snatch a few winks of sleep in my room. I often say there is nothing so pleasant as a nap in front of a crackling fire in a country-house bedroom. Off you go.'

Pongo did not set out with enthusiasm, but he set out, and Lord Ickenham made his way to his room. The fire was bright, the armchair soft, and the thought of his nephew trudging four miles along the high road curiously soothing. It was not long before the stillness was broken by a faint, musical noise like a kettle singing on the hob.

But these good things do not last. A little sleep, a little slumber, a little folding of the hands in sleep, and along comes somebody shaking us by the shoulder.

Lord Ickenham, sitting up, found that the person shaking his shoulder was Horace Davenport.

CHAPTER 16

HE ROSE courteously. To say that the sight of this unexpected apparition had left him feeling completely at his ease would be to present the facts incorrectly. For an instant, indeed, his emotions had been practically identical with those of the heroine of a pantomime when the Demon King suddenly pops up out of a trap at her elbow in a cascade of red fire. But his nervous system was under excellent control, and there was nothing in his manner to indicate how deeply he had been stirred.

'Ah, good evening, good evening!' he said. 'Mr Davenport, is it not? Delighted to see you. But what are we doing here? I thought we had decided to go and take a rest cure at Bournemouth. Did something happen to cause us to change our mind?'

'Hoy!' said Horace.

He had raised a protesting hand. His eyes were the eyes of one who has passed through the furnace, and he was vibrating gently, as if he had swallowed a small auxiliary engine.

'I beg your pardon?'

'That "we" stuff. Cut it out. Not in the mood.'

Something seemed to tell Lord Ickenham that this was not the delightfully receptive Horace Davenport of their previous meeting, but he persevered.

'My dear fellow, of course. I'm sorry if it annoyed you. Just one of those professional mannerisms one slips into. Most of my patients seem to find it soothing.'

'They do, do they? You and your bally patients!'

The undisguised bitterness with which the young man spoke these words confirmed Lord Ickenham in his view that there had been a hitch somewhere. However, he continued to do his best.

'I beg your pardon?'

'Don't keep begging my pardon. Though, my gosh,' said Horace shrilly, 'you jolly well ought to. Pulling my leg like that. It may interest you to learn that I know all.'

'Indeed?'

'Yes. You're not Sir Roderick Glossop.'

Lord Ickenham raised his eyebrows.

'That is a very odd statement to make. I confess I do not like the sound of it. It suggests a feverishness. Tell me, do we—'

'Will you stop it! Listen. You're Valerie's Uncle Fred. I've met someone who knows Glossop, and have had him described to me in pitiless detail.'

Lord Ickenham was a man who could accept the inevitable. He might not like it, but he could accept it.

'In that case, as you suggest, it is perhaps hardly worth while to try to keep up the innocent deception. Yes, my dear fellow, you are perfectly right. I am Valerie's Uncle Fred.'

'And it was Pongo Twistleton and Polly Pott that I met in the hall that time. It wasn't a – what's the word? A nice thing that was you three blisters did to me, making me think I was off my rocker. I realize now that there was absolutely nothing wrong with me at all.'

'No doubt you are feeling much relieved.'

'What I'm feeling, if you want to know, is considerably incensed and pretty dashed shirty.'

'Yes, I can appreciate your emotion, and I can only say that I am sorry. It went to my heart to do it, but it was military necessity. You were in the way, and had to be removed by such means as lay to hand. Let me explain what we are all doing, visiting Blandings Castle incognito like this. Believe me, it was no idle whim that brought us here. We are hoping that Polly may succeed in winning the Duke's heart, without him knowing who she is, thus paving the way for her marriage to your cousin Ricky. You know that pumpkin-headed old man's views on class distinctions. If Ricky told him that he wanted to marry a girl of dubious origin – and I defy anyone to think of an origin more dubious than dear old Mustard – he would forbid the banns without hesitation. We are trying to put something over by stealth, and we could not trust your open, honest nature not to give the show away.'

Horace's just wrath gave way momentarily to bewilderment.

'But I thought Ricky and Polly had split up.'

'Far from it. It is true that after that affair at the Ball there was a temporary rift, but Polly's womanly tact smoothed the thing over. He is once more one hundred per cent the devout lover.'

'Then why does he want to murder me?'

'He doesn't.'

'He does, I tell you.'

'You're thinking of someone else.'

'I'm not thinking of someone else. I found him on the back of my car just now, and he distinctly stated that he was going to tear me into little shreds and strew me over the local pasture land.'

'On the back of your car, did you say?'

'Yes. As I climbed down from the front, he climbed down from the back and made a dive at me.'

'I appear not to be abreast of the Stop Press situation,' said Lord Ickenham. 'You had better tell me your story – one, I can see, that promises to be fraught with interest.'

For the first time, Horace brightened. It was plain that some pleasing thought had occurred to him.

'It's going to interest you, all right. Yes, by Jove, you're going to sit up and take notice, believe me. A pretty nasty spot you're in. The curse has come upon me, said the Lady of Shalott. What, what?'

Lord Ickenham found him obscure.

'You speak in riddles, my boy. A little less of the Delphic Oracle. Let your Yea be Yea and your Nay be Nay.'

'All right. If you want the thing in a nutshell, then, Valerie is in full possession of the facts concerning your goings-on, and is coming here tomorrow at the latest.'

Here was something Lord Ickenham had not anticipated. And though it was his habit to present on all occasions an impassive front to the blows of Fate, he started perceptibly, and for an instant his jaunty moustache seemed to droop.

'Valerie? Coming here?'

'I thought that would touch you up.'

'Not at all. I am always glad to see my dear niece, always. You have run into her again, then?'

Horace's manner became more friendly. He was still resentful of the trick that had been played upon him and by no means inclined to accept as an adequate excuse for it the plea of military necessity, but he found it impossible not to admire this iron man.

'I met her at a restaurant last night. I had gone there in pursuance of that idea we discussed of having the binge of a lifetime before tooling off to Bournemouth. You remember agreeing with me that it would be a good thing to go on a binge?'

'Ah, yes. So I did.'

'You also recommended me to steep myself in a beverage called May Queen.'

'That's right. The binge-goer's best friend. Did you like it?'

'Well, yes and no. Peculiar stuff. For a while it makes you feel as if you were sitting on top of the world. But, as you progress, a great sorrow starts to fill you. Quart One – fine. Joy reigning supreme and blue birds singing their little hearts out. The moment you're well into Quart Two, however, the whole situation alters. You find yourself brooding on what a rotten world this is and what a foul time you're having in it. The outlook darkens. Tears spring to the eyes. Everything seems sad and hopeless.'

'This is most interesting. In my day, I never went into the thing as thoroughly as you appear to have done. One-Pint Ickenham, they used to call me.'

'And I had just reached this second stage, when who should come in but Valerie, accompanied by an elderly female who looked as if she might have something to do with breeding Pekingese. They sat down, and the next thing I knew, I had squashed in between them and was telling Valerie how miserable I was.'

'This must have interested her companion.'

'Oh, it did. She seemed absorbed. A decent old bird, at that. I owe everything to her. As soon as she got the hang of the situation, she started advocating my cause in the most sporting fashion. Valerie, I should mention, wasn't frightfully sympathetic at the outset. Her manner was cold and proud, and she kept telling me to take my elbow out of her lap. But this fine old geezer soon altered all that. It seemed that there had been a similar tragedy in her own life, and she told us all about it.'

'You revealed the facts about your broken engagement to this Pekingese-breeder, then?'

'Oh, rather. Right away. There's something about this May Queen of yours that seems to break down one's reserve, if you know what I mean. And when I had given her a full synopsis, she related her story. Something to do with once long ago loving a bloke dearly and quarrelling with him about something and him turning on his heel and going to the Federated Malay States and marrying the widow of a rubber planter, all because she had been too proud to speak the little word that would have fixed every-thing. And years afterwards there arrived a simple posy of white violets, together with a slip of paper bearing the words: "It might have been."'

'Moving.'

'Very. I cried buckets. She then leaned across me and told Valerie that the quality of mercy was not strained but dropped like something or other on something I didn't catch. I couldn't quite follow it all, but the effects were excellent. I saw Valerie's eye soften, and a tear stole into it. The next moment, we were locked in a close embrace.'

'And then?'

'Well, the long evening wore on, so to speak. The female Pekingese told us more about her Federated Malay Stater, and I went on crying, and Valerie started crying, too, and presently the Peke was also weeping freely, and it was at about this time that the head waiter came up and suggested that we should take our custom elsewhere. So we all went back to my flat and had eggs and bacon. And it was while I was doling out the dishfuls that I suddenly remembered that I was a loony and so had no right to marry a sweet girl. I mentioned this to Valerie, and then the whole story came out.'

'I see.'

'The Peke, it appeared, knew Sir Roderick Glossop well, her cousin Lionel having been treated by him for some form of loopiness, and her description of the man made it clear that you couldn't be him. So it seemed pretty obvious that you must be you.'

'Remorseless reasoning.'

'And when I speculated as to your motives for leading me up the garden path, Valerie snorted a bit and said it was plain that you were up to some kind of hell in this ancient pile and had wanted to get me out of the way. Which you admit to have been the case. She's a most intelligent girl.'

'Most. I have sometimes thought that it would be an admirable thing if she were to choke.'

'And the outcome of the whole affair was that she went down to Ickenham this morning, just to make sure you weren't on the premises – her intention, having ascertained this, being to breeze along here and expose you to one and all. And I saw that what I had got to do was make an early start and get here before she did. Because you see, though all is forgiven and forgotten between us, so to speak, and love has, as it were, come into its own again, there is just one small catch, that she seems a bit curious about Polly.'

'You mean about your relations with her?'

'Yes. She said in rather a sinister way that she supposed Polly was a very pretty girl, and my statement to the effect that she was a plain little thing whom I had taken to the Ball purely out of pity was none too cordially received. Her manner struck me as that of a girl who intended to investigate further.'

'So your desire to have her arrive here and meet Polly and see what she really looks like is slight?'

'Almost nil,' confessed Horace frankly. 'As soon as I could manage it, therefore, I drove here in the car to tell Polly to clear out while there was yet time.'

'Very shrewd.'

'I 'phoned her from the Emsworth Arms, arranging a meeting at the castle gate. I then hopped into the car and went there. And conceive my astonishment when, alighting from the prow, I observed Ricky alighting from the stern.'

'It must have given you a start.'

'It did. A flying start. I was off like a jack rabbit. And after I had gone about three-quarters of a mile, touching the ground perhaps twice in the process, I found myself outside the castle and stopped and reviewed the situation. And I saw that having missed Polly, the best thing I could do was to get hold of you. I knew which your room was, of course, and I sneaked up with the idea of waiting till you came to dress for dinner. That I should have found you first crack out of the box like this is the one bit of goose I have experienced in the course of a sticky evening.'

'You wish me, I take it, to find Polly and tell her not to be among those present when Valerie arrives?'

'Exactly.'

'She shall be removed. Indeed, I rather think that none of us will be here to welcome the dear girl. I remember telling my nephew Pongo not long ago that the Twistletons do not clear out, but there are exceptions to the rule. If Valerie were in a position to report to GHQ that she had found me at Blandings Castle posing as a brain specialist, the consequences might well be such as would stagger humanity. But if I am gone before she gets here, it seems to me that I am up against nothing that stout denial will not cover. So rest assured, my boy, that I will lose no time in collecting my young associates, and you shall drive us back to London in your car. Unlike the Arabs, who paused to fold their tents before silently stealing away, we will not even stop to pack.'

'But how can I get at the car? I left Ricky standing guard over it.'

'I think I shall be able to adjust your little trouble with Ricky satisfactorily. My first move shall be to go and explain things to him. I would suggest that you remain here till my return. If you prefer to hide in the cupboard in case your uncle happens to look in, by all means do so. Make yourself quite at home.'

The evening was cool and fragrant and a soft wind whispered in the trees, as Lord Ickenham made his way down the drive. Despite the peril that loomed, his mood was serene. He was sorry to be obliged to leave Blandings Castle, which he had found a pleasant spot full of interesting personalities, but he could see that the time had come to move on. And, after all, he reflected, his work was done. Polly had her money, Pongo had been promised his, and the Empress was safe from the Duke's clutching hand. There was really, he felt, nothing to keep him. All he had to do now was to speak a few soothing words to this explosive young poet of Polly's, and an agreeable episode might be considered closed.

He was about half-way to the castle gate when he heard the sound of footsteps. A small figure was coming towards him through the dusk.

'Polly?'

'Hullo.'

It seemed to Lord Ickenham that there was a flat note in the girl's usually musical voice, and as he halted beside her he detected in her bearing a listlessness which struck him as odd.

'What's the matter?'

'Nothing.'

'Don't be evasive, child. The visibility may not be good, but I can see that you are drooping like a tired flower. Your depression is almost Pongoesque. Come on, now, what has happened?'

'Oh, Uncle Fred!'

'Hullo! Here, I say! Dash it, what's all this about?'

It was some moments later that Polly drew away, dabbing at her eyes.

'I'm sorry. I've been making a fool of myself.'

'Nothing of the kind. A good cry is what we all want at times. I shall recommend it to Pongo. I think I can guess what is wrong. I take it that you have been having a talk with your young man. You went to meet Horace at the gate, and found Ricky. And from your manner, I gather that the plugugly rather than the poet was uppermost in him.'

'He was awful. Not that you can blame him.'

'Of course not, bless his heart, the little pet.'

'I mean, I can understand how he must have been feeling. I had promised I would never see Horace again, and there I was, sneaking off to him.'

'Don't be so infernally broadminded, child. Why the devil shouldn't you see Horace as often as you like? What right has this sweet-singing baboon to tell you whom you shall see and whom you shan't see? What happened?'

'He raved and yelled at me. He said everything was over.'

'So he did a couple of days ago, after that Ball. But you smoothed him down.'

'I couldn't this time.'

'Did you try?'

'No. I lost my temper, and started being as beastly as he was.'

'Good girl.'

'It was horrible. He hated me.'

'Do you hate him?'

'Of course I don't.'

'You mean that in spite of everything you love him still?'

'Of course I do.'

'Women are amazing. Well, I'll soon fix things. I'm on my way to interview him now.'

'It won't be any use.'

'That's what they said to Columbus. Don't you worry, my dear. I can handle this. I know my potentialities, and sometimes they absolutely stun me. Are there no limits, I ask myself, to the powers of this wonder-man? I am still completely unable to comprehend why you should want the chap, but if you do you must have him.'

He walked on, and coming presently to the gate found the Bingley standing at the roadside. Pacing up and down in its vicinity like a tiger at feeding-time he perceived a sturdy figure.

'Mr Gilpin, I presume?' he said.

CHAPTER 17

SO MANY disturbing things had happened to Ricky Gilpin in the course of this April day that it is scarcely to be wondered at that his mood was not sunny. In a world congested with dukes and Potts and Horace Davenports and faithless girls, it is only an exceptionally philosophical man who can preserve his amiability unimpaired, and Ricky had never been that. He scowled darkly. He did not know who this elegant stranger was, but he was prepared to dislike him.

'Who are you?'

'My name is Ickenham.'

'Oh?'

'I see that it is familiar. No doubt Polly has spoken of me?'

'Yes.'

'Then in reciprocal spirit I will now speak of Polly.'

A quiver passed through Ricky Gilpin's solid body.

'No, you won't. I've finished with her.'

'Don't say that.'

'I do say that.'

Lord Ickenham sighed.

'Youth, Youth! How it flings away its happiness like a heedless child,' he said, and, pausing for a moment to think what heedless children flung away, added 'blowing bubbles and throwing them idly into the sunlit air. Too bad, too bad. Shall I tell you a little story, Mr Gilpin?'

'No.'

'Years ago' – it would have taken a better man than Ricky to stop Lord Ickenham telling stories – 'I loved a girl.'

'You haven't by any chance seen Horace Davenport, have you?'

'Loved her dearly.'

'If you do, tell him it's no use his skulking away. I intend to wait here for weeks, if necessary.'

'We quarrelled over some trivial matter. Bitter recriminations ensued. And finally she swept out of the room and married a rubber planter.'

'Sooner or later he will have to present himself and be torn into little pieces.'

'And years afterwards there arrived a simple posy of white violets, together with a slip of paper bearing the words: "It might have been." Tragic, eh? If you will allow an old man to advise you, Mr Gilpin – an old man who has suffered – an old man who threw away his happiness just because he was too proud to speak the little word that—'

There was a metallic clang. Ricky Gilpin appeared to have kicked the fender of the car.

'Listen,' he said. 'I may as well tell you at once that you're wasting your time. I know Polly sent you to try to talk me round—'

'Sent me to talk you round? My dear fellow! You little know that proud girl.'

Lord Ickenham paused. Ricky had moved into the golden pool spread by the headlights, and for the first time he was able to see him as more than an indistinct figure in the dusk.

'Tell me,' he said, 'was your father a chap named Billy Gilpin? In some Irish regiment?'

'His name was William, and he was in the Connaught Rangers. Why?'

'I thought so. You're the living spit of him. Well, now I know that, I'm not so surprised that you should have been behaving in this idiotic way. I used to know your father, and I wish I had five pounds for every time I've sat on his head in bars and restaurants in a painstaking effort to make him see reason. Of all the fly-off-the-handle asses that ever went about with a chip on the shoulder, taking offence at the merest trifles—'

'We won't discuss my father. And if you're suggesting that it's the merest trifle, the girl who's supposed to love you going and hobnobbing with Horace Davenport after she had promised—'

'But, my dear boy, don't you understand that it was precisely because she loved you that she did hobnob with Horace?... Let me explain, and if when I have finished you are not bathed in shame and remorse, you must be dead to all human feeling. In the first place, nothing but her love for you could have dragged her to that Ball at the Albert Hall. You don't suppose a girl enjoys being seen in public with a fellow wearing the costume of a Zulu warrior and tortoiseshell-rimmed spectacles, do you? Polly went to that Ball because she was prepared to endure physical and spiritual agony in order to further your interest. It was her intention to catch Horace in mellow mood and plead with him to advance you the sum which you require for that onion soup bar of yours.'

'What!'

'For weeks she had been sedulously sweetening him by giving him dancing lessons, and that night was to have marked the culmination of the enterprise. She was hoping to be able to come to you and tell you that the weary waiting was over and that you and she could get married and live happy ever after, dishing out onion soup to the blotto survivors of bottle-parties. By your headstrong conduct you ruined her plans that night. A girl can't try to borrow money from a man while he's being taken off to Marlborough Street Police Station. Her instinct tells her that he will not be in the mood. So she had to wait for another opportunity. Learning that Horace was expected here, she came, too. She met him. She got the money—'

'She – what?'

'Certainly. It's in her possession now. She was bringing it to you.'

'But how did she know I was here?'

For perhaps a third of a split second this question had Lord Ickenham in difficulties.

'Woman's intuition,' he suggested.

'But—'

'Well, there it is,' said Lord Ickenham bluffly. 'What does it matter how she knew you were here? Suffice it that she did know, and she came running to you with the money in her hand like a child about to show some cherished treasure. And you – what did you do? You behaved like a cad and a scoundrel. I'm not surprised that she feels she has had a lucky escape.'

'Oh, my gosh! Does she?'

'That is what she was saying when I saw her just now. And I don't blame her. There can be no love without trust, and a pretty exhibition of trustfulness you gave, did you not?'

To Horace Davenport, could he have seen it at this moment, Ricky Gilpin's face would have come as a revelation. He would scarcely have been able to believe that those incandescent eyes had it in them to blink so sheepishly, or that that iron jaw could have sagged so like a poorly set blancmange. The future Onion Soup

King was exhibiting all the symptoms of one who has been struck on the back of the head with a sock full of wet sand.

'I've made a fool of myself,' he said, and his voice was like the earliest pipe of half-awakened birds.

'You have.'

'I've mucked things up properly.'

'I'm glad you realize it.'

'Where is Polly? I must see her.'

'I wouldn't advise it. You don't appear to understand what it means, behaving to a girl of spirit as you have behaved to Polly. She's furious with you. It would be madness to see her. There is only one thing you can do. When are you returning to London?'

'I had meant to catch the evening train.'

'Do so. Polly will be back at her home shortly. As soon as she arrives, go and buy her chocolates – lots of chocolates – and send them round with a grovelling note.'

'I will.'

'You might then plead for an interview. And when I say plead, I mean plead.'

'Of course.'

'If you display a sufficiently humble and contrite spirit, I see no reason for you to despair. She was fond of you once, and it may be that she will grow fond of you again. I will talk to her and do what I can for you.'

'That's awfully kind of you.'

'Not at all. I would like to do a good turn for the son of an old friend. Good evening, Gilpin, my boy, and remember… chocolates – humble, remorseful chocolates – and plenty of them.'

It was perhaps fortunate that Pongo Twistleton was not present when his uncle, rejoining Polly, concluded the recital of what had passed between Ricky Gilpin and himself, for there ensued an emotional scene which would have racked him to the foundations of his being.

'Well, there you are,' said Lord Ickenham, at length. 'That is how matters stand, and all you have to do is sit tight and reap the strategic advantages. I'm glad I told him to send you chocolates. I don't suppose a rugged he-man like that would ever dream of giving a girl chocolates in the ordinary course of things. He struck me as a fellow lacking in the softer social graces.'

'But why wouldn't you let him see me?'

'My dear child, it would have undone all the good work I had accomplished. You would have flung yourself into his arms, and he would have gone on thinking he was the boss. As it is, you have got that young man just where you want him. You will accept his chocolates with a cool reserve which will commit you to nothing, and eventually, after he has been running round in circles for some weeks, dashing into his tailors' from time to time for a new suit of sackcloth and ashes and losing pounds in weight through mental anguish, you will forgive him – on the strict understanding that this sort of thing must never occur again. It doesn't do to let that dominant male type of chap think things are too easy.'

Polly frowned. In a world scented with flowers and full of soft music, these sentiments jarred upon her.

'I don't see why it's got to be a sort of fight.'

'Well, it has. Marriage is a battlefield, not a bed of roses. Who said that? It sounds too good to be my own. Not that I don't think of some extraordinarily good things, generally in my bath.'

'I love Ricky.'

'And very nice, too. But the only way of ensuring a happy married life is to get it thoroughly clear at the outset who is going to skipper the team. My own dear wife settled the point during the honeymoon, and ours has been an ideal union.'

Polly halted abruptly.

'It's all nonsense. I'm going to see him.'

'My dear, don't.'

'Yes.'

'You'll regret it.'

'I won't.'

'Think of all the trouble I've taken.'

'I do, and I can't tell you how grateful I am, Uncle Fred. You've been wonderful. You've picked me up out of the mud and changed the whole world for me. But I can't treat Ricky like that. I'd hate myself. I don't care if he does go on thinking he's the boss. So he is, and I like it!'

Lord Ickenham sighed.

'Very well, if that's the way you feel. "His fair large front and eye sublime declared Absolute rule." If that's the sort of thing you want, I suppose it's no use arguing. If you are resolved to chuck away a heaven-sent opportunity of putting this young man in his place, go ahead, my dear, and God bless you. But you can't

see him now. He has gone to catch his train. You must wait till
tomorrow.'

'But it's such ages. Couldn't I send him a telegram?'

'No,' said Lord Ickenham firmly. 'There are limits. At least
preserve a semblance of womanly dignity. Why not get Horace to
drive you to London tonight in his car?'

'Would he, do you think? He's had one long drive already
today.'

'It is his dearest wish to have another, provided you are at his
side. Pongo and I can come on in the morning by that eight-
twenty-five train of which everybody speaks so highly.'

'But are you leaving, too?'

'We are. Get Horace to tell you all about it. You will find
him in my bedroom. If you don't see him, look in the cupboard.
I, meanwhile, must be getting in touch with Pongo and commu-
nicating the arrangements to him. The news that we are flitting
should please him. For some reason, Pongo has not been happy
at Blandings Castle. By the way, did you meet him?'

'Yes. As I was coming back after seeing Ricky.'

'Good. I was only wondering if you had got that money all
right.'

'He did offer me some money, but I gave it back to him.'

'Gave it back?'

'Yes. I didn't want it.'

'But, my good child, it was the purchase price of the onion
soup bar. Your wedding portion!'

'I know. He told me.' Polly laughed amusedly. 'But I had just
had that frightful row with Ricky, and we had parted for ever, and
I was thinking of drowning myself, so I didn't want a wedding
portion. Will you tell him I should like it, after all.'

Lord Ickenham groaned softly.

'You would not speak in that airy, casual way, if you knew the
circumstances. Informing Pongo that you would like it, after all, is
not going to be the pleasant task you seem to think it. I dare say
that with the aid of anæsthetic and forceps I shall eventually be
able to extract the money from the unhappy young blighter, but
there will be a nasty, hacking sound as he coughs up. Still, you may
rely on me to protect your interests, no matter what the cost. I will
bring the stuff round to the Pott home tomorrow afternoon. And

now run along and find Horace. I know he would appreciate an early start.'

'All right. Uncle Fred, you're an angel.'

'Thank you, my dear.'

'If it hadn't been for you—'

Once more Lord Ickenham found his arms full and behaved with a warmth far greater than one of his nephew's austere views would have considered either necessary or suitable. Then he was alone, and Polly a voice in the darkness, singing happily as she went on her way.

It was some ten minutes later that Lord Ickenham, sauntering along the high road in the direction of Market Blandings, heard another voice, also singing happily. He recognized it with a pang. It was not often that Pongo Twistleton cast off his natural gloom in order to carol like a lark, and the thought that it was for him to wipe this unaccustomed melody from the lips of a young man of whom he was very fond was not an agreeable one.

'Pongo?'

'Hullo, Uncle Fred. I say, what a lovely evening!'

'Very.'

'The air! The stars! The scent of growing things!'

'Quite. Er – Pongo, my boy, about that money.'

'The money you gave me to give to Miss Pott? Oh, yes – I was going to tell you about that. I offered it to her, but she would have none of it.'

'Yes— But—'

'She told me that owing to her having parted brass rags with Ricky, she had no need of it.'

'Precisely. But since then—'

'So I trousered it, and toddled along to Market Blandings, and breezed into the post office, and shoved two hundred quid into an envelope addressed to George Budd and fifty into an envelope addressed to Oofy Prosser and sent them off, registered. So all is now well. The relief,' said Pongo, 'is stupendous.'

It was not immediately that Lord Ickenham spoke. For some moments he stood fingering his moustache and gazing at his nephew thoughtfully. He was conscious of a faint resentment against a Providence which was unquestionably making things difficult for a good man.

'This,' he said, 'is a little awkward.'

'Awkward?'

'Yes.'

'How do you mean? It seems to me...'

Pongo's voice trailed away. A hideous thought had come to him.

'Oh, my aunt! Don't tell me she's changed her mind and wants the stuff, after all?'

'I fear so.'

'You mean she's made it up with Ricky?'

'Yes.'

'And needs this money to get married on?'

'Exactly.'

'Oh, my sainted bally aunt!'

'Yes,' said Lord Ickenham, 'it is awkward. No getting away from that. I told Ricky the money was actually in her possession, and he went off to catch his train with golden visions of soup-swilling multitudes dancing before his eyes. I told Polly I would bring her the stuff tomorrow, and she went off singing. It is not going to be pleasant to have to reveal the facts. Disappointment will be inevitable.'

'Would it be any good to ring up Budd and Oofy and ask them to give the money back?'

'No.'

'No, I suppose not. Then what?'

Lord Ickenham's face brightened. He had seen that all was not lost. That busy brain was seldom baffled for long.

'I have it! Mustard!'

'Eh?'

'Mustard Pott. He must handle this for us. Obviously, what we must do is unleash Mustard once more. I think he may be a little annoyed when he learns that his former donation, instead of ensuring the happiness of a loved daughter, has gone to ease the financial difficulties of a comparative stranger like yourself, but I have no doubt that a few minutes of my eloquence will persuade him to forget his natural chagrin and have another pop.'

'At Bosham?'

'Not at Bosham. People who play Persian Monarchs with Mustard in the afternoon are seldom in a frame of mind to play again in the evening. Emsworth is the man.'

'Old Emsworth? Oh, I say, dash it!'

Lord Ickenham nodded.

'I know what you mean. You feel that one ought to draw the line at nicking a kindly host, with whose bread and meat we are bursting, and considering the thing as a broad general proposition I agree with you. It will undoubtedly tarnish the Ickenham escutcheon, and I wish it hadn't got to be done. But in a crisis like this one must sink one's finer feelings. I don't believe I told you, did I, that your sister Valerie is expected here shortly?'

'What!'

'So Horace informs me, and you may look on him as a reliable source. This means that we have got to get out of here by tomorrow's eight-twenty-five train without fail, so you will see that we cannot loiter and dally, if we are to secure funds for Polly. It is not a question of asking ourselves "Is it right to take it off Emsworth?" and "Are we ethically justified in skinning this good old man?" but rather "Has he got it?" And he has. Emsworth, therefore, shall give us of his plenty, and I will be going along now and putting the thing in train. I will look in at your room later and report.'

CHAPTER 18

IT WAS a sombre, preoccupied Pongo Twistleton who dressed for dinner that night in the small apartment which had been allotted to him on the second floor. As a rule, the process of transforming himself from the chrysalis of daytime to the shimmering butterfly of night was one that gave him pleasure. He liked the soothing shave, the revivifying bath, the soft crackle of the snowy shirt-front and the general feeling that in a few minutes he would be giving the populace an eyeful. But tonight he was moody and distrait. His lips were tight, and his eyes brooded. Even when he tied his tie, he did it without any real animation.

The news that his sister was on her way to join the little circle at Blandings Castle had shaken him a good deal. It had intensified in him the sensation, which he had been experiencing ever since his arrival, of being beset by perils and menaced by bad citizens. A cat in a strange alley, with an eye out for small boys with bricks, would have understood how he felt. And this nervous apprehension would alone have been enough to take his mind off his toilet.

But far more powerful than apprehension as an agent for wrecking his mental peace was remorse. Ever since he had fallen in love at first sight with Polly Pott, he had been dreaming that an occasion might arise which would enable him to make some great sacrifice for her sake. He had pictured himself patting her little hand, as she thanked him brokenly for that astounding act of nobility. He had seen himself gazing down into her eyes with one of those whimsical, twisted, Ronald Colman smiles. He had even gone so far as to knock together a bit of dialogue for the scene – just in case – starting 'There, there, little girl, it was nothing. All I want is your happiness' and getting even more effective as it went on.

And what had actually happened was that, unless her Persian-Monarchs-playing father intervened and saved the situation at the eleventh hour, he had ruined her life. It takes an unusually well-tied tie to relieve a mind tottering under a reflection like that, and his, he found, looking in the mirror, was only so-so. Indeed, it seemed to him to fall so far short of the ideal that he was just about to scrap it and start another, when the door opened and Lord Ickenham came in.

'Well?' cried Pongo eagerly.

Then his heart sank far beyond what a few moments before he had supposed to have been an all-time low. One glance at his uncle's face was enough to tell him that this was no exultant bearer of glad tidings who stood before him.

Lord Ickenham shook his head. There was a gravity in his manner that struck a nameless chill.

'The United States Marines have failed us, my boy. The garrison has not been relieved, the water supply is giving out, and the savages are still howling on the outskirts. In other words, Mustard has let us down.'

Pongo staggered to a chair. He sat down heavily. And some rough indication of his frame of mind may be gathered from the fact that he forgot to pull the knees of his trousers up.

'Wouldn't he take it on?'

'He would, and did. As I had anticipated, there was a certain huffiness at first, but I soon talked him round and he assented to the plan, saying in the most sporting spirit that all I had got to do was to provide Emsworth, and he would do the rest. He pulled out his pack of cards and fingered it lovingly, like some grand old warrior testing the keenness of his blade before a battle. And at this moment Emsworth entered.'

Pongo nodded heavily.

'I see where you're heading. Emsworth wouldn't play?'

'Oh yes, he played. This is a long and intricate story, my boy, and I think you had better not interrupt too much, or it will be dinner-time before we can get down to the agenda.'

'What agenda?'

'I have a scheme or plan of action which I propose to place before you in due course. Meanwhile, let me relate the sequence of events. As I say, Emsworth entered, and it was plain from his manner that he was in the grip of some strong emotion. His eyes goggled, his pince-nez were adrift and he yammered at me silently for a while, as is his habit when moved. It then came out that his pig had been stolen. He had gone down to refresh himself with an after-tea look at it, and it was not there. Its sty was empty, and its bed had not been slept in.'

'Oh?'

'I should have thought you could have found some more adequate comment on a great human tragedy than a mere "Oh?"' said Lord Ickenham reprovingly. 'Youth is very callous. Yes, the pig had been stolen, and Emsworth's suspicions immediately leaped, of course, to the Duke. He was considerably taken aback when I pointed out that the latter could scarcely be the guilty person, seeing that he had been in his room all the afternoon. He retired there immediately after lunch, and was not seen again. And he could not have gone out into the garden through his bedroom window, because we find that Baxter was sitting on the lawn from one-thirty onwards. You may recall that Baxter was not with us at lunch. It appears that he had a slight attack of dyspepsia and decided to skip the meal. He testifies that Dunstable did not emerge. The thing, therefore, becomes one of the great historic mysteries, ranking with the Man in the Iron Mask and the case of the *Mary Celeste*. One seeks in vain for a solution.'

Pongo, who had been listening to the narrative with growing impatience, denied this.

'I don't. I don't give a single, solitary damn. Dash all pigs, is the way I look at it. You didn't come here to talk about pigs, did you? What happened about Pott and the card game?'

Lord Ickenham apologized.

'I'm sorry. I'm afraid we old fellows have a tendency to ramble on. I should have remembered that your interest in the fortunes of Emsworth's pig is only tepid. Well, I suggested to Emsworth that what he wanted was to take his mind off the thing, and that an excellent method of doing this would be to play cards. Mustard said that curiously enough he happened to have a pack handy, and the next moment they had settled down to the game.'

Lord Ickenham paused, and drew his breath in reverently.

'It was a magnificent exhibition. Persian Monarchs at its best. I never expect to witness a finer display of pure science than Mustard gave. He was playing for his daughter's happiness, and the thought seemed to inspire him. Generally, I believe, on these occasions, it is customary to allow the mug to win from time to time as a sort of gesture, but it was clear that Mustard felt that in a crisis like this old-world courtesy would be out of place. Ignoring the traditions, he won every coup, and when they had finished Emsworth got up, thanked him for a pleasant game, said that it was fortunate that they had not been playing for money or he might have lost a considerable sum, and left the room.'

'Oh, my gosh!'

'Yes, it was a little disconcerting. Mustard tells me he was once bitten by a pig, but I doubt if even on that occasion – high spot in his life though it must have been – he can have been more overcome by emotion. For about five minutes after Emsworth's departure, all he could do was to keep saying in a dazed sort of way that this had never happened to him before. One gets new experiences. And then suddenly I saw his face light up, and he seemed to revive like a watered flower. And, looking round, I found that the Duke had come in.'

'Ah!'

Lord Ickenham shook his head.

'It's no good saying "Ah!" my boy. I told you at the beginning that this story hadn't a happy ending.'

'The Duke wouldn't play?'

'You keep saying that people wouldn't play. People always play when Mustard wants them to. He casts a sort of spell. No, the Duke was delighted to play. He said that he had had a boring afternoon, cooped up in his room, and that now he was out for a short breather a game of Persian Monarchs was just what he would enjoy. He said that as a young man he had been very gifted at the pastime. I saw Mustard's eyes glisten. They sat down.'

Lord Ickenham paused. He seemed to be torn between the natural desire of a raconteur to make the most of his material and a humane urge to cut it short and put his nephew out of his suspense. The latter triumphed.

'Dunstable's claim to excellence at the game was proved to the hilt,' he said briefly. 'Mark you, I don't think Mustard was at his best. That supreme effort so short a while before had left him weak and listless. Be that as it may, Dunstable took three hundred pounds off him in ten minutes.'

Pongo was staring.

'Three hundred pounds?'

'That was the sum.'

'In ready money, do you mean?'

'Paid right across the counter.'

'But if he had all that on him, why didn't he give it to Miss Pott?'

'Ah, I see what you mean. Well, Mustard is a peculiar chap in some ways. It is difficult enough to get him to part with his winnings. Not even for a daughter's sake would he give up his working capital. One dimly understands his view-point.'

'I don't.'

'Well, there it is.'

'And now what do we do?'

'Eh? Oh, now, of course, we nip into the Duke's room and pinch the stuff.'

That strange nightmare feeling which had grown so familiar to Pongo of late came upon him again. He presumed he had heard aright – his uncle's enunciation had been beautifully clear – but it seemed incredible that he could have done so.

'Pinch it?'

'Pinch it.'

'But you can't pinch money.'

'Dashed bad form, of course, I know. But I shall look upon it as a loan, to be paid back at intervals – irregular intervals – each instalment accompanied by a posy of white violets.'

'But, dash it—'

'I know what you are thinking. To that highly trained legal mind of yours it is instantly clear that the act will constitute a tort or misdemeanour, if not actual barratry or socage in fief. But it has got to be done. Polly's need is paramount. I remember Mustard saying once, apropos of my affection for Polly, that I seemed to look on her more like a daughter than a whatnot, and he was right. I suppose my feelings towards her are roughly those of Emsworth towards his pig, and when I have the chance to ensure her happiness I am not going to allow any far-fetched scruples to stand in my way. I am a mild, law-abiding man, but to make that kid happy I would willingly become one of those fiends with hatchet who seem to spend their time slaying six. So, as I say, we will pinch the stuff.'

'You aren't proposing to lug me into this?'

Lord Ickenham was astounded.

'Lug you? What an extraordinary expression. I had naturally supposed that you would be overjoyed to do your bit.'

'You don't get me mixed up in this sort of game,' said Pongo firmly. 'Dog Races, yes. Crashing the gate at castles, right. Burglary, no.'

'But, my dear boy, when you reflect that but for you Polly would have all the money she needs—'

'Oh, golly!'

Once more, remorse had burst over Pongo like a tidal wave. In the agitation of the moment, he had forgotten this aspect of the affair. He writhed with shame.

'You mustn't overlook that. In a sense, you are morally bound to sit in.'

'That's right.'

'Then you will?'

'Of course. Rather.'

'Good. I knew you would. You shouldn't pull the old man's leg, Pongo. For a minute I thought you were serious. Well, I am relieved, for your co-operation is essential to the success of the little scheme I have roughed out. What sort of voice are you in these days? Ah, but I remember. When we met in the road, you were warbling like a nightingale. I mistook you for Lily Pons. Excellent.'

'Why?'

'Because it will be your task – your simple, easy task – I will attend to all the really testing work – to flit about the lawn outside Dunstable's window, singing the "Bonny Bonny Banks of Loch Lomond".'

'Eh? Why?'

'You do keep saying "Why?" don't you. It is quite simple. Dunstable, for some reason, is keeping closely to his room. Our first move must be to get him out of it. Even a novice to burglary like myself can see that if you are proposing to ransack a man's room for money, it is much pleasanter to do it when he is not there. Your rendering of Loch Lomond will lure him out. We know how readily he responds to that fine old song. I see your role in this affair as a sort of blend of Lorelei and Will-o'-the-Wisp. You get Dunstable out with your siren singing, and you keep him out by flitting ahead of him through the darkness. Meanwhile, I sneak in and do the needful. No flaws in that?'

'Not so long as nobody sees you.'

'You are thinking of Baxter? Quite right. Always think of everything. If Baxter sees us slip away on some mysterious errand, his detective instincts will undoubtedly be roused. But I have the situation well in hand. I shall give Baxter a knock-out drop.'

'A what?'

'Perhaps you are more familiar with it under the name of Mickey Finn.'

'But where on earth are you going to get a knock-out drop?'

'From Mustard. Unless his whole mode of life has changed since I used to know him, he is sure to have one. In the old days, he never moved without them. When he was running that club of his, it was only by a judicious use of knock-out drops that he was able to preserve order and harmony in his little flock.'

'But how do you propose to make him take it?'

'I shall find a way. He would be in his room now, I imagine?'

'I suppose so.'

'Then after paying a brief call on Mustard I will look in on him and enquire after his dyspepsia. You may leave all this side of the thing to me with every confidence. Your duties will not begin till after dinner. Zero hour is at nine-thirty sharp.'

It was plain to Lord Ickenham, directly he thrust his unwanted society on him a few minutes later, that Rupert Baxter was far from being the stern, steely young fellow of their previous encounters. The message, conveyed by Beach the butler to Lady Constance shortly after noon, that Mr Baxter regretted he would be unable to lunch today had been no mere ruse on the secretary's part to enable him to secure the solitude and leisure essential to the man who is planning to steal pigs. The effect of his employer's assignment had been to induce a genuine disorder of the digestive organs. There is always a weak spot in the greatest men. With Baxter, as with Napoleon, it was his stomach.

He had felt a little better towards evening, but now the thought that there lay before him the fearful ordeal of removing the Empress from her temporary lodging in the Duke's bathroom to the car which was to convey her to her new home had brought on another and an even severer attack. At the moment of Lord Ickenham's entry, wild cats to the number of about eighteen had just begun to conduct a free-for-all in his interior.

It was not to be expected, therefore, that he should beam upon his visitor. Nor did he. Ceasing for an instant to massage his waistcoat, he glared in a manner which only the dullest person could have failed to recognize as unfriendly.

'Well?' he said, between clenched teeth.

Lord Ickenham, who had not expected cordiality, was in no way disconcerted by his attitude. He proceeded immediately to supply affability enough for two, which was the amount required.

'I just dropped in,' he explained, 'to make enquiries and offer condolences. You will have been thinking me remiss in not coming before, but you know how it is at a country house. Distractions all the time. Well, my dear fellow, how are you? A touch of the collywobbles, I understand. Too bad, too bad. We all missed you at lunch, and there was a great deal of sympathy expressed – by myself, of course, no less than the others.'

'I can do without your sympathy.'

'Can any of us do without sympathy, Baxter, even from the humblest? Mine, moreover, takes a practical and constructive form. I have here,' said Lord Ickenham, producing a white tablet, 'something which I guarantee will make you forget the most absorbing stomach-ache. You take it in a little water.'

Baxter regarded the offering suspiciously. His knowledge of impostors told him that they seldom act from purely altruistic motives. Examine an impostor's act of kindness, and you see something with a string attached to it.

And suddenly there came to him, causing him momentarily to forget bodily anguish, an exhilarating thought.

Rupert Baxter had no illusions about his employer. He did not suppose that the gruff exterior of the Duke of Dunstable hid a heart of gold, feeling – correctly – that if the Duke were handed a heart of gold on a plate with watercress round it, he would not know what it was. But he did credit him with an elementary sense of gratitude, and it seemed to him that after he, Baxter, had carried through with success the perilous task of stealing a pig on his behalf, the old hound could scarcely sack him for having attended a fancy-dress Ball without permission. In other words, this man before him, beneath whose iron heel he had been supposing himself to be crushed, no longer had any hold over him and could be defied with impunity.

'I see you have a tumbler there. I place the tablet in it – so. I fill with water – thus. I stir. I mix. And there you are. Drink it down, and let's see what happens.'

Baxter waved away the cup with a sneer.

'You are very kind,' he said, 'but there is no need to beat about the bush. It is obvious that you have come here in the hope of getting round me—'

Lord Ickenham looked pained.

'Yours is a very suspicious nature, Baxter. You would do well to try to overcome this mistrust of your fellow-men.'

'You want something.'

'Merely to see you your old bonny self again.'

'You are trying to conciliate me, and I know why. You have begun to wonder if the hold you suppose yourself to have over me is quite as great as you imagined.'

'Beautifully expressed. I like the way you talk.'

'Let me tell you at once that it is not. You have no hold over me. Since our conversation in the billiard-room, the whole situation has altered. I have been able to perform a great service for my employer, with the result that I am no longer in danger of being dismissed for having gone to that Ball. So I may as well inform you here and now that it is my intention to have you turned out of the house immediately. Ouch!' said Baxter, rather spoiling the effect of a dignified and impressive speech by clutching suddenly at his midriff.

Lord Ickenham eyed him sympathetically.

'My dear fellow, something in your manner tells me you are in pain. You had better drink that mixture.'

'Get out!'

'It will do you all the good in the world.'

'Get out!'

Lord Ickenham sighed.

'Very well, since you wish it,' he said and, turning, collided with Lord Bosham in the doorway.

'Hullo!' said Lord Bosham. 'Hullo-ullo-ullo! Hullo-ullo-ullo-ullo-ullo!'

He spoke with a wealth of meaning in his voice. There was, he felt, something pretty dashed sinister about finding the villain of the piece alone with Baxter in his room like this. An acquaintance with mystery thrillers almost as comprehensive as his brother Freddie's had rendered him familiar with what happened when these chaps got into rooms. On the thin pretext of paying a formal call, they smuggled in cobras and left them there to do their stuff. 'Well, good afternoon,' they said, and bowed themselves out. But the jolly old cobra didn't bow itself out. It stuck around, concealed in the curtain.

'Hullo!' he added, concluding his opening remarks. 'Want anything?'

'Only dinner,' said Lord Ickenham.

'Oh?' said Lord Bosham. 'Well, it'll be ready in a minute. What was that bird after?' he asked tensely, as the door closed.

Baxter did not reply for a moment. He was engaged in beating his breast, like the Wedding Guest.

'I kicked him out before he could tell me,' he said, as the agony abated. 'Ostensibly, his purpose in coming was to bring me something for my indigestion. A tablet. He put it in that glass. What he was really leading up to, of course, was a request that I would refrain from exposing him.'

'But you can't expose him, can you? Wouldn't you lose your job?'

'There is no longer any danger of that.'

'You mean, even if he tells old Dunstable that you were out on a bender that night, you won't get the boot?'

'Precisely.'

'Then now I know where I stand! Now the shackles have fallen from me, and I am in a position to set about these impostors as impostors should be set about. That's really official, is it?'

'Quite. Ouch!'

'Anguish?'

'Oo!'

'If I were you,' said Lord Bosham, 'I'd drink the stuff the blighter gave you. There's no reason why it shouldn't prove efficacious. The fact that a chap is an impostor doesn't necessarily mean that he can't spot a good stomach-ache cure when he sees one. Down the hatch with it, my writhing old serpent, with a hey nonny nonny and a hot cha-cha.'

Another twinge caused Baxter to hesitate no longer. He saw that the advice was good. He raised the glass to his lips. He did not drain it with a hey nonny nonny, but he drained it.

It was then too late for him to say 'Hey, nonny nonny,' even if he had wished to.

Down in the hall, like a hound straining at the leash, Beach the butler stood with uplifted stick, waiting for the psychological moment to beat the gong. Lady Constance, as she came downstairs, caught a glimpse of him over the banisters, but she was not accorded leisure to feast her eyes on the spectacle, for along the corridor to her left there came a galloping figure. It was her nephew, Lord Bosham. He reached her, seized her by the wrist and jerked her into an alcove. Accustomed though she was to eccentricity in her nephews, the action momentarily took her breath away.

'Gee-ORGE!' she cried, finding speech.

'Yes, I know, I know. But listen.'

'Are you intoxicated?'

'Of course I'm not. What a dashed silly idea. Much shaken, but sober to the gills. Listen, Aunt Connie. You know those impostors? Impostors A, B, and C? Well, things are getting hot. Impostor A has just laid Baxter out cold with a knock-out drop.'

'What! I don't understand.'

'Well, I can't make it any simpler. That is the bedrock fact. Impostor A has just slipped Baxter a Mickey Finn. And what I'm driving at is, that if these birds are starting to express themselves like this, it means something. It means that tonight's the night. It signifies that whatever dirty work they are contemplating springing on this community will be sprung before tomorrow's sun has risen. Ah!' said Lord Bosham, with animation, as the gong boomed out below. 'Dinner, and not before I was ready for it. Let's go. But mark this, Aunt Connie, and mark it well – the moment we rise from the table, I get my good old gun, and I lurk! I don't know what's up, and you don't know what's up, but that something is up sticks out a mile, and I intend to lurk like a two-year-old. Well, I mean to say, dash it,' said Lord Bosham, with honest heat, 'we can't have this sort of thing, what? If impostors are to be allowed to go chucking their weight about as if they'd bought the place, matters have come to a pretty pass!'

CHAPTER 19

AT TWENTY minutes past nine, the Duke of Dunstable, who had dined off a tray in his room, was still there, waiting for his coffee and liqueur. He felt replete, for he was a good trencherman and had done himself well, but he was enjoying none of that sensation of mental peace which should accompany repletion. Each moment that passed found him more worried and fretful. The failure of Rupert Baxter to report for duty was affecting him much as their god's unresponsiveness once affected the priests of Baal. Here it was getting on for goodness knew what hour, and not a sign of him. It would have pained the efficient young secretary, now lying on his bed with both hands pressed to his temples in a well-meant but unsuccessful attempt to keep his head from splitting in half, could he have known the black thoughts his employer was thinking of him.

The opening of the door, followed by the entry of Beach bearing a tray containing coffee and a generous glass of brandy, caused the Duke to brighten for an instant, but the frown returned to his brow as he saw that the butler was not alone. The last thing he wanted at a time like this was a visitor.

'Good evening, my dear fellow. I wonder if you could spare me a moment?'

It was about half-way through dinner that the thought had occurred to Lord Ickenham that there might be an easier and more agreeable method than that which he had planned of obtaining from the Duke the money which he was, as it were, holding in trust for Polly. He had not developed any weak scruples about borrowing it on the lines originally laid down, but the almost complete absence of conversation at the dinner-table had given him time to reflect, and the result of this reflection had been to breed misgivings.

Success in the campaign which he had sketched out would depend – he had to face it – largely on the effectiveness of his nephew Pongo's performance of the part assigned to him, and he feared lest Pongo, when it came to the pinch, might prove a broken reed. You tell a young man to stand on a lawn and sing the 'Bonny Bonny Banks of Loch Lomond', and the first thing you know he has forgotten the tune or gone speechless with stage fright. Far better, it seemed to him, to try what a simple, straightforward appeal to the Duke's better feelings would do – and, if that failed, to have recourse to the equally simple and straightforward Mickey Finn.

That glass of brandy there would make an admirable receptacle for the sedative, and he had taken the precaution, while tapping Mr Pott's store, to help himself to a couple of the magic tablets, one of which still nestled in his waistcoat pocket.

'It's about that money you won from that man – Pott is his name, I believe – this evening,' he went on.

The Duke grunted guardedly.

'I have been talking to him, and he is most distressed about it.'

The Duke grunted again, scornfully this time, and it seemed to Lord Ickenham that an odd sort of echo came from the bathroom. He put it down to some trick of the acoustics.

'Yes, most distressed. It seems that in a sense the money was not his to gamble with.'

'Hey?' The Duke seemed interested. 'What do you mean? Robbed a till or something, did he?'

'No, no. Nothing like that. He is a man of the most scrupulous honesty. But it was a sum which he had been saving up for his daughter's wedding portion. And now it has gone.'

'What do you expect me to do about it?'

'You wouldn't feel inclined to give it back?'

'Give it back?'

'It would be a fine, generous, heart-stirring action.'

'It would be a fine, potty, fatheaded action,' corrected the Duke warmly. 'Give it back, indeed! I never heard of such a thing.'

'He is much distressed.'

'Let him be.'

It began to be borne in upon Lord Ickenham that in planning to appeal to the Duke's better feelings he had omitted to take into his calculations the fact that he might not have any. With a dreamy look in his eye, he took the tablet from his pocket and palmed it thoughtfully.

'It would be a pity if his daughter were not able to get married,' he said.

'Why?' said the Duke, a stout bachelor.

'She is engaged to a fine young poet.'

'Then,' said the Duke, his face beginning to purple – the Dunstables did not easily forget – 'she's jolly well out of it. Don't talk to me about poets! The scum of the earth.'

'So you won't give the money back?'

'No.'

'Reflect,' said Lord Ickenham. 'It is here, in this room – is it not?'

'What's that got to do with it?'

'I was only thinking that there it was – handy – and all you would have to do would be to go to the drawer... or cupboard...'

He paused expectantly. The Duke maintained a quiet reserve.

'I wish you would reconsider.'

'Well, I won't.'

'The quality of mercy,' said Lord Ickenham, deciding that he could not do better than follow the tested methods of Horace's Pekingese breeder, 'is not strained—'

'The what isn't?'

'The quality of mercy. It droppeth as the gentle rain from heaven upon the place beneath. It is twice blessed—'

'How do you make that out?'

'It blesseth him that gives and him that takes,' explained Lord Ickenham.

'Never heard such rot in my life,' said the Duke. 'I think you're potty. Anyhow, you'll have to go now. I'm expecting my secretary at any moment for an important conference. You haven't seen him anywhere, have you?'

'I had a few words with him before dinner, but I have not seen him since. He is probably amusing himself somewhere.'

'I'll amuse him, when I see him.'

'No doubt he has been unable to tear himself away from the fascinations of the backgammon board or the halma table. Young blood!'

'Young blood be blowed.'

'Ah, that will be he, no doubt.'

'Eh?'

'Someone knocked.'

'I didn't hear anything.'

The Duke went to the door and opened it. Lord Ickenham stretched a hand over the brandy glass and opened it. The Duke came back.

'Nobody there.'

'Ah, then I was mistaken. Well, if you really wish me to go, I will be leaving you. If you don't feel like making the splendid gesture I proposed, there is no more to be said. Good night, my dear fellow,' said Lord Ickenham, and withdrew.

It was perhaps a minute after he had taken his departure that Mr Pott entered the corridor.

Of all the residents of Blandings Castle who had been doing a bit of intensive thinking during dinner – and there were several – Claude Pott was the one who had been thinking hardest. And the result of his thoughts had been to send him hastening to the Duke's room. It was his hope that he would be able to persuade him to play a hand or two of a game called Slippery Joe.

The evening's disaster had left Mr Pott not only out of pocket and humiliated, but full of the liveliest suspicion. How the miracle had been accomplished, he was unable to say, but the more he brooded over the Duke's triumph, the more convinced did he become that he had been cheated and hornswoggled. Honest men, he told himself, did not beat him at Persian Monarchs, and he blamed himself for having selected a game at which it was possible, apparently, for an unscrupulous opponent to put something over. Slippery Joe was open to no such objection. Years of experience had taught him that at Slippery Joe he could always deal himself an unbeatable hand.

He was just about to turn the corner leading to the Garden Suite, hoping for the best, when the Duke came round it, travelling well, and ran into him.

For some moments after Lord Ickenham had left him, the Duke of Dunstable had remained where he sat, frowning peevishly. Then he had risen. Distasteful and even degrading though it might be to go running about after secretaries, there seemed nothing for it but to institute a search for the missing Baxter. He hastened out, and the first thing he knew he was colliding with the frightful feller.

Then he saw that it was not the frightful feller, after all, but another feller, equally frightful – the chap with the wedding-portion daughter, to wit – a man for whom, since listening to Lord Ickenham's remarks, he had come to feel a vivid dislike. He was not fond of many people, but the people of whom he was least fond were those who wanted to get money out of him.

'Gah!' he said, disentangling himself.

Mr Pott smiled an ingratiating smile. It was only a sketchy one, for he had had to assemble it in a hurry, but such as it was he let the Duke have it.

'Hullo, your Grace,' he said.

'Go to hell,' said the Duke and, these brief civilities concluded, stumped off and was lost to sight.

And simultaneously a thought came to Mr Pott like a full-blown rose, flushing his brow.

Until this moment, Mr Pott's only desire had been to recover his lost money through the medium of a game of Slippery Joe. He now saw that there was a simpler and less elaborate way of arriving at the happy ending. Somewhere in the Duke's room there was three hundred pounds morally belonging to himself, and the Duke's room was now unoccupied. To go in and help himself would be to avoid a lot of tedious preliminaries.

Though stout of build, he could move quickly when the occasion called for speed. He bounced along the passage like a rubber ball. Only when he had reached his destination did he find that he need not have hurried. Preoccupied the Duke might have been, but he had not been too preoccupied to remember to lock his door.

The situation was one that might have baffled many men, and for an instant it baffled Mr Pott completely. Then, his native ingenuity asserting itself, he bethought him that the door was not the only means of access to the room. There were French windows, and it was just possible that on a balmy evening like this the Duke might have left them open. Reaching the lawn after a brisk run, rosy and puffing, he discovered that he had not.

This time, Mr Pott accepted defeat. He knew men in London who would have made short work of those windows. They would have produced a bit of bent wire and opened them as if they had been a sardine tin, laughing lightly the while. But he had no skill in that direction. Rueful but resigned, with some of the feelings of Moses gazing at the Promised Land from the summit of Mount Pisgah, he put an eye to the glass and peered through. There was the dear old room, all ready and waiting, but for practical purposes it might have been a hundred miles away. And presently he saw the door open and the Duke came in.

And he was turning away with a sigh, a beaten man, when from somewhere close at hand a voice in the night began to sing the

'Bonny Bonny Banks of Loch Lomond'. And scarcely had the haunting refrain ceased to annoy the birds roosting in the trees, when the French windows flew open and the Duke of Dunstable, shooting out like a projectile, went whizzing across the lawn, crying 'Hey!' as he did so. To Mr Pott, the thing had been just a song, but to the Duke it seemed to have carried a deeper message.

And such was indeed the case. The interpretation which he had placed upon that sudden burst of melody was that it was Baxter who stood warbling without, and that this was his way of trying to attract his employer's attention. Why Baxter should sing outside his room, instead of walking straight in, was a problem which he found himself at the moment unable to solve. He presumed that the man must have some good reason for a course of conduct which at first glance seemed merely eccentric. Possibly, he reflected, complications had arisen, rendering it necessary for him to communicate with headquarters in this oblique and secret society fashion. He could vaguely recall having read in his boyhood stories in which people in such circumstances had imitated the hoot of the night-owl.

'Hey!' he called, trying to combine the conflicting tasks of shouting and speaking in a cautious undertone. 'Here! Hi! Hey! Where are you, dash it?'

For his efforts to establish contact with the vocalist were being oddly frustrated. Instead of standing still and delivering his report, the other seemed to be receding into the distance. When the 'Bonny Banks' broke out again, it was from somewhere at the farther end of the lawn. With a muffled oath, the Duke galloped in that direction like the man in the poem who followed the Gleam, and Mr Pott, always an excellent opportunist, slid in through the French windows.

He had scarcely done so, when he heard footsteps. Somebody was approaching across the grass, and approaching so rapidly that there was no time to be lost if an embarrassing encounter was to be avoided. With great presence of mind he dived into the bathroom. And as he closed the door, Lord Ickenham came in.

Lord Ickenham was feeling well pleased. The artistry of his nephew's performance had enchanted him. He had not supposed that the boy had it in him to carry the thing through with such *bravura*. At the best he had hoped for a timid piping, and that full-throated baying, a cross between a bloodhound on the trail and a Scotsman celebrating New Year's Eve, had been as unexpected as it was agreeable. Technical defects there may have been in Pongo's vocalization, but he had certainly brought the Duke out of the room like a cork out of a bottle. Lord Ickenham could not remember ever having seen a duke move quicker.

And he was just settling down to a swift and intensive search for the wedding portion, when his activities were arrested. From behind the bathroom door, freezing him in his tracks, there came the sharp, piercing scream of a human being in distress. The next moment, Mr Pott staggered out, slamming the door behind him.

'Mustard!' cried Lord Ickenham, completely at a loss.

'Coo!' said Mr Pott, and in a lifetime liberally punctuated by that ejaculation he had never said it with stronger emphasis.

Normally, Claude Pott was rather a reserved man. He lived in a world in which, if you showed your feelings, you lost money. But there were some things which could break down his poise, and one of these was the discovery that he was closeted in a small bathroom with the largest pig he had ever encountered.

For an instant, after he had entered his hiding–place, the Empress had been just an aroma in the darkness. If Mr Pott had felt that it was a bit stuffy in here, that was all he had felt. Then something cold and moist pressed itself against his dangling hand, and the truth came home to him.

'Mustard, my dear fellow!'

'Cor!' said Mr Pott.

He was shaking in every limb. It is not easy for a man who weighs nearly two hundred pounds to quiver like an aspen, but he managed to do it. His mind was in a whirl, from which emerged one coherent thought – that he wanted a drink. An imperious desire for a quick restorative swept over him, and suddenly he perceived that there was relief in sight – if only a small relief. That glass of brandy on the table would be of little real use to him. What he really needed was a brimming bucketful. But it would at least be a step in the right direction.

'Mustard! Stop!'

Lord Ickenham's warning cry came too late. The lethal draught had already passed down Mr Pott's throat, and even as he shook his head appreciatively the glass fell to the floor and he followed it. If twenty pigs had bitten Claude Pott simultaneously in twenty different places, he could not have succumbed more completely.

It was with a sympathetic eye and a tut-tut-ing tongue that Lord Ickenham bent over the remains. There was nothing, he knew, to be done. Only Time, the great healer, could make Claude Pott once more the Claude Pott of happier days. He rose, wondering how best to dispose of the body, and as he did so a voice spoke behind him.

'Hullo-ullo-ullo-ullo-ullo!' it said, and in the words there was an unmistakable note of rebuke.

Faithfully and well Lord Bosham had followed out his policy of lurking, as outlined to his Aunt Constance before dinner. He was now standing in the window, his gun comfortably poised.

'What ho, what ho, what ho, what ho, what ho, what, what?' he added, and paused for a reply.

This Lord Ickenham was not able to give. Man of iron nerve though he was, he could be taken aback. The sudden appearance of Horace Davenport earlier in the evening had done it. The equally sudden appearance of Lord Bosham did it again. He found himself at a loss for words, and it was Lord Bosham who eventually resumed the conversation.

'Well, I'm dashed!' he said, still speaking with that strong note of reproof. 'Here's a nice state of things! So you've put it across poor old Pott now, have you? It's a bit thick. We engage detectives at enormous expense, and as fast as we get them in you bowl them over with knock-out drops.'

He paused, struggling with his feelings. It was plain that he could not trust himself to say what he really thought about it all. His eye roamed the room, and lit up as it rested on the door of the cupboard.

'You jolly well get in there,' he said, indicating it with a wave of the gun. 'Into that cupboard with you, quick, and no back chat.'

If Lord Ickenham had had any intention of essaying repartee, he abandoned it. He entered the cupboard, and the key turned in the lock behind him.

Lord Bosham pressed the bell. A stately form appeared in the doorway.

'Oh, Beach.'

'M'lord?'

'Get a flock of footmen and have Mr Pott taken up to his room, will you?'

'Very good, m'lord.'

The butler had betrayed no emotion on beholding what appeared to be a corpse on the floor of the Garden Suite. Nor did the two footmen, Charles and Henry, who subsequently carried out the removal. It was Blandings Castle's pride that its staff was well trained. Mr Pott disappeared feet foremost, like a used gladiator being cleared away from the arena, and Lord Bosham was left to his thoughts.

These might have been expected to be exultant, for he had undoubtedly acted with dash and decision in a testing situation. But they were only partly so. Mingled with a victor's triumph was the chagrin of the conscientious man who sees a task but half done. That he had properly put a stopper on Impostor A was undeniable, but he had hoped also to deal faithfully with Imposter B. He was wondering if the chap was hiding somewhere and if so, where, when there came to his sensitive ear the sound of a grunt, and he realized that it had proceeded from the bathroom.

'Yoicks!' cried Lord Bosham, and if he had not been a man of action rather than words would have added 'Tally ho!' He did not pause to ask himself why impostors should grunt. He merely dashed at the bathroom door, flung it open and leaped back, his gun at the ready. There was a moment's pause, and then the Empress sauntered out, a look of mild enquiry on her fine face.

The Empress of Blandings was a pig who took things as they came. Her motto, like Horace's, was *nil admirari*. But, cool and even aloof though she was as a general rule, she had been a little puzzled by the events of the day. In particular, she had found the bathroom odd. It was the only place she had ever been in where there appeared to be a shortage of food. The best it had to offer was a cake of shaving-soap, and she had been eating this with a thoughtful frown when Mr Pott joined her. As she emerged now, she was still foaming at the mouth a little and it was perhaps this that set the seal on Lord Bosham's astonishment and caused him not only to recoil a yard or two with his eyes popping but also to pull the trigger of his gun.

In the confined space the report sounded like the explosion of an arsenal, and it convinced the Empress, if she had needed to be convinced, that this was no place for a pig of settled habits. Not since she had been a slip of a child had she moved at anything swifter than a dignified walk, but now Jesse Owens could scarcely have got off the mark more briskly. It took her a few moments to get her bearings, but after colliding with the bed, the table and the armchair, in the order named, she succeeded in setting a course for the window and was in the act of disappearing through it when Lord Emsworth burst into the room, followed by Lady Constance.

The firing of guns in bedrooms is always a thing that tends to excite the interest of the owner of a country house, and it was in a spirit of lively curiosity that Lord Emsworth had arrived upon the scene. An 'Eh, what?' was trembling on his lips as he entered. But the sight of those vanishing hind-quarters with their flash of curly tail took his mind instantly off such comparative trivialities as indoor artillery practice. With a cry that came straight from the heart, he adjusted his pince-nez and made for the great outdoors. Broken words of endearment could be heard coming from the darkness.

Lady Constance had propped herself against the wall, a shapely hand on her heart. She was panting a little, and her eyes showed a disposition to swivel in their sockets. Long ago she had learned the stern lesson that Blandings Castle was no place for weaklings, but this latest manifestation of what life under its roof could be had proved daunting to even her toughened spirit.

'George!' she whispered feebly.

Lord Bosham was his old buoyant self again.

'Quite all right, Aunt Connie. Just an accident. Sorry you were troubled.'

'What – what has been happening?'

'I thought you would want to know that. Well, it was like this. I came in here, to discover that Impostor A had scuppered our detective with one of those knock-out drops of his. I quelled him with my good old gun, and locked him in the cupboard. I thought I heard Impostor B grunting in the bathroom and flung wide the gates, only to discover that it was the guv'nor's pig. Starting back in natural astonishment, I inadvertently pulled the trigger. All quite simple and in order.'

'I thought the Duke had been murdered.'

'No such luck. By the way, I wonder where he's got to. Ah, here's Beach. He'll tell us. Do you know where the Duke is, Beach?'

'No, m'lord. Pardon me, m'lady.'

'Yes, Beach?'

'A Miss Twistleton has called, m'lady.'

'Miss Twistleton?'

Lord Bosham's memory was good.

'That's the girl who gave Horace the raspberry,' he reminded his aunt.

'I know that,' said Lady Constance, with some impatience. 'What I meant was, what can she be doing here at this hour?'

'I gathered, m'lady, that Miss Twistleton had arrived on the five o'clock train from London.'

'But what can she want?'

'That,' Lord Bosham pointed out, 'we can ascertain by seeing the wench. Where did you park her, Beach?'

'I showed the lady into the drawing-room, m'lord.'

'Then Ho for the drawing-room is what I would suggest. My personal bet is that she supposes Horace to be here and has come to tell him she now regrets those cruel words. Oh, Beach.'

'M'lord?'

'Can you use a gun?'

'As a young lad I was somewhat expert with an air-gun, m'lord.'

'Well, take this. It isn't an air-gun, but the principle's the same. You put it to the shoulder – so – and pull the trigger – thus. . . . Oh, sorry,' said Lord Bosham, as the echoes of the deafening report died away and his aunt and her butler, who had skipped like the high hills, came back to terra firma. 'I forgot that would happen. Silly of me. Now I'll have to reload. There's a miscreant in that cupboard, Beach, a devil of a chap who wants watching like a hawk, and I shall require you to stay here and see that he doesn't get out. At the first sign of any funny business on his part, such as trying to break down the door, whip the weapon to the shoulder and blaze away like billy-o. You follow me, Beach?'

'Yes, m'lord.'

'Then pick up the feet, Aunt Connie,' said Lord Bosham, 'and let's go.'

THE FRUITLESS pursuit of Loreleis or will-o'-the-wisps through a dark garden, full of things waiting to leap out and crack him over the shins, can never be an agreeable experience to a man of impatient temperament, accustomed to his comforts. It was a puffing and exasperated Duke of Dunstable who limped back to his room a few minutes after Beach had taken up his vigil. His surprise at finding it occupied by a butler – and not merely an ordinary butler, without trimmings, but one who toted a gun – was very marked. Nor did the sight in any way allay his annoyance. There was a silent instant in which he stood brushing from his moustache the insects of the night that had got entangled there and glaring balefully at the intruder. Then he gave tongue.

'Hey? What? What's this? What the devil's all this? What do you mean, you feller, by invading my private apartment with a dashed great cannon? Of all the houses I was ever in, this is certainly the damnedest. I come down here for a nice rest, and before I can so much as relax a muscle, I find my room full of blasted butlers, armed to the teeth. Don't point that thing at me, sir. Put it down, and explain.'

In a difficult situation, Beach preserved the courteous calm which had made him for so many years the finest butler in Shropshire. He found the Duke's manner trying, but he exhibited nothing but a respectful desire to give satisfaction.

'I must apologize for my presence, your Grace,' he said smoothly, 'but I was instructed by Lord Bosham to remain here and act as his deputy during his temporary absence. I am informed by his lordship that he has deposited a miscreant in the cupboard.'

'A what?'

'A miscreant, your Grace. Something, I gather, in the nature of a nocturnal marauder. His lordship gave me to understand that he discovered the man in this room and, having overpowered him, locked him in the cupboard.'

'Hey? Which cupboard?'

The butler indicated the safe deposit in question, and the Duke uttered a stricken cry.

'My God! All in among my spring suits! Let him out at once.'

'His lordship instructed me—'

'Dash his lordship! I'm not going to have smelly miscreants ruining my clothes. What sort of a miscreant?'

'I have no information, your Grace.'

'Probably some foul tramp with the grime of years on him, and the whole outfit will have to go to the cleaner's. Let him out immediately.'

'Very good, your Grace.'

'I'll turn the key and throw the door open, and you stand ready with your gun. Now, then, when I say "Three". One.... Two.... Three.... Good Lord, it's the brain chap!'

Lord Ickenham had not enjoyed his sojourn in the cupboard, which he had found close and uncomfortable, but it had left him his old debonair self.

'Ah, my dear Duke,' he said genially, as he emerged, 'good evening once more. I wonder if I might use your hairbrush? The thatch has become a little disordered.'

The Duke was staring with prawnlike eyes.

'Was that you in there?' he asked. A foolish question, perhaps, but a man's brain is never at its nimblest on these occasions.

Lord Ickenham said it was.

'What on earth were you doing, going into cupboards?'

Lord Ickenham passed the brush lovingly through his grey locks.

'I went in because I was requested to by the man behind the gun. I happened to be strolling on the lawn and saw your windows open, and I thought I might enjoy another chat with you. I had scarcely entered, when Bosham appeared, weapon in hand. I don't know how you feel about these things, my dear fellow, but my view is that when an impetuous young gentleman, fingering the trigger of a gun, tells you to go into a cupboard, it is best to humour him.'

'But why did he tell you to go into the cupboard?'

'Ah, there you take me into deep waters. He gave me no opportunity of enquiring.'

'I mean, you're not a nocturnal marauder.'

'No. The whole thing is very odd.'

'I'm going to get to the bottom of this. Hey, you, go and fetch Lord Bosham.'

'Very good, your Grace.'

'The fact of the matter is,' said the Duke, as the butler left the room like a stately galleon under sail, 'the whole family's potty, as I told you before. I just met Emsworth in the garden. His manner was most peculiar. He called me a pig-stealing pest and a number of other things. I made allowances, of course, for the fact that he's as mad as a hatter, but I shall leave tomorrow and I shan't come here again. They'll miss me, but I can't help that. Did Bosham shoot at you?'

'No.'

'He shot at someone.'

'Yes, I heard a fusillade going on.'

'The feller oughtn't to be at large. Human life isn't safe. Ah, here he is. Here, you!'

Through the door a little procession was entering. It was headed by Lady Constance. Behind her came a tall, handsome girl, in whom Lord Ickenham had no difficulty in recognizing his niece Valerie. The rear was brought up by Lord Bosham. Lady Constance was looking cold and stern, Valerie Twistleton colder and sterner. Lord Bosham looked merely bewildered. He resembled his father and his brother Freddie in not being very strong in the head, and the tale to which he had been listening in the drawing-room had been of a nature not at all suited to the consumption of the weak-minded. A girl claiming to be Miss Twistleton, niece of the Earl of Ickenham, had suddenly blown in from nowhere with the extraordinary story that Impostor A was her uncle, and she had left Lord Bosham with such brain as he possessed in a whirl. He was anxious for further light on a puzzling situation.

'What the devil do you mean....' The Duke broke off. He was staring at Lady Constance's companion, whom, owing to the fact that his gaze had been riveted on Lord Bosham, he had not immediately observed. 'Hey, what?' he said. 'Where did you spring from?'

'This is Miss Twistleton, Alaric.'

'Of course she's Miss Twistleton. I know that.'

'Ah!' said Lord Bosham. 'She *is* Miss Twistleton, is she? You identify her?'

'Of course I identify her.'

'My mistake,' said Lord Bosham. 'I thought she might be Impostor D.'

'George, you're an idiot!'

'Right ho, Aunt Connie.'

'Bosham, you're a damned fool!'

'Right ho, Duke.'

'Chump!'

'Right ho, Miss Twistleton. It was just that it occurred to me as a passing thought that Miss Twistleton, though she said she was Miss Twistleton, might not be Miss Twistleton but simply pretending to be Miss Twistleton in order to extricate Impostor A from a nasty spot. But, of course, if you're all solid on the fact of Miss Twistleton really being Miss Twistleton, my theory falls to the ground. Sorry, Miss Twistleton.'

'George, will you please stop drivelling.'

'Right ho, Aunt Connie. Merely mentioning what occurred to me as a passing thought.'

Now that the point of Miss Twistleton's identity – the fact that she was a genuine Miss Twistleton and not a pseudo Miss Twistleton – had been settled, the Duke returned to the grievance which he had started to ventilate a few moments earlier.

'And now perhaps you'll explain, young cloth-headed Bosham, what you mean by shutting your father's guests in cupboards. Do you realize that the man might have messed up my spring suits and died of suffocation?'

Lady Constance intervened.

'We came to let Lord Ickenham out.'

'Let who out?'

'Lord Ickenham.'

'How do you mean, Lord Ickenham?'

'This is Lord Ickenham.'

'Yes,' said Lord Ickenham, 'I am Lord Ickenham. And this,' he went on, bestowing a kindly glance on the glacial Valerie, 'is my favourite niece.'

'I'm your only niece.'

'Perhaps that's the reason,' said Lord Ickenham.

The Duke had now reached an almost Bosham-like condition of mental fog.

'I don't understand all this. If you're Ickenham, why didn't you say you were Ickenham? Why did you tell us you were Glossop?'

'Precisely,' said Lady Constance. 'I am waiting for Lord Ickenham to explain—'

'Me too,' said Lord Bosham.

'– his extraordinary behaviour.'

'Extraordinary is the word,' assented Lord Bosham. 'As a matter of fact, his behaviour has been extraordinary all along. Most extraordinary. By way of a start, he played the confidence trick on me in London.'

'Just to see whether it could be done, my dear fellow,' explained Lord Ickenham. 'Merely an experiment in the interests of science. I sent your wallet to your home, by the way. You will find it waiting there for you.'

'Oh, really?' said Lord Bosham, somewhat mollified. 'I'm glad to hear that. I value that wallet.'

'A very nice wallet.'

'It is rather, isn't it? My wife gave it me for a birthday present.'

'Indeed? How is your wife?'

'Oh, fine, thanks.'

'Whoso findeth a wife findeth a good thing.'

'I'll tell her that. Rather neat. Your own?'

'Proverbs of Solomon.'

'Oh? Well, I'll pass it along, anyway. It should go well.'

Lady Constance was finding a difficulty in maintaining her patrician calm. This difficulty her nephew's conversation did nothing to diminish.

'Never mind about your wife, George. We are all very fond of Cicely, but we do not want to talk about her now.'

'No, no, of course not. Don't quite know how we got on to the subject. Still, before leaving same, I should just like to mention that she's the best little woman in the world. Right ho, Aunt Connie, carry on. You have the floor.'

There was a frigidity in Lady Constance's manner.

'You have really finished?'

'Oh, rather.'

'You are quite sure?'

'Oh, quite.'

'Then I will ask Lord Ickenham to explain why he came to Blandings Castle pretending to be Sir Roderick Glossop.'

'Yes, let's have a diagram of that.'

'Be quiet, George.'

'Right ho, Aunt Connie.'

Lord Ickenham looked thoughtful.

'Well,' he said, 'it's a long story.'

Valerie Twistleton's eye, as it met her uncle's, was hard and unfriendly.

'Your stories can never be too long,' she said, speaking with a metallic note in her voice. 'And we have the night before us.'

'And why,' asked Lord Bosham, 'did he lay out Baxter and our detective with knock-out drops?'

'Please, George!'

'Yes,' said Lord Ickenham rebukingly, 'we shall never get anywhere, if you go wandering off into side issues. It is, as I say, a long story, but if you are sure it won't bore you—'

'Not at all,' said Valerie. 'We shall all be most interested. So will Aunt Jane, when I tell her.'

Lord Ickenham looked concerned.

'My dear child, you mustn't breathe a word to your aunt about meeting me here.'

'Oh, no?'

'Emphatically not. Lady Constance will agree with me, I know, when she has heard what I have to say.'

'Then please say it.'

'Very well. The explanation of the whole thing is absurdly simple. I came here on Emsworth's behalf.'

'I do not understand you.'

'I will make myself plain.'

'I still don't see,' said Lord Bosham, who had been brooding with bent brows, 'why he should have slipped kayo drops in—'

'George!'

'Oh, all right.'

Lord Ickenham regarded the young man for a moment with a reproving eye.

'Emsworth,' he resumed, 'came to me and told me a strange and romantic story—'

'And now,' said Valerie, 'you're telling us one.'

'My dear! It seemed that he had become sentimentally attached to a certain young woman ... or person ... or party ... however you may choose to describe her—'

'What!'

Lord Bosham appeared stunned.

'Why, dash it, he was a hundred last birthday!'

'Your father is a man of about my own age.'

'And mine,' said the Duke.

'I should describe him as being in the prime of life.'

'Exactly,' said the Duke.

'I often say that life begins at sixty.'

'So do I,' said the Duke. 'Frequently.'

'That, at any rate,' proceeded Lord Ickenham, 'was how Emsworth felt. The fever of spring was coursing through his veins, and he told himself that there was life in the old dog yet. I use the expression "old dog" in no derogatory sense. He conceived a deep attachment for this girl, and persuaded me to bring her here as my daughter.'

Lady Constance had now abandoned altogether any attempt at preserving a patrician calm. She uttered a cry which, if it had proceeded from a less aristocratic source, might almost have been called a squeal.

'What! You mean that my brother is infatuated with that child?'

'Where did he meet her?' asked Lord Bosham.

'It was his dearest wish,' said Lord Ickenham, 'to make her his bride.'

'Where did he meet her?' asked Lord Bosham.

'It not infrequently happens that men in the prime of life pass through what might be described as an Indian Summer of the affections, and when this occurs the object of their devotion is generally pretty juvenile.'

'What beats me,' said Lord Bosham, 'is where on earth he could have met her. I didn't know the guv'nor ever stirred from the old home.'

It seemed to Lord Ickenham that this was a line of enquiry which it would be well to check at its source.

'I wish you wouldn't interrupt,' he said, brusquely.

'Yes, dash it, you oaf,' said the Duke, 'stop interrupting.'

'Can't you see, George,' cried Lady Constance despairingly, 'that we are all almost off our heads with worry and anxiety, and you keep interrupting.'

'Very trying,' said Lord Ickenham.

Lord Bosham appeared wounded. He was not an abnormally sensitive young man, but this consensus of hostile feeling seemed to hurt him.

'Well, if a chap can't say a word,' he said, 'perhaps you would prefer that I withdrew.'

'Yes, do.'

'Right ho,' said Lord Bosham. 'Then I will. Anybody who wants me will find me having a hundred up in the billiard-room. Not that I suppose my movements are of the slightest interest.'

He strode away, plainly piqued, and his passing seemed to Lord Ickenham to cause a marked improvement in the atmosphere. He had seldom met a young man with such a gift for asking inconvenient questions. Freed of this heckler, he addressed himself to his explanation with renewed confidence.

'Well, as I say, Emsworth had conceived this infatuation for a girl who, in the prime of life though he was, might have been his granddaughter. And he asked me as an old friend to help him. He anticipated that there would be opposition to the match, and his rather ingenious scheme was that I should come to Blandings Castle posing as the Sir Roderick Glossop who was expected, and should bring the girl with me as my daughter. He was good enough to say that my impressive deportment would make an excellent background for her. His idea – shrewd, however one may deplore it – was that you, Lady Constance, would find yourself so attracted by the girl's personality that the task of revealing the truth to you would become a simple one. He relied on her – I quote his expression – to fascinate you.'

Lady Constance drew a deep, shuddering breath.

'Oh, did he?'

The Duke put a question.

'Who is this frightful girl? An absolute outsider, of course?'

'Yes, her origin is humble. She is the daughter of a retired Silver Ring bookie.'

'My God!'

'Yes. Well, Emsworth came to me and proposed this scheme, and you can picture my dismay as I listened. Argument, I could see, would have been useless. The man was obsessed.'

'You use such lovely language,' said Valerie, who had sniffed.

'Thank you, my dear.'

'Have you ever thought of writing fairy stories?'

'No, I can't say I have.'

'You should.'

The look the Duke cast at the sardonic girl could scarcely have been sourer if she had been Lord Bosham.

'Never mind all that, dash it. First Bosham, now you. Interruptions all the time. Get on, get on, get on. Yes, yes, yes, yes, yes?'

'So,' said Lord Ickenham, 'I did not attempt argument. I agreed to his proposal. The impression I tried to convey – and, I think, succeeded in conveying – was that I approved. I consented to the monstrous suggestion that I should come here under a false name and bring the girl as my daughter. And shall I tell you why?'

'Yes, do,' said Valerie.

'Because a sudden thought had struck me. Was it not possible, I asked myself, that if Emsworth were to see this girl at Blandings Castle – in the surroundings of his own home – with the portraits of his ancestors gazing down at her—'

'Dashed ugly set of mugs,' said the Duke. 'Why they ever wanted to have themselves painted...However, never mind that. I see what you're getting at. You thought it might cause him to take another look at the frightful little squirt and realize he was making an ass of himself?'

'Exactly. And that is just what happened. The scales fell from his eyes. His infatuation ceased as suddenly as it had begun. This evening he told her it could never be, and she has left for London.'

'Then, dash it, everything's all right.'

'Thank Heaven!' cried Lady Constance.

Lord Ickenham shook his head gravely.

'I am afraid you are both overlooking something. There are such things as breach of promise cases.'

'What!'

'I fear so. He tells me the girl took the thing badly. She went off muttering threats.'

'Then what is to be done?'

'There is only one thing to be done, Lady Constance. You must make a financial settlement with her.'

'Buy her off,' explained the Duke. 'That's the way to handle it. You can always buy these females off. I recollect, when I was at Oxford...However, that is neither here nor there. The point is, how much?'

Lord Ickenham considered.

'A girl of that class,' he said, at length, 'would have very limited ideas about money. Three hundred pounds would seem a fortune to her. In fact, I think I might be able to settle with her for two hundred and fifty.'

'Odd,' said the Duke, struck by the coincidence. 'That was the sum my potty nephew was asking me for this afternoon.'

'Curious,' said Lord Ickenham.

'Had some dashed silly story about wanting it so that he could get married.'

'Fancy! Well, then, Lady Constance, if you will give me three hundred pounds – to be on the safe side – I will run up to London tomorrow morning and see what I can do.'

'I will write you a cheque.'

'No, don't do that,' said the Duke. 'What you want on these occasions is to roll the money about in front of them in solid cash. That time at Oxford... And I happen, strangely enough, to have that exact sum in this very room.'

'Why, so you have,' said Lord Ickenham. 'We were talking about it not long ago, weren't we?'

The Duke unlocked a drawer in the writing-table.

'Here you are,' he said. 'Take it, and see what you can do. Remember, it is imperative to roll it about.'

'And if more is required—' said Lady Constance.

'I doubt if it will be necessary to sweeten the kitty any further. This should be ample. But there is one other thing,' said Lord Ickenham. 'This unfortunate infatuation of Emsworth's must never be allowed to come out.'

'Well, dash it,' said the Duke, staring. 'Of course not. I know, and Connie knows, that Emsworth's as potty as a March hare, but naturally we don't want the world to know it.'

'If people got to hear of this,' said Lady Constance, with a shiver, 'we should be the laughing stock of the county.'

'Exactly,' said Lord Ickenham. 'But there is one danger which does not appear to have occurred to you. It is possible, Valerie, my dear, that you have been thinking of telling your aunt that you met me here.'

Valerie Twistleton smiled a short, sharp smile. Hers was at the same time a loving and a vengeful nature. She loved her Horace, and it was her intention to punish this erring uncle drastically for the alarm and despondency he had caused him. She had been looking forward with bright anticipation to the cosy talk which she would have with Jane, Countess of Ickenham, on the latter's return from the South of France.

'It is,' she said, 'just possible.'

Lord Ickenham's manner was very earnest.

'You mustn't do it, my dear. It would be fatal. You are probably unaware that your aunt expressed a strong wish that I should remain at Ickenham during her absence. If she discovered that I had disobeyed her instructions, I should be compelled, in order to put things right for myself, to tell her the whole story. And my dear wife,' said Lord Ickenham, turning to Lady Constance, 'has just one fault. She is a gossip. With no desire to harm a soul, she would repeat the story. In a week it would be all over England.'

The imperiousness of a hundred fighting ancestors descended upon Lady Constance.

'Miss Twistleton,' she said, in the voice which Lord Emsworth would have recognized as the one which got things done, 'you are not to breathe a word to Lady Ickenham of having met Lord Ickenham here.'

For an instant, it seemed as if Valerie Twistleton was about to essay the mad task of defying this woman. Then, as their eyes met, she seemed to wilt.

'Very well,' she said meekly.

Lord Ickenham's eyes beamed with fond approval. He placed a kindly hand on her shoulder and patted it.

'Thank you, my dear. My favourite niece,' he said.

And he went off to inform Pongo that, owing to having received pennies from heaven, he was in a position not only to solve the tangled affairs of Polly Pott but also to spend nearly three weeks in London with him – with money in his pocket, moreover, to disburse on any little treat that might suggest itself, such as another visit to the Dog Races.

There was a tender expression on his handsome face as he made his way up the stairs. What a pleasure it was, he was feeling, to be able to scatter sweetness and light. Especially in London in the springtime, when, as has been pointed out, he was always at his best.

FROM OVER SEVENTY

AN AUTOBIOGRAPHY WITH
DIGRESSIONS

FOREWORD

THERE IS a rare treat in store for the reader[1] of this book. Except in the Foreword,[2] which will soon be over, it is entirely free from footnotes.

I am not, I think, an irascible man,[3] but after reading a number of recent biographies and histories I have begun to feel pretty sore about these footnotes and not in the mood to be put upon much longer.[4] It is high time,[5] in my opinion, that this nuisance was abated and biographers and essayists restrained from strewing these unsightly blemishes[6] through their pages as if they were ploughing the fields and scattering the good seed o'er the land.[7]

I see no need for the bally things.[8] I have just finished reading Carl Sandburg's *Abraham Lincoln, The War Years*, and Carl manages to fill four fat volumes without once resorting to this exasperating practice.[9] If he can do it, why can't everyone?[10]

Frank Sullivan, the American writer,[11] has already raised his voice[12] on this subject,[13] being particularly severe on the historian Gibbon for his habit of getting you all worked up, thinking now that you are going to hear full details of the vices of the later Roman emperors, and then switching you off to a Latin footnote

---

1 Or readers. Let's be optimistic.
2 Sometimes called Preface. See *Romeo and Juliet*, Act Two, Scene One – 'A rose by any other name would smell as sweet'.
3 Sunny Jim, many people call me.
4 See *King Lear*, Act One, Scene Two – 'Some villain hath done me wrong'.
5 Greenwich Mean or, in America, Eastern Standard.
6 Footnotes.
7 Hymns A. and M.
8 Footnotes.
9 Bunging in a footnote every second paragraph.
10 Answer me that.
11 One of the Saratoga, N.Y., Sullivans.
12 A light baritone, a little uncertain in the upper register.
13 Footnotes.

which defies translation for the ordinary man who forgot all the Latin he ever knew back in 1920.[14]

I know just how Frank feels. It is the same with me. When I read a book I am like someone strolling across a level lawn, thinking how jolly it all is, and when I am suddenly confronted with a^1 or a^2 it is as though I had stepped on the teeth of a rake and had the handle spring up and hit me on the bridge of the nose. I stop dead and my eyes flicker and swivel. I tell myself that this time I will not be fooled into looking at the beastly thing,[15] but I always am, and it nearly always maddens me by beginning with the word 'see'. 'See the *Reader's Digest*, April 1950,' says one writer on page 7 of his latest work, and again on page 181, 'See the *Reader's Digest*, October 1940.'

How do you mean, 'See' it, my good fellow?[16] Are you under the impression that I am a regular subscriber to the *Reader's Digest* and save up all the back numbers? Let me tell you that if in the waiting-room of my dentist or some such place my eye falls on a copy of this widely circulated little periodical, I wince away from it like a salted snail, knowing that in it lurks some ghastly Most Unforgettable Character I Ever Met.

Slightly, but not much, better than the footnotes which jerk your eye to the bottom of the page are those which are lumped together somewhere in the back of the book. These allow of continuous reading, or at any rate are supposed to, but it is only a man of iron will who, coming on a^6 or a^7, can keep from dropping everything and bounding off after it like a basset hound after a basset.[17]

This involves turning back to ascertain which chapter you are on, turning forward and finding yourself in the Index, turning back and fetching up on Sources, turning forward and getting entangled in Bibliography and only at long last hooking the Notes; and how seldom the result is worth the trouble. I was reading the other day that bit in Carrington's *Life of Rudyard Kipling* where

14 Or, in my case, earlier. The sort of thing Sullivan dislikes is when Gibbon says you simply wouldn't believe the things the Empress Theodora used to get up to, and tells you in the footnote that she was in *tres partes divisa* and much given to the *argumentum ad hominem et usque ad hoc*.

15 The footnote.

16 The man's an ass.

17 What *is* a basset? I've often wondered.

Kipling and his uncle Fred Macdonald go to America and Kipling tries to sneak in incog. and Fred Macdonald gives him away to the reporters. When I saw a[7] appended to this I was all keyed up. Now, I felt, we're going to get something good. The footnote, I told myself, will reveal in detail what Kipling said to Fred Macdonald about his fatheadedness and I shall pick up some powerful epithets invaluable for use in conversations with taxi-drivers and traffic policemen.

Here is[7] *in toto*:

F. W. MACDONALD

If that is not asking for bread and being given a stone, it would be interesting to know what it is. The only thing you can say for a footnote like that is that it is not dragged in, as are most footnotes, just to show off the writer's erudition, as when the author of – say – *The Life of Sir Leonard Hutton* says:

> It was in the pavilion at Leeds – not, as has sometimes been stated, at Manchester – that Sir Leonard first uttered those memorable words, 'I've been having a spot of trouble with my lumbago.'

and then with a[6] directs you to the foot of the page, where you find:

> Unlike Giraldus Cambrensis, who in *Happy Days at Bognor Regis* mentions suffering from measles and chickenpox as a child but says that he never had lumbago. See also Caecilius Status, Dio Chrysostom and Abu Mohammed Kasim Ben Ali Hariri.

Which is intolerable.[18]

No footnotes, then, in this book of mine, and I think on the whole no Dedication.

Nobody seems to be doing these now, and it just shows how things have changed since the days when I was starting out to give a shot in the arm to English Literature. At the turn of the century the Dedication was the thing on which we authors all spread ourselves. It was the *bonne bouche* and the *sine qua non*.

We went in for variety in those days. When you opened a novel, you never knew what you were going to get. It might be the curt, take-it-or-leave-it dedication:

---

18 It is what Shakespeare would have called a fardel. See *Hamlet*, Act Three, Scene One – 'Who would fardels bear?'

To
J. Smith

and the somewhat warmer:

To
My friend Percy Brown

one of those cryptic things with a bit of poetry in italics:

To
F.B.O.

Stark winds
And sunset over the moors
Why?
Whither?
Whence?
And the roll of distant drums

or possibly the nasty dedication, intended to sting:

To
J. Alastair Frisby
Who
Told Me I Would Never Have A Book Published
And
Advised me
To
Get a job selling jellied eels

SUCKSTOYOU, FRISBY

It was all great fun and kept our pores open and our blood circulating, but it is not difficult to see why the custom died out. Inevitably a time came when there crept into authors' minds the question, 'What is there in this for me?' I know it was so in my own case. 'What is Wodehouse getting out of this?' I asked myself, and the answer, as far as I could see, was, 'Not a thing.'

When the eighteenth-century author inserted on page 1 something like

To
The Most Noble and Puissant Lord Knubble of Knopp
This book is dedicated

By
His very Humble Servant, the Author

My Lord,
It is with inexpressible admiration for your lordships transcendent
gifts that the poor slob who now addresses your lordship presents
to your lordship this trifling work, so unworthy of your lordships
distinguished consideration,

he expected to do himself a bit of good. Lord Knubble was
his patron and could be relied on, unless having one of his attacks
of gout, to come through with at least a couple of guineas. But
where does a modern author like myself get off? I pluck – let us
say – P. B. Biffen from the ranks of the unsung millions and make
him immortal, and what does Biffen do in return? He does
nothing. He just stands there. I probably won't get so much as a
lunch out of it.

So no Dedication and, as I say, none of those obscene little fly-
specks scattered about all over the page.[19]

I must conclude by expressing my gratitude to Mr P. G.
Wodehouse for giving me permission to include in these pages
an extract from his book, *Louder and Funnier*. Pretty decent of him,
I call it.[20]

Here ends the Foreword. Now we're off.

19 Footnotes.
20 The whitest man I know.

I INTRODUCING J. P. WINKLER

I

INTERESTING LETTER the other day from J. P. Winkler.

You don't know J. P. Winkler? Nor, as a matter of fact, though he addresses me as friend, do I, but he seems to be a man of enterprise and a go-getter.

He says, writing from out Chicago way:

> Friend Wodehouse,
>
> For some time I have been presenting in newspapers and on radio a feature entitled *Over Seventy*, being expressions on living by those who have passed their seventieth year, and I should like to include you in this series.
>
> Here are some of the questions I would like you to answer. What changes do you notice particularly in your daily life now? What changes in the American scene? Have you a regimen for health? Are you influenced by criticism of your books? Have you ever written poetry? Have you ever lectured? What do you think of television and the motion pictures?
>
> I see you are living in the country now. Do you prefer it to the city? Give us the overall picture of your home life and describe your methods of work. And any information concerning your experiences in the theatre and any observations on life in general, as seen from the angle of over seventy, will be welcome.
>
> You have been doing much these last fifty years, perhaps you can tell us something about it.

Naturally I was flattered, for we all know that it isn't everybody who gets included in a series. Nevertheless, that 'fifty years' piqued me a little. Long before fifty years ago I was leaving footprints on the sands of time, and good large footprints at that. In my early twenties it would not be too much to say that I was the talk of London. If you had not seen me riding my bicycle down the Strand to the offices of the *Globe* newspaper, where I was at that time employed, frequently using no hands and sometimes bending over to pick up a handkerchief with my teeth, it was pretty generally agreed that you had not seen anything. And the public's memory must be very short if the 22 not out I made for the printers of the *Globe* against the printers of the *Evening News* one Sunday in 1904 has been forgotten.

However, I get the idea, Winkler. You want to start the old gaffer mumbling away in the chimney corner over his clay pipe in the hope that something will emerge which you can present in newspapers and on radio. You would have me survey mankind from China to Peru, touching now on this subject, now on that, like a butterfly flitting from flower to flower, and every now and then coming up with some red-hot personal stuff by way of supplying the human interest.

Right ho. Let's get cracking and see what we can do about it.

2

I am relieved, old man, that you do not insist on the thing being exclusively autobiographical, for as an autobiographer I am rather badly handicapped.

On several occasions it has been suggested to me that I might take a pop at writing my reminiscences. 'Yours has been a long life,' people say. 'You look about a hundred and four. You should make a book of it and cash in.'

It's a thought, of course, but I don't see how I could do it. The three essentials for an autobiography are that its compiler shall have had an eccentric father, a miserable misunderstood childhood and a hell of a time at his public school, and I enjoyed none of these advantages. My father was as normal as rice pudding, my childhood went like a breeze from start to finish, with everybody I met understanding me perfectly, while as for my schooldays at Dulwich they were just six years of unbroken bliss. It would be laughable for me to attempt a formal autobiography. I have not got the material. Anything on the lines of

Wodehouse, The Story of a Wonder Man starting with

Chapter One: The Infant
Chapter Two: Childhood Days
Chapter Three: Sturm und Drang of Adolescence

is, I feel, out of the question.

Another thing about an autobiography is that, to attract the cash customers, it must be full of good stories about the famous, and I never can think of any. If it were just a matter of dropping names, I could do that with the best of them, but mere name-dropping is not enough. You have to have the sparkling anecdote as well, and any I could provide would be like the one Young Griffo, the boxer, told me in 1904 about his meeting with Joe Gans, the then lightweight champion. Having just been matched to fight Gans, he was naturally anxious to get a look at him before the formal proceedings began, and here is how he told the dramatic tale of their encounter.

'I was going over to Philadelphia to see a fight,' he said, 'and my manager asks me would I like to meet Joe Gans. He asks me would I like to meet Joe Gans, see, and I said I would. So we arrive in Philadelphia and we start out for one of the big sporting places where the gang all held out, and my manager asks me again do I want to see Joe Gans, and I say I do. So we go to this big sporting place where the gang all held out, and there's a big crowd standing around one of the tables, and somebody asks me would I like to meet Joe Gans, he's over at that table. Would I like to meet Joe Gans, he says, he's over at that table, he says, and I say I would. So he takes me to the table and says "Here's Young Griffo, Joe," he says. "He wants to meet you," he says. And sure enough it was Joe all right. He gets up from the table and comes right at me.'

I was leaning forward by this time and clutching the arms of my chair. How cleverly, I thought, just as if he had been a professional author, this rather untutored man had led up to the big moment.

'Yes?' I gasped. 'And then?'

'Huh?'

'What happened then?'

'He shakes hands with me. "Hullo, Griff," he says. And I say "Hullo, Joe." '

That was all. You might have thought more was coming, but no. He had met Gans, Gans had met him. It was the end of the story. My autobiography would be full of stuff like that.

I had long wished to make the acquaintance of Mr (now Lord) Attlee, but it was not for some years that I was enabled to gratify this ambition. A friend took me to the House of Commons, and we were enjoying tea on the terrace when Mr Attlee came by.

'Oh, Clem,' said my friend, 'I want you to meet Mr Wodehouse.'
'How do you do?' said Mr Attlee.
'How do you do?' I replied.

You can't charge people sixteen bob or whatever it is for that sort of thing.

Still, I quite see, J.P., that I must give you something personal on which your radio public can chew, or we shall have them kicking holes in their sets. I could mention, for instance, that when I was four years old I used to play with an orange, but I doubt if that would interest them, and that at the age of six I read the whole of Pope's *Iliad*, which of course they wouldn't believe. Better, I think, to skip childhood and adolescence and go straight to the Autumn of 1900, when, a comely youth of some eighteen summers, I accepted employment in the Lombard Street office of the Hong Kong and Shanghai Bank. Reluctantly, I may mention. As the song says, I didn't want to do it, I didn't want to do it, but my hand was forced.

The trouble in the Wodehouse home at the beginning of the century was that money was a good deal tighter than could have been wished. The wolf was not actually whining at the door and there was always a little something in the kitty for the butcher and the grocer, but the finances would not run to anything in the nature of a splash. My father, after many years in Hong Kong, had retired on a pension, and the authorities paid it to him in rupees. A thoroughly dirty trick, in my opinion, for the rupee is the last thing in the world – or was then – with which anyone who valued his peace of mind would wish to be associated. It never stayed put for a second. It was always jumping up and down and throwing fits, and expenditure had to be regulated in the light of what mood it happened to be in at the moment. 'Watch that rupee!' was the cry in the Wodehouse family.

The result was that during my schooldays my future was always uncertain. The Boy, What Will He Become? was a question that received a different answer almost daily. My brother Armine had got a scholarship and gone to Oxford, and the idea was that, if I got a scholarship too, I would join him there. All through my last term at Dulwich I sprang from my bed at five sharp each morning, ate a couple of *petit beurre* biscuits and worked like a beaver at my Homer and Thucydides, but just as scholarship time was approaching, with me full to the brim with classic lore and just spoiling for a good whack at the examiners, the rupee started creating again, and it seemed to my father that two sons at the University would be a son more than the privy purse could handle. So Learning drew the loser's end, and Commerce got me.

You are probably thinking, Winkler, that this was a nice slice of luck for Commerce, but you are wrong. Possibly because I was a dedicated literary artist with a soul above huckstering or possibly – this was the view more widely held in the office – because I was just a plain dumb brick, I proved to be the most inefficient clerk whose trouser seat ever polished the surface of a high stool. I was all right as long as they kept me in the postal department, where I had nothing to do but stamp and post letters, a task for which my abilities well fitted me, but when they took me out of there and put me in Fixed Deposits the whisper went round Lombard Street, 'Wodehouse is at a loss. He cannot cope.'

If there was a moment in the course of my banking career when I had the foggiest notion of what it was all about, I am unable to recall it. From Fixed Deposits I drifted to Inward Bills – no use asking me what inward bills are. I never found out – and then to Outward Bills and to Cash, always with a weak, apologetic smile on my face and hoping that suavity of manner would see me through when, as I knew must happen 'ere long, I fell short in the performance of my mystic duties. My total inability to grasp what was going on made me something of a legend in the place. Years afterwards, when the ineptness of a new clerk was under discussion in the manager's inner sanctum and the disposition of those present at the conference was to condemn him as the worst bungler who had ever entered the Hong Kong and Shanghai Bank's portals, some white-haired veteran in charge of one of the departments would shake his head and murmur, 'No, no, you're wrong. Young Robinson is, I agree, an almost total loss and ought to have been chloroformed at birth, but you should have seen P. G. Wodehouse. Ah, they don't make them like that nowadays. They've lost the pattern.'

Only two things connected with the banking industry did I really get into my head. One was that from now on all I would be able to afford in the way of lunch would be a roll and butter and a cup of coffee, a discovery which, after the lavish midday meals of school, shook me to my foundations. The other was that, if I got to the office late three mornings in a month, I would lose my

Christmas bonus. One of the great sights in the City in the years 1901–2 was me rounding into the straight with my coat-tails flying and my feet going pitter pitter pat and just making it across the threshold while thousands cheered. It kept me in superb condition, and gave me a rare appetite for the daily roll and butter.

Owing to this slowness of uptake where commerce was concerned, I was never very happy in the bank, though probably happier than the heads of the various departments through which I made my stumbling way. What I would have liked to do on leaving school was to dig in at home and concentrate on my writing. My parents were living in Shropshire – lovely scenery and Blandings Castle just round the corner – and nothing would have suited me better than to withdraw to that earthly Paradise and devote myself to turning out short stories, which I used to do at that time at the rate of one a day. (In the summer of 1901 I contracted mumps and went home to have them in the bosom of my family. I was there three weeks, swelling all the time, and wrote nineteen short stories, all of which, I regret to say, editors were compelled to decline owing to lack of space. The editors regretted it, too. They said so.)

Putting this project up to my parents, I found them cold towards it. The cross all young writers have to bear is that, while they know that they are going to be spectacularly successful some day, they find it impossible to convince their nearest and dearest that they will ever amount to a row of beans. Write in your spare time, if you really must write, parents say, and they pull that old one about literature being a good something but a bad crutch. I do not blame mine for feeling that a son in a bank making his £80 a year, just like finding it in the street, was a sounder commercial proposition than one living at home and spending a fortune on stamps. (The editor is always glad to consider contributions, but a stamped and addressed envelope should be enclosed in case of rejection.)

So for two years I continued to pass my days in Lombard Street and write at night in my bed-sitting-room, and a testing experience it was, for all I got out of it was a collection of rejection slips with which I could have papered the walls of a good-sized banqueting hall. The best you could say of these was that some of them were rather pretty. I am thinking chiefly of the ones *Tit-Bits* used to send out, with a picture of the Newnes' offices in an attractive shade of green. I like those. But what I always feel about rejection slips is that their glamour soon wears off. When you've seen one, I often say, you've seen them all.

The handicap under which most beginning writers struggle is that they don't know how to write. I was no exception to this rule. Worse bilge than mine may have been submitted to the editors of London in 1901 and 1902, but I should think it very unlikely. I was sorry for myself at the time, when the stamped and addressed envelopes came homing back to me, but my sympathy now is for the men who had to read my contributions. I can imagine nothing more depressing than being an editor and coming to the office on a rainy morning in February with a nail in one shoe and damp trouser legs and finding oneself confronted with an early Wodehouse – written, to make it more difficult, in longhand.

H. G. Wells in his autobiography says that he was much influenced at the outset of his career by a book by J. M. Barrie called *When A Man's Single*. So was I. It was all about authors and journalists and it urged young writers to write not what they liked but what editors liked, and it seemed to me that I had discovered the prime grand secret. The result was that I avoided the humorous story, which was where my inclinations lay, and went in exclusively for the mushy sentiment which, judging from the magazines, was the thing most likely to bring a sparkle into an editor's eyes. It never worked. My only successes were with two-line He and She jokes for the baser weeklies.

At The Servants' Ball

COUNTESS (waltzing with her butler): I'm afraid I must stop, Wilberforce. I'm so danced out.
BUTLER: Oh, no, m'lady, just pleasantly so.

I got 1s. for that, and I still think it ought to have been 1s. 6d.

The curious thing about those early days is that, in spite of the blizzard of rejection slips, I had the most complete confidence in myself. I knew I was good. It was only later that doubts on this point began to creep in and to burgeon as time went by. Today I am a mass of diffidence and I-wonder-if-this-is-going-to-be-all-right-ness, and I envy those tough authors, square-jawed and spitting out of the side of their mouths, who are perfectly sure, every time they start a new book, that it will be a masterpiece. My own attitude resembles that of Bill, my foxhound, when he brings a decaying bone into the dining-room at lunch-time.

'Will this one go?' he seems to be saying, as he eyes us anxiously. 'Will my public consider this bone the sort of bone they have been led to expect from me, or will there be a sense of disappointment and the verdict that William is slipping?'

As a matter of fact, each of Bill's bones is just as dynamic and compelling as the last one, and he has nothing to fear at the bar of critical opinion, but with each new book of mine I have, as I say, always that feeling that this time I have picked a lemon in the garden of literature. A good thing, really, I suppose. Keeps one up on one's toes and makes one write every sentence ten times. Or in many cases twenty times. My books may not be the sort of books the cognoscenti feel justified in blowing the 12s. 6d. on, but I do work at them. When in due course Charon ferries me across the Styx and everyone is telling everyone else what a rotten writer I was, I hope at least one voice will be heard piping up, 'But he did take trouble.'

3

I was getting, then, in the years 1901–2, so little audience response from the men in the editorial chairs that it began to seem that I might have done better to have taken up in my spare time some such hobby as fretwork or collecting bus tickets. But if only a writer keeps on writing, something generally breaks eventually. I had been working assiduously for eighteen months, glued to my chair and taking no part in London's night life except for a weekly dinner – half a crown and 6d. for the waiter – at the Trocadero grill-room, when somebody started a magazine for boys called the *Public School Magazine*, and on top of that came another called *The Captain*, and I had a market for the only sort of work I could do reasonably well – articles and short stories about school life. Wodehouse Preferred, until then down in the cellar with no takers, began to rise a bit. The *Public School Magazine* paid 10s. 6d. for an article and *The Captain* as much as £3 for a short story, and as I was now getting an occasional guinea from *Tit-Bits* and *Answers* I was becoming something of a capitalist. So much so that I began to have thoughts of resigning from the bank and using literature not as a whatever-it-is but as a crutch, especially as it would not be long now before I would be getting my orders.

The London office of the Hong Kong and Shanghai Bank was a sort of kindergarten where the personnel learned their jobs. At the end of two years, presumably by that time having learned them, they were sent out East to Bombay, Bangkok, Batavia and suchlike places. This was called getting one's orders, and the thought of getting mine scared the pants off me. As far as I could make out, when you were sent East you immediately became a branch manager or something of that sort, and the picture of myself managing a branch was one I preferred not to examine too closely. I couldn't have managed a whelk-stall.

And what of my Art? I knew in a vague sort of way that there were writers who had done well writing of life in foreign parts, but I could not see myself making a success of it. My line was good sound English stuff, the kind of thing the magazines liked – stories of rich girls who wanted to be loved for themselves alone, and escaped convicts breaking into lonely country houses on Christmas Eve, when the white snow lay all around, and articles for *Tit-Bits* and school stories for *The Captain*. Could I carry on with these, enclosing a stamped addressed envelope in case of rejection, if I were out in Singapore or Sourabaya?

I thought not and, as I say, toyed with the idea of resigning. And then one day the thing was taken out of my hands and the decision made for me.

Let me tell you the story of the new ledger.

4

One of the things that sour authors, as every author knows, is being asked by people to write something clever in the front pages of their books. It was, I believe, George Eliot who in a moment of despondency made this rather bitter entry in her diary:

> Dear Diary, am I a wreck tonight! I feel I never want to see another great admirer of my work again. It's not writing novels that's hard. I can write novels till the cows come home. What slays you is this gosh-darned autographing. 'Oh, *please!* Not just your *name*. Won't you write something *clever*.' I wish the whole bunch of them were in gaol, and I'd laugh myself sick if the gaol burned down.

And Richard Powell, the whodunit author, was complaining of this in a recent issue of *The American Writer*. 'I begin sweating,' he said, 'as soon as someone approaches me with a copy of one of my books.'

I feel the same. When I write a book, the golden words come pouring out like syrup, but let a smiling woman steal up to me with my latest and ask me to dash off something clever on the front page, and it is as though some hidden hand had removed my brain and substituted for it an order of cauliflower. There may be authors capable of writing something clever on the spur of the moment, but I am not of their number. I like at least a month's notice, and even then I don't guarantee anything.

Sometimes the quickness of the hand will get me by, but not often. When I am not typing I use one of those pen-pencil things which call for no blotting paper. The ink, or whatever the substance is that comes out at the top, dries as you write, so I take the book and scribble, 'Best wishes, P. G. Wodehouse' and with equal haste slam the lid, hoping that the party of the second part will have the decency not to peer inside till I am well out of the way. It seldom happens. Nine times out of ten she snaps the thing open like a waiter opening an oyster, and then the disappointed look, the awkward pause and the pained, 'But I wanted something *clever*.'[1]

The only time I ever wrote anything really clever on the front page of a book was when I was in the cash department of the Hong Kong and Shanghai Bank and a new ledger came in and was placed in my charge. It had a white, gleaming front page and suddenly, as I sat gazing at it, there floated into my mind like drifting thistle-down the idea of writing on it a richly comic description of the celebrations and rejoicings marking the Formal Opening of the New Ledger, and I immediately proceeded to do so.

It was the most terrific 'piece', as they call it now. Though fifty-five years have passed since that day, it is still green in my memory. It had everything. There was a bit about my being

1 I'm frightfully sorry, but I must have just one footnote here. I have recently taken to inscribing these books with the legend:

'You like my little stories do ya?

Oh, glory glory hallelujah.'

It sometimes goes well, sometimes not.

presented to his Gracious Majesty the King (who, of course, attended the function) which would have had you gasping with mirth. ('From his tie he took a diamond tie-pin, and smiled at me, and then he put it back.') And that was just one passing incident in it. The whole thing was a knock-out. I can't give the details. You will have to take my word for it that it was one of the most screamingly funny things ever written. I sat back on my stool and felt like Dickens when he had finished *Pickwick*. I was all in a glow.

Then came the reaction. The head cashier was rather an austere man who on several occasions had expressed dissatisfaction with the young Wodehouse, and something seemed to whisper to me that, good as the thing was, it would not go any too well with him. Briefly, I got cold feet and started to turn stones and explore avenues in the hope of finding some way of making everything pleasant for all concerned. In the end I decided that the best thing to do was to cut the pages out with a sharp knife.

A few mornings later the stillness of the bank was shattered by a sudden yell of triumph, not unlike the cry of the Brazilian wild cat leaping on its prey. It was the head cashier discovering the absence of the page, and the reason he yelled triumphantly was that he was feuding with the stationers and for weeks had been trying to get the goods on them in some way. He was at the telephone in two strides, asking them if they called themselves stationers. I suppose they replied that they did, for he then touched off his bombshell, accusing them of having delivered an imperfect ledger, a ledger with the front page missing.

This brought the head stationer round in person calling heaven to witness that when the book left his hands it had been all that a ledger should be, if not more so.

'Somebody must have cut out the page,' he said.

'Absurd!' said the head cashier. 'Nobody but an imbecile would cut out the front page of a ledger.'

'Then,' said the stationer, coming right back at him, 'you must have an imbecile in your department. Have you?'

The head cashier started. This opened up a new line of thought.

'Why, yes,' he admitted, for he was a fair-minded man. 'There is P. G. Wodehouse.'

'Weak in the head, is he, this Wodehouse?'

'Very, so I have always thought.'

'Then send for him and question him narrowly,' said the stationer.

This was done. They got me under the lights and grilled me, and I had to come clean. It was immediately after this that I found myself at liberty to embark on the life literary.

2 GETTING STARTED

I

FROM MY earliest years I had always wanted to be a writer. I started turning out the stuff at the age of five. (What I was doing before that, I don't remember. Just loafing, I suppose.)

It was not that I had any particular message for humanity. I am still plugging away and not the ghost of one so far, so it begins to look as though, unless I suddenly hit mid-season form in my eighties, humanity will remain a message short. When I left the bank and turned pro, I just wanted to write, and was prepared to write anything that had a chance of getting into print. And as I surveyed the literary scene, everything looked pretty smooth to me, for the early years of the twentieth century in London – it was in 1902 that the Hong Kong and Shanghai Bank decided (and a very sensible decision, too) that the only way to keep solvent was to de-Wodehouse itself – were not too good for writers at the top of the tree, the big prices being still in the distant future, but they were fine for an industrious young hack who asked no more than to pick up the occasional half-guinea. The dregs, of whom I was one, sat extremely pretty *circa* 1902. There were so many morning papers and evening papers and weekly papers and monthly magazines that you were practically sure of landing your whimsical article on 'The Language of Flowers' or your parody of Omar Khayyám somewhere or other after say thirty-five shots.

I left the bank in September, and by the end of the year found that I had made £65 6s. 7d., so for a beginner I was doing pretty well. But what I needed, to top it off, I felt, was something in the way of a job with a regular salary, and I was fortunate enough to have one fall right into my lap.

There was an evening paper in those days called the *Globe*. It was 105 years old and was printed – so help me – on pink paper. (One of the other evening sheets was printed on green paper. Life was full then, very rich.) It had been a profitable source of income to me for some time because it ran on its front page what were called turnovers, 1000-word articles of almost unparalleled dullness which turned over on to the second page. You dug these out of reference books and got a guinea for them.

In addition to the turnovers the *Globe* carried on its front page a humorous column entitled 'By The Way', and one day I learned that the man who wrote it had been a master at Dulwich when I was there. Sir W. Beach Thomas, no other. These things form a bond. I asked him to work me in as his understudy when he wanted a day off, and he very decently did so, and when he was offered a better job elsewhere, I was taken on permanently. Three guineas a week was the stipend, and it was just what I needed. The work was over by noon, and I had all the rest of the day for freelancing.

What you would call the over-all picture, Winkler, now brightened considerably. There was quite a bit of prestige attached to doing 'By The Way' on the *Globe*. Some well-known writers had done it before Beach Thomas – E. V. Lucas was one of them – and being the man behind the column gave one a certain standing. A parody of Omar Khayyám submitted to a weekly paper – as it might be *Vanity Fair* or *The World* – by P. G. Wodehouse, 'By The Way', the *Globe*, 367 Strand, was much more sympathetically received than would have been a similar effort by P. G. Wodehouse, 21 Walpole Street, Chelsea.

My contributions appeared from time to time in *Punch*, and a couple of times I even got into the *Strand* magazine, which for a young writer in those days was roughly equivalent to being awarded the Order of the Garter. My savings began to mount up. And came a day when I realized that I was sufficiently well fixed to do what I had always dreamed of doing – pay a visit to America.

Why America? I have often wondered about that. Why, I mean, from my earliest years, almost back to the time when I was playing with that orange, was it America that was always to me the land of romance? It is not as though I had been intoxicated by visions of cowboys and Red Indians. Even as a child I never became really cowboy-conscious, and to Red Indians I was definitely allergic, I wanted no piece of them.

And I had no affiliations with the country. My father had spent most of his life in Hong Kong. So had my Uncle Hugh. And two other uncles had been for years in Calcutta and Singapore. You would have expected it to be the Orient that would have called to me. 'Put me somewheres east of Suez,' you would have pictured me saying to myself. But it didn't work out that way. People would see me walking along with a glassy look in my eyes and my mouth hanging open as if I had adenoids and would whisper to one another, 'He's thinking of America.' And they were right.

The *Globe* gave its staff five weeks' holiday in the year. Eight days crossing the Atlantic and eight days crossing it back again was going to abbreviate my visit, but I should at least have nineteen days in New York, so I booked my passage and sailed.

This yearning I had to visit America, rather similar to that of a Tin Pan Alley song-writer longing to get back, back, back to his old Kentucky shack, was due principally, I think, to the fact that I was an enthusiastic boxer in those days and had a boyish reverence for America's pugilists – James J. Corbett, James J. Jeffries, Tom Sharkey, Kid McCoy and the rest of them. I particularly wanted to meet Corbett and shake the hand that had kay-oed John L. Sullivan. I had a letter of introduction to him, but he was in San Francisco when I landed, and I did not get to know him till a good many years later, when he was a charming old gentleman and one of Broadway's leading actors.

But I did meet Kid McCoy. I went out to the camp at White Plains where he was training for his championship fight with Philadelphia Jack O'Brien, and it was at the end of my afternoon there that I made what I can see now – in fact, I saw it almost immediately then – was a rash move. I asked him if I could put on the gloves and have a round with him. I thought it would be something to tell the boys back home, that I had sparred with Kid McCoy.

He assured me he would be delighted, and as we were preparing ourselves for the tourney he suddenly chuckled. He had been reminded, he said, of an entertaining incident in his professional career, when he was fighting a contender who had the misfortune to be stone deaf. It was not immediately that he became aware of the other's affliction, but when he did he acted promptly and shrewdly. As the third round entered its concluding stages he stepped back a pace and pointed to his adversary's corner, to indicate to him that the bell had rung, which of course was not the case but far from it.

'Oh, thank you so much,' said the adversary. 'Very civil of you.'

He dropped his hands and turned away, whereupon Kid McCoy immediately knocked him out.

It was as my host concluded his narrative, laughing heartily at the amusing recollection, that, in Robert Benchley's powerful phrase, I developed a yellow streak which was plainly visible through my clothing. The shape of things to come suddenly took on a most ominous aspect.

'Is this wise, Wodehouse?' I asked myself. 'Is it prudent to go getting yourself mixed up with a middleweight champion of the world whose sense of humour is so strongly marked and so what you might almost describe as warped? Is it not probable that a man with a mind like that will think it droll to knock your fat head off at the roots?'

Very probable indeed, I felt, and that yellow streak began to widen. I debated within myself the idea of calling the whole thing off and making a quick dash for the train. It was an attractive scheme, in which I could see no flaw except that the strategic rearward movement I was planning would put an awful dent in the pride of the Wodehouses. I had never gone much into the family history, but I assumed that my ancestors, like everybody else's, had done well at Crécy and Agincourt, and nobody likes to be a degenerate descendant. I was at a young man's crossroads.

At this moment, as I stood there this way and that dividing the swift mind, like Sir Bedivere, there was a clatter of horse's hooves and a girl came riding up. This was the Kid's wife – he had six of them in an interesting career which ended in a life sentence for murder in Sing-Sing prison – and she caused a welcome diversion. We all became very social, and the McCoy–Wodehouse bout was adjourned *sine die*.

I remember that girl as the prettiest girl I ever saw in my life. Or maybe she just looked good to me at the moment.

2

Right from the start of my sojourn in New York I don't think I ever had any doubts as to this being the New York of which I had heard so much. 'It looks like New York,' I said to myself as I emerged from the Customs sheds. 'It smells like New York. Yes, I should say it was New York all right.' In which respect I differed completely from Sig. Guiseppe Bartholdi, who, arriving on the plane there from Italy the other day, insisted against all argument that he was in San Francisco.

What happened was that the signor was on his way to visit his son in San Francisco and was not aware of the fact that to get to that city from Italy you have to change at New York and take a westbound plane. All he knew was that his son had told him to come to Montgomery Street, where his – the son's – house was, so when his plane grounded at Idlewild, he hopped out and got into the airport bus, shouting the Italian equivalent of 'California, here I come', and in due course the bus deposited him at the terminus, where he hailed a cab and said, 'Montgomery Street, driver, and keep your foot on the accelerator.'

Now it so happens that there is a Montgomery Street in New York, down on the lower east side, and the driver – Jose Navarro of 20 Avenue D., not that it matters – took him there, and pretty soon Sig. Bartholdi, like Othello, was perplexed in the extreme. Nothing the eye could reach resembled the photograph his son had sent him of the house for which he was headed, so he decided to search on foot, and when he had not returned at the end of an hour Mr Navarro drove to the Clinton Street police station and told his story.

About seven p.m. Sig. Bartholdi arrived at the police station escorted by Patrolman J. Aloysius Murphy, and that was where things got complex and etched those deep lines which you can still see on the foreheads of the Clinton Street force. For, as I say, the signor stoutly refused to believe that he was not in San Francisco. Hadn't he seen Montgomery Street with his own eyes? The fact that some men of ill-will had spirited away his son's house had, he said, nothing to do with the case. Either a street is Montgomery Street or it is not Montgomery Street. There is no middle course.

After about forty minutes of this Mr Patrick Daly, the courteous and popular police lieutenant down Clinton Street way, drew Patrolman Murphy aside. There was a worried expression on his face, and his breathing was rather laboured.

'Look, Aloysius,' he said, 'are you absolutely sure this *is* New York?'

'It's how I always heard the story,' said Patrolman Murphy.

'You have no doubts?'

'Ah, now you're talking, Lieut. If you had asked me that question an hour ago – nay, forty minutes ago – I'd have said "None whatever", but right now I'm beginning to wonder.'

'Me, too. Tell me in your own words, Aloysius, what makes – or shall we say used to make – you think this is New York?'

Patrolman Murphy marshalled his thoughts.

'Well,' he said, 'I live in the Bronx. That's in New York.'

'There may be a Bronx in San Francisco.'

'And here's my badge. Lookut. See what it says on it. "New York City".'

The lieutenant shook his head.

'You can't go by badges. How do we know that some international gang did not steal your San Francisco badge and substitute this one?'

'Would an international gang do that?'

'You never can tell. They're always up to something,' said Lieutenant Daly with a weary sigh.

Well, it all ended happily, I am glad to say. Somebody rang up the signor's son and put the signor on the wire, and the son told him that New York really was New York and that he was to get on the westbound plane at once and come to San Francisco. And there he is now, plumb spang in Montgomery Street, and having a wonderful time. (On a recent picture postcard to a friend in Italy he asserts this in so many words, adding that he wishes he, the friend, were there.) It is a great weight off everybody's mind.

The whole episode has left the Clinton Street personnel a good deal shaken. They are inclined to start at sudden noises and to think that they are being followed about by little men with black beards, and I am not surprised, for they can never tell when something like this may not happen again. And, really, if I were the city of New York, I honestly don't see how I could prove it to a sceptical visitor from Italy. If I were London, yes. That would be simple. I would take the man by the ear and lead him into Trafalgar Square and show him those Landseer lions.

'Look,' I would say. 'Lions. Leeongze. Dash it, man, you know perfectly well that you would never find leeongze like those anywhere except in London.'

Upon which the fellow would say, '*Si, si. Grazie*,' and go away with his mind completely set at rest.

3

From 1904 to 1957 is fifty-three years, and I see that you ask in your questionnaire, Winkler, what changes I have noticed in the American scene during that half-century and a bit. Well,

I should say that the principal one is the improvement in American manners.

In 1904 I found residents in the home of the brave and the land of the free, though probably delightful chaps if you got to know them, rather on the brusque side. They shoved you in the street and asked who you were shoving, and used, when spoken to, only one side of the mouth in replying. They were, in a word, pretty tough eggs.

One of my earliest recollections of that first visit of mine to New York is of watching a mob of travellers trying to enter a subway train and getting jammed in the doorway. Two subway officials were standing on the platform, and the first subway official said to the second subway official (speaking out of the starboard side of his mouth), 'Pile 'em in, George!'

Whereupon the two took a running dive at the mass of humanity and started to shove like second-row forwards. It was effective, but it could not happen today. George and his colleague would at least say, 'Pardon us, gentlemen,' before putting their heads down.

For in recent years America has become a nation of Chesterfields, its inhabitants as polite as pallbearers. It may be Emily Post's daily advice on deportment that has brought about this change for the better. Or perhaps it is because I have been over here, setting a good example.

You see it everywhere, this new courtesy.

A waitress in one of the cheaper restaurants on the west side was speaking highly of the polish of a regular customer of hers. 'Every time I serve him anything at the table,' she said, 'he stops eating and raises his hat.'

A man I know was driving in his car the other day and stalled his engine at a street intersection. The lights changed from yellow to green, from green to red, from red to yellow and from yellow to green, but his car remained rooted to the spot. A policeman sauntered up.

'What's the matter, son?' he asked sympathetically. 'Haven't we got any colours you like?'

It is difficult to see how he could have been nicer.

Boxers, too, not so long ago a somewhat uncouth section of the community who were seldom if ever mistaken for members of the Vere de Vere family, have taken on a polish which makes their society a pleasure. They have names like Cyril and Percy and Clarence and live up to them. I can remember the time when, if you asked Kid Biff (the Hoboken Assassin), what in his opinion were his chances in his impending contest with Boko Swat (the Bronx's answer to Civilization), he would reply, 'Dat bum? I'll moider him.' Today it would be, 'The question which you have propounded is by no means an easy one to answer. So many imponderables must be taken into consideration. It is, I mean to say, always difficult to predict before their entry into the arena the outcome of an encounter between two highly trained and skilful welterweights. I may say, however – I am, of course, open to correction – that I am confident of establishing my superiority on the twenty-fourth prox. My manager who, a good deal to my regret, is addicted to the argot, says I'll knock the blighter's block off.'

There was a boxer at the St Nicholas Rink a few weeks ago who came up against an opponent with an unpleasantly forceful left hook which he kept applying to the spot on the athlete's body where, when he was in mufti, his third waistcoat button would have been. His manager watched pallidly from outside the ropes, and when his tiger came back to his corner at the end of the round, was all concern and compassion.

'Joey,' he asked anxiously, 'how do you feel, Joey?'

'Fine, thank you,' said the boxer. 'And you?'

One can almost hear Emily Post cheering in the background.

Even the criminal classes have caught the spirit. From Passaic, New Jersey, comes the news that an unidentified assailant plunged a knife into the shoulder of a Mr James F. Dobson the other day, spun him round and then, seeing his face, clicked his tongue remorsefully.

'Oh, I beg your pardon,' he said. 'I got the wrong guy.'

Frank and manly. If you find yourself in the wrong, admit it and apologize.

Nobody could be more considerate than the modern American. In the Coronet motel outside the town of Danvers, Massachusetts, there is a notice posted asking clients to clean out their rooms before leaving. 'Certainly, certainly, certainly, by all means,' said a recent visitor, and he went off with two table lamps, an inkstand and pen, a mahogany night-table, an ashtray, four sheets, two pillow-cases, two rubber foam pillows, two blankets, two bedspreads, two bath towels, two tumblers and a shower curtain. It was as near to cleaning out the room as he could get, and it must have been saddening to so conscientious a man to be compelled to leave the beds, the mattresses and a twenty-one-inch console television set.

Yes, Manners Makyth Man is the motto of the American of today, though, of course, even today you come across the occasional backslider, the fellow who is not in the movement. A 'slim, elderly man wearing a grey Homburg hat' attracted the notice of the Brooklyn police last week by his habit of going to the turnstile of the Atlantic Avenue subway station, pulling the bar towards him and slipping through the narrow opening, thus getting a free trip, a thing the subway people simply hate. And what I am leading up to is this. Appearing before Magistrate John R. Starley at the Flatbush Police Court, he continued to wear his Homburg hat. When a court official removed it, he put it on again, and kept putting it on all through the proceedings, though he must have been aware that this is not done. ('Unless you are a private detective, always *always* take your hat off indoors'... Emily Post.)

It is a pleasure to me to expose this gauche person in print. Michael Rafferty (67) of 812 Myrtle Avenue, Brooklyn. That'll learn you, Mike.

3 BRING ON THE EARLS

I

BACK IN London, I found that I had done wisely in going to New York for even so brief a visit. The manner of editors towards me changed. Where before it had been, 'Throw this man out,' they now said, 'Come in, my dear fellow, come in and tell us all about America.' It is hard to believe in these days, when after breakfasting at the Berkeley you nip across the ocean and dine at the Stork Club, but in 1904 anyone in the London writing world who had been to America was regarded with awe and looked upon as an authority on that *terra incognita*. Well, when I tell you that a few weeks after my return *Tit-Bits* was paying me a guinea for an article on New York Crowds and *Sandow's Magazine* 30s. for my description of that happy day at Kid McCoy's training camp, I think I have made my point sufficiently clear.

After that trip to New York I was a man who counted. It was, 'Ask Wodehouse. Wodehouse will know,' when some intricate aspect of American politics had to be explained to the British public. My income rose like a rocketing pheasant. I made £505 1s. 7d. in 1906 and £527 17s. 1d. in 1907 and was living, I suppose, on about £203 4s. 9d. In fact, if on November 17th, 1907, I had not bought a secondhand Darracq car for £450 (and smashed it up in the first week) I should soon have been one of those economic royalists who get themselves so disliked. This unfortunate venture brought my capital back to about where it had started, and a long and dusty road had to be travelled before my finances were in a state sufficiently sound to justify another visit to America.

I was able to manage it in the spring of 1909.

2

At the time of this second trip to New York I was still on the *Globe* doing the 'By The Way' column, and had come over anticipating that after nineteen days I would have to tear myself away with many a longing lingering look behind and go back to the salt mines. But on the sixth day a strange thing happened. I had brought with me a couple of short stories, and I sold one of them to the *Cosmopolitan* and the other to *Collier's* for $200 and $300 respectively, both on the same morning. That was at that time roughly £40 and £60, and to one like myself whose highest price for similar bijoux had been ten guineas a throw, the discovery that American editors were prepared to pay on this stupendous scale was like suddenly finding a rich uncle from Australia. This, I said to myself, is the place for me.

I realized, of course, that New York was more expensive than London, but even so one could surely live there practically for ever on $500. Especially as there were always the good old *Cosmopolitan* and jolly old *Collier's* standing by with their cornucopias, all ready to start pouring. To seize pen and paper and post my resignation to the *Globe* was with me the work of an instant. Then, bubbling over with hope and ambition, I took a room at the Hotel Duke down in Greenwich Village and settled in with a secondhand typewriter, paper, pencils, envelopes and Bartlett's book of *Familiar Quotations*, that indispensable adjunct to literary success.

I wonder if Bartlett has been as good a friend to other authors as he has been to me. I don't know where I would have been all these years without him. It so happens that I am not very bright and find it hard to think up anything really clever off my own bat, but give me my Bartlett and I will slay you.

It has always been a puzzle to me how Bartlett did it, how he managed to compile a volume of 3 million quotations or whatever it is. One can see, of course, how he started. I picture him at a loose end one morning, going about shuffling his feet and whistling and kicking stones, and his mother looked out of the window and said, 'John, dear, I wish you wouldn't fidget like that. Why don't you find something to *do*?'

'Such as…?' said John Bartlett (born at Plymouth, Mass., in 1820).

'Dig in the garden.'

'Don't want to dig in the garden.'

'Or spin your top.'

'Don't *want* to spin my top.'

'Then why not compile a book of familiar quotations, a collection of passages, phrases and proverbs, traced to their sources in ancient and modern literature?'

John Bartlett's face lit up. He lost that sullen look.

'Mater,' he said, 'I believe you've got something there. I see what you mean. "To be or not to be" and all that guff. I'll start right away. Paper!' said John Bartlett. 'Lots of paper, and can anyone lend me a pencil?'

So far, so good. But after that what? One cannot believe that he had all literature at his fingers' ends and knew just what Aldus Manutius said in 1472 and Narcisse Achille, Comte de Salvandy, in 1797. I suppose he went about asking people.

'Know anything good?' he would say, button-holing an acquaintance.

'Shakespeare?'

'No, I've got Shakespeare.'

'How about Pliny the Younger?'

'Never heard of him, but shoot.'

'Pliny the Younger said, "Objects which are usually the motives of our travels by land and by sea are often overlooked if they lie under our eye."'

'He called that hot, did he?' says John Bartlett with an ugly sneer.

The acquaintance stiffens.

'If it was good enough for Pliny the Younger it ought to be good enough for a pop-eyed young pipsqueak born at Plymouth, Mass., in 1820.'

'All right, all right, no need to get steamed up about it. How are you on Pliny the Elder?'

'Pliny the Elder said "Everything is soothed by oil."'

'Everything is what by *what*?'

'Soothed by oil.'

'How about sardines?' says John Bartlett with a light laugh. 'Well, all right, I'll bung it down, but I don't think much of it.'

And so the book got written. In its original form it contained only 295 pages, but the latest edition runs to 1254, not counting 577 pages of index, and one rather unpleasant result of this continual bulging process is that Bartlett today has become frightfully mixed. It is like a conservative old club that has had to let down the barriers and let in a whole lot of rowdy young new members to lower the tone. There was a time when you couldn't get elected to Bartlett unless you were Richard Bethell, Lord Westbury (1800–73) or somebody like that, but now you never know who is going to pop out at you from its pages. Gabriel Romanovitch Dershavin (1743–1816) often says to Alexis Charles Henri Clerel de Tocqueville (1805–59) that it gives him a pain in the neck.

'Heaven knows I'm no snob,' he says, 'but really, when it comes to being expected to mix with non-U outsiders like P. G. Wodehouse and the fellow who wrote *The Man Who Broke the Bank at Monte Carlo*, well, dash it!'

And Alexis Charles Henri says he knows exactly how Gabriel Romanovitch feels, and he has often felt the same way himself. They confess themselves at a loss to imagine what the world is coming to.

Nevertheless and be that as it may, Bartlett, with all thy faults we love thee still. How many an erudite little article of mine would not have been written without your never-failing sympathy, encouragement, and advice. So all together, boys.

'What's the matter with Bartlett?'

'He's all right!'

'Who's all right?'

'Bartlett! Bartlett! Bartlett! For he's a jolly good fellow, for he's a jolly good fellow, for he's a jolly good fe-hellow....'

And no heel-taps.

3

I was down having a nostalgic look at the Hotel Duke the other day, and was shocked to find that in the forty-seven years during which I had taken my eye off it it had blossomed out into no end of a high-class joint with a Champagne Room or a Diamond Horseshoe or something like that, where you can dance nightly to the strains of somebody's marimba band. In 1909 it was a seedy rookery inhabited by a group of young writers as impecunious as myself, who had no time or inclination for dancing. We paid weekly (meals included) about what you tip the waiter nowadays after a dinner for two, and it was lucky for me that the management did not charge more. If they had, I should have been in the red at the end of the first few months.

For it was not long before I made the unpleasant discovery that though I had a certain facility for dialogue and a nice light comedy touch – at least, I thought it was nice – my output was not everybody's dish. After that promising start both *Collier's* and the *Cosmopolitan* weakened and lost their grip. If it had not been for the pulps – God bless them – I should soon have been looking like a famine victim.

I have written elsewhere – in a book called *Heavy Weather*, if you don't mind me slipping in a quick advert – that the ideal towards which the City Fathers of all English country towns strive is to provide a public house for each individual inhabitant. It was much the same in New York in 1909 as regards the pulp magazines. There was practically one per person. They flooded the bookstalls, and it was entirely owing to them that I was able in those days to obtain the calories without which it is fruitless to try to keep the roses in the cheeks.

Not that I obtained such a frightful lot of calories, for there was nothing of the lavishness of *Collier's* and *Cosmopolitan* about the pulps. They believed in austerity for their contributors, and one was lucky to get $50 for a story. Still, $50 here and $50 there helps things along, and I was able to pay my weekly bill at the Duke and sometimes – very occasionally – to lunch at a good restaurant. And after a year or so a magazine called *Vanity Fair* was started and I was taken on as its dramatic critic.

I blush a little as I make that confession, for I know where dramatic critics rank in the social scale. Nobody loves them, and rightly, for they are creatures of the night. Has anybody ever seen a dramatic critic in the daytime? I doubt it. They come out after dark, and we know how we feel about things that come out after dark. Up to no good, we say to ourselves.

Representing a monthly magazine, I was excluded from the opening performance and got my seats on the second night. This of course was rather humiliating and made me feel I was not really a force, but I escaped the worries that beset the dramatic critic of a morning paper. The inkstained wretches who cover the new plays for the dailies have a tough assignment. Having to rush off to the office and get their notice in by midnight, every minute counts with them, and too often they find themselves on a first night barred from the exit door by a wall of humanity.

The great thing, according to John McLain of the *NY Journal-American*, is to beat the gun, and with this in mind he employs two methods. One is to keep his eye on the curtain, and the minute it

starts to quiver at the top, showing that the evening's entertainment is about to conclude, to be off up the aisle like a jack-rabbit.
The other is to anticipate the curtain line, but here too often the
dramatist fools you. At a recent opening the heroine, taking the
centre of the stage at about five minutes to eleven, passed a weary
hand over her brow and whispered, 'And that ... is all.' That seemed
good enough to Mr McLain and he was out of the theatre in a whirl
of dust, little knowing that after his departure the hero entered (l.)
and said, 'All what?' and the play went on for another half-hour.

Having two weeks in which to write my critique, I missed all
that.

So what with my $50 here and my $50 there and my salary
from *Vanity Fair*, I was making out fairly well. All right so far,
about summed it up.

But I was not satisfied. I wanted something much more on the
order of a success story, and I would be deceiving your newspaper
and radio public, Winkler, if I were to say I did not chafe. I chafed
very frequently.

You know how it is, J.P. You ask yourself what you are doing
with this life of yours, and it is galling to have to answer, 'Well, if
you must pin me down, not such a frightful lot.' It seemed to me
that the time had arrived to analyse and evaluate my position with
a view to taking steps through the proper channels. I was particularly anxious to put my finger on the reason why slick-paper
magazines like the *Saturday Evening Post* did not appear to want
their Wodehouse.

Quite suddenly I spotted what the trouble was. It came to me
like a flash one day when I was lunching on a ham sandwich (with
dill pickle) and a glass of milk.

My name was all wrong.

This matter of names is of vital importance to those who
practise the Arts. There is nothing about which they have to be
more careful. Consider the case of Frank Lovejoy, the movie star,
who for a time was not getting anywhere in his profession and
couldn't think why till one morning his agent explained it to him.

'We meet producer resistance,' the agent told him, 'on account
of your name. The studio heads don't think Frank Lovejoy a
suitable name for a movie star. You'll have to change it. What
they want today is *strong* names, like Rock Hudson, Tab Hunter
and so on. Try to think of something.'

'Stab Zanuch?'

'Not bad.'

'Or Max Million?'

'Better still. That's got it.'

But a week later Mr Lovejoy had a telephone call from his agent.

'Max Million speaking,' he said.

'It is, is it? Well, it better not be,' said the agent. 'The trend has changed. They don't want strong names any more, they want *sincere* names.'

'How do you mean, sincere names?'

'Well, like Abe Lincoln.'

'Abe Washington?'

'Abe Washington is fine.'

'Or Ike Franklin?'

'No, I think Abe Washington's better.'

For some days Abe Washington went about feeling that prosperity was just around the corner, and then the telephone rang once more.

'Sorry, kid,' said the agent, 'but the trend has changed again. They want *geographical* names, like John Ireland.'

So Frank Lovejoy became George Sweden, and all seemed well, with the sun smiling through and all that sort of thing, but his contentment was short-lived. The agent rang up to say that there had been another shift in the party line and the trend was now towards *familiar* names like Gary Stewart, Clark Cooper and Alan Gable. So Frank Lovejoy became Marlon Ladd and might be so to this day, had not he had another call from the agent.

'There's been a further shake-up,' the agent said. 'What they want now are *happy* names suggestive of love and joy.'

'How about Frank Lovejoy?'

'Swell,' said the agent.

But I was telling you about my name being wrong. All this while, you see, I had been labelling my stories.

BY

P. G. WODEHOUSE

and at this time when a writer for the American market who went about without three names was practically going around naked. Those were the days of Richard Harding Davis, of Margaret

Culkin Banning, of James Warner Bellah, of Earl Derr Biggers, of Charles Francis Coe, Norman Reilly Raine, Mary Roberts Rinehart, Clarence Budington Kelland and Orison Swett – yes, really, I'm not kidding – Marden. And here was I, poor misguided simp, trying to get by with a couple of contemptible initials.

No wonder the slicks would not take my work. In anything like a decent magazine I would have stood out as conspicuously as a man in a sweater and cap at the Eton and Harrow match.

It frequently happens that when you get an inspiration, you don't stop there but go right ahead and get another. My handicap when starting to write for American editors had always been that I knew so little of American life, and it now occurred to me that I had not yet tried them with anything about English life. I knew quite a lot about what went on in English country houses with their earls and butlers and younger sons. In my childhood in Worcestershire and later in my Shropshire days I had met earls and butlers and younger sons in some profusion, and it was quite possible, it now struck me, that the slick magazines would like to read about them.

I had a plot all ready and waiting, and two days later I was typing on a clean white page.

SOMETHING FRESH
BY
PELHAM GRENVILLE WODEHOUSE

and I had a feeling that I was going to hit the jackpot. It seemed incredible to me that all this time, like the base Indian who threw away a pearl richer than all his tribe, I should have been failing to cash in on such an income-producing combination as Pelham Grenville Wodehouse. It put me right up there with Harry Leon Wilson, David Graham Phillips, Arthur Somers Roche and Hugh McNair Kahler.

If you ask me to tell you frankly if I like the name Pelham Grenville Wodehouse, I must confess that I do not. I have my dark moods when it seems to me about as low as you can get. I was named after a godfather, and not a thing to show for it but a small silver mug which I lost in 1897. But I was born at a time when children came to the font not knowing what might not happen to them before they were dried off and taken home. My three brothers were christened respectively Philip Peveril, Ernest

Armine and Lancelot Deane, so I was probably lucky not to get something wished on me like Hyacinth Augustus or Albert Prince Consort. And say what you will of Pelham Grenville, shudder though you may at it, it changed the luck. *Something Fresh* was bought as a serial by the *Saturday Evening Post* for what *Variety* would call a hotsy $3500. It was the first of the series which I may call the Blandings Castle saga, featuring Clarence, ninth Earl of Emsworth, his pig Empress of Blandings, his son the Hon. Freddie Threepwood and his butler Beach, concerning whom I have since written so much.

4

Too much, carpers have said. So have cavillers. They see these chronicles multiplying like rabbits down the years and the prospect appals them. Only the other day a critic, with whose name I will not sully my typewriter, was giving me the sleeve across the windpipe for this tendency of mine to write so much about members of the British peerage. Specifically, he accused me of an undue fondness of earls.

Well, of course, now that I come to tot up the score, I do realize that in the course of my literary career I have featured quite a number of these fauna, but as I often say – well, perhaps once a fortnight – why not? I see no objection to earls. A most respectable class of men they seem to me. And one admires their spirit. I mean, while some, of course, have come up the easy way, many have had the dickens of a struggle, starting at the bottom of the ladder as mere Hons., having to go into dinner after the Vice-Chancellor of the Duchy of Lancaster and all that sort of thing. Show me the Hon. who by pluck and determination has raised himself step by step from the depths till he has become entitled to keep a coronet on the hat-peg in the downstairs cupboard, and I will show you a man of whom any author might be proud to write.

Earls on the whole have made a very good showing in fiction. With baronets setting them a bad example by being almost uniformly steeped in crime, they have preserved a gratifyingly high standard of behaviour. There is seldom anything wrong with the earl in fiction, if you don't mind a touch of haughtiness and a tendency to have heavy eyebrows and draw them together in a formidable frown. And in real life I can think of almost no earls whose hearts were not as pure and fair as those of dwellers in the lowlier air of Seven Dials. I would trust the average earl as implicitly as I trust bass singers, and I can't say more than that. I should like to digress for a moment on the subject of bass singers.

What splendid fellows they are, are they not? I would think twice before putting my confidence in the tenor who makes noises like gas escaping from a pipe, and baritones are not much better, but when a man brings it up from the soles of his feet, very loud and deep and manly, you know instinctively that his heart is in the right place. Anyone who has ever heard the curate at a village concert rendering 'Old Man River', particularly the 'He don't plant taters, he don't plant cotton' passage, with that odd effect of thunder rumbling in the distance, has little doubt that his spiritual needs are in safe hands.

Am I right in thinking that nowadays the supply of bass singers is giving out? At any rate, it is only rarely today that a bass singer gets a song to himself. As a general rule he is just a man with a side shirt-front who stands on one side and goes 'Zim-zim-zim' while the tenor is behaving like Shelley's skylark. It was not like this in the good old days. When I was a boy, no village concert was complete without the item:

6. Song: 'Asleep on the Deep' (Rev. Hubert Voules)

while if one went to a music-hall one was always confronted at about ten o'clock by a stout man in baggy evening dress with a diamond solitaire in his shirt-front, who walked on the stage in a resolute way and stood glaring at you with one hand in the armhole of his waistcoat.

You knew he was not a juggler or a conjurer, because he had no props and no female assistant in pink tights. And you knew he was not a dramatic twenty-minute sketch, because he would have had a gag along with him. And presently you had him tabbed. He was a – bass, naturally – patriotic singer, and he sang a song with some such refrain as:

> For England's England still.
> It is, and always will.
> Though foreign foes may brag,
> We love our dear old flag,
> And old Enger-land is Enger-land still.

But where is he now? And where is the curate with his 'Asleep on the Deep' (going right down into the cellar on that 'So beware, so beware' line)?

This gradual fading-out of the bass singer is due, I should imagine, to the occupational hazards inseparable from his line of work. When a bass singer finds that night after night he gets his chin caught in his collar or – on the deeper notes – makes his nose bleed, he becomes dispirited. 'Surely,' he says to himself, 'there must be other, less risky ways of entertaining one's public', and the next time you see him he has taken to card tricks or imitations of feathered songsters who are familiar to you all. Or, as I say, he just stands in the background going 'Zim-zim-zim' – this is fairly free from danger – and leaves the prizes of the profession to the sort of man who sings 'Trees' in a reedy falsetto.

I was very touched the other day when I read in one of the papers the following item:

> Montgomery, Alabama. Orville P. Gray, twenty-seven-year-old bass singer serving a sentence at Kilby prison, has turned down a chance for parole. Gray told Parole Supervisor E. M. Parkman that he does not want to break up the prison quartette, of which he is a member.

Would you get a tenor making that supreme sacrifice? Or a baritone? Not in a million years. It takes a man who can reach down into the recesses of his socks and come up with

> He must know sumfin', he don't say nuffin',
> He just keeps rollin' along.

to do the square thing, with no thought of self, on such a majestic scale.

But to get back to earls (many of whom, I have no doubt, sing bass). They are, as I was saying, fine fellows all of them, not only in real life but on the printed page. English literature, lacking them, would have been a good deal poorer. Shakespeare would have been lost without them. Everyone who has written for the theatre knows how difficult it is to get people off the stage unless you can think of a good exit speech for them. Shakespeare had no such problem. With more earls at his disposal than he knew what to do with, he was on velvet. One need only quote those well-known lines from his *Henry VII, Part Two*:

My lord of Sydenham, bear our royal word
To Brixton's earl, the Earl of Wormwood Scrubbs,
Our faithful liege, the Earl of Dulwich (East),
And those of Beckenham, Penge and Peckham Rye,
Together with the Earl of Hampton Wick
Bid them to haste like cats when struck with brick,
For they are needed in our battle line,
And stitch in time doth ever save full nine.

(Exeunt Omnes. Trumpets and hautboys.)

'Pie!' Shakespeare used to say to Burbage, and Burbage would agree that Shakespeare earned his money easily.

A thing about earls I have never understood, and never liked to ask anyone for fear of betraying my ignorance, is why one earl is the Earl of Whoosis and another earl just Earl Smith. I have an idea – I may be wrong – that the 'of' boys have a social edge on the others, like the aristocrats in Germany who are able to call themselves 'Von'. One can picture the Earl of Berkeley Square being introduced to Earl Piccadilly at a cocktail-party.

The host says, 'Oh, Percy, I want you to meet Earl Piccadilly,' and hurries off to attend to his other guests. There is a brief interval during which the two agree that this is the rottenest party they were ever at and that the duke, their host, is beginning to show his age terribly, then the Earl of Berkeley Square says: 'I didn't quite get the name. Earl of Piccadilly, did he say?'

'No, just Earl Piccadilly.'

The Earl of Berkeley Square starts. A coldness creeps into his manner. He looks like Nancy Mitford hearing the word 'serviette' mentioned in her presence.

'You mean *plain* Earl Piccadilly?'

'That's right.'

'No "of"?'

'No, no "of".'

There is a tense silence. You can see the Earl of Berkeley Square's lip curling. At a house like the duke's he had not expected to have to hobnob with the proletariat.

'Ah, well,' he says at length with a nasty little snigger, 'it takes all sorts to make a world, does it not?' and Earl Piccadilly slinks off with his ears pinned back and drinks far too many sherries in the hope of restoring his self-respect.

Practically all the earls who are thrown sobbing out of cocktail-parties are non-ofs. They can't take it, poor devils.

NOTE. (Not a footnote, just a note.) A friend, to whom I showed the manuscript of this book, does not see altogether eye to eye with me in my eulogy of bass singers. You get, he reminded me, some very dubious characters who sing bass. Mephistopheles in *Faust*, for one. Would you, he said, trust Mephistopheles with your wallet? And how about Demon Kings in pantomime?

There is, I must admit, a certain amount of truth in this. I don't suppose there is a man much lower in the social scale than the typical Demon King. Not only does he never stop plotting against the welfare of the principal boy and girl, but he goes in for loud spangles and paints his face green, thus making himself look like a dissipated lizard. Many good judges claim that he is the worst thing that has happened to England since the top hat. And yet he unquestionably sings bass. One can only assume that he is a bass singer who went wrong in early youth through mixing with bad companions.

4 GOOD-BYE TO BUTLERS

I

THE SAME critic who charged me with stressing the Earl note too determinedly in my writings also said that I wrote far too much about butlers.

How do you feel about that, Winkler? Do you think I do? There may be something in it, of course.

The fact is, butlers have always fascinated me. As a child, I lived on the fringe of the butler belt. As a young man, I was a prominent pest at houses where butlers were maintained. And later I employed butlers. So it might be said that I have never gone off the butler standard. For fifty years I have omitted no word or act to keep these supermen in the forefront of public thought, and now – with all these social revolutions and what not – they have ceased to be.

I once read an arresting story about a millionaire whose life was darkened by a shortage of pigeons. He had the stuff in sackfuls, but no pigeons. Or, rather, none of the particular breed he wanted. In his boyhood these birds had been plentiful, but now all his vast wealth could not procure a single specimen, and this embittered him. 'Oh, bring back my pigeon to me!' was his cry. I am feeling these days just as he did. I can do without pigeons – Walter Pidgeon always excepted, of course – but it does break me up to think that I have been goggled at by my last butler.

It is possible that at this point, J.P., you will try to cheer me up by mentioning a recent case in the London courts where a young peer was charged with biting a lady friend in the leg and much of the evidence was supplied by 'the butler'. I read about that, too, and it did cheer me up for a moment. But only for a moment. All too soon I was telling myself cynically that this 'butler' was probably merely another of these modern makeshifts. No doubt in many English homes there is still buttling of a sort going on, but it is done by ex-batmen, promoted odd-job boys and the like, callow youngsters not to be ranked as butlers by one who, like myself, was around and about in the London of 1903, and saw the real thing. Butlers? A pack of crude young amateurs without a double chin among them? Faugh, if you will permit me the expression.

A man I know has a butler, and I was congratulating him on this the last time we met. He listened to me, I thought, rather moodily.

'Yes,' he said when I had finished, 'Murgatroyd is all right, I suppose. Does his work well and all that sort of thing. But,' he added with a sigh, 'I wish I could break him of that habit of his of sliding down the banisters.'

The real crusted, vintage butler passed away with Edward the Seventh. One tried one's best to pretend that the Georgian Age had changed nothing, but it had. The post-First World War butler was a mere synthetic substitute for the ones we used to know. When we septuagenarians speak of butlers, we are thinking of what used to lurk behind the front doors of Mayfair at the turn of the century.

Those were the days of what – because they took place late in the afternoon – were known as morning calls. Somewhere around five o'clock one would put on the old frock-coat (with the white piping at the edge of the waistcoat), polish up the old top hat (a drop of stout helped the gloss), slide a glove over one's left hand (you carried the other one) and go out and pay morning calls. You mounted the steps of some stately home, you pulled the bell, and suddenly the door opened and there stood an august figure, weighing seventeen stone or so on the hoof, with mauve cheeks, three chins, supercilious lips and bulging gooseberry eyes that raked you with a forbidding stare as if you were something the carrion crow had deposited on the doorstep. 'Not at all what we have been accustomed to,' those eyes seemed to say.

That, at least, was the message I always read in them, owing no doubt to my extreme youth and the fact, of which I never ceased to be vividly aware, that my brother Armine's frock-coat and my cousin George's trousers did not begin to fit me. A certain anaemia of the exchequer caused me in those days to go about in the discarded clothes of relatives, and it was this that once enabled me to see that rarest of all sights, a laughing butler. (By the laws of their guild, butlers of the Edwardian epoch were sometimes permitted a quick, short smile, provided it was sardonic, but never a guffaw. I will come back to this later. Wait for the story of the laughing butler.)

My acquaintance with butlers and my awe of them started at a very early age. My parents were in Hong Kong most of the time when I was in the knickerbocker stage, and during my school holidays I was passed from aunt to aunt. A certain number of these aunts were the wives of clergymen, which meant official calls at the local great house, and when they paid these calls they took me along. Why, I have never been able to understand, for even at the age of ten I was a social bust, contributing little or nothing to the feast of reason and flow of soul beyond shuffling my feet and kicking the leg of the chair into which loving hands had dumped me. There always came a moment when my hostess, smiling one of those painful smiles, suggested that it would be nice for your little nephew to go and have tea in the servants' hall.

And she was right. I loved it. My mind today is fragrant with memories of kindly footmen and vivacious parlour-maids. In their society I forgot to be shy and kidded back and forth with the best of them. The life and the soul of the party, they probably described me as, if they ever wrote their reminiscences.

But these good times never lasted. Sooner or later in would come the butler, like the monstrous crow in *Through The Looking Glass*, and the quips would die on our lips. 'The young gentleman is wanted,' he would say morosely, and the young gentleman would shamble out, feeling like 30¢.

Butlers in those days, when they retired, married the cook and went and let lodgings to hard-up young men in Ebury Street and the King's Road, Chelsea, so, grown to man's estate, I found myself once more in contact with them. But we never at that time became intimate. Occasionally, in a dare-devil mood, encountering my landlord in the street, I would say, 'Good morning, Mr Briggs' or Biggs, or whatever it might be, but the coldness of his 'Good morning, sir' told me that he desired no advances from one so baggy at the trouser-knee as myself, and our relations continued distant. It was only in what my biographers will speak of as my second London period – *circa* 1930 – when I was in the chips and an employer of butlers, that I came to know them well and receive their confidences.

By that time I had reached the age when the hair whitens, the waistline expands and the terrors of youth leave us. The turning point came when I realized one morning that, while I was on the verge of fifty, my butler was a Johnny-come-lately of forty-six. It

altered the whole situation. One likes to unbend with the youngsters, and I unbent with this slip of a boy. From tentative discus-
sions of the weather we progressed until I was telling him what
hell it was to get stuck half-way through a novel, and he was
telling me of former employers of his and how the thing that sours
butlers is having to stand behind their employer's chair at dinner
night after weary night and listen to the funny noise he makes
when drinking soup. You serve the soup and stand back and
clench your hands. 'Now comes the funny noise,' you say to
yourself. Night after night after night. This explains what in my
youth had always puzzled me, the universal gloom of butlers.

Only once – here comes that story I was speaking of – have
I heard a butler laugh. On a certain night in the year 1903 I had
been invited to dinner at a rather more stately home than usual
and, owing to the friend who has appeared in some of my stories
under the name of Ukridge having borrowed my dress clothes
without telling me, I had to attend the function in a primitive suit
of soup-and-fish bequeathed to me by my Uncle Hugh, a man
who stood six feet four and weighed in the neighbourhood of
fifteen stone.

Even as I dressed, the things seemed roomy. It was not,
however, until the fish course that I realized how roomy they
were, when, glancing down, I suddenly observed the trousers
mounting like a rising tide over my shirt-front. I pushed them
back, but I knew I was fighting a losing battle. I was up against the
same trouble that bothered King Canute. Eventually when I was
helping myself to potatoes and was off my guard, the tide swept up
as far as my white tie, and it was then that Yates or Bates or
Fotheringay or whatever his name was uttered a sound like a
bursting paper bag and hurried from the room with his hand
over his mouth, squaring himself with his guild later, I believe,
by saying he had had some kind of fit. It was an unpleasant
experience and one that clouded my life through most of the
period 1903–4–5, but it is something to be able to tell my grand-
children that I once saw a butler laugh.

Among other things which contributed to make butlers
gloomy was the fact that so many of their employers were
sparkling raconteurs. Only a butler, my butler said, can realize
what it means to a butler to be wedged against the sideboard, unable
to escape, and to hear his employer working the conversation

round to the point where he will be able to tell that good story of his which he, the butler, has heard so often before. It was when my butler mentioned this, with a kindly word of commendation to me for never having said anything even remotely clever or entertaining since he had entered my service, that I at last found myself understanding the inwardness of a rather peculiar episode of my early manhood.

A mutual friend had taken me to lunch at the house of W. S. (Savoy Operas) Gilbert, and midway through the meal the great man began to tell a story. It was one of those very long deceptively dull stories where you make the build-up as tedious as you can, knowing that the punch line is going to pay for everything, and pause before you reach the point so as to stun the audience with the unexpected snaperoo. In other words, a story which is pretty awful till the last line, when you have them rolling in the aisles.

Well, J.P., there was Sir William Schwenk Gilbert telling this long story, and there was I, tucked away inside my brother Armine's frock-coat and my cousin George's trousers, drinking it respectfully in. It did not seem to me a very funny story, but I knew it must be because this was W. S. Gilbert telling it, so when the pause before the punch line came, thinking that this was the end, I laughed.

I had rather an individual laugh in those days, something like the explosion of one of those gas mains that slay six. Infectious, I suppose you would call it, for the other guests, seeming a little puzzled, as if they had expected something better from the author of *The Mikado*, all laughed politely, and conversation became general. And it was at this juncture that I caught my host's eye.

I shall always remember the glare of pure hatred which I saw in it. If you have seen photographs of Gilbert, you will be aware that even when in repose his face was inclined to be formidable and his eye not the sort of eye you would willingly catch. And now his face was far from being in repose. His eyes, beneath their beetling brows, seared my very soul. In order to get away from them, I averted my gaze and found myself encountering that of the butler. His eyes were shining with a doglike devotion. For some reason which I was unable to understand, I appeared to have made his day. I know now what the reason was. I suppose he had heard that story build up like a glacier and rumble to its conclusion at least fifty times, probably more, and I had killed it.

And now, Gilbert has gone to his rest, and his butler has gone to his rest, and all the other butlers of those great days have gone to their rests. Time, like an ever-rolling stream, bears all its sons away, and even the Edwardian butler has not been immune. He has joined the Great Auk, Mah Jong and the snows of yesterday in limbo.

But I like to think that this separation of butler and butler-*aficionado* will not endure for ever. I tell myself that when Clarence, ninth Earl of Emsworth, finally hands in his dinner pail after his long and pleasant life, the first thing he will hear as he settles himself on his cloud will be the fruity voice of Beach, his faithful butler, saying, 'Nectar or ambrosia, m'lord?'

'Eh? Oh, hullo, Beach. I say, Beach, what's this dashed thing they handed me as I came in?'

'A harp, m'lord. Your lordship is supposed to play on it.'

'Eh? Play on it? Like Harpo Marx, you mean?'

'Precisely, m'lord.'

'Most extraordinary. Is everybody doing it?'

'Yes, m'lord.'

'My sister Constance? My brother Galahad? Sir Gregory Parsloe? Baxter? Everybody?'

'Yes, m'lord.'

'Well, it all sounds very odd to me. Still, if you say so. Give me your A, Beach.'

'Certainly, m'lord. Coming right up.'

5 CRITICS AND THE CRITICIZED

I

THOSE STRAY thoughts on earls and butlers which I have just recorded were written as a dignified retort to a critic dissatisfied with the pearls which I had cast before him, and I see, Winkler, referring to your questionnaire, that you want to know if I am influenced by criticisms of my work.

That, I suppose, depends on whether those who criticize my work are good or bad critics. A typical instance of the bad critic is the one who said, 'It is time that Mr Wodehouse realized that Jeeves has become a bore.' When my press-cutting bureau sends me something like that, an icy look comes into my hard grey eyes and I mark my displeasure by not pasting it into my scrapbook. Let us forget this type of man and turn to the rare souls who can spot a good thing when they see one, and shining like a beacon among these is the woman who wrote to the daily paper the other day to say that she considers Shakespeare 'grossly materialistic and much overrated' and 'greatly prefers P. G. Wodehouse'.

Well, it is not for me to say whether she is right or not. One cannot arbitrate in these matters of taste. Shakespeare's stuff is different from mine, but that is not necessarily to say that it is inferior. There are passages in Shakespeare to which I would have been quite pleased to put my name. That 'Tomorrow and tomorrow and tomorrow' thing. Some spin on the ball there. I doubt, too, if I have ever done anything much better than Falstaff. The man may have been grossly materialistic, but he could crack them through the covers all right when he got his eye in. I would place him definitely in the Wodehouse class.

One of the things people should remember when they compare Shakespeare with me and hand him the short straw is that he did not have my advantages. I have privacy for my work, he had none. When I write a novel I sit down and write it. I may have to break off from time to time to get up and let the foxhound out and let the foxhound in, and let the cat out and let the cat in, and let the senior Peke out and let the senior Peke in, and let the junior Peke out and let the junior Peke in, and let the cat out again, but nobody interrupts me, nobody comes breathing down the back of my neck and asks me how I am getting on. Shakespeare, on the other hand, never had a moment to himself.

Burbage, I imagine, was his worst handicap. Even today a dramatic author suffers from managers, but in Shakespeare's time anybody who got mixed up in the theatre was like somebody in a slave camp. The management never let him alone. In those days a good run for a play was one night. Anything over that was sensational. Shakespeare, accordingly, would dash off *Romeo and Juliet* for production on Monday, and on Tuesday morning at six o'clock round would come Burbage in a great state of excitement and wake him with a wet sponge.

'Asleep!' Burbage would say, seeming to address an invisible friend on whose sympathy he knew he could rely. 'Six o'clock in the morning and still wallowing in hoggish slumber! Is this a system? Don't I get no service and co-operation? Good heavens, Will, why aren't you working?'

Shakespeare sits up and rubs his eyes.

'Oh, hullo, Burb. That you? How are the notices?'

'Never mind the notices. Don't you realize we've gotta give 'em something tomorrow?'

'What about *Romeo and Juliet*?'

'Came off last night. How long do you expect these charades to run? If you haven't something to follow, we'll have to close the theatre. Got anything?'

'Not a thing.'

'Then what do you suggest?'

'Bring on the bears.'

'They don't want bears, they want a play, and stop groaning like that. Groaning won't get us anywhere.'

So Shakespeare would heave himself out of bed, and by lunchtime, with Burbage popping in and out with his eternal 'How ya gettin' on?' he would somehow manage to write *Othello*. And Burbage would skim through it and say, 'It'll need work,' but he supposed it would have to do.

An author cannot give of his best under these conditions, and this, I think accounts for a peculiarity in Shakespeare's output which has escaped the notice of the critics – to wit, the fact that while what he turns out sounds all right, it generally doesn't mean anything. There can be little doubt that when he was pushed for time – as when was he not? – William Shakespeare just shoved down anything and trusted to the charity of the audience to pull him through.

'What on earth does "abroach" mean, laddie?' Burbage would ask, halting the rehearsal of *Romeo and Juliet*.

'It's something girls wear,' Shakespeare would say. 'You know. Made of diamonds and fastened with a pin.'

'But you've got in the script, "Who set this ancient quarrel new abroach?" and it doesn't seem to make sense.'

'Oh, it's all in the acting,' Shakespeare would say. 'Just speak the line quick and nobody'll notice anything.'

And that would be that, till they were putting on *Pericles, Prince of Tyre*, and somebody had to say to somebody else, 'I'll fetch thee with a wanion.' Shakespeare would get round that by pretending that a wanion was the latest court slang for cab, but this gave him only a brief respite, for the next moment they would be asking him what a 'geck' was, or a 'loggat', or a 'cullion' or an 'egma' or a 'punto' and wanting to know what he meant by saying a character had become 'frampold' because he was 'rawly'.

It was a wearing life, and though Shakespeare would try to pass it off jocularly by telling the boys at the Mermaid that it was all in a lifetime and the first hundred years were the hardest and all that sort of thing, there can be little doubt that he felt the strain and that it affected the quality of his work.

So I think the woman who wrote to the paper ought to try to be kinder to Shakespeare. Still, awfully glad you like my stuff, old thing, and I hope you don't just get it out of the library. Even if you do, 'At-a-girl, and cheers.'

2

This episode had rather an unpleasant sequel. A letter was forwarded to me from the paper – addressed to the editor and signed 'Indignant' – which began:

> Sir – I was completely confounded to read in this morning's —— the statement by your correspondent 'Highland Lassie' that P. G. Wodehouse is a better writer than Shakespeare. As an authority on

the latter I can definitely state he was the greatest genius of his time, to be compared only with Riley, Drake and Nelson.

These names convey very little to me. Drake, I suppose, is Alfred Drake, the actor who made such a hit in *Kismet* and was the original Curly in *Oklahoma*, but who is Nelson? Does he mean Harold Nicolson? And as for Riley, we know that his was a happy and prosperous career – we still speak of living the life of Riley – but I never heard of him as a writer. Can 'Indignant' have got mixed up and be referring to the popular hotel proprietor O'Reilly, of whom a poet once wrote:

> Are you the O'Reilly
> Who keeps the hotel?
> Are you the O'Reilly
> They speak of so well?
> If you're the O'Reilly
> They speak of so highly,
> Gawblimey, O'Reilly,
> You are looking well.

But I never heard of him writing anything, either. Evidently some mistake somewhere.

The letter continues:

I have followed the arts for some time now and can definitely state that even the work of Joshua Reynolds was not up to Shakespeare's standard.

He has stymied me again. I recall a reference to, I presume, Joshua Reynolds in a music-hall song by Miss Clarice Mayne, the refrain of which began:

> Joshua, Joshua,
> Sweeter than lemon squash you are

and gather from that that he must be an attractive sort of fellow with lots of oomph and sex appeal, whom I should enjoy meeting, but I can't place him. There is a baseball player named Reynolds who used to pitch for the New York Yankees, but his name is Allie, so it is probably not the same man. I shall be glad to hear more of this Joshua Reynolds, if some correspondent will fill in the blanks for me.

Up to this point in his letter 'Indignant', it will be seen, has confined himself to the decencies of debate and it has been a pleasure to read him. But now, I regret to say, he descends to personalities and what can only be called cracks. He says:

> It is not my disposition to give predictions on this dispute, but let's see how Wodehouse compares with the great bard in 2356.

Now that, 'Indignant', is simply nasty. You are just trying to hurt my feelings. You know perfectly well that I have no means of proving that in the year 2356 my works will be on every shelf. I am convinced that they will, of course, if not in the stiff covers at 12s. 6d., surely in the Penguin edition at two bob. Dash it, I mean to say, I don't want to stick on dog and throw bouquets at myself, but if I were not pretty good, would Matthew Arnold have written that sonnet he wrote about me, which begins:

> Others abide our question. Thou art free.
> We ask and ask. Thou smilest and art still,
> Out-topping knowledge.

When a level-headed man of the Matthew Arnold type lets himself go like that, it means something.

I do not wish to labour this point, but I must draw Indignant's attention to a letter in *The Times* from Mr Verrier Elwyn, who lives at Patangarth, Mandla District, India. Mr Elwyn speaks of a cow which came into his bungalow one day and ate his copy of *Carry On, Jeeves*, 'selecting it from a shelf which contained, among other works, books by Galsworthy, Jane Austen and T. S. Eliot'. Surely a rather striking tribute.

And how about that very significant bit of news from one of our large public schools? The school librarian writes to the school magazine complaining that the young students will persist in pinching books from the school library, and, he says, while these lovers of all that is best in literature have got away with five John Buchans, seven Agatha Christies and twelve Edgar Wallaces, they have swiped no fewer than thirty-six P. G. Wodehouses. Figures like that tell a story. You should think before you speak, 'Indignant'.

I suppose the fundamental distinction between Shakespeare and myself is one of treatment. We get our effects differently. Take the familiar farcical situation of the man who suddenly discovers that something unpleasant is standing behind him. Here is how

Shakespeare handles it. (*The Winter's Tale*, Act Three, Scene Three.)

> ...Farewell!
>
> > The day frowns more and more: thou art like to have
> > A lullaby too rough. I never saw
> > The heavens so dim by day. A savage clamour!
> > Well may I get aboard! This is the chase:
> > I am gone for ever.
>
> *Exit, pursued by a bear.*

I should have adopted a somewhat different approach. Thus:

> I gave the man one of my looks.
> 'Touch of indigestion, Jeeves?'
> 'No, sir.'
> 'Then why is your tummy rumbling?'
> 'Pardon me, sir, the noise to which you allude does not emanate from my interior but from that of the animal that has just joined us.'
> 'Animal? What animal?'
> 'A bear, sir. If you will turn your head, you will observe that a bear is standing in your immediate rear inspecting you in a somewhat menacing manner.'
> I pivoted the loaf. The honest fellow was perfectly correct. It was a bear. And not a small bear, either. One of the large economy size. Its eye was bleak, it gnashed a tooth or two, and I could see at a g. that it was going to be difficult for me to find a formula.
> 'Advise me, Jeeves,' I yipped. 'What do I do for the best?'
> 'I fancy it might be judicious if you were to exit, sir.'
> No sooner s. than d. I streaked for the horizon, closely followed across country by the dumb chum. And that, boys and girls, is how your grandfather clipped six seconds off Roger Bannister's mile.

Who can say which method is the superior?

3

It has never been definitely established what the attitude of the criticized should be towards the critics. Many people counsel those on the receiver's end to ignore hostile criticism, but to my thinking this is pusillanimous and they will be missing a lot of fun. This was certainly the view taken by the impresario of a recent revue in New York which got a uniformly bad press. He has instructed his lawyers to file an immediate damage suit against each

of his critics 'to cover the costs of their undisciplined and unwarranted remarks'. With special attention, no doubt, to the one who
said, 'The only good thing about this show was that it was raining
and the theatre didn't leak.' This, one feels, would come under the
head of that 'slanderous volley of humourless witticisms that defies
the most vivid imagination' to which the impresario alludes.

The case, when it comes to court, will no doubt be closely
watched by the New Orleans boxer, Freddie Biggs, of whom
reporting his latest fight, Mr Caswell Adams of the *NY Journal-
American* said that he flittered and fluttered as if he were performing
in a room full of wasps. 'The only thing bad so far about the
Louisiana Purchase in 1803,' added Mr Adams, 'was that we
eventually got Freddie Biggs.'

I would not, perhaps, go so far as the impresario I have quoted,
but I do think that an author who gets an unfavourable review
should answer it promptly with a carefully composed letter, which
can be either (*a*) conciliatory or (*b*) belligerent.

Specimen (a) The Conciliatory

Dear Mr Worthington,
Not 'Sir'. 'Sir' is abrupt. And, of course, don't say 'Mr Worthington' if the fellow's name is John Davenport or Cyril Connolly.
Use your intelligence, Junior. I am only sketching the thing out
on broad lines.

Dear Mr Worthington,
I was greatly impressed by your review in the *Booksy Weekly* of my
novel *Whither If Anywhere*, in which you say that my construction is
lamentable, my dialogue leaden and my characters stuffed with
sawdust, and advise me to give up writing and start selling catsmeat.

Oddly enough, I am, during the day, a professional purveyor of
catsmeat. I write in the evenings after I have disposed of the last
skewerful. I should hate to give it up, and I feel sure that now
I have read your most erudite and helpful criticisms I can correct
the faults you mention and gradually improve my output until it
meets with your approval. (And I need scarcely say that I would
rather have the approval of Eustace Worthington than that of any
other man in the world, for I have long been a sincere admirer of
your brilliant work.)

I wonder if you would care to have lunch with me some time and go further into the matter of my book and its many defects. Shall we say Claridge's some day next week?

Yours faithfully,
G. G. Simmons

PS. What an excellent article that was of yours in the *Licensed Victuallers Gazette* some weeks ago on 'The Disintegration of Reality in the Interest of the Syncretic Principle'. I could hardly wait to see how it all came out.

PPS. If you can make it for lunch, I will see if I can get Mrs Arthur Miller to come along. I know how much she would like to meet you.

This is good and nearly always makes friends and influences people, but I confess that I prefer the other kind, the belligerent. This is because the Wodehouses are notoriously hot-blooded. (It was a Wodehouse who in the year 1911 did seven days in Brixton Prison – rather than pay a fine – for failing to abate a smoky chimney.)

Specimen (b) The Belligerent

Sir,
Not 'Dear Sir'. Weak. And not 'You potbellied louse', which is strong but a little undignified. Myself, I have sometimes used 'Listen, you piefaced child of unmarried parents', but I prefer 'Sir'.

Sir,
So you think my novel *Storm Over Upper Tooting* would disgrace a child of three with water on the brain, do you? And who, may I ask, are you to start throwing your weight about, you contemptible hack? If you were any good, you wouldn't be writing book reviews for a rag like the one you befoul with your half-witted ravings.

Your opinion, let me add, would carry greater authority with me, did I not know, having met people who (with difficulty) tolerate your society, that you still owe Moss Bros. for a pair of trousers they sold you in 1946 and that the lady who presides over the boarding-house which you infest is threatening, if you don't pay five weeks' back rent soon, to throw you out on the seat of them. May I be there to see it. That you will land on something hard and sharp and dislocate your pelvis is the sincere hope of

Yours faithfully,
Clyde Weatherbee

PS. *Where were you on the night of* 15*th June?*

Now that's good. That cleanses the bosom of the perilous stuff that weighs upon the heart. But don't send this sort of letter to the editor of the paper, because editors always allow the critic to shove in a reply in brackets at the end of it, thus giving him the last word.

4

The critics have always been particularly kind to me. As nice a bunch of square-shooters as I ever came across, is how I regard them. And one gets helpful bits of information from them every now and then. John Wain, reviewing a book of mine the other day in which one of the characters was an impecunious author living in dingy lodgings, said that this was quite out of date. Nowadays, he said, impecunious authors do not live in dingy lodgings. Where they do live, I have not ascertained – presumably in Park Lane – though as to how they pay the rent I remain vague. Still, thanks, John. A useful tip, if I ever do another impecunious author.

Of course, there are black sheep in every flock and, like all other writers, I occasionally find a brickbat mixed in with the bouquets. I was roughly handled not long ago by the man who does the book reviews on the *Daily Worker.* He called Jeeves a 'dim museum-piece' and 'a fusty reminder of what once amused the bourgeoisie'. Harsh words, these, and especially hard to bear from a paper of the large circulation and nationwide influence of the *Daily Worker.* But against this put the very complimentary remarks of the *Berlingske Tidende* of Denmark.

Its critics says (in part):

> Skont Wodehouse laeses af verden over, betyder det dog ikke, at alle hat det i sig, at de er i Stand til at goutere ham. Jeg ved, at der er dannede Mennesker, som ikke vil spilde deres kostbare Tid paa hans Boger. Hvis man ikke er for Wodehouse, er man nodvendigvis imod ham, for der er kun Undskyldning for at laese ham, og det er, at man kan klukle over ham.

That is the sort of thing that warms an author's heart, but, come right down to it, I suppose the best and simplest way of getting a good notice for your book is to write it yourself. The great objection writers have always had to criticism done by outside critics is that they are too often fobbed off with a 'Quite readable' or even a '8½, 233 pp', which, they feel, do not do complete justice to their work. Getting the Do-It-Yourself spirit, the author of a novel recently published in America starts off with a Foreword in which he says:

> This book is a major work of prose, powerful, moving, trenchant, full of colour, crackling with wit, wisdom and humour, not to mention a rare gift for narrative and characterization perhaps never before equalled. It is a performance which stands alone among the books of the world.

The book in question, by the way, is the story of the life of Mona Lisa and is to be published in nine volumes. The first consists of 1267 pages, and at the end of page 1276 Mona Lisa has not yet been born. But one feels that she is bound to be sooner or later, and when she is, watch for the interest to quicken.

6 RAW EGGS, CUCKOOS AND PATRONS

I

And now, Winkler, we come to rather a moot point – to wit. Where do we go from here?

I know you are waiting with ill-concealed impatience for me to resume the saga of my literary career and asking yourself why I don't get on with it, but I am hesitating and fingering the chin, wondering if it would not be better for all concerned if we let it go and changed the subject. Here is the position as I see it, J.P. I have held you spellbound – or fairly spellbound – with the narrative of my early struggles, but with the publication of *Something Fresh* in the *Saturday Evening Post* those struggles ceased abruptly. Its editor, George Horace Lorimer, liked my work, and except for an occasional commission from some other magazine everything I wrote for the next twenty-five years appeared in the *SEP*. All very jolly, of course, and I would not have had it otherwise, but you do see, don't you, that it does not make a good story. Suspense and drama are both lacking.

It was at about this time, too, that I started to clean up in the theatre. Just after the appearance of my second *Post* serial, *Uneasy Money*, while I was writing my third serial, *Piccadilly Jim*, I ran into Guy Bolton and Jerome Kern. I had worked with Jerry for Seymour Hicks at the Aldwych Theatre in 1906, and the three of us now wrote a series of musical comedies, as Guy and I have related in *Bring on the Girls*, which were produced at New York's Princess Theatre and were very successful. At one time we had five shows running simultaneously on Broadway, with a dozen companies on the road.

So you see what I mean, J.P. All the zip has gone out of the thing, and I think we should take my activities from now on as read. To my mind there is nothing so soporific as an author's account of his career after he has got over the tough part and can look his bank manager in the eye without a quiver. I have known novelists, writing the story of their lives, to give not only a complete list of their novels but the plots of several of them. No good to man or beast, that sort of thing. A writer who is tempted to write a book telling the world how good he is ought to remember the reply made by Mr Glyn Johns to an interviewer at Fort Erie, Ontario, last spring.... Ah, Fort Erie, Ontario, in the springtime, with the chestnut trees a-blossom ... on the occasion of his winning the raw-egg-eating championship of Canada by getting outside twenty-four raw eggs in fourteen minutes.

A thing I never understand, when I read an item like that in the paper, is how these fellows do it. How, I mean, does a man so shape himself that he becomes able to eat twenty-four raw eggs in fourteen minutes?

One feels the same thing about performers at the circus. How did the man who dives through a hole in the roof into a small tank first get the impulse? One pictures him studying peacefully for the Church, without a thought in his mind of any other walk in life, when suddenly, as he sits poring over his theological books, a voice whispers in his ear.

'This is all very well,' says the voice, 'but what you were really intended to do was to dive through holes in the roof into tanks. Do not stifle your individuality. Remember the parable of the talents.'

And he throws away his books and goes out to see an agent. Some sort of spiritual revelation like this no doubt happened to Mr Johns.

From his remark to the interviewer, 'I owe it all to my mother,' I piece his story together like this. His, as I see it, was a happy home, one of those typical Canadian homes where a united family lives its life of love and laughter, but he found the most extraordinary difficulty in getting any raw eggs. No stint of boiled, and on Sundays generally a couple poached on toast, but never raw. And all the time he was conscious of this strange power within him.

'If only they would let me get at the raw eggs!' he would say to himself. 'There, I am convinced, is where my genius lies.'

And one day he found his mother had forgotten to shut the door of the larder — ('I owe it all to my mother') — and saw on a lower shelf a whole dozen smiling up at him, seeming to beckon to him. It was as he wolfed the last of the twelve that he knew he had found his life's work.

'Stick to it, boy,' said that inward voice. 'Lead a clean life and practise daily, and the time will come when you will be able to manage twenty-four.'

And from that moment he never looked back.

But I was going to tell you about the reply he made to the interviewer. Asked after the final egg how he had done it, he said, 'I ate twenty-one in twelve minutes, and then I ate another three, making twenty-four in all.'

'No, I mean how did you *start*?'

'With the first egg. Call it Egg A or (1). I ate that egg, then I ate another egg, then I ate another egg, then I ate another egg, then I ate another egg, then I ate another egg, then I ate another egg and, if you follow me, so on.'

Substitute 'wrote' for 'ate' and 'book' for 'egg', and an author with a bank balance has said everything about his career that needs to be said. I, to take the first instance that comes to hand, wrote *Something Fresh*, then *Uneasy Money*, then *Piccadilly Jim*, and after that I wrote another book, then I wrote another book, then I wrote another book, then I wrote another book, and continued to do so down the years.

They are all there on my shelves – seventy-five of them, one for each year of my life – and I would love to name them all, but for the reader it would be too tedious. It is not as if I had ever written one of those historic best-sellers which everybody wants to hear about. When Noel Coward gave us the inside story of *The Vortex* and *Cavalcade*, I drank in every word, as I suppose all the readers of *Present Indicative* did, but there has never been anything dramatic and sensational about any of my productions. I have always run a quiet, conservative business, just jogging along and endeavouring to give satisfaction by maintaining quality of output. *The Inimitable Jeeves*, it is true, sold 2 million copies in America, but that was in the 25¢ paperback edition, which really does not count, and apart from that I have never stepped out of the status of a young fellow trying to get along. I would call myself a betwixt-and-between author – not on the one hand a total bust and yet not on the other a wham or a socko. Ask the first ten men you meet, 'Have you ever heard of P. G. Wodehouse?' and nine of them will answer 'No.' The tenth, being hard of hearing, will say, 'Down the passage, first door to the right.'

For the benefit of the small minority who are interested in statistics I will state briefly that since 1902 I have produced ten books for boys, one book for children, forty-three novels, if you can call them novels, 315 short stories, 411 articles and a thing called *The Swoop*. I have also been author or part author of sixteen plays and twenty-two musical comedies. It has all helped to keep me busy and out of the public houses.

There was once a millionaire who, having devoted a long life to an unceasing struggle to amass his millions, looked up from his death-bed and said plaintively, 'And now, perhaps, someone will kindly tell me what it's all been about.' I get that feeling sometimes, looking back. Couldn't I, I ask myself, have skipped one or two of those works of mine and gone off and played golf without doing English literature any irreparable harm? Take, for instance, that book *The Swoop*, which was one of the paper-covered shilling books so prevalent around 1909. I wrote the whole 25,000 words of it in five days, and the people who read it, if placed end to end, would have reached from Hyde Park Corner to about the top of Arlington Street. Was it worth the trouble?

Yes, I think so, for I had a great deal of fun writing it. I have had a great deal of fun – one-sided possibly – writing all my books. Dr Johnson once said that nobody but a block-head ever wrote except for money. I should think it extremely improbable that anyone ever wrote anything simply for money. What makes a writer write is that he likes writing. Naturally, when he has written something, he wants to get as much for it as he can, but that is a very different thing from writing for money.

I should imagine that even the man who compiles a railway timetable is thinking much more what a lark it all is than of the cheque he is going to get when he turns in the completed script. Watch his eyes sparkle with an impish light as he puts a very small *a* against the line

4.51 arr. 6.22

knowing that the reader will not notice it and turn to the bottom of the page, where it says

(*a*) On Mondays only

but will dash off with his suitcase and his golf clubs all merry and bright, arriving at the station in good time on the afternoon of Friday. Money is the last thing such a writer has in mind.

And how about the people who write letters to the papers saying they have heard the cuckoo, Doc? Are you telling me they do it for money? You're crazy, Johnson.

2

Although it is many years since I myself gave up writing letters to the papers, I still keep in close touch with the correspondence columns of the press, and it is a source of considerable pain to me to note today what appears to be a conspiracy of silence with regard to the cuckoo, better known possibly to some of my readers as the *Cuculus canorus*. I allude to the feathered friend which puzzled the poet Wordsworth so much. 'O Cuckoo! Shall I call thee bird or but a wandering voice?' he used to say, and I don't believe he ever did get straight about it.

In my young days the cuckoo was big stuff. Thousands hung upon its lightest word. The great thing, of course, was to be the first to hear it, for there was no surer way of getting your letter printed. The cuckoo always wintered in Africa – lucky to be able to afford it – returning to the English scene around the second week in April, and you never saw such excitement as there was from 9th April on, with all the cuckoo-hearers standing like greyhounds in the slips, one hand cupped to the right ear and the fountain-pen in the top left waistcoat pocket all ready for the letter to the editor at the first chirp.

Virtually all the men at the top of the profession – Verb Sap, Pro Bono Publico, Fiat Justitia and the like – had started their careers by hearing the first cuckoo and getting the story off to the *Daily Telegraph* while it was hot. It was the recognized *point d'appui* for the young writer.

'My boy,' I remember Fiat Justitia saying to me once after he had been kind enough to read some of my unpublished material, 'don't let editorial rejections discourage you. We have all been through it in our time. I see where you have gone wrong. These letters you have shown me are about social conditions and the political situation and things like that. You must not try to run before you can walk. Begin, like all the great masters, with the cuckoo. And be careful that it is a cuckoo. I knew a man who wrote to his daily paper saying he had heard the first reed-warbler, and the letter was suppressed because it would have given offence to certain powerful vested interests.'

I took his advice, and it was not long before editors were welcoming my contributions.

But how changed are conditions today. I quote from a letter in a recent issue of the *Observer*:

> Sir,
> If the hypothesis be accepted without undue dogmatism in the present rudimentary state of our knowledge that brain is merely the instrument of mind and not its source, the term soul and spirit could plausibly be regarded as redundant.

Pretty poor stuff. Not a word about hearing the cuckoo, which could have been brought in perfectly neatly in a hundred ways. I should have handled it, I think, on something like the following lines:

> Sir,
> If the hypothesis be accepted without undue dogmatism in the present rudimentary state of our knowledge that brain is merely the instrument of mind and not its source, good luck to it, say I, and I hope it has a fine day for it. Be that as it may, however, I should like your readers to know that as early as the morning of Ist January this year, while seeing the New Year in with some friends in Piccadilly, I distinctly heard the cuckoo. 'Hark!' I remember saying to the officer who was leading me off to Marlborough Street. 'The cuckoo!' Is this a record?

That, I fancy, is how Ruat Coelum and the others would have done it, but the letter which I have quoted is evidently the work of a beginner. Notice how he plunges at his subject like a man charging into a railway station refreshment room for a gin and tonic five minutes before his train leaves. Old hands like Verb Sap and Indignant Taxpayer would have begun:

> Sir,
> My attention has been drawn....

Before I broke into the game I used to think of the men who had their attention drawn as unworldy dreamers living in some ivory tower, busy perhaps on a monumental history of the Ming dynasty or something of that sort and never seeing the papers. But when I became a correspondent myself and joined the well-known Fleet Street club, The Twelve Jolly Letter-Writers, I found I had been mistaken. Far from being dreamers, the 'My-attention-has-been-drawn' fellows were the big men of the profession, the top-notchers.

You started at the bottom of the ladder with:

Sir,
I heard the cuckoo yesterday....

then after some years rose to a position where you said:

Sir,
The cuckoo is with us again, its liquid notes ringing through the
countryside. Yesterday...

and finally, when the moment had come, you had your attention
drawn.

There was, as I recollect it, no formal promotion from the
ranks, no ceremony of initiation or anything like that. One just
sensed when the time was ripe, like a barrister who takes silk.

I inadvertently caused something of a flutter in the club,
I remember, soon after I got my AD, and was hauled over the
coals by that splendid old veteran Mother of Six (Oswaldtwistle).

'Gussie,' he said to me one morning – I was writing under the
name of Disgusted Liberal in those days, 'I have a bone to pick with
you. My attention has been drawn to a letter of yours in *The Times*
in which you say that your attention has been called to something.'

'What's wrong with called?' I said. I was young and headstrong then.

'It is not done,' he replied coldly. 'Attentions are not called, they
are drawn. Otherwise, why would Tennyson in his well-known
poem have written:

Tomorrow'll be the happiest day of all the glad new year,
Of all the glad new year, mother, the maddest merriest day,
For my attention has been drawn to a statement in
the press that I'm to be Queen of the May, mother,
I'm to be Queen of the May.

I never made that mistake again.

3

Returning to Dr Johnson, I am sorry that a momentary touch of
irritation caused me to tick him off so harshly. I ought to have
remembered that when he said that silly thing about writing
for money he was not feeling quite himself. He was all hot and
cross because of the Lord Chesterfield business. You probably
remember the circumstances. He had wanted Lord Chesterfield

to be his patron and had been turned down like a bedspread. No wonder he was in ugly mood.

In the days when I was hammering out stories for the pulp magazines and wondering where my next buckwheat cakes and coffee were coming from I often used to think how wonderful it would be if the patron system of the eighteenth century could be revived. (I alluded to it, if you remember, in the Foreword.) No blood, sweat and tears then. All you had to do was to run over the roster of the peerage and select your patron.

You wanted somebody fairly weak in the head, but practically all members of the peerage in those days were weak in the head and, there being no income tax or super tax then, they could fling you purses of gold without feeling it. Probably some kindly friend put you on to the right man.

'Try young Sangazure,' he said. 'I know the nurse who dropped him on his head when a baby. Give him the old oil and you can't miss. Don't forget to say "My Lord" and "Your lordship" all the time.'

I have never been quite clear as to what were the actual preliminaries. I imagine that you waited till your prospect had written a poem, as was bound to happen sooner or later, and then you hung around in his ante-room till you were eventually admitted to his presence. You found him lying on the sofa reading the eighteenth-century equivalent of *Reveille*, and when he said 'Yes?' or 'Well?' or 'Who on earth let *you* in?' you explain that you had merely come to look at him.

'No, don't move, my lord,' you said. 'And don't speak for a moment, my lord. Let me just gaze at your lordship.'

You wanted, you said, to feast your eyes on the noble brow from which had proceeded that *Ode to Spring*.

The effect was instantaneous.

'Oh, I say, really?' said the young peer, softening visibly and drawing a pattern on the carpet with his left toe. 'You liked the little thing?'

'*Liked it*, my lord! It made me feel like some watcher of the skies when a new planet swims into his ken. That bit at the beginning – "Er, Spring, you perfectly priceless old thing." I'll bet you – or, rather, I should say your lordship – didn't want that one back. However did your lordship do it?'

'Oh, just thought of it, don't you know, and sloshed it down, if you see what I mean.'

'Genius! Genius! Do you work regular hours, my lord, or does your lordship wait for inspiration?'

'Oh, well, sometimes one, as it were, and sometimes the other, so to speak. Just how it happens to pan out, you know. But tell me. You seem a knowledgeable sort of bloke. Do you write yourself by any chance? I mean, write and all that sort of rot, what?'

'Why, yes, my lord, I am a writer, my lord. Not in your lordship's class, of course, but I do scribble a bit, my lord.'

'Make a good thing out of it?'

'So far no, my lord. You see, to get anywhere these days my lord, you have to have a patron, and patrons don't grow on every bush, my lord. How did that thing of your lordship's go? Ah, yes. "Oh Spring, oh Spring, oh glorious Spring, when cuckoos sing like anything." Your lordship certainly gave that section the works.'

'Goodish, you thought? I must say I didn't think it bad-dish myself. I say, look here, harking back to what you were saying a moment ago. How about me being your patron?'

'Your lordship's condescension overwhelms me.'

'Right ho, then, that's all fixed up. Tell my major-domo as you go out to fling you a purse of gold.'

4

Recently I have seemed to detect welcome signs indicating that the patron is coming back. I wrote an article the other day, in which I gave my telephone number.

'In the life of every man living in New York and subscribing to the New York telephone service' (I wrote) 'there comes a moment when he has to face a problem squarely and make a decision. Shall he – or alternatively shall he not – have his name in the book? There is no evading the issue. Either you are in the book or you are not. I am in myself. I suppose it was wanting to have something good to read in the long winter evenings that made me do it. For unquestionably it reads well.

Wodehouse, P. G. 1000 PkAv. BUtrfld 8–5029

Much better, it seems to me, than Wodak, Norma L. 404 E. 51. MUryhl 8–4376, which comes immediately before it, and

Wodicka, Geo. D. 807 ColbsAv. MOnumnt 6–4933, which comes immediately after. Both are good enough in their way, but they are not

Wodehouse, P. G. 1000 PkAv. BUtrfld 8–5029

In moods of depression I often turn to the well-thumbed page, and it always puts new heart into me. 'Wodehouse, P. G.,' I say to myself. '1000 PkAv.,' I say to myself. 'BUtrfld 8–5029,' I say to myself. 'Pretty good, pretty good.'

But – or as we fellows in the book say, BUt – there is just one objection to having your name listed – viz. that you thereby become a social outcast, scoffed at and despised by the swells who have private numbers, the inference being that you can't be very hot if you aren't important enough to keep your number a secret confined to a small circle of personal friends.

Nevertheless, I shall continue to instruct the brass hats of the system to publish my name, address and telephone number. (Wodehouse, P. G. 1000 PkAv. BUtrfld 8–5029, in case you have forgotten.) A fig, if I may use the expression, for the snobs who will look down on me. What is good enough for Aaklus, Valbourg E., for the AAAAA–BEEEE Moving and Storage Company, for Zwowlow, Irving, for Zyttenfeld, Saml., and for the ZZYZZY Ztamp Zstudio Corpn is good enough for me.

Well, for weeks after the article appeared no day passed without two or three people ringing up to ask if that really was my telephone number. One of them rang up from Pasadena, California. He said – this seems almost inconceivable, but I am quoting him verbatim – that he thought my books were drivel and he wouldn't read another of them if you paid him, but he did enjoy my articles and would I like a coloured Russell Flint print of a nude sitting on the banks of the Loire. I said I would – you can't have too many nudes about the home, I always say – and it now hangs over my desk. And the point I am making is this. Whatever we may think of a man who does not appreciate my books, we must applaud what is indubitably the right spirit.

We authors live, of course, solely for our Art, but we can always do with a little something on the side, and here, unless I am mistaken, we have the patron system coming into its own again. It should, in my opinion, be encouraged.

If any other members of my public feel like subsidizing me, what I need particularly at the moment are.

> Golf balls
> Tobacco
> A Rolls-Royce
> Dog food suitable for
>> (*a*) A foxhound
>> (*b*) A Pekingese
>> (*c*) Another Pekingese
> Cat food suitable for
>> A cat (she is particularly fond of peas)
> and
> Diamond necklace suitable for
>> A wife

I could also do with a case of champagne and some warm winter woollies. And a few shares of United States Steel would not hurt.

I

WELL, TIME marched on, Winkler, and, pursuing the policy of writing a book, then another book, then another book, then another book and so on, while simultaneously short stories and musical comedies kept fluttering out of me like bats out of a barn, I was soon doing rather well as scriveners go. Twenty-one of my books were serialized in the *Saturday Evening Post*. For the second one they raised me to $5000, for the third to $7500, for the fourth to $10,000, for the fifth to $20,000. That was when I felt safe in becoming 'P. G. Wodehouse' again.

For the last twelve I got $40,000 per. Nice going, of course, and the stuff certainly came in handy, but I have always been alive to the fact that I am not one of the really big shots. Like Jeeves, I know my place, and that place is down at the far end of the table among the scurvy knaves and scullions.

I go in for what is known in the trade as 'light writing', and those who do that – humorists they are sometimes called – are looked down upon by the intelligentsia and sneered at. When I tell you that in a recent issue of the *New Yorker* I was referred to as 'that burbling pixie', you will see how far the evil has spread.

These things take their toll. You can't go calling a man a burbling pixie without lowering his morale. He frets. He refuses to eat his cereal. He goes about with his hands in his pockets and his lower lip jutting out, kicking stones. The next thing you know, he is writing thoughtful novels analysing social conditions, and you are short another humorist. With things going the way they are, it won't be long before the species dies out. Already what was once a full-throated chorus has faded into a few scattered chirps. You can still hear from the thicket the gay note of the Beachcomber, piping as the linnets do, but at any moment Lord Beaverbrook or somebody may be calling Beachcomber a burbling pixie and taking all the heart out of him, and then what will the harvest be?

These conditions are particularly noticeable in America. If as you walk along the streets of any city there you see a furtive-looking man who slinks past you like a cat in a strange alley which is momentarily expecting to receive a half-brick in the short ribs, don't be misled into thinking it is Baby-Face Schultz, the racketeer for whom the police of thirty states are spreading a dragnet. He is probably a humorist.

I recently edited an anthology of the writings of American humorists of today, and was glad to do so, for I felt that such publications ought to be encouraged. Bring out an anthology of their writings, and you revive the poor drooping untouchables like watered flowers. The pleasant surprise of finding that some-body thinks they are also God's creatures makes them feel that it is not such a bad little world after all, and they pour their dose of strychnine back into the bottle and go out into the sunlit street through the door instead of, as they had planned, through the seventh-storey window. Being asked for contributions to the book I have mentioned was probably the only nice thing that had happened to these lepers since 1937. I am told that Frank Sullivan, to name but one, went about Saratoga singing like a lark.

Three suggestions as to why 'light writing' has almost ceased to be have been made – one by myself, one by the late Russell Maloney and one by Wolcott Gibbs of the *New Yorker*. Here is mine for what it is worth.

It is, in my opinion, the attitude of the boys with whom they mingle in their early days that discourages all but the most deter-mined humorists. Arriving at their public school, they find them-selves placed in one of two classes, both unpopular. If they merely talk amusingly, they are silly asses. ('You *are* a silly ass' is the formula.) If their conversation takes a mordant and satirical turn, they are 'funny swine'. ('You think you're a funny swine, don't you?') And whichever they are, they are scorned and despised and lucky not to get kicked. At least, it was so in my day. I got by somehow, possibly because I weighed twelve stone three and could box, but most of my contemporary pixies fell by the wayside and have not exercised their sense of humour since 1899 or thereabouts.

Russell Maloney's theory is that a humorist has always been a sort of comic dwarf, and it is quite true that in the middle ages the well-bred and well-to-do thought nothing so funny as a man who was considerably shorter than they were, or at least cultivated a deceptive stoop. Anyone in those days who was fifty inches tall or less was *per se* a humorist. They gave him a conical cap and a stick with little bells attached to it and told him to caper about and amuse them. And as it was not a hard life and the pickings were pretty good, he fell in with their wishes.

Today what amuses people, says Mr Maloney, is the mental dwarf or neurotic – the man unable to cross the street unescorted, cash a cheque at the bank or stay sober for several hours at a time, and the reason there are so few humorists nowadays is that it is virtually impossible to remain neurotic when you have only to smoke any one of a dozen brands of cigarette to be in glowing health both physically and mentally.

Wolcott Gibbs thinks that the shortage is due to the fact that the modern tendency is to greet the humorist, when he dares to let out a blast, with a double whammy from a baseball bat. In order to be a humorist, you must see the world out of focus, and today, when the world is really out of focus, people insist that you see it straight. Humour implies ridicule of established institutions, and they want to keep their faith in the established order intact. In the past ten years, says Gibbs, the humorist has become increasingly harried and defensive, increasingly certain that the minute he raises his foolish head the hot-eyed crew will be after him, denouncing him as a fiddler while Rome burns. Naturally after one or two experiences of this kind he learns sense and keeps quiet.

2

Gibbs, I think, is right. Humorists have been scared out of the business by the touchiness now prevailing in every section of the community. Wherever you look, on every shoulder there is a chip, in every eye a cold glitter warning you, if you know what is good for you, not to start anything.

'Never,' said one of the columnists the other day, 'have I heard such complaining as I have heard this last year. My last month's mail has contained outraged yelps on pieces I have written concerning dogs, diets, ulcers, cats and kings. I wrote a piece laughing at the modern tendency of singers to cry, and you would have thought I had assaulted womanhood.'

A few days before the heavyweight championship between Rocky Marciano and Roland La Starza, an Australian journalist who interviewed the latter was greatly struck by his replies to questions.

'Roland,' he wrote, 'is a very intelligent young man. He has brains. Though it may be,' he added, 'that I merely think he has because I have been talking so much of late to tennis players. Tennis players are just one cut mentally above the wallaby.'

I have never met a wallaby, so cannot say from personal knowledge how abundantly – or poorly – equipped such animals are with the little grey cells, but of one thing I am sure and that is that letters poured in on the writer from Friends of The Wallaby, the International League for Promoting Fair Play for Wallabies and so on, protesting hotly against the injustice of classing them lower in the intellectual scale than tennis players. Pointing out, no doubt, that, while the average run-of-the-mill wallaby is perhaps not an Einstein, it would never dream of bounding about the place shouting 'forty love' and similar ill-balanced observations.

So there we are, and if you ask me what is to be done about it, I have no solution to suggest. It is what the French would call an impasse. In fact, it is what the French do call an impasse. Only they say amh-parrse. Silly, of course, but you know what Frenchmen are. (And now to await the flood of strongly protesting letters from Faure, Pinay, Maurice Chevalier, Mendès-France, Oo-Là-Là and Indignant Parisienne.)

3

They say it is possible even today to be funny about porcupines and remain unscathed, but I very much doubt it. Just try it and see how quickly you find your letter-box full of communications beginning:

Sir,
With reference to your recent tasteless and uncalled-for comments on the porcupine....

A writer in one of the papers was satirical the other day about oysters, and did he get jumped on! A letter half a column long next morning from Oyster Lover, full of the bitterest invective. And the same thing probably happened to the man who jocularly rebuked a trainer of performing fleas for his rashness in putting them through their paces while wearing a beard. Don't tell me there is not some league or society for the protection of bearded flea trainers, watching over their interests and defending them from ridicule.

There is certainly one watching over the interests of bearded swimming-pool attendants and evidently lobbying very vigorously, for it has just been ruled by the California State Labour Department that 'there is nothing inherently repulsive about a Vandyke beard'. It seems that a swimming-pool attendant in Los Angeles, who cultivated fungus of this type, was recently dismissed by his employer because the employer said, 'Shave that ghastly thing off. It depresses the customers,' and the swimming-pool attendant said he would be blowed if he would shave it off, and if the customers didn't like it let them eat cake. The State Labour Department (obviously under strong pressure from the League for the Protection of Bearded Swimming-Pool Attendants) held that the employer's order 'constituted an unwarranted infringement upon the attendant's privilege as an individual in a free community to present such an appearance as he wished so long as it did not affect his duties adversely or tend to injure the employer in his business or reputation'. And then they went on to say that there is nothing inherently repulsive about a Vandyke beard.

Perfectly absurd, of course. There is. It looks frightful. A really vintage Vandyke beard, such as this swimming-pool attendant appears to have worn, seems to destroy one's view of Man as Nature's last word. If Vandyke thought he looked nice with that shrubbery on his chin, he must have been cockeyed.

And if the League for the Protection of Bearded Swimming-Pool Attendants and the Executors of the late Vandyke start writing me wounding letters, so be it. My head, though bloody, if you will pardon the expression, will continue unbowed. We light writers have learned to expect that sort of thing.

'What we need in America,' said Robert Benchley in one of his thoughtful essays, 'is fewer bridges and more fun.'

And how right he was, as always. America has the Triborough Bridge, the George Washington Bridge, the 59th Street Bridge, auction bridge, contract bridge, Senator Bridges and Bridgehampton, Long Island, but where's the fun?

When I first came to New York, everyone was gay and lighthearted. Each morning and evening paper had its team of humorists turning out daily masterpieces in prose and verse. Magazines published funny short stories, publishers humorous books. It was the golden age, and I think it ought to be brought back. I want to see an A. P. Herbert on every street corner, an Alex Atkinson in every local. It needs only a little resolution on the part of the young writers and a touch of the old broad-mindedness among editors.

And if any young writer with a gift for being funny has got the idea that there is something undignified and anti-social about making people laugh, let him read this from the *Talmud*, a book which, one may remind him, was written in an age just as grim as this one.

> ... And Elijah said to Berokah, 'These two will also share in the world to come.' Berokah then asked them, 'What is your occupation?' They replied, 'We are merrymakers. When we see a person who is down-hearted, we cheer him up.'
>
> These two were among the very select few who would inherit the kingdom of Heaven.

20 MY METHODS, SUCH AS THEY ARE

I

And now, to conclude, I see that you ask me to tell you what are my methods of work, and I am wondering if here your questionnaire has not slipped a cog and gone off the right lines. Are you sure your radio and newspaper public want to know?

I ask because I have never been able to make myself believe that anything about my methods of work can possibly be of interest to anyone. Sometimes on television I have been lured into describing them, and always I have had the feeling that somebody was going to interrupt with that line of Jack Benny's – 'There will now be a slight pause while everyone says "Who cares?"' I should have said that if there was one subject on which the world would prefer not to be informed, it was this.

Still, if you really think the boys and girls are anxious to get the inside facts, let's go.

I would like to say, as I have known other authors to say, that I am at my desk every morning at nine sharp, but something tells me I could never get away with it. The newspaper and radio public is a shrewd public, and it knows that no one is ever at his desk at nine. I do get to my desk, however, round about ten, and everything depends then on whether or not I put my feet up on it. If I do, I instantly fall into a reverie or coma, musing on ships and shoes and sealing wax and cabbages and kings. My mind drifts off into the past and, like the man in the Bab Ballads, I wonder how the playmates of my youth are getting on – McConnell, S. B. Walters, Paddy Byles and Robinson. This goes on for some time. Many of my deepest thoughts have come to me when I have my feet up on the desk, but I have never been able to fit one of them into any novel I have been writing.

If I avoid this snare, I pull chair up to typewriter, adjust the Peke which is lying on my lap, chirrup to the foxhound, throw a passing pleasantry to the cat and pitch in.

All the animal members of the household take a great interest in my literary work, and it is rare for me to begin the proceedings without a quorum. I sometimes think I could concentrate better in solitude, and I wish particularly that the cat would give me a word of warning before jumping on the back of my neck as I sit trying to find the *mot juste*, but I remind myself that conditions might be worse. I might be dictating my stuff.

How anybody can compose a story by word of mouth face to face with a bored-looking secretary with a notebook is more than I can imagine. Yet many authors think nothing of saying, 'Ready, Miss Spelvin? Take dictation. Quote No comma Sir Jasper Murgatroyd comma close quotes comma said no better make it hissed Evangeline comma quote I would not marry you if you were the last man on earth period close quotes Quote Well comma I'm not comma so the point does not arise comma close quotes replied Sir Jasper comma twirling his moustache cynically period And so the long day wore on period. End of chapter.'

If I had to do that sort of thing I should be feeling all the time that the girl was saying to herself as she took it down, 'Well comma this beats me period. How comma with homes for the feebleminded touting for custom on every side comma has a man like this succeeded in remaining at large as of even date mark of interrogation.'

Nor would I be more happy and at my ease with one of those machines where you talk into a mouthpiece and have your observations recorded on wax. I bought one of them once and started *Right Ho, Jeeves* on it. I didn't get beyond the first five lines.

Right Ho, Jeeves, as you may or may not know, Winkler, begins with the words:

'Jeeves,' I said, 'may I speak frankly?'
'Certainly, sir.'
'What I have to say may wound you.'
'Not at all, sir.'
'Well, then—'

and when I reached the 'Well, then—' I thought I would turn back and play the thing over to hear how it sounded.

There is only one adjective to describe how it sounded, the adjective 'awful'. Until that moment I had never realized that I had a voice like that of a very pompous headmaster addressing the young scholars in his charge from the pulpit in the school chapel, but if this machine was to be relied on, that was the sort of voice I had. There was a kind of foggy dreariness about it that chilled the spirits.

It stunned me. I had been hoping, if all went well, to make *Right Ho, Jeeves* an amusing book – gay, if you see what I mean – rollicking, if you still follow me, and debonair, and it was plain to me that a man with a voice like that could never come within several million light-miles of being gay and debonair. With him at the controls, the thing would develop into one of those dim tragedies of the grey underworld which we return to the library after a quick glance at Chapter One. I sold the machine next day, and felt like the Ancient Mariner when he got rid of the albatross.

2

My writing, if and when I get down to it, is a combination of longhand and typing. I generally rough out a paragraph or a piece of dialogue in pencil on a pad and then type an improved version. This always answers well unless while using the pad I put my feet up on the desk, for then comes the reverie of which I was speaking and the mind drifts off to other things.

I am fortunate as a writer in not being dependent on my surroundings. Some authors, I understand, can give of their best only if there is a vase of roses of the right shade on the right spot of their desk and away from their desk are unable to function. I have written quite happily on ocean liners during gales, with the typewriter falling into my lap at intervals, in hotel bedrooms, in woodsheds, in punts on lakes, in German internment camps and in the Inspecteurs room at the Palais de Justice in Paris at the time when the French Republic suspected me of being a danger to it. (Actually, I was very fond of the French Republic and would not have laid a finger on it if you had brought it to me asleep on a chair, but they did not know this.) I suppose it was those seven years when I was doing the 'By The Way' column on the *Globe* that gave me the useful knack of being able to work under any conditions.

Writing my stories – or at any rate rewriting them – I enjoy. It is the thinking them out that puts those dark circles under my eyes. You can't think out plots like mine without getting a suspicion from time to time that something has gone seriously wrong with the brain's two hemispheres and that broad band of transversely running fibres known as the *corpus callosum*. There always comes a moment in the concoction of a scenario when I pause and say to myself, 'Oh, what a noble mind is here o'erthrown.' If somebody like Sir Roderick Glossop could have read the notes I made for my last one – *Something Fishy* – 400 pages of them – he would have been on the telephone instructing two strong men to hurry along with the strait-waistcoat before he was half-way through. I append a few specimens:

> *Father an actor? This might lead to something.*
> (There is no father in the story.)

> *Make brother genial, like Bingo Little's bookie.*
> (There is no brother in the story.)

> *Crook tells hero and heroine about son.*
> (There is no crook in the story, either.)

> *Son hairdresser? Skating instructor?*
> (There is no son in the story.)

> *Can I work it so that somebody – who? – has told her father that she is working as a cook?*

> (This must have meant something to me at the time, but the mists have risen and the vision faded.)

> *Artist didn't paint picture himself, but knew who painted it. Artist then need not be artist.*

> (Who this artist is who has crept into the thing is a mystery to me. He never appears again.)

And finally a note which would certainly have aroused Sir Roderick Glossop's worst suspicions. Coming in the middle of a page with no hint as to why it is there, it runs thus:

> *An excellent hair lotion may be made of stewed prunes and isinglass.*

The odd thing is that, just as I am feeling that I must get a proposer and seconder and have myself put up for Colney Hatch, something always clicks and the story straightens itself out, and after that, as in the case of Otis Quackenbush, all is gas and gaiters, not to mention joy and jollity. I shall have to rewrite every line in the book a dozen times, but once I get my scenario set, I know that it is simply a matter of plugging away at it.

To me a detailed scenario is, as they say, of the essence. Some writers will tell you that they just sit down and take pen in hand and let their characters carry on as they see fit. Not for me any procedure like that. I wouldn't trust my characters an inch. If I sat back and let them take charge, heaven knows what the result would be. They have to do just what the scenario tells them to, and no larks. It has always seemed to me that planning a story out and writing it are two separate things. If I were going to run a train, I would feel that the square thing to do was to provide the customers with railway lines and see that the points were in working order. Otherwise – or so I think – I would have my public shouting, as did the lady in Marie Lloyd's immortal song:

> Oh, mister porter,
> What shall I do?
> I want to go to Birmingham
> And they're taking me on to Crewe.

Anyone who reads a novel of mine can be assured that it will be as coherent as I can make it – which, I readily agree, is not saying much, and that, though he may not enjoy the journey, he will get to Birmingham all right.

3

Well, I think that about cleans the thing up, J.P., does it not? You will have gathered, in case you were worrying, that in my seventy-sixth year – I shall be seventy-six in October – 15th, if you were thinking of sending me some little present – I am still ticking over reasonably briskly. I eat well, sleep well and do not tremble when I see a job of work. In fact, if what you were trying to say in your letter was, 'Hullo there, Wodehouse, how *are* you?' my reply is that I'm fine. Touch of lumbago occasionally in the winter months and a little slow at getting after the dog next door when I see him with his head and shoulders in our garbage can, but otherwise all spooked up with zip and vinegar, as they say out west.

All the same, a letter like yours, with its emphasis on 'over seventy', does rather touch an exposed nerve. It makes one realize

that one is not the bright-eyed youngster one had been considering oneself and that shades of the prison house are beginning, as
one might put it, to close upon the growing boy. A rude awakening, of course, and one that must have come to my housemaster
at school (who recently died at the age of ninety-six) when he said
to a new boy on the first day of term:

'Wapshott? Wapshott? That name seems familiar. Wasn't your
father in my form?'

'Yes, sir,' replied the stripling. '*And* my grandfather.'

Collapse of old party, as the expression is.

PUBLICATION DETAILS OF THE SHORT STORIES
IN THIS ANTHOLOGY

'Jeeves Takes Charge' originally published in the *Saturday Evening Post* (US) in November 1916 and in *Strand* magazine (UK) in April 1923. First book publication in *Carry On, Jeeves*, Herbert Jenkins, 1925; George H. Doran, New York, 1927. Copyright © 1925 by P. G. Wodehouse, renewed 1953 by P. G. Wodehouse.

'Jeeves and the Impending Doom' originally published in *Strand* magazine (UK) in December 1926 and in *Liberty* (US) in January 1927. 'The Love that Purifies' originally published in *Cosmo* (US) in November 1929 and as 'Jeeves and the Love that Purifies' in *Strand* magazine (UK) in November 1929. 'Jeeves and the Yule-tide Spirit' originally published in *Strand* magazine (UK) in December 1927 and in *Liberty* (US) in December 1927. First book publication of all three stories was in *Very Good, Jeeves!*, Herbert Jenkins, 1930; Doubleday, Doran, Garden City, 1930. Copyright © 1930 by P. G. Wodehouse, renewed 1958 by P. G. Wodehouse.

'The Great Sermon Handicap' originally published in *Strand* magazine (UK) in June 1922 and in *Cosmo* (US) in June 1922. First book publication in *The Inimitable Jeeves*, Herbert Jenkins, 1923; US title *Jeeves*, George H. Doran, New York, 1923. Copyright © 1923 by P. G. Wodehouse, renewed 1951 by P. G. Wodehouse.

'Uncle Fred Flits By' originally published in *Red Book* (US) in July 1935 and in *Strand* magazine (UK) in December 1935. 'The Amazing Hat Mystery' originally published in *Cosmo* (US) in August 1933 and in *Strand* magazine (UK) in June 1934. First publication for both stories was in *Young Men in Spats*, Herbert Jenkins, 1936; Doubleday, Doran, Garden City, 1936. Copyright © 1936 by P. G. Wodehouse, renewed 1964 by P. G. Wodehouse.

'The Crime Wave at Blandings' originally published in the *Saturday Evening Post* (US) in October 1936 and in *Strand* magazine (UK) in January 1937. First book publication in *Lord Emsworth and Others*, Herbert Jenkins, 1937; US title *Crime Wave at Blandings*, Doubleday, Doran, Garden City, 1937. Copyright © 1937 by P. G. Wodehouse, renewed 1965 by P. G. Wodehouse.

'Honeysuckle Cottage' originally published in the *Saturday Evening Post* (US) in January 1925 and in *Strand* magazine (UK) in February 1925. First book publication in *Meet Mr Mulliner*, Herbert Jenkins, 1927; Doubleday, Doran & Co., New York, 1928. Copyright © 1927 by P. G. Wodehouse, renewed 1955 by P. G. Wodehouse.

'Ukridge Rounds a Nasty Corner' originally published in *Cosmo* (US) in January 1924 and in *Strand* magazine (UK) in February 1924. First book publication in *Ukridge*, Herbert Jenkins, 1924; US title *He Rather Enjoyed It*, George H. Doran, New York, 1928. Copyright © 1924 by P. G. Wodehouse, renewed 1952 by P. G. Wodehouse.

'The Nodder' originally published in *Strand* magazine (UK) in January 1933 and as 'Love Birds' in *American Magazine* (US) in January 1933. First book publication in *Blandings Castle*, Herbert Jenkins, 1935; Doubleday, Doran, Garden City, 1935. Copyright © 1935 by P. G. Wodehouse, renewed 1963 by Lady Ethel Wodehouse.

'The Heart of a Goof' originally published in *Red Book* (US) in September 1923 and in *Strand* magazine (UK) in April 1924. First book publication in *The Heart of a Goof*, Herbert Jenkins, 1926; US title *Divots*, George H. Doran, New York, 1927. Copyright 1923, 1924, 1925, 1926, 1927 by P. G. Wodehouse.

'A Bit of Luck for Mabel' originally published in the *Saturday Evening Post* (US) in December 1925 and *Strand* magazine (UK) in January 1926. 'The Editor Regrets' originally published in *Strand* magazine (UK) in September 1930 and in the *Saturday Evening Post* (US) in July 1939. First book publication of both stories was in *Eggs, Beans and Crumpets*, Herbert Jenkins, 1940; Doubleday, Doran, Garden City, 1940. Copyright 1925, 1926, 1928, 1931, 1935, 1937, 1939, 1940 by Pelham Grenville Wodehouse.

This book is set in BEMBO which was cut
by the punch-cutter Francesco Griffo
for the Venetian printer-publisher
Aldus Manutius in early 1495
and first used in a pamphlet
by a young scholar
named Pietro
Bembo.